The Rebels

Book Two
Of
The Eleusis Cycle

D. Brumbley

Content Warning

This book contains content that some readers might find
triggering, such as:

Combat violence
Mass casualty events
Sexual content (explicit)
Dom/Sub dynamic
CnC
Arranged marriages
Infidelity
Sexual assault / rape (implied, off-page)
Genetic experimentation
Medical trauma
Terminal illness
Mentions of pregnancy complications
Apocalyptic scenarios
Pandemic / disease
Institutional gaslighting / emotional
manipulation
Forced pregnancy
Persecution based on sexuality
PTSD / trauma responses

Read with Care

To all of you
who know who you are
but can't quite be that person.
Yet.

CONTENTS

1

Thousands of people moved slowly toward the exits, heading into the rest of the station in small packs or artificially-matched pairs. Many had their heads down, looking at communicators for directions to their assigned housing units. All of them had their eyes on the person with whom they'd been matched, either in furtive, nervous glances or outright appreciative stares. The low buzz of awkward conversation echoed through the halls, making the assembly feel more alive than the stark sterility of their surroundings would have suggested.

Logan, Mercury, Anna, and Orion were still standing in their row near the front of the room, each looking back and forth through the other three. An hour ago, it had been each of them and their spouse against the world. New entrants into the Eleusis Initiative, their entire lives left behind them for the sake of building something new. Building a new world for humanity on Eleusis. A better world.

But there was nothing better about the world. Not if the Initiative's matching program was going to try and force them away from the person they had chosen to spend their life with.

"There's no way they reviewed this." Orion said finally, since one of them had to speak first. "There were thousands of people matched, and like they said, adjustments had to be made at the last second. There's no way any of the actual administrators of the program reviewed this kind of match."

"Well, then let's fucking talk to someone about it and get it fixed." Anna was nearly growling as she responded, but her jealousy was off the charts. "They didn't say anything about Petri dishes, and I'm not interested in fucking around on my husband."

"No one here is interested in fucking around on anybody." Orion agreed, moving past the woman he had supposedly been matched with so he could get back to Mercury. "Let's go see what the sixteen-year-old has to say about this. You said she's done a lot of the work with the program, right?"

Mercury nodded, but she didn't seem to be in a talking mood, unlike the short and talkative Mrs. Bickford. She followed after Anna and Orion as they led the way toward the stage where the officials were still talking, even though the whole room had mostly cleared out except for the four of them and a few others.

"Dr. Santos? Could we speak to you?" Mercury asked politely as soon as they were close enough to be heard.

Maria Santos turned around at the sound of someone saying her name, her bright eyes and the smooth, severe control of her dark hair bouncing a bit in the motion, in time with the click of her heels as she approached the edge of the stage. "Hello. Certainly. I'm here to answer questions, after all."

"Your program cross-matched two married couples." Logan said from near the back of the group. His tone was clipped, but not so far as to be rude. Their quarrel was with technology, not with leadership. "We came here married, and we were given assurances previously that that would be respected."

"And it is." Dr. Santos said without even a flicker of change in her expression or tone. "No one is forcing you to divorce your spouse or even to do anything but procreate with the person that you have been matched with. Of course we would like for you to have a cordial relationship with your match, but that's not always possible." Dr. Santos looked from one face to the next in the group of four. "This is a hard thing to ask of all of you, I understand that. Here, let me pull up your files."

As the doctor grabbed a large tablet to pull up their information, all Anna could think about was finding something in the room and throwing it at the doctor's head. She made it sound like having a baby was simple, as if the existence of a human being growing inside a person should have no effect, emotional or otherwise. As if sleeping with someone still didn't mean something. However much she had slept around before Logan, she hadn't treated them as though they were a cock to ride and nothing more. "Your files aren't going to say anything that will convince any of us that breaking up two marriages is a good idea."

Dr. Santos looked over her tablet at Anna as she ironically had pulled up Anna's file. She stared at the earthborn woman for a cold moment before she looked at the device again. "I would think that you, of all women, would understand that furthering the human race is important, Ms. Prince."

"Bickford." Anna corrected sharply, since she could tell the doctor was trying to get under her skin. "I know what that file says, I gave you the information to fill it with when I filled out my application."

"More than thirty sexual partners and still not a single child." Dr. Santos continued as though she hadn't been corrected about Anna's name, or even that Anna had spoken at all. "That doesn't include female partners, of course." She finally looked up from the information and turned her attention directly to Anna again.

"Your genetics and Logan's are compatible to create a child, though the tests show that it hasn't happened yet, and that it may be a struggle to do so. Regardless, both of your families have spent a significant amount of time in the Midwest district of North America. You're both of similar descent, even though your family lines haven't actually crossed previously. When you agreed to be a part of this project, you agreed to participate in supporting its genetic diversity. I have your signatures, I have recorded, verbal agreement from not only you, but all four of you." She looked away from Anna and looked around the group again. "Are you telling me those records were falsified?"

"Supporting genetic diversity is one thing." Logan spoke up again, an immediate and intense dislike for the woman apparent in his tone. "We talked about that in the past month since we got our letters. So if the giant over here needs to fill up a cup to be used later, that's one thing. You've all got technology coming out your ears up here, so don't tell me that's not feasible. But if you're gonna try and tell us that agreeing to support genetic diversity is the same thing as cheating on our spouses, then I've got a list of things you can do with those signatures, none of which you'd find pleasant."

Dr. Santos smiled at Logan before she responded. Clearly she was unaffected by his attempt to take control over the situation. "I assure you that a veiled threat isn't going to get you anywhere, Mr. Bickford." She moved on to pull up another file, this time it belonged to Mercury.

"Doctor Finnegan." Maria scanned over the file quickly and looked up at her colleague with a warmer smile. "You're the baby expert here. Tell me. How *feasible*," she said as she flicked her glance to Logan once before she looked back at Mercury. "Is it that we can monitor and administer the collection of specimen, monitor and regulate the cycles of all of the women that have been matched today, and also have the support staff and medical facilities to perform the creation of embryos and then the implantation of all of those embryos, on a newly colonized planet where we will be dealing with immediate needs like food and shelter?"

She turned slightly to point a hand at the screen that had been lit up during the matching process, but was now dark. "Even with the lives that were lost, we have well over two thousand people in this program."

Mercury didn't like being put on the spot by anyone, even though she could answer her colleague's question easily enough. She didn't like the fact that she didn't have the realization on her own, especially knowing their training was only a year. She didn't consider they would want trainees to go into full procreation mode before they were even on Eleusis.

"It would take a medical staff of hundreds to monitor every step of that procreative process efficiently and far more time to implement than a year." Mercury replied softly. "But you're crazy to think you have the staff or the facilities to handle that many pregnant women in the first place." She added quickly, since that was just as crazy.

"That's true, but we can be assured that not everyone will get pregnant immediately or quickly. And once we've reached a number of what this facility *can* handle, then we can cease the push for procreation and wait until the first round of babies are born. Regardless, that's not a concern for us right now. Getting enough babies to take to Eleusis is our concern. Not having too many."

Dr. Santos looked over Mercury's file again. "It also says here that you and your husband, while well-matched, may face a greater hurdle in procreating than Logan and Anna. Your blood types are highly incompatible, and your children face a much higher risk of genetic abnormalities than children you would naturally produce with Logan. Since we don't have the staff to monitor the conception of children, we certainly don't have the staff to correct genetic abnormalities. Not here. And certainly not when you get to Eleusis. It is preferable to minimize the risk."

Orion had started feeling hopeful when Mercury mentioned they wouldn't have the staff to support a thousand pregnant women in the first place, but by the time Dr. Santos was finished speaking, his eyes were wide again. "Right. Sure. It's a math equation. Simple."

He and Mercury had been matched. Why wouldn't the program have told them about some kind of possibility for abnormality when that happened? More to the point, why would it have matched them at all? Even as he wondered, though, he already knew the answer. Procreation was common in orbit, even encouraged, to a point, but it was far from universal. His family had been incredibly strange for having three children, and neither he nor Mercury had placed having children high on their list of priorities in submitting their profiles to be matched.

"I guess the four of us will just be late having children, then, and they'll offer Eleusis what they can offer." Orion had no doubt that most of the other Initiates would follow the program as outlined, since they had signed up for it without reservations, after all. "The rest of the Initiative can provide plenty of children without the four of us making it a top priority."

"I see. So that's how your attitude is going to be toward this entire program? Whatever suits you best, regardless of what is needed?" Dr. Santos pulled up Orion's file next and read over it. "I would not have guessed that of you, Lieutenant. Everything in your file shows you to be dedicated to the causes you choose." She looked around the group and looked back toward Director Vance and Manager Kaplan. "Maybe you're not suited for this project after all. I can certainly talk to the Director to see about sending you home. Doctor Finnegan has worked very hard to make it this far, I'm certain that she'll do well regardless."

"What was it you *just* said about threats not working? At all?" Orion shot back without missing a beat.

"Just to be clear," Logan interjected before Orion could say anything else to dig himself in deeper, "going home is an option, then? Being released from the program and returned to our place of origin?"

"His home is Station Three. Going back to Earth is an option for no one. All transportation except vital transport between Orbit and Earth has been halted due to the attacks earlier today."

Logan's jaw tightened at that, even though he knew he should have been expecting it. They had known there was no way back to Earth once they left, or at least that it was possible they would never return. But hearing someone state it as a fact was a very different experience than assuming it.

"I see." His tone was his best mimicry of her own professional politeness. "Well, Doctor, you've clearly given us quite a lot to consider. While we do that considering, we all have quarters to find and I'm sure you have a great deal to do." It was clear they weren't going to get any kind of resolution or change out of Santos, and Logan had never seen the point in continuing to beat a brick wall. They would have to sort things out on their own, somehow.

"And what about you, Doctor?" Anna said with as much acid in her tone as she could muster. "Are you exempt from having to fuck someone you didn't choose?" She said it loudly enough for the director and manager to look over at them. "Kaplan too? Must be nice."

Kaplan's eyes widened a little, but he was smiling at the woman's attack, and he nodded afterward, stepping up closer to Dr. Santos and the obvious hostility of the discussion underway. "You know, that's curious, Maria, I completely forgot to submit my profile. Did you submit yours?"

"I forgot to submit mine as well." She looked up at Kaplan. They had been colleagues for some time while working on the Eleusis Initiative, and they had gotten to know each other fairly well. Not everyone had been matched due to some recalculation needed for the lives lost, so there was a small pool of possible matches remaining.

"But it's prepared, right? If there's anyone in the world the program knows best, it's you, right?" He completely ignored the temperature of the preceding discussion to smile at her, then pulled out his communicator. "What do you say? Count of three? Small drum-roll?"

Maria gave him a small glare she hoped no one else would notice. "No theatrics necessary, Mr. Kaplan." Maria pulled up her own device and navigated to the 'submit to be processed' button. She tapped it without the countdown, giving him a look that was anything but encouraging.

He tapped his own at the same time, and changed the display so it would project the hologram of the screen in front of him for easy manipulation. "I don't have to explain how this works to you two," he nodded at Orion and Mercury, both of whom were giving him dark looks in spite of his smile. "But for those of us who didn't grow up in near-zero gravity, it can take some adjustment. System is rigged to account for all kinds of factors. Kind of shit you wouldn't find out about a person till you'd been married to 'em for years, it already knows. Knows how you'd deal with it, if you'd let it ride, if it'd be a deal-breaker, all of it. Things like the genetics you were talking about. It already knows, it's already taken into consideration."

"Maybe you should get matched to the computer." Orion suggested before he could stop himself. "You're clearly already a fan, I'm sure you two would be very happy together."

"The first *real convincing* artificial intelligence that comes along that isn't throttled by the Consortium? Absolutely. Sign me up." Kaplan said with a laugh, as if he couldn't feel the heat of the glares all four of them were giving him.

"Isn't that romantic." Anna said sarcastically as the big screen lit up again, this time with Dr. Maria Santos on one side. It looked like it was still processing her match for another minute before Kaplan's face appeared next to hers.

Maria was clearly surprised, but relief quickly followed. At least with Stephen, he was as deeply a part of the Initiative as she was, and they were both going to be busy keeping the Initiates in line. "It seems there's a reason we work well together, Stephen."

Anna just stared at the screen and started to laugh. Loudly. "All you've done right now is prove that the fucking thing is rigged."

"Well, if you call working within available parameters rigged, then sure." Stephen was clearly happy about it, and he smiled over at Maria before he changed the screens to show the names and photos of all the remaining single members of the Initiative. There were half a dozen men and ten women remaining to be matched, all of them younger and all of them from Earth.

"This was the available pool against which it attempted to match us. Not really an easy goal, I think you'll agree. None of these have the education or the background me and Maria here have in common, none of them are from orbit, it looks like at least two of the women are dominantly interested in more passive partners . . . I could go on. There are plenty of reasons."

He turned back to the four of them with the same bright smile on his face, motioning to their pockets. "The same information is available to you on your devices. This isn't private record. Well, ours is, but yours is available to you, your own match information, the reasons behind the system's choice, all of it." He paused and clasped his hands in front of him. "Unless you'd rather we re-ran the match program against everyone in the Initiative? Possibly shuffle around some new matches a bit? What do you think, ladies, would one of you prefer me over the two men you've already got? There's a chance."

"I have *one* man." Anna replied immediately and looked over at Logan before she continued ranting. She looked Kaplan up and down once before she narrowed her eyes at him. "I don't think you could handle me. *Sir.*"

"There's no need to re-run anything." Mercury finally responded, since she really didn't even want to think about the situation anymore. "I think there have been enough waves today."

"At last. Reason is seen." Kaplan sounded sarcastically relieved, and flicked away the images up on the screens before turning back to face the four of them again. "You four are some of the best we've got. I've seen your profiles and your aptitude scores. Bickford and Bickford, I don't imagine either of you will stay long where you've been put, it's just a matter of seeing where you're needed most. You'll do some excellent things for this Initiative. Just keep your heads on straight."

Logan glared at the man, who had the single most smug smile Logan had ever seen in his life. He took Anna's hand and pulled her away without waiting for Mercury and Orion to join them. Logan had seen enough.

Anna tripped and bounced after him as he pulled her along in the weird gravity, but clearly she wasn't interested in hanging around. She attempted to use her communicator to find her unit, but it kept telling her how to get to a shared unit for her and Orion Al-Jabbar. There were supposed to be *options*. "The fuck. What does yours say about a unit? It's telling me how to get to a shared one with the fucking pilot."

"Mine's telling me the same, with the doctor. Deck seven, hall three, I don't even know." He sighed and returned the communicator to voice function, which he had figured out it could do on the way up in the shuttle. "Locate my individual unit, not the one shared with Finnegan. Everybody else in the damn Initiative's gotta have one, show me mine."

A path lit up for him to follow, and Anna relaxed just a little bit as soon as she saw they actually had a place they could go. "Thank god."

Once they reached the unit and had sealed themselves inside, Anna threw herself full-force into Logan's chest. Angry tears stung her eyes, but she didn't care.

"Logan . . ." She could feel his name breaking her inside just a little, fear clutching every nerve in her body even if she hadn't allowed herself to show it in the face of the fuckers responsible.

"I know." He held onto her, arms tightening around her shoulders as he closed his eyes. He didn't want to see the unit, didn't want to see the place where he and Anna would be hiding out from the rest of the Initiative staff or trying to remind themselves that they still had each other. All he wanted to do was hold his wife.

Hot, traitorous tears slid down her cheeks as she kept her face buried against his chest and her fingers dug into his back. "I won't do it. I waited so long . . . I only want you."

"I don't want anyone else." She could hear the anger in his voice as he said it. She knew him much too well to mistake quiet for calm where Logan was concerned. "We could take a shot at a shuttle. Pilot it to some other station where they're not complete fucking manipulative assholes."

"I don't know enough yet." Anna shook her head, though she would have gladly piloted anywhere but where they were. "They would send someone after us and probably shoot us out of the sky and call us terrorists." She gripped his shirt even tighter. "I saw her face and when she sat down near you, I wanted to lose my shit. She's gorgeous." They hadn't been together long enough for her insecurities to fall away, especially because she had seen Logan with other women before.

"I don't care if she's Helen of fucking Troy. She's not you." Logan said sharply, letting her go just enough to look her in the eye. "All I care about on this entire damn station is you."

Anna put her hands on the sides of his face and pulled him into a rough kiss, even as the tears continued to fall. "I love you. I'm not going to let them force me into anything. I'm not sleeping with anyone else. Just you. You're the only person that matters to me."

He kissed her until it felt less like the world was about to break apart beneath his feet. With one arm still around her, he turned back to the door and looked around for something that equated to a lock, but he had to settle for a handprint plate along one side. The panel lit up and there was a low ding, but nothing else actually appeared, so Logan took it as his cue to speak. "Okay, if this is voice activated, I'm gonna tell you to lock this fucking door so that nobody else can get in. You understand that?"

"Door locked." The computer affirmed, giving Anna the only

cue she needed to start clawing at the ridiculous clothes he was wearing. She hated the way the orbital suits looked on both of them. "We'll just stay in here. You and me."

"Fine by me." He reached for the top latch of her suit and broke it with one hand, along with part of the zipper it was attached to. "Let them just forget we're in here. I've got no problem with that." He had no trouble ripping down her zipper to expose the rest of her, walking her backward into the unit without even knowing where he was going.

It didn't matter. All that mattered was Anna.

* * * * *

Mercury had a much easier time finding a unit where she and Orion could go without having to worry about who was assigned where. The medical halls nearby were nearly empty, except for those tending to the injured from the debacle of shuttle launches.

Both of them were quiet as they walked and after Mercury closed the door behind Orion, she quickly moved to the nearest chair and buried her face in both hands.

Orion was the practical one who decided to lock the door and make sure they were secured against anyone else coming in and ruining their day, but he stayed beside the door to heave a sigh, both in relief and resignation.

When he'd allowed himself a moment to dwell on things, he moved to her chair and went to his knees in front of her with his hands on the arms of the chair. At first, all he did was lean in to kiss her once, but then he went the rest of the way down to his knees and began untying the laces of her boots.

Mercury started to cry softly by the time he got both boots off her feet and she slowly lifted her heavy head from her hands. "What are we going to do, Orion?"

He set the boots aside precisely and looked back up at her with his arms resting on her thighs. He was so tall that he was still nearly her height on his knees when she was sitting down, and his lips were only a heartbeat from hers.

"What we're *not* going to do is what they want. We're going to get ourselves back together and we're going to find a way through this. You're going to look into the 'genetic abnormalities' shit she just shoveled on us and verify everything she's saying, see if there's loopholes she hasn't seen. And we're gonna figure it out. The way we said we were going to when we decided to come into this."

Mercury looked into his eyes quietly before she kissed him gently. "I'll look into it, but I wouldn't be surprised if the genetic abnormalities part is true. There's no reason for them to lie about it, and there's no reason that it would have mattered before. If we had wanted to have children and it would have been a problem, we would have just gone to a geneticist and chosen an embryo without any abnormalities. It's a little more difficult to make those decisions with a natural conception."

She sighed, pressing her forehead to his. "My parents chose most of my traits before I was born. That's how it goes most of the time, so far as I have seen. It can create difficulties down the line, but no one worries about that anymore. Not usually, anyway."

"My siblings and I were the same way." He shook his head and moved in to kiss her again anyway, resting his cheek against hers. "Genetics and probabilities didn't have anything to do with the beginning of this. The beginning of us. I don't feel any need for it to have anything to do with the rest of us. I want you. I want this. Nothing else."

She nodded, but it didn't stop more tears from sliding down her cheeks. "I want you too. I want this. Only us." Mercury felt fairly confident, though, they wouldn't be able to fight what had been handed to them. "I'll try to find a way out, but after the response we were given . . ." She heaved a heavy breath as a few more tears fell.

"If we don't at least make it look like we're getting along with the other two, things could get really bad. We're in an entirely closed environment. They've cut us off for our protection, but that also means that we can't reach out for help. Or get out. These are powerful people running this program, they could keep us apart even if we left the program. The way Dr. Santos reacted to our questions and concerns . . . "

Orion had always taken what Mercury said seriously, and that moment was no exception. But Mercury had a medical background. He had been in the military since he was ten. "So if we're trapped here, with people in charge who have all or most of the control over this situation, then we're backed into a corner. You can't plan for something like that. All you can do when it happens is refuse to give up, refuse to give them what they want, and get creative." His hands moved to her sides to hold her. "We came here for Eleusis and each other. Not their games."

She wiped at her eyes and sniffled a few times before she grabbed onto his hands and got up out of the chair. Afterward she hugged herself tightly to him and buried her face against his shoulder. "Can we just snuggle and go to sleep? I'm exhausted and I just don't . . . I just want to be with you."

"That sounds like a plan to me." He massaged her back in the hopes of smoothing away some of the situation, if only for a while, then headed away with her toward the bedroom.

The unit was plain, the walls nothing but the steel grey of the prison it was. There were directives on the walls that instructed them to customize the place to their own preferences, but Orion shook his head at them.

It would still be a prison, no matter how it was decorated. And they had walked right into it.

Mercury stripped down to her underclothes and slid under the blankets wordlessly. As soon as Orion joined her, she curled into his embrace and buried her face into the side of his neck. The scent of his skin was comforting, at least, and she closed her eyes as she savored being close to him.

"I love you, Orion. This is worth keeping. This is worth fighting for. You are worth fighting for."

2

Gordon turned around once he and Jessie got out of the main hall. He tugged lightly on her hand to spin her through the air in the low gravity, clearly savoring the moment, and her.

When she stumbled a little on the landing, he caught her with a chuckle and settled for only holding her hand on the way to the lift. "Okay," he said once they were relatively alone in the corridor. "Twenty questions. I know you've got them. And now you're my match, officially and completely under the sacred auspices of the holy and sanctified Consortium. So you're entitled to answers. Hit it."

"Maybe we should wait until we get to the unit?" Jessie looked both ways along the corridor, since there were people everywhere trying to find their way. "Though, to be honest, I'm nervous about the unit too, so that might not help." They got to the lift and she turned her gaze back to Gordon. "I guess there are safe questions to ask. Where you're from, favorite color, favorite food . . ."

"Where I'm from is complicated." Gordon smiled and pulled her into the corner of the lift as a few other people joined them to head down to levels where gravity meant a little more than it did so close to the docks. "I was born in Sweden, as close as I've ever been able to find out. Grew up in the Montana territory till I was six, then ended up in the Dakotas till I was sixteen. Been hopping around since then."

"And your family?" She looked around a little bit again, since she was a little uncomfortable in a corner with him looking at her like he wanted to devour her. "That can't have been fun, moving around all of the time."

"I don't mind most of the time." He cleared his throat before he answered her first question, and the unspoken answer pulled down his smile. "I have . . . I had fourteen brothers, once. At last count, I have six left. That I know of."

"Fourteen brothers? Six left?" Jessie's shock showed plainly on her face, since that was a number she didn't think was possible on Earth. "Wow. That's a lot of family." She watched people get off on the same floor they were supposed to, but they were the last ones off the lift.

Jessie chewed on her bottom lip as he led her toward the unit they were assigned to share. "Are you sure you want me instead of whoever you were supposed to be with?" She replied in a low voice as they drifted toward their unit.

He smiled at the question, and shook his head to himself before he looked back over at her. "Yes, I'm sure. Just tell me up front how many times you're going to ask, so I know. However many times it is, the answer is going to be yes. Unless you're hiding an awful lot that I'm for some reason not going to be into. You're the one who's likely to start running here in a minute."

"Me? Why would I run?" Her stomach twisted into more knots as they reached their shared unit. Jessie was too nervous to put her hand up to the scanner, but Gordon chuckled and scanned his hand, tugging her inside. Their bags had been delivered, and she immediately went to hers so she could make sure everything was there. Anything for a distraction.

Gordon smiled as she went to her things, but he didn't try to stop her. Instead, he went to take his boots off by the door and gave her the space to be nervous if she wanted to be. He stepped up to the door and placed his hand to the plate once he was finished with his shoes.

"Lock, please. Full privacy. And send up some water bottles and snack bars, please." He waited for confirmation of his request, then headed back into the unit to get a look at the whole place. "Looks like they gave us a smaller unit. Must not think we're very important."

"We're not." Jessie confirmed as she went through her things, pulling out clothes that were more comfortable than a flight suit. She retreated to the small bathroom in the unit and looked around, since she wasn't exactly sure how things worked. It couldn't actually have running water, right? Would the water float, or just bounce around like they did? Instead she found some sanitary gel and used it on her hands, though she really wanted to wash her face before she changed into comfortable pajamas.

By the time she got back out into the room, Gordon had gotten out of his flight suit as well, though he had gotten re-dressed, after a fashion. He had apparently either brought a long robe with him into space, or had ordered one and it had arrived already while she was getting changed. Either way, he was barefoot and sitting on the side of the bed.

Their bed.

It was low to the ground, covered in the same grey as the rest of the walls, but it looked fairly comfortable, with big pillows at the head of it waiting for them. He looked over at her once he heard her come out, and smiled. "You look comfortable."

"I, um . . . we're matched and everything, but I didn't want to assume . . . we barely know each other, right?" Even though they were essentially 'married' by being matched, she wasn't going to jump into anything. They were still strangers. Mostly. "I couldn't leave home without some of my own things."

"None of us could." He smiled at her pajamas, and stood up slowly. The fabric he wore wasn't silk, but the cotton moved easily as he walked, and it was warm to her touch when he moved to kiss her gently. "I've had this since I was . . . fifteen, I think? Didn't seem right to go anywhere without it."

Jessie kissed him eagerly as soon as he initiated a kiss, then nodded in agreement. Nothing about leaving home had felt wrong, but it wouldn't have been right to leave every single thing behind. She ran her hands over his arms, above and below the loose sleeves of the robe, her fingers caressing tentatively over his wiry grip on her. "You're right, I do have a lot of questions, but I'm too distracted to ask any questions. Do you have questions?"

"One to begin with. And it's fairly important." His hands moved up over her body freely to cradle her face in his fingertips for one last kiss. He stepped back afterward and reached up to take the necklace he wore with the data core on it out from under the neckline of his robe. He set it gingerly on the table next to what was apparently going to be his side of the bed.

"I um, I wish there was something I could say or do to sufficiently warn you, but I'm afraid there really isn't. I just . . ."

Was he . . . nervous? Everything about the man since she had met him had been overflowing, frankly annoying, self-assurance. And now he was mumbling?

"I need to know if this is something you can tolerate." He continued, finally getting his speech back in order. "If you can't, believe me when I tell you, I will understand." Once the data core was out of his hand, he reached up to untie the belt of his robe, clearly lacking the hesitation she was feeling about herself for the time being.

He wasn't looking at her when he finally pulled the robe aside and let it fall over his arms to the floor. He was still wearing boxers beneath it, but his underwear was far from the first thing she noticed about him once the bathrobe was gone. The rest of him told a story too loud and violent to be ignored.

More of Gordon's body, his torso, legs, and arms, was covered by scars than by unblemished skin. There were long, angry gashes over his chest in particular that looked like they had all come from the same source, raised and badly healed, but the cuts crisscrossed over his entire form, no part of him left sacred or safe from whatever had caused them.

Beneath the marks, she could see from the outline of his stomach that he was missing part of at least one rib, and another one had been broken long ago and healed incorrectly, leaving a small protrusion on one side. Looking closely at his stomach brought to her attention just how skinny the man really was. He looked lean while he was wearing clothes, but without them, the only thing that stopped him from looking emaciated was the clear muscle definition of his abs and chest. He seemed well-enough nourished to develop an impressive musculature beneath the scars, but not enough to gain weight otherwise.

Where the incisions weren't, he had small burns or more jagged marks that looked like bites, especially on his arms. None of them were particularly discolored, and they were all obviously long-healed, but they had left their print on him in a way that would never truly leave.

Jessie didn't move at first, but when she did, she moved toward him instead of away from him. She reached out to touch his arms and chest, and her fingers moved lightly over his scars. She looked horrified but she still met his eyes. Clearly she wasn't horrified by him, but *for* him. "My god, what happened to you? Who did this to you?"

"More complicated answers." He smiled weakly, but he didn't move away from her exploration or flinch at her touch. It took some time for him to meet her eyes again, but eventually he did. "The majority of them I got when I was six. The rest I've collected over the years since, a few at a time."

"Six?!" She said as she recoiled slightly, but she immediately met his eyes again. "Who would do this to a little boy?" Jessie felt sick at the very idea and she moved her hand to his face, tentatively touching his cheek. "I hope they're dead, whoever they are. No one should do this to an innocent child. God, that makes me sick."

"Some of them are. Others will follow." There was a promise behind his tone, but his expression didn't change. "It would take a long time to kill everyone who was involved. It's important to have priorities when you're plotting revenge on my kind of scale."

He turned his face to kiss her hand as she touched him, grateful, for her sake, that the scars had never reached his face or his hands and feet, though those were the only scar-free parts of him. "I'm aware of what they look like. I wanted you to see them so you could know that I'm not interested in pity. I only want to know if they're something you think you can tolerate or not. That's all."

"I'm sorry, I'm not trying to pity you, even though I do feel terrible that you had to endure whatever you endured. I don't know if you'll ever want to talk about it, but you can. If you want to." Jessie looked away from him and down at her own feet when he asked her if she could tolerate the scars. "I know it sounds cliche, but I really don't care about scars. Even though yours are pretty intense." She chewed on her bottom lip before she looked up at him again briefly. "The last man I was with wasn't exactly the prettiest man in the world. And clearly I'm not one to talk. Don't worry about your scars. They don't scare me."

Gordon watched her eyes for the truth of what she was saying, then reached out to hold her by her waist with the ghost of a smile creeping back onto his face. "Yeah, I've seen pictures of your brother-in-law. Not the most dreamy-looking fellow. He didn't deserve you."

Jessie laughed and shook her head before she looked him in the eye. "I think you mean he didn't deserve my sister." Her sister was beautiful, thinner, less plain in her coloring, while Jessie had brown hair and eyes and somewhat tanned skin. Her curves meant that she had an ass and breasts to be proud of, though, which was the main reason why her brother-in-law had pursued her in the first place. He was an ass-man, and her sister didn't have those particular goods like she did. "I can't complain. I would probably be a virgin without him."

"Is he the only one you've been with, then?" His eyebrows rose in confusion, since that was incredibly strange among those from Earth. His hands weren't idle as he asked, moving over her shirt and even dipping beneath the hem of it to caress the bare skin of her waist.

"The only man I've slept with, yes. Mostly because I come from a wealthy family but as soon as other men found out that I won't inherit, they moved on. The only person who inherits is whoever has children first, but it's still their responsibility to take care of the direct family. I would have been my sister's responsibility if my mother died before I left, but instead my mother hung around to berate me until I left the planet."

"Well, she's not around to berate you now." His fingers worked at the hem of the pajama pants she had on, tugging them down slightly on her waist as he kissed her again. "Probably for the best. No mother should ever see her daughter in the kind of positions I mean to put you in."

Jessie sucked in a clipped, nervous breath as he pulled at her pants, and when they fell away from her waist to her ankles, her cheeks turned deep crimson. Clearly the sass that she liked to flaunt was in hiding, and she was all nerves. Jessie's skin was warmly tanned and her legs were silky. She was concerned about her curves, but every part of her was voluptuous and plush. She couldn't convince herself to look at him again. "Can we turn the lights off?"

His hands moved over her newly-exposed hips in a slow caress before he answered, still holding her close against him. "I would rather see you if the choice is up to me. But I won't do anything to make you uncomfortable. You don't have to ask me what you can and can't do, you can do as you please. With me and with just about everything else."

In an effort to compromise, Jessie asked the computer to only lower the lighting instead of turning them off, though she still found it impossible to look at him directly. He was touching her like he wanted her, but she didn't want to see it in his expression if he didn't actually want her.

Jessie moved toward the bed and sat on the edge, though she didn't know if he would pursue her to help her out of the rest of her clothes.

He followed her slowly, looking her over in the small space between them, until he came to stand between her parted knees and nudged them yet further apart with his own. He reached down to tilt her chin up to look at him, then ran his fingers through her loose brown hair to smooth it all away from her face. Once she was looking at him, if only furtively, he leaned down to kiss her and spoke against her lips afterward as his hands moved down to caress her through her shirt. "I've wanted you from the second you opened your mouth at that meeting, Jessie. Haven't stopped since, and I don't intend to. I hacked the matching system because I wanted you to myself. I'll hack whatever other systems I have to hack to keep you mine, and do whatever else needs doing."

"I want you too. I know I put on a lot of show . . ." She was getting a *little* bit braver about meeting his eyes. Small steps. She pushed herself to kiss him again and again, her arms working up his bare sides to pull him down to her. Each kiss came with more need, more urgency. "Acting like I'm brave. I have a hard time believing you would really want me, but you're saying that you do, and I don't think you would lie. I don't think you have any reason to lie to me, but maybe you do. I don't know. Even if you're lying to me, I still want you."

"I'm not lying to you." He said between kisses, returning the hunger in her kisses as it rose between them both. "I can't promise that I'll always give you the full and unabridged truth right away. I have a lifetime of secrets to share, and they'll take some time for us to get through, but I can promise you that I won't lie to you."

He made sure she was looking at him as he promised, but afterward he leaned down and grabbed the hem of her shirt with both hands to pull it up over her head, leaving her bare beneath him. He pressed her onto the bed in the kiss that followed, until her back came down on smooth grey sheets and the lean, scarred weight of him settled on top of her. "We can share our insecurities, I'm comfortable with that. So long as we're sharing more than just them."

"Mhm." Only her whimper agreed, and she couldn't help but squirm as his hands wandered over her bare skin. A low groan escaped her as his hands grabbed onto her ample breasts and his fingers caressed her nipples. Her nipples pebbled instantly and ached for more of his attention, peaking at the smallest touch. Her hands wandered down to the waist of his boxers, tugging at them in a silent command.

"You don't have to be insecure." Her fingers wandered over his abs again as he rolled to one side of her to accommodate, allowing her to pull his boxers down and away. Jessie took a good look at the cock bared before her. "Your cock definitely looks better than any other one that I've seen up close."

"Says the woman whose only other experience belonged to an

accountant." Gordon grinned in spite of himself at the compliment, and let her take in the sight of him for just a breath longer before he kissed her, taking one of her hands and placing it on him firmly so she could feel what the sight of her was doing to him. She could doubt what he said, but that kind of response left no room for confusion about his attraction to her. "Fate's been a bitch to me in half a hundred ways, but she's thrown a few things my direction to try and make amends, this cock being one of them."

"Clearly." Jessie replied breathily as her hand slid up and down the length of him slowly. He was already rock hard, but her fingers teased and explored eagerly. He was amazingly patient as she indulged her curiosity. "It always drove me crazy he never knew what he wanted. Like sex was this confusing, complicated thing." Jessie looked into Gordon's eyes as he hovered over her, mostly because she was having a hard time believing that she was turning him on so much by being naked and not in complete darkness. "Probably because he was married to my sister. I hope you know what you want."

"I do." He growled, kissing the breath out of her with a desire in his touch that was intent on devouring her. His fingers were all over, but mostly teasing her nipples as often as he could. Jessie's hips bucked a few times in response as he tortured her breasts. "I want you under me, exhausted and begging for mercy because you can't take me making you come even one more time. That's what I want."

Of all the things she'd imagined hearing from him, that had not been one of them. She gasped between kisses as his hands branded her skin. "Is that even possible? Usually I . . . take care of myself."

"Do you?" He grinned as his hips moved him against her hand and his own touch slid south over her waist. "Well, no reason to let me stop you. But from now on, if you're taking care of yourself because I'm not doing a good enough job of it for you, you should let me know, and I'll be sure to up my game."

She nodded as if she agreed, but there was no way she would feel comfortable telling Gordon if she felt like he was 'doing a good enough job' or not. Instead she let his hand wander until it found her core and she gasped. He hadn't spent that much time exploring her, but she was slick from his attention.

Jessie squirmed when his fingers slid through and her pulse

skipped several times, since she couldn't believe it was actually happening. They were still strangers, but she'd thrown caution to the non-existent wind. She took quick breaths as his fingers stroked her slowly. He eased one finger around her clit as though he knew what she wanted and she only ached for more.

"You don't have to . . ." She gasped between strokes, since she didn't want him to think he had to please her. They were matched together, but she certainly didn't want to give him any reason to turn her away.

He gave a moan of his own at the way her grip tightened on his cock in response to what he was doing to her, but her unfinished statement only made him grin. She was distracted by his adept fingers, but she didn't stop her erratic stroking. "Life . . . is filled with things . . . I don't have to do. All the more reason to enjoy doing them."

Jessie whimpered as his fingers teased her clit and then slid into her. She was so wet she almost felt embarrassed, but he kept going. Jessie wanted to make him feel good in return, so she focused on stroking him quickly instead of erratically. "You're so hard . . ."

"Yeah, well, you're to blame for that." He said with another violent kiss, moving away from her to get farther up the bed. He pulled her with him, throwing her around easily in the low gravity, then attacked her again with his lips, but this time along her neck and breasts, his hands roaming all over her to take her in hungrily.

His tongue laved at her neck and traced along her breasts before he took a nipple into his mouth. Every time he touched her, every time his cock grazed her leg, she could feel the heat running through him, the need he was feeling for her now that he actually had her. There was nothing feigned about it, nothing that made the encounter feel like he was doing her some kind of favor by spending time with her. The only thing in his eyes when he looked at her was desire, the likes of which she'd never seen before, even from her own reflection in the mirror.

Eventually Jessie's thoughts were swimming in lust and desire and she couldn't think about being self-conscious. She also couldn't control all the noises escaping her lips as he tortured her, and her kisses turned frantic as she edged closer to orgasm. How was she so close already?

"Gordon . . ." She moaned his name in a worship, since he was about to undo her. "I'm going . . . to . . ." His mouth didn't stop with her breasts, and between sucking on her pink nipples, he teased them with a heated breath across her skin.

His fingers moved against her as if they had been pleasuring her for years, pressing her right to the edge over and over again, teasing her with it, driving her insane with it as he moved to position himself against her. There was an eager triumph waiting behind his eyes as his fingers circled her clit, but just as her moans escalated and her hips started to twitch against his hand, his touch stopped completely and he slid himself inside her, one delicious, rock-hard inch at a time.

By the time he was all the way inside of her, the pressure and the feeling of him inside of her was enough to push her over the edge into an amazing orgasm. Her body clenched around his cock and her hips kept moving to keep the pleasure pulsing through her body.

All the hesitancy in her demeanor had been banished by the spine-tingling orgasm, and she arched her back beneath him, fanning her hair back on the covers behind her before she reached up to tug him against her boldly.

"More." She begged, since he was still buried inside of her. "I need more."

He had a grin on his face and from the way he slammed himself into her in answer to her begging, she could feel just how much he had enjoyed watching her come undone for him. "All you want." He promised in a growl, then pulled back from her just enough to grasp her hips and brace his knees on the bed to get the leverage he wanted to piston himself into her. If she wanted more, he was absolutely going to give it to her.

Jessie enjoyed seeing his smile but she could barely focus on it as he drove into her with such force. She was being well and truly fucked, and she liked it a little too much. Her previous lover had been careful and uncertain in bed, but Gordon had no such uncertainty. She could already feel her body building up to another orgasm again. "This is . . . so . . . fucking . . . good . . ."

From the fervor in him, she could tell it had been a while since he'd been with anyone as well, but he was still fixed on making her come again as he groaned down against her. He leaned down to tease along her neck and her breasts as he plunged himself into her with abandon, licking and nipping at her skin as she felt him get closer to his own orgasm.

"Fuck, Jessie . . ." He groaned against her nipple and drove himself into her fully so he could feel the entirety of him buried into her, staving off his orgasm just a little longer. "You're even better than I imagined."

"You imagined?" She couldn't refrain from asking, even though they were both so close to orgasm, her for a second time. Jessie wrapped her legs around him as soon as the entirety of him was thrust inside of her, and his growl against her nipple sent chills down her spine. Her sensitive and pert nipples enjoyed every bit of attention, and the realization he had fantasized about her only turned her on more.

"Damn right I did." He could only hold himself off for so long, and he had no desire to try very hard in the first place. He gave her nipple one final lick and leaned back again with one hand on her shoulder for leverage as he drove himself into her. His shaggy brown hair fell wildly around his face, but it couldn't hide the need in his eyes. She could see it in his face when he passed the point of no return. That didn't stop the rest of him from going wild on her until she felt him reach his own climax, with a cry that knew nothing of restraint.

It was only moments later as his movements slowed that she climaxed again, simply because her body had built up the tension so much that any kind of movement sent her over the edge. Jessie's nails bit at his shoulders as the warmth of the orgasm rippled through her body, wringing every heartbeat from him before her body relaxed slowly.

"Mmmm." It was the only thing she could say for a long time, but it summed up exactly how she felt.

For his part, Gordon just laid on top of her trying to catch his breath, his lips moving over her breasts as they heaved beneath him. His hips continued to grind against hers even after his body spent itself, as if he already wanted her again the moment he'd been satisfied by her. The sweat they had between them was heated with his quick breaths against her chest, and his arms worked under her shoulders to hold her tightly. "Mmmm is right."

Jessie reached up to run her fingers lightly across his face, and she pushed some of his hair out of the way so she could see his eyes better. "Did you really mean what you said about imagining what it would be like to be with me?"

He nodded under her touch and leaned down to kiss the inner curve of her breasts without breaking eye contact. "I hacked your family's phones after that first meeting. Wasn't looking for anything like it at the time, but I ran across some of the pictures you sent the accountant." He grinned and moved his hips against hers one more time to savor the way she felt so exposed against him. "Been jerking off to you every time since."

Jessie was definitely stunned by that kind of revelation, but she loved it at the same time. Feeling sexy, or empowered, was a new feeling for her, but she was quickly finding out just how much she enjoyed both. "That is wildly inappropriate." Jessie chewed on her bottom lip for a moment before she pulled his face toward hers and her lips dove into his. "I don't usually do that, send photos. I don't like my body." But amazingly enough, it seemed that Gordon did.

He finally moved away from her with a groan, but fell on the sheets beside her with a deep sigh of satisfaction. He rested on his side to look at her, and continued to run one hand over every part of her he could reach. "I meant what I said back on the ground too. You are gorgeous, Jessie. You've got nothing to be ashamed of, and nothing not to like."

"If that were true, I wouldn't have ended up as someone's dirty little secret." His fingers exploring her skin gave her chills. "I'm definitely softer in places where I shouldn't be. But as long as you're okay with it, I'll try to be less obsessed about it." Jessie turned toward him as well, which only pressed her breasts together and pushed them closer to him. "I want to know more about you. Who you are, what you like, what you don't, sexually and otherwise. I'm a pleaser when it's people that matter."

That comment made him laugh, and he laid back on the bed with an arm around her shoulders to keep her and her exquisite breasts close. "I'm glad to know I fall into that category." He looked into her eyes and brushed some hair out of her face as she laid against him. "Who I am, what I like . . . you ask some seriously complicated questions." He teased her with a whispery kiss, but sighed afterward.

"Who I am . . . you're going to have to wait a little while for the answer to that. What I like is easier. More than anything, I like seeing people get what they want. So I want you to tell me what it is you want as often as possible, so that I can make sure you get it and watch when you do. Sexually and otherwise."

"What I want more than anything, I've already told you. I want a life on Eleusis with someone who wants me, and only me." Jessie felt like the conversation was a little too serious all too quickly, but maybe it needed to be serious. Everything around them was serious, people were trying to kill them, for crying out loud. "And you may or may not have just put a baby in me, but you don't want to tell me who you are?"

His eyes flicked down to her stomach as he grinned. "I want to. It's a matter of being certain I'm not overheard doing it." His eyes flicked up to the ceiling and the walls around them, as if he could look at the eyes and ears the Initiative planted into the residential units.

Jessie looked around in paranoia, since she hadn't even thought about the possibility of someone listening or watching. "Well someone just got a show, didn't they?" She actually crossed her arms over her chest, since she was feeling insecure again with the thought of being watched planted in her mind. "I think I had three orgasms. That's a record for me."

"Only three? Good thing I'm just getting warmed up." He pulled her into his body, the back of his fingers tracing a caress down her breast. "If they're gonna watch, they're gonna watch. I'm not going to let that possibility stop me from doing as I please."

* * * * *

Aiko fell asleep as she sat in the waiting room after everyone had been released from the meeting. Hours had passed. People had encouraged her to go back to her unit, but she had already been there to put her things away and to change into more comfortable clothing. Kazuo had hesitated to leave her, but he had his own match and Aiko was stubbornly staying put.

She had barely met the man before, but Aiko had Kazuo who would have sat vigil and Carl didn't have anyone but her. Her parents told her before she left that she shouldn't get too attached to her match, since it was a manipulated program, but she didn't care about that. They might all be dead if it weren't for the giant of a man. He deserved to have someone waiting for him to wake up.

Well into her first night on the station, (observable only by the fact that the lights in the hallway were dimmed to simulate nighttime conditions) a man stepped out whom she recognized, but only vaguely, as having been on her flight earlier that day. He was wearing a white coat and carrying a tablet in one arm.

"Ms. Tanaka? I'm Dr. Woods. They tell me you're here for Mr. Espinoza, is that right?"

Aiko nodded as she jumped up from her chair at the sound of someone calling out her name. She regretted it immediately, sore from sleeping in an awkward position, but she stretched herself out quickly before she approached the doctor. "Yes, I'm here waiting for him. He's my match. He's going to be okay, right? They said he was stable."

Dr. Woods smiled amiably and started walking back down the corridor, motioning for her to follow. "Carl is harder to kill than most, don't worry. He'll be fine. We'll tell him to take a few days off, he won't listen, and he'll still be in fine shape in a couple days. My boss has been treating him for years, and he's been through worse than this. I'm just surprised they didn't let you sit with him. There's a bed in the same room for you, just in case."

"Well, he doesn't really know me. We only met very briefly down on Earth before the accident. He doesn't know we're matched yet. They kept telling me to go to my unit and when he was well, he would join me there, but I didn't want to just leave him. He saved our lives down there." Aiko said the last bit softly, since she knew that maybe not everyone believed that Carl did as much as he did, but she did. "He was kind to me. It deserved kindness in return."

"That's very dutiful of you, on such short acquaintance." He smiled back at her, and held open a door for her to get back into the critical care section of the ward. "As his match, you're entitled to all medical records and histories, so just a quick update on what to expect from him at this point. He's still unconscious, but that's mostly because we've kept him sedated all night, to let his natural healing start to do some of the groundwork he needs."

"The knife he was stabbed with was a wicked piece of work, and it did a lot of damage to his kidney on the way in and out, not to mention leaving him bleeding like crazy. Dr. Finnegan did well to help him as much as she did. He had some touchy moments in surgery, but it's Carl. So he pulled through like a champ and he's resting now, still not quite conscious. But yes, he's stable and we expect a full recovery. Probably a whole lot sooner than you might expect."

"Access to his medical records? Histories? Just because I'm his match? Would he even want me to know that information?"

That question made Woods laugh, even though he knew she

meant it seriously. "I haven't known Carl myself for very long, but I've heard of him plenty of times. He's done security on just about every station in orbit. He once told an angry mob his payroll number and then dared any of them to use it. Crazy bastard repeated it twice for those who missed it the first time. So I doubt he'd have much of a problem with us giving out his current condition. And yes, just because you're his match. Carl was pretty excited about going into the matching program when the Initiative finally got together. I'm sure when he wakes up he'll be pissed that he missed the first meeting."

"Sounds like quite a character." Aiko said with a slight note of concern in her tone, since she didn't know what she would do with a man so rough. She had experience with men that were more like her brother; quiet, usually shy. Since she was usually fairly quiet herself, it drew her to the like-minded and similar personalities.

"What kind of medications are you giving him?" She could look at his file now that she had access, but she would rather hear it from a doctor. "I study plants and pharmaceuticals."

"Oh, excellent. Always happy to talk to an apothecary." He was clearly in an incredibly good mood in spite of their setting and the situation, but eventually Aiko remembered seeing him on the screen earlier with his wife. So he'd been matched with the woman he'd already been matched with. No wonder he was in a good mood.

"Carl's had a long history of medical treatment for us to go by, so don't be alarmed when you see some of the stuff we're giving him. He's been through pretty much everything ever created. Right now, we have him on Oritavancin and a new Morphine derivative I've been working on, in addition to a secondary shot of his usual daily cocktail. They had to stitch him in with some mesh on account of all the damage, but he's already more or less healed through that in just the past few hours."

Daily cocktail? Healing so quickly? Aiko nodded but she really did need to look into his file to see exactly what kind of man she had been matched with. This was the same man who was supposed to father her children, after all, according to the Initiative. Even though her parents told her to avoid that possibility as well. "He sounds like he's near indestructible."

"He's plenty destructible. He's just stubborn enough to get back up again every time."

Carl's was a private room, and the operating table took up the entire center of it. He seemed even more massive when he was lying down, somehow, his eyes closed and his entire body covered in what was obviously the largest size of gown they had. He looked like he was resting peacefully enough, as Woods had said, but Aiko could see the stab wounds in his side. They were open to the air, but not bleeding.

One machine was dropping medicine directly into the wound and another was hovering over it with some kind of beam that pulsed into the wound every few seconds to assist his body in healing. As he'd said, though, it was much closer to being healed than it should have been, for having happened only a few hours before. The wound was closing up from the inside out, almost visibly as she watched. In any event, it was close to the surface of his skin, and therefore nearly finished with stitching itself closed.

Aiko moved closer to him but carefully dodged all of the equipment so she wouldn't get in the way. She looked him over carefully before she grazed one of his hands lightly with her fingertips. "So you said I can stay here with him?"

"Of course. Big guy's all yours. He's not due for any rounds for a while, just once the stitching over here finishes up we'll be back in to check on him and do some final scans. Other than that, he just needs to rest up. Not that he actually will, I expect." He went to the side of the room and hit a latch along the wall that pulled down a mattress with sheets wrapped in plastic waiting to be used. "Best projections, knowing Carl, is that he'll be up and walking around by morning, pretty well back to normal in a day and a half or so. Any other questions?"

Aiko shook her head as she continued to stare down at Carl, but then she turned and looked back at the doctor once he started to move away. "Actually, yes. If I look over his file and think there might be better medications for him, can we discuss his options? I'm not a doctor, of course, but maybe he won't have to take so many synthetic medications if I can find other things."

"We don't get much by way of herbal remedies up here." He said with a patient smile and a shrug. "I mean, yes, we've got the entire hydroponics bay down on the outer ring, but our medications are typically shipped in from Prime and Seven. But yes, of course, I'd be happy to discuss any ideas you have. He has a fairly long medical history to sort through, though, you'll find. Treating him gets trickier every year. There aren't many things left that his body hasn't already been exposed to and learned how to resist. That's why we had to go to the Oritavancin for him this time, it's not something he's had before, so his body didn't know how to break it down yet."

She knew a smile like that, since most of the time people thought 1 the medications she developed were ridiculous, but her brother was living proof that she knew what she was doing. If it wasn't for all of her research, her brother never would have made it long enough to make it up to the space station in the first place.

Aiko just nodded. Being underestimated was sometimes better than being understood.

"Thank you for being willing to discuss his medications with me, should the situation arise." She looked away from the doctor and back at Carl, and instead of going to the open bed, she decided to grab a chair and pull it close to the side of his bed. "I don't have any more questions."

"Well, if you need anything, the call button's right there. We're not far away." He waved pleasantly as he made his exit, obviously already moving on to the next item on his to-do list before he even finished closing the door behind him.

Once Aiko was alone with Carl, she looked over him closer. It was insane how his body healed almost in front of her eyes. Even though he was unconscious, she grabbed one of his hands to hold onto it as she got comfortable in the chair with a tablet from her bag. There was a lot in her bag that she didn't want anyone to have access to, but the tablet was issued by the Initiative after the first meeting, so she wasn't worried about being on it as long as she kept her searches low-key.

She pulled up Carl's medical file to look over, but she was still exhausted from being up for nearly twenty-four hours with little sleep in the lobby. It wasn't long before sleep won out over everything else.

Before she was even fully conscious again upon waking up, she heard somebody groaning nearby in a voice that was so deep it shook the table she'd laid her head down on. The table shook a little and finished the process of waking her up, but by the time her eyes were open again, Carl had pushed himself up to a mostly-sitting position on the operating table.

He reached over to switch off the stitching machine that was still working on him with a grunt as if it had offended him. It had clearly done its work, from the first glance she got of his dark skin that had grown back over the stab wound. The drips of antibiotic fell past his side onto the table until he shut that machine off too and shook his head to clear the grogginess.

His hand was still holding hers as he tried to get up, but he didn't seem to realize it until he was finished with the machines and started looking around the room. "Um, hi." He said awkwardly as he looked down at her in confusion. "Are you . . . one of my doctors? Because that's some pretty intense bedside manner you've got going for you there."

Aiko laughed nervously as she pulled her hand away before she sat up and cleared her throat. "No, I'm not." She wasn't surprised that he didn't remember her from their brief encounter on Earth. He'd been stabbed and drugged since then. "I'm your match. Aiko Tanaka. They let me in here a little while ago. I was waiting for you to wake up."

"You're my . . ." he looked her over a second and then a third time at that announcement, his eyebrows nearly leaping off his face in the process. "I . . . holy shit! I've never been religious, but if you're my match, then I'm pretty sure there *is* a god, and he must really, *really* like me." He swung his legs off the side of the table to face her, moving a little gingerly at first but then apparently deciding that caution wasn't warranted as he adjusted his position to face her directly. "Carl Espinoza. But I'm guessing you already knew that."

She winced on his behalf as he moved around haphazardly and she eyed him carefully to make sure that he wasn't going to start bleeding again. "Interesting thing to say about someone you just met." Aiko sat up straighter in the chair next to him and she put her tablet back in her bag. "You might want to be a little more careful, you're supposed to rest."

"Are you sure you're not one of my doctors? Because that's what they always tell me." He looked down at the IV in his arm and reached up to stop the flow of fluids before yanking it out himself, with no regard for either the medications it was dispensing or the pain involved in doing so. "Oh wait, I remember you and your brother from St. Louis. So I'm guessing everybody made it up to orbit alright?"

"Mostly. I don't know what happened to the other guard, um, Johnson was her last name." Aiko frowned at the fact that he yanked the IV out of his arm, so she got up quickly to retrieve some gauze and a bandage to stop the bleeding. She didn't even ask permission to bandage him up, she just went to the edge of his bed and attended to the puncture wound the IV left behind. "Please be a little more careful."

He was taken aback by her taking care of him so immediately, but he stayed still to let her do her work, staring at her the entire time. "Sorry. Old habits. I've actually never been able to stand needles." He watched her closely as she worked on him and nodded to her once she was finished. "Thank you. You didn't have to do that. Or, you know, come and sit with me for . . . however long you were here." He looked himself over and gave her a tentative smile as he tugged at the hospital gown briefly. "Also not exactly the first impression I really wanted to make on my match."

She shrugged, since the current state of his dress didn't really bother her after what he'd done for the entire ship. "You're a hero. You risked your life to protect a bunch of strangers from Earth. We probably wouldn't have made it up here if you hadn't jumped in when you did. That's quite a first impression." She gave him a small smile and looked around for a glass of water or something, but she didn't see anything. "Are you hungry? Thirsty? I can get you something."

"Let's get something on the way out. Hospital food always ends up tasting like sanitizer." He moved to get off the bed, moving slowly for her benefit. He put a hand over the spot where he'd been stabbed, which was obviously still a little sore, but nothing started bleeding again and the rest of him seemed to be alright as he stretched. Standing up, even in a hospital gown, he dominated the room, though he didn't seem to know it. "You wouldn't happen to know where they put my clothes, would you?"

"You bled through most of what you were wearing." She grabbed a bag she brought from their unit and held it out to him. "They delivered our things to our unit. I put some clean clothes in here for you. I intended to drop it off because I didn't think they would let me stay, but then I stayed in the lobby and now here . . ."

She shook her head, since she was repeating herself. "Do you need some help?" Aiko knew it sounded ridiculous she was offering to help the giant man with getting dressed, but she truly was concerned that he was going to bust open a wound. "I don't want them to change their mind about releasing you if you hurt yourself getting dressed."

He looked confused at first, but took the clothes from her with an amused smile. "They know better than to change their minds about releasing me, don't worry. Thank you, though." He clearly didn't fit her usual type of shy, since he sifted through the clothes and started pulling on the boxers right in front of her. The fact that he was still wearing the oddly-shaped hospital gown hid most of him from view but Aiko did get the occasional flash of the large man underneath. Once he had his boxers on, he did away with the hospital gown entirely, and she got her first good look at the man she'd been matched with.

When Dr. Woods had mentioned Carl's previous hospitalizations, the man had sounded both reckless and dangerous, but looking him over was an entirely different testament to both possibilities. Most of his past wounds had been gunshots, that much was obvious at a glance. He had four in one arm alone, at least six in some part of his shoulders and chest, three in the stomach and a few in each leg. The stab wound he had suffered the day before had been stitched up perfectly, leaving the slightest hairline scar that she could barely notice.

Next to many of the bullet scars, there were tattoos in small black print, almost invisible against the perfect darkness of his skin. Other than those small marks, the only significant tattoo he had anywhere to be seen had been done in white ink along one of his shoulders, a pattern that looked like a fire spiralling out from a central point.

Beneath the scars and the tattoos, the man was built like a tank. He wasn't just tall, everything about him was huge, from the size of his arms to the breadth of his shoulders and the torso that looked like it could have been carved out of marble by the ancient world.

He saw her looking him over once the hospital gown was off, so he moved slower, pulling on his jeans, letting her look her fill. "The first few times I needed looking after, they tried to do the whole song and dance. 'Stay in bed, take your meds, watch reruns, just sleep.' Fuck that."

He caught himself and looked back up at her quickly. "Sorry about the language if you're sensitive about that kind of shit. Stuff." He censored again quickly, then returned to getting his pants up over his waist. "I just don't stay still. They know that by now. If I really needed to stay in bed any longer than I already have, they would've kept me sedated."

Aiko tried not to embarrass herself by gawking at the rest of him any more than a few glimpses here and there. She gave him a reassuring smile as soon as he started talking again. "I'm tougher than I look, even though I realize saying that to a man who has survived multiple bullet wounds is pretty worthless. Just be yourself. Don't censor yourself for me. But also don't be crazy reckless? It would be unfortunate if our match was short-lived because you're so restless."

"I promise you, walking out of a hospital will be the craziest thing I do today. Unless there are extenuating circumstances that call for added crazy. Then I might top it." He gave her a tentative smile and pulled his boots on while disregarding his shirt. "So you're . . . I remember something with plants and drugs. It's a little fuzzy. Mostly I was just wondering how two Japanese siblings ended up in St. Louis, of all places."

"Well, my parents are actually from Japan, but my father is a botanist and wanted to work on Eleusis research. They have a big facility in St. Louis, so he and my mother moved there when I was about three." She could see him struggling with the bending over part of getting his boots on, so she went and knelt in front of him to help him with tying them up.

"Kazuo, my brother, was five. My mother stayed home and raised us. I have three younger siblings, but I'm the only one who turned into a botanist. My mother teaches Japanese at an extended-learning school in St. Louis." Universities didn't exist anymore, there weren't the people or the staff (or, usually, the time) for it, but in some of the bigger cities, there were 'extended learning' schools. It was as close to post high-school education as anyone could get on Earth.

"Five of you, wow. That's a lotta Tanaka." He clearly wasn't accustomed to getting help with his shoes, but he gave her a grateful smile once he could get back on his feet. The world felt like a slightly better place the more he got away from his hospital appearance. "They sound pretty great. Mom, Dad, siblings, the whole bit. I hope I get to meet them someday."

He took the shirt she'd found for him and pulled it on over his head, leaving it to hang loose around the bulk of his torso. The garment would have drowned at least two of Aiko without a trace. "You don't have to worry about anything like that with me. Never had parents or siblings, unless you count fosters, which I don't."

"I got dropped off at a clinical wing on Twelve when I was about a week old. They tried to track down my parents, genetic testing and profiling, found out they had their profiles burned out of the system a week before I was born, nobody could get any more information on them. Best guess is they were station-hoppers who wouldn't want their information in the system and couldn't be bothered to take care of a kid." He shrugged as he said it, though, and didn't sound too upset about the circumstances he was describing. "So yeah, no need to worry about meeting my family. One less thing."

That sounded a little suspicious to Aiko, but she didn't say anything about it out loud. "I would have been glad to meet whoever you wanted me to." She couldn't imagine not having family, even if her parents were extremely controlling. Her parents had exceptionally high expectations, but Aiko did her best to live up to every single one. "It's not unusual to have big families on Earth. I don't even think about it, most of the time." She went back to pick up her bag and she slung it carefully over her shoulder, since she cared about most of the contents. "Are you sure they're going to let you leave? You just woke up."

"They'll let me leave." He tossed the hospital robe on the bed and looked around the room for anything else of his that might have been left, then headed out into the hall with her, opening the door for her in the process.

He smiled when he saw Mercury, of all people, at the far end of the hall reviewing someone's chart on the screens in front of her, and he headed her direction even though he didn't know who he had been assigned to. "Good morning, Doctor. Think you could take care of my discharge?"

Mercury looked him up and down with narrowed eyes as she thought about how to respond. "You know, Orion asked me to check on you several times. I really don't think you should leave, but I know it's unlikely that I can stop you." She sighed as she pulled up his chart on her tablet. "If you leave, are you going to promise me that you'll take it easy?"

"That depends on your definition of easy." He couldn't help himself when it came to doctors, and his grin was everything ornery. "I'm glad Orion didn't have to take any of the heat off those idiots. Did we end up getting any other intel on them?" He looked back and forth between Mercury and Aiko for an answer, since he had just assumed everyone made it up to orbit safely after the altercation with the crazy in the parking lot.

"I haven't heard anything about intel." Mercury said softly as she looked between Aiko and Carl, but it was clear that she was distracted by something. Carl didn't know what had happened, and she didn't want to talk about it. "You might want to talk to Orion about everything, he knows more about it than I do."

"I'll do that." He could see that all wasn't well with her at the moment but he wasn't going to bother her. "I'm sorry, Aiko, this is Mercury, my best friend's wife. Her husband is Orion, you probably saw him back on the ground. He was the one who kept banging his head on the stratosphere everywhere he went. Tall guy, light brown coloring."

Aiko was quiet as she nodded but her glance over at Mercury was sympathetic. "I remember." She looked up at Carl and while she wanted to say something to him, she didn't want to say it in front of the Doctor. "I'll take good care of him, Dr. Finnegan. I'll make sure he takes it easy."

He waited on Mercury's reluctant nod, then smiled and patted her on the shoulder on his way by. "Don't work too hard, Doc. And thanks for patching me up down there. I appreciate the assist in staying alive."

Mercury nodded and looked Carl over once more. "Get some rest, Carl. If you need anything, let me know." She gave him a small smile and then went back to work, clearly seeking some kind of distraction.

When Aiko and Carl moved far enough away from the doctor, Aiko touched his arm lightly to get his attention. "She was matched with someone else." Aiko glanced back, but the doctor had already disappeared, off to do something else. "And the man she was matched with is also already married. Logan Bickford, from Earth."

"What the fuck?!?" He yelled loudly at that, making a few people nearby jump out of their skins with the violence of his reaction. He waved a half-hearted apology at a few of them and brought his tone down slightly as he kept walking with Aiko. "What kind of bullshit is that? She just got matched to Orion a month ago! Why would it . . . that makes no damn sense. I thought they weren't eligible to be re-matched if they were already matched with somebody from the program?"

"I don't know." Aiko replied softly, since she hadn't stayed around to see any fireworks as soon as everyone was dismissed. She wanted to get to her unit and check on him, even though he had been unconscious. "Most of the married couples, even though there weren't many, were kept together. I don't know why they split them up. It was rough to watch."

"God, Orion's gotta be a mess." He shook his head as he tried to wrap his mind around it. "I just went to their wedding. Kind of wedding I actually like going to. Kind where they actually look like they like each other. World doesn't see enough of those." He reached up to rub at his forehead and scratch his fingers through the short hair against his scalp. "So who'd they end up pairing Orion with, then? Fitch? That would be the only thing I can think of that would make less sense."

"No, Kameron Fitch was matched with my brother, actually." Aiko looked down at his free hand between them and thought about holding his hand, because it had felt nice to do so, but decided against it. "Orion was matched with Logan's wife. They swapped the two couples."

"Well, I hope your brother has better luck with Kam than my imagination thinks he will." He looked down at her incredulously, but his initial explosion had clearly been the only one he needed to get out of his system. He rubbed at his eyes instead. "That just doesn't make any damn sense. I also can't see him or Mercury going along with it. That's so fucked up." He turned his attention back to her, though, as she led him down a corridor toward their unit, since she apparently knew her way around already. "I'm not married, for the record. Never have been. Not even a serious girlfriend for the past . . . what is it, two years and change?"

"Not interested or you just traveled that much? Even if you were, I would be understanding. In fact, my parents told me not to get too attached to anyone. They don't believe in the matching program, but I think that it has enough data to make reasonable matches. It's the undeniable tampering that really bothers me. I don't find it convincing that a computer broke up two marriages and swapped the spouses. That's too coincidental."

"Why would they do something like that, though?" He kept his voice down as they talked about it, even though he couldn't imagine they were the only ones having the conversation if the mis-match had happened in front of the entire Initiative. "What's wrong with just leaving two marriages together if they're obviously happy about it? Even if there was some kind of fertility problem like they kept yapping about in the intros over and over, who the fuck cares? There's thousands of us and we can get back and forth to Eleusis in two years round trip now. What does it matter who's fertilizing who?"

Aiko looked down at the floor as they slowly made their way toward their shared unit, and she kept one of her hands on the strap of her bag. "Why do people do anything? Why do doctors do experimental trials, why do medications go through several rounds of testing, why do farmers cross-breed different kinds of cows or crops? Humankind has always wanted something bigger, better, stronger, prettier, tastier, the list goes on. If you have a group of some of the strongest and brightest people on Earth and in space in an experimental program, why not push them to the limit?" Aiko whispered the entire thing to Carl, since she was aware they were probably being monitored though it was hard to predict how much.

He caught her implication and her tone, and he was quiet for several twists and turns as he followed her lead through the corridors.

"I'm nobody's lab rat." He finally said in a low rumble, then reached out with one hand to take hers, even though hers nearly disappeared in his grip. "And neither are you. Somebody puts me in a maze to find some cheese, they'd best be sure the maze is fucking bulletproof. Whole reason I volunteered for this project is to help keep people from manipulating and abusing each other on another world. If somebody's already fucking with us and my friends, we need to stop that shit before it even gets started."

Aiko didn't say anything else until they arrived at their unit, and she scanned her hand to open the door. She took off her shoes before she stepped inside, and put them on a mat by the door. Clearly, even in her rush, she had made the place a little more homey. There were plants anchored in the small windows. There were a few small paintings on the walls, and her things were on her side of the bed except for the bag she had over her shoulder. He hadn't brought many things with him, but his other clothes and suits were already hanging in a small closet.

"I have a question for you." She looked over at him once before she went to put her bag down on the table in their small eating area. "Do you even know what is in the medications they give you?"

He gave her a startled look, since that had been far from the first question he had expected from her, but he leaned back against the door to take off his shoes. He followed her lead in the home she had already started for them. "I take it one of the doctors gave you the rundown on my heart condition?" He got his shoes off with some effort and set them next to hers on the mat. "Honestly, I used to ask, but it's changed so many times I stopped trying. I've been taking them since I was a baby. Orphanage told me when I was a kid they thought that might be the reason I got left. Heart works too hard, lungs work too hard, nervous system is always too high-strung. I was just glad when I turned ten and they stopped having to give it to me in an injection every day. Stuff tastes terrible, but it's better than getting stabbed every morning."

Aiko was clearly distressed by the idea of him guzzling down even half the things that she'd seen on his file before she had fallen asleep looking it over. She watched him quietly before retrieving a small bottle of water for him from the unit fridge. Without saying anything, she took his hand and led him to a chair to sit down, even if clearly she couldn't force him to do so if he was disinclined. "I'm going to look over what they're giving you, and why. I'll see what I can do. Maybe I can figure out a better solution."

He sat where she led him, but he didn't let go of her hand afterward. There was a brief flicker of lingering pain when he actually sat down, but only when he had to bend or readjust himself. Otherwise, he looked her in the eye with a flicker of suspicion.

"I'm trying to think of a better way to ask this, but there really isn't one, so I'm just gonna ask. Why do you care? You don't know me. I mean, I get the whole 'grateful for kicking somebody else's ass' thing, I do, but for that, you could've just sent a card. All this? Waiting up for me at the hospital, making this place more like a home than any place I've ever even lived when you've been here all of ten seconds, looking after me, why do you care what happens to me? Especially if the match that put you with me is bullshit?"

"I didn't say that the matching program was complete . . . bullshit." Clearly she wasn't someone who cursed very often. "Just that I thought it could be manipulated." Aiko sighed as she looked down at his hand, where she could see a few scars here and there on his dark skin.

"Do you care what happens to me? You don't know me either. If someone came in here and offered you a one-way jump to all the riches in the world in exchange for me, would you stop them? Or would you let them do whatever they wanted?" Aiko had done as much research as she could on Carl as soon as they were matched, even before she knew she had been given access to his file. He had been a hero more than once. Often.

He narrowed his eyes in a sarcastic glare. "No, because I'm not a complete piece of shit. But there's a difference between not being willing to sell somebody out and wanting to take care of somebody."

"Despite what my parents told me before I left, I want to make my match work." Aiko admitted as she pulled the other chair around, though it meant letting go of his hand. "I want to believe that we were put together because we could be good together, even if I know there's a chance that isn't the truth. And I like taking care of people, especially good people who deserve it." She wasn't good about meeting people's eyes, but when she met his again, he could see that hers were an unnatural hue, a light lilac color, instead of a blue or grey. She tucked back a few loose strands of her dark hair behind her ear. "So is it okay with you if I care, even if you don't think I should?"

He watched her after she asked the question, looking back and forth between her eyes with wheels turning behind his own. She had seen in his file that whatever else Carl had been given, a superior intellect was not among his gifts, with terrible marks in any kind of education that wasn't physical. But he wasn't a dumb brute either, and she could feel him looking for any kind of lie behind what she was saying. The inspection only lasted a few moments, but felt much longer.

"I don't mind if you care." He reached over to take her hand again, and pulled her out of the chair she had pulled close, into his lap, drawing her in against him on the side that hadn't been stabbed the day before. "So long as you don't mind if I do."

Aiko was immediately nervous about bumping an injury, and her cheeks flushed when he pulled her into his lap, but she didn't try to get away. She didn't think he would trap her, but she was surprised that he wanted to pull her close. "You are . . . incredibly strong." She commented as one of his arms wrapped around her loosely. Aiko could feel the muscles of his arms easily through her clothes, rippling sinews of pure power. "I feel even smaller than I normally do."

"Well, this is what I get for working out down on the outer rim of the station at one and a quarter gravity." He laughed once and ran his hand up and down her back as he held her. She was a small woman, but especially at that kind of proximity, it was obvious that she was no child. "I can make sure to stay sitting down or laying down whenever we're here, if that would help. Don't want you to bust your neck looking up at me all the time." He made the joke tentatively, but moved his fingers up her spine to the back of her neck, massaging gently as if to make amends for his height.

She chuckled in amusement and shook her head. "I don't want you to do anything to make yourself uncomfortable just to accommodate me. Sitting down all of the time would get incredibly boring." Aiko was surprised again by his tender touch on the back of her neck, and her cheeks remained flushed as he explored her. "I hope you don't find us a disappointing match. Especially because I'm sure I sound like a crazy conspiracy theorist."

"You don't sound crazy. You sound like you've got a lot more sense than I do, jumping into this thing without looking or thinking twice." He shook his head with mixed emotion and looked her over again, never one to hide his interest in anyone or anything. "And hell no, you are in no way disappointing to me. You're obviously smarter than I'm ever likely to keep up with, and you're a damn sight more gorgeous than I'm ever gonna deserve. Only thing I'm disappointed about is that I've been unconscious for the first day of our match. Pretty rude of me, really."

Aiko's shoulders relaxed a little. "You're a flirt if I ever met one." She leaned in and gave him a chaste kiss on the cheek, since he still had her in his lap. She knew she wasn't unfortunate-looking, but she was thin and small, though at least she wasn't flat-chested and she had a little bit of a backside. She looked every part a woman. "Are you hungry? We didn't stop anywhere to get anything to eat."

"I am. But we can get something from the catering slot." He said without letting go of her. He looked her in the eye for another moment, then leaned in to return the chaste kiss she'd given him, his arms tightening around her in the process.

"I want our match to work too, Aiko." He did his best to replicate the way she'd said her own name, though he had clearly never studied Japanese, and his vowels were going to take some work. "I've been saying for the past year coming up to this thing that I'm looking forward to being matched with somebody instead of being left to my own idiot devices to figure things out on my own and get myself killed in the process. If we're on the same page in wanting to make this whole Eleusis thing happen for the world, then whatever it is you need me to do to make this work, I can work on. Can't promise I'll be much good at this whole match thing, but I can learn."

"All relationships start out rocky, there's a learning curve for everyone." She assured him, since she didn't want him to think that he was inadequate. Aiko was lucky to be matched with someone who was as loyal and kind as she felt Carl was, from everything that she could find about him. "I want someone who will be faithful, someone who can and will protect me, and someone who is a good man with a good heart." Aiko smiled brighter before she caressed the side of his face lightly with her fingertips. "What do you want?"

There was more hesitation in Carl's eyes as he thought about the question, not because he was uncertain of the answer, but because he was uncertain about how honest to be with her. Eventually, he seemed to decide on full disclosure, since his dark eyes looked like they were unaccustomed to handling a lie.

"Somebody to call home. Somebody who'll call me on my bullshit when I get things wrong, which is frequently. Somebody who doesn't start trouble for no reason. Somebody who's gonna be happy to see me at the end of the day." His hands moved over her waist as he spoke, leaving caresses over the comfortable clothing she'd worn down to the hospital to wait on him without getting too frisky for the time being. "Somebody who isn't scared of me. I've had about enough of having that effect on people."

Aiko nodded. "Good to know." She smiled before she kissed his lips very lightly, almost too lightly, but she was still nervous. They were strangers, after all, but she did want to jump into it with both feet. Carl was someone she hoped she could fully trust, and trust was something that needed to be built, starting somewhere. "I don't usually start trouble, and I'm already happy to see you, alive and healing."

"I'll be back to fully okay within another day or so, unless somebody else tries to stab me in the meantime. I'll try not to piss you off quite that quickly." He smiled under the kiss, and pulled her back in for another, fingers sliding along her back as he held her, though he didn't push for anything more than that. "Let's go see what kind of food we can get out of the establishment, shall we? I'm starving, but the longer you stay this close, the less I'm gonna care about being wounded." He kissed her again after he said so, making no motion to get up in spite of what he'd said.

She caressed his cheek again but slid off of his lap, since she was uncertain about tempting anything at the moment. "I care about you being wounded, don't make yourself worse. Let's eat."

3

When Anna woke, she found Logan was already awake, lying beside her, his eyes open and flicking from place to place as if something was darting around their ceiling. Through half-open eyes, she could see that there was, in fact, a holographic projection of the station layout up on the ceiling, which Logan was manipulating with the arm and hand that wasn't presently occupied holding onto her as she slept.

He would zoom in on one section, zoom back out, zoom in again, examining different sections of the station one by one as if he was looking for something. His gestures were slow and smooth, obviously doing everything he could not to disturb her.

Anna's first reaction upon waking was to scoot closer to Logan's side so there was no space between her body and his. After that, though, she pressed her lips to the side of his neck and nibbled at his skin. They were both naked underneath the sheets, and she liked tasting him first thing in the morning. If morning ever meant anything in space. "What are you doing, babe?"

"Checking out what they do and don't want us looking at in terms of the station design." His hand moved down over her back to press her body against him, but he zoomed the hologram out completely until it was just a spinning star against their ceiling. "Interesting place. Not as interesting as you naked next to me, though. I'd much rather study that."

"Mmmm. I'd much rather you study that, too." She replied with a sleepy grin before she moved just enough so she was kissing his lips instead of his neck. "I don't know if it's possible for us to break out of here." She said after the kiss broke, but she was a little worried about ruining the moment. "And if it is, we can't do it alone."

"I'm figuring that out, yeah." He glanced back up at the suspended image and waved it away. He was worried the computers would be too advanced in space for him to use, but really, it seemed like they were just sensitive. He could get used to that.

Once it was off, he turned toward her to return her sleepy kisses. They had made a run of the place the night before, but if Logan knew anything, it was that he would never get enough of his wife. "You sleep alright? I know it's low gravity, but you would think they could at least get beds right. Thing feels like a rock."

"I slept on you, mostly, so I didn't even notice." She laughed softly and continued one slow kiss after another. "You're the best bed there is. The best ride too." Anna teased. It was easier to believe nothing was wrong in their own little world.

At least until both of their fancy new communicators went off simultaneously.

"I dreamed about breaking it." She growled and glared at her communicator, across the room on the floor but unbroken. "But then they would just give me another one." Anna held tighter to Logan as if someone was going to show up and snatch him away. "Computer, read the incoming alert." She snapped at no one.

The incoming message for Anna Bickford and Logan Bickford is the same. Please report to the medical wing for your daily treatment. You are due within the hour. End of message.

Anna buried her face against Logan's chest. "I was hoping we could just lock ourselves in here."

He took a deep breath to keep himself from growling at the programmatically-pleasant tone of the computer. It wasn't the machine's fault. "We can, for another forty-five minutes or so, it sounds like." He shook his head and rolled them to her side so he could rest his face against her breasts. "We're going to have to pick our battles when it comes to being disobedient up here. Find out slowly what happens when we go against the grain."

"I don't think we should start with the treatments. We do kind of need those to keep from dying." His stubble against her breasts made her groan as he scraped his chin along her sensitive skin. "Don't do that. It drives me crazy."

"It drives you crazy so you say don't? Right, like that's gonna stop me." He nuzzled even further as he pushed her onto her back. The bed was hard, but it was still warm from them sleeping in it together, and he planned to enjoy that warmth for as long as possible before returning to the cold of the rest of the station.

After enjoying each other thoroughly, Anna was breathless beneath him, and she laughed softly. "God, I love having sex with you. You are the best lover."

There was no one on Earth or in Orbit who didn't enjoy hearing something like that, and Logan was no exception. One of her legs was still up over his shoulder, and he turned his stubbled cheek to kiss along the inside of her ankle as he worked on recovering his breath. "I keep wondering when I'm gonna get to the bottom of your bag of tricks in bed. I'm starting to think that's just never gonna happen. That'd be fine with me too."

"Gotta keep you guessing, Sexy." She replied breathily as a chill ran down her spine from his teasing stubble.

Report to the medical wing within the next twenty minutes. The computer reminded.

Anna tossed a pillow at the ceiling.

"Fucking computer." She growled, since she didn't want to go. "We can come right back here after, right?"

Negative. The computer's voice continued, since it seemed to think she was still talking to it instead of Logan. *The remaining shuttles belonging to the Initiative will arrive in one hour and thirty-nine minutes. All able members of the Initiative have been requested to attend to greet the newcomers.*

"Requested." Logan confirmed. "So we can decline this request?"

The computer hesitated at that, since it hadn't expected to be contradicted. *Yes.*

"Then we decline to attend. In the future, when addressing either Anna or me, you will make it clear which meetings have been labeled compulsory and which have not been given negative consequences for attending. Is that clear?"

Directive saved. Attendance at the greeting of the final shuttles is not compulsory. Initial treatments for the Crisis Virus are compulsory.

"Well, I'm glad we got that straightened out." Logan went back to lie down next to Anna with a sigh, running his hands back through his hair. "Better go shower off if you're going to, baby. Wouldn't want to keep our 'compulsory' waiting."

Anna pouted but gave him a wickedly scandalous kiss before she climbed over him to get out of the bed. "Come with me?"

"Didn't I just do that?" He grinned and slapped her ass to get her moving. "Go on, get it warm for me. I'll break our clothes out of our bags and be in there in a minute."

Anna squealed excitedly after he smacked her backside, rushing for the bathroom. Anything for more fun with Logan.

They were nearly late for their appointments. They moved as quickly as they could through the corridors, bouncing like gazelles through the hallways until they arrived at the medical wing. Their names were checked in as soon as they walked in the door, which was a little disconcerting, but Anna was called first and she hurried away to get her treatment.

Logan was called back just a few minutes later, but he noticed that a few people who came in after him were taken before him, which he thought was a little strange. Even so, when his name lit up, he followed the indicator lights like an obedient sheep until he headed into the relevant room where Doctor . . .

Of course. Those were the first two words that went through his mind as he got in the door and shut it behind him. Of course he and Anna would be required to get their treatments when she was on duty. "Good morning, Doctor." Logan said in the most formal tone he could manage. "How are you?"

A chill ran through Mercury as she heard *his* voice. She didn't even have to look at her tablet to know what chart would show up next. "Mr. Bickford. Good morning." She barely glanced at him before she started punching information into his chart so she could get his CV treatment. "I've been better, but I'm sure you can agree with that sentiment."

"I can." He agreed with an equally formal nod, glancing around the room to look anywhere but at her. "Do you need me sitting, standing, lying down? Is there a preference?"

"However you're most comfortable." She waited for the vial and sighed when there seemed to be a delay. "Do you have any questions? About the treatment, I mean."

"It's compulsory and necessary. No questions I have would alter that." He was wearing short sleeves in the first place, but he reached up to shove his sleeve farther up onto his shoulder as they waited.

"It's interesting how it works, really." Mercury didn't know why she felt it was necessary to fill the silence, but she couldn't just sit there quietly with this man in the room. "The treatment is a mixture of medications that boost your immune system and attack the virus directly. After a month of daily treatments, the CV is gone. I'm trying to find a way to make it permanent so that it can be used as a cure, but I need a lot more time, data, and research to break that code. It's not easy."

He looked at her for the first time as she detailed the process, but he held his silence while he considered what she'd said. It seemed almost like he was determined not to engage even in casual conversation, but he did finally speak.

"You're the first person I've met who might be able to answer this question, actually. My physician back in the Midwest was never able to find a satisfactory answer." He looked down at his own arm, considering the question, since it meant he could look somewhere other than at her. Anna hadn't been wrong about how gorgeous the doctor was. She was beautiful, objectively and subjectively flawless in every way. He'd never seen her like on Earth, and didn't imagine he ever would have.

"It's my understanding that human immune response is supposed to be something like four thousand percent stronger in the descendents of Crisis survivors, since they were the only ones who could survive the initial outbreak. I remember learning in school that amplifying immune response even further is often fatal. So then why does the CV treatment amplify what's already working harder than it should for our species?"

"The treatment is very specific in the way that it works against CV. You're right, if it boosted your immune system generally, it could be very bad, but since the immune booster is mixed with the CV-targeted medication, it really only boosts your immunity by directing it toward destroying the CV. That's why a lot of people feel tired after treatment, because all of your antibodies are focused on destroying something that has been present since conception." She grabbed the vial as soon as it showed up, and slowly pulled the liquid into a syringe.

"The treatment is partially a virus that has been manipulated and perfected to target and destroy CV in the body, but it's a short-lived virus if it's not boosted by your immune system. It becomes completely worthless on Earth because of the abundant presence of CV, so even once destroyed, people become reinfected. CV has endless, mutating strains, much like influenza or covid. The anti-virus is deadly to CV but short-lived, so it has to be intensely monitored during treatment."

She tapped the syringe and cleaned off his arm before she briefly met his eyes and continued her medical explanation and administration. The treatment included large needles and they definitely weren't painless. "I've conducted simulated trials to manipulate the anti-virus, but it's a fickle thing. It dies too easily or it mutates quickly into something dangerous or something worthless. I don't even know how they discovered it in the first place, to be honest with you."

"Must have been a miracle." His voice dripped with cynicism and he didn't watch her work since doing so put her squarely in his field of vision, which was something he intended to avoid. "I thought you were an obstetrician, not a virologist?"

"I am." She finished his first treatment and held the gauze in place to make sure the bleeding stopped. "You have to stay here for fifteen minutes after each treatment for the first week so I can monitor your vitals. Sometimes recipients have troubling reactions." Mercury looked him over without meeting his gaze, but she checked his pupils as she monitored him.

"Part of my research is focused on babies who are born with CV immunity. I want to study them more so that maybe I can find a way to help more babies, but it's hard to find CV-immune people who live past childhood. In fact, I haven't found any. They are incredibly rare, and they all die. It's a little disturbing, really. But I'm going to figure out the answer. Somehow."

That sounded incredibly suspicious to Logan, and it almost distracted him from the fact that he was going to be medically detained every day, each time undoubtedly with the woman he least wanted to spend time with in the universe. He went across the room to a chair to sit down and get comfortable if he had to wait it out. "How do they die? Immune over-response?"

"Mostly from commonplace accidents." She tapped through her tablet and and walked over to him, even though she was sure that he had walked away to avoid her. Mercury didn't want to spend time with him either, but her nerves kept her talking. Mercury handed him her tablet with her research pulled up. "This table has all the data I've collected about babies that tested CV-immune at birth. As you can see, there aren't many. But their cause of death is listed there too." Once she handed him the tablet, she backed away to give him his desired space.

He took his time looking over the data trying to see any kind of pattern but he eventually looked back up in confusion. "Fifteen percent of these are Earth-births, at best. You don't have data collected on Earth pregnancies? I thought we were all tested at birth for susceptibility as well."

"I was told that you were, but that doctors have become somewhat unreliable on Earth to keep this kind of information. There are bigger issues that they care about on a daily basis."

Mercury shrugged, since she didn't know if she believed that or not. "I was told that one doctor alone might cover a large area or support a large population on a daily basis. It doesn't give them much opportunity to keep diligent records."

"That much is true." Logan said absently as his eyes scanned the data, rearranging it a few different ways to try and get a good visual of it or pick out a pattern, if there even was one. "My family physician back home lived an hour and a half away. She told me once that she had case files on six hundred people, from up to about four hours away from her home. She was angry at the time, so she might have been exaggerating, but not by much."

"Wow. Six hundred people?" Mercury couldn't imagine having that many active patients at once, and it was hard to imagine how busy she would be if she had that many people depending on her. "You need more doctors on Earth." Mercury kept her distance until she absolutely had to check his vitals again, and she was careful about listening to his pulse and breathing, which seemed normal, if a little quickened. Mercury bent down in front of him so she could check his pupils. "Are you feeling warm? Your pulse is a little quick. It's normal, but I just need to know how you're feeling."

"Slightly warmer than usual, I would say, but I've had that since I got on board the shuttle. Even if this place is as big as a city, I'm still aware that I'm spinning in a metal box." He shrugged slightly, but couldn't keep his eyes from reacting out of long-ingrained habit and looking down her blouse as she bent in front of him. From what little he knew of the doctor, he imagined she had no idea she was even exposing herself, so he didn't take it as some kind of intentional tease, but it was a tease nonetheless.

"I'll get you some water." She finished checking his pupils and moved away to the same dispensing slot. Mercury gave him a polite smile when she handed him the cup. "Halfway there, and then you can go on your way." She took her tablet back and went to his chart to enter his vitals.

He stared into the cup for what seemed like a small, awkward eternity after he downed the contents, before he spoke again. "I have a suggestion for your research." He said quietly. "Look into the histories of the direct blood relatives of the immune children you're researching. Siblings and cousins especially. The genes that made them immune are in their family somewhere. If they resurface, there will have to be some kind of pattern that could help isolate them."

Mercury considered his suggestion silently at first and then nodded, since she was appreciative of any ideas that might help her research. "I haven't done that. Thank you, I'll make a note to look into it."

With that suggestion passed on, Logan lapsed back into silence for what felt like the longest five minutes of his entire life. He felt fine, aside from a slight headache that felt like it was building from his shoulders toward the crown of his head, but he didn't say anything to Mercury about it. If the symptoms of the treatment would pass, he would just wait it out.

When he saw that fourteen minutes of his observation time had elapsed, he got up and headed toward the door, careful of his steps just to make sure he didn't suddenly feel dizzy or nauseous. He had slight pangs of both, including fatigue that she had warned about, but he stood firm near the door before turning to face her. "You and your husband seem like good and decent people. That's more rare than most people admit. I think under different circumstances, the four of us could have been friends."

Mercury nodded in quiet agreement before she picked up a small packet from a table nearby, which looked like a piece of clear plastic with a few pills inside. "For your nausea and dizziness. The sleepy feeling will go away with a nap." She looked into his eyes briefly, for almost the first time during the appointment.

"You know, maybe that's the solution to all of this. Maybe we should just try to be friends, and that will appease them into thinking that we're not resisting. I have a feeling if we resist even speaking to each other, situations like this will just keep happening." Clearly Mercury was also under the impression that being assigned as his doctor was no coincidence. "Talking to each other isn't terrible. And you gave me a suggestion for my research."

Logan nodded, sticking the pills in his pocket so he could pretend he was going to take them later. "We'll see if that's possible. For now, with other recruits coming in, I think they should have bigger things to worry about."

She nodded again and stepped past him to open the door so he could leave. "Have a nice day, Mr. Bickford."

"And you, Doctor." He didn't smile on the way out the door, and he even managed to hold his breath until he got around the corner to let out the sigh he'd been bottling up. Anna was nowhere in sight, but he was determined to wait.

After her treatment, Anna was led by her doctor to another room where she was told to wait, since an official wanted to speak with her. She felt restless and uneasy as she sat in a small room by herself, but she twirled around in a chair as she waited for someone to show up. She spent most of the time brainstorming less and less-polite ways of telling someone to fuck off so she could get back to Logan.

It was almost ten minutes before the door opened, and she knew just by the silhouette of the man's arm as he opened the door that it was attached to a ridiculously tall person. Orion came through and shut the door behind himself with a sigh, nodding to Anna to acknowledge that he was the one there to talk with her. "Morning. How's the treatment treating you?"

She stopped cold in her spinning and just stared at him before she let out a sarcastic laugh. "You've got to be fucking kidding me. What the hell are you doing here? You're an official now?"

"I'm an officer. We're pretty official people, so if that's how it announced me, I'm not surprised." He shook his head and sighed without getting any closer. "I won't stay long. I'm here to offer you the piloting classes if you're interested in them. After losing shuttles and having some of our other pilots injured in the attacks, the program has identified a need for more trainees. So I identified you as someone with interest and aptitude."

Anna opened her mouth to say something extremely rude and sarcastic, but she stalled as she thought about what Logan said about taking a shuttle and getting the fuck away from the station. She needed to know how to drive the damn things if they were ever going to get away. "If I agree, do I have to take lessons from you?"

"I have no idea. But considering the fact that I was instructed by the computer to come down here and talk to you without being given a name, I'm gonna guess that yes, that would end up happening at some point." He leaned back against the door with his hands in his pockets. "If you say no, there are a lot of other technical jobs I'm sure you'll get picked up for. It won't be the end of the world."

"You know that I wanted to learn how to fly a shuttle." She snapped at him, since his last comment pissed her off. He knew she wanted to learn to fly, and yet he was being dismissive. Callous, even. Their situation was fucked up enough and he was being a dick. "No. Does that make you feel better? No, I don't want you to teach me shit." Anna got up and walked toward him, but only because he was standing by the the only exit.

"Good. That makes that visit easier." He stood aside and opened the door, looking everywhere else but at the small woman on a warpath headed past him. "If you change your mind later, I'm not the only one who's going to be running training classes. I'm just one of three. So the odds are plenty high for the system to fuck with."

"The computer tell you to say that too?" She spat at him, since he was being an asshole, but she knew she was being a bitch too. "It doesn't matter what I want, really, does it? But lucky you, you're an Orbital. You could find a way to fly your ass out of here, but the rest of us are stuck here."

"Fly my ass out of here and go where, exactly?" He spat right back at her once she got into the hallway. "Home? The home that's run by all the same systems that run this place? Right, that's an option. Don't try to act like your will is the only one somebody tried to take away yesterday. Because we are all right there."

Anna scoffed at him. "So you're trying to tell me we're on the same side, but you're here acting like an asshole to me? You're wasting your time and mine by showing up here hoping that I won't do something you don't want me to do. I thought you were pretty decent before, but now you just seem like an ass."

"I didn't know you were on the other side of this door. If I had, I would've stayed home, or gone to recruit somebody else." He jabbed a finger at the door as if it had been personally responsible for him being forced to talk to her. "And I'm giving you the odds so that you'll have some idea of how to play them if you have to. I can imagine the conversation that you and your husband had last night when you went back to your unit after the meeting. I can imagine it because Mercury and I had the same fucking conversation, I'm thinking. So yeah, in that way, we're absolutely on the same side. And that side is that we want to stay on opposite sides. Real simple."

"Logan and I don't have to discuss staying on the same side." She responded with a glare up at the giant that was supposed to be her genetic match. What bullshit. "Fucking each other seemed like a much better option than talking about shit that didn't need to be talked about. Logan and I have been best friends for most of our lives. No one is going to change that."

"Good. Keep it that way." Orion threw up his hands and headed away from her down the hall, even though he wasn't sure he could get out of the medical sector that way. All he cared about was getting away from the woman he had wanted nothing to do with in the first place.

Anna stormed her way all the way to the lobby to find Logan, who was clearly waiting for her. She went up and grabbed his hand, but she looked more frustrated than angry. "Can we go?"

"Yes, we can." He was already on his feet as soon as he saw her, but the level of frustration in her voice was a lot higher than he had expected. "What happened?"

"The giant showed up." She held Logan's hand in a death grip. "To offer me flying lessons that he didn't really want me to learn. Asshole."

He walked next to her in silence until her pace began to return to normal, then squeezed her hand once. "My appointment was with Dr. Finnegan. Apparently in an absence of babies, she does general practice and virology as well." He shook his head and checked both ways before taking the turn he was pretty sure would take them back to their unit. "I can't imagine this is the last time we're gonna get crossed like this. What did you tell the giant?"

"It's not going to be the last time if 'the computer told me so' is going to happen again." She did nothing to moderate the vitriol in her tone. "I told him that I don't want anything to do with him. What do you think I said? I'm not giving in to this bullshit. Even though I really do want to learn to fly a damn shuttle. What did you say to the doctor?"

"I asked her about CV, she seems to have studied it for a long while. I took my shot, waited around in awkward silence for fifteen minutes for observation, then left. If their computer program, or the people behind it, are going to play childish games about trying to put us with the two of them, then I'm not going to be dragged into participating."

He shook his head as they walked, looking around at every part of the corridor in the context of the structural schematics. He wanted to understand as much about the place as possible, if he was going to have to live there for a while. Anything could be helpful in figuring out a way to get off. "Be nice if you could learn how to fly without having him be the one to teach you."

"I think if I agreed to learn how to fly, I wouldn't have any choice. They'd put him with me." Anna was clearly pissed about it, but there was nothing she could do to change it. "So I won't. I'm not going to let them push me around."

They were given several more reminders about the meeting with the new initiates on their way back to their room, but Logan finally ordered the computer to stop telling them about it. He halfway expected the door to be locked when they got there, but they got in and locked it again behind them without further interference. "Computer, what's the next thing that we've been 'requested' to attend after this meeting with the last shuttles?"

During the last meal of the day, there is a social event where all Initiates are requested to attend. The computer reported, then Anna looked it up to get further explanation.

"It's supposed to be a get-to-know you event, so we can get friendly with the rest of the people trapped on this spinning tin can." Anna flipped through the message on her communicator. She saw something else come in after she read the notice, her scowl dissolving instantly. "Hey, I got something from Cory."

"Oh yeah?" That dissolved his frustration as well, and he stood behind her as she pulled up the message, his hands on her hips. "We've only been gone a day and a half, he can't have burned too many things down just yet."

Anna read over the short message several times as her heart pounded excitedly. "He's saying they heard about the attack on the shuttle, but they were informed that we're okay, and he just wanted to get something from me for his own peace of mind." There were a few pictures attached to the email of her family being goofy, except for Ben, who rarely smiled in the first place unless Susan was the cause.

"I love that kid." Anna wasn't sure how a day and a half could feel like a year, but the pictures of her family calmed her significantly. "Look, Larissa is in this one with Cory."

Logan smiled at how comfortable the two of them looked together, and ran his hands up over Anna's sides as she flipped through them. "That was one of your better ideas, those two together. I hope they decide to make it permanent." He leaned down to kiss the back of her neck and sighed against her skin, his smile dimming. "Do we send them back a happy picture of ourselves and tell them everything's fine, or do we tell them how things actually are? Happy picture seems like it makes more sense to me. It's not like any of them can be of help up here."

"Lots of happy pictures." She agreed, even though things were definitely rough at the moment. "Anyway, if Ben and Liam knew, they'd try to do something really stupid, and we don't need that. Ben has to worry about Susan and everyone else, and Liam has three new wives. We can handle this shit, right?" Anna turned to look at Logan, wanting just as much to be reassured as they were about to attempt with their families.

"We can handle this shit." He echoed with a smile he thought he would have to force, but ended up being completely genuine, just because there was no one he would rather be going through problems with than Anna. So long as they were on the same side, nothing in the world would get to him.

They took a couple of silly pictures and one with a scandalous kiss that was sure to get groans, but Anna was in a much better mood by the time she went to respond to Cory's email. She wrote a quick message about floating everywhere and already missing the food on Earth before she signed off a mushy 'I miss you guys', and sent it off.

She turned her attention back to Logan while she waited for the message to go through to Earth. "Did anyone send you anything? I would think if Cory sent me something, Larissa would have sent you one too."

He hadn't thought to look for himself, but he took out his communicator anyway. When he pulled up his messages, though, there were a few introductory formal messages from the Initiative network and some station memos, but nothing else at first. One message came up as a "communications error" due to corrupted data. "Mine looks like it's on the fritz, but of course station messages are still coming through just fine. Figures."

Anna frowned at that, but when she looked back at her own, an error popped up telling her the message she was trying to send could not be sent. She tried to send it again but it popped up with an error yet again.

An invitation for her and Orion to attend the social, however, *did* come through.

"I'm not going to the fucking social with the giant." She growled at her communicator before she looked at Logan again. "I guess I'll have to try again later."

The look on Logan's face was skeptical, though, as she was getting an error of the same type but they were both still getting other messages. He tapped the button on his communicator to enable voice commands. "Are all the other members of the agricultural group on board yet? I'd like to send a message to all of them, if we're going to be working together."

Members of the agricultural group are all aboard the station.

"And is there any problem with me sending a message to them?"

The agricultural group consists entirely of approved contacts. The computer replied.

"Uh huh." Logan said as he looked over at Anna, since that confirmed his suspicion. "Can you tell me on whose authority or for what reason my contacts have been limited?"

All default settings have been approved by Initiative policy. The reason for the restriction is not known. Would you like the list of your approved contacts?

"Just make sure they're marked obviously. And if the rest of the agricultural workers in the Initiative aren't currently on my list of approved contacts, submit a request to whatever fuckwad restricted my access to get them unrestricted. They want me here and working, they'd better give me the room to do my fucking job in the process. And yes, you can quote me directly in that request."

He tossed his communicator on the table next to him just because he didn't want to be touching the thing anymore. "They didn't exactly put in the brochure that we were gonna be incommunicado when it comes to Earth."

"Maybe they thought we would all play by the rules." Anna put aside her communicator and sat down in Logan's lap. She put her head on his shoulder as she draped her legs over one of the arms of the chair. "It's going to get worse, isn't it? More than just random run-ins and restricted messages."

Logan nodded, though he wanted very much to lie, if only to himself. "Depending on just how crazy the fuckers in charge of this place are? Yeah, I'm guessing it's gonna get worse." He kissed her once without being able to put the fire behind it that they normally shared.

In the silence, though, Logan could feel the slight humming vibration of the ship's systems, reminders they were no longer on Earth but constantly falling in a tenuous circle around the planet. "But they're gonna have to take their time with it. There's too many people in this program to piss us all off at once. They're gonna have to make sure the majority of people are happy with the way things are, then they'll be more free to pick off the rest of us who won't cooperate."

"The majority of people didn't come here already married." Anna held tighter to Logan. "I'm sure the giant and his goddess wife are just as mad as we are. They're probably the two people who understand how we feel more than anyone else. Even if he is a dick."

"So the two people who might actually be sympathetic are precisely the two people we least want to see right now." He shook his head against her hair, running one hand up over her legs. There was no way he could ever have Anna so close without touching her extensively. "Maybe that's the whole reason they did it in the first place. The only other married couple I saw broken up was the two British men they called out, but that's . . . I mean, I'm sure they're no more happy about being separated than we are but they had to have been given the same kind of buy-in that Santos threw in our faces yesterday. Genetic diversity and all that bullshit. No matter what, nothing gives the Initiative the right to fuck with people's lives like this."

"The way they barged in on my family after what happened to this station should have been a clue, but I didn't want to think the worst." Anna never tired of Logan's touches, even when things seemed terrible.

"There's gotta be some good that can come out of this. If we can just find a way to get them to either ignore us or ease off on us while we're here, we can make it to Eleusis and forget all this fucked up mess." She kissed along his jaw lightly and then sighed against his skin. "Maybe we should just talk to them. They're from here, for fuck's sake. Maybe they know how we can get out. The giant can fly a shuttle better than anyone else, according to his co-pilot. Talking to them doesn't mean we have to get naked."

"No, there's plenty of folks I've talked to in my life without getting naked." He groaned at the concession, but he knew she was right. "We need to stretch things out as much as possible, if we're going to knuckle under for the sake of keeping things steady. We're going to see them again tomorrow for sure, during treatments. Or I am, anyway. Let's see about scheduling out your flying lessons a few days, see if that forces the system to ease up on us, then we can go from there."

Anna's expression was pinched, like she'd just eaten something sour, but she nodded. "Maybe I shouldn't yell so much or call him an asshole. But he was being one." She went back to kissing Logan since that was what she would rather do than anything else. "Wanna be my date to the social? I think they want me to bring someone else, but I kinda like you, Bickford."

"Good. I'm a fan of you too, *missus* Bickford." He smiled under her kisses and raked a hand up and down her back as he held her against him. "I will absolutely be your date to the social. In the meantime, you and I need to see what this station will give us when it comes to some kind of food. That treatment this morning left me fucking starving for some reason."

"Really? It made me feel the opposite." She replied as she glanced at her arm. "Also, that doctor really tried to convince me to get stabbed in my ass, and I don't think it was for medical reasons." Anna slid off of Logan's lap so he could get something to eat. "I'm gonna put some pictures up that I brought. That'll be something, at least."

"It's a start." He agreed as he got up, but he didn't let go of her. Instead, he ran his hand up over her shirt to her neck to pull her into a fiery kiss before he glanced around the room. "Of course, it's not gonna feel completely like home until I've fucked you on every single piece of furniture, but we'll run down that checklist pretty quick, I'm guessing." He smiled as he stepped toward the tiny kitchen, his stomach growling the whole way.

"You can't just say that and walk away! You're mean." She said with a pronounced pout as she let him get away, since she could definitely hear his stomach growling. "Such a tease." Anna watched his backside before she went to her bag to dig for pictures. He had such a nice ass. Everything. Nice everything.

Logan managed to find the settings that would send along some protein bars, since that was the only thing he felt like he could trust out of the long list of prepared foods. Even when they arrived, he looked over the packaging with suspicion, but he had to remind himself that he had no way of knowing what was going into their food or the treatments being shoved into their arms. All he could do was keep going.

As he waited for more food to come through and Anna worked on the pictures, he reluctantly scrolled through his contact list. He was not surprised to find Mercury's name on it, but when he looked through it again, he realized it had been moved to the very top as his first-priority contact. He shook his head at the little games the computer seemed to enjoy before he selected her name and typed out a brief message.

Anna and I have decided it's in our best interests to attend the social tonight in the observatory gallery. Can we plan to see you and Orion there as well?

When Mercury received a message from Logan Bickford, she almost fell out of her chair. She and Orion had met for a meal during a break in their busy day. She hadn't planned to go to the social, but Orion also thought it was better to be compliant than not. "I just got a message from Logan Bickford." She put down her fork and looked across the table at Orion before she let him read the message.

Orion took the communicator for a quick look, then handed it back to her with a resigned sigh. "Maybe they tried to call home too." He stabbed at his food, but he suddenly wasn't hungry. He brought the meal over to the clinical wing even though the computer told him Mercury wasn't going to get any time to herself to take a lunch. He figured he was going to be ignoring the computer's advice a lot in the days and months to come. "I don't know why else they would decide to make an appearance. Them not attending the greeting with the other shuttles was pretty clear."

Mercury did no more than poke at her own food the same as he was. "I talked to him today, I had to give him his treatment." She hadn't told Orion, but she was a little nervous about admitting that she had been in a room alone with the man who had been slated as her match, even though it wasn't her choice. "Mostly I just jabbered on about CV. I didn't know what to say."

Orion was quiet, unsure what to make of the fact that she hadn't mentioned meeting with Logan while he had immediately sent her a message about being tricked by the computer into meeting with Anna. He wasn't going to let stupid little things make him wonder about his wife. "Did he seem interested?" He asked eventually, finally working another bite of food onto his fork. "In CV, I mean."

"He made a suggestion to look at the families of the children who are born immune. It's a good suggestion." She poked at her food some more. "I'm sorry I didn't tell you sooner. It felt wrong, being trapped in a room with him. I felt guilty about it, even though I had no idea I would even be treating him. I should have told you immediately. It was silly not to."

"You're doing your job. Nothing to apologize for." He reached over and ran his hand over her back as they sat across a corner from each other to eat. "What do you think about the social? If it's all two and a half thousand of us in one room, I would think it should be pretty easy not to mingle with them any longer than we absolutely have to. We can focus on seeing Carl and your friend Barry and the others, see how things are going for them. I'd be willing to bet good money Fitch has got some pretty hilarious stories by now."

Mercury nodded and moved closer, abandoning her meal. "I told you about Carl. I don't think he should have left, but he seemed eager to get out with his match. She does not seem his type at all. Quiet. Overly helpful. Nice, though."

"Yeah, I'm not sure putting him with someone quiet was a good idea. That doesn't seem right at all." He shook his head and held her close against his shoulder, his fingertips scratching up and down her spine in ways he had learned she liked. "Maybe it'll work out, though. I told you when we first got together, you're nothing like the women I used to date. So if somebody had known me before, they wouldn't have said you were my type either. I have since discovered, however, in a thoroughly scientific study, that you are very much my type. It's a fact. I have evidence."

"You have evidence?" She teased as she leaned into him even more. Mercury had seen a lot of patients that day and almost all of them had recognized her, not because she was a good doctor, but because of what had happened with the matching program. She had heard the word 'mistake' uttered in reference to her and Orion together more than once, since she had been rematched.

Was it a mistake? Could the computer make mistakes? Had they put all of their faith in something that had put them together by error?

"What evidence is that?"

He held onto her for a while in silence, then took her hand and pulled it up to rest it on his chest. She could feel his heart beating strongly against her hand. Mercury had remarked once that because he was so lean it was easier to feel his heartbeat, and that was just as much the case now as it was while they were naked on Three. "This evidence. Go on, shove me under one of your scanners in there, you'll see two ventricles, two atria, four valves, and your name stamped on the whole mess, prefaced with the words 'property of' in big, friendly letters."

That made Mercury chuckle, despite her overall dour mood. "I don't know if I would want to see that. It might make me concerned for your health." She leaned in and brushed her lips against his before she hungrily dove in for more and tugged on his shirt. "I've heard more than once today that we're the couple the matching program got wrong." She whispered against his lips, her nose touching his. "Even if it was wrong, I still love you. I don't care about that now."

"I've never been conflicted about how I feel toward a machine before I got here." He said with a chuckle, laying his long-fingered hand over hers to hold it against his chest. "I've been pretty fond of them, on the whole. They help me fly my ships, bring me food, pump oxygen into the air, so yeah, generally I'm a fan. And the matching program gave me you. I'm fond of it for that reason. This . . . this feels different. So no, this version of the program, I'm not a fan of. And I don't care what it says now. It got me to you, and that's all I want. Just the woman I love. I'm not sure why that particular computation seems to be one it's having trouble with."

She responded to his declaration by pressing her lips into his, the warmth of his mouth, the taste of him forever a comfort. Especially now. "I should get back to work for a little while before the social. Tomorrow will be just as busy." Mercury ran her fingers over his face several times, since she really didn't want him to go. It was supposed to be lunch but instead she felt like she had stepped into an Orion-shaped haven. "I'll go back to the unit in a little while so I can get cleaned up and out of scrubs for the social."

"I like the 'out of scrubs' part. I'll make sure I'm around to help out with that bit." He grinned and kissed her fingertips without making any move to get up. "I volunteered for some duty work since they tasked you at the clinic for the day, so I'm running inspections on the shuttles if you need me. But I'll make sure to be back when you finish your shift."

Mercury stole a couple more kisses. "I brought some new clothes with me. I hope you like them." She smiled coyly and moved out of his lap. "I'll see you back at the unit as soon as I can. Thank you for bringing me a warm meal."

"Wha . . ." he put his hands up in exasperation as she got up to walk away. "You can't tell a guy that and then just walk away! That is just mean. You're a mean person." He pointed at her accusingly, but he was smiling anyway as he cleaned up their lunch.

4

Mercury was surprised when she returned to the unit and found that Orion hadn't made it back before she did. She took one of the fastest showers of her life and pinned up her hair into an immaculate bun on the top of her head with a few loose tendrils before she pulled out one of her new dresses. It was a forest green that flattered her curves and her eyes, and while she wasn't used to wearing dresses that went to mid-thigh and exposed cleavage, she was learning what Orion liked and she wanted to look good for him.

Her announcement of Orion's return was a whiff of oil and something burnt as the doors opened for him. He seemed unscathed, but he also seemed somehow deflated.

"If I ever volunteer to try and help out on actual mechanical duty again, please, sedate me or shoot me or . . ." he finally turned around and saw her step out of the kitchen area and his eyes went wide. "Ho . . . ly . . . *shit,* you look amazing." For his part, he was covered in singed pieces of fabric with grease marks on his arms and face.

Mercury didn't even hesitate to rush up to him, bringing a hint of a sugary vanilla scent with her, which smelled as divine as she looked. She looked him over for any bleeding, touching him gingerly. "I told you, I bought new clothes because I wanted to look good for you. I'm realizing that scrubs aren't very flattering, though they're much more comfortable than this dress. Are you alright? Are you bleeding? Burned? I have a kit in the kitchen . . ."

"I'm fine, just a little scalded. Nothing major, I promise." He stripped off the burnt fabric and left it by the door so that he could bag it up and dispose of it later. "I went through one of the engines with a mechanic who's also from Three. Never met the guy, but he's pretty great. Hell of a lot better at actually working on those things than I am."

"I ended up sparking an ignition core and got myself flashed for it. Nothing major." Once he was naked, she could see for herself that he was unharmed, but his arms and face still looked like they could use some work. "Seriously, you look incredible, Mercury. I don't even want to get in the shower and get cleaned up, I just want to stand here and look at you for the rest of the night."

She rolled her eyes and tried not to show the blush that crept into her cheeks. "Go, get showered. I'll wait here for you. Are you sure you're alright? I don't care about looking pretty if you're hurt."

"I'm fine, I promise. Just got a little messed up. I'll clean up in a hurry." He leaned in carefully to give her a light kiss, since his lips at least hadn't been compromised by his afternoon, then headed toward the shower. "Should I go with the uniform or something else? Normally I would go with the uniform, but the last time somebody called me Lieutenant, I wanted to punch her in the face, so I'm feeling like I might need to go civilian for a change."

"I think you look very good in your uniform, but I also think you look very nice when you're naked, so I'm not the best person to ask." Mercury smiled at him and nodded toward their small closet. "I'll find you something civilian if you want."

"Sure, let's go for that, at least for tonight. If a CO comes to the social and yells at me for being out of uniform, I'll just tell them I didn't know what rank to wear, so I didn't want to make the mistake." He was already in the bathroom by that point, with the water running, but he popped out at that.

"Oh yeah, wanted to let you know that happened today. We all got notified that our current ranks have been nullified. We're all going to be placed in Eleusis ranks according to the assessment of the military commanders. So I'm not a lieutenant anymore, as of yesterday when we got here."

"They are changing quite a lot, very quickly." Mercury commented with a frown. "The next thing you know, they'll be telling me I'm not a doctor anymore." She shook her head as she went to retrieve her shoes and his clothing. "I'll be out here, possibly peeking in on you."

"Peek all you like. Everything in here belongs to you." He winked at her before he got in the shower, then kept yelling to be heard over the water. "You're one of the best doctors they've got. What are there, twenty of you with us now? Out of more than two thousand people? Yeah, they need everybody they can get. Besides, you're obstetrics director. You're completely fine."

"An obstetrics doctor who is doing routine work all day long. They could have anyone administering the treatments after the first week. Though I suppose with all the new matches, they'll have use for me soon enough." She picked out some dark pants and a grey shirt, but it was the kind of fit that would show off his lean body. "I saw some very enthusiastic matches in the corridors today. You and I have some competition out there for the sexiest kisses."

"What? No. That cannot be allowed to stand. We will claim our title and none shall take it from us." He sounded suitably scandalized, and she could just imagine the sarcasm on his face as he said it. "Who's holding the title, would you say? I like hearing about happy couples."

"I don't know, there's quite a few. I saw a Mister White today with a Miss Rogers. They were rather attached by the lips." She went to stand by the shower once she had picked out his clothes and once her shoes were by the door. "It was a long day without you, and I think seeing any happy couples made me miss you even more."

He smiled at her through the walkspace between the rest of the bathroom and the shower. There was a rod for a curtain, but neither of them had seen the point in hanging one, since they enjoyed looking at each other too much. He was already a lot cleaner than he had been, and she could see that he did have a few minor cuts along his hands and one on the side of his neck, all of which had already begun to heal.

"I didn't get to see any happy couples, just heard about them all day long. I thought pilots were bad with gossip, but mechanics are worse. I think they've all been so pent up waiting for it that they were all just glad to finally get with somebody. The ones who got laid last night, anyway."

"I'm betting a lot of people did last night." She continued to watch him with a smile, glad he didn't mind her gawking. "I'm glad that most people seem happy, at least. It restores a *little* faith in the Initiative. They may have made a mistake with us, but I'm glad that's not the overall feeling. I still want Eleusis to be a success, you know?"

"So do I." He looked her over again and turned the water off, checking out his face and hands in the mirror nearby just to make sure he'd actually gotten everything. "So long as what's going on with us is actually a mistake. I hope it is."

Mercury's smile disappeared. She grabbed some ointment stored behind a mirror and put it on a few of his burn spots without asking before he completely dried himself off. "Are you saying that you think someone tampered with it, or are you saying that the new matches might be correct?"

"No, of course I don't think the new matches are correct." He looked horrified at even the prospect, but he stood still for her to put the ointment on his cuts. "I think the new matches were tampered with somehow, I just don't know why."

"But it is possible that the results weren't tampered." She confirmed as she ran her fingertips lightly over his freshly-cleaned skin. "Not that it matters. I've made my choice, and I don't want anyone other than you. But it is *possible* that these people have actually been matched with us based on the compatibility algorithms built into the program and the computer determined that these new people are better matches for us than each other." Mercury looked him up and down before she leaned in and planted a kiss on his jaw, since she didn't want him to think she was contemplating someone else.

"It's possible." He conceded, towelling off his legs and returning the kiss she had given him, finally clean enough to put a hand on the waist of her dress to hold onto her. "But like you said, not that it matters. He can't have you. I said so."

Mercury's smile returned to her lips and she stepped in closer, the pull between them was magnetic. She felt like her body was meant to be plastered against his, and their lips fused together. Every velvet kiss, every sweep of the tongue, and she was more an addict than the day before. "I didn't know you were so possessive."

"I'm new at possessive, but I've got a damn good reason to be." He had no trouble returning the heat in her kisses, moaning quietly under them after being separated for most of the day. "I told you before I was gonna be greedy with you. That doesn't change because we actually have to work for a living. Probably only gonna make it worse."

"I'm okay with greedy." She whispered between kisses before her hand tentatively trailed down his body, moving lower until she grazed his manhood. "I should have waited out there."

"Should you, though?" His voice cracked with sarcasm, but he was grinning anyway, and certainly wasn't moving away from her touch. Just a few kisses from her already had him beginning to get hard, and she could feel as soon as her fingers even grazed him that his body began responding immediately. There were all kinds of questions about the state of their match and the future of the Initiative, but his absolute attraction to her was not in question.

When he moved his kisses to the side of her neck, she let out a small moan. Mercury still smelled strongly of sugary vanilla, especially in the steam from his shower, and with her hair up it gave him plenty of opportunity to kiss along her sweet, porcelain skin. Her hand wrapped around his hardened cock and stroked slowly.

"I read about something that I wanted to try. With my mouth." She was already dressed and didn't want to get undressed, but he was still naked and she couldn't get the curiosity out of her mind.

"Did you?" She could tell he was surprised, but from the way he gripped her waist and ran his hands over her dress, it was surprise of the pleasant variety. "You know I love it when you read. What did you read about, exactly?"

She was glad to see he was eager, but from what she read, there didn't seem to be many men that were opposed to what she was hoping to try. Mercury moved closer to him, but she turned more of her attention to his penis. "I read about how a woman can please a man by sucking and licking his penis. There were a lot of techniques I read about and I would like to try it. I saw a lot of diagrams and read detailed explanations, so I think I'm prepared."

As always, Orion smiled at her clinical description of what she wanted to try, and he kissed her again before he led her back to the bedroom with a cushioned bench where he could sit down. "I've never once been able to stay on my feet during . . . that." For some reason, it didn't quite feel right to call it a blowjob when she was standing there in front of him looking like a goddess come to life. That felt too cheap for someone like her, but he wasn't going to go clinical himself and call it fellatio either. That wasn't him.

Mercury felt a little more shy about it once she realized that he'd experienced it before. She wasn't surprised by him, but she was surprised at herself for not remembering that he had much more experience than she did. "Oh, okay." She followed him until he sat down and she easily went to her knees in front of him. "If I'm doing something wrong you'll tell me, right?"

He leaned in and kissed her once she was down in front of

him, one hand sliding down over the smooth fabric of the dress to caress her freely, even if she wasn't looking to get out of it. "Baby, there's no such thing as something wrong when it comes to the things you do to me. You do as you please."

Mercury focused on touching him and stroking him until he was harder, and only then did she convince herself not to be nervous. She leaned in to wrap her lips around just the head at first, suckling it lightly. Orion was not a small man and she wasn't sure how much of him she could take in her mouth, but she was determined. Mercury also wasn't sure what she would do when he was near ejaculation, but she figured that would be an in-the-moment decision as well. She was curious about the taste as well as what his face would look like. So far, he just smelled like Orion, clean and fresh, and so she slid her mouth slowly down his shaft while her hands followed the instructions of her research and stimulated him toward the base.

His groans were plenty of guide to go by as she took him into her mouth, and his long fingers rested at first along her shoulder and then on the back of her neck. It had been a long while since he'd last had a woman's mouth around his cock, and just the fact that it was Mercury was an incredible turn-on.

When she started to move her mouth faster on him, his groans got a great deal louder, and his hand actually slowed her down with its light grip on the back of her neck. "Easy, baby. You keep on like that and we're gonna be . . . early to the social, not late." She could hear the smile in his voice, but it was quickly overtaken by his moans as her lips and tongue continued to stroke him.

From the first time she met Orion, she was surprised how attracted she was to him and the effect he had on her, but this was a new level for her. Hearing him groan and moan like he was having the time of his life because of something that she was doing was intoxicating and emboldening. It made her want to do more research about how in the world she could please him. It was such a turn-on that she couldn't even think about anything other than Orion. She was also grateful for his simple instruction by his touches here and there. The salty taste of him in her mouth and the feel of his silky skin along her tongue lit her body with need.

At one point when she moved to adjust herself between his knees, she saw his free hand was beside him clutching a hand-towel that he'd grabbed from the bathroom, but he wasn't paying attention to the towel or to anything in the room as she worked at him. "Holy . . . shit that's good . . ."

Mercury could feel her own arousal between her legs, but she certainly wasn't going to stop because she had soaked through her underwear. She racked her brain for every trick that she'd read about, and even though she knew she wasn't doing them perfectly, her enthusiasm more than made up for her lack of experience. It wasn't long before she didn't care about when it happened, as long as it happened. She wanted him to reach that delicious point of no return, she wanted to hear him groaning her name. She needed it.

Sleeping with Orion for a little over a month had given her plenty of experience in judging when he was about to reach climax, and that time was only more obvious, if anything. He managed to grab one of her hands and place the hand towel in it as his fingers shook with the impending orgasm, but he was clearly leaving what she wanted to do up to her. She could feel what happened to him both more scientifically and more specifically as she stroked him through the last moments, felt his entire body tense up in anticipation of his release, and above her he couldn't even open his eyes as his face twisted in the pleasure she was giving him.

Mercury dropped the towel to his feet as she kept going with both of her hands on his thighs as she pushed him over the edge. His muscles were taut in his legs and her fingers dug into his skin and as soon as he climaxed she felt like she'd won the lottery.

Orion's hands clenched at the cushions on either side of him as he cried out, his legs shaking on both sides of her as she took him in her mouth. It had all happened so fast that his orgasm didn't last long, but it still left him panting afterward as he slumped back on the bench, his hands moving up and down over her arms and shoulders as she finished him off. "Good . . . god . . ." he said as his chest heaved.

Her skin was flushed and she was so turned on she was nearly panting. God, she loved it. The salty taste of him was on her lips and she licked over them slowly after she slid him out of her mouth. Her green eyes devoured him as much as her mouth had, and she wanted to burn the sight of him into her memory. "That was fun." Mercury said sincerely as she leaned back on her feet. "And sexy. I love all of the noises you make."

He looked at her with a breathless chuckle, still not quite able to move. "If that was your first try doing that, then god help me, I am a dead man." He gave a contented sigh, then leaned forward to kiss along her cheek down to her neck while she remained in front of him. "You can try out anything on me you like. I fully support this whole research thing."

Mercury laughed, since there was little in the entire universe that could stop her from reading and researching whenever she wanted answers. "I'm glad that my research was useful." She gave a tiny moan of her own when he teased along her neck. She was hypersensitive with arousal. "I wonder what else I can discover that will make you this pleased."

"Oh no. No no. It's very much your turn to be the pleased one in this relationship." He continued his kisses over her neck as his hands wandered over her. "If you think you're getting out of this without payback, you'd be very wrong about that."

She wanted to tell him that they shouldn't really linger and they should get moving, but it seemed like every part of her body was aching for him. Every time he touched her, it made her feel the magnetic pull all over again. "I'm a little embarrassed." She admitted before he could explore any part of her below the waist. "About how aroused that made me."

"Really?" He asked with an obvious grin, obviously more to do with the effect it had had on her than the fact that she was embarrassed about it. "That . . . is a very interesting result of that experiment." He pulled her slowly up to her feet and parted her legs a little as he looked up to her. His hands moved up over her legs slowly to smooth themselves beneath the dress she was wearing, and he pushed it up slowly, making sure not to wrinkle or distress the fabric as he exposed more of her. "Nothing wrong with getting into what you do."

Every whisper of a touch had her heart pounding and she chewed on her bottom lip as his hand skimmed up the inside of her leg. "Everywhere you touch me makes me feel like I'm on fire." She laughed at how ridiculous it sounded until his fingertips grazed the outside of her underwear, and a whimper escaped her lips.

Once her dress was pushed up above her waist and still unscathed, he took her by the waist and spun her to sit on the very edge of the bench beside him, leaning in to kiss along her exposed cleavage on his way down her torso. He slid down beside her first, his fingers hooking into her underwear and tugging it down over her thighs as his kisses continued down her chest. Once he dropped it over her knees to the floor, he tossed her underwear aside and knelt down to trail kisses along the inside of her thigh. "I'm comfortable with you on fire. You keep me warm, it's the least I can do to return the favor."

It wasn't the first time Orion had gone after her with his mouth, but she was nervous every time because she felt so out of control. Her whole life was about control, and giving any of it up to Orion was both nerve-wracking and blissful. His teasing kisses fried her brain, and the excitement she felt at his nearness was infuriatingly irrational but incredible at the same time. This time, though, she was even more nervous because of how turned on she was already and he had barely touched her at all. "You don't have to." She blurted out of obligation, but she really didn't want him to stop.

"Oh, but I want to." He said very nearly against her core itself, with a smile she could both feel and hear. His fingers moved up over her skin to push her knees just a little farther apart before his tongue's assault on her began.

Mercury had absolutely no control of the noises that escaped her lips. The way she already felt, the orgasm that built would be intense, and it wouldn't take long to get there. Her fingers gripped his shoulders, and she bit down hard on her lip just to try and quiet herself. "Orion . . ." She moaned as often as she could, since it was the only word her mouth could form.

Orion's experience, in contrast to Mercury's research, had been entirely practical. He knew how to tease a woman when he wanted to thoroughly shatter her. He held off allowing her to have her orgasm for as long as he could restrain himself. His tongue circled her clit slowly, torturously, and her legs trembled. Mercury's head tilted back against the wall as he slid his tongue up and down her folds, tasting her sweetness while he drove her mad. When he felt that she was right on the edge, he slipped a single long finger inside her to send her sailing over the edge with teasing strokes both inside and out.

Mercury shattered almost a little too easily once his finger slid inside of her, and she certainly wasn't quiet. Her hips ground against his mouth and his hand shamelessly. Her body shook as the orgasm tore through her, but it was so delicious she didn't care. About anything.

"Oh . . . god . . . Orion . . ." She wasn't really known for using terms of endearment, but she definitely wanted to start after this. Even if it would sound silly. "Baby . . ." She said tentatively, though it still sounded strange to her.

The term got a full grin from him as he teased out the last remnants of her climax, making sure she rode it all the way through to the end. He kissed his way back down along her inner thigh afterward, the stubble on his cheeks scratching playfully at her skin before he looked up. "Seems to me you needed that the same as I did after a day like today."

"Mhm." She replied simply since it was the only thing that came to mind as she attempted to recover. "That . . ." Mercury tried to think, but it was a jumble. "That was great. Thank you." Being grateful for it was the least she could do. Especially if she wanted him to do it again.

He grinned provocatively up at her as he ran his hands over her thighs possessively, his thumbs grazing the most sensitive parts of her to keep pleasure thrumming in her veins. "I'll have to wake you up with my tongue. Really get your day started off right."

"That would be quite a surprise." She replied breathily as she attempted to recover from his assault, the best kind of assault to exist. "Now we're really going to be late." Mercury teased, but her tone made it quite clear that she didn't really care. "That was the best reason to be late for something."

"We'll have to be late more often." He pushed himself up to his feet, but enjoyed the sight of her all askew and bothered as she laid back. "I doubt anyone will notice us walking in, even late. If you can walk right now, that is." He teased before he offered his hand.

Mercury stumbled a little as he pulled her up, but he tugged her into his chest, stabilizing her quickly. She immediately kissed along his jaw and gave him a quick hug before she shimmied her dress back into place. Her underwear was still discarded on the floor. "You better go get dressed or we'll never leave."

"And that would be a bad thing?" He grinned, holding her tightly in the hug before he finally let her go with a smack to her backside. "Alright, public appearance, here we come. Even if I am just gonna be fantasizing about getting you out of that dress all night."

She was still flushed as she went to retrieve her underwear and put it down the laundry chute. She grabbed a fresh pair from the bedroom, brushed her teeth quickly as he finished getting dressed, and hoped he was right about no one noticing they were half an hour late.

He had his own quality time with a toothbrush when he was dressed, and he got out just as she was pulling on her underwear. "Could've left those off and made it a really interesting evening." He teased with a raised eyebrow, since she quickly put them on and pushed her dress back into place.

"You want me to not wear underwear?" Mercury hadn't even considered not wearing underwear, and she wondered why that would be so exciting to him as she slid into her heels. "That's not very sanitary, is it?"

He laughed loudly and pulled her sharply into a kiss. "Maybe some other time, with a longer dress." He twirled her around once just to get another good look at her, then headed out.

The social was full and loud, but it was a 'requested' event and there was food and alcohol being served. Mercury didn't look around to see if she saw her new match, clinging instead to Orion's arm as they wandered. "Do you see Carl? I was hoping to see how he is healing."

"Well, he should stand out in a crowd, let's see." He squeezed her hand and put his arm around her shoulders as he stood to his full height and scanned the massive room. He had a distinct advantage when it came to looking for people, since he was head, shoulders, and half a torso taller than the majority of people in the Initiative.

It didn't take long for him to spot his friend, and he raised a hand over the crowd to grab Carl's attention and tell him to stay where he was. "Well, he's upright, at least, that's a start. He's over by the food. Typical." He was smiling as he led her over toward the buffet, though, since the last time he'd seen his friend, it had been on a stretcher.

Mercury relaxed a little as they made it up to the food, though she wasn't particularly hungry. She was just glad to see a friend, even though she didn't know if Carl was up to date on current events. "Look at you two." She said with a polite smile as she looked between Carl and Aiko. "You look better, Carl."

Carl had apparently gone the same civilian route as Orion, since he hadn't been military prior to the Initiative. He was in black slacks and boots with a bright white shirt over his torso that just barely covered his massive arms. Aiko was tucked in against his side as Orion and Mercury approached, nearly disappearing against the man, but he let go of her to say hello to Mercury.

"Told you I would be, Doc. Being hospitalized is a special gift of mine." He gave Mercury a brief hug, but then turned to Orion and took him in a tighter hug that looked like he was trying to snap Orion in half. "They told me you got out of there without getting shot. I couldn't believe it. Had to ask twice."

"Thanks for the vote of confidence." Orion rolled his eyes before he glanced over at Aiko.

"Oh, right. You weren't there earlier." Carl said hastily, looking down at his new match. "This is my giant friend I was telling you about earlier. Aiko, Orion, Orion, Aiko."

"Nice to meet you officially." Aiko said as she held out her hand to shake Orion's, even though she did have to crane her neck to look up at him. He was nearly twice her height. "Even if it means breaking my neck to talk to you." She said with a small, playful smile.

"Yeah, I get that a lot." Orion smiled as he shook her hand, glad that she wasn't intimidated by him. Though if she wasn't intimidated by Carl, she wasn't going to be intimidated by anyone. "This guy treating you alright so far?"

Aiko's smile was reserved, but spoke volumes. "It's been nice to get to know each other. I'll feel a little more comfortable when I know for sure that he's better and not about to bleed out or die."

"Eh. I've seen him worse. I'm pretty sure I'd have to dump this guy out an airlock to actually get rid of him." Orion settled with an arm around Mercury's shoulders and a smile over at Carl.

"Even then. I'd just freeze and come back the next loop and bust through your window to haunt you for dumping me out there." Carl took Aiko under his arm the same as Orion and Mercury. "So yeah, don't do that."

Mercury smiled at the banter between the two friends, happy to be in Orion's embrace, though she knew that they weren't far from an awkward confrontation lurking somewhere in the room.

It was a few drinks and some snacks from the buffet table later when Orion and Mercury finally caught sight of Anna and Logan meandering through the crowd, but it was Logan that Mercury saw first. It was obvious the clothes they were wearing had been requisitioned just that day, since they were dressed in styles that were popular in space rather than some of the dingy and functional patterns that seemed to pervade life on the ground.

Logan was in a full black suit and looked like he had been born to wear it. The shirt buttoned up to his neck and had no collar to it, but he wore a black stone covering the top button, per the current fashion. His black vest was buttoned most of the way up his chest and the black coat he wore was open, making his impressive appearance all the more obvious as he moved through the crowd.

Most striking was the intensity of his eyes that Mercury had seen herself earlier in the day. Eyes that took in everything with a single glance, hard clouds set in a face that was pleasant only for the sake of appearances The anger beneath the surface was clear, and barely restrained. It came through in everything about his posture and the tightness of his interactions, like a disease that was all too easy for Mercury to diagnose.

They didn't seem to notice Orion and Mercury at first, and Orion was too distracted by the conversation with Carl and Aiko to be looking around for anybody. As soon as Logan and Anna stopped to talk to someone they apparently knew, Logan looked up as if he heard someone call his name, and turned to look through the press of people directly at Mercury.

Mercury felt her breath catch in her lungs as he looked at her, since it felt like she was caught, though she wasn't doing anything wrong by looking around the room and noticing him with Anna. She held his gaze, though, and wondered what he was thinking as he looked at her, if he had any idea how they could all get out of this mess, or if his apparent anger just consumed everything. Somehow they would all have to figure out how to coexist in order to make things work, or they were really going to find themselves in trouble.

He held her eyes only briefly, but immediately afterward, he looked her up and down to take in the full view of the dress she was wearing and the rest of her self-presentation. The look in his eyes didn't change as he met her eyes again, but he didn't look away. Only after that appraisal did he turn back to the conversation he and Anna had been having with their friend, and he didn't look back.

Mercury turned her attention back to Orion and Carl who were laughing about something, but she had missed it entirely. She listened for a brief moment before she felt like she needed to walk to clear her mind. "Does anyone want a drink?" She waited for a lull in the conversation before interjecting, but it still felt abrupt.

Carl and Aiko shook their heads awkwardly, but Orion squeezed her hand and nodded. "Sure, baby. I don't think we're close enough to the center for Shine, but if you want to grab me a beer, that'd be great. Thanks."

Mercury kissed him with more gusto than she normally would have publically. After the kiss she leaned in to whisper into his ear. "They're nearby. I just need to walk a little bit to loosen up my anxiety."

Understanding moved across Orion's features, but he nodded and kissed her again to send her on her way. "Don't be long." He asked with a comforting look before he let go of her.

Mercury walked away to get Orion's drink but took a route around the outside perimeter so that she could take her time and avoid almost everyone in the room. It was something, at least, to distract her from the intense, unexplained look Logan Bickford had given her.

Anna was close to Logan's side as they talked with Gordon and Jessie. The conversation was a little strange, partially because Gordon was just that twitchy or sketchy, Anna wasn't sure which, and partially because they seemed like they were high on being close to each other. They were touching each other constantly, and Anna was a little disturbed at how quickly most people had grown fond of their match. After a day.

"This is quite an event." Anna was in an actual dress, which was rare for her, but it was clearly uncomfortable from the way she kept tugging at it to try and get it to fit right. "Some of these people are dressed like they're going to some million-dollar meal or something. I would have been happy at a bar with loud music."

"They have those too, I checked." Gordon was saying as the four of them moved lazily through the gathering. The hall they were in was something in itself, a broad corridor on the outside of the arm that was, at the moment, angled so that the moon in all its full radiance was looking down on them from a distance. It was beautiful, and more lavishly appointed than most other places on the station. The glass edges of the windows were worked in patterns that caught the moonlight and reflected it in varied patterns along the floor and ceiling. "The best bars are up by the docks, but they've got a couple others scattered through. Deck six is a good one too." Gordon shrugged. "Always know where the alcohol is. Rules I live by."

"I'm glad someone does. I'm a fan of alcohol." Anna said as she looked away from the group just to try and spot the alcohol table. "Speaking of, I need to get a bit buzzed in order for this dress to stop annoying the hell out of me. Who's with me?"

"I absolutely am." Logan said quickly, since he was in dire need of a drink after realizing that Mercury and Orion were close. "What about you two, anything?"

"No, I don't drink." Gordon said, then smiled to show that he knew exactly what kind of contradiction that conveyed. He turned to Jessie without any explanation of himself. "What about you? Thirsty?"

"Why the fuck do you care about where the alcohol is if you don't drink?" Anna interrupted with a laugh before Jessie could respond, but she watched as Jessie just shook her head at the invitation. "Two non-drinkers? That's no fun."

Logan went with Anna toward the bar, and shook his head as he glanced back over his shoulder at Gordon and Jessie. "We've got some weird company up here, that's for damn sure. Not sure what to make of those two."

"Well, they definitely fucked. That's for sure. He's all sorts of grabby and she likes it, so whatever their deal is, it seems to be working for them." Anna glanced back at Gordon and Jessie once more, but then the giant and his almost-equally-giant friend caught her eye. "So they really did show up."

He followed Anna's look to where Orion and a few others were standing, and she could feel him sigh. "Looks that way. Though I don't see his wife anywhere." He said it flatly, turning away from Orion to keep his eyes forward, in hopes that Mercury might have suddenly decided to abandon the social altogether. That would make things much easier. "Maybe they had the same idea we did. Cooperate to a point and hope for the best."

"Maybe so." Anna walked up to the table where there was a variety of alcohol in clear containers with straws so that the liquid wouldn't just float around in the air. "Maybe I should at least apologize to the giant for being a bitch. Especially if playing nice means I can send Cory that email so he knows we're okay. They need to know we're okay."

Logan hesitated with another look back at Orion, but he pulled Anna into a possessive kiss and nodded. "Alright. I'm just . . . gonna be here not looking in that direction and having the strongest drink I can find."

"I'm just going to talk to him. It's no different than me talking to that crazy guy back there, Gordon. I don't want to fuck either of them." She gave him another kiss just to reassure him and she grabbed a beer to take to the giant, since she figured it could be a peace offering.

She drank her entire blue drink on the way over, though, which was poor planning on her part, since it left her without a drink. "Uh, hey. Hi. Hello." Anna shook her head at herself and then held up the beer. "Thirsty?"

Orion was clearly taken off guard by Anna coming back instead of Mercury, and he had actually started to reach out instinctively to pull her close when she spoke so close to him, assuming it would be his wife. He stopped the motion before he actually touched her, though, dropping his hand awkwardly. "Um . . . yeah, actually." He took the beer from her, then looked back and forth between it and her a few times before he started to raise the bottle to his lips. "Is it poisoned? Because I don't think I've racked up sick time to take off just yet."

Anna raised her eyebrow as he inched the bottle closer to his lips. "Unfortunately I haven't made any friends who have access to poison. Yet. So you're in the clear." She crossed her arms as she stared up at him. "I was a bitch to you earlier, and while I'd like to lie and say that's not my normal setting, it is. I should not have directed it at you, though. Sorry."

He still didn't quite take a sip, and he looked down at the bottle in his hand, raising it toward her in some kind of toast. "So this is how you apologize? Bringing people alcohol? Because if so, then I'm pretty sure we can be friends. I just want to make sure this is a regular occurrence I can count on in the future."

"If I can involve alcohol in any number of things, I typically like to do that. Apologies included. But, in all fairness, you were being an asshole too. Just sayin'." She held up her hands after that and kept her distance. "Don't count on the regular occurrence of booze. I'm not a waitress."

"That's fair. Apology accepted." He raised the bottle again and sighed when he saw that the glass she was holding was empty. "Cheers." He took a drink and took half a step back, just to maintain the space between them. "How, um, how did the rest of your day go?"

"It was alright." She glanced over at the giant's friends as they eyed her silently, but she kept talking. "Did you get a block on your contacts? We couldn't send shit through and the computer said someone did it on purpose."

Orion nodded. "Communications restriction to all external recipients. Mercury and I both have it. We haven't been getting anything in either, and I know my sister's been sending me stuff, since she never stops."

"We should do something about that." She replied without further explanation. She looked over at his friends before she stepped closer to them and stuck out her hand. "Anna Bickford. Apparently some computer program thinks I'm supposed to be sexually entwined with your giant friend here."

Carl looked down at the woman briefly and burst out laughing in spite of himself as he took her hand. "Carl Espinoza. We met briefly down on the ground." He motioned to Aiko and introduced her with a smile. "The computer told us the same thing about each other, we just don't happen to have the complications you do. Aren't you and your husband the ones who were right at the impact site of the arm when it came down?"

Carl's laughter relaxed her just slightly as she nodded. "Close to it. It landed on a nearby farm, we were the first ones to show up." Anna held out her arm and traced a faint line, the only evidence left of the incident. "I tried to wander through the wreckage and sliced the hell out of my arm. I was hoping . . ." Anna shook her head mid-sentence, since remembering what she saw was traumatic. "It was fucked up. I hope that never happens again."

"That makes all of us." Orion agreed as he sipped at his beer, looking Anna over appraisingly. He had known from the moment he met her that she was far from the quiet or reserved type, but she was definitely more ballsy than he had first guessed. "But considering it's never happened before, I'd say our odds are pretty good."

A humorless laugh escaped her lips as she thought about odds. "Well, I don't seem to have the best luck recently, except marrying Logan, so I'm holding my breath about what my odds actually look like." Talking about her husband encouraged Anna to look back at him, but when she did, she saw him talking to the redheaded doctor by the alcohol. It felt like a punch in the gut, even though it wasn't like she was witnessing anything scandalous. Logan was having a conversation the same as she was. She couldn't help feeling jealous anyway. "You seem to have decent luck, though, your wife is unrealistically attractive."

"You are not wrong about that. She definitely is." He followed her look back at the bar, but she could see the same punch in his expression when he saw Logan sitting near Mercury, and he watched them for longer than he really needed to. "I um, yeah, I've definitely been sending my lucky stars some love letters this past month. She's amazing." He forced himself to turn away from the bar, since he wasn't going to be the guy who felt like he had to watch his wife at all times. He wasn't. "What's the story with you two? I know you guys don't really buy into the matching program down there."

"Logan and I have been best friends since we could walk, pretty much." She didn't allow herself to look back at the bar again, but her confidence and bravado had definitely deflated a bit. "It was a story of multiple missed opportunities to be with each other, and once he married someone else, I applied to Eleusis to get away from it. His wife died last year and then a month ago, after a piece of a space station fell out of the sky, we realized that nothing should stand in the way of being with someone you want to be with."

Orion couldn't help but smile at the snark in the woman's voice, and he told himself he shouldn't feel bad about smiling, since it was a good thing that she was talking about. That was all they were doing. Talking. "Yeah, I guess if somebody had dropped a station on my head, I'd be thinking pretty hard about priorities too. Sounds like you've been missing each other a while. I'm glad it worked out."

"Me too. At least before we decided to come up here." She added acidically. "We came up here because we want to get to Eleusis and we want our families to get there too. You and the doctor, similar things, I can only assume. We should work together to make it happen."

"I think everyone in this room is on the same page when it comes to wanting to get to Eleusis." He glanced around quickly, but stopped before he glanced over at the bar, since he didn't want to see what was happening over there. "Getting there is going to be tricky if they're already trying to lock us down on the first day, though. What kind of 'working together' are you suggesting?"

"Well, no one else is getting fucked over *quite* like we are." Anna looked over at Carl and Aiko. "You two look like you're getting along well enough. I don't think you're feeling the same kind of drive that I am. No offense."

"None taken. If I was in your situation, I'd be pissed too." Carl had moved over the course of the conversation to stand behind Aiko, with his hands still loosely clasped around her to hold her against him. "Anybody tries to tell me I'm supposed to spend any time with *that* hideous freak, I'd punch them in the face." He nodded to Orion with a smile that Orion didn't entirely return.

Anna laughed but she looked Orion up and down. "You're genetically altered. You're not hideous. Trust me, I've seen hideous." She didn't want to imagine for even a second what he would look like shirtless or naked, though the fact that she was supposed to sleep with the guy made it hard not to think about it. Just a little bit. Anna had spent years jumping from partner to partner, and only a month married. Some habits were a little hard to break. "That's not the problem."

"No, it's not." Orion agreed, and finally allowed himself to look back at the bar, where Logan and Mercury had kept precisely the same distance between them, even though that fact didn't comfort him the way he knew it probably should have.

When he spoke again, he turned away from Carl and Aiko and kept his voice low, for only Anna to hear. "Mercury and I don't have any intention of complying with the match that they've given us. We came here tonight so that we would be seen talking to you two, kind of like we are now. If we do things like this, see each other, interact, we want to see what the system does. If it eases up, we'll know we're being manipulated by somebody and that the new matches are rigged. I just don't understand why."

"I was hoping that you two would know a little more about what's going on than we do." Anna answered just as quietly, but oddly, she felt more comfortable standing closer to him than she did about seeing Logan near the doctor. "I guess we'll have to figure out more along the way."

"I wish we did." He shook his head and then turned his attention back to his beer to keep from checking on Mercury. "The match program has a lot of history behind it, so most people up here trust it. Mercury and I were matched, and things have been great until we got here. Even a lot of your people from down below seem to be pretty comfortable with it. But that's just more of a reason why I think it was tampered with in our case."

"My money would be on Santos, she seems like the type to treat people like lab rats. But without knowing why, there's not much we can do about it. If she just enjoys fucking with people, then she could've done that anywhere, with anyone. Not sure why she decided to do it with just us and just inside the Initiative. It doesn't make any sense. Especially if we're all gonna be on the other side of the galaxy in a year."

"They've altered enough shit already that I wouldn't be surprised if they were lying about the timeline too." Anna said flatly before she looked down at the empty drink in her hands. "Even if the program wasn't tampered with, I think we both agree that we're happy the way we are with our spouses. Just from the flight over here, I would be stupid not to acknowledge the fact that you and I get along easily. And sure, I'd probably be interested if I wasn't married. You're attractive. But I am married, and you are too. So maybe the program knows how to put compatible people together, but that doesn't mean shit when people have free will. If we even have that anymore."

"Nobody's planted a match program in my head, and if anybody comes at me with a scalpel to do so, I'll make sure they choke on it." He sounded angrier than someone as easygoing as Orion was usually capable of, but it was a crap situation and they all knew it.

"We've still got a choice about this, even if they're gonna try and encourage things to go their way. While we're working on finding out why, the four of us can plan to see each other at stuff like this, in between other things if we have to. See if that eases things up. If not, then I'll make sure you get flying lessons. Not like it's gonna take you long to pick it up, from the way you were grabbing things yesterday."

Anna's expression softened a little when he said that he would make sure she got flying lessons. "Thanks. I really do want to learn how to fly one of those things. I just . . . I was really angry."

"Yeah, I'm guessing that happens to you a lot." He said with an expression that was probably teasing, but she didn't know the man well enough to be absolutely certain. "Gonna have to start calling you Sparky like this one kid in my training class who kept getting pissed off and trying to punch the instructor."

"Sparky?" She laughed and shook her head before she realized that Logan and the doctor weren't standing by the alcohol anymore. It made her instantly thirsty for more booze. "If I punch you, you'll remember it. I pack a mean one." Anna tugged at her dress uncomfortably, since it was still bothering her, but she was even more uncomfortable with Logan MIA. "I'm going to get another drink. Or ten. Do you want to come with me?"

He looked over at the bar as well, but didn't see Mercury anywhere, which meant she wasn't immediately on her way back to him. He tried very hard to ignore that fact, but consequently didn't ignore it at all. "Sure. I doubt they'll let you hit ten, since they normally cut off after four or five, but you're welcome to try."

5

The last person Mercury wanted to run into while getting a drink for Orion was Logan Bickford, but somehow it happened. "Hello, Mr. Bickford." She kept her distance and held the bottle tightly in her hand as she glanced his way.

Logan tensed up visibly at the sound of her voice, but he looked over and nodded to her just as politely. "Dr. Finnegan. I hope the rest of today was a little less interesting than this morning?"

"It was busy, of course. Though it will be like that for the next month, at least. Adults are not nearly as fun or cute to handle as my usual patients." She replied with a plastered polite smile before she turned her attention back to the drink in her hand. Mercury saw Orion with Mrs. Bickford, so she grabbed a water bottle for herself. "You and your wife look very nice tonight, though it must be different not to wear your own clothes."

"Space fashions don't make much sense to me." He admitted freely, then nodded back to Anna. "Or to her. I've always tried to be practical when it comes to clothes, and these . . ." he looked down at himself and the getup he was in. "They're plenty formal, I'm just not seeing the point of most of it." He finally looked back over at her, and glanced down at her dress the same way he had a few minutes earlier. "You look very nice as well."

"Thank you." She looked down at herself before she drank from the water bottle. "I'm used to more practical clothing as well, mostly scrubs. I suppose it isn't terrible to look nice every now and again, though." Mercury took another sip of water before she just stared at the bottle in her hand. "I'm curious, does the water taste different here than it does on Earth? I imagine it must, but even when we touched down on Earth to pick up passengers, we only drank what we brought with us."

Logan nodded as he looked down at his own glass, which was filled with what they tried to call whiskey, rather than water.

"Everything is different." He said thoughtfully, staring into the liquid as if it would answer some of his questions.

"My impulsive brother bought a set of atomically-sanded glasses on a whim once, said they would make a nice addition to our glassware in the kitchen. None of us could stand to drink out of them after more than a day or so. Just didn't feel right. Everything up here is the same way. Glasses are too smooth, floors are too clean, everything's too simple. Even the whiskey tastes like somebody described what whiskey tastes like and somebody tried to synthesize the flavor."

He nodded over at her bottle with a slight shrug. "The water's fine, though. Bottled water's never the same as it's gonna be from the tap out of the well, but it's water. One of the better constants between the two places."

"Everything is too simple." She repeated as she thought about her surroundings and how she had never once thought of everything as simple, but she rarely paid attention to her surroundings. There was too much that went on in her head to pay attention to her surroundings unless she was doing something like taking a photo or painting. "That's an interesting view. Earth felt so vast and massive. It was overwhelming. Beautiful, though." Mercury glanced back at Orion and sighed as she watched Mr. Bickford's animated wife. "How does she have so much . . . passion? Her facial expressions and body language have so much emotion behind them."

That question actually brought a smile out of Logan and he looked back over his shoulder at Anna. She seemed to be talking with Carl about something the massive man thought was funny. "Just the way she's built. You think she's energetic now, just try and swap a generic brand in for her corn flakes in the morning. She goes completely feral. It's hilarious."

Mercury laughed softly, though she was watching Orion as he talked with Anna while Carl and Aiko stood by. "It's nice that you know things like that about her. I don't even know if I know my parents that well. I've spent a large portion of my life away from them in training. I don't know if I know *anyone* that well."

Logan looked over at her in spite of himself, his eyebrows knitted in a way that completely altered his face. He had pleasant features, if a little on the rough side, but they were typically smooth and fairly calm. One little raise of the eyebrows, though, and his look could have been taken for either worry or anger.

Apparently there was no middle ground with the man. "Grief, how long have you been in training? Did they let you get out of diapers first, or would that have delayed things too much?"

Mercury laughed again. "I started when I was about eight. I officially started my medical training at fourteen. My father is a government official, so he travels a lot. Once I started my medical training, I lived on a different station than my parents. So I never saw them much after that. My mother tells me it's a miracle I retained any of my accent at all."

"By fourteen, that kind of thing is pretty well fixed, as I understand it." He seemed to be timing his glances, careful not to look at her for too long at once. "Goes with the hair."

Mercury tugged on one of the loose strands of her hair. "It sure does. On my home station, there are quite a few. It's where a lot of the Irish population who survived CV settled together." She finished her water and refused to allow herself to look back at Orion again. "If you don't mind, I think I'm going to sit down. I don't want to take up any more of your time. I'm just going to sit and wait for Orion." She knew it was an abrupt response, but she was feeling more and more uncomfortable.

Logan hesitated before he responded and picked up his drink reluctantly. "Would you mind if I joined you? If we've been matched, and the administration expects us to at least act as if we're considering their twisted ideas, we ought to know who it is we've been rematched with, at minimum."

Mercury looked into his stormy eyes and gave a small shrug. "If you want to, feel free." She took Orion's drink with her as she grabbed another water and sat down at a nearby table. "I'll answer any questions you like. I'm a fairly open person."

He followed her to the low table along the wall of the gallery and immediately hated the fact that the tables' entire purpose seemed to be allowing people to be private without actually being private at all. They were still exposed on one side to the gallery at large, but the table was set into a hollow in the wall, which left them in their own alcove away from the rest of those gathered. But maybe an impression of seeking privacy without actually being private would be enough for the powers that were blocking them from speaking to their families.

"I wish I had more creative questions, but since I don't really know anything about you, I'd have to start with the most basic ones. If you've been in some kind of training since you were eight, what was it that made you want to be a doctor, two thirds of your life ago?"

"I told you that my father is a government official. At one point in time he was also a liaison for people that came up from Earth. Until they were treated and could be housed appropriately, families often stayed with us or near us for several days. I often heard stories about people dying, or people being left behind, and whenever there were children my age, they were always so sad about leaving home."

"I asked my father several times the reason why people had to leave Earth and why people were dying, and eventually he told me it was because people on Earth got sick and it made them die very young but that no one had come up with a way to fix it. So I wanted to come up with a way to fix it. I have always been curious about CV, but eventually babies also became a fascination of mine, so I took the practical route of gynecology and obstetrics and decided to study CV in that field so that I could get support for my research. If you try to research CV without working in a particular field, most of the time you hit a dead end because no one will sponsor your work."

That clearly got Logan's attention. "Why's that? Because everyone assumes it's a dead end or because it's just Earth people dying instead of Orbital ones?"

"It has been centuries since CV hit Earth, and no one has found a cure or a reason. They don't think anyone ever will." Mercury admitted honestly, and she didn't recoil from the venom in his tone. He wasn't the first person from Earth who hated people from space on principle, and he wouldn't be the last. "There is little recent research involving CV, but I do all I can to dig up whatever I can find. It would be helpful if I had more access to information from Earth, but that doesn't really happen much either. The Consortium has a lot of restrictions on the data they deem usable."

"That's funny, Doc Weber always described it as being the other way around." He sipped at his drink as he watched his strange match. The woman was incredibly intelligent, just from how much she knew about everything. Logan could tell he was barely scratching the surface of what her mind was doing behind the scenes. "She said she could get medical data from some of the wilderness retreats in Nepal more easily than she could get any kind of census data from orbit."

Mercury's expression definitely clouded at that, since she wasn't pleased to hear that. "Maybe you can give me contact information for your doctor and she and I can share information? I've never met a doctor who was trained on Earth."

"She was trained in space, actually. But her daughter's been trained by her entirely on Earth." He actually remembered Dr. Weber's information by heart, so he pulled out his communicator and sent it to Mercury while he was thinking about it. "If they actually let you correspond with her, especially now, I'll be incredibly surprised."

"Well, I can try." She smiled when he sent her the information. "You're one of my patients, right? Maybe under that guise I can get some information from her."

"Devious." He gave her an approving smile in return, but it didn't stay on his face long before guilt at even smiling in her presence turned him back to his drink. "Hopefully it gets through. Wouldn't want you to have to go without my vaccination history or something."

Mercury drank her water in silence awhile, though she was starting to feel quite bored of water. Her caloric restrictions weren't as strict under the Initiative as they were on Seven, but if that day had been any indication, she would be too busy to eat most of the time. "Is it wrong to behave friendly toward each other?" She eventually asked, since his guilt was written clearly across his face. "We're not doing anything wrong by attempting to be friends. If you feel guilty, then by extension I should feel guilty too, but I don't. I haven't wronged my husband by talking to you."

"I haven't wronged Anna either. But our ability to be just friends was compromised the moment we were matched." He didn't sound happy or angry about it, it just sounded like it was something he had already gotten himself to accept. "We've been tasked by the Initiative with wronging our spouses, and they've made it pretty clear already that they don't really give a damn about our own feelings on the subject."

"So that's it for you, then?" She was surprised he was just going to fall in line with the ridiculous idea of having intercourse with a stranger. "If you think we can't be friends and in the end we're just going to have to have intercourse together, then why ask to know my personal feelings and thoughts? If you just wanted to look chatty and avoid being friends, you could have asked about things that don't matter. Favorite color, favorite food, favorite holiday." She stared at him across the table from her and he could see the annoyance in her features. "Don't ask me about how my dream to be a doctor developed and then tell me we cannot be friends."

"That wasn't my intention." He shook his head and met her eyes for once, the storm in his look wasn't backing down at her annoyance. "We're in a crossed situation, is what I'm saying. No matter what we become to each other, what we do or don't do, we're crossed against something or someone. Whatever we are or aren't, it's complicated."

"I know that." Mercury replied simply, since saying it was complicated was as if he was saying there was no air in space. It was obvious. "It is complicated. However, no matter what they do, we still have a choice in how we behave. I don't intend to have intercourse with you, but even if I did, I still belong to Orion. I still love him. They can't change how I feel about him or my devotion to him."

"Or how I feel about Anna." He agreed, and finished off his whiskey. "I'm not known for my obedient tendencies. I've never had to be and never felt any compulsion to be. I was taking care of my brother and sister by ten years old, and taking care of business with the help of family friends who I had to outthink just to keep on top of it. So I don't have much talent in taking orders. Not something I intend to gain, either. I want what I want, and that's Anna, and that's finding a way to get to Eleusis and get to work without anyone trying to fuck with my life or anyone else's. But I don't know enough about what's even going on up here to know if that's possible anymore."

"We'll work together to try and get the information you need, and we'll all try to figure things out." Mercury said calmly as she continued to stare at him across the table. "As a doctor, I have certain access to things that other people don't. Is there something you would like me to try and find for you?"

He considered that offer quietly for a while before he said anything. "Yes, there is. I'd like personal histories and information on as many of the top brass as possible. If someone's pulling the strings on my life, I'd like to know the character of the people doing the pulling, so far as that's possible."

"I'll see what I can get for you. I can give it to you at your treatment." She finished off her second bottle of water and looked at the beer she was still keeping close for Orion. "It was interesting to speak with you, Mr. Bickford. I should get back to my husband." Mercury didn't want to talk about the situation anymore, since it made her feel dirty, but not because she had any romantic interest in Logan. She felt dirty because she was trying to be friendly and he didn't care a bit about it, only about appearances.

Mercury had gotten up and started away from the table before he spoke. "Dr. Finnegan." He stopped her and got up himself, carrying his empty whiskey glass. "I hope I'm wrong. I hope that we can be friends through this."

"I hope so too." Mercury replied in a clipped response. She didn't really think it was possible, based on his attitude alone. "I will see you tomorrow for your treatment. Have a nice evening, Mr. Bickford." Mercury didn't wait to see if he would say anything else and hurried to find Orion. Everything would make sense again when she was with Orion, and that was all that mattered.

Logan went back to the bar to get a refill on his whiskey, and was glad to see Anna nearby, though he was less glad to see Orion not far off. He went to Anna and sighed as he met her eyes. "It was my turn tonight to be the one pissing somebody off. How did yours go?"

"It was alright. I have a shining sense of humor that makes me quite endearing." She said with a sarcastic laugh before she grabbed another drink, but a holographic image popped up out of thin air, showing her blood-alcohol level. Apparently she was over the limit. Anna swatted at the image like a bug, but it only flickered and she went about destroying another drink anyway. "What did you do to piss her off? Tell her that a hair was out of place?"

"No, even worse, I spoke realistically about what's happening." He rolled his eyes at his own comment and clinked his glass with hers. "Here's to appearances."

She sighed dramatically before she guzzled more of her glass, even though the room was getting a little hazy. "Can we get the fuck out of here, Logan? I've been socialized enough."

"You and me both." He downed his whiskey in a hurry and set the glass upside down on the bar. The moon was making another obvious pass through the gallery windows, but Logan couldn't bring himself to give it more than a passing glance. "Come on."

Anna jumped up, even in her dress, so she could end up in his arms if he would catch her. "Whisk me away, dear husband."

He caught her and her playfulness finally managed to put a smile back on his face. "As you command, my love." He edged through the crowd cautiously, and used her feet to kick a few people out of the way if they lingered in the wrong place too long. They had most of the people they passed laughing as they went by, but Logan was just glad to be back out in the hallway where they could be more or less alone.

As she leaned into the corner of the lift, he took out his communicator and his smile fell. "Five new messages. Two each from Liam and Larissa and one from Doc Weber asking how the trip was."

Anna cursed before she kissed him again anyway. "Orion talked about setting up 'dates' if this fucking worked, and I'm pissed that it did. Because that really means they're going to manipulate us into doing whatever the hell they want, and I don't like that kind of precedent."

Logan couldn't disagree with that, and he just held her as they slowly moved farther out from the center of the station and their bodies began feeling closer to their normal accustomed weight. "What it means is that they created a situation, we responded, and they listened. All it means is that we know they're listening. How the conversation goes from here is still up to us."

Anna slipped her hand into Logan's and held tightly. "Why does she have to be so pretty? God, I hate it. I hate it because what if you do have to get all naked with her and then I'll be this sub-par country mouse compared to that woman. She's got boobs like every woman wants and an ass to back it up with. It's not fair."

"The only ass I want backing anything up against me is this one." He grabbed her by her backside to hold her up in a sizzling kiss. "She could be Helen of Troy with whiskey fountains for nipples and I would still choose you. No contest."

"You're so romantic." She said with a groan as he grabbed her ass and held her up. "I'm glad to hear that you're not tempted by whiskey nipples." Anna mumbled against his lips before she leaned into his ear. "And I'm not wearing any underwear."

"Mmmm . . ." Logan growled against her neck. "I knew I liked you."

* * * * *

Jessie and Gordon wandered as some people started to filter out of the social. Soon after they finally sat down at a table, she noticed he was watching a nearby group with one of his more intense stares. A thin, willowy woman with platinum blonde hair was the center of conversation, half a dozen men around her. As soon as Jessie saw the woman she felt jealous of Gordon's attention on the group, but she tried not to jump to a possibly-erroneous conclusion. "Friends of yours?"

Gordon nodded without looking back immediately, picking up the mixed non-alcoholic drink he had acquired from the bar after receiving some amused looks for it. "Old friends, some of them. Well, people I'm friendly with. I'm not sure I actually have any friends in the classical definition of the term." He smiled over at her and took her hand, looking back at the group to point them out.

"The three tall ones are with us, the short one with the crazy sleeves, he's also with us. The rest might be, but they're new, I don't know them. The one in the middle is with us. Her name's Tatyana." His voice audibly dropped when he mentioned her, and he looked back at Jessie before continuing. "My ex. The only one of the three of them still alive."

"Of course she is." Jessie muttered only halfway to herself, even though she knew he would hear her. "Your ex is a model?"

"She actually hates getting her picture taken. Or being on camera in any way. Which is why I was surprised she actually came up here, to say the least." He shook his head and looked away from Tatyana, back to Jessie with a reassuring smile, though there were ghosts behind it. "I was the one who broke it off with her, a little over a year ago."

"So she probably still has feelings for you." Jessie replied before she got up from the table, since she wasn't going to sit around and watch him reminisce about his ex-girlfriend. "I guess I better go meet her, then." She didn't even look back at him as she moved away from the table, since she wanted to stake her claim even before the woman had a chance to realize that Gordon was in the room.

Gordon opened his mouth to answer, but instead thought better of it and closed it again, smiling as he watched her go. He leaned back in his seat as she headed across the room and put his arm up along the back of the bench he was sitting on, taking his drink in his other hand to sip at it as he watched.

"Well," he muttered to himself against the rim of the cup, "this should be interesting."

Jessie had no problem marching up to the group and making her presence known, fueled by jealousy and anger. She wasn't going to sit idly by when she finally had someone she thought was hers. Of all the people to show up and be a part of the Initiative, why did one of his exes have to show up?

"Excuse me." She said loudly, and a few of the men around Tatyana looked back at her. "New arrivals?"

All of the men looked at her as if she was a little touched in the brain for randomly approaching them, eyebrows raised, their expressions faintly amused. Up close, she could tell from their bearing they were the rough kind of men, accustomed to violence and certainly not afraid of a challenge. One of them seemed to take it as his job to get rid of her, and he turned a little away from the group to face her.

"We're all new here, aren't we?" He was about her height, tall as she was, and was in jeans and a tight button-down shirt. He looked her up and down with a grin. "You don't look quite as new as I generally prefer, though." That got a laugh from a few of the men around him, all of whom were looking Jessie over the exact same way.

"Figures." She pinned him with a poisonous glare. "Anyone who's already had their cherry popped would know to stay away from someone like you. I bet you can't even last five minutes, can you, big guy?"

"Things you'll never know, Bessie." The name got another round of laughs from his friends, which only encouraged the man further. "Are you lost, bitch? Or has the lower gravity made you forget you're still the same size and there's still no one interested?"

"I'm not lost." She inched closer to the man as though she was going to take a swing at him herself. "And I'm not here to talk to you, asshole. I'm here to talk to the blonde twig you're guarding, probably because she would snap in half if there was a single breeze in this place."

That seemed to confuse the man quickly, and he turned back toward Tatyana, clearly not afraid of Jessie or her potential swings, and spoke in Russian. "You know this bitch, T?"

Tatyana turned her icy blue eyes on the stranger and replied, also in Russian. "I've never seen her before, but I suppose that doesn't mean everything." Tatyana narrowed her eyes at the woman before she tucked her nearly-white blonde hair behind her ear. "What do you want with me?" She responded in English.

"It seems that you're intimately acquainted with my match." She motioned backward in the general direction of Gordon's table. "I just wanted to meet you and clear the air. Because whatever history you have with him, it stays there. In the past."

Tatyana smirked, even though she hadn't looked around to see who the woman was talking about. "I see." She eventually spotted Gordon and smiled even brighter. "He mentioned me, did he?"

The ex's smile and the still-stinging comment by the meathead made her more angry and insecure at the same time. "He did. Which is why I'm here, clearly."

Tatyana pushed past some of the men and the jabbering woman as though Jessie didn't even exist, and made a beeline toward the table where Gordon was still sitting.

As Tatyana approached the table, the expression on the face of the meathead who had taken it upon himself to play guard-dog had completely changed. All trace of cockiness or amusement had fled from his face and the faces of the other men around him. "You're matched with White?" The man asked quietly, naked fear evident in his eyes and in the eyes of all the men around him.

Jessie was still stunned that Tatyana had just pushed past her. "Unless he changes his mind, yes." She was clearly worried that he was going to change his mind now that Tatyana was gliding toward the table, and her stomach twisted in knots.

"Hey, all that shit about Bessie was just about looking out for Sery, alright? I'm sorry. That doesn't need to get back to White. Please." She could hear the man's voice almost trembling as he spoke. All the other men in the small circle had started edging back from her and from King Meathead slowly, trying to dissociate themselves as much as possible.

She clearly didn't think his apology was genuine, though his fear clearly was. Jessie eventually shook her head. "No, it wasn't looking out for anyone, it was just an asshole being an asshole." Jessie was still feeling the sting from his insults, but she wasn't about to go running to Gordon even if the man next to her clearly feared her match for some reason or another. "And I don't need Gordon to deal with it." She spat at the man before she convinced herself to follow after the twiggy blonde.

Tatyana sat down across from Gordon easily and smiled at him across the table. "Interesting match you have there." She didn't look back, she just stared at him, still smiling. "Not even two days up here and you're talking to your match about me? Do you miss me?"

He responded in Russian, the same as she had begun, though his accent wasn't quite as natural as hers. "I mentioned to her during our introductions that I had an ex who might be joining us in the Initiative. You showed up just now with the rest of your dogs, and I indicated who you were. That's the extent of the conversations you've been a part of."

He sipped at his drink, not bothered by her presence, even if she knew him well enough to see when he was internally squirming. He switched back to English as he looked back up at her, glancing out at the group she'd left behind. "You've trained a few more to fetch and heel since I saw your roster last. Do they know you'll want them to roll over and play dead before long too, or are you saving those tricks for later?"

"You know me better than anyone." She reached across to take his drink and to take a sip for herself without breaking eye contact. "You know I don't hide the dangers, and if I don't run from them, I don't expect anyone else to run either." She held onto his drink, hoping that he would reach out for it himself. "They know the risks. Same as you."

Instead of taking his drink back from her, he just picked up Jessie's beside him and sipped at it instead. "Risks can be mitigated." He set the drink back down beside him where Jessie could get to it when she got back, and he smiled faintly to see her heading through the crowd to get back to their table before looking back at Tatyana. "But that's why I'm here. To mitigate risks and ensure the best outcome. At least you and I still seem to agree on what that is, even if that's the last thing left in that category."

"We still want the same things." She tilted her head back to finish off his drink quickly before she turned her icy gaze back to his face. "Still don't consume alcohol, I see." She quirked an eyebrow as she watched his gaze flit to his new match and then back to her. "She's not your usual."

"Neither were you." He said casually, and actually smiled, though it had nothing to do with actually being happy to see Tatyana. "Of course, considering my 'usual' would be either a pedophile or a cougar depending on time frames, I'd say most things are an improvement."

He looked up as Jessie approached the table, and slid her drink over toward her side of the bench, motioning to the space beside him with his arm along the back of it. "Welcome back. I missed you."

Jessie hesitated for a moment before she sat down, clearly not expecting such a comment. "That, um, that didn't go quite the way I had hoped." She glared across the table at the ex, who was still fucking smiling. It made her skin crawl. "You can't have him back." She finally said, since that was the whole point of her approach in the first place.

"I can't?" Tatyana said as she looked from Jessie to Gordon. Jessie could tell she hadn't been the one to end things. It was crystal clear in the way that she looked at him. "We'll see."

"We're here to work, Tatyana." His fingers began moving along the back of Jessie's shoulder, just to let her know he was there with her, not with the tiny woman with the coloring of an ice queen. "And I wouldn't be here if I didn't have to be. I'm glad to see that you're well, but I hope we can leave personal matters behind us and concentrate on the present. And the future."

"So we're simply keeping up appearances, then." Her gaze skipped over to Jessie and then she gave Gordon a nod before she switched back to Russian. "I'm glad you're here, whatever your reason, White." She tapped his cup on the table and left it behind as she slid out from the booth and went back to the men waiting for her without saying another word.

All of Tatyana's looks and her last statement slithered inside Jessie's mind and she didn't like feeling as though she was being used for appearances. She didn't say anything about it, though, since her ego was wounded enough as it was. "I think I want to go back to the unit."

"You and me both." He said with a sigh before getting up to follow her out of the booth and out of the gathering.

Once they weren't weaving between people to get out, he took her hand again as they went to the lift. "What do you want to know about all that back there?"

"Are you going to change your mind?" She asked almost too quickly once they were in the lift, but luckily, they were alone. "Now that you saw her and she's here and she wants you back. Are you going to change your mind?"

"She's wanted me back since I left. That's not a change. And no, I'm not going to change my mind." He selected the number for their level and turned to lean against the back of the lift facing her. "I told you, I walked away from her. And I had reasons enough that I've never once looked back."

Jessie looked at him without saying anything for at least a minute before her gaze dropped to her feet. "Those men with her reminded me that it's hard for me to find someone who will want to stay with me. I just . . . she looked at me like I was nothing. They all did. I don't want you to think that."

He didn't do or say anything in the silence that followed, but when he did reach out for her, he ran the back of his fingers up from her waist over her chest to her chin, lifting it to look at him. Normally, when she looked at Gordon and he was looking at her, she could see all the secrets he held like walls behind his eyes, an entire life grown accustomed to not being known, not being seen, accustomed to hiding any of his real thoughts or feelings in case they were discovered by the wrong people.

The only time she had ever seen those walls fall completely was when they were in bed together the past day since their matching, completely fixed on her and devoted to her in the throes of what they did to each other. As she looked at him in that moment, though, there were no walls, no secrets. Only a deep-burning and dangerously secretive rage in the midst of an otherwise calm face.

"Which one of them was it?" He said slowly, forming each word carefully to keep himself from growling.

She was surprised by the amount of anger she saw in his expression and his eyes, and she quickly remembered the fear on the men's faces as soon as they realized she was with Gordon. Jessie didn't know why the men were so afraid of him, but now she saw a reason why they might be. "It doesn't matter." Jessie said quickly. "I don't know their names, and it's all been said to me several times before. I try not to let it get to me, but with her here and how new everything is between us. . . I just didn't want you to suddenly remember that you could have someone better."

He eventually nodded, but she could tell he wasn't just going to let something like that go so easily. He took a handful of the front of her dress and pulled her in closer to him so he could rest his forehead against hers.

"I went shopping before the informational meeting." He said quietly, working hard to get away from the anger she could still feel in his grip. "Not seriously, just browsing the database of the accepted, once the letters went out. They sent almost five thousand acceptance letters to people on Earth, and got only a little over fifteen hundred who actually decided to come up here. Tells you a lot about the smarts of Earth people, I think." He shook his head.

"There's a lot of very beautiful women here. They had their own selection bias when they went through and approved everyone, obviously, so I'm guessing Kaplan was the one who did most of the work on that front. A few ex-models, a few models from orbit too, though they always look even less healthy than the ones from Earth. There are some true knockouts up here, objectively speaking. I'm aware of who's here, and I'm aware of what my options could have been if I had wanted them to be. Could've had any of them, could've had any two or three of them if I had decided to institute polygamy protocols. Those are written into the Initiative's coding, they just didn't end up being necessary. I'm aware of all that."

He ran his hands up over her significant breasts to her face as he kissed her, and then back down again to hold her against him. "I'd much rather be aware of you, given whatever options you want to throw at me. And if I can be a little blunt here, Ms. Rogers, I am going to fuck you until you believe me when I say so." He was smiling by the end of the speech, but only because he had her so close and she wasn't pulling away.

Her cheeks were flushed after the last bit of his speech, but she only responded by kissing him hastily and desperately. She was breathing a little heavily by the time she stopped kissing him when the lift stopped. "I don't want you to 'keep up appearances' with me. I want to be someone you trust. I barely know you, and I understand that developing that trust takes time. Especially because I know that you must be hiding something big. But I'm on your side. Whatever it is. Because I believe that you want what I want."

"I believe I do." They had to prompt the doors to open again because they had taken their time with each other inside it rather than getting off immediately. "And when she said we were keeping up appearances, she was talking about her and me. I'm not just staying with you so I can blend in with the rest of the Initiative. I don't do that very well, so it's never been something I rely on heavily. I'm with you because I want you. It really is that simple, though like you said, I know it takes time to believe that." Their hands swung between them as they walked, and he spun her once as they rounded a corner, just to see her loose skirt fly up a little in the process.

Back in their unit, they stopped when they heard the computer pinging to let them know a message was waiting. Nothing had come through on her communicator, though, so Jessie was surprised to hear an alert.

"Did you get a message on your communicator? The computer isn't identifying a recipient." All they could hear over and over in their unit was that a message had been received and was waiting to be opened.

Gordon narrowed his eyes and took his communicator out of his pocket, but there was nothing chiming there. "Direct to the unit, it looks like." He tossed the communicator on a nearby table and looked up at the wall where visual messages from the computer were generally displayed. "Computer, play the pending message, please."

There was no voice or hologram that appeared, but as the message appeared on the wall, it typed out slowly instead of appearing all at once, to chilling effect. It was as though someone was waiting for them to appear, and had somehow bypassed their official contact via their communicators.

Your shuttle made it with only one casualty. You do surprise me from time to time. I did warn you. Kill count for the simultaneous launches was 294. Still not high enough to stop their big plans.

Gordon froze as he watched the words scroll out, and Jessie could see the anger from before begin to burn again in his eyes the longer it went on. There was no surprise in them, but whoever was on the other end of the message, Gordon knew them, and was not a fan. "Computer, has the sender provided a return package whereby a response can be sent?" He asked out loud, then continued under his breath. "Or are you gonna make me hunt you down to reply. Again."

Sender is standing by for a reply.

Jessie got another chill that forced her to look around as if she expected to see cameras pointed at her. "What the hell is going on? Who sent that?"

Gordon sighed, and just moved to take Jessie's hand to hold it for a brief second of reassurance, then turned back to look at the computer screen. "Send reply text. '294 unnecessary and wasteful casualties. Many of them innocent of involvement in the Consortium's games. If you truly wanted to stop them, you should never have left.'"

Jessie's hand was still hanging in the air between them from when he grabbed it to hold it while she waited. She watched the screen in confusion and horror as a reply came back through one letter at a time after his response.

There's only one way to stop them. We will continue until they shut it down. More people will need to die in order for that to happen.

Gordon's jaw was set in a hard glare as he stared at the screen, and Jessie could see his fists begin to clench at his sides. "Send response. 'Our goals have nothing to do with death and everything to do with life, Carmina. Continue fighting this war your way and the people who will die will be your own. You can still choose to support our methods in useful ways. All you're doing now is giving them more power.'"

Jessie was frozen in place as she waited for some kind of response, but it seemed like nothing was going to come again. She didn't know if that was a good thing or if it was worse. She was just about to attempt to speak again when another message started coming through on the wall.

Deliver the information we need and you will buy yourself a little more time to do it your way. Otherwise we will continue as planned.

Gordon's fists were clenched so tight it looked like any moment he might draw blood from his palms, and Jessie could see his face starting to get red, though no other hint of emotion broke through his expression. "Send . . . response." He managed to say through clenched teeth. He took his time formulating a response, but when he did answer, it was smooth and unhurried in spite of the rage in his face.

"You are no better than those we seek to destroy. A child without understanding, throwing a temper tantrum on the floor." He took a deep breath and then waved away the computer's display altogether. "If further messages arrive by that channel, computer, respond with a random selection of classical music and document the message for my review later. Confirm understanding of last order."

Order confirmed, procedure is now saved.

Jessie's heart was racing in her chest as Gordon cut off further communication. She tried to start several sentences, but they all caught in her throat until she cleared it. "There are going to be more attacks? Here?"

He took several measured breaths before he even moved, and when he did, it was to lean on the table with his fists as he focused on his breathing to keep himself calm before he responded. "Yes. There almost certainly will be." He finally began to relax as his breathing got a little easier, and he stood back up to flex his hands and stop clenching his fists. "But not tonight. Giving warning isn't much Carmina's style, and she'll know that with that kind of message, I'll be on alert for her and her thugs."

Jessie walked across their unit to the bed and sat on the edge. "How do we stop it?"

"We don't." He followed her into the bedroom. "We just prepare for it."

He stayed by the wall near the door for just long enough to let the situation sink in, then walked over to his bedside table, reaching below his shirt to pull out the data core he always wore and place it in its accustomed place.

"Hyacinth." He said quietly, which elicited a response from the data core and a bright display of its interface hologram. "Package the transcript of the conversation that just took place between me and the supposedly-unknown sender. Send the package to Grey, Green, Gold, Red, and Black, with the following accompanying message. 'Just had this conversation waiting for me in my room when we got back from the social. Everyone on alert and maintain current parameters. Green, see what you can find out, and Gold, get a message to Blue.' Send message and go to standby."

He waited until the hologram quickly confirmed it did as he ordered and it disappeared again before he turned to go back to Jessie, taking off his shirt as he went.

When he got to her, he tossed his shirt aside, and reached out a hand to caress along her cheek and neck until she looked up at him. He looked in her eyes so she could see l his anger had faded to a low boil, then nodded toward the bathroom. "Come on. Shower's got plenty of room for the both of us."

Jessie didn't ask about the message he sent, but it was obvious that the colors were people.

People like him. White.

She nodded and stood up slowly before she kissed him and ran her fingers over his chest slowly. "Will it help you? Being in the shower with me?"

"Always." He said with a smile, leaning in to kiss her gently in return, his voice low. "It's also the only place in the station where I know for certain we can talk without being overheard. There's a lot of history behind what just happened, and you need to know it."

Jessie nodded feebly and undressed quickly so they could head into the shower together. She needed to know more. She needed to know if someway, somehow, there was a chance that they weren't going to die.

6

The dinging in the unit didn't stop until Anna acknowledged it, and the message that followed informed her of a meeting that was organized that morning at which her attendance was required. It was labeled an "Aviation Audition," and had Orion's name printed as one of the main organizers.

She was, on account of having put off the message for so long, likely to be late, but she still somehow managed to make it up to the docks only a few seconds after the appointed time.

The docks were a confusing place, to say the least, since it was difficult to maintain any kind of orientation in near-zero gravity, but it was easy to spot the group she was supposed to join. They were all drifting near a door marked "Pod Access," just over a dozen men and women all looking every bit as confused as she was.

She floated past a man with olive skin and short black hair, a disparaging attitude painted clearly across his face. "Hopefully you're the last one. I don't mind a little friendly competition, but the crowd is starting to get a little thick." His accent was thickly South American, but his English was smooth. "You here to learn how to fly too?"

"Hell yes. And I wouldn't worry too much about the competition." She nodded to the others. "If they can't even decide which way to float, there's no way they're staying at a ship's controls very long." Anna held out her hand with a smile, though it was more like a grimace through her hammering hangover. She really should have listened to the annoying hologram. "Anna Bickford."

The man smiled at her comment and took her hand. "Pablo Gutierrez. Pleased to meet you, Mrs. Bickford." Clearly he remembered the detail of her marriage as well, but if the social the night before had taught her anything, it was that she and Logan and their supposed matches had quickly become the headline of the Initiative gossip column. "So what do you think? I count at least three who have absolutely no hope."

"Oh at least." She pointed at a few, one who was nearly floating away before their eyes. "Five, Six . . ."

Pablo chuckled beside her, easily keeping himself balanced and oriented with his feet casually hooked through a handle on the column. "If nobody else comes to join us, I'm gonna put my money on them eliminating five of us right off the bat. You willing to put yours on six? Or you gonna lowball me and go with four?" There was something both flirtatious and incredibly lackadaisical in Pablo's manner, his arms crossed and everything about him perfectly at ease. His confidence was almost like a physical presence surrounding him, but his genuine smile made it entertaining rather than obnoxious.

"Go big or go home, Pablo." She responded with a grin of confidence. "I'll go with six. I'm hungover and I'm still managing better than they are. I'm not even from this place. I like my chances."

"Six then. Stakes are ten seconds' head start in whatever crazy audition they've got in mind for us. You up for it?" If six people were eliminated, it would still leave them with seven other competitors besides the two of them, but it certainly went a long way toward thinning the playing field.

"Cutthroat. I like it." Anna pondered her odds and she nodded just as she saw some of the actual pilots headed down a corridor toward them. It wasn't easy to ignore Orion, since he was towering over the rest, and her eyes immediately went to him. "I'm up for it, Pablo."

Pablo just grinned, and spun in mid-air to shake her hand, though it jostled them both around quite a bit in near-zero gravity. "I believe we are going to be friends, Mrs. Bickford. May the best potential pilot win."

"Good morning, possibilities." Orion stopped himself smoothly on a column near the group. "As your invitation should have indicated, you're here this morning because either you've shown an aptitude for navigation or you indicated an interest in learning. You're the first round out of three that we'll be teaching between now and liftoff for Eleusis. If you do well and learn fast enough, maybe some of you will be helping us teach the second and third rounds. We'll see. I'm not impressed yet. You want me to be impressed."

In spite of his drill sergeant tone, Orion was still smiling, his eyes jumping from one of the prospects to the other. "There'll be two tests today, and you'll be scored based on how well you execute those two tests. Please note, it's possible to finish the tests first and still not get the best score. Despite popular belief, being a pilot, especially in space, is about how well you fly, not how fast."

He had to stop mid-speech as one of the others floating nearby lost his grip on the column nearby and began floating in mid-air without any kind of purchase within reach. He flailed in panic, setting himself spinning wildly in mid-air, and Orion just shook his head.

Nearby, Fitch moved to grab the man and put him back on a column, but Orion still looked at him with a sigh. "Some of you clearly need a little more time in zero gravity before working with actual vessels, I'm thinking. You can go. You'll be included in the auditions for the second round of training in a couple months." He pointed at the man who had started to float away, as well as two more who were clinging tightly to the column as if they were going to fall away into nothing. "And you and you, and you, with the . . . yeah. Are you alright? Still hung over?"

The man nodded, turning both a little red in embarrassment and a little green, apparently about to be sick.

"Yeah, go, quickly, before you throw up all over my dock. Anybody else?" He looked around and waved off another woman who raised her hand and volunteered to wait until the next round, making five that had already been eliminated. "The rest of you alright?"

Anna frowned a little at that, since she had been keeping count and she was down one. "Aw, come on." She muttered as she looked over at Pablo. "One more. There's gotta be *one*."

"Alright, looks like the rest of you think you're ready to try and fly something." Orion announced when it didn't appear there were any other takers on his offer of an out. "How many have we got, eight? Good, that'll simplify things. Follow me, please." He and the other four instructors took hold of the columns and, strangely, headed down toward the exit to the docks, the landing plate near the lifts they had come in on.

The docks were empty aside from their group and a minimal stream of people coming and going from the lifts near them to one or another of the areas that were available in zero gravity. The space was more than a hundred meters across, a perfect sphere that was shot through with navigation and support columns, dotted with pods here and there for a bar, storage, tiny hotel pods, and a long panel along one wall for Nav Control, populated with a dozen workers watching flight paths all around the station, including small debris in the path of their orbit.

"Look at it this way." Pablo and Anna followed the pilots down toward the lift platform, tossing themselves from one column to the next in long, fluid movements, "you'll have ten more seconds to kick that headache before you have to jump into whatever they have us doing."

Anna glared and managed to elbow him and set him off balance, which made her feel a little better. "I'll still beat you."

Fitch managed to look back and witness Anna land an elbow on a guy she didn't know, and Kam chuckled. "Not that you want to hear this, Al-Jabbar, but I would have guessed that one was way more your type in the first place."

Orion just rolled his eyes. "You're mostly saying that because she's *your* type. My wife is type enough for me and then some."

Fitch laughed some more as she watched Anna longingly and she sighed as she looked back at Orion. "If they wanted to separate her from her husband, it should have been with me. I had sex with a man last night. It wasn't terrible, but it really wasn't fun either. I swore the last time I had sex with a man that I would never put myself through that again no matter what my parents wanted. But he looked so sad and we're in this no matter what I want. I'm such a pushover sometimes."

"Seriously? Sad was all it took? I never took you for the type to stoop to pity-fucking somebody. Excuse me while I re-evaluate everything I've ever known about you."

Fitch elbowed him hard but she grabbed onto him so he would have to absorb the whole blow instead of flying off somewhere because she hit him. "Listen here, asshole. I'm trying to make this shit work so I can get to Eleusis. If that means fucking someone out of pity to get knocked up so I can finally get back to a vagina and tits, then that's what I'm going to do. Maybe you just don't have the balls to do what actually needs to be done, but the rest of us apparently want Eleusis more than you do. And don't be a fucking ass about it because you're here with a spouse. Not many of us have the luxury of having a partner in crime here, so sack up."

"You know what, maybe the rest of you do want it more than

I do. And if I'm supposed to be bothered by that, too bad. I'm not." One of the other instructors gave directions to the trainees about their first test, which was to get from the platform where they were standing to the Nav Control desk, grab a flag that was sitting there waiting for them, then to the bar where there was a second flag, and then back to the lift platform. "I made a promise and I gave my word. That means more to me than any assignment anyone else is gonna give me. It's that simple."

"More than the future?" Fitch asked incredulously. "Didn't you say you worked your whole life for Eleusis? And more importantly, didn't you say that Mercury has dreams about what she can accomplish for Eleusis? And for Earth? Aren't those important? Or just fuck that shit because you're more worried about hurting each other's feelings over fucking someone that doesn't matter to you anyway? It's just sex. You're making it into something else."

"It's allowing somebody else to decide what I do with my private life." Orion clearly wasn't backing down from her arguments, even if they touched on more nerves than he wanted Kameron to know about. "You think if they've instituted this kind of bullshit here, while we're all in training, that it's just gonna evaporate once we get to Eleusis? Vance and Gehrig and most of the other director staff might not be going, but the Kaplan brothers and Santos are, along with some of the others. If they're pairing us up and dictating who we fuck and don't fuck here, what exactly makes you think they're gonna let Eleusis be any different?"

"Dude, we talked about this before you even met the redhead. We talked about all the shit that happened back when we had to deal with rebels on Twenty. The Consortium has been fucking with us since the day we were born, Orion. None of that was gonna change just because you went and fell in love. But getting to Eleusis, that can mean change for us. Even if the Kaplans and Santos are there. That's a whole planet we're talking about, for crying out loud."

Orion shook his head as he watched the trainees take whatever positions they thought would be best prior to the start of their test. Anna was down in position ready to launch herself into motion, but she seemed angry about it, for some reason. "Maybe the problem isn't that I'm not as dedicated to Eleusis as I should be. Maybe the problem is that I don't have the hope for it that you do."

"Maybe you should ask your wife how she would feel if she never made it to Eleusis." Kam looked at the trainees right before the bell sounded, and felt puzzled when they all started moving except the hot brunette who was just counting loudly. "Okay, maybe she's a little touched in the head."

Orion was similarly confused, since she looked plenty ready to jump off, she just hadn't. "Something wrong, Bickford?"

"Five . . . lost a bet!" She yelled up as she glanced over at Orion. "Six . . . I'm trying not to be pissed about it, I mean, seven, you're my match, couldn't you . . . eight . . . have kicked out six instead of five? What good are you? Nine."

Orion rolled his eyes and immediately calmed a little. "You want me to collude with you in corruption, you've gotta at least clue me in beforehand. How long a head start did you give up?"

"You didn't tell me I could cheat!" She stared intently at the rest of the trainees to see what she could do to make up for lost time. She was going to need to push off as hard as she could without losing control. "Ten!" Anna finally yelled out before she hurled herself forward with impressive force for her size.

Orion smiled in spite of himself as he watched her fly, and he took out his tablet to take notes on each trainee's performance. Pablo was clearly in the lead, with the best balance, best accuracy, and fewest corrections needed, but Anna's initial jump was much riskier than it should have been. If she ran into something at that kind of speed, it was possible she would break something. But her trajectory looked good, so Orion wasn't worried. Yet. "Interesting bunch we've got here. Pablo's the only one from orbit, right?"

"In this group, yeah." Fitch replied as she watched carefully. "There are more in the second . . . shit!" Fitch said as Anna barely managed to make it to grab the first flag. Anna had hurled herself directly at the flag, which was risky in the first place, and then she had used the flag to whip around and hurl herself toward the second flag, but pulling the first one out had slowed her down a bit.

"She moves like she's got the mind for it." He said with approval in his voice, though he forced himself to take his eyes off her to point out the others. "Kipling and Adams are a little more cautious, but they're at least taking routes that make sense. Nothing wrong with being careful in unknown terrain."

"Mhm." Kameron said as she kept her eyes on Anna. "But risk

is so much sexier." Since Anna had lost speed, Fitch was watching how Anna would make up for it, and just when Anna looked like she was going off course into a wall, she did a flip and then pushed off just as she had turned herself in the right direction and was picking up speed. "We should have made them do this naked. We can haze them, right?"

"Down, girl. I'm pretty sure there's some kind of policy against naked hazing of new recruits somewhere. If there isn't, maybe I'll write it myself, since I'm supposed to be all commander-ish." He was impressed with Anna too, though, and obviously so were a couple of her colleagues whom she was finally overtaking.

The only person Anna was paying attention to was Pablo. She knew she was being watched, that was the whole point, but she had to keep it a game or she would care too much about the outcome. She didn't want to get kicked out of the program before she even had a chance to get into it.

"On your left, Gutierrez!" She yelled out as she scanned the area for her next move. The game was hard but she threw herself around like it didn't matter. That was just how she did it. She didn't want to come out of it with a broken arm, though she was aware it could definitely happen.

It took a while for Pablo to even spare a glance backward as he spun himself around a support column, but he was smiling, since she was still behind. "Not fast enough, *bonita!*" He moved like a fish in water, and that alone was enough to tell her that he was actually from orbit, which might have been considered an unfair advantage in the game if anyone had been paying attention. He grabbed the flag from the bar and took two hops to make sure of his vector before launching into the next leg. "You're going to get somebody killed, you know that, right?"

"You scared it'll be you?" When she got to her second flag she stopped sharply to catch her breath before she looked around. Anna saw a couple of bottles behind the bar and took the chance to bounce over and grab one before she used the bartop to launch herself, her beer, and two flags toward the third flag. As she drifted through the air, she took a drink. She had to chase the hangover with something, after all.

Orion laughed back on the lift platform and shook his head as he made a note in his tablet. Drinking or not, he could see the vector she had chosen and the route it would put her through. There was one other Earth-born recruit between her and Pablo, but that youngling hadn't chosen as well as Anna had when re-orienting himself, and was going to lose some seconds because of it.

Those behind her had actually taken to following her lead, since she had cleared the air and shown that her routes worked. "Incoming. Somebody got the timer?"

"Thank god someone was keeping time." Fitch said over to Orion, but she was still watching the recruits. "I just wanted to watch. Couldn't even pay attention. I mean, she's drinking a beer! What the hell!"

"Fitch, if you soak through your panties before we even get started on this test, so help me . . ." he shook his head, unable to look over at his longtime friend. He backed away from the final flags a little to give the recruits space to land, and was glad he had when Pablo came down harder than expected, giving a grunt as he braced his feet against the platform and fumbled to grab the third flag. The fumble and the difficult landing had been enough to allow the second flier to come in right behind him and grab the flag a little more smoothly, but Orion could see Anna was only a few seconds behind.

Anna didn't want to run into anyone, but she didn't see any way not to. She re-capped her beer and pushed herself into a flip, altering her path so she could tumble onto the platform just to the side of the other two. She had to reach out as far as she could to reach the flag, and even after she grabbed it, the struggle to yank it out sent her skidding across the floor. Anna crashed into a wall but she didn't break anything, including the glass in her hand. "Didn't spill any! We're good!"

That comment had all of the pilots in attendance shaking their heads, but they were all smiling as well, making notes in their tablets about her time and her performance. She had landed close to a lift door that opened to produce a group of highly confused Earth-born Initiates, all of whom darted out of the way with variously terrible results as the last few trainees came crashing down unceremoniously to grab at their flags. Orion observed the carnage dispassionately until everyone seemed to be more or less settled on the platform, a few of them nursing some obvious bruises. "Anybody bleeding?"

"I did see some blood. Not mine." Anna made her way over to the rest of the training group, but she was headed right toward Orion until Fitch reached out to prevent the collision.

"Thanks." She coughed a bit as the woman helped her regain her equilibrium.

"No, thank *you*." Kameron kept ahold of Anna, ostensibly to make sure she was alright. "That was a show. I'm going to remember that."

"You do that." Anna laughed, since she hadn't forgotten the few comments from the shuttle ride. Obviously the giant's friend was way more into her than he was. If that didn't show how fucked up the matching program was, Anna didn't know what would. "If I pretend your hand isn't grazing my tit, does that give me more points?"

"She's a junior pilot. She's here to help instruct, not to score trainees." Orion was still laughing as he finished his notes. "She also doesn't call assignments. Though she does beg for them to go her way, occasionally. We'll see how this one goes." He finished what he was doing and looked up.

"Alright, Mr. Sandrino, Mr. Hutchins, we'll have you scoot back to the second training class. Thank you for your time this morning. Adams, Kipling, Bickford, Gutierrez, Ramsay, and Krauss, dust off and follow along." He tapped off the platform and floated up toward the pod corridor at a sedate pace, especially compared to the race they had just witnessed and its rough ending.

When they got into the pod portion of the dock, Orion waited for everyone to join him, and tucked the tablet into a large pocket along his chest. "The second part of today's test is going to be taken live in a pod. They're the most agile and maneuverable birds available to the Consortium at the moment, max occupancy of three people who preferably know each other really well. Each of you will be flying with one of us as backup, just to make sure nobody blows anyone else up."

"Your objective, from the starting position, will be to complete three full circuits of the station's perimeter, aligned with the current rotational axis of the station's arms. Bonus points if you actually manage to get it back to the dock afterward without assistance. Questions?"

"So we're supposed to fail? We're not supposed to make it back?" Anna replied, obviously confused as she looked at Orion. "That doesn't sound very fair."

"Failure is never an expectation. But docking gets tricky." Orion answered with a patient smile. "One of us will be with you the whole time, like I said. None of us expect you to be immediate professionals at this. It's expected that you'll have questions, but part of the evaluation is to see how quickly and how thoroughly you learn, not just how well you fly once you do."

Anna didn't say anything else and looked around over the rest of the group before she looked back at the instructors. She didn't know who she would end up sharing a pod with. Orion had already proven to be a patient teacher with her before, but that was before they were matched. Now she would be lucky if he ever actually looked at her, let alone teach her anything useful. "I think we're all ready when you are, Cap."

That got a strange smile from Orion. "Our ranks have all been revoked, actually. Maybe you'll end up outranking me by the time this is over, Mrs. Bickford." He pulled out his tablet to look down the names again, but his smile dimmed. "Fitch, take Gutierrez, Rosetti, take Adams. Ascuncion, take Kipling. Brasseaux and Wells, take Ramsay and Krauss. Bickford, looks like you're with me. We'll review once we're all at the starting position. Best of luck to everybody."

Anna was silent as she followed after Orion to a pod and just as the doors started to open, she finally said something. "You're a good teacher. I'd be glad to learn from you. Though you don't have to, just swap with the horny lesbian."

He gave her a look that implied he was rolling his eyes at her on the inside. "She would try and convince you that she had to adjust your crotch straps by hand, and take her time doing it. No chance."

Now it was Anna's turn to roll her eyes, except she made no secret about it. "I'm not into women. Had my fair share, but I'm not into it. It's not like I would make out with her, I'm trying to actually learn here."

"All the more reason for you to stay with me." He reaffirmed as their pod presented itself in the loading bay in front of them. "Let me know if you have trouble with the straps. You're flying solo, as far as you can."

"I'll manage. I don't want to get angry again, it's just not worth it over this." She turned her attention to the pod and climbed inside. Clearly she didn't care what he chose, but she was giving him an out since she wanted to keep things civil between them. Anna was still tugging the straps into place, even though they were complicated, as he poked his head inside. "How many straps do these things have?"

"At least three more than absolutely necessary." He looked her over, pointing at the ones she had missed without moving his hands to help. "I've only crashed one once, and I was glad of the extra straps at the time. Kept me from freaking out and tossing myself into the black."

"The last place I'm going out is in the black. I'm either getting to Eleusis or I'm going back to Earth. If extra straps will help me there, then whatever." She said as she tugged the others in place after his instruction. "Let's go, then, Giant."

He checked over her restraints again, and gave her an approving nod before he swung her board around to face the controls, then anchored her in place. "I've got a set of backups over here, so I'll be making sure we don't crash into anything that'll kill us." She heard him get strapped in quickly, and before she could believe he was finished, his board spun to anchor him in place. The panel behind him closed and sealed itself shut, with an ominous rush of clicks and air. "And if you keep calling me Giant, I'm gonna have to start calling you Shortie. Choose wisely."

"There are worse names. Giant." Anna added with a smirk, though she was still impressed by his speed and skill. There was also no way she was going to call him by his name. Calling him Giant meant keeping him at a distance. She was all about that. "Okay, so do I just start pressing buttons or are you going to give me a quick rundown?"

"There will be no rundown, Shortie. It's all you."

The pod was taken by the station machinery out to the edge of the pod storage area and out through an airlock before the dark of space became visible again right in front of them. There was a whirr of machinery behind them that was a little ominous, and they were jettisoned out into the nothing, with no sound, no light, and no context to orient by, at least at first. They spun as they went, and the guidance systems of the pod became active once they were clear of the station, lighting up parts of the glass capsule to show different objects to be aware of and different navigation tools.

Anna was swiping through all sorts of screens as she attempted to make sense of all the information the shuttle was throwing at her. After pushing a few buttons that ended up thrusting them out farther, she just laughed. "Okay, I'm getting there. Don't worry." He hadn't said a word to her, but she wasn't the type to stay quiet for long.

"Take your time. It's gonna take a few minutes to get everybody out here and get set." He chuckled afterward, watching her around the corner of the boards. There was no more than a few centimeters between them once they were in position, and the way they were situated, they could see each other only if they craned their necks. "Only word of advice you get from me is not to press the big red button that says 'Eject' on it."

She hovered her finger over the button teasingly. "This one? What fun are you? You don't want to just float out there in space?"

"And instantly freeze to death while simultaneously exploding? No thank you. Finger off the button." He glared down at her, though he wasn't sure if she could see him or not.

"Bossy." She teased as she moved her hands elsewhere to flip through screens. Anna looked over at Orion, staring as she considered whether or not to speak. As usual, she chose to speak. "Thanks for making this happen. I've always wondered what this would be like."

"Well, go on and get creative with it. You've got about forty-five seconds before I take over and get you into position." Orion said teasingly, then immediately grimaced. "That . . . could have been phrased better."

Anna laughed started moving the controls to get a feel for them. "I'm no Barbie doll. I can position myself, big guy."

"I'm sure you can." He said quietly in an attempt to drop the subject and leave it as much alone as possible. They got jerked around a few times as she got accustomed to what went where and how incredibly sensitive the controls were, which got a few grunts and groans from him as he did his best just to hold on and keep from getting whiplash.

"Alright, over to the starting line." A line showed up on her controls in the distance, and she could see a few other white dots for the other capsules moving toward designated starting positions.

She moved them closer to the starting line until she had them right on top of the line and while they waited, Anna busied herself with the computer until she found a radio. "Hey! This makes it a little less creepy in here." She turned on the radio and went through the stations until she found some rock music. "Logan hates rock. Country for that man."

"There are people who hate rock? How do you hate rock? I could never get into country, but I don't hate it. Just not for me."

Out of the corner of her eye, she could see him making notes on the ways she handled the controls and the initial shot over to the starting line, but he did have to step in to adjust her alignment once she got close, bringing them in line with the others with a few effortless hits to the maneuvering thrusters. "Come on, Adams, move your ass. First out of the dock, last in line. Not okay."

Anna chuckled at his bossiness and waited quietly for the signal. What she didn't expect was that something sent them off without her knowledge and scared her shitless as she attempted to regain control. The giant didn't seem phased, though, so she figured it was part of the test. "A little warning would have been nice!"

"Sure. Because we get warnings about every little thing that's ever gonna happen up here. That always happens." Orion was chuckling as he said so, just making notations as they spun through the blackness, with lights flickering and spinning on every side of them to indicate the state of her competitors. "Less yelling, more recovery action."

"If I could smack you, I would." She said with a growl as she swiped through screens and pushed buttons to get them oriented enough so she wasn't spinning around aimlessly. Eventually she had them stopped, but she was trying to figure out which way they needed to go. Clearly she was struggling after being flung around, but at least she was figuring out the controls quickly. The music was helping her focus. "I love this song. You can feel it in your veins. I saw them live about five years ago. Great concert."

"You saw them live? I saw where we picked you up. There was nothing there. How far did you have to go?" She was about ready to get moving again when their pod jerked violently to one side. A few seconds later, another pod came careening past them, and Anna got a quick view of one of the other trainees in a panic, obviously not in control of his craft. "That wasn't a reflection on you, that was on Krauss."

"Shit." Anna hissed as she shook her head after being jerked that hard in one direction. She wasn't actually in a dangerous situation, so she answered his question. "I, uh, Logan, his brother, and some of our friends, we all carpooled to St. Louis. It's actually pretty busy in comparison to the rest of the Midwest region. It's kind of a central hub for us."

She attempted to engage the thrusters, but only after they

started moving did she realize that she had them going the wrong way. "We stayed out there for a week, drank like fish, slept in tents under the stars, listened to a different band every night. It was awesome. Logan and I weren't dating, but we still had fun as a group. He was with someone else, but somehow we were always together for the good memories. He let me sit on his shoulders for this band so that I could see even though he doesn't like them. It was incredible."

"Sounds like a good time." Orion's tone was clearly jealous of the memory. "Only concerts I've been to were back on Three while I was in training. Some bands would play the larger clubs. But of course we never get anybody from down below. They do on Prime, but that's about it."

"That sucks. Maybe things will be different once we somehow convince the assholes to stop fucking with us." Anna finally got them in the right direction and tapped on the thrusters carefully, building up momentum. "Have you really been training most of your life? Your file said you were ten. That's fucking crazy. Didn't you want to just be a kid sometimes?"

She could see him shaking his head out of the corner of her eye. "I was a kid until I was ten. Then I had the chance to get into a pilot training program five years ahead of most other kids. No way I was gonna pass that up. Acceptance like that, if I pulled it off, meant I'd never go without a placement the rest of my life. Meant I had already found something I was good at and could make a living for myself up here. Meant I'd never be a drifter, trying to scratch a few credits selling other people's shit in the back markets on Three."

"That's still a lot for a kid to take on at ten. I guess we both had things forcing us to grow up too soon." This time when the shuttle jerked, she was the one to make it happen, since another person was out of control but she had seen it coming. "I was pretty lucky. My dad is still alive, so I got to be a kid longer than most. Logan wasn't as lucky."

Orion wasn't sure how to respond to that, since he had just seen both his parents a few days before and they were perfectly fine. "You ask around to enough people, they'll tell you I make up for it by still being a kid no matter how old I get. I see it as having fun with life any way I can get it, but that works some days better than others."

"You mean like when you sign up for something you believed

in and it turned out to be a shit show?" She replied with a laugh, but she still meant what she said. "We're not really sure what we do to get out of this. Either we somehow get to Eleusis or we go back to Earth. At least that's what Logan and I think are our options." She hit the acceleration before she glanced at him. "What do you think?"

He didn't know if she had meant the question to be about him and Mercury both or just him, but any chance he could include Mercury in the conversation, he was going to take. "We mostly want to know the why. I don't trust what Santos told us. Until we know why, there's not much way for us to know how to get around it."

He pressed a button and her fuel gauges flashed on the screen, drawing her attention to them as he continued speaking. "If it was really about genetic abnormalities and all that, they could've made an exception and done the usual gene modification and in-vitro fertilization on you two and been done with it. Let us worry about the rest on Eleusis."

"My guess is that this is part of some twisted experiment, and whoever makes it to the end, even if they get fucked up on the way, they are the *lucky* ones who get to go to Eleusis." Anna punched the acceleration again even though he was showing her the low fuel levels. "I'm worried about my family. I don't want anything to happen to them just because someone told me to dance and I didn't."

"I've thought about that too." He admitted reluctantly. "I've got two parents, a sister, a sister-in-law, and a nephew. None of whom need to be roped into anything if I don't dance the right steps." He sighed in frustration but highlighted the button she was looking for to show her the reiteration of the required course she was supposed to be taking around the station. "This just isn't the kind of world I thought I was walking into. Same for you, I'm sure."

"We had our doubts. Lots of them. We should have listened to them, but we got greedy." She admitted as she went off course without his permission, attempting to shorten the path so that her fuel, or at least her momentum, would get them back. "We wanted more than twenty years together. We wanted fifty. Sixty. Silver hair and wrinkles. But it got all fucked up as soon as we stepped out of the truck."

She could see him shrug in his reflection on the glass. "I don't know. You seemed to make it through the check-in process without things going sideways. After that, it's been pretty much downhill, though, you're right."

Anna punched even harder on the accelerator as soon as she had a clear view of the path she wanted. When the fuel ran out and the boosters sputtered, she still felt confident they could make it. So long as she didn't have to dodge anything. "Logan and I just barely got together." The music in the background had turned angry, and it seemed appropriate for their conversation. "I want nothing more than the rest of my life with him. But now that we're here and we're stuck with this shit, I've had times where I wonder if everything would have just been better if he and I had never admitted our feelings. Then this wouldn't hurt the way it does. Then fucking government couldn't control us like this."

"Or if I had waited to be matched until I actually got here. The way Carl did. The tall guy you met last night. He and I disagreed about how to approach the whole matching thing coming up on the start of the Initiative. He said it was better to wait. I said better to get matched, get a connection with that person established, and move forward together once we got started with the Initiative. That was the plan. It was a pretty damn good plan."

"Until someone tries to use it to rip your heart out." She replied softly, despite the angry music. Anna eventually turned the music off as they drifted through on her new projected path. "You're a decent guy, it seems like. It wouldn't have been terrible to be matched to you if the situation wasn't like this. I've always been in love with Logan, but I didn't know he loved me back. You're attractive and funny. It could have worked out in a different situation."

"In a different situation." He repeated and re-emphasized. "You've got emergency backup thrust buried in the contingency menu. Don't use it all, it'll eat through the power for the life support if you do. At worst, they can tow us back if it's not enough. I don't want to freeze."

"I'm not using emergency anything. We'll get there." She watched them move closer to the station through the front window. "We should get together. The four of us. And talk about what we are gonna do."

"You're still thinking like gravity means anything. Getting there is good, but we're gonna have to stop afterward, otherwise we'll head down into the atmosphere. Stopping takes just as much effort up here as getting moving." He said it casually, since he wasn't that worried about it, obviously, but he sighed afterward as he thought about the rest of her comment. "I don't want the Initiative thinking I'm going to let them dictate what I do and don't do in my personal life. I'm happy to train you on how to be a pilot, happy to hang out and have drinks once in a while, whatever. But that's not what they're interested in. They're interested in twisting the match program to do . . . whatever it is they're doing."

He shook his head again as he thought back over the conversations he'd had with Mercury. "Honestly, the worst part of all of it is thinking about what it means if the program really wasn't even tampered with. It selects the most ideal match based on current parameters, and as far as I know, it would never have needed to be programmed to account for who's married and who isn't. Everyone who submits their name to the matching program is available, by definition. So marital status is a complete non-issue. If they just changed the parameters to account for greatest possible fertility and lowest instance of genetic abnormalities, while also maintaining the priorities of personal compatibility and everything it already does . . . then yeah. It's possible that it's just doing its job. I'd rather think it was tampered with."

"Why?" She swiped through screens again to try and figure out what to do now that he had reminded her that she was piloting a spacecraft, not an aircraft. "So what if it wasn't tampered with? Logan and I weren't a part of your matching program when you were matched with your wife. It's not like your match with her is any less compatible or less important if someone else shows up and would have been a better match."

"Hell, I don't know what it would have said if I had asked about my compatibility with Logan before we hooked up. It's not all about commonalities and shared goals and interests. Even though that's important. But there's chemistry too. You're in love with your wife. You have great chemistry with her. There's no reason to doubt that just because a computer program says that you might have had that with someone else too."

"The real mindgame, it seems, is that they know that they can fuck with people who are programmed to put that much faith in a system. In hierarchy, in computers, in the government. When this is the same government that fucked people over even before CV wiped out most of the world in the first place."

"Government's always done that. Always will." Orion agreed, though it sounded like he was trying to contradict her at the same time. "Eleusis was supposed to be something different. Starting with this whole project."

"Yeah, I know. I hoped it would be different too." Anna agreed as she maneuvered them to try and slow them down, but it wasn't really working. "I'm really jacking this docking thing up, aren't I?"

"You're not terrible, actually. Your instincts are improving, your technique is just for shit. But don't sweat it. I'm told gravity takes a while to let go of." Orion's hands were already on the controls as the ship began giving them warnings about a possible collision with the station itself. The alarms shut off quickly once he had them back in hand, setting the pod in a spin to match that of the station, after which it was easier to adjust to get into position.

"Not bad for a first run, you're actually the first one back. If this were an actual set of maneuvers, your dock master would rip you a new one for inefficient use of fuel, but you managed pretty well. A few hours on a simulator so you don't have to go searching for the command you want and I think you'll get right into the physics of it."

Anna was pleased to hear that she wasn't a total lost cause, and she smiled as the shuttle started to dock and they were greeted with mechanical noises and hissing from pressurization. "I'm glad I didn't mess anything up too bad. I'd hate to miss out on learning something like this." She forced herself to look over at him again, and now he felt a lot closer once she wasn't distracted by everything else. "You're a patient teacher."

"I had a lot of patient teachers. They were the only ones who actually managed to accomplish anything with their students. The rest mostly just liked to hear themselves talk." As soon as they were back in the clutches of the station machinery, he swung his board around to unbuckle himself deftly. He pointed out the latch to swing herself back around as well, but she clearly needed some help with the latches. Orion helped her, specifically those around her thighs and at her waist that were sometimes tricky to get to.

"You um, you figure things out quickly, which is a bonus, I thought I'd be getting a lot more questions. But you do need to work on maintaining balance between the fuel you've got and the maneuvers you still need to execute, get in the habit of thinking just a little further ahead. That would be the only major note that I've got for you from this. Everything else will come with practice. Just need to be looking at your flight a little more on the long-term."

Anna nodded as she watched his fingers, since she knew she needed to learn how to get in and out of the damn things without needing help like a toddler. She avoided looking at him except for once, and looked away quickly. He really was just too close to her. Attractive men needed to stay away except for Logan. "Thanks. I'll work on that. That's kind of important." She added with a laugh as she attempted to diffuse the tension of their closeness.

Once he was finished with her restraints, he didn't linger, but there wasn't far he could go in the close quarters of the pod. He leaned back against his own back-board until the pod was locked in place and the entry hatch at their feet opened up to allow them to exit. "After you." He gestured down for her into the empty hallway.

"I don't think you have any option other than to let me out first, Giant. You're gonna have to fold yourself like origami just to get back out." She teased with a small jab to his arm with her finger before she propelled herself out of the shuttle and out into the hallway.

Orion just sighed as she slid past him, and shook his head. It was just to give flying lessons. That was all. Just to give flying lessons. He just had to ignore the incredibly close quarters. He also needed to see if Mercury was going to be free for their lunch date that day. They were going to need to take that back to their quarters.

7

Logan stopped briefly when he entered the room, since there were only two occupants so far, for what he had assumed would be a sizable meeting. There were a few steps down from the door into the sunken room, and a large oval table with chairs all around it. Gravity was close to non-existent at their level, so Logan stepped off the platform and fell lightly the few feet to the ground.

He had obviously interrupted a conversation between Gehrig and Santos. "I didn't think I was that early. The meeting invitation did say ten."

Maria Santos looked back when Logan spoke up, giving him a warm smile as soon as she saw him. "Welcome, Mr. Bickford. It doesn't look like you're that early, but perhaps others aren't as punctual as you are." She motioned toward a chair. "How have you been adjusting? It's difficult to go from living on Earth to living up here, I've been told. Many of my prior patients often had homesickness to the point of requiring medication to cope for the first six months after arrival."

"I won't be requiring any more drugs than you're already pumping into me every morning, Doctor." He bounced behind Santos and Gehrig on the way to his seat, taking his time about it. "And I'm not sure you could call what I'm feeling at the moment homesickness, exactly. Though there was this very strange glitch my first day here with my communicator being unable to receive any communications from home. Very strange. But I've gotten a few back and forth now, so it must have corrected itself." He took a seat and immediately leaned back in the chair to appear more comfortable than he felt.

"I'm glad to hear that." She replied just as pleasantly as her smile implied. "It's important to maintain contact with those we love." Maria watched him as he sat down and then her attention was drawn to the doorway again. "Dr. Finnegan. Nice to see you this morning." She turned her attention back to Logan. "See? You aren't that early. Everyone will be arriving shortly."

Logan's look darkened as he looked up at Mercury, but the only indication of his thoughts was a slight tightening of his jaw. Of course they would manipulate the situation any way they could in order to put the two of them together. Especially with Anna out getting private lessons from the giant. "Good morning, Doctor. I apologize for missing my treatment window this morning. I was still violently hung over from last night's social. I planned to stop by once this meeting was concluded, if that's acceptable."

"Of course." Mercury said politely, even though she had no interest in speaking with Mr. Bickford after their conversation the night before. She sat down next to him, though. She knew she was supposed to, even though there was no assigned seating. "Next time, if you would like some help with a hangover, there are medications I can provide for you."

"I'll keep that in mind for next time. Since I'm sure there will be a next time." It was just the four of them in the room for a few seconds of awkward silence, but others began coming in by ones and twos, and they seemed to take the attention of Santos and Gehrig for the time being.

Logan turned slightly toward Mercury, though he still didn't look at her. "I was rude to you last night for no reason that you were at fault for. I thought at the time that it was a good method for helping to keep distance in this situation, but I've realized that there's no excuse for being an asshole to you, no matter the circumstances. That's allowing them to influence me just as much as doing anything else would be. It was short-sighted, and I'm sorry."

Mercury's expression softened slightly, but she was grateful for his apology. "This isn't easy for any of us." She wasn't afraid to look into his eyes, even if he was avoiding her gaze. "I don't want to make an enemy of someone over something we have no control over."

"Neither do I." He agreed, finally meeting her eyes briefly before he glanced around the room. "I imagine we'll have enemies aplenty here shortly without manufacturing any more of them ourselves. Anna and I are on your side. Yours and your husband's. Whatever that side ends up being."

Mercury nodded and she glanced around the room at the rest

of the group that settled in around them. "Then we need to discuss things together so we know what we're going to do. They're prepared, and we're not. That's never a good way to be."

"They're prepared to be obeyed." He agreed, glaring over at Santos and Gehrig as conversation continued to buzz around the room. "No one is ever prepared for every possibility. But you're right, we do need to talk this through. Because if this is how they've started, it's only going to get worse."

She looked down at the tablet and she looked up at him again. "I really want to get to Eleusis. I've worked my whole life for it. I love my husband." She said very quietly, as if she was afraid if Dr. Santos heard her more would go wrong. "But I've loved being a doctor for longer."

Logan looked over at her as she spoke, just to see the look on her face when she said it. He saw how serious she was about what she was saying, and he nodded in acknowledgement, though he had to look away afterward. "I have a brother and sister down on Earth. My brother just got married and hopefully my sister won't be too far behind with the man Anna and I arranged for her. Anna's younger brother, as a matter of fact."

"I want Eleusis for them. For their kids. For Anna's dad, so he doesn't have to waste away at barely forty years old. I want Eleusis for the same reason most people do, I imagine. I just want our people to have a home that isn't trying to kill us." He took in a deep, quiet breath, his chest rising and expanding as he let it out slowly. "I love Anna. I have for a long time. But Eleusis is bigger than any of us."

Mercury turned her attention back to the tablet and the meeting agenda. She hated herself for what she admitted to Logan, but it was the truth. And so was his. "At least we're on the same page." She conceded, though she felt guilty about that too. She'd spent her life sacrificing to get to where she was already. This was no different.

Logan looked as though he was about to respond, but Director Vance came through the door, and everyone turned in a wave to look over at him.

"Forgive me for being late." Vance said as he came down the stairs into the room, though he made no move toward any of the seats. "I will not be staying long, I only wanted to come and introduce the purpose of this assembly, at which point you are all free to do as you wish." He smiled around the room, though there were only a few returning the expression.

"As you all know here, Vice Director Gehrig and myself will not be accompanying you on your voyage to Eleusis. At least not immediately. What that means for all of you, and what I'm sure most of you already knew coming up here, is that you'll be governing yourselves, both during the trip to Eleusis and the initial stages of colonization after arrival. The purpose of this meeting is so that you can all get to know each other as the appointed heads of your various departments, and begin the process of choosing your own colony leadership. Everything else might be different on Eleusis, from the plants to the air to the weather, but things always function better when there is effective leadership in charge. That never changes."

Mercury's rust-colored eyebrow rose slightly as she heard him explain they would choose their own leadership and she had to wonder how far they would be allowed to set their own parameters. "Is this only effective once we arrive on Eleusis? Or are we able to establish laws that will go into effect here as well?"

"That will have to depend on the kind of rules being established, but some of them may be implemented before launch." Vance's tone didn't seem suspicious or in any way defensive. The man was either truly an open and honest individual or a complete sociopath with decades of practice.

Smart money was on the latter.

"At any rate, once the launch is effected and you are all in the process of transiting the galaxy, all governing decisions will be enacted by the committee or persons you select. A separate judiciary will be set up later on in the training process, to provide impartial review of laws and act to hold trials based on the laws that are decided, but all of that will be drawn from you, the members of the Initiative. Think of it as the beginning of the self-reliance this group will need to hold onto when you arrive."

"We'll need *something* to hold onto."

Mercury wasn't sure who said it, but when she looked around, all eyes fell onto the silvery-blonde-haired woman with icy blue eyes and a thick Russian accent.

Director Vance just smiled over at the woman, then looked around the rest of the room with the same pleased expression. "I would like to lie to you and say you will be going to Eleusis with a full community already established. I would like to tell you the area where you'll be landing is known to be safe. There are many things

I would like to lie and tell you I know about Eleusis, but there are still many, many variables involved with colonizing a planet on the other end of the galaxy. Any one of them could be fatal or catastrophic."

"It will be your job, as the leaders of your various departments, and eventually those of you who are selected as the governing administrators of the colony itself, to manage those situations. So yes, you will need *something* to hold onto, and that something will be each other. Until you can build a home on that planet, establish a base of operations, wake up in the morning in a sturdy home, having gotten a good night's sleep, with food ready to hand, you will be relying on each other for survival. That is the community some of you will have to manage. That is the reality of colonization. It's never pretty, but it's more tolerable if you're prepared."

"Thank you, Director." Dr. Santos said with a similarly pleasant smile, and she looked around at the group. "Any more questions for the Director before he steps away? This is up to us, as he said."

"You're asking us to choose the first government of an entire planet." Logan said from the opposite side of the room, looking perfectly comfortable as he stared down Vance. "Assuming that happens, and assuming we create a code of laws for the planet by which people are expected to live, what guarantee is there that the next batch of colonists will agree to the laws we decide on? They might have their own ideas about what government should be doing and go to form their own colony on the other side of the world. I don't relish the thought of Eleusis becoming just a copy of Earth, with different factions on every side. If we're going to build a new government on a new planet, not only do we need to do it right, but we need assurance that it's going to stick. The Consortium controls transportation to and from Eleusis at the moment. We would need assurance that future colonists will come through us."

Vance seemed genuinely shocked by a speech like that, as did many of the others in the room, some of whom were looking at Logan suspiciously and others with new respect. "That is an interesting perspective, Mr. Bickford. We hadn't thought so far ahead to consider that as of yet."

"Which, I'm assuming, is why you hired us. To do the kind of thinking you don't." Logan's stare was even, but more of the room was looking back at Vance, waiting for him to find some ice to apply to the burn.

Vance thought for a moment, but then clasped his hands in front of him. "I can speak on behalf of the Consortium board of directors when I say that so long as relations between the Orbital Consortium and the Eleusis Colony remain amicable and open, colonists will not be taken to establish rival colonies."

"I've heard veiled threats before, Director. If you intended to hide that one, you should've used a thicker curtain." Logan shot back with a smile that could have been interpreted as teasing, but nothing in his eyes was amused. "You want us to appoint a governing body for the Eleusis Colony? We can do that. But that body's decisions will be respected, both here and on Eleusis itself, once they're decided upon. That means dealing with us as a sovereign entity."

"Way to put the revolution before the founding, Bickford." Kaplan interjected with a laugh. "You're trying to declare independence when you're not even on the ground yet. You won't be getting to Eleusis without the Consortium in the first place. They control the air you're breathing right now, let alone everything else about this project."

"And they never let us forget it." Logan snapped back, only glancing at Kaplan before looking back at Vance. "The Consortium was founded with a mission statement to improve life for all of humanity. Eleusis will do that better than anything else the Consortium has done in its entire history. And yes, I would rather declare independence now and have it accepted now, instead of people needing to die for it later when the colony gets its feet under it and the self-reliance to do so, as you said yourself."

Vance was no longer looking around the room, but staring directly at Logan, his hands still clasped quietly in front of him. "The governing body of Eleusis Colony will be treated as a distinct and sovereign entity from the Orbital Consortium." He agreed in slow, measured syllables.

"I assume that's on tape." Logan motioned up and around the room without breaking eye contact. "Make that statement public record while we're making our deliberations and we'll make sure we choose wisely."

Mercury was impressed by Logan's attitude about the entire thing, as well as his methods in making sure no one was going to change whatever they decided as a governing body. "It makes sense." She supported vocally, which wasn't easy for her, mostly because Mercury was used to doing as she was told. But her father's advice was ringing in her ears. "And anything we decide is useless until we have absolute assurance, publicly known, that what we decide will be what goes, on Eleusis."

Vance was clearly just as impressed by the exchange as the rest of them were, but he nodded anyway. "We'll be certain it's clarified in our next full-Initiative meeting here and communicated publicly soon thereafter. Our intention is to make this colony a successful one. I'm glad it seems we've tapped some of the right people for the job." He was only looking at Logan and Mercury, though, ignoring everyone else in the room who was still looking back and forth between the ends of the table to follow what was going on. "We'll let you all get to it. Unless you have more questions about the terms, of course."

Logan shook his head, though no one in the room had given him permission to speak for everyone. "Not right now. We'll get in contact with more questions and clarifications as they come up. You can go."

Mercury was a little aghast he was actually dismissing the director, but she was impressed at the same time. She watched to see what would happen, but before either man could respond, the silvery-blonde haired woman just started laughing.

"Well, then, Director. Thank you for your time. It seems that we have a new leader here with us." Tatyana looked over at Logan with a smirk before she looked around the room, her eyes lingering on Kaplan a little more than most. "At least for now. We'll keep you updated about the things we decide upon."

Vance remained where he was standing with the same uncommitted half-smile on his face as he watched Logan. No one in the room was able to ignore the staring contest, and the fact that Vance lost it was lost on no one. "I look forward to it." He said before he turned to Gehrig and walked out of the room with the older woman not far behind.

"Where I come from," a dark-skinned man with a thick Kenyan accent said from a seat near the door, eyeing Logan intensely, "if people speak like that to those in authority, they are often killed."

Logan just reached for the water bottle he'd brought with him to the meeting and uncapped it with a nonchalant smile. "Aren't you glad you left?"

The man looked at Logan until he could be sure the farmer was being serious, then a slow smile spread across his face and he picked up a water bottle of his own. "Jela Koskei. Hydroponics. I like a man with a death wish. Whatever it is we are voting on here today, I vote for Bickford." There were a few mumbles of agreement around the large table, but there were two dozen people present from every department of the ship. It would be a lot of people to win over.

"Why don't we get to know each other a little bit first?" Tatyana spoke again, even though she knew most of the people in the room didn't know her. "We obviously know Kaplan, Santos, and Bickford, and I'm Tatyana Sery. Military strategist, specifically technology operations and data analysis. Once we start talking, we can decide how to organize ourselves." She looked over at Logan and raised a blonde eyebrow. "Unless you have something you'd like to pitch right now. You look like you're itching to become the first president of Eleusis."

"Logan is the only person who actually stood up for us just now. I don't know why you're choosing to mock him for it." Mercury said firmly at Logan's side, but she didn't look over at him even once.

"The only itch I have," Logan said without moving in his chair or even sitting closer to the table, looking every bit the politician sitting on a throne, "is to do things for ourselves. All of us together. I came up here thinking the Consortium was going to hand us some kind of colony charter that we were gonna have to swallow even if we choked on it, same as they seem to do everything else up here. But if they're gonna give us the acreage, then I say we better build a damn good fence around it."

"Your farmer's tan is showing, Bickford." One of the other men said with a cautious smile, of middling height and middling appearance, one side of his face pockmarked with scars while the other was more or less unscathed. "But I get the message. If we've supposedly got the freedom to organize ourselves, no reason why we shouldn't do it our way. Though I'm not a fan of presidents. Usually ends up being a popularity contest to choose the person who sucks least. The Balkan coalition uses an Executive Council. Seemed to be working out pretty well for them." He looked around quickly before retreating back into his seat, but leaned forward again quickly. "Oh, Tarmo Valk. Architectural design and renewable energy systems."

"We should probably wait to discuss specifics once we've actually been given the power publicly to do so." Mercury spoke up again, as she looked around the table with her green eyes. "Mercury Finnegan, Medical Operations."

The rest of the table seemed to concur with that, but everyone went around and briefly introduced themselves, representatives from educational services, transportation, geology, botany, textiles, mechanical engineering, communications, zoology, meteorology, the list seemed to go on and on until it came back around to Santos and Kaplan, who seemed to have calmed down significantly during the introductions.

"As the only person here who appears to have a legal background, I can tell you that waiting for public confirmation is a good idea." Kaplan's agreement didn't seem entirely enthusiastic. "But we should also have something prepared to announce along with that once Vance decides to go public with the information about our sovereign treatment. Some kind of a structure to offer the rest of the Initiative."

"So some form of government to put in place." Koskei clarified. "Something that we can expect their input on deciding. Some kind of election."

"Among more than two thousand strangers?" Valk sounded skeptical at best. "If we're being tasked with appointing our officials, at least to begin with, then that's what we should do. Say that we can hold a more full election once we reach Eleusis, or after a year on Eleusis or something. State right up front that we're selecting a temporary government just to get things started. Emphasis on temporary."

"Make the structure of the government more important than the people in it." Logan agreed with a nod. "That would encourage stability and promote the idea that we're all in this together. Which we are, in case anyone was confused."

Santos glanced over at Kaplan before she looked back at Logan. "How about a council of ten? Or eleven for the sake of majorities?" She smiled at Logan. "I think you are a lock for one of the spots, Mr. Bickford. I would nominate you."

Mercury looked over at Logan again and nodded. She knew it was public knowledge about her and her match and how terrible it had been so far, but she was supporting him now. "I agree. Logan should be a part of whatever council is formed." It was the first time she called him by his first name and it felt almost intimate, but she ignored that feeling as best she could.

He looked back over at her when she seconded her support, and actually met her eyes. He wasn't smiling, and didn't even look happy behind his expression, but he did nod to her once in gratitude before he looked around the rest of the table. "Koskei, your vote from earlier makes three. Are there nine more of you who think I would do a halfway decent job on this governing council of ours?"

Tatyana raised her hand and nodded. "Yes, I think you would do well."

Valk raised his hand as well, as did a few others in quick succession. Kaplan ended up being one of the few who didn't raise his hand to support the motion, but it carried by clear numbers anyway. "Anyone here interested in being the interim secretary of the Executive Council? All of this is going to need to be documented." Logan asked with a sarcastic grin over at Kaplan. "Feeling administrative, Steve?"

Most of the room laughed, both at Logan's suddenly flippant tone and the flash of anger that went through Kaplan's eyes at being caught off guard. He opened his mouth to respond, but he didn't get the chance.

"I'll take note for now." Koskei interjected, pulling up an interface in front of his part of the table. He accessed a quick roster of the meeting attendees and immediately took note of those who had voted for Logan's inclusion. "The first member of the Eleusis Colony Executive committee is so named. Logan Bickford, First Chair. Entered in the records this twenty-third day of October, 2476." He made the entire thing sound ominous and parliamentary, but he was smiling the entire time.

"So it begins." Santos's smile was pleasant as she looked around the group, then pulled out her own tablet to make notes.

By the end of the meeting, both Santos and Kaplan were also on the council, but Logan's match was not. Ultimately, they had decided that the bigger group would narrow down laws and ideas and the council would ultimately vote on the ideas and final say until an official body of government had been formed by a vote of the people.

As everyone got up to leave, Logan lingered on his side of the table, looking around the room and waving goodbye to the other members of the group that had shown themselves to be friendly to him, either passively or overtly. It felt like it had been a long meeting, but it had only been a little over two hours. Logan felt drained by the weight of everything happening, but he tried not to let it show.

Mercury got up from her chair and held her tablet to her chest as she stood nearby. "Are you alright?"

He let out a quiet laugh as the last few of the group filed out of the room. "Sure. Just became the chief executive of an entire planet I've never been on. Just your average day."

"You don't have to do it alone. I'm sure your wife will be a great support for you, and I'm on your side." She reached over and gave him a brief squeeze on the shoulder before she pulled her hand back. "You seem like you were born to lead. It's no mistake, I can tell. You'll be good, and fair."

"Which, if you look at history, means I won't lead for very long." He said sardonically, but then shook his head and turned to face her more directly. "Thank you. For speaking up for me. I would have nominated you as well, but I hope I'm not presuming too much when I say you don't seem like the type who would enjoy that kind of paperwork."

"I would rather spend my time doing medical research than governing, certainly. I think I am of much better service to the people as an active doctor than a Councilor." She nodded toward the doorway. "Do you want to get a bite to eat? You still need your treatment as well."

"Sure. Food would be good." He took up his water bottle and tossed it into a reclamation chute on the way out, holding the door for her in the process. "But food first, then treatment. I don't really want to do that again on an empty stomach."

"That's for the best." They passed Kaplan and Santos as they walked away from the room. Mercury looked back at the two of them, and while they didn't look cozy, Mercury did wonder if they decided to follow their own match, as they said they had.

Once Maria and Steven were alone in the hallway, Maria shook her head slowly. "That was interesting, to say the least. Logan has responded quickly to the pressure. His anger has escalated more than I expected it would by this point."

"How does it feel to be wrong once in a while?" He asked with a subdued smile. He hadn't expected Logan either, but he was chiding himself for his own lack of foresight regarding the man. "I had my money on Sery trying to take over. Short-girl syndrome. She seems like the type. As it is, our provisional first-chair isn't going to make the rest of our life any easier."

"I'm happy to be wrong sometimes." Maria said as she looked back toward the empty hallway. "It means I have more to learn." She chewed on her bottom lip as she thought about the entire interaction. "I was concerned that you and I wouldn't make it onto the council. We need to make ourselves more likeable."

He actually snickered at that, since he had no illusions about himself. "There are two ways assholes like me ever make themselves more likeable. Either they find more like-minded assholes with less personal ambition to hang around and be their posse, or they get shit done. The second part I can do. I've got no patience for the first. We need to talk to Vance anyway about this whole sovereign declaration thing. If I help push that through, maybe some more of the board will start to think I'm not a waste."

Maria didn't reply right away. "They don't trust us because we look like we're outside of everything they're dealing with. They think we're exempt. We should spend more time socializing in the places where they gather. Together. That's the biggest hang-up for a lot of them. Accepting their new match and developing a relationship with them. We should spend more time together. Publicly."

He was obviously skeptical as to whether that would work or not, but he looked her up and down anyway. "Maybe that's so. A little forced public display of affection while we're at it might help that go the distance." He stepped up closer to her without an invitation, and put a hand along her waist to press her back against the wall behind her. "You would definitely get some sympathy votes for being paired with the biggest asshole in the room."

Maria smirked as she looked up into his eyes, since she knew he liked to push buttons, even hers, if he was given the opportunity. She liked to think she wasn't easily rattled. "You made yourself known as such as soon as you could. It's not my fault you decided to show your true colors. I'm a little more secretive."

"A little?" He laughed aloud at that, since it was the understatement of the century. As far as he knew, even Vance and Gehrig weren't entirely sure of every detail about their beloved medical director. They assured him they were all on the same side and encouraged him not to piss her off.

That was advice he almost categorically ignored.

He moved his hand along her waist up under the hem of her

blouse, since she hadn't seemed bothered by the initial touch. He looked forward to seeing what *would* bother her. "One of these days you're gonna have to start unloading all your secrets on me. Especially if we're matched for the rest of this enterprise."

She let him get a touch of her skin before she put a hand on his arm to stop his exploration with a smirk still on her lips. "I'm going to need to be thoroughly convinced of a good reason to let you get that personal, Stephen."

He let her stop his hand for a moment as he looked down in her brown eyes, but then he stepped in a little closer to her, his hand pushing past her restraint just a little to leave an uninvited caress along her side just beneath the curve of her ample breasts. "You want to understand these people, see how they tick, predict their moves, prepare for the *real* test? Getting involved in your own experiment is the only way to do it. Your program put you with me, and that's all the convincing you should need."

He leaned down almost close enough to kiss her, but stopped abruptly and started backing away without breaking eye contact. "Or maybe I'll tweak the station systems to make your life a little less comfortable until you do. See how your own reactions fall along the spectrum of expected response."

Maria's eyes studied his as he backed away, and she tugged her clothing back into place before she said anything. "I'll admit, I'm curious about why we were matched, since that was not . . . a customized variable. But I would suggest you don't attempt any experimenting on me. You'll regret it." She promised without sounding threatening, but she clearly meant what she was saying. "You won't know your own name by the end of it if you toy with me."

The threat made him grin as he stepped back. "It shouldn't be too hard to remember. You'll be screaming it by the time I'm finished *toying* with you."

She eyed him for a moment longer at that particular promise in response to hers, and she walked away from him even though her curiosity begged her to stay. It had been some time since she'd last taken a lover, but that was because she needed to tread lightly. Especially with someone like Stephen Kaplan. They still had to work together, after all. "We'll see."

8

Kameron Fitch was not generally considered soft or gentle, but most people didn't know her the way her lovers knew her. She had been with her last girlfriend over a year before she broke up with her to apply for Eleusis, and Kam had been floating in relationship limbo ever since. The last thing she wanted, though she had been aware of it, was to get matched up with a man. Even if she understood the logistics of it. It didn't matter how much sex she had with a woman, it was never going to produce a baby. Even if the sex was amazing. After watching Anna Bickford during training, Kameron was definitely missing a woman's body as she walked back to her unit.

The man she'd been matched up with wasn't terrible, and he was actually kind of funny in a self-deprecating kind of way. He made her laugh, but it made her feel a little uncomfortable as well. He was well aware of her sexual preferences, and he didn't seem to mind not topping the list of her varied appreciations.

His understanding was nice, but it didn't make any difference when it came down to it. She still had to figure out how to deal with a man, but she thought she was doing as well as could be expected, so far.

Until she showed up in her unit and found him nearly unconscious on the floor.

Kameron dropped her bag and rushed to him as soon as she saw him, white as a sheet and sweating. They were about the same size, and she was able to pick him up easily to move him to their bed. "What the fuck have you been doing, Kaz?" Her nickname for him made the situation lighter, but right now she didn't think humor would help.

He was breathing heavily, but at least he was breathing, and he looked like he was recovering from whatever had happened rather than in the middle of it. He rolled to one side, his arms cradled along his rib cage as he actually laughed once without opening his eyes.

"Oh, nothing much, Kam. I was just standing there looking through some residential unit models and I suddenly thought the floor looked lonely. The sweating and feeling like my lungs are about to explode, that's just coincidence, I'm sure."

"What happened? Did you eat something bad?" She looked around the room as though she expected to see poison, but she spotted his bag instead and she left his side to go get it. "Do you have medication?"

"Nothing that's gonna make a difference." He groaned from the pillow, then slowly pushed himself up so that he was sitting with his back to the wall at the head of their bed. "But I appreciate you caring. Honestly." He was still favoring his ribs, but he was breathing easier the longer he sat up. "It's not the kind of thing that gets better. Unless Dr. Patel comes back and gives me a different story than the one I'm expecting, anyway."

"Story? What story?" Kameron dug through his bag and found some pills labeled THC. "You have the good stuff, don't you? I'm gonna take this stuff if you don't."

That got another laugh from him. "Help yourself. Aiko tells me they've already got the plants on board to manufacture more where that came from. She's got her own process she's been using since we were kids." He closed his eyes in pain, but it wasn't as bad as it had been before she got home. "I'll bet you're a box of giggles when you're stoned."

"Probably so." She brought the bottle to him and sat down on the edge of the bed next to him. "Here, we're not on shift the rest of the night. I'll take one if you do. Then you can tell me this story you mentioned."

"It's not a great story." He took one of the pills from her anyway, and tapped it comically against the one she plucked out before popping it in his mouth and taking it without a drink. "Have you never done THC before? First time can be pretty weird. Especially if you're with a stranger who might take advantage of you." He smiled across the bed at her, since the way they seemed to be settling into life with each other was to joke about everything in the world.

"Just once. Swiped it from a delivery." She popped the pill easily and crawled over him so she could lie back on her own pillow. "I don't remember what happened, so I can't even warn you what High Me is like."

Kazuo rolled his eyes, but still laughed as he looked over at her. It was surprisingly easy to just hang around with her, even in such an intimate position as lying together in bed. He had thought, when she gave him a very abrupt and up-front disclosure, that things would be perpetually awkward between them or she would end up resenting him, but she had actually been amazing. "Believe me, whatever happens, I won't be judging you. Though if there is stripping and dancing involved, you will be filmed. Fair warning."

"Filmed? That's not fair. You should have told me that before I took the pill." She teased as she turned toward him. "If you do film it, keep it to yourself. I don't need the rest of my pilot friends making fun of me."

"Not a problem. I can be greedy like that." He looked down and looked her over, because she was a beautiful woman in his opinion, whether she was actually attracted to him or not. He scooted down on the bed so he was lying next to her, and kicked the shoes off his feet to let them fall beside the bed.

"Story starts before I was born. Geneticists on Earth work a little differently than they do up here. Up here, they modify people to be . . . whatever the parents order, I guess. Down there, they try to build us to be CV-resistant. Sometimes it works, sometimes it doesn't. Most of the time, it blows things up, and it's all very sad."

"In the case of my sister, it works really well, and she's classified as near-immune. She's never shown any signs of her systems succumbing to CV's effects. But she was the second draft. I was the first." He reached up over the bed and gestured to wake up the computer, which displayed a hologram above the bed in front of them. A few gestures later, his medical records were pulled up, and it showed a full-body scan of him that had been taken just a few days before. As the hologram loaded and showed different parts of the medical report, Kameron could see some very obvious reasons why Kazuo might have collapsed.

There were spots and masses highlighted in red all over Kazuo's body. There were spots on every major organ, in both his arms and legs, threaded through his spine like it had been stitched into it over time. It was so widespread that the system hadn't even been sure what to recommend to work on first, so it had defaulted to his heart.

It had also displayed a message showing that he shouldn't be alive.

"That's my favorite part, I think." He reached up and pointed to that particular warning message. "You know it's a good day whenever you can confuse a machine."

Kameron's eyes were wide and she didn't even know what to say as she stared up at the hologram and the message. He was a decent man, as far as men went. He didn't deserve whatever the hell she was looking at. It was like an internal war had left all of his organs nearly nonfunctional. "How the hell did you even get up here? I mean, I had to take all sorts of physical exams and blood tests and shit. How . . . are they going to fix you? Is there something to fix you?"

"Not down on Earth." He dismissed most of the hologram, but he left the interface open in case he needed to look at it again. It was nothing he hadn't seen before. "The low gravity up here actually helps, for some reason, so that was a selling point. But I can still do pretty much everything a guy my age should be able to do, unless I'm too busy collapsing on the floor once every few days."

"I confuse doctors because it's not killing me as quickly as it should be, so I'm a fun medical guinea pig for people to poke and sample from. I went and saw Dr. Patel our second day here, and she said she would meet with the rest of the medical staff and see what they're willing to do." He shrugged, shaking his head as he looked over at her. "I've been dying since I was ten. I'd like to say it's not a big deal to me anymore, but it still is. I didn't come up here because I'm suicidal, this is just the only place where they've got the tools to start fixing me, if they're in the mood."

"If they're in the mood? They *have* to fix you." She swiped away anything hanging in the air between them. "You're supposed to be my partner in this shit show."

"I hope they do." He didn't sound entirely hopeful as he said it, though. He turned toward her, and she could see that the color had returned to his face, his breathing even and steady as he leaned his head on his hand to look at her. "I want to live. Want to see Eleusis, see some of my designs take shape out there. But there's a lot circling around this Initiative, and if they decide not to commit the resources to fix me, I'll be less than surprised."

Kameron frowned and looked him over before she sighed and laid her head back against the pillow instead of facing him. "I want to say I disagree, but I guess there's a chance they won't. Cuz they're motherfucking bastards sometimes." She ran her fingers through her hair that she had loosed from her ponytail and covered her eyes with both hands. "This death conversation is really harshing the high I feel coming on, Kaz."

"Hey, you asked for the story." He chuckled beside her and reached up to begin undoing her uniform, just because he knew already she was never going to be the one to initiate things between them, and if she was already starting to feel the effects of the purified drug moving through her system, he was going to make sure she could take advantage of it. "Not my fault if it's not the greatest one. But I'm glad you're not the type to get all mopey about it. Like I said, I've been dying since I turned ten and got my first tumor. I'm more interested in living until I can't anymore."

"You're rather gung-ho about nudity for someone I just scraped up off the floor." She raised an eyebrow at his fingers working on her clothing. "You know my no-underwear policy. Don't tell me you're unprepared to see that again."

"I have no problem with your no-underwear policy." He pulled down the zipper of her uniform to bare her chest, but he didn't get immediately sexual about the touch. "And I'm the one you're not that 'gung-ho' about seeing naked. I could look at you all day. You're gorgeous. So I fully support the no-underwear policy. Underwear in general is overrated."

Kameron rolled her eyes and shrugged her arms out of her uniform, since she wasn't used to being undressed. Usually she was the one doing the undressing. "You're attractive for a man. There's nothing wrong with the way you look. Unless we're looking at your organs. That was fucked up."

"Sorry. I'm a visual person, so that's always been the way I understand it best. No need to look at any more of my organs unless you actually go looking for them." He promised with a laugh. "Flip over. If you've never had a stoned massage, we need to change that fact in your life."

"You're giving me a massage? Are you sure you're okay to do that? I mean, you looked pretty bad." She reminded him for the fiftieth time, but she kicked her uniform out of the way once she'd wiggled the rest of the way out, rolling onto her stomach. "Does getting high give me superhuman smell? It smells like you're wearing cologne and I didn't smell anything before. It smells nice."

"I'm glad you like it." Once she was comfortable, he moved to kneel over her backside and leaned down to get started on her back and shoulders. He wasn't the strongest man she'd ever hung around in her life, but he was fit rather than just scrawny, and his long fingers were plenty strong enough to dig into her muscles.

"THC changes a lot of things about the brain, but it's a little different for everyone. Some people are more audio-visual in their hallucinations and heightened perceptions. For me it's usually just that colors turn super-bright and sounds get super-detailed. Maybe you're more about smell and taste. Hopefully feeling comes in there somewhere too." His hands worked along her neck to get her relaxed into the pillow, but they roamed up and down her back to make sure he hit all of her as intensely as he could.

Kameron closed her eyes so she could focus on the feeling of his hands working along her back, and admittedly, it did feel really good. Especially after getting jerked around in a shuttle by an inexperienced dumbass who ended up getting cut anyway. "Are you scared to die? Even if you've been dying for a long time?"

"Now who's killing the buzz?" He asked with a laugh, but the massage continued, moving freely over her back and arms as they spoke. "I don't think anyone gets free of being afraid to die. I've gotten about as close as I imagine is possible. If somebody wants to die, that's one thing. It's harder to be afraid of something you want. But even though I don't, I know it won't be long, without intervention. So no, I don't lose much sleep over it anymore."

She was quiet a while until he moved up closer to her neck, and she couldn't prevent the groan that escaped her lips. It felt really damn good. "Does your sister know?"

He hesitated before answering that. "She knows it's gotten worse. She doesn't know how bad it is. Most of the drugs I take, she designed. She's the only reason I've lived this long."

"I can tell how much she loves you by the way she looks out for you. I've been watching women for years, I'm decent at reading their expressions." She chuckled, but then groaned again in pleasure. "I'm gonna talk to Doctor Patel, see what I can do, not that I have any influence. But if you knock me up in this place, you can't ditch me to go off and die."

"Hm. That's a tough one." He chuckled above her, his hands still working their slow, constant magic along the muscles of her spine and shoulders. "Die, or put up with you pregnant. I'm not sure which one would be worse. You're gonna be six different kinds of moody. It's gonna be insane."

"What are you talking about? I'm fucking pleasant." She attempted to look back at him, but it was hard to do so from where he was over the back of her. "Moody, my ass."

"No, your ass always seems to have its mind made up. It either wants to be grabbed or it wants to be in a flight seat. Nothing tricky about that." He was kneeling over the ass in question, and he moved a little against her as his massage moved down over her lower back and her sides. "And you have been very fucking pleasant. I hope things stay that way between us."

She turned her head to the side and opened her eyes, but she was looking at a very interesting version of the room, since she knew the THC was messing around with her senses. Closing them again made things a little easier.

"I knew when I signed up for this gig that they wouldn't put me with another woman. It's the reason my parents celebrated when I got accepted. They're religious fanatics. They think my acceptance into this program was God's answer to their prayers to get me back on the *straight* and narrow. Not a chance. I can't change who I am, but I do want to go to Eleusis. And I was a total slut with men before I admitted to myself and my parents that it just wasn't me. I guess I was trying to change myself too, to make them happy. Didn't work."

"Never seems to." He continued the massage down to the small of her back, but then moved off her to begin working down over her legs. He was a thorough man, whatever else he was, and as the THC took effect more strongly in her senses, the massage got that much more interesting. "Only time anyone ever changes is if it's something you really want, and even then, it's not always possible. I'm glad you don't seem like you completely hate being with me, at least. I'm not sure how I'd be if our situation was reversed and I was forced to be with a man while up here. That . . . Yeah, I don't have any experience with that, never had any interest in getting any."

"Good luck making a baby that way either." She replied with a laugh before she continued. "One of my friends is one of the people here with his spouse. He's all torn up about it, and I get that. But I'd rather just accept what is and try to make the best of it, you know? You have a dick. It's a downside to this relationship, but it's not the worst thing in the world. Not for me, anyway."

"And this means I don't have to go through some crazy medical shit to get a baby up in here. My last girlfriend was all against having a baby since she said it would ruin her figure. Probably true, but I would not have cared. Anyway, so she looked into it for us and hell no to them taking some fucking probe . . . I hate hospitals. I'd rather just deal with man mess and a few sloppy orgasms and get it done that way."

"Man mess. Way to make it sexy." He laughed, but he knew she wasn't wrong. He looked her up and down as he continued his massage, and eventually worked his way down over her long legs to her feet, at which point he flipped her onto her back again. His hands had been good on her back and expert on her legs, but his touch on her feet was something completely different. It might have been unfairly augmented by the high that was moving through her, but whatever the reason, the man was good. And the only one of the two of them still wearing clothes.

"You might have to put up with more than a few messes before you actually manage to get knocked up, you know. But I hope it's soon, for your sake. Then I'll just go back to grabbing increasingly shameful porn off the station network and keeping my 'man mess' to myself."

"What about your sake?" He was not what she would have chosen for sexy time, and she knew it, but the massage helped. And the drugs. "I know we only had sex the once, but it wasn't bad, right? And your porn isn't that shameful. You and I could probably enjoy the same stuff."

That got a full belly laugh from him, which was a rare thing with her somewhat-reserved match. "You're right, we probably could. I didn't think about it that way. I was also told by one of the guys at lunch today in my Engineering department meeting that we should go looking through the rest of the roster to see if we can find some other woman who'd be up for joining us. Certainly nothing in the bylaws against that. So long as we're working on getting pregnant, you might as well enjoy that part of it a little more than I know you enjoy my part. Little much to talk about after we've only had sex the once, I know, but it was an idea I thought I'd pass along." His hands were half-massage and half-caress along her ankles and calves, still working to remove the last of the tension from her muscles.

"Hell yeah, I'm down with that." She stretched out as his hands continued to wander. "You didn't answer the good part. It's good for you, right?"

"Um, hell yes." He hadn't answered because he didn't think clarification was necessary, but he could absolutely reassure her if she was looking for it. "I haven't had that many girlfriends before coming up here, only slept with two different women. Neither of them were quite as, um, intense, as you are. I know some of that might have been you wanting things to be over in a hurry, and I get that, but goddamn."

"Fly fast, ride hard." She replied with a laugh. "So then what are you waiting for? I'm all naked and relaxed, thanks to your drugs and your hands. Why are you still wearing glowing clothes? Wait, why are your clothes glowing?"

He looked down at them and his eyes went a little wide. "I don't know. They weren't doing that earlier. That is so weird." He actually paused at that and pulled at them for a minute to examine them before he took his shirt off. The few scars on his torso had a different story to tell now that she knew where they had come from, but his eyes were still on his shirt as it floated away in the low gravity.

"I swear they don't normally do that. That's amazing." He watched until the clothes hit the floor on the far side of the room, then turned back to her with an admonishing look. "You're not allowed to glow. You would freak me out if you started glowing right now. So don't." He turned on the bed to kiss the inside of her knee, his lips moving upward as his hands resumed their caresses on her legs.

Fortunately for her, Kazuo was clean-shaven, so she didn't have to worry about facial hair getting personal with her and his lips actually felt good on her skin. The guy had a decent knowledge about pleasing women, but she had no problem telling him what to do when she wanted something. "No glowing. Got it." She replied with a soft moan as she looked up above them before she closed her eyes again. "I might glow if your lips get adventurous, though. Just saying. I know my smooth lady bits are pretty enticing."

"No glowing!" He reiterated as he continued kissing up along her thigh, his lips obviously headed for the core of her. "You can glow when you come, but that's the only time. Those are the rules."

"Man, I hate rules." She mumbled until his mouth definitely found the right spot. "God. We should've done this before . . ."

He might not have had many lovers before her, but they had not been shy about making sure their man knew how to please them. Kazuo didn't mind a bossy woman. His tongue was every bit as deft with the most sensitive parts of her as his hands had been with the rest of her, and he was nothing if not persistent.

* * * * *

Aiko had been working most of the day on her computer instead of directly with the plants that she loved so much, and by early afternoon, she was desperate for a break. She headed back to her unit knowing that Carl was just as busy with security as she was with her work, so she expected the silence she found when she walked in.

She flipped through a menu of catering options, smiling when she saw a hamburger, thinking of Carl's admission that he'd never had a real one. She smiled and ordered it and decided to take him a late meal. He was a big man, and even if he'd had a midday meal, she hoped he wouldn't mind being surprised with another.

She was questioned on her way into the security station where Carl worked, but as soon as she mentioned she was Carl's match, she was admitted quickly. The deck where he worked was closed off right from the lift exit, since it also served as the offices for the Initiative brass on that arm. She passed Vance and Gehrig's offices on her way to Carl's, and saw them cloistered in holographic meetings, though she didn't recognize any of the other participants.

When she got to Carl's office, the door was open and there was music playing from one corner of the room, just loud enough to be heard inside. Carl himself was pacing along one wall with a tablet in one huge hand and the rest of the wall lit up with what looked like people's profiles. Faces and relevant information covered most of the room, and he kept looking back and forth between the holograms and the information on the tablet.

His tendency to mumble to himself (which extended to his sleep, she had quickly discovered) was in full force as he paced, talking to all of the people in front of him seemingly at once. "No, no, you couldn't be more boring if you tried. You? You might have one or two interesting bones in your body, but no, not quite enough. You, definitely. You're absolutely going under watch. No two ways about it."

"Carl?" Aiko said after looking over some of the faces from where she stood in the doorway. "Is this a bad time?" She didn't like that she saw some faces she knew, but she tried not to think about it.

"Hm?" He turned around as if it was perfectly natural for her to be standing there in his doorway, and shook his head. "No, it's not a . . . oh, hey!" His delayed surprise brought a smile to his face, and he set down his tablet before crossing the room to get to her. "Wasn't expecting to see you here. Did you sneak past the guards? Please tell me you snuck past the guards." He leaned down to give her a quick, tentative kiss as soon as he was close enough.

Aiko gave him a kiss in response to let him know that the kiss was alright with her and smiled at him afterward. "Sorry, no, I didn't sneak past. I'll try to do that next time if it will make you happy." She kissed him once more. "I told them that I was your match and they let me in to see you. I brought a late lunch, I hope that's alright. I wanted a break from staring at reports on my computer. Watching grass grow *is* more fun than that."

"Only for you." He gave her a teasing look and took one of the bags she'd brought from her. "Thank you for this. I got this project laid on me halfway through the morning and haven't stopped since."

There wasn't much room to sit in the office, just one decent chair and a stool, but Carl took the chair and put his feet up on the stool, pulling Aiko into his lap beside the desk so they could dig into the food. "Are your reports not doing what you thought they'd be doing? With the . . . the Eleusis specimens and whatnot?"

"They're working just fine, but they're just projection reports from elsewhere. I don't really care so much about projections right now, I want to get into the dirt and look at things for myself." She knew that didn't sound pleasant for most people, and certainly not sexy, but she enjoyed her work. Mud and all. "There are always boring parts to every job, I suppose."

"They'll let you get into it soon enough, I'm sure. I think everybody's still just kind of settling in around here. Figuring out how everything's gonna work." He shook his head and worked through a massive bite of hamburger, even if it was entirely synthetic. "First time I've ever had an office. Most I ever had was a desk back at the first station I worked at. So this kinda feels like I'm occupying somebody else's space and waiting for them to come back and kick me out of it."

She leaned back into his shoulder as she sat on his lap so he could eat without her getting in his way. Aiko just picked at some fries. "You're a leader of security. No one is going to kick you out of anything." Sitting in his lap felt more intimate than anything else they'd yet done, even more than sleeping next to each other, though sleep was all it had been. Kissing him was fun, though. She definitely liked that part. "Am I allowed to ask what you're working on?"

"Yeah, of course." He pointed back over to the board he'd been pacing in front of and the several faces still pulled up on it. "Me and a couple other guys are going back and cross-checking all the background reports of everybody on board. Verifying backstories, biographical details, stuff like that. We want to prevent another 'Jeffrey' situation." He actually used air quotes on the man's name, and was obviously a little frustrated about it.

"Still don't know that guy's real fucking name. He's a piece of work. They're gonna give me a shot at him later this week. Nobody's been able to get a damn thing out of him yet. Brass figures if he managed to make it onto the shuttle, others might have too, so we're digging."

Aiko shifted a little in his lap as she looked at some of the photos, but she was relieved not to see her face up there. "You don't think it was just a fluke?"

"That guy getting on? No. He had help and setup. We've already found some falsifications on his file, but it's a thorough job." Carl didn't seem particularly concerned about it as he ate. Security was just a part of his job. He only devoted one hand to the hamburger, keeping the other on Aiko's waist to hold her close. "I still hope he was the only one to make it on, but it's still possible he wasn't. Finding it is gonna be a needle in a big damn haystack. We're starting with the cases that have suspect profiles and we'll work our way out from there. A couple ex-cons, a few with some minor felony convictions that could be exactly who they say they are but influenced by somebody else, that kind of thing. It's gonna be pretty tedious."

The fry in her mouth felt like she was chewing sawdust, but she kept chewing. "What if you do find more people? What's going to happen?"

"What, more people who aren't who they say they are?" He seemed to think that was a fairly obvious question, but he still didn't seem to mind it. "Well, at this point, I'm pretty sure the brass would just put a closer eye on them. You can find the ends of a whole lot of strings as long as you get a hand on just one. If they're tied to others, you can follow the associations until you're fairly sure you've got the whole knot."

He nodded back up at the screen. "Only found a couple other shaky stories on our shuttle coming up, but I've already chased down a couple and they actually check out. One guy lied on his application about having kids, he's got two with some other guy's wife. That was a fun conversation. Imagine most of it is gonna be stupid shit like that."

Aiko nodded before she swallowed down the rest of her food and then she turned so that she could look at him. "I'm sure you're right. Hopefully you don't find anyone else." She felt heat creeping up her neck before she looked back at the photos again. "Who is the most suspicious?"

"Why, you want to take a spin with a weapon?" He teased with a chuckle at just the thought of Aiko holding a gun. A quick gesture at the screen brought some of his other files back into focus, and the face front and center on the screen was one she knew well. "Right now, this is the guy my gut keeps telling me to chase a little more closely, but I can't find anything on him. That's what worries me."

Gordon's lips weren't smiling in the picture he had submitted to the Consortium, but it was so emotionless and cold that it was almost chilling on its own. "I mean, I get the narrative on him, orphan from the age of five, couple adoptions, then a registered vagrant ever since he was seventeen. The fact that somebody like this was registered off the grid but comes up here and is immediately assigned into data processing with no recorded experience . . . people can pick up skills anywhere, I get that, but it's just unnerving. So until we fill in the pieces on his story, he's at the top of my list."

She couldn't find her voice as she stared at Gordon's picture for a little bit longer before she cleared her throat. "Well, what's the saying? You can't always judge a book by its cover?" She turned again to look back at Carl. "Sometimes even when you are right about people, the story isn't what you think. I already don't trust everything here, you know that. Maybe some people snuck up here for good reasons?"

He seemed genuinely confused by that statement, and it showed on his face. "Good reasons to sneak into a place that's colonizing another planet? We're already up here trying to work for the good of humanity. The people in the Initiative if not everybody in the Consortium, I'm with you on that one. What kind of good would people be doing if they had to sneak into something like that?"

"The Consortium has an agenda, don't they? They picked the people who turned around and picked us. That says something, doesn't it?"

Carl was finally catching on at that, and he turned to nod back at the board with Gordon's face on it. "So you think somebody might be up here with a better idea of how to handle a new planet than the Consortium? A better agenda?"

"Maybe. I'm just saying that some of the people who might be bad for the Consortium might not be bad for us." She was saying too much, she knew it, but she couldn't stop herself.

It took a while, but eventually Carl nodded. "I could see that." He was finished with the hamburger, but he grabbed a fry anyway, then leaned back in his chair and held her close.

"Did you hear some of the trickle down from the one committee meeting yesterday? One of the agro leaders took Vance to task and demanded recognition of sovereignty for us colonists. I'm gonna be looking into him pretty hard because of it, but he's got a point. And especially with something like that, I could see that there might be some people on our side who aren't exactly fans of the guys who currently sign our checks."

"So does that mean that you're going to be looking at Orion's match, too? Isn't that her husband?" Clearly she had heard gossip. Or something like gossip. "Is he suspicious of his match?"

"I haven't asked him, actually. And I probably won't. If I do end up digging something up on her, I'm gonna need to take care of it without him knowing about it. I hope that's not something that needs to happen." He heaved a sigh, heavy with the work. "Starting to think I should've been a botanist. Trees don't resist when you arrest 'em."

Aiko kissed him again before she said anything else. "What if it was me? Would you arrest me?"

He gave her a look that was accompanied by a grin. "You? Please. I can find records of what you had for breakfast on your thirteenth birthday. You and your brother are the walking definition of on-the-grid living." He put both arms around her waist to kiss her again, leaning back to pull her tightly against him. "Besides, you don't scare me. If I found out that you came up here with some kind of freedom-fighter movement or whatever, I would at least listen to what you had to say. Though there might have to be handcuffs involved later one way or another."

It gave her a little bit of relief to hear that he would at least listen to what she had to say, because she had a feeling there would come a time when she would have to tell him things he might not want to hear. If for no other reason than his own safety. "Handcuffs? Really? You haven't even seen me naked yet and you want to handcuff me somewhere?"

"Not for you, for me. I've never been arrested, so I've never actually been in a pair. Could be fun to be at your mercy for a while." He teased her and kissed her soundly as his hands wandered up her back. "Unless you're into the whole getting-restrained thing. My job kinda comes with all the right paraphernalia for that, so just say the word."

Aiko laughed against his lips before she allowed herself to get lost in his touch. Every one of Carl's kisses made her feel every bit of his desire, and it made her feel like a queen. "I'm into making people happy. So you tell me what would do that, and I'll do my best."

He looked her up and down once as he held her, smiling at that comment. "I'm either gonna make you very happy you said that or very sorry. You might have just created a monster." His hands wandered down to her backside to hold her against him and he scooted her higher on his lap so the entirety of her could be pressed into him.

Aiko's cheeks flushed but this time for a very different reason. She could feel his manhood pressed into her, but not only that, the door was open behind them. "I hope I don't disappoint you. I'm certainly not a woman like your friend's wife. She was blessed by some kind of goddess to look like that."

Carl just rolled his eyes. "Everybody's going on and on about Mercury. I need to tell Orion there's a whole pool started about her in the general public. One of the guys on the force here has had to crack down on some of the geeks trying to hack the cameras in their room to get nude shots of her to sell to everybody else. Just makes me dizzy."

He chuckled once and reached up to brush Aiko's hair back from her face with another kiss, then ran his hand down over her body, tracing her curves down over her hip. "You are beautiful, Aiko. Stand next to any other woman in this Initiative, and I'd take you. Not just for looks, but seriously, it's not possible to get better than a woman who brings you a hamburger in the middle of the afternoon. I want *you*."

Aiko felt all kinds of warm emotion in her chest before she leaned in and kissed him again. Aiko was flattered that he was so interested in her. It was certainly something she did not expect. "There's a whole lot of you. What if we don't . . . fit?"

"That's crossed my mind." He admitted with a chuckle and another quick kiss. "Not gonna know if there's something to worry about until we know, though. I'm not gonna hurt you." He promised with a caress along the side of her face. "Not like that or any other way. Last thing I ever want to do."

"I'm not sure you are well enough to try." She could feel his body thought he was well enough, though, the way his hardness pressed into her. "I don't want you to overdo it."

"I told you I heal faster than most." He reminded her with a low groan, since they were nearly fused together. "Especially when I've got a damn good reason. But if it would make you feel better, I'll stop by the medic station on my way home tonight to get a once-over."

"It would make me feel better." She replied, but she kept tasting his lips. Between kisses, she attempted to continue the conversation. "Should I go so you can work?"

"See, that question started by asking if you should go." He said between kisses, his hands wandering down over her backside as she flattened herself against him. "Day I say yes to a question like that, shoot me."

"You have work to do." Aiko said instead of asked, since she knew they all had work to do. "I didn't think you'd want anything to happen here. Where you work."

He glanced around as if seeing the space for the first time. "Just a room." He looked back at her with a teasing smirk. "Just a bunch of walls, a floor, a ceiling and some tech. You're you. Easy choice. Plus, the door locks. I checked."

She hesitated because she was clearly nervous about the entire situation but she could also tell that he was eager. Aiko looked back at the door and told the computer to close and lock the door before she started to pull off her shirt.

Carl clearly hadn't been expecting that response, but his grin was a permanent fixture on his face as he watched her. He was dressed casually himself, and it was easy for him to undo the first two buttons on his shirt and pull it off over his head. The sight of her once her shirt was on the floor, perfect dark hair spilling down over perfect pale skin, was enough to take his jeans from painfully tight to miserably constricting. "Oh, I knew I liked this office."

"You thought about this in your office?" She asked as she unclasped her black bra and let it fall to the floor. Aiko was a small woman, and everything about her was small, but she didn't look like a child. Her small breasts were still round and full and clearly her nipples were begging for Carl's attention. She bit her bottom lip as she sat on top of his lap for his inspection, her eyes roaming his dark skin. "You are a *wall* of muscle."

"My nickname in school was Tank." He leaned in to kiss down her chest as her hands wandered over him, his lips teasing at her perfect breasts until his tongue could flick over one of her nipples. "Mmmm . . . that's a taste I'm gonna need a steady supply of." His voice seemed even deeper when it was pressed right up into her chest, growling in satisfaction at just the first sample of her.

Aiko couldn't stop the whimper that escaped her lips at the feeling of his tongue flicking out across her nipple. She really did hope that no one would burst into his office on them, especially if he was going to keep doing that, but she had no intention of leaving. "I'm not going to call you Tank, but I think it's appropriate."

"Nobody's called me that in years. I sent the last guy who did to the hospital. He hadn't earned the right." He kissed his way back up to her lips, but his huge hands took the place of his lips on her breasts, calloused from work but still warm and well acquainted with the right way to handle a woman.

"You . . . are bolder than I gave you credit for. And I like that. I'll do my best not to underestimate you." One of his hands moved down her spine to press her into him with a moan, even though they were both still wearing pants and for the life of him he wasn't sure why.

"Is it a bad thing?" Aiko was focused on pleasing him, even though she still didn't know him very well. Her hands slid between their bodies and unbuckled his belt slowly, but she pulled it out of the loops with flourish. "I don't think I'm particularly bold, but I want to make you happy."

"Well, everything you're doing right now, very much on the happy side. These pants are killing me right now." He didn't want to put any distance between them, but once she stood up, he pushed himself up out of the chair he'd been in so she could get his pants off. There was nothing particularly fancy or surprising about his standard-issue boxers underneath, but as soon as they were off . . .

There was nothing standard-issue about the man's cock.

Aiko was sure she looked surprised or shocked, because she had certainly never tangoed with a penis that large. Not even close. Her nervousness spiked, partly killing her libido. "I, um . . ." She stared at it for a moment before she decided to distract herself by taking the rest of her clothes off, but then she decided to move in closer and touch him. Touching him was safe, it wasn't trying to fit a monster cock inside of her.

Carl groaned at her touch, but he could see the nervousness in every move. She could feel him getting harder in her hand now that he was out of his pants, and he groaned as he put his arms around her to hold her in against him. "Come here." He sat back down on the chair and pulled her back onto him, straddling his parted knees. He leaned back in it and leaned her down with him to kiss her, but he made no move to take her hand off the growing hardness of him between them. Instead, as he kissed her, he ran one hand up over the inner curve of her thigh until his fingers brushed the core of her.

Her breath hitched as his fingers brushed over the intimate part of her, and her breathing quickened after she let out the breath that had caught. "I told you that I'm not a virgin, and that's true, but I don't have a lot of experience either. I know that seems strange for someone from Earth, but it's true."

"Was it good experience, at least?" His fingers started working slowly against her. Nothing about him was in a hurry or insistent, just gradually teasing at the most sensitive pieces of her. She wasn't the first woman he'd ever seen get nervous about his cock once she saw it, and even though most men would have laughed at him for saying so, it had caused problems before.

He didn't want it to cause problems with Aiko, and he knew a lot of preventing those problems meant making sure she was almost begging for him before she tried to take him. That kind of need took time, but it was time he was willing to take. She was worth it.

"It wasn't terrible." She admitted as his fingers started playing her like an instrument she didn't realize he was so talented at playing. "How . . . how do you know . . ." She moaned as his fingers changed up their pattern and it tightened the tension building inside of her. "How to do . . . that?"

"Oh what, that? Or do you mean this?" He changed up the

way he was touching her again, and began actually rocking his hand against her as he stroked her, one of his strong fingers slipping inside her just to accentuate the sensation.

"All of it." She replied with another moan, since he seemed to know exactly how he should touch her, but he'd never touched her before. Aiko squirmed on his lap but kept a firm hold on his cock, moving her hand along with her body, squirming around and sliding up and down just to make sure he stayed hard. "I can't think." Her head tilted back as one of his large fingers circled her clit deftly.

"Good. Means I'm doing something right." He was a little more breathless as she stroked him, and he groaned every time she tightened her grip on him, but his assault on her own body was relentless. She could feel the easy strength in him from the way he held her, the way she could feel every bit of the steel from which he seemed to be carved when her breasts pressed into him. He took his time with her, toying with her to push her body to want more, but his touch refused to be rushed. Instead it became a slow, heated kind of torture inside her as a second finger joined the first, beckoning against her insides at every masterful stroke.

Aiko felt like her whole body was bathed in heat, but she was afraid she was going to fall right off of his lap. The feeling of his fingers inside her wasn't as pleasurable as his attention to her clit until he curved one of his fingers and changed the sensation. Aiko nearly came as soon as he did that, and her whole body shook with pleasure. God, she was going to embarrass herself, if she hadn't already. His lips somehow continued to tease along her skin as his fingers stroked her, her hips responding to every flick of the finger.

He grinned and held her a little tighter to keep her right there with him, but soon he wasn't kissing her any longer because she was moaning with every breath. He had gotten into more of a steady rhythm against her, pressing her closer and closer to an orgasm with every passing moment. "I want all of it, baby. Give me all of it."

She felt like she couldn't breathe. If she took even one deep breath, she was going to shatter into a million pieces, but she didn't care. Aiko held her breath until his fingers broke her anyway. She cried out too loudly for an office, but she couldn't stop herself. Sweat had broken out across her forehead and she leaned back just enough that her breasts were heaving in front of him as she fell apart.

Instead of stopping immediately, his hand rode her straight through the orgasm to make sure she was thoroughly and completely satisfied, then he kissed her again when she finally tried to catch her breath. His hand didn't move away, as if he had taken possession of her with the touch and was holding tightly to what was his. "Something tells me you haven't had as much of that in your life as you should have. I'm gonna fix that. With extreme prejudice."

"Yes, please." It was the only way she could respond as she came down slowly from her orgasm, but she tried to kiss him several times between panting breaths. She felt so wet and slick after such intense attention, but she definitely didn't want to stop. "I haven't had much." She kissed wildly as she wrapped her arms around his neck. "And I've never . . . had a lover as attractive . . . as you are."

"You're easily the most beautiful woman I've ever been with. No contest." He finally drew his hand away from her slowly, but not without sending echoes of pleasure scorching through her. "I'm also gonna make sure you're the most satisfied. That's a promise."

She still couldn't breathe consistently as she sat there on his lap, but her oddly-colored lilac eyes met his dark eyes again. "What if I can't satisfy you?"

"I'm not worried." He said with his hands roaming all over her again, pulling her in against him so that the heat of his cock was pressed between them. "Not even a little."

Aiko went back to kissing him and squirming against him, the heat of her core teasing his straining cock. Any trace of her usual reserve had evaporated, surprising even her. Hunger for Carl had replaced it with a vengeance. Eventually she grabbed onto his hands and slid them to her waist so that he could pick her up. "I don't want to wait. Please."

He certainly didn't need to be asked twice, and he slid his hands beneath her backside easily, picking her up with no effort whatsoever. He slid her up against his torso until the tip of him moved to tease against the parts of her that were still ringing with pleasure. He started to let her down on top of him, but she had enough control to take as much or as little of him as she could.

Fortunately all of his torture had definitely prepared Aiko for the adjustment, but she still moved slowly so her body would adjust for him, as much as she could. She was vocal with her groans as his cock slowly filled her. She didn't know why she was being so loud, she was never noisy during sex. "Is it okay?" She asked breathily. "Are you okay?"

"I'm fucking amazing." He said breathlessly as she took him, the grip of his hands on her ass intensifying the more of him she took. "God, you feel incredible, Aiko . . ." he buried his face against her neck as his hips rocked slightly beneath her just out of instinct he couldn't help.

Aiko moaned and hummed in pleasure as she continued to drop slowly, rocking down on him bit by bit. She seriously doubted she could fit all of him inside of her, no matter how much her body attempted to accommodate. "Carl . . . You're so . . ." She replied with a moan as she gripped his arms tightly. Aiko could feel the stretch and the tightness inside of her as her heat gripped his cock, since she was a tight fit, especially for someone like him.

Once she'd taken all of him that she could, Carl leaned back in the tilting chair and rocked her against him without allowing any distance between their bodies. It kept things as tight and close between them as possible, and allowed him to taste the moans that hummed past her lips while he rocked inside her.

She was perfect. From the way she felt to the sounds she was making as she took him, everything about her, he wanted more. And when she unexpectedly started rocking against him herself, her hips taking on every bit of him that she could take, he gave a loud growl and had to close his eyes against how amazing it felt. "Mmmm, go on, get it like that, get whatever you want. That's all yours."

She definitely liked hearing that and she rocked herself harder against him at his encouragement. Aiko busied herself by kissing along his neck between every movement. The size of him had the added benefit of involving her clit, which lit up with every stroke. "I want to please you. I'll do whatever you want."

He let her ride him a little longer there on the chair, but then leaned her back to kiss along her neck and breasts, both his arms wrapped around her back to hold her as his thrusts pulsed inside her. He couldn't even talk as he took her slowly, still not wanting to rush things and hurt her.

After a while, he slowed to focus on her breasts, his hot mouth teasing each nipple in turn. After, he picked her up completely clear of his cock, before spinning her around in mid-air to face away from him with her legs spread on either side of his own. He laid her back against his chest with her black hair spilling past one shoulder, and one of his hands found her needy clit again, teasing her ruthlessly until he could lower her back onto him.

From that angle, she could take just a little more of him than she had the other way, but one of his hands could hold her across her breasts while the other hand moved down over her heat with fingers on either side of her clit. Every time he rocked her against him, every part of her body could feel it, every part of her was bound against his and claimed by him, and that was exactly the way he liked it.

It wasn't much longer before Aiko couldn't take it anymore and her body clenched around his as she cried out in pleasure, moaning his name between her breaths and whimpers. She didn't know what to grab onto, but she made the best of whatever was within range, mostly his legs and arms. "Carl . . . " She moaned a few times. "Oh, babe . . ."

Her orgasm on top of him was clearly the last straw for him too, and his grip on her showed as much as he rocked her through the last vestiges of her climax. As large as he was, she could feel every tiny detail about what happened to him as he came, not to mention him crying out almost right against her ear as he did.

"Aiko . . ." he groaned as his hips continued to rock, apparently of their own volition. Every one of his considerable muscles locked up all at once against her, his arms clenched around her chest and waist as his climax ran its course, and it was a delicious kind of imprisonment there on his chair. His lips were pressed against her hair near her ear, but he couldn't speak. All he could do was moan and growl, and he had no desire to do anything else.

All he wanted was Aiko.

* * * * *

Jessie and Gordon hadn't talked about what she witnessed, not in much detail. He assured her he would do what he could to keep them safe, but he hesitated every time she asked to know more. By the time another two days had passed, Jessie's patience had worn out.

She was always back at the unit before he was, but this time when he got home, she was theatrical about barring the door with a chair. His meal was waiting and ready at the table, but clearly she had more in mind. "You have to tell me more about what's going on. You have to tell me about the messages and Tatyana, but not as your girlfriend. You have to trust me."

He looked back at her for a while in silence, but eventually put down the bag he carried near the door. He took out the data core around his neck and walked to the dinner table to set it down and activate it. "Hyacinth, when is the security station's next sweep of surveillance on me taking place?"

Two hours, six minutes, thirteen seconds. The core replied simply.

Jessie moved to sit at the table, even though she didn't have any food for herself. "Well, that's plenty of time, I think."

Gordon agreed. "Give me a notification ten minutes prior and loop video and audio of other days here at home to all surveillance outlets starting ten minutes ago." He waited for the core to acknowledge his command, then moved to stand next to where she'd sat down, running a hand down the side of her face before he kissed her.

"I'm sorry I've put it off. It hasn't been out of distrust, there are just a lot of moving pieces that seem to be changing by the hour." He pulled out a chair next to her for himself and pulled his plate of food to the new seat, obviously unwilling to put much distance between them. "Where would you like me to start?"

"I don't know." She said quickly, since she was still a little flustered, especially because he was good at making her forget about it by touching her in the right way. "Did you really get accepted into this project? Why are you really here?"

"No, I didn't." He answered straightforwardly. "A man named Gordon White, with a carefully engineered profile to make him agreeable to the Initiative's criteria, was accepted. He's one of my better forgeries, if I do say so myself. He doesn't exist, except in their databases."

He took a deep breath before he continued, and glanced over at his data core to make sure it was showing a successful blocking of all monitoring to his unit.

"The name I was given as a child is Jason William Montgomery. I haven't used it regularly in nearly six years. Under that name, I am wanted for nine counts of terrorism in four countries, twenty-seven separate acts of vandalism, and five counts of murder. Even with all that, I'm something of an annoyance to world governments because no one can seem to track down a reliable picture of me in any system. The best they have is some artist renderings, which get fairly close but don't quite do me justice."

That kind of explanation wasn't something that she was expecting, and she was too shocked to say anything else for a solid minute. "Murder? Have you really murdered people?"

"Yes, I have." He didn't sound like he was remorseful about it, but he wasn't exactly bragging either. It was just a fact of his existence. "Their numbers are wrong, through. The number of people I've killed either directly or whose death was in some way my responsibility is closer to twenty."

"Did you pick me because you wanted to recruit me for something? You still haven't told me why you're here." All the statistics he had rattled off were still swimming in her mind and she was trying to process it. "I assume I'm not to call you by your name, obviously."

"Not while we're on the station, please." He said softly, since he could tell she was getting a little angry with him. "If all goes to plan, we won't be here forever, so once we're away from here, you can call me whatever you like best. I've answered to Gordon for so long it feels like it's almost as much mine as the other." He reached out along the table to take her hand, hoping she wouldn't pull away because of what he'd already told her.

"I'm here because I'm one of three people on the side of Earth who understands the technology that's making it possible for the Consortium to get to Eleusis. We're here to find it, to steal it, to fuck the Consortium in the ass, and take it back down to Earth where it belongs. Where it can be used to really and truly help the world instead of stoking the Consortium's monopoly on power."

Jessie looked down at his hand holding hers and eventually pulled hers away from him slowly. "Were you ever going to tell me if I didn't demand to know? If I didn't overhear that fucked up email conversation?" She didn't care about the Consortium being fucked over, they'd already done that to her before she was even conceived, as far as she was concerned. But she didn't like the idea she might not have meant anything to Gordon/Jason, though she didn't know why it made her so angry. She hadn't known him for very long. Maybe he *did* want to use her in the beginning. "I mean, I guess I don't have much to contribute working in food service."

"I've executed two of my own people in the few days we've

been here." He said just as quietly as he'd spoken before, still not certain of what she would say or how she would react. "Tatyana and I discovered they were working with Carmina, feeding her as much information as they could. We've been reviewing the rest of those who came with us, about three dozen people altogether. Your boss, Clark, is one of them. I wanted somebody close to you who was able to see any kind of threat to you coming when you might not."

He shook his head. "My point is, I haven't even been able to trust my own people in the past few days. Bringing you in, telling you everything, introducing you to everyone, puts you in the center of whatever danger the rest of us are in from traitors already among us. As of this morning, we're reasonably sure the rest of our people are loyal and committed. So yes, I've wanted to tell you everything about what I'm doing here ever since the informational meeting. But things have been complicated. I had to be sure."

"So you're here to steal technology. How? What are you trying to steal? Where are you going to take it? The Consortium has a lot of resources to track people, if you haven't noticed." She still didn't reach out to touch him again and to resist any temptation, she crossed her arms. "They're even monitoring what people are eating and how much they're allowed to eat ever since the social. I can't change restrictions, but I see them." Which was why she wasn't eating while he was, she'd been allotted chicken broth for the evening, and she'd opted not to drink down fake broth.

He hadn't realized that part, clearly, but he also hadn't been paying attention, and there was no way any computer program was going to restrict his own intake, since he was considered underweight by most standards. He looked down at the table again and at his food, and pushed the plate closer to her side of the table. "One of the more ridiculous things the Consortium does to their people in orbit, if you ask me. But it's like everything they do. Cold and calculated and apathetic to anything approaching human understanding. Please."

He tapped the plate, breaking off a small piece of the potato that had been waiting there for himself, indicating for her to share the rest. "They consider their reliance on superior technology a strength, and it's managed to keep them in power ever since the Crisis. They've got technology to monitor everything just about everywhere, like you said. But technology can always be fooled. Always. No matter how much of it they have at their disposal."

She shook her head and kept her arms crossed, she didn't need his pity. "It can be fooled by people, but that doesn't mean the output from the technology is wrong." Jessie sighed as she looked over at him again. "I'm still on your side. But I don't want to be left out. I can help, I'm not useless."

"I never once thought you were. I kept you out because if someone was sent up here to kill me, I didn't want them coming after you next." He could feel how angry she was, and he didn't blame her, but instead of touching her again he got up and moved the data core a little closer to them so he could work with it.

"This . . ." he said when he got to a visualization and expanded it so that it took up most of the dining room, "is what I came here to steal."

The image in light looked like a narrow oval laid on its side, surrounded by complex machinery and anchored to a wall behind it in a dozen places. A hologram of a featureless person was standing in front of it for scale, and the entire thing looked just a few meters long and two meters tall.

"They call it a Twist, and it's how the Consortium is able to get to Eleusis."

Jessie stared at the image and she looked more confused than angry. "Wait, what? You're here to steal a machine?" When he said technology, she thought he meant some kind of chip or data core or something that would be the answer, not some machine. "I thought it was a year-long trip by ship?"

"You thought that because that's what they told you." Gordon looked longingly at the machine in the hologram then turned more fully to face her with the image still active behind him.

"About seventy years ago, one of the first near-light probes the world sent out right before the Crisis finally reached the Eleusis system and started sending back information. They were calling it Proxima Centauri B back then, before habitability was confirmed. But it took centuries for it to get there, and by the time it got to us, the information was years old already. Fortunately, it kept broadcasting and scanning and sending back information, and the Consortium's teams were able to give it a few new sets of instructions before it passed out of range of the system. That's when we learned about Eleusis and about how frankly perfect it is for human habitation."

"I've seen the data myself, it wasn't tampered with. Eleusis is real, even if pretty much everything else about this project is a lie."

He pulled up an image of Eleusis with its star, a system jam-packed with planets, more than Earth's own neighborhood.

"So the Consortium finally decided we wanted to go there. And they scrambled their brains trying to figure out how to get people there. Just build a big generational ship and set out, hoping that the colonists' descendants still have the right ideas? Freeze everyone? Autopilot never ends well. There didn't seem to be many good options."

"So they started putting out contests asking for better ideas. Some brilliant pilots were able to shave the trip to a mere seventy-plus years using modern acceleration methods. That was almost acceptable. And then, just when they were about to start building their generational ship and announce the plan to the world, one of the contest participants took a completely different approach and created this beautiful piece of machinery." He indicated the hologram again, and the image changed so that the area contained by the oval of the Twist became a window onto a beautiful grassy landscape rather than the blank wall behind it. The featureless human figure stepped through, and the image vanished, including the person themselves.

"Getting to Eleusis won't take a year." Gordon concluded as he looked back at Jessie. "It'll take about three steps. And there are maybe a few dozen people in all of humanity who know it. Including you."

"Oh my god." She stared at the image in front of her and soaked in what he explained. "So why did they lie to us? What else did they lie about? What are we doing here for training if we can go there tomorrow?" It was a lot of questions all at once, but she couldn't stop herself.

He actually smiled at her questions, though it obviously wasn't a happy subject, and he leaned over to kiss her on the cheek once without any explanation before he sat back in his chair.

"Imagine. You're in control of an organization that controls or maintains just about every facet of the supports that are keeping humanity afloat. You have millions of people living in space stations completely under your thumb and, as you said earlier, vast resources to maintain this level of control over the population."

"Not only that, but you have your fingers in every single major government left standing on Earth, and you control, indirectly, just about everything that goes on with the skeleton population struggling to live on a planet that's constantly trying to kill them.

You can do anything you want, with impunity, because you are the highest authority, and no one can break your monopoly on power."

He poked a thumb back toward the hologram. "And then someone discovers another habitable planet. Not just that, but they discover a means to just hop, skip and jump their way right over to that planet. An escape hatch for all of your subjects from all of the things that are trying to limit them. From you. If you're in that position, and you're the kind of person or group of people who will do anything in their considerable power to maintain that considerable power, then what do you do with a new and picture-perfect world like Eleusis?"

"You try to find like-minded people or manufacture like-minded people before you go." She thought about all of the people that were a part of the Initiative, just like the two of them. "Except people aren't entirely on board. They're bound to start a rebellion before they get anyone on their side."

"Case in point." He pointed to himself. "And the people they've drafted for this Initiative aren't exactly the most cooperative bunch. You've heard about the waves Bickford made, and there's a few couples already starting to break down and despise each other, predictably enough, but the leadership isn't budging." He knew she had already heard about all of those things, but the recap had a point to it.

"They didn't bring us up here because they intend to send us to Eleusis. They brought us up here because they want a rebellion, and they want to be sure the measures they have in place to deal with rebellious types are effective, before they try to apply it to the general population. They fully intend to take people to Eleusis, so long as they remain thoroughly under Consortium control."

"And if a rebellion does happen within the year they've told us we'll be here? What, they'll swipe the babies we make and kill us?" She thought it sounded far-fetched, but his expression wasn't changing.

He still didn't contradict her as the silence stretched on. "Now you understand the stakes." He said quietly. "My goal here, and Tatyana's, and that of all those who came here with us, is to retrieve the Twist, escape to Earth, and take as many Initiative members with us as possible when we go, to aid in the rebellion that has to follow. If we get the Twist, we can take the fight to them on Eleusis itself, claim it for the rest of humanity, and keep the Consortium from gaining a foothold in a paradise they don't deserve."

Jessie was quiet and she nodded but she still didn't move closer to Gordon. She was still angry it took her pushing against the silence to get anything from him. "This relationship isn't something that I consider temporary, no matter what the hell the Initiative thinks. I want to be with you. Whatever that means."

"No less than I want from you." He reaffirmed. "I didn't choose you so that I could use you or keep you in the dark or just to have someone to keep the bed warm. But getting involved in this makes you as much a target as I am. I care about you, Jessie. Hopefully you can forgive me for hesitating to paint a target on your back, whether the Consortium knows it's there yet or not."

"If I'm in this, I'm in it." She finally relaxed just a little bit. "If I do get pregnant, they're going to come after me no matter what, if they have a reason to go after you. I should at least know why."

"You're right. You should." He sat in silence for another few breaths and turned off the holograms. "There's more to the story, more to the history and the current state of things, but those are the main things to understand. Carmina, the woman whose threats you witnessed the other day, got her start as one of us, just like Tatyana and myself. Her designation with us was Violet. But about a year ago, she decided our methods were working too slowly, and she took some of us away with her to become more . . . militant."

Jessie nodded since she wasn't sure she could take any more information at the moment anyway. She got up to get herself a drink of water and brought him a glass. "Just let me be a part of this. That's what I want. To be a part of it and to support you. Is that alright?"

"That's more than alright." He took the water from her when she got back to the table. "You're one of the smarter people I've run into here on the station so far. What I'd like you working on, if you're willing, is contingency plans, to prepare for the various ways things could go south with what we're trying to do. Clark is actually a part of that team already. There's a lot that can go wrong in what we're trying to do, obviously, and we want to be as prepared as we can be for whatever happens and whatever the Consortium throws at us."

"I'll do that. The best I can." She finally uncrossed her arms and then reached out for his hand before she leaned over the table to kiss him. "I'm glad you trust me. I won't let you down."

He held tight to her hand and pulled her around the table in the middle of the kiss until he could draw her into his lap. "I know you won't." His hands on her sides were as hungry as ever for the feel of her, and his kisses felt the same way. "You also need to let me know when you've had enough of working for catering. I can get you assigned anywhere else in the station you want, with whoever you want to work with. I'm magical like that."

"Wouldn't that get suspicious?" Jessie knew of some of his magical ways already, and his lips were already promising more.

"Depends on where you want to go. If I were to jump in there and replace your job title with Vance's, yeah, sure, that would turn a few heads." He smiled at that thought, since he really did think she would have done a better job than Vance at leading the entire Initiative. "But I could start by making sure you get named to the Judiciary Council that's about to be formed in a few days, to answer the Executive. Once you're on there and you're a part of guiding things there, I could get you reassigned someplace like Communications, or Station Operations, somewhere they're already training dozens of people from Earth to help out with things and where it wouldn't turn any heads that you're being transitioned there with no background in them."

He smiled again after a few more kisses. "Plus, Communications is right up by the tech labs where my cave is. We wouldn't have the whole arm between us every time I go looking for you on our lunch break."

"Are you saying that you want to shuffle me around so that you can come looking for a booty call whenever you want?" She laughed, but clearly she wasn't offended by the idea. "You really want to see me that often?"

"I'm sorry, have I been in any way unclear about just how much I want you?" He asked sarcastically as his hands moved up beneath her shirt to caress along bare skin. He had said before that touching her with clothes on was just never going to be enough for him after having her without. "If I had my way in designing a perfect world, I would design it so that you and I would never have to go anywhere public, so that I could have you wrapped around me at least twelve out of the twenty-four hours of the day. Have to stop to eat and sleep every once in a while, after all."

Jessie just shook her head in disbelief. She was still waiting for the time when he would tell her that he had enough of her, it had happened in every other aspect of her life. People always had enough of her. "We'll see if you still want me that much in a couple of weeks. I'll be old news by then."

"Old news? Why, do you have a birthday coming up that I don't know about?" He grinned as he kissed along her neck. "Someday you'll be convinced that my interest in you is genuine, Jess. Until then, I'm perfectly content to keep on working to convince you."

"Jess, huh?" She said with a slight moan as his kisses teased along her neck. "Only you can call me that."

"Damn right." He said with another kiss farther down along her neckline, and his teeth got into the action with a gentle sharpness against her skin.

"You are insatiable." She replied with a groan. "Except for your food. You should eat."

"So should you." He said with a playful glare up at her. "I'm going to take a look at whatever restrictions you're on and blow them to hell. Also, if you see the asshole who tormented you the other night, give him my regards. I found him on the surveillance footage."

"You looked on surveillance?" She pulled back from his lips so that she could look at him fully. "I told you, it's nothing I haven't heard before. And he told me he did it because he was protecting Tatyana." She shrugged, but she didn't want to dwell on it. "And if the computer says I should drink fake chicken broth, then I probably should."

Gordon just rolled his eyes as he leaned back in his seat. "No, you shouldn't. The dietary restrictions on their computers are usually set to try and bring everyone to what they consider healthy body weight. I've seen what you can do with the body you've got, and I don't see any reason for it to be anything else. If people want to do something and ask the computer for help doing it, that's one thing. I'm not gonna have something imposed on you like a fucking slave."

Jessie ran her fingers along the side of his face slowly. "I love that you love me the way I am." She paused as soon as she realized what she said. "I mean, I love that the way that I am doesn't bother you. I didn't mean to say that you love me. That's a little soon."

He just smiled under her caress, clearly not bothered by what she'd said. "I can't honestly say that I was in love with any of the women I've been with so far in my life." He said quietly, returning the caress along her face before his touch trailed down freely over her body. "The first . . . well, that was a pretty fucked-up situation even by Earth standards, even if it took me until after she died to realize it. And Tatyana . . . you have to really know someone in order to really love them. It turns out I didn't, not like I should have."

He undid the top button on the casual dress she wore but he didn't go any farther than that, taking his time with teasing her. "I like to think I'm just a little wiser now. From what I know of you so far, Jessie, I can see myself loving you. The way people ought to love each other. Hopefully the rest of what you learn about me won't convince you that's impossible."

"I want to love you. It's too soon, but I already know I'm in trouble." Jessie stole another kiss. "But we don't need to talk about any of that right now. We need to have make-up sex right now."

"I do love a woman with an agenda." He grinned under another violent kiss, and had no difficulty turning things very intense very quickly. The table was fairly utilitarian, but there was plenty of space for him to stand up and lay her back on it beside his plate of uneaten food. If she wanted make-up sex, he was damn well going to make it up to her.

9

Logan found it difficult to relax in the pods, but in its own way, the near-zero gravity was almost soothing. Weightlessness had its advantages. He took the water pouch he'd gotten from the bar and drained it quickly, since he was thirsty after the morning's work, which had mostly consisted of him talking. Not only had he been voted the first president of the Executive Council, but he was also the head of the Agricultural department, and the rest of his subordinates were almost as pigheaded as he was.

He was reading over the dispatch on his communicator for the tenth or eleventh time while he waited for Anna, the feeling of disbelief still lingering as he glanced over the words.

It is declared by the Orbital Consortium that the governing bodies of the Eleusis Initiative and all governing bodies established on Eleusis itself shall be sovereign entities, their right to govern and administer the affairs of Eleusis and all their territories recognized by international treaty under Article Seventeen of . . .

Logan always trailed off a little after that, since it devolved into legalese that he didn't completely understand. He was going to have to draft someone to dig into it for loopholes, but it sounded pretty airtight to him.

That, however, was the only message he had received that morning, which was beginning to worry him. Larissa almost always sent him at least a quick update message every morning without fail, but he'd seen nothing from Earth since the day before, even though he was keeping up his appointments with Mercury and had even met her for lunch a few times in the past week to have some casual conversation and be seen together publicly.

When Anna showed up, she looked flustered, and worse, she looked a little bit irritated. She was in a sports bra and spandex shorts, her hair pulled into a high ponytail. "Here you are." She was glistening with sweat, so clearly she had been working hard.

"I invited you to come work out with us, but never heard back. Then when I just sent you a message to meet up with you back at the unit, it sent back the message and told me you were unreachable. I had to ask around to find you here. I thought something was wrong, so I didn't even get a shower."

She could see the confusion on his face, and he looked down at his communicator again, only to turn it around and show her the lack of messages from her, only the one from Director Vance. "I've been sitting here for half an hour, just about. I just figured your flight training went long. I didn't get any of that."

Anna looked at her communicator and then pulled up the messages she'd sent as well as she tried again in front of him only to get another error. "Fuck." She growled as she looked between their communicators. "I got a message from Orion this morning when our training changed to a group workout, but I haven't gotten anything else. Are they restricting us again?"

Logan sighed and shoved his communicator back into his pocket, worthless as it was. "Looks that way." He grabbed another pouch of water he brought along from the bar and handed it to her before he started unwrapping his food. He'd gotten hers as well, but it was cold from how long he'd been there waiting for her. "What about carrier pigeons? You think they could reprogram them to be selective about delivering messages too? We should see about getting some of those."

"They would probably do something." She sighed and went to sit down in Logan's lap. "I heard you got a fancy title this morning. All I got was my ass kicked. I need to work on my upper body strength."

"I like your upper body just the way it is. Especially in this thing that's just asking to get tossed in a corner somewhere." He leaned in and kissed her exposed cleavage, but then settled back to eat since he was hungry, and it wasn't a moment to really start pushing intimacy, if they were starting to get restricted again. "And you know I could care less about titles. All I care about is having the leverage to make sure shit gets done right. Maybe even influence some of the rules around here eventually. Like the ones that keep fucking with our communications."

"That's a long time before you'll be able to have that much power, though." She shook her head and drank her water instead of eating. "I'm going to send a message to Orion. We need to talk about this shit."

"I'll see if Mercury is around this afternoon." He agreed, pulling his own communicator out. When he did, though, there was a new message waiting for him, and he heard Anna's chime in her hand as she began to pull up Orion. The first few lines of his own message sent chills down his spine.

This is an automated system message. A connectivity issue has been identified with external communications systems. Technicians have been assigned to work on this issue, and we hope to resolve it soon. Your communications with family members outside this station have been analyzed, and the following details provided, in order to reassure you of the well-being of your frequent contacts during this outage. We thank you for your patience.

What followed was a series of pictures, of stunningly good quality, showing the Bickford manor grounds, Liam, each of Logan's new sisters-in-law, Larissa, and Cory, each of them in the middle of various activities around the house and on the estate grounds. A few of the pictures seemed to have been taken from inside the manor itself, and in none of the images did his family members seem to know that they were being photographed, since none of them were ever looking at the camera. Logan couldn't stop flipping through them as his blood started turning first to ice, then to magma in his veins.

Anna turned to look at his communicator when hers chimed right after his, and when she looked over the pictures that were attached, she felt sick to her stomach. Ben and Susan were there, sitting out on a swing, but the photo was skewed as though the photographer was laying on the bench next to them, looking up at them. She saw a photo of her father reading the paper, and even of her youngest sister, taken from afar, as if she was running away from something but she was laughing, playing.

"They tapped their devices." She flipped through the photos almost desperately. "The angles are all weird. They didn't take these, and they didn't know they were being photographed. They tapped their tech!"

Logan seethed in the seat beneath her, and he wanted to crush his communicator in his fist as he looked through the pictures. "They'll tap more than that if we don't play along with their fucking game." Logan knew a threat when he saw one, and the pictures, coupled with the way Eleusis officials had just shown up out of nowhere to interview and interrogate Anna's family, meant the Consortium wanted the two of them to know just how easily they could get to their loved ones back on Earth.

"I don't know what they want from us." He eventually said as his knuckles turned white on his communicator. "I don't know what they want or why, but the last thing I want is to give it to them."

"What they want? They want to be obeyed." She deleted the message. "We're not obeying them, so they're targeting us until we do. Except it's not just us. It's fucking Ben and Liam and Susan and . . ." Anna had to pause to take a deep breath before she looked back at Logan. "I love you. But I don't know if I have the strength to keep fighting them if they're going to do this fucking shit. I . . . What if the next pictures are worse? What if someone gets hurt? Jailed? My family's farm would fall apart without Ben and Cory there. My dad would die if he got thrown into some shitty facility somewhere. If they're going to make me fuck some stranger to keep my family safe . . ."

Logan closed his eyes, but he nodded at that, not wanting her to actually finish the sentence. He opened his eyes just to delete his own message. He had acknowledged what she was saying, and he agreed, but the fact that he agreed didn't make it any easier for him to admit to what they needed to do.

"We should never have come here." He finally said without looking at her. "I want to say that out loud, just once. Maybe they would've found some way to threaten us into something even down on the ground, I don't know, but at least down there, we would've had somewhere to run. Some resources to deal with the problem. Up here . . . it's their world. We're just the rats running around in it."

"You're right. We never should have." She didn't say anything else for a moment before she turned so that she was facing him as she sat on his lap and straddled his legs. "It doesn't mean anything, though. They don't mean anything." Anna hated he wouldn't even look up at her, and so she reached in and grabbed his chin. "Look at me. Please."

It took him some time, but he finally did look her in the eye, and he tightened his arms around her waist as he did. "No, they don't mean anything. They're decent people in the same shitty situation as we are, and they love each other. I don't want to come between that any more than either of them wants to come between us."

He ran his hands up over her back and eventually pulled her down into a quiet kiss before he sighed, leaning his head back against the wall. "We just need to find a way out of this. Some kind of endgame that puts us beyond their reach. Whether that's on Eleusis, or back on Earth, or somewhere else in orbit, I really don't give a shit anymore. All I care about right now is finding some way back to the life where I can wake up next to you in the morning without worrying about some cocksucker in a three-piece suit ordering some other cocksucker to put a gun to my sister's head for it."

"If they put us through all this hell for Eleusis, we're going to Eleusis. I don't care if we leave bodies behind for this." She knew that she was probably being recorded as she sat there with Logan, but she didn't care. "You are my husband. No one is going to change that." Anna pressed both of her hands to his cheeks and sealed her lips to his. "I just never thought I'd have to share you again." She responded heavily, since she really hated the idea of the redhead's paws on her husband. "I mean, she's not even your type."

"No, she's really not." He said with a subdued smile, since he knew she was trying to lighten the situation any way she could, even if that didn't really seem possible. Melanie had been roughly Anna's size, just a little on the skinnier side and a touch taller than his feisty wife, but neither of them would have been considered by anyone to be large or full-bodied women. Mercury was a very different class of woman altogether, and nothing like any of the women Logan had ever once been involved with. Too flawless and too soft by half. "He's not yours either. I don't recall anyone taller than me for at least a few hundred kilometers in any direction."

"He's like twice my size!" She said incredulously as she thought about how ridiculous the entire thing was. "And we have this thing where I call him Giant and he calls me Shortie. It's not romantic in the slightest. I mean, seriously. There's no way I could think of him that way. He can't handle me. That's why he has a softie."

"Speaking of which, I have no idea how that woman's gonna handle me either. The giant might as well have been her first, from the way she talks. That's . . . about as far from what I'm used to as Eleusis is from here." He shook his head just thinking about the possibility of being with Mercury, since the woman didn't seem to know the meaning of the word sexy. She was beautiful, there was no living soul who could deny that. But beautiful and sexy were two very different things. Every time Anna moved, her body told everyone she knew exactly how to use it. Mercury couldn't have been farther from that if she tried.

Just thinking about what they were talking about was giving Anna a headache, and she didn't even know what the giant and the redhead would think about it. She wasn't going to attempt to seduce the giant, so if it didn't happen, then it didn't.

"If it happens," she was still going with 'if.' "If it happens, we don't talk about it, agreed? We keep the fucking psychos from killing our families, we move on, we're still the best couple in this universe. You and me. I'm still Anna Bickford. I belong to no one else."

It took an effort for Logan to convince himself to even nod when it came to a pronouncement like that. "You know I'm yours." He said with another lingering kiss, looking in her eyes afterward with deadly seriousness in his own. "No one owns me unless I say so, and I say I belong to you. No one else. I'll do whatever it takes to protect our family. Cory and Danny and Ben are my brothers as much as Liam. No one's laying a finger on them if I can prevent it."

Anna slid in closer to him, since it was too much to think about anyone else kissing him. He was hers, he'd just told her so, but she still had to think about him with someone else. It made her sick, but kissing him helped her to forget about it. "Let's go back to the unit. Fuck the rest of this shit right now."

* * * * *

Orion was sitting back in his chair when Mercury came back from the restroom to join him for lunch. They had made it into a near-daily event at the same time and place, as much as they were both able to be present for it, but that day, Orion almost wished there had been something to keep him from joining her. Not because he didn't want to see her, but because he didn't want to hear the confirmation from her of what he had just seen a few minutes ago himself.

The food he'd brought to the clinic for their lunch was still wrapped up on one side of the exam table they had jokingly taken for themselves days before, untouched. Orion was leaning on the table with his forehead in one hand, his communicator on the table in front of him. He only looked up when he heard her close the door behind her. "Did you get one too?" If she had, he would have no need to specify what he was talking about.

Mercury looked confused, since she hadn't taken her communicator with her to the restroom, but when she picked it up, she opened the message and just stared. "There are photos of my parents." She sounded confused as she slowly ticked through the photos. "But they didn't send them. They aren't even looking at the camera. Is someone watching them?"

Orion nodded with resignation on his features, and slid his own communicator toward her. There were no pictures, only a short video of Misha and young Ahmed, playing in a zero-gravity playground back on her home station, completely unaware that anyone was filming them. "I haven't gotten anything from Khadi in three days. She's pretty self-centered most of the time, but she did seem pretty faithful in writing, and my parents haven't responded since I wrote to them last night. That's not like them at all."

She looked like she was going to cry as she turned off both of their communicators and closed her eyes. "Why are they doing this?" She was a respected doctor and researcher in her field. Always working hard to do her best for the Consortium. "I've been a law-abiding citizen all my life. I work hard every single day. Why are they treating us like this?"

"I don't know." He answered honestly, staring at the blank screen of his communicator and seeing the image of his sister-in-law and her child running over and over again through his mind with chilling implications. "I've earned commendations my whole life, helped write some of the basic navigational code for this damn trip, and now . . . I don't know why. I feel like this whole Initiative is some huge inside joke and nobody bothered to clue us in on the punchline. In no world could it possibly matter this much who fucks who or who has kids by who. There's no way you can convince me of that. I just don't know what they really want from us."

She sank down to the floor next to the exam table and buried her face in her hands as she thought about what could possibly force the Initiative to treat them like they didn't matter. They were the best, the brightest, the most inventive and imaginative.

Why were they being conditioned to respond to negative

stimuli? Why were they being backed into a corner repeatedly?

"Stephen Kaplan is on the council with me. Talking to Maria was useless and has been useless. But maybe I can talk to him. There has to be some kind of explanation for all of this. There is absolutely no need for them to threaten us."

"Kaplan is a notorious asshole." Orion didn't sound optimistic about her chances, but he wasn't going to tell her no either. "I mean, if you think you can talk to him and get some answers, then by all means, go for it. I just . . . I just want to know what kind of game they're playing. Whether or not you and I sleep with the Bickfords should not, in any kind of fucked-up world, involve threats like this against our families. I don't understand the point of that at all."

"Me either." She took a deep breath before she lifted her head from her hands and reached for her communicator so that she could attempt to schedule a meeting with Stephen Kaplan. "I'll contact Stephen." Mercury typed out a quick message before she would even look at Orion again. "If no one can be reasoned with . . ."

"I know." He cut her off before she had to finish the thought, since it was the same thought that had been running through his mind off and on since they were first handed the communication restrictions after coming to Nine. He let the weight of that reality settle on him, and closed his eyes briefly before he looked at Mercury. He reached out with one hand to caress along her cheek and draw her in to rest the side of her head against him. "I love you, Mercury. No one's threats and no amount of duress is going to change that. I'm here with you, for you, and for Eleusis. They can push all the buttons they want, they're not going to change that."

Mercury eventually convinced herself to get up and she buried her face into his chest. "You won't change your mind? What if the match is right? What if it *is* a better match?" Normally she would convince herself that it didn't matter, but she was truly worried.

"No match that we're getting forced into is going to be better than the one we chose with each other. Whatever potential the program might have seen in the two of us with the Bickfords, it got shot to hell by the fact that we're being pushed into it by a gun to our heads." He put his arms around her to hold her, as if that could keep anything else from happening. "If they're willing to threaten our families, then they're willing to threaten us if we don't do whatever they're telling us to do. I don't know what I would do if anything happened to you."

Mercury tucked her head under his chin and took a deep breath of the scent of him. It was calming to have him hold her, it made her feel secure. If only for a moment. "I don't want anything to happen to anyone, least of all you." She closed her eyes again briefly as she clung to his chest. "I love you too, Orion. I know I probably don't say it often enough, and I'm sorry."

"You've got nothing to be sorry about." He ran his fingers through her hair. "No matter what happens from here. As long as we're together at the end of the day, that's what matters. That's the only thing that matters."

She nodded as she held onto him, only disturbed by the sound of her communicator letting her know that she had received a message. When she grabbed it again and looked down at it, she let out a heavy breath. "Logan is asking to meet me for dinner. I imagine if we received messages like this, they did too." She didn't know how or when she had made the switch from calling him Mr. Bickford to Logan, but the change suddenly became glaring after she said his name out loud.

"I'm sure they did." He said without looking at the communicator. "I'll . . . send a message to Anna and see what her plans are for the day." Saying Anna's name was strange to him as well, but mostly because he had been consistently calling her Short Stuff or Shortie the entire time. Giant no longer sounded precisely like an insult or even a nickname, it was just what she called him.

Mercury didn't like thinking about him making plans with Anna, but she was about to agree to see Logan for dinner. "Hopefully Kaplan answers my message soon and we can avoid this mess. I don't . . . I don't even want to think about it."

As if on cue (Orion wondered if they really were being monitored so tightly as to make such a coincidence possible), Mercury's communicator chimed again, with a response from Stephen.

I'm free now. I'd be delighted to have you for lunch. I'm in the dining area near hydroponics.

Mercury read the message out loud to Orion and she responded that she would take her lunch break now and meet with him. "The sooner the better so we can avoid all of this. There's no need for this. I'm sure I can convince him to see reason."

"I hope so." He pulled her into a lingering kiss with his arms around her back, pressing his forehead to hers afterward. "I'm going to get back up to the dock, but I'll wait to hear from you before doing anything else."

She nodded as she held onto him a little bit longer and she kissed him once more. "I love you." Mercury said again to emphasize how she felt, and she pulled away from him slowly. "I better go. Stephen Kaplan is not a man of patience."

Orion nodded, but he held onto her hand as she moved away from him. In any other circumstances it might have been him being playful, and it was the kind of thing he would have done at any other time, holding onto her just to tug her back at the last second. But all the playfulness had been drained out of them both, and as she stepped away from him toward the door, he let his fingers slide from hers.

Orion watched her as she headed out to meet with Kaplan, smoothing the fingers of his dropped hand against each other as if to savor the smooth touch of her for just a little longer.

*****

Stephen was eating alone in the dining area, which wasn't surprising. People generally ate either by themselves or with their match, as very few of them had sufficient time to really make friends, let alone large groups of them. He was sitting on a bench with his feet up on the rest of its unoccupied length and a finished plate in front of him while he read something on his communicator. He didn't even look up as Mercury approached the table.

"Dr. Finnegan, always a pleasure." He finished reading whatever had so gathered his attention, then gestured to the seat across from him for her to sit down. "Have you eaten? I'd recommend something good from here, but it's roughly the same as everything else in space. Just a selection between different configurations of shit."

"I'm not hungry, thank you." She sat down across from him in the indicated seat. "I wanted to talk to you about the matching situation between Orion, myself, and the Bickfords. This morning we received some rather disturbing photos of our families from back home, but I'll take the message at face value and assume they were sent with good intentions. I don't understand, however, why it is necessary only weeks after our arrival to rush anything with the matching situation. Relationships aren't built overnight. Even if they were, the methods employed are rather extreme. Orion and I have been great contributors to this Initiative. I don't see why the matches are taking precedence over our work."

"You're referring to the genetic diversity requirements, right?" He skipped right past the comments about the photos she had received, either unaware of them or completely apathetic to whatever impact such pictures might have had. "Didn't you already talk this over with Maria? I could have sworn I was there for a conversation just like that."

"Yes, but clearly the Initiative has more of an agenda about people sleeping together than I ever thought likely. Since when does the government deem it absolutely necessary to dictate when people have intercourse and who they have intercourse with? And if the subjects don't comply, they threaten them or cut them off from communicating with family and their own spouse? You can't tell me that this is appropriate behavior for the Initiative."

"Appropriate behavior." He repeated as if he was tasting the way the words moved through his mouth. "I wonder what that would be like, to behave appropriately?" He turned on the bench to face her directly, and clasped his hands on the table as if he was about to give her a job interview.

"Well, let's consider that. Appropriate is a relative term. What's appropriate in a library is inappropriate in a boxing ring and what's appropriate for a manager would be inappropriate for a subordinate. What is and isn't appropriate clearly changes, then, based on who and where someone is in the greater order of things. The Initiative has been tasked with ensuring that Eleusis is populated with people who can contribute effectively to its development. A demonstrated unwillingness to do that would seem to be the appropriate stimulus for corrective actions. Speaking hypothetically, of course."

The look on his face was such a mixture that it was difficult to read. She had seen him nearly lose his temper with Logan in meetings before, when his emotions had been plain and simple for everyone to see, but this was different. He seemed both thoroughly genuine and thoroughly sarcastic, to the point where either could have been possible.

"You grew up on Seven, Dr. Finnegan. You and I both know

from personal experience how harsh the restrictions and expectations there can be. You're required to conceive with Bickford, not develop a relationship with him. Just the same as we were ever required to keep up with our PT on Three, or take our vitamins in the morning."

"This isn't about personal health, nor is it about saving someone's life. Even if it was, the Initiative could use some work on their bedside manner." Mercury was typically slow to anger, but apparently he had a knack for it. "I have contributed nearly my entire life to Eleusis, and I did it with dignity. This isn't entirely about genetic diversity. I've read Dr. Santos' work. I know what she does to get the results she wants, but I never would have imagined they would allow her to play with people like this."

Mercury mimicked how he folded his hands and she placed them on the table in front of her as well. "You know who my father is. Do you really want to push this?" Clearly when the mouse was backed into a corner, she had claws.

The smile that crawled across Kaplan's face answered her question before he even spoke, and he didn't look the least bit frightened. "We've met, your father and I. For the first time a very, very long time ago. My brother was three, I was a little older than five, but I remember your father. The accent made an impression. I'd never heard it before."

He sat back on the bench, the perfect image of relaxation with one arm stretched out beside him. "He was also the best-dressed person I'd ever seen walk into the orphanage. That helped him stick in my memory. Of course, given the rest of what happened that day, those things leave a mark on a person too, that isn't soon erased."

He gestured down to her side where he assumed she was carrying her communicator. "You should have access to file a report with your father, if you'd like. You may be surprised by his response. He's been working behind the scenes to help Eleusis become a reality for even longer than you have. I know he'd hate to see your chances of being a successful part of it ruined by your lack of conviction."

"Lack of conviction." She repeated as she looked away from Kaplan. Mercury didn't know if she wanted to know what he was talking about, what behind-the-scenes work that her father may have done. However, she was also very aware of how much her parents hadn't wanted her to marry Orion in the first place. She wasn't sure that her parents would be on her side. "I wanted to be a part of this to help people, not to become someone's plaything."

Kaplan chuckled at the defiance in her beautiful eyes. "If, Dr. Finnegan, you have ever, even for a brief flicker of time, believed that you, or that any of us are anything but playthings, it is only because you have managed to delude yourself into that belief. Humanity has no kings or queens or knights. Not anymore, at least, if it ever did in the first place. We are all pawns to one player or another."

"If you want to continue to help Eleusis, if you want to have a chance at living in peace with your husband and seeing your children grow up beneath a friendly sun, with free air in their lungs, then you have been informed of the requirements. Comply or concede." He picked up a water pouch on the table between them and uncapped it in a toast to her as he got up from the bench, the conversation clearly over as far as he was concerned. "Tell your father that Stephen and Byron Kaplan send their regards."

Mercury watched him as he got up and left, sitting in momentary silence before she eventually pulled out her communicator. She looked at the message from Logan that she had left unanswered and opened it first.

No one among the Initiative brass was going to help her, but Logan was certainly rising in authority. Maybe he could fix this, but right now, they had no choice but to comply.

I would find your company for dinner quite pleasant. I'll schedule your treatment for later in the day, and we can find a good meal together afterward.

She sent off the message and sighed before she pulled up a blank message and tapped in Orion's contact.

No luck. We'll find another way to fight this.

Orion was the one who responded first, apparently waiting by his communicator for any word back from her.

Yes we will.

She hadn't been married to Orion for long, and the one and only time she'd seen him really angry was when he was in the process of destroying the man who had tried to assault her in the nightclub, but she could imagine the look of resolution on his face as he read her message. Her communicator let her know that he was working on a reply as well, but it took him longer to get it across.

I love you. If I don't see you after dinner, I'll understand, and I'll wait to hear from you. Anna said that she was free for dinner as well.

Mercury cringed at the very idea of not going back to her unit with Orion after dinner, but she also realized that if she wanted to minimize contact with Logan Bickford, she would have to see him at the right time. She'd been tracking her ovulation cycle ever since the reproduction blocks had been removed, and she knew she was in the right window. Even if it was not something she wanted to do.

I don't expect there should be any reason why I won't be home after dinner. I love you. I'll see you soon.

Just because they realized they had to bend to the Initiative for now, that didn't mean that she was going to jump into it right away, or jump at all. They were pulling her into it, feet dragging all the way.

10

Orion knew he should have been working harder that afternoon, especially with all of them under such tight surveillance, but if there had ever been a time when he wasn't in the mood, it was that day.

He did some of his work, laying out flight plans for all the supply ships that were supposed to come in and out of the station in the next few days, but he had to pass it off to Fitch to have it re-checked, since he wasn't honestly sure if he had been paying attention. All he could think about was Mercury's plan to have dinner with Logan and his own plans with Anna.

Every time he turned a corner and saw one of the Initiative officials moving through the station in uniform, he had to bite back a glare. None of those people individually had done what was being done to him and to Mercury. At least not that Orion could prove. There was someone, somewhere, with their finger on that particular trigger. Someone who had ordered people to take discreet video of the people who mattered most to him, just so he would remember that they could.

Someone, somewhere, was calling the shots. Or at the very least, someone had set something in motion previously and there were a whole host of people deciding collectively to do nothing about it.

Well, he wasn't going to be one of those people.

Halfway through the afternoon he became much more engaged in his tasks, and he started analyzing the flight paths of other ships that would pass within a few hundred kilometers of Station Nine over the next week. It was possible one of them would end up stopping. It was possible that one of them would need maintenance or some kind of aid from Nine's own fleet of pods and ferry-craft. There were all kinds of possibilities, and he needed to be prepared for all of them. His research began expanding by the window of opportunity and the nature of the ships coming by and before long, he was thoroughly absorbed in his work, his hands flitting from one screen to another.

After a couple attempts to contact Orion with no success and being stood up for dinner, Anna managed to convince the computer to show her how to find him, and she showed up at his office without warning. Since she was his assigned match, all of the computer protocols let her through doors to get to him without special permission. The reminder was as convenient as it was painful.

When she showed up at his office and he was staring at flight plans in the air, she rolled her eyes. "You ditched me to look at maps? Thanks, dude." She looked fierce with her hands on her hips, even though he was twice her size. Anna was dressed in casual clothes that were obviously from Earth, since the jeans were all sorts of ripped. An Orbital might have incinerated them a long time ago. She liked her 'fashionable' jeans to have a little wear and tear. She had a band t-shirt on, like most of her shirts from Earth.

"Huh?" He looked shocked when he looked up at her, then spun around to look at the time, appearing suitably embarrassed. "Oh, for the fucking love . . . I'm sorry. I lost track of time." He turned in his chair to look at her, floating there on the edge of his cubicle with her feet spread as if she was trying to plant them and look intimidating, even in zero gravity. She had gotten better at near-zero quicker than any of her other Earth-born colleagues, that was for sure.

"I'm running flight paths and patterns for the ships that are slotted to pass close in the next few days." He admitted quietly, giving her a knowing look. "I mean, sure, it's a long shot that any of them would have to stop here, but it's best to be prepared for all contingencies, I think."

She nodded and sighed before she relaxed her stance. "So do you just want to reschedule dinner for another time, then? I can leave you to it and head back to my unit."

"No, it's fine, I need to get out of here anyway. I'm getting nowhere." He closed down his programs and unhooked himself from the chair before gliding away, clearly frustrated. "If I could convince them to let you trainees run some everyday operations, that would be one thing." He said quietly as they moved away from Nav Control. "I could engineer it so that the four of us are plugged into the same tin can and off we'd go. There's a thousand ways to go dark out here. But the very first time, I got an automatic denial."

"That's because they want to keep control." She shook her head as she stayed close to him while they made their way out through the twisty hallways. Interesting place, Nav Control. "Apparently there are a lot of people obsessed with the relationship between your penis and my vagina."

"Which is strange, when you think about the fact that so far in our entire lives, there's been no relationship there whatsoever." He met her sarcasm for sarcasm, like always. "Also, my penis has never been even remotely under somebody else's control unless they're busy steering me through a handjob. So this is definitely new territory for me."

"Handsies are boring unless you're out in public." She didn't look over at him as they half-walked, half-floated on their way. Anna, however, was much more bitingly sarcastic and quicker to anger than Orion, who seemed more playful than anything else. "We don't need to talk about sex. Sorry I brought it up with the whole penis/vagina mention. What do you want to get for dinner?"

"Here the bar actually serves decent food. Have you started getting into orbital alcohol yet?" He opened the last door out of Nav Control and closed it in the same motion as he headed out behind her, floating at a casual pace toward the bar across the dock where she'd stolen a beer a few days earlier.

"Only at the social." Anna thought back to that night, half of which she didn't even remember except in random pieces. "I got pretty drunk by the end of it. Wicked hangover the next day, remember? Or maybe I didn't actually admit that to you, since you're a *teacher*."

"Oh no, I could tell. You still had some of it on your breath, and I was stuck with you in a pod for a while. Plus, beer at nine in the morning? I know hair of the dog when I see it. Who do you think you're talking to?" He smiled back over at her to try and lighten the mood between them, but when he looked back at the bar, his smile faded quickly.

He caught himself on one of the columns leading up to the round opening for the bar itself. "Hey, Lila." He said with an attempt at a nervous smile. "Long time no see."

"Hey, big guy." Lila said with a strained smile, though she looked over at the woman next to him curiously. "Long time no see." She repeated. "Who's this lovely lady?"

"Oh this here? This is Shortie. She's um," he sighed as he looked Anna over, though it was nothing but the truth. "She's my match."

"Did you rig the system so that you can take all the pretty ones?" Lila said teasingly, though the look on his face told her he wasn't happy about it. She'd heard about married couples getting separated, though she never thought he'd get parted from his rockin' redhead. She mixed him up the drink he ordered and then floated it his way before she said anything else. "I thought you'd come find *me* if you decided that you were looking around again after the redhead. I'm hurt."

"Well that was definitely the plan, no doubt about that." He smiled at her and thanked her before taking an appreciative sip. "This . . . was not according to the plan." He shook his head and motioned to Anna anyway. "She's from down below. Give her some Shine and make it the good kind. We're also gonna need food, I'm starving. What's good today?"

Lila moved away again to get some Shine and nodded toward the board where she'd just written up the meal specials. "We have pizza today, it's fresh, delicious if you ask me." She poured a shot of Shine and made her way back. "Gotta pay the toll, sweetheart."

Anna raised an eyebrow and looked back and forth between Orion and the bartender. "Toll? What toll? He didn't pay anything."

"I paid mine a while back. It's a one-time deal, unless she decides she likes you." He smiled over at Lila, feeling a little more comfortable in the banter. He plucked the shot of Shine Lila had brought out of the air and placed it in Anna's hand. "Shine first, then toll."

Anna tipped it back and drank from the glass bottle quickly. It burned at the back of her throat, but the risk of it, the novelty of it, felt like a familiar place. She knew from experience if she wanted the burn to go away quicker, she had to drink faster. "That was spicy." Anna looked at Orion again with a raised eyebrow.

"It's a secret recipe." Lila teased before she leaned across the bar with a smirk. "Can I have my toll now?"

Anna looked at how close the bartender had gotten to her and then she actually started laughing. "Do I have to pay the toll to get more booze?"

"Yes." Lila said immediately, without hesitation. "I'm the bartender, after all, and I'll even fight off the big guy if I have to."

"He's not gonna fight for me." Anna said as she focused her attention on the bartender. It was hard to know what was meant, if she meant that Orion wouldn't protect her or fight to have her, both were applicable. She ignored him and planted a kiss right on the bartender's lips.

The rest of those dining nearby started whooping and clapping and when she was finished even Orion was smiling. "Ah, the customs of orbit. Well, mostly the customs of Lila, but nobody's complaining." He took his drink and motioned for another. "We'll take the pizza, once you're done putting out the flames from popping Shortie's toll-cherry."

Lila grinned and licked her lips afterward since she could taste the Shine from Anna's kiss. "Girl can kiss. Damn. Pizza it is, big guy."

Orion was still grinning as he led Anna back to one of the semi-private pods and he hooked one of his feet deftly into the slots to steady himself as he tilted some of his drink into his mouth. "Apparently I'm destined to hang around while women everywhere throw their vaginas at you. Interesting life to be a spectator on."

"She's a bartender, she probably samples everything she wants." Anna said with a laugh as she steadied herself next to him in the pod. Fortunately they weren't that close, but it was still strange. "I don't know what to say about your co-pilot. She wants more than a kiss."

"Yeah, Kam is an all-or-nothing kind of girl." He chuckled and briefly wondered what kind of crap he would catch from Kam for spending more time with Anna, after everything else he'd said on the subject. "Apparently she got matched with a singularly understanding guy, though. He already suggested they find some girl for a threesome to help her feel more comfortable with things. Isn't that sweet?"

"Sweet? That sounds like every man's fantasy." Anna laughed again but she had more than enough experience and stories to know what she liked and what she didn't. "I've done that twice. Girls are much more attentive lovers, but it gets messy with three people."

"It can get pretty messy with two, if you're doing it right." He shrugged and tried not to think of all the experience she had on the subject. "Had a guy early on in flight school who was interested in me, made out with him a few times, but it never went anywhere. I figured out pretty early on which way I lean. Never have done a threesome, that I can remember. Definitely had it on my to-do list for a while, though. Had to scratch it off unfinished when I decided to get matched."

"No shit, you made out with a guy? That's awesome." She grinned since she couldn't imagine the giant next to her kissing a man, but it was interesting anyway. "I did all my experimenting before I got married. That's how I coped, terribly, with Logan getting married the first time." She shook her head again. "Santos wasn't wrong when she called me out on all my partners. I had to guess."

"I . . . don't think I have a number right off the top of my head either. High twenties? Low thirties?" He shrugged, since obviously that was one competition neither of them particularly wanted to win. "Most of them weren't one-and-dones. I was usually with them for a few weeks at least. That's when the crazy generally set in and I had to find ways to break up."

"I had some clingers, but men deal with the no-strings-attached sex much easier than women do." Anna looked over when Lila showed up with the pizza, and her eyebrows raised slightly. "That was fucking fast."

"This is orbit, gorgeous." Lila smiled and winked at Anna before she looked up at Orion. "More drinks?"

"And water to go with them, beautiful. Thank you." He tipped his bottle toward her and finished off the one she'd given him before tossing it to her.

Anna was all about the pizza in front of them and she grabbed a piece and folded it in half to eat it. After one bite, she groaned. "At least this tastes more or less normal. The cheese is a little off, but hey, it's pizza."

"That's what I've heard. And having had real cheese once or twice in my life, I have to agree. But it is close." He took a slice for himself and then placed it back in one side of the box it had come in so that it was his and wouldn't float away. Eating in zero gravity could be tricky sometimes, but it was also often lots of fun. "I had a steak once, right after I graduated from flight school. Best fucking thing I think I've ever tasted. Good thing I don't live on the ground. I'd be a bovine serial killer."

"Cows could use a little more population control down there, there aren't enough people to handle the slaughtering in most places. Logan grills the best steak. I'm a terrible cook unless I follow a recipe religiously. Even then . . ." Anna shrugged and took a couple more bites.

"Good, more things we have in common." He took a small bite of his pizza, still not feeling comfortable even though he also thought it was crazy they couldn't just eat a pizza in peace. They were friends, or they had started to become friends, anyway. They should have been able to eat without it being awkward. "Terrible in the kitchen, decent hands behind the controls, a love of dead cows correctly seasoned. No wonder we're supposed to be soulmates."

Anna laughed again but talking about it again made her think about Logan. Out of instinct she checked her communicator. Nothing. She shoved it away quickly and looked at Orion again. "I don't know how we're not supposed to talk about this stuff. I mean . . ." She shook her head and heaved a sigh. "He's never gonna want to be with me again if he's with her. Your wife is unreal."

"She's plenty real." He said weakly, but he understood what she was saying. "But I don't think that's going to be an issue. He loves you. Otherwise he wouldn't be walking around so pissed off all the time. He's getting a serious reputation for his temper. I have to think the reason for that is because all this is taking him away from you."

"Maybe for now." She knew Logan loved her, but he had loved Melanie too. It was possible for one person to love multiple people. She, however, had been so stuck on Logan that she had never allowed herself to be with anyone long enough to love them. "I think you're a decent guy. You're hot and you know it. But in no way could you actually handle me. I don't know how we would work it out."

He gave her a quizzical look at that, midway through a bite of pizza. "You know, that's not the first time you've said that, and I get the impression you're not joking. What about you could I not handle, exactly?"

"I'm nothing like your wife. Quiet, reserved, academic. A thinker. I'm a doer. I say shit I shouldn't say. I think you and I could make good friends, but I think you'd find me annoying as hell after a while. Logan is patient and quiet, usually, so he just thinks I'm entertaining."

"You know, I figured most of that out after talking to you for about two and a half minutes. You're not exactly blowing my mind with new revelations, here." He looked her over, but kept most of his attention on his pizza.

"I'm with you, though. I already consider you a friend, even as fucked-up as the situation's been. You've got the makings of a good pilot, you can take shit from people, and you've got the right attitude to kick the shit out of any problem you're put up against. You're the kind of person I'd want on my team if we're picking sides."

He pointed to himself as he worked through a bite, shaking his head. "But I'm nothing like your husband, either. Patient, sure, maybe, if I've got a reason to be, but nobody's ever accused me of being quiet. I want to get shit done, I want to get from A to B and have as much fun as I can. B in this case happens to be Eleusis, though the fun is definitely lacking so far."

"No kidding. We left it down on Earth." Lila came back with drinks, but was on her way again quickly. Anna took her new drink and downed half of it, forgoing the water. "So what do we do? Have a sleepover in our jammies and hope the Initiative thinks we went all the way?"

Orion gave her a sarcastic look. "You really think that would convince them? Seriously? You've been here two weeks, you've already seen what kind of toys we have up here. They know whatever they want to know about us, when they want to know it."

"What if you and your hand have some personal time in the bed and then we just cuddle? Then a bioscan would at least pick up semen, right?" Anna didn't have anything against sex, as long as it was good, but Orion wasn't her husband.

"My hand and I haven't needed personal time since I was seventeen, for one thing." He attempted to keep his tone joking, but he was afraid they were past that. "They sent me a video earlier, of my sister-in-law and her son. Three years old. Cute kid. Always in trouble, you'd like him." He shook his head and popped the top on his new drink. "They didn't waste any time in making the threats personal. I thought they would just tighten the restrictions a little more, bit by bit, but no, they went straight for the bloodline."

"They sent me pictures of my family too. My dad reading the paper. My baby sister playing. My brother and his wife." She took another gulp of alcohol. "I'm here for them. I'm here for Logan and myself too, but I'm also here for them." Anna grabbed another slice of pizza and she folded it like the first. "All of them are reasons I never should have come, too."

"I know exactly what you mean." The world wasn't what they had been taught it was, and it never would be again. "Mercury and I could've done just fine for ourselves back on Seven, or maybe on one of the nicer parts of Three, where I'm from. Would've been a good life."

He finished off his drink thoughtfully, unable to look at Anna. "I came here to go to Eleusis, but now all I care about is making it off this station alive with all the people I care about safe. I don't know how to make that happen, but I do know, after today, how to guarantee that won't happen, and that's if I fuck with the Initiative's idea of what I ought to be doing with myself."

Anna just kept eating her pizza and had most of it eaten before she responded again. "I'm going to need way more booze than this."

"I'm flattered." He took a few more bites with a look down at himself. "I pride myself on being the kind of man a woman could meet at a bar and not require beer goggles to find attractive. I would put you well and truly in that category too."

"It's got nothing to do with your attractiveness, Giant. You're hot. I said that. I love the tats." She had tattoos herself, though most weren't visible at the moment. "It's not you. It's the whole married thing. Even though that's a new development in my life, I like being married."

"I actually like it too. Better than I thought I would." He said matter-of-factly. "It's a lot less to worry about, for one thing. And it's just . . . a lot more you can get out of a relationship, if you've both decided to go the distance. I like that." Talking about how much they liked being married wasn't going to help their current situation much, he realized a little too late, but there was no taking it back. "I like being married, *and* I like knowing that my family is still out there somewhere breathing. They've already shown us that they're willing to push us as far as threats against them. I'm normally all about pushing back against the man, but in this case?" He shook his head and went back to drinking.

"Yeah, I know." She finished her drink and was grateful for the fact that being in space made her get drunk faster. Anna didn't want to analyze why, she didn't want to think about much of anything at all. "How about this. We finish this pizza, we order a shit ton of booze to go and then we just hang out together. If shit happens, then it does. I don't want to sit here and plan some fucked up moment where we agree to cheat on our spouses."

"I can do that." He agreed quickly. "I got notice a while ago that apparently your forward-thinking husband commissioned two separate rooms, for the four of us, split the way the Initiative seems to think we should be." He rolled his eyes and pulled out his communicator to program the path to their shared room while he was still sober enough to do it on purpose. "Pizza first, though. You like video games?"

Anna's stomach twisted as she thought about Logan in a room with the redhead and suddenly her pizza was not sitting right in her stomach. "Video games?" She said out loud as she attempted to clear her mind. "Oh, yeah. I have brothers, of course I like video games." She smiled over at him, though there wasn't true emotion behind the smile. "You better have some good ones. Not just a bunch of racing games. I'm talking combat. Guns, guts, the whole thing."

"The only kind I play is the kind where I'm shooting something. Which is the kind I definitely have a craving for right now. There's one that's set post-Crisis, where you're in one of the crews trying to survive in the big urban centers while everybody's losing their minds. It got a lot of shit for being in poor taste, mostly on Earth, but it's got the best system and the best feel of all the ones I've played lately."

"Sounds great. Let's do it." She waved Lila back over to their table and gave the woman a tight smile. "Hey, Lila. Can we get all the booze that you're allowed to give us?"

Lila laughed until she realized that Anna was being serious. "You know, it's not really recommended . . ."

"Please?" Anna said with a pout, hoping it would work. "I'll pay the toll again. I just need some quality booze in high quantities."

Lila sighed and looked over at Orion, but when he shrugged, she reluctantly agreed. "Alright. But be careful. Don't get yourself killed. People still die from that shit up here, you know."

"Death is for amateurs. We're professionals. We go for minor hospitalizations." He smiled at Lila with a sigh. "But we'll try and avoid that too. No promises. I'll send you the unit number, if you could authorize whatever we've got access to for the rest of the night, we'd be grateful."

"Yeah, I'll see what I can do." Lila looked back and forth

between them before she sighed. "Could be worse, you know."

"Well, don't jump the gun on that yet. She hasn't seen how badly she's about to get her ass beat at Crisis Corps. She might wind up hating me after that." Orion's smile was strained, but clearly he wanted to maintain the banter between them.

As long as they were teasing each other, they were still just friends. Right?

* * * * *

When the time came for Logan's late afternoon treatment, it had been a trying day, with the images of his family lingering in the back of his mind. He came into the physician offices dressed in jeans and a worn grey t-shirt, incredibly out of place in the sea of uniforms coming in and out of Mercury's office all day long. The dark brown coat over his clothes looked uncharacteristically earthy and alive compared to the steel grey and glass surroundings of the station, falling to his knees with pockets into which his hands were presently tucked. "Afternoon, Doctor."

Mercury hated that his voice actually made her jump, since it meant he was real in her exam room, and that all four of them, her husband and his wife included, were on the same page. She didn't like that page, even if she was a little curious how the computer had put them together, unless it was tampered.

"Good afternoon, Logan." She turned around and gave him the same polite smile as always. She was in light green scrubs, her hair pulled up as usual. She had a more colorful selection of clothing than most, but it never varied in style. "How was your day?" She could guess how his day had been, but she had to make some kind of conversation.

"It's been . . . varied." He took off the coat he was wearing, folding it almost lovingly before he laid it on the exam table beside him. "The morning wasn't my favorite time of life, but the afternoon did its best to make up for it. I spent most of it reading international response to the declaration of sovereignty. If they're forgeries, they're elaborate ones."

"Sounds like an interesting way to spend your afternoon." She pulled the liquid for his treatment into the needle and approached him, looking up into his eyes briefly before she turned her attention back to the needle. "I met with Stephen Kaplan." She was careful, as always, as she inserted the needle and injected slowly. "It didn't make any difference."

He shook his head and looked across the room as she injected the daily treatment. "I wish I was more surprised by that." He took the small patch to cover the injection site from her out of force of habit established over the past week. "I've had a standing request for another meeting with Vance, but given how our first conversation went, I can't say I'm surprised that he continues declining. Koskei thinks it's funny. He's the one who keeps sending the requests, all of them phrased just differently enough to not get blocked as a duplicate. Not that I think meeting with him would make much of a difference either, but I'll keep trying."

"If I get pregnant, then it won't matter." She checked to make sure he stopped bleeding, even though it was only a pinprick. Mercury looked up at him again and didn't move away after she removed the gauze and he placed the patch. "But still, something should be done to prevent something like this from ever happening again." She glanced at the time and went about checking his vitals as she was supposed to. "Now is the right time for it. Maybe we can minimize the pain of this entire situation sooner rather than later." She had to be logical about it. It was the only way to think about the entire situation.

Logan could only nod to show that he understood what she was saying, but he didn't move otherwise as she finished her checks. "I wish I could do that." He finally said when she finished checking his lungs. "Just see the logical course of action and proceed with it, without looking back. You have a lot more practice with that than I do. I mean that entirely as a compliment. All I've wanted to do since the initial meeting is destroy something, but that method wouldn't help anything."

It didn't really sound like a compliment, even though he said it was, but she didn't think he had any reason to want to offend her. "It's my profession. Sometimes, if you let it, it can destroy you. It's good to care, it's bad to care too much. It's a strange balance to maintain, but bad things happen. Sometimes you can stop them and that's a good day. Sometimes you can't, and that's a bad day. But there will always be both."

She checked his blood pressure and looked up at him again, even though he wasn't looking at her. "One way to deal with this would be to get mad at you, even though that's not the right way. You're not doing this, you're not attempting to break up my marriage, nor do I believe you have any ill will toward me. The second way is to accept it insofar as I have to accept it, and attempt to enjoy the company of someone who understands my pain a little too well. Before I met Orion, I engaged in intercourse only twice, and those times were mostly for my curiosity. I'm not going to make this worse by crying or getting upset, especially when that can be psychologically damaging if it inadvertently becomes associated with sexual behavior. Sex is enjoyable, and is meant to be enjoyed. There's no reason to let it be otherwise."

Logan nodded slowly as he listened to her, and rolled his sleeve back down when he knew she was finished with the vitals she needed. "I'm a long way from being puritanical when it comes to sex." She had given her attitude on the subject, so he figured he might as well give his. "I can't give an honest accounting of the number of women I've slept with. I started when I was fourteen and the last five years have been a little insane. The first two, mostly, before I got engaged to Melanie. I was with her until she died a little over a year ago. After that, I went on a month-long trip up to Vancouver and spent most of it one kind of fucked-up or another. Came back and I was celibate as a stump until Anna and I got together a month and a half ago. Sex has been a lot of things to me, but it's never been meaningless. Either it brings you closer to someone or it takes you farther away from somebody else."

"I don't want to take you away from your wife, and I don't want to be taken away from my husband." She went to sit on a stool halfway across the room. The gravity within the medical wing was near Earth-norm, since they didn't want to poke and prod at people who might float away. "So it looks like we need to find a way to avoid that."

There were two chairs bolted to the floor on the side of the room with the exam table, and Logan sat down in one. They had to stay in the room for a while to expend his observation time post-treatment, after all.

"You're suggesting that we find some way to make the single most personal activity in existence less personal." That was the least affecting kind of sex that he could think of, and it reminded him more of Vancouver than he was readily willing to admit. "Some way to make it so that even though I know you, and I'm going to know that it's you, it will somehow be distanced enough from my marriage with Anna and my friendship with you that it won't affect either relationship."

"Sounds about right." She looked at him for a moment and her eyebrows pulled in slightly before she grabbed her communicator from a nearby table. "I read something in my research that might work."

Mercury pulled up some of her saved files and tapped a few times on the screen until it popped the screen out of her communicator and cast it in the air in a hologram. Mercury swiped through and opened and closed a few folders, all of which contained far too much research and information about sexual practices.

"There are some strange fetishes with masks and elaborate costumes, but I read about something called roleplaying. That's a step of removal from reality, correct?" Logan didn't say anything, so she pulled up the folder and several articles popped up, but what stood out were the passages she'd highlighted. "I don't know how I feel about costumes. Or pretending that I'm something that I'm not. I'm not a fairy witch or something similarly ridiculous."

"Nor am I a police officer or fireman. I think those are among the usual stand-ins." He looked over some of the passages she had highlighted, and reached out to draw the hologram a little closer to get a better look at a few of the quotes. "I've never taken the roleplaying bit very far. There was a girl who used to show up at my house when I was younger in a french maid outfit, crotchless pantyhose, all that, spent a lot of time dusting my hallway with her ass in the air. My brother ended up spending a lot more time with her than I did."

He flipped through the research, scanning some of the relevant points, then flicked the articles away. "If you take the roleplaying far enough, I've heard it can give you some kind of freedom, just to be something you're not normally. Invent a character, act the part, change your expectations both of yourself and of your partner, set the rules and turn into a completely different person, if only for an afternoon."

Mercury looked over what she had highlighted and thought about the things she had found most interesting. She never had a chance to go into detail with Orion, but now she wondered if that was for the best. At least in this instance. "Of all of it, the most attractive option was to try the submissive/dominant relationship. I thought it sounded appealing to be told what to do, told how to please . . . someone." Mentioning Orion's name would be bad in that moment, since she was trying to distance herself from herself.

"I like giving pleasure, but I don't like fumbling around to figure it out. Being told is far more appealing."

That certainly wasn't the kind of thing he had expected to hear from a woman like Mercury, and it set his eyebrows up a notch or two as he looked her over again. "Those relationships can sometimes get quite complicated." His tone was cautious, thinking over the role she wanted to play. "I've never participated in one, but from what I understand, they also involve consequences. For disobedience. Though unlike other situations I could mention, those consequences could be agreed upon."

"I read about it. I understand that there could be consequences." She knew her cheeks were flushed just from talking about it, but she not only found the idea attractive but quite . . . appealing. She just never thought it would be with someone other than her husband, not that she thought Orion would actually agree to such a thing. He seemed far too playful for it, which was part of the reason it had been difficult for her to approach the topic.

"I accept that there might be consequences for disobedience. Complicated or not, I find that the type of relationship suits our needs and I think it could work very well for us. You have a commanding personality, and in order to develop a relationship very unlike the one I already have, this would be that kind of relationship. I make life and death choices too often. It would be nice to make fewer choices."

Logan was quiet as he considered it, but the majority of his thoughts were consumed by the fact that he hated himself for considering it at all. Everything she said made sense, in a way he knew he needed to recognize. "It would certainly take us away from ourselves and the other relationships we want to preserve. For a while." He agreed, since he did want her to know that he was still on her side.

As he said so, his communicator chimed in his coat on the table beside him. He took it out and looked over the message, then slid it back into the pocket it had come from. "Earlier, after you accepted my invitation to dinner, I sent a message to maintenance ordering a second set of units prepared for us. I thought it was best to keep the units where we've been staying so far . . . apart from the rest of this. For us and for them. That was maintenance notifying me that they've finished cleaning and furnishing them."

The implications of that fact weren't lost on either of them, and he suppressed a sigh at the steps they were beginning to take. "Our unit is up two decks, just off the gallery, where we had the gathering the night after we got here. I'm told it was allocated to me as befitting my current position."

Mercury looked at the time and realized that it was well past the fifteen minutes he needed to stay. "You're my last appointment and you are free to go. Would you like to go to dinner or . . . what would you like to do, Logan? Mr. Bickford?"

Logan felt like he had been harpooned and then anchored to the floor as he looked back at her, half a dozen different directions pulling at him to lash him into a set course of action. He had no personal interest in the woman in front of him. All of that was reserved for Anna.

But every time he thought about that devotion to his wife, the images of his brother and sister floated through his mind, their laughs echoing in chilling monotone, drowned out by the glaring threat in the images themselves. Eleusis drew him another direction, his anger at the Consortium in another, and through all of it, he was bolted to the floor with a simple question hanging in the air waiting for his answer. What, given all the constraints and conflict in his mind, would he like to do?

"Logan." He finally stood up, taking his coat and laying it over one arm as he looked across the room at her. "Or Sir, will do, depending on what seems most appropriate. At least for the time being." He didn't look away from her as he shoved his hands into his pockets, but even in such a nonchalant pose, he still exuded authority. "Let's go see if the unit is acceptable. What else do you have left to do here to close up?"

Was she really going to go through with this? Was she really going to agree to this kind of relationship with this stranger she barely knew? She didn't have a choice, not really, and this would remove her from even thinking about Orion. "I just need to clean up a little bit and submit my reports. It should take no longer than fifteen minutes."

He nodded back to her without moving. "I'll wait for you up in the gallery. I don't know you yet well enough to know if you're one of those doctors who actually prefers scrubs or if you have a different preference in clothing. If you don't . . ." he caught himself, since he had been just about to give her the option the way he would have given it to Anna, and he closed his mouth to set his jaw before he opened it to speak again. "When you've finished here, change into whatever you prefer that's casual and comfortable. If the point of this is to be something other than ourselves, then I'm not a farmer, and you are not a doctor. Temporarily."

Mercury nodded and looked down at her scrubs before she looked up at him and gave him a tentative smile. "I'll change and meet you up at the unit." She allowed herself to look him over once, mostly because she needed to accept the fact that she was going to be intimate with someone who wasn't her husband and despite the fact that he wasn't her husband, he was still an attractive man. One who was locked into the same threats she was. Maybe together they could do something about their situation, but they had to play along first.

"Sir."

11

Anna hadn't wanted to assume anything, but she brought a bag of her things to her shared unit with Orion anyway. When she showed up she was in shorts and a t-shirt, one in worse shape than most that she owned, clearly too big for her. Someone else's shirt. "I thought I'd show up in my PJs. One less step to worry about when I'm drunk."

"You sleep in clothes?" Orion was similarly casual, and she could see a well-worn bag of his own things tossed down by the door. He was wearing shorts that went down just past his knees (they'd have been pants on anyone else), with a multitude of pockets and a tight black tank top that hugged his chest and abs, showing off the fractal tattoo for his unit on one shoulder. He was already in the living area with holograms pulled up all around him, apparently picking out his gear for their game. He had pushed all the furniture to the sides of the room to make space, and there were several bottles of alcohol in the delivery slot with a bucket of ice next to the rest of their pizza. "Honestly, I wouldn't have called that."

"Are you saying you would have preferred I show up here naked? That would have been incredibly presumptuous. And everyone on the way here would have gotten a show." Anna tossed her bag down and went to grab a beer. "I'm gonna kick your ass, Giant."

"Just didn't picture you as the type, that's all." He picked out a few more guns and added them to his inventory. He started up a profile for her so she could just walk into it and get to work, and he smiled when she walked into it without any hesitation. "If I was playing in my pajamas, I'd either be in just boxers or nothing, so no jammies for me. I've played my share of video games naked, but like you said, a little presumptuous."

"I guess it wouldn't be the worst way to handle this fucked up situation." She picked a couple wicked-looking weapons and looked over at him. "Okay, what if we did this like strip poker? Every time one of us loses a round, we strip."

He looked back and forth between the two of them, since neither of them was heavily clothed. "That's gonna be a pretty short game." He chuckled, but his eyes rested on her for a little longer than absolutely necessary. "But you're on. Shouldn't take me more than . . ." he scanned her again, pointing a holographic revolver at her and counting, "four rounds? Yeah, that should be long enough for you to concede to the better player."

"Psh. We'll see. You're gonna end up naked and I'm gonna be juuuuuust fine." She swiped at the air to get herself into the game. "Let's go."

The game began in what had once been Tokyo, which left even Anna taller than the majority of the holographic enemies around them. He started them at the beginning, with information scrolling through from actual historical newspapers and articles detailing the timeline since the Crisis outbreak itself. In the game, it had been only three months since the first reported cases of CV, and eleven billion people had already been reduced to just over six in that time. In the next two years, the time period the game stated it would cover, the world's population would fall beneath just one hundred million. Would they be among them? That was up to them.

The game had them attempting to fight for their lives to get out of a crowded market where someone had stumbled in like a zombie, changed somehow by CV, and a small army followed. Orion jumped in quickly and started laying people out, in a dash to get out of the market. It was strange to be running through a place while also standing more or less in one place, but the holographics made it work, and the people they were fighting were certainly not set on easy.

Anna was incredibly good with a gun, at least in the game. Her kill-count was keeping up with Orion's easily. "I heard CV used to fry people's brains, they would get like 115 degree fevers and just go fucking crazy. They didn't eat people, though." She shot a crazed woman in the head and she whipped around and kicked a man down, breaking his neck. "It doesn't really do that anymore. If it ever actually did in the first place. That's some rabies shit."

Orion ran out of ammunition and switched to more hand-to-hand fighting, since he didn't seem to really need or even prefer the gun. He had to avoid getting bitten or clawed by the people who were running after them, but that wasn't terribly difficult. His height gave him so much of an advantage against the crowd that he was almost faster when killing them barehanded.

"That's almost disappointing." He snapped someone's spine and came up with a knee to someone else's face. "I was picturing this continuous zombie outbreak in little bits and pieces. I could've sworn I heard something about," he paused to grab a handful of rice from a nearby stall and throw it in a crazed man's face to distract him, then finally drew another gun and put a bullet between his eyes, "some outbreak of mass hysteria and mayhem. Just a few months ago, in Greece, if I'm remembering right."

"Those people took an experimental CV drug and went crazy because of it. People do everything they can to try and gain another five or ten years before they get sick." She nailed another man in the head before she missed the fact that someone was sneaking up behind her. Before she knew it, she'd been shot in the head. "Fuck! Damn it."

The level ended shortly after that, and with her having gotten shot in the head, it placed her about seven kills behind him as the bodies cleared away, the scenery turning into an artistic scramble as it loaded the next level. He stowed his guns to reload them and grabbed his beer, tipping it in her direction. "You called the stakes."

"Yeah, I know." She growled before she grabbed her beer again and chugged the entire thing. Once she finished her drink, she leveled a glare. "But it won't happen again." She didn't even look down at herself before she grabbed the hem of her t-shirt and pulled it over her head to toss it aside. For a shorter woman, Anna was well stacked. Her lacy black bra accentuated everything, even though the lace didn't fit with her persona. Her tattoos were all on display now. "Okay, round two, then."

Orion held onto his beer as the next level loaded, and looked her over more than once. She was a heck of a lot shorter than most of the women he'd been with in his promiscuous life before Mercury, but she was fit, that was for damn sure. And the tattoos were very much a plus. "Don't see many women go for the barbed wire." He drew one of his holographic weapons and tapped it on her shoulder. "It suits you, though. You've got a good artist back home."

"Thanks." She looked down at her own arm. "Someone I knew in St. Louis. Gorgeous, covered in ink. Total bad-boy type.

He actually did most of it for free because we were good friends once my mouth was done with him."

His eyebrows shot up at that but the round started up again and they were plunged into darkness, having apparently spent the night somewhere underground only to be attacked in their sleep. "If I was the right kind of artist, I guess I wouldn't mind working for that kind of currency either. Give somebody a free lift from one place to the next so long as they pay the fare on the way, yeah, I could probably have handled that. In a life before this one." He got three kills in a row, which got him a bonus, and one of them had been about to bite into Anna's arm.

The game did require a lot of movement, and Anna was almost glad to be rid of her shirt to cool down. "I really wanted the ink. And I had a bit of a reputation down on Earth." She shrugged as she shot through a couple of crazies and went running to find the tunnel. "We need to find some light. It's too fucking dark."

She could see him nod out of the corner of her eye, and the game did a good job of keeping things as dark as possible as they moved through the imaginary terrain. "I'll draw, you cover. Should be some more open patches outside." He ran up a set of steps ahead of her, taking them two at a time, and waited at the top to make sure she was headed up after him before he ran. Sure enough, people started shooting at him as soon as he was out in view. He kept to cover as much as possible, but he still got tagged several times in one arm and was forced to switch hands.

"You are brave, aren't you?" She ran in front of him in the room as she did in the game, but she didn't look back at him. "Maybe we can find the medic and you can get your arm fixed."

"There's a station near the end of this level. Two streets over, south side." Obviously the wounds came with no actual pain, but he did hate having to shoot left-handed. When they got to a point where they could stop to regroup a little, he explored the alley until he found a tiny abandoned car. He did a few things that seemed to make sense to the game system, and the hood of the car came detached, becoming something he could hold on his uninjured arm to use as a shield and a weapon. "Plus, there's a difference between being brave and spending a lot of your free time playing video games. There's a pack of knives on the body next to the dumpster if you want them."

"Hell yeah." She went to pick up the knives and the body turned out not to be dead. Anna had someone lunging at her and was tackled to the ground and bitten her before he got a shot in. Anna's health was in the red and beeping loudly. "That's the last time I listen to your advice, Orion!" She glanced back at him and glared, but her expression changed as soon as she realized that she had called him by name. That required a game pause for a beer.

"In my defense, that guy is usually dead when I get to this point. Not always, but usually." He wasn't above being a little sneaky to win the game, but he took a sip of his own beer. "Or maybe the guy just got a good look at your tits in that bra and thought they were worth coming back from the dead to take a shot at. I'd take it as a compliment, if I were you."

Anna's death-stare was not convinced. "Sure. Zombie wants my tits. Great compliment." She grabbed a slice of pizza before taking the game off pause, but she was dead before they made it to the medic. Anna was cursing again as she took off her pants and he could see the matching black panties that went with the bra. "Now you really have to die. Even if I'm the one to kill you."

"Oooh, threats. I love threats." He grinned as the game loaded the next level, but they both were hitting the drinks hard. Hanging out was turning out to be more fun than he thought it would be, and the entire reason why they were hanging out seemed to be both fuzzy in his mind and exactly at the forefront, at the same time. "Double or nothing on the next level, then? If you're feeling trigger-happy?"

"Double or nothing? I'd end up naked!" She looked over at him, fully clothed, and she went to get yet another beer. "Fine. I'm never one to back down from a challenge, Giant. Bring it on." Anna drank quickly and ran back to get into place so she would be ready to fight. "You better watch your back."

The next level was more or less a single bridge, filled with stopped and abandoned cars, which they had to cross to get to some modicum of safety, all of which took place at night. It seemed like a hundred kilometers, given the number of people who suddenly came out of their cars to attack them, yelling for help even as they began to turn crazed and claw at them. Orion mopped up, even pausing in the middle of one killing spree to pour himself a pair of shots, both of which he threw back between killings.

Halfway through the bridge, though, he ended up shooting the lock off a bus door, and several dozen of the freaks poured out at once. "Oh, shit! I always wondered why that thing was locked!"

He started running, but she was well ahead of him, and the freaks were moving fast.

"I'm not helping you this time!!" She was laughing as she was running, though she did shoot back at some of the freaks, but not before some of them caught up with him.

"Traitor!" He called out as he was swarmed. He definitely went down fighting and she could see his kill count skyrocketing as he flailed to fend them off, but his health did eventually fade to black, and he laid on the floor of the living room panting for breath as the freaks finally started rushing past him to go after Anna instead.

She actually moved back to look at his dead body but she was still nailing freaks left and right. "Now YOU have to strip!!" She was laughing, but eventually she was overpowered, too drunk and distracted to care. "That was so gratifying."

He just glared at her for gloating, but when he got back to his feet, he was grinning as he stripped. He had only been wearing three things to begin with, so when he took off his shirt and his shorts, he was down to his boxers. His dog tags gleamed black against his chest. It was the first look she'd gotten at the full extent of his tattoos, including the Arabic on his abs and the praying hands on his back, but it was also the first good look she'd gotten at his physique.

He wasn't just tall and pretty, for a guy, he was also clearly toned and lithe, even mostly-drunk as he was. His boxers went farther down his thighs than those of most guys she'd seen out of their pants, but as soon as he started moving around, she could see through the thin fabric exactly why that was. He needed more boxers to contain more of him. "Alright. Next round is gonna have to be winner-take-all. Let's see what you've got."

"Not as much as you do." She glanced down at his boxers again before she paused to bend over and pile her hair on top of her head again, since it had gotten loose. Anna stood back up and wobbled a little with how drunk she was, which made her giggle. "I like your tats. Sexy. I told you, tats are hot."

"Glad you like them." He poured himself one more shot while the level was loading, which put him over next to her. "Am I gonna find more on you once I get the rest of this off you?" He hooked the back of her panties and snapped the band against the base of her spine.

She yelped when he snapped the panties and she whipped around to face him, which only put her breasts that much closer to him. "What are you hoping to find, exactly? A 'welcome' sign?"

"I don't know, I've seen some pretty kinky shit decorating women's happy places." He didn't back away from her, and tipped back his shot with an appreciative groan as it burned down his throat. "Saw one girl had an actual cat curled around it. Thought she was clever."

"Was she bare like a little girl then? Cuz I'm no little girl, Giant. I mean, I keep things respectable down there, but I'm a woman. Not a girl." She looked up into his dark eyes. They were captivating. "Are you hiding a welcome sign by your junk?" Anna similarly reached out and snapped his waist of his boxers teasingly.

He jerked a little as she did, but it was a slightly delayed response, since he was more than a little buzzed. "Not a chance. Needles are unwelcome in the proximity of my dick. My artist keeps begging me to let her do some work on it, though. Had some idea for a dragon that would admittedly look pretty cool, but that's . . . no. Not happening."

"Probably for the best." She teased, but as drunk as she was, she didn't feel so twisted up about what they needed to do. Anna reached out to run her fingers over his tattoo on his ribs since he was so close to her. "Is the level loaded yet? Sure is taking a long time."

"It's the last one for the head-to-head." He put out his own hand to touch the barbed wire along her arm, twisted in ways that were strong and sharp while still curling along her muscles in a way that was distinctly feminine. "I think you'll like it, if I remember it right. Been a long time since I played somebody one on one."

She eventually pulled her fingers away from his skin. Damn his muscles and his tattoos. "Yeah. Sounds fun."

He took a little longer pulling his own caress away from her, but when he did, he took a few steps back to get to the other side of the room, and the reason quickly became clear. The stage loaded on a hospital room where they had both been picked up as survivors of the bridge, but they were both shown evidence that said the other had been infected with CV, and they had to shoot the other person to get out. Orion was standing behind a set of cabinets as the instructions for the level concluded, one of his guns drawn but not yet pointed at her. "I've never lost this level. That I can remember. Just so you know." He grinned at her past his cover, only part of his deliciously-exposed body showing.

"You know, I actually do have CV and I'm not a crazy person." Anna said as she moved to take cover. "I mean, clearly I'm getting my treatments like a good girl, but still. This game is extreme."

"With underwear like that, your treatments are the only thing you're doing like a good girl." He let off a shot that hit just a whisper from her head past the cover she had taken, but he didn't let off any more shots.

"Hey!!" She was shouting about the shot, not the comment, and she sent a couple of answering shots back at him to let him know that she wasn't going to take his shit. "You're right about the underwear. I'm not a good girl, so they're an excellent reflection of my character."

"I'm not sure what reflects my character." He rolled from the cabinets to one of the beds, which he kicked over to serve as cover for him. "I used to think the uniform did. Now I'm not so sure." He let off a couple more shots in her direction, but they went wild since his aim wasn't doing very well. "What kind of fashion says 'rebel,' exactly? Ripped jeans and bad sunglasses?"

"That's a start." She ducked into a closet and peeked out a few times, though he was still extremely hard to spot. Not to mention the game was a lot more blurry now than it had been when they started. "I'm not sure drunk gaming was the best idea. You're blurry."

"I thought you said I was hot. Blurry hurts my feelings." He let off a few more shots in her direction that were a little more precise, but still didn't hit her. "My vision can't get blurry. Genetically engineered. So no matter how drunk, I'm still gonna see those perfect tits of yours in better than twenty-twenty."

"They're not perfect, but thanks." She glanced down at her own breasts, clearly distracted by his comment. "They are pretty nice, though. Not genetically engineered. These are courtesy of my Momma." Anna looked up again only to see a shot nearly hit her in the face. "Hey again! Stop cheating with your genetically-engineered perfect sight. That's not fair."

"You set the terms." He fired off a few more, but he exposed himself a little more to do so, trying to get at the lock of the closet to get through to her. "Those panties and bra look pretty good on you, but they're about to look better in a pile on the floor." Apparently being intoxicated took him back to classic but tired pickup lines.

"And what if I resist? Are you going to tackle me to the ground and rip them off of me?" She teased right back before she aimed the best she could and fired back at him. Anna took the risk of running from her cover to take a couple clearer shots at him and she narrowly missed his arm.

When she took off running, he set off half a dozen shots, one of them taking out her leg. His gun was empty and he had no more ammunition so he just set off after her, stumbling along the way. "Maybe I will!"

Anna actually took off running away from him in the living room, shooting her gun back at him a few times, but the game had locked up her leg when she was hit, and she ended up stumbling to the ground straight onto the floor. She rolled over quickly only to see him hovering over her, except his gun was empty. It was strange to look up at him and see the holographic image of his game uniform but then his mostly-naked body past the computer pixels. "Hi."

He reached up quickly to grab her gun hand and pin it to the floor, but he fumbled with it a few times before he got it right, and he was, after all, only holding her actual hand, wrestling with her actual nearly-naked body against the floor. The longer he stayed there above her, breathing heavily from the exertion of the game, the more his body seemed to realize that fact. "Hi yourself."

"You shot my leg." She said matter-of-factly as he kept her arm pinned to the ground, though she only stopped moving momentarily. His large body was hovering over hers in just his boxers, the tension between them palpable. She loved Logan, but being exclusive was a relatively new concept to her. Anna couldn't ignore the fact that attractive men were still attractive even after she was married. "That was rude."

"I did." He reached up to take the holographic gun from her fingers, and he moved to press it between her breasts, pointed right into her heart. "I should shoot you again. Win the game honorably, get these bits of cloth off you."

"Do you really want to see me naked?" She asked a little too seriously, but the way he threatened her with the holographic gun made her wonder if he was just that competitive or if he really did want her to take the rest of her clothes off.

He nodded slowly, and she could see in his eyes that he was definitely a little tipsy, but not so much that he was actually completely drunk. He was a big man, and it would take more than a few drinks to put him on his ass. "Do you really want to see me?"

"I know I shouldn't." She said as she looked him over anyway, at least the parts of him she could see as he kept the gun aimed at her heart. Anna never had any interest in cheating on Logan, but now that she was being forced into a rough situation, she was grateful, at least, that Orion was sexy. The ridges of his abs begged to be touched. Licked. "But yeah."

"Alright, then." He moved above her, and she could feel him against her leg, getting hard. He pushed himself away from her a little just to give the situation in his boxers more room, then pulled the holographic trigger and put a bullet straight through her heart, ending the level and the multiplayer match with a smile. "You first."

"You asshole." She said aghast, since she had been manipulated into getting naked first. Anna reached out to smack his shoulder and to send him off rolling onto his back before she managed to get herself up. Anna was facing away from him once she was standing again, and while she hesitated at first, she eventually just slid her panties down and then tossed them toward her bag before she unclasped her bra and tossed it away as well.

She wasn't at all ashamed of her body, but the situation was too complicated to be completely comfortable. She didn't turn around, but she knew he was getting an eyeful of her ass. "Okay. There. I'm naked."

Orion took in the eyeful he was getting for a while in silence, but when she felt him come up behind her, the touch of him against the small of her back told her he had done away with his boxers as well. His hands moved to rest along her sides, his long fingers raking up over her waist. "You're gorgeous, is what you are. Even though you did lose, so I'm not impressed with these video game skills you claimed to have."

"I'm blaming the booze. Rematch later." She looked down at his hands on her waist and turned slightly to look up at him. Anna slowly turned to face him, her eyes locked with his for a moment. "You have like, the most gorgeous eyes."

He shrugged, but his hands didn't leave her and from the way they were working caresses along her sides, she could tell he knew exactly what to do with them. "You have your Momma to blame for some things, I have mine. I'm glad I got her eyes and not her tits, though. That would've been awkward."

"I'm a little hesitant to ask where you got your cock from, though." Her eyes slowly wandered from his dark eyes down his body to the beast that she knew was already lurking, since she'd watched him in his boxers. Even though he was tall and lanky, every bit of him was delicious muscle, coiled and ready to pounce. "I've seen a lot of cock. You should be impressed with yourself."

"I am, as a general rule." He moved back slightly so she could get a good look at him, and so he could look down at the beauty of her in return. "Causes as many problems as it does parties, though. We'll have to see which it is for you." He enjoyed a beautiful woman when he saw one, and Anna was certainly that. Her breasts were large with dusky pink nipples, already peaked from his touch, her tanned skin was warm and inviting, her hips curved enough to beckon a touch.

His body responded with or without the conflict in his mind, and his fingers trailed up along the outer curves of her breasts in a caress headed for her neck. "I admit, your tattoo story's got me curious as to exactly what you Earth women are capable of when you put your mouth to it."

Despite herself, Anna smirked. "Oh, babe. You have no idea what I can do." She looked down at his cock again as though she was figuring it out simply by looking at it, and then she daringly reached out to stroke him. The confidence in her touch said a little about what she knew. "I told you I had a reputation, and part of that was that I gave the best blow jobs in the entire midwest. That's a lot of land." She looked up into his eyes again and smiled. "I practiced a lot with a lot of different men. All shapes and sizes. Do you want me to show you?"

He groaned a little as she stroked him, then backed up a few steps into one of the armchairs. "I think I do. I've always had a weakness for a good blowjob, and I've had them from women who've said they're the best in orbit." And if the woman was going to offer, there was no way he would ever be crazy enough to say no.

There was no way Anna was going to get shown up by some Orbital women who thought they knew something about sex when she had spent years learning about it in every way that she could. Anna smiled at Orion as though she had some sort of secret before she knelt down between his legs. He wasn't quite hard enough for her liking, so she continued to stroke him a little bit more before she felt like he was ready for her to put her lips on him. Anna didn't ask him what he wanted or if he had any particular requests, she just licked the tip of him first before she wet her lips and started to take him into her mouth. His moans would let her know what he liked and what he wanted.

At first, he moaned at the feeling of a woman, any woman, taking him to task in such a way, but as she continued, his moans intensified and he laid his head back along the stiff chair cushion. "Holy . . . sh . . ." he couldn't even quite finish cursing. The woman had a mouth like a black hole, and he had never once thought of black holes as being sexy before. He would never theorize about them again without thinking of Anna. When she said she was good, it was no idle boast. And if she was this good while mostly drunk, he couldn't even imagine how lethal she would be when she was sober.

Anna knew how to make a man last longer, so when his moans would get louder, she would back off and leave him wanting. Men could play women like a fiddle that way, slowing down, changing things up, so she thought it was justified to do the same thing to men. Anna popped off a couple of times to tease him with just her tongue. "You're good and hard now." She said with a silly grin as she continued to lick his shaft. "How long do you think I can torture you before you start to go crazy?"

He groaned loudly and reached down to run his fingers through her hair with a rough touch, both given how buzzed he was and how riled up she had gotten him. "I'm pretty crazy to start with, that's gonna be hard to judge. But if your mouth is this good, then I want to know how good the rest of you is."

Anna paused a moment but she started to take him back into her mouth again, despite what he told her about wanting to know what the rest of her was like. It was easier for her to focus on giving him a blowjob he would never forget than to worry about getting all up close and personal with his dick and her vagina. Between him probably thinking about his wife anyway and now Logan . . . she just wanted to be memorable in some way, at least. The redhead had just about everything memorable locked down as it was.

As she tormented him with her mouth, stroked him with deeply talented fingers, it was her name that he was moaning. Not Mercury, not even Shortie, but "holy fuck, Anna . . ." His fingers stayed in her hair as her lips stroked him, but eventually they wandered down, clearly hungering for every other part of her. He was a tall man, and just as his dick was longer than most, so were his arms. His caresses went to her breasts, beckoning her upward closer to him.

Eventually his insistence pulled her away and up into his lap, but he could tell that she was still feeling a little insecure about it. Anna was a confident woman in what she could do, but that was a different thing entirely than who she was, or what she looked like. She knew she was attractive enough but she was more plain than some, and certainly more plain than what he'd been with. She hated it made her feel vulnerable, especially because she knew it was in her head. "I didn't finish." She complained as he pulled her in, straddling his legs. "You could have let me finish."

"If you had finished, then so would I." His hands moved to grip her backside as she settled herself in his lap, his fingertips seeking out a nipple and tracing idle caresses around it with a fingernail. "And where would that have left you? Me finished and you not even started? Some friend I'd be."

Anna laughed and shook her head, since this was already one of the strangest friendships she'd ever had. "I was trying to prove a point and keep my title." She looked back down to his straining cock between them, and she couldn't help but stroke him again, her mouth watering for more. "I've never had a fuck buddy before. Plenty of people that I've fucked, but not that I've kept friendships with. Not really."

"Neither have I. I'm not really sure how it works." He groaned as she stroked him, since she was nearly as good with just her hand as she was with her mouth. He reached down between her legs to tease her and when he slid a finger into her heat he was a little surprised to find that she was already wet.

"The way I understand it . . ." he said between groans, his eyes rolling back in his head as she handled him, "fuckbuddies can be frank, and honest with each other. Open about things, no strings attached, no drama, no . . . oh, right like that, the whole thing, yeah . . ." he groaned again, and didn't stop for a while as she clearly got what he wanted exactly right, "no bullshit."

"Definitely no bullshit." She smiled as she watched his face and listened to his groans, it was incredibly satisfying to watch, especially when his fingers continued to explore her core, teasing her clit, making her wetter. "You tell me what you want, I'll tell you what I want . . . it will be great."

"And whatever it is you end up wanting . . . I've heard

weirder." His long fingers slipped inside her, sliding with her arousal. He'd handled plenty of women in his time, and most of them had the same weaknesses. He hoped Anna would be the same, just so he could see the pleasure on her face the way she'd written it on his. "Probably done weirder too, so just be aware, you can't scare me."

"I'm . . ." She paused to moan. "A little more to the left . . . not like, yes . . . like that." She moaned even louder when he got it right, and he could see that a chill of pleasure in goosebumps and the fact that her nipples perked up again. "I'm a bit . . . of an exhibitionist. I don't . . . fuck. That's good." What was she thinking about? Oh, right. "I don't like people to watch . . . I just like the idea of getting caught. Being overheard works too."

"Oh, so a public places pervert?" He chuckled, but groaned at the same time, his hips thrusting against her hand as the pace between them increased. "Let's see . . . slow down a little, that's . . . yeah, that's good." He pulled her in close with his free hand so he could kiss along her neck, his tongue laving between kisses. "Most public place I've ever been fucked . . . gotten head in a restaurant, fucked an ex in a dressing room . . . those pods are practically designed for it, so half a dozen of . . . god, woman, your hands are fucking dangerous."

"You better believe it." She teased his neck on the opposite side he was kissing hers, and it made everything that much hotter. Anna worked her way up to his ear and started nibbling on his earlobe. "I just like being heard. And caught. Without anyone seeing."

"We can make that happen." He slid his fingers deeper into her, careful to follow the direction she'd given him earlier as he toyed with her. He loved the way her entire body moved with everything she did, her breasts bounced, her hips swiveled.

"I had a reputation." He growled through the moans, every stroke of both their hands drawing the most intimate parts of them closer together. "I had a reputation in the modeling agencies back on Three. Well, that cock you've got in your hand did, anyway. Everybody knew about it, talked about it, gave me every kind of come-fuck-me look every turn I took." His kisses moved closer along her jawline, his cheek nuzzling hers as they talked and teased each other. "I enjoyed that. People knowing. So when we get caught, and word gets around as to how I make you scream . . . that's gonna be fun."

The thought was both thrilling and terrifying, since she didn't need people talking about her and Orion getting caught together, especially if Logan were to hear people talking about it. She couldn't help it, though, that she thought it was naughty and hot, getting caught. "Where are we getting caught, big guy?"

"Mmmm . . ." he leaned back in the chair and brought her with him, her breasts straining against his chest as she continued to slide her hand up and down his length. It made her want to lick him again, to taste his salty flavor. "Arm is mostly empty, there's a thousand places waiting to get fucked in. Start with the storage rooms . . . off the dining areas. Work our way up to the brass offices. See what we can get away with in one of those pods off the bar, maybe."

"That sounds like so much fun." She said sincerely, especially as she thought about being fucked on top of someone's desk, official paperwork flying everywhere. "Fuck." She groaned as he teased her, his finger stroking her inside and drawing out to circle her clit. "Enough fingers. I want your cock."

"Better be sure about that." He cautioned as he drew his fingers away from her with a final attentive stroke to her now-explosive clit. "Be careful what you wish for, but come and get it anyway."

"I'm sure we can figure this out. Giant cock or not." Anna wrapped her arms around his neck to help support herself as she lifted herself up and positioned herself above his cock. She slid down slowly on top of it, so slow she was torturing herself. "Fuckkkkk, yes."

His hands returned to her gorgeous ass as she took him into her, encouraging her along but certainly not forcing her. "God, you're tighter than I thought you'd be." He grinned up at her as she started to ride him, her body getting accustomed to his. "When you talked about being some kind of super-slut, I had expected differently, but god, go on, dig in on it . . . just like that."

"Super-slut." She chuckled and moaned as his hips bucked against hers, and she waited some more for her body to adjust before she started riding him harder. Anna gripped his shoulders and her eyes devoured every sexy inch of his body and his cock. Anna's fingers traced over muscles and tattoos and everything else while her pussy gripped his dick. "You are so fucking hot."

"And you . . ." he leaned back to enjoy the feeling of her riding him and slapped her ass hard. "I can already tell . . . are a sex goddess." His hands raked up over her breasts as she moved expertly on top of him, every single move worthy of a groan or an outright cry of pleasure from him. "There's beautiful women in the world . . . and there are sluts . . . and there are sex goddesses. It's fucking rare . . . to find a woman who's all three. Even rarer to get to fuck her."

"You know just what to say." She teased before she moaned loudly in her own throes of pleasure, since riding a cock like his, while it wasn't easy for a woman of her size, it was a fucking blast. "God . . . you are hung like a horse."

"Now who's sweet-talking?" He leaned back and let her ride for a while, both impressed and immensely satisfied by just how much of him she was able to take. Anna was eager as hell and undeterred by anything. "Tell me more about what gets you off. I already know you're gonna . . . mmm, do that again. Not that, the other thi . . . fuck, yeah, that's the one . . . Shit, that's good . . . You're gonna wring me out like a fucking fire hose. I wanna know how you like the favor returned."

"Well, the dirty talk? That's fucking sexy as hell." Anna moaned loudly as he thrust up into her, which sent more chills down her spine. He was bouncing her on his lap and she could feel him as deep inside of her as he could go. "Put your hand . . ." She put one of his hands at the small of her back and then shoved his other one between their bodies. "My clit. That's . . .. Mmmm . . . The best . . ."

It took some coordination on both their parts as she rode him, but his long fingers eventually settled in a rhythm to either side of her clit, stroking her with every buck of her hips against him. She didn't lose control or get distracted by the touch either, which he continued to be impressed by. Most women were completely helpless with a man who actually knew what to do, since they so rarely ever met one. Anna was taking everything he knew how to give her and still begging for more. "You'd better rock me right through it." He ordered playfully as his fingers shook against her, driving her wild. "Go on now, come on it and come get seconds."

Anna tilted her head back, which changed the angle slightly, but in a good way. She was moaning loudly already, but as his fingers pushed her over, it felt incredible. "Fuck . . . Orion . . ."

"There it is." He growled in satisfaction as he felt her body spasming with pleasure, and continued his assault on her throughout the orgasm as it moved through her. He smiled at the way her face twisted, and thrust up into her just that much more insistently to prolong the feeling for her. "Always glad to fuck a screamer."

Anna was grateful for his efforts to prolong her orgasm and that he even knew how to try in the first place. Most men she'd been with weren't so considerate. It made her want to fuck him harder, even while the ripples of her orgasm were still ringing in her muscles. Anna gripped his perfect torso, tattoos and all, and kept fucking him while her legs felt numb from pleasure. "Let's . . . hear . . . you."

He let her ride out the orgasm but then pulled her down on his dick as far as she could take him before leaning forward and standing up, with her legs still clutching his waist. Thankfully, he didn't have far to go to get to the couch, but he wasn't gentle about laying her down. He dropped her onto her back while still inside her, and started attacking her neck with his kisses as he pounded himself into her. When she drew her knees back to change their position, he groaned all over again. "Woman, I am going to fucking keep you." He leaned back so that the angle he was taking her at would hit most women's g-spots, and it was his hips' turn to show her exactly how dangerous he could be.

Anna wasn't expecting him to change his angle, and when he did, it only took a couple of thrusts before she was moaning his name all over again. He'd definitely found her number, and she was perfectly okay with that. "Good God . . ." she whimpered as his large cock pounded her relentlessly. Anna was still reeling from his comment about keeping her, but she tried to ignore it. The orgasm high was helping. "Harder." She begged as he groaned with her. "Fuck me harder, Orion." She didn't yell, but she did demand.

He had been trying to take it a little easier on her, since he knew his size was a problem for some women, but a demand like that was one he wasn't going to ignore, and his moans escalated quickly as he complied. It wasn't often that he had even had rough sex in his life for that exact reason, so the freedom to do so was a high that he couldn't ignore. "Sweet mother of fuck, woman, you're . . . mmmm . . . you gonna come with me?" He said breathlessly, leaning over her to put a hand on her shoulder for leverage. Her tits were still bouncing, and he licked one in the moment. "You gonna . . . are you . . . I'm . . ."

Anna came hard right before he did, and she was crying out

his name yet again until her voice almost sounded worn and hoarse from her noises. "Hell yeah, baby."

His orgasm was not over quickly, and he wasn't quiet about it as she felt his climax deep inside her. The touch of his hands on her breasts and sides was frantically rough, and there was a wildness to his eyes that wasn't there during the rest of his mild-mannered life. He was left gasping for breath as his orgasm ran its course, but he didn't pull away from her afterward. Instead, he leaned down and kissed along her shoulder to her jaw.

After a panting look in her eyes to see the echoes of her own pleasure there, he took her lips in a lingering kiss that was surprisingly gentle, considering how rough things had been between them only moments before.

He groaned against her lips as his hips continued to grind against her out of instinct, savoring the feel of her tight around him and her legs wrapped tight around his waist.

Anna continued the kiss for longer than she knew she should, but she was a sucker for a good kisser. After the kissing was over, she caressed the side of his face with hers, which felt a little too intimate, but she didn't care. He had fucked her like a champ. "I'm going to be so sore until I get used to your monster cock." Clearly she was okay with the sacrifice, though.

That got a laugh from him, which pulled a follow-up groan and another round of kisses from them both, since it shook him against her. "Hey, you're the one that wanted it harder. I did warn you to be careful what you wish for." His hands moved up over her breasts as he got back just a little more self-control, but even though he knew he should move away, he didn't really want to. "You a cuddler afterward, or what's your usual preference?"

"Yeah." She met his dark eyes again and she kissed him a couple more times, each more gentle than the last. "I want to cuddle."

He nodded with his forehead against hers, and moved on the couch so that he was lying beside her, though he moved them carefully enough that she still held him inside her, mostly on top of him as he pressed her into the cushions. His kisses never ceased, and neither did his caresses all over her body, since he could reach every part of her. "I'm gonna say something that most women might not take as a compliment, but you absolutely should. You fuck like a professional. Seriously."

Anna smiled, though it was subdued, since she knew that she

was skilled in the art of sex. She'd gotten that way for one person, because she told herself if she ever had the chance to sleep with Logan Bickford, he'd never forget it. Now she was with someone else. Again. She curled into Orion's side anyway, since it felt nice to cuddle, even if it wasn't with the person that she wanted to be with. Feeling desired helped her to cope, at least.

"I'm glad you enjoyed it. I hoped you would." She kissed his cheek and closed her eyes as the guilt settled into her chest sooner than she hoped. This wasn't her fault, this wasn't Orion's or Logan's or Mercury's, but they were still the ones who had to deal with the emotional turmoil of it all. "We're going to stay good friends, right? I need a good friend."

"Yeah, I'd say we're pretty good friends, at this point." He shot back sarcastically, but he didn't laugh, since he was feeling the same way. He did look down over himself with a shrug. "The majority of my friends haven't seen me naked. So, you know, different kind of friendship, maybe, but no, you're not getting rid of me. Besides, if we stopped being friends, who would my co-pilot fantasize about? I'm just thinking of other people, here."

That made her laugh and roll her eyes at the same time but she was grateful for his humor. "Are you going to describe this to her? Cuz that would be mean."

His laugh joined hers and he rolled his eyes. "I'm not gonna have to go out of my way. I'm sure she's gonna ask me how you were as soon as she finds out we're actually doing this. Especially since she's stuck riding a dick for a while, she'll live vicariously wherever she can get it."

"You better make me sound good." She smiled before she yawned, since it had been a long day and she needed some rest. "I mean, goddess level."

"Won't be hard to make you sound like that, since that's exactly what you are." He finally moved just the slightest bit away from her, since she was looking sleepy, and he spun her around in his arms so that her ass was against him and his arm was across her chest to hold her against him. "You want to nap out here or on the bed? Either way, you're probably in for a very horny awakening. Just saying."

"I'm not moving. If you want to go to bed, you better carry me." She didn't even open her eyes as he spun her around, but she did wiggle her backside against him. "I'm already halfway asleep. If you wake me up, you better be good and ready."

"I thought that was supposed to be the guy's job." He moved backward off the couch, and did actually pick her up in both arms to carry her toward the bedroom. He was stronger than his lean frame would suggest, she had felt that from him before, but being picked up by him was a different testament to that fact entirely. "Fall asleep right after sex. And no, on second thought, I'm not the couch-sleeping type. They're really not built for guys like me." He leaned down to tear the sheets back from the bed once they got to it, and he deposited her the same way he'd been pressed against her on the couch, his recently-satisfied manhood along the back of her thighs threatening further satisfaction when she woke.

* * * * *

Mercury's communicator led her through the gallery itself, down the long hall made entirely of glass that ran the length of the station along one side of the arm. Earth was in full view, but by the time she got to the end of it where Logan was waiting for her, night was starting to fall on the planet below, leaving the station to orbit above the dark side of the world.

There was a set of double doors just past him that obviously led to residential quarters, but the entire place was decorated with bolted-down plants and glass sculptures adorning each panel of the walls. He was standing by the window, watching the sparse lights of the world below rather than standing and watching for her, with his hands clasped behind his back and his feet slightly parted. He might as well have been a lord looking over his kingdom.

"Hi." She said sheepishly as she approached. Mercury had changed into a simple black dress that fell to her knees and was otherwise modest. The only skin revealed was her arms and her legs past her knees. Mercury's hair was up in a bun on the top of her head and she was wearing modest flats. She was slightly shorter than Logan, but it was hard to tell even that much when she stood near him. "I hope I didn't keep you waiting too long."

"No more than expected." He turned his head to take in her appearance, and nodded his approval. "You look beautiful." The look in his eyes was just as hard to read as it had been earlier in her exam room, but eventually he moved to face her, his hands still clasped behind him. "Whenever we're out in public together, I'm fond of this kind of conservative style. I've heard too many people talking about the lengths they'd like to go to in order to get a more scandalous look at you."

Mercury looked confused. "You've heard people talking about me? Scandalously?" She really was surprised about that, since she clearly spent most of her time working. In scrubs. Giving people shots. "Yes, of course, I'll dress however you like."

"Good." He managed to give her a subdued smile. "I'll be certain not to place you in anything that would embarrass you. At least not in public." He moved his hands to the front pockets of his jeans, and started toward the residential hallway. He paused beside her with one elbow extended toward her, looking down at her as he waited expectantly.

Mercury took his arm and walked easily at his side, even though it felt so strange. "They gave you a unit with a beautiful view."

He agreed, and took out his communicator to verify the number of the unit that was supposed to be his. Theirs. He had to think of it as something shared between them, something that existed only in the fictitious space they were agreeing to occupy together. "It comes with a view and what I'm told are extended amenities, whatever that means."

The corridor itself was noticeably nicer than most of the rest of the station, but the doors to the units were the same as the other residential access, and there was nothing to indicate who was living in any of the other doors to either side of the hall, if anyone lived there at all. They reached the one his communicator indicated near the end of the hall where it terminated in another, smaller observation gallery, and the door unlocked at Logan's handprint to admit them.

The "unit" was the closest thing orbit had to a palace, as far as Logan could tell. The ceilings were higher than most of those Logan had in his manor back home, and the facilities were thorough in ways that nothing else Logan had seen from space would dream of being. The kitchen was tiled in an impressive counterfeit of granite if it wasn't the real thing, and the living room had couches he could already tell were upholstered in some form of silk. One whole wall that they could already see consisted of glass that looked out on Earth, with a small sliver of another arm of the station in the distance. The glass obviously continued through into the bedroom area, Logan could already see through the open door, but he couldn't convince himself to go exploring yet.

The door closed behind them, and Logan shook his head. "If the toilet in there is made of solid gold, there's no coming back from that. The whole Consortium will be certifiably batshit crazy at that point."

"They already are." She looked around, her arm still looped with his. Mercury did pause shortly to take her shoes off, though she thought afterward that she didn't know if he wanted her to ask permission to do something like that. "You are in a position of power now. This is how the powerful live up here."

"This is how the powerful live everywhere." He said almost under his breath. He paused after she did to put one boot at a time up on a chair near the door and undo the laces, leaving them beside her flats. A brief tap on the panel beside the door locked it behind them, and he had her take his arm again so they could tour the expansive unit.

"I'm fairly easy to please when it comes to food." He said as they did a lazy circle through the kitchen, equipped with every specialized cooking tool a chef could dream of in addition to the standard slot for automated food delivery. "So long as there's plenty of it, I haven't found many styles I'm not fond of."

"I like to hear that. I like to cook, whenever I have time to do so. I realize our ingredients here probably don't come anywhere near the quality of what you have on Earth, but I find that things taste better when I make them myself." She glanced around the kitchen, and she would be glad to use some of the tools when she had the opportunity. "Hopefully you'll tell me if I make something you particularly enjoy so I can remember the things you like."

"I'll do that." He promised as they finished the quick tour, and he stopped briefly to look over at her. "When you do start cooking in here, start with your favorites, so I can know what they are."

Mercury nodded and she gave him a small smile as he stopped to look at her. "I will admit that I have a little bit of a sweet tooth. I love chocolate, but it's very hard to find, and usually my dietary restrictions don't allow for the indulgence."

He looked around the unit again with a sarcastically-raised eyebrow before they continued through the living area. "I doubt there's much a person living in a place like this is restricted from. I'll see what I can do."

She thought about mentioning he was the one the unit was really for, since he was the one with all of the authority, but she didn't say anything about it. "Thank you, that's kind of you." Mercury looked him over again and then she turned her attention back to the unit. "Does it come with everything we need? Clothing included?"

"I didn't request any stock of clothing, besides two bathrobes that I initially ordered as a joke, but they said they would provide them." There wasn't much to see in the living area, just a few couches and a perfectly smooth wall for videos of all kinds. There was no point avoiding the bedroom, so he walked in with her to get a good first look at the king-size bed and the massive wall of glass looking down on Earth. There was a bathroom visible through a door off the bedroom that was every bit as opulent as the rest of the unit, and sure enough, there were two bathrobes hanging from hooks on the wall.

"I see they delivered." He looked at the robes just to keep from doing anything else, but then looked back at her. "Anything else we require, I'm sure they won't have any difficulty providing. Relationships like this often come with a few bits of paraphernalia." He moved the arm she still had her own looped through, and took her gently by the wrist, holding it up between their bodies. "Ties. Restraints. Whips, depending on people's tastes."

Mercury looked at her wrist and up at his eyes again, even though he seemed distracted by looking at her wrist. "It's all worth a try. I found many things very interesting during my research. We can't know what we will or will not like until we try it, right?"

Logan thought he had a fairly good idea of what he did and didn't like, but he had to remind himself that he was dealing with a relative novice when it came to sex. She was obviously still excited, on some level, to explore and try new things, especially in a context that was rendered safe by virtue of not being with her husband, whom she'd have to see all the time. "I'm not sure the bed is sturdy enough for restraints right now." He nodded back toward it and released her wrist, walking through the room as if he was continuing the tour on a house he was considering buying. "Headboard looks a little . . . flimsy."

She really couldn't believe they were talking about sex, since she kept thinking that she was in the middle of a very strange game of cat and mouse, but . . . it was all very real. Mercury remembered the message she sent to Orion, the message that she would be back after dinner, but he would know soon enough that she wasn't going to make it back.

She walked up next to the bed and examined the headboard before she sat down on the edge and looked at Logan across the room. She had to push Orion out of her mind. He couldn't be here with her in her thoughts. It would make everything so much more painful. "The bed seems nice enough, even if you think the headboard looks flimsy."

"I'm sure it is." He walked around the far side of the bed from where she was sitting, running his fingers over the comforter on top of it and laughing inwardly that something like it was included in such a situation. The irony was too much for him to ignore.

He looked over at her across the mattress and turned a lock inside of himself. He was there with her, and there was no point anymore batting around what was happening. If it got the Consortium off their collective backs, if it gave him a chance at the life with Anna that he wanted, then he wouldn't allow himself to look back. He couldn't.

"There is one thing that needs to change." He said finally, one hand still on the comforter and the other in his pocket as he looked at her. "Come here."

Instead of getting up and walking around the bed to get to him, Mercury crawled across the bed to get to him. She didn't know what he wanted to change, but she didn't say anything as she moved across the bed to get to him. He could change her however he liked, it was all part of the act, the game, whatever they were doing.

He waited until she got over to him, then pulled her up to her knees on the bed with a single finger beneath her chin, so that she was nearly his height again. When she was looking him in the eye, the finger moved along her face in a slow caress until it reached her neck, and continued downward from there, a single fingertip tracing down over the fabric of her dress.

"When we are spending time here, more than just to come and grab something we may have left but to really take our time here, however often that happens, there are some things you will do as soon as you come in." He spoke gently, but his tone left no room for argument, and his fingertip continued to move down over the slope of her breasts along the center of her chest.

"First, you will wear only the robe that's hanging in the bathroom for you right now, unless I change my mind later about what I want you to wear. Second, you'll make sure there are water bottles and some form of snacks available in the cupboards so that we don't have to wait on things while we're here unless they're more complex. Third . . ." his caress moved back up over her body until it arrived at her temple again, and his eyes flicked up to the bun on top of her head briefly. "Your hair is to be worn down in my presence at all times. You're too beautiful and too free a woman to be restrained in any way, unless I am the one doing the restraining."

"I understand." She nodded her agreement to his terms, and without much hesitation, reached up and pulled her hair free of the bun she had it in. Her hair was long, which was why she usually kept it tied in some way, and the deep red tumbled over her shoulders as soon as it was loose. Pulling her hair down was the easiest of the three things for her to handle. "Would you like me to change out of my clothes now?" Somehow she said it without sounding nervous, but she was.

He shook his head. "No. Just remember for next time." His hand moved to pull some of her hair forward over her shoulder, running it through his fingers just to get a more complete experience of her. Afterward, he brushed it back with the rest of her hair, and his caress along her neck led his hand to the zipper on her back between her shoulder blades, artfully hidden in the folds of the fabric.

"I had a chance to think about the kinds of rules that I would expect to be obeyed while I was waiting for you just now." He began pulling the zipper down slowly, which didn't affect anything about the way the dress held itself to her at first, but it did let her feel just how much more exposed she was getting by the minute. "Some of them I'll require most of the time but not always, and others will come with consequences if they aren't obeyed. I hope that you'll enjoy them. It's my intention that you do."

Mercury could only nod at first, and when the zipper couldn't move any lower down her back and his fingers stopped, she shivered a little at the exposure of her skin to the cool air around them. "I am certain I can remember any rules that you give me, and consequences are appropriate when rules are not obeyed." She replied as she remained unmoving, wondering what his hand would do next. Mercury was getting turned on, and while she hated herself for it, she was not going to think about it. "I hope I can please you too, Sir."

Logan nodded slowly, but his hand moved over her dress

instead of just leaving the moment half-finished in front of him. He wanted to adjust the growing tension in his jeans, but he didn't want to move, didn't want to break the stillness they had found between them or the pristine moment before everything was lost. Want or no want, though, eventually his hand moved to the neckline of the dress and he raked it slowly down over her torso, letting it fall eventually to her knees on the bed, since she was still kneeling to face him.

He made no secret of staring at her perfect breasts as they were exposed, and the same hand that had disrobed her moved to leave gentle, almost teasing caresses along the curve of them, his fingertips only grazing one of her already-attentive nipples in the process. "Mercury doesn't sound right for you, I don't think. Not here." His touch on her lingered, but his eyes moved back up to meet hers. "Not while you're mine." A finger brushed more purposefully over the tender skin of her nipple as he said so, but he just watched for flickers of emotion in her own eyes. "I have to consider what to call you."

His touches were a stark contrast to the tension of the moment between them, and it made her heart race to feel his calloused fingers touching such a sensitive part of her. He knew what he was doing, she could tell that, even though he'd already told her that he'd been with many women before. Her breath hitched when he did it again after she didn't give him a response, but eventually his touch forced a moan to escape her lips. It felt so good. She couldn't fight it, and obviously, she wasn't going to.

It was as if her slight moan set off a pile of tinder that he hadn't been aware he was dancing around, but after she groaned, his large hand moved to cup her breast completely, teasing her nipple along his palm. "I can see in your eyes, every time I tell you how beautiful you are, you don't know it already. You know, but you don't really know. You don't get what I mean when I say that women as beautiful as you are shouldn't be real. But you are."

When she started to look away from the compliment he was giving her, he reached up with his free hand and pulled her back to look him in the eye. "I think your parents were one planet off when they named you." He leaned a little more into her against the side of the bed, letting her lean into him, still clothed as he was, with one knee up on the bed. "They should have called you Venus instead. It suits you better."

"Venus." She repeated, though it wasn't easy for her to speak while his hand palmed her breast. "I can be your Venus." He said he needed a name for her while she was his, and in that moment, she was certainly his. She didn't spend much of her time worrying about beauty, certainly not her own. She spent most of her time worrying about how to rid the universe of CV. "I'm glad you think I'm beautiful. And that you know that I'm real."

His face came closer to hers, until she could feel the roughness of his cheek against hers and the heat of his breath along the sensitive skin of her neck and shoulder as his fingertips continued to tease her breast. His lips came close to kissing hers, but instead whispered past, as if testing her resolve not to initiate things and just be the passive responder of what was happening. "Get me out of these clothes, Venus." He ordered quietly. "Let's see what you think of the rest of me."

Mercury wanted to kiss him and didn't want to kiss him at the same time, and so she thought the safest route was to do as she was told, even though all of her senses were on fire with need as he teased her. She reached out for his shirt and grabbed the hem of the t-shirt he wore to pull it over his head. As soon as he was shirtless she paused, and her fingertips were slow to move, but eventually her fingers slid slowly down his chest and torso while they made their descent toward his belt and pants.

"Don't be shy." He said once she got there and started fumbling with his belt. "You can take that as an order. Never be shy about doing what I tell you to do, and never be shy about doing what you want, within my rules. I've got no interest in shy. When we're in this, I don't want you holding anything back."

"That's a little difficult for me." She admitted, but she figured out the belt and finally pulled it off of him and tossed it away. "I grew up in a very reserved and restricted environment. I'm used to holding myself back in a lot of things. But I will do my best."

"We're both doing things a little differently." He agreed, offering no help with his pants as she undid the clasp and carefully pulled down the zipper, her fingers brushing the straining bulk of him that the pants were holding back. Once she had pushed them to the floor, his boxers did a much worse job of hiding anything about him than the jeans had.

Before she could get to the boxers, he reached down and plucked at the dress that was still bunched around her knees. "Get rid of this. You seem to like it, and if it stays on the bed, it will be compromised."

Mercury was learning quickly not to hesitate, since hesitation meant thinking about things, and the whole point of something like this was not to think. That was what made it enjoyable. She pulled the dress the rest of the way off and tossed it aside, which left her in only her underwear, but she didn't know if he wanted her to take that off already as well. She turned her attention back to his boxers, but she looked up at him before she made any move to remove them. "You're so hard." She sounded a little bit surprised, but she was pleased at the same time, since that meant she wasn't the only one enjoying the situation.

"I have a lot to look forward to." He eyed her again as she knelt on the bed, and put his hands on her sides, exploring her slowly. His rough hands took her breasts firmly in hand to draw her in against him, then moved down over her underwear to grip her backside and press her into him so she could feel his hardness for herself. "You didn't finish." His voice was a low rumble that she could feel through her own chest, then took her hands and placed them on the waist of his boxers. "I told you to get a good look at the rest of me."

Her heart picked up pace at that kind of command, and her skin flushed as she felt him against her, but she was quick to respond to his command. Mercury's fingers dipped under the band of his boxers and pulled the fabric down slowly. She slid her body down his to remove the boxers completely, then looked down at the length of him. Mercury hadn't allowed herself to think of any other man, and it was fairly easy, because her first thoughts were never sexual. Even after marrying Orion. But seeing Logan naked in front of her was a different story, and her desire spiked just as it had when she saw Orion for the first time. Apparently the two men previous to Orion were very low quality men, since she'd felt nothing for either of them physically.

He stood there under her inspection, but eventually took her hands by the wrists as if he was going to restrain her. He waited until she was looking him in the eye again, then took both her hands and placed them on his newly-freed cock, watching the flush rise in her cheeks as she wrapped her fingers around it. Orion was something of a freak of nature, but she couldn't bring herself to call either one larger or smaller than the other, even with her hands around him. Logan was noticeably thicker than Orion, which set off some scientific inquiries in the back of her mind. Those instincts had been pushed to the rear of her consciousness by the other instincts of the present, but she already knew she'd be spending some time thinking about them, and the cock in her hands, later.

"One more requirement." He set her hands to stroking him and turned his own attention to letting his hands wander over her instead. "When I ask you a question, I want a true answer. At all times, in all things. No matter the question."

Mercury nodded and continued to stroke him, since she enjoyed getting familiar with him. It was all new and exciting even though she knew it shouldn't be exciting at all. She couldn't help herself. He was so masculine, and she was starting to wonder if that was what had been lacking up until Orion, the need for a masculine man. Commanding, possibly violent . . . "I'm a terrible liar, and lying is never my first instinct anyway. Softening the truth, maybe, but that's what doctors do. I will not lie to you, though."

"Good." Without teasing her about it or giving her much warning, one of his hands gave a final caress to her breast and then ran down her stomach to dip into her underwear. His fingers knew exactly where to go, exactly what to look for as they slid against her, and she was so wet already that the warmth of his hand hit the most sensitive parts of her like a lightning strike. "As part of that honesty, you're going to tell me every time you come for me, and you will never fake enjoying something if you don't."

Mercury gasped when his fingers found her clit, and she couldn't help but groan as he started to tease and torture her. It was as though he already knew her, the way he touched her so confidently. "Yes, Sir." She replied in another moan.

His fingers played against her until he could feel her hips begin to twitch of their own accord, and he slowed his pace to delay the satisfaction he knew he could give her just a little longer. "Honest answers." He reminded her as he reached up with his free hand to cradle the side of her face so she could look him in the eye. "Do you want me, Venus?" There was still no trace of a smile on his face, but she'd heard quiet groans escaping him ever since she'd gotten her hands on his cock. He knew it was a complicated question for a complicated moment, but the way he was stroking her and the hardness of him in her hand certainly served as answers.

Complicated emotions flooded through her thoughts but she knew for certain that she *did* want Logan, even though she shouldn't. It made things easier for that moment, but she knew it would make things harder when they were apart. She was unbelievably wet, and that was certainly evidence. "Yes." Mercury whimpered as he kept her from the orgasm that she wanted. No, needed. "Yes, I want you. So much."

At that admission, and the fact that he could tell she wasn't lying, he pulled his fingers away slowly, though it made her whimper again. He pulled her underwear down over her hips, then forcibly shoved her onto her back on the bed with a single push. Once she hit the mattress, he grabbed her underwear and yanked it the rest of the way off to leave her bare on her back for his inspection. "Put your arms up over your head." He ordered as his hand lingered along her inner calf. He was moving up onto the bed slowly, but was more focused on looking at her than moving quickly to satisfy her. It left her aching, left the need still burning between her legs, but that seemed to be the way he wanted her.

Mercury did as she was told and stretched her arms above her head after she landed on her backside, which both surprised her and thrilled her. He looked hungry for her and it made her want him even more. The entire situation was so intense, she felt like she was ready to burst into flames with desire. Mercury certainly didn't stop herself from looking him over, her eyes devouring the look of him. Logan had muscles born of hard work, ridges along arms, thighs, torso, scars and skin that was evidence of a hard-working life. His skin was a golden tan from the sun, and there were slight smatterings of hair along his navel and chest. The look of his hardened features, his incredible body, and his even harder cock made it difficult to keep her hands above her head and follow his command. Hopefully he would let her touch him soon.

He moved up onto the bed slowly, swatting away one of her legs to spread them wide and lay her open in front of him. He took hold of her knees once he was closer, and she could feel the strength in his hands as they worked up her thighs. Thoughts of Orion were placed at a distance with Logan's grip on her thighs shocking her system again by pulling her close to him instead of coming the rest of the way himself.

She was a vision out of a fantasy, any man's fantasy, splayed out and panting in front of him, breasts tight with anticipation and brilliant red hair fanned out on the bed beneath her. He wished there was some way to freeze the moment in his memory, the look in her emerald eyes that was begging for him. Her lips, prim and as pink as her nipples, the rest of her as pale and porcelain as a fantasy. That was the life they had chosen to live while they were together, a fantasy. It would be nothing more, he told himself for the thousandth time, but it would be a fantasy.

When he'd gotten a good look at her and saw her hips begin to arch up and beg to be taken by him, he took her legs by the back of the knees, then leaned down so that he could look her in the eye. He didn't even need to reach between them to guide himself into her, he was so hard and she was so ready and begging for him. His mouth gaped open at the incredible heat of her as she took him, and though the claiming was almost gentle, the way his muscles were drawn tight in his torso above her promised anything but gentleness to come.

Mercury had no idea it could be like this, and she never expected that she would melt under his touch and his commanding nature. Once he was inside of her, she couldn't think about anything but Logan as he towered over her, and the need burning in her body demanded to be satisfied by this man. Keeping her arms above her head was difficult, since she wanted to grab onto him, but Mercury reacted as she could with the rest of her body and her hips. "You feel so good . . ." She moaned at the fullness she felt once he was buried deep. "Oh . . . god . . ."

Logan shoved away the conflict he felt, which became worlds easier once he was inside her. His hands raked up from her waist over her breasts to her shoulders before he leaned back and slammed himself into her again, setting her whole body trembling. The moans coming from her were escalating the more he teased her, and just seeing the normally-reserved doctor so vulnerable, so needy, was a turn-on he hadn't expected. He took the sheets to either side of her beautiful, full breasts in his fists and watched her face as he slammed himself into her slowly, each one a shock, each one lighting every nerve in her core on fire, until eventually his hips picked up the pace and owned her body completely with his own.

Mercury was normally quiet unless Orion told her he wanted to hear her make noise, but she couldn't help her moans and whimpers. Orion knew what he was doing, but somehow Logan seemed to know exactly what to do to her, specifically, and he didn't even know her. The way that he slammed into her, the look on his face was intoxicating. She liked to think she was the one who made him look just as hungry and needy as she felt. He still hadn't let her climax, and it was making her crazy with need. Was she allowed to talk? Did he want her to be quieter? She still had so much to learn about what he wanted or liked, and while she didn't know if this would be the one and only time they were together, she found herself hoping that it would happen again. Mercury lowered her arms slightly because she was desperate to do something with them, but she had to fight her own need because of his command. "Can I touch you? Please?"

He knew she was close, he could tell that much just from the way she felt as he slammed into her, and he considered telling her no, but he eventually nodded and pulled her arms down from over her head to make sure she knew she had his permission, though it didn't stop him thrusting inside her or slow his pace.

Mercury groaned even louder as soon as she could touch his chest and she slid her hands along his muscled body. His body was toned differently than anyone she had ever seen, the difference of someone who was from Earth versus from Orbit. His body was made of labor and not daily visits to the gym. She swiveled her hips and gripped his back as he slammed into her, since she desperately needed release. Mercury knew whenever it hit her, she was going to see stars. He'd delayed her so long that the tension was making her crazy.

Instead of getting more violent with his movements as she rocked against him, Logan laid himself completely against her so that the bulk of his weight was pressing her into the mattress, his arms locked around her back and shoulders. The louder she moaned, the higher he stoked the need in her, the slower he moved against her, the tighter he pressed himself into her. He was riding every blazing pleasure center she had, her nipples pressed into his rock-solid chest, every part of her firmly and completely in his control. The grind of his hips into her perfect pussy hit every part of her at once, and he looked down into her eyes with a growl of pleasure as her moans climbed in pitch. "Come for me, Venus. And don't stop until I give you permission."

There was a relief that came with permission itself, amplified a hundred times when she finally had his permission to climax. It took only a couple of movements after he gave her permission for her to fall apart in his arms, and as tightly as they were pressed together, there was no way that he didn't feel what he did to her. While she had done her best to call him 'Sir' at every moment, she was moaning Logan's name as her head tipped back in complete bliss.

Something about the way he pressed himself into her when she came intensified the sensation and seemed to forbid her body from even coming down from it. The tight grinding of his hips against hers set off firework after firework in her senses, and just when she might have been expecting her body to try and recover, another quick movement from Logan sent her spinning all over again. He kept up the small, tight movements until her own body lost count of what had happened, and he remained still as he finally gave her implicit permission to begin to recover, while he leaned down to run his lips over her breasts, glistened with sweat from the exertion.

Mercury made little noises that let him know how utterly pleased she felt, the rest of the time she was gasping to catch her breath. The scrape of his facial hair against her tender breasts sent sparks through her with every kiss. "You . . ." She tried to talk, but she was really struggling. Mercury could feel how hard he still was, and the whole point of what they were doing was to make a baby, though clearly it had turned into more than that. Quickly.

He groaned at just how extreme everything seemed to have been for her, since there were few things in life that he enjoyed more than looking down at a thoroughly satisfied woman when he was the cause. "I what?" He teased as his tongue flicked over her breasts. He held himself off her with his fists in the sheets at her sides, but he made no motion of getting away from her, even if his hips were mercifully still for the time being to let her begin to recover.

"So good." She mumbled as he held himself off of her, and she lifted one of her hands from his side so that she could run it through her own hair. Mercury couldn't do much more than mumble, though, and she wondered if she was even still speaking in English. "You didn't . . ." She attempted to talk but it wasn't working, so she just hooked one leg around his waist to keep him tight and close and buried inside of her. "You didn't finish."

Logan shook his head, but he didn't seem bothered as his hands roamed over her. "My job is you. Your job is me." With the encouragement of her leg hooked around him, he ground himself into her again slowly, and moved on the bed so that they could roll together to one side, without him ever leaving the heat of her. Once he was on his back, he adjusted himself once to get straightened out, but it only served to heat things up all over again between them. His hands rested along her sides as she got settled, and he pulled her down so that he could kiss her neck, his hands roaming her back. "Come and get me."

It shocked her how his words immediately made her want to please him, and once she was on top, it was a lot easier for her to take control. Mercury flipped some of her hair back over her shoulder but the rest fell into her face as she moved slowly and ground her hips into his, moving up and down on top of him with slowly increasing speed.

It was Logan's turn to lie back on the mattress and put his hands behind his head to let her ride him, and she could see from the hunger on his face he wanted his climax every bit as much as she had wanted hers. The sight of her on top of him, still moaning in the echoes of her orgasms, was something he knew more than a few men in the world would have killed for. She was perfect. He knew it, everyone who saw her knew it. As far as he could tell, she was the only person in the world who didn't seem to know it, but none of that mattered. All that mattered was the way she was rocking against him, watching his face for all signs of pleasure.

He reached up after a while and took hold of her ass when she got into a particular rhythm that pulled a loud moan from him with her leaning over him with her breasts bare inches from his chest and her hips slowly making him lose his mind. "Oh, *fuck* that's good . . ."

That was exactly what she wanted to hear, and it encouraged her to work harder. His moans and groans, his profanity, his face, it was so sexy she could feel that it was building up the tension in her body all over again. Mercury's face got closer to his, and even though he hadn't given her permission, he didn't tell her that she couldn't kiss him. Mercury kissed his cheek tentatively a few times and moved closer to his lips slowly as a few moans escaped her.

He knew it wouldn't take her long to get him where he needed to be once she had him on his back. A woman who took control was a favorite weakness of his, and Mercury was no exception. "You . . ." he devolved into more groans, and his arms latched around her back as he began to thrust up into her in steady answer to her own rhythm. His lips were only a breath away from hers as his moans escalated, and as he came, his arms locked around her back to press her against him hard. In blind instinct and a blind fury to have her in every way he could, he kissed her, his moan of release and satisfaction hummed through their lips.

Mercury kissed him back with just as much force and hunger,

and she didn't stop moving her hips, which made her body tremble with need until she moaned into his lips with another orgasm.

For a small moment of eternity, the world turned to a shared explosion of darkened stars in their shared vision. Their senses screamed their satisfaction in a language only their bodies understood. The perfect heartbeat of escape held them both aloft, weightless as a satellite in orbit, suspended in the momentum of their ecstasy. Some part of them knew re-entry would follow, but there was a world of power in that brief infinity.

Once he recovered from the initial paralysis of his orgasm, his hands wandered over her smooth, perfect skin. The last thing he wanted was to move away from her or have her move away from him. He pulled her voluminous hair off to one side so he could kiss along the porcelain skin of her neck and shoulder, still moaning at the small sensations that shot through his body as she writhed against him. "You . . ." he heaved when he could speak again, kissing up behind her ear as his hands massaged over her back, "are amazing."

"Hmmm." She purred as she rested her head against his shoulder, her whole body settled against his as she laid on top of him. Mercury could hear his heartbeat, and she smiled when she heard how quickly it was beating. She traced imaginary lines over his skin as they attempted to recover. "I've never . . . that was . . . incredible." Obviously sex with Orion was wonderful, but this was very different. And she was perfectly okay with that, at least at the moment. "You're amazing too."

He was curious to know what part she'd never done before, but he would wait to ask those questions later, when his brain won back the majority of his blood supply. For the time being, his hands wandered lazily, until one drew back in a slap to her ass that left a sting but didn't exactly hurt. He tilted his head to look up at the Earth, which was finally lit by the sun again, both celestial objects shining up at them. "Somebody with a strong enough telescope could have just gotten a hell of a show."

Mercury laughed since she didn't think anyone was watching, though she realized there definitely could have been *someone* watching. How else would they have gotten into this mess in the first place, unless people knew they hadn't had intercourse before now? Mercury kissed along his jaw before she said anything else. "Hopefully it was only you watching." She lifted her head slightly so she could kiss his lips once more. "I hope I don't sound too selfish when I say I want to do that again. Once we've recovered."

"You can sound as selfish as you want." He put one arm back behind his head as his other around her. "When we're here, when it's just us, that falls under your order not to be shy. Come up to me and get some whenever you want it, and I will do the same to you." He moved slightly so he would slide out of her with a final groan, but he didn't move her off him. "If I end up leaving you sore, though, or you're otherwise indisposed for some reason, tell me that. Otherwise if we're here, I'm going to have you whenever I want you. Which, judging by the last hour, is going to be a fucking lot of the time."

"I hope that's true." She said softly as her fingers trailed along his golden skin. "It was amazing. I didn't realize I would enjoy it so much, it felt so freeing." Mercury nipped slightly at his bottom lip before she looked into his stormy eyes. "This is fun." She smiled even though he wasn't really smiling back at her. "Do you do this very often? Smile?"

His smile widened just a little. "When I don't have other things on my mind." There was obviously a whole host of things to complicate his emotions, but they weren't in that world. They were there specifically not to talk about it. "Am I what you expected?" He wondered if there was anything about him that would come as a surprise to anyone upon seeing him naked for the first time.

"Your touch is gentler than I thought it could be, when you want to be." Her hand trailed down his abs before she ran her hand over his. She opened his hand slowly and then traced a fingertip along his palm and fingers. "After the first conversation we had, even since, I thought you would always be angry and it would be directed at me."

"It was never directed at you. Though it may end up being taken out on you at some point in the future." He said it simply, without a threat or a promise, only a statement of fact. "I've been called out previously by my partners for being an expert at angry sex. Usually makes for great make-up sex, but if I come in here in a bad mood, you can expect me to be rougher. I won't hurt you," he reassured her quickly, "but I can and will throw you around as I like."

"I'm not easily broken." She also reassured, "And if I get tossed onto my backside, there's cushion enough there."

Another smile tugged at his lips and he reached down to grip the 'cushion' in question as he kissed her intensely onto her side, then rolled her onto her back. "If you stay here much longer, I'm gonna get you screaming again. Go find us some dinner from the dispenser. Quickly."

Mercury turned her head to smirk at him before she sat up and then scooted herself to the edge of the bed. She thought about going to get the robe he mentioned, but unless he told her otherwise, she thought it was best to stay as she was. "Yes, Sir. Right away."

12

Gordon always had trouble sleeping, but being with Jessie had gone a long way toward alleviating that problem, even in just two weeks. Still, there were some nights when he woke up in the quiet hours of the morning. He sighed as he stared up at the ceiling, his familiar nightmare playing through his brain. He managed to banish it with thoughts of Jessie, staring at her as she slept in order to accomplish such a banishment.

Pulling the sheet down over her chest was slow going without waking her. A single brush of his fingertips over her nipple was enough to draw it to attention without disturbing her further. She had been thoroughly tired when they finally fell asleep, though, so he didn't want to disturb her before morning. He just preferred her to the nightmares. He would have preferred anything to the nightmares, but Jessie best of all.

When he actually allowed himself to get up from the bed and go to his communicator, he saw that there was a notification outside of his actual messages. It was a message direct to his communicator but had bypassed the network. He tried to push down the feeling of dread that came with that understanding, but he went to a chair in the living area before he opened it, steeling himself for whatever might come through.

Are you aware how easy it is to watch you? I'm a little impressed with your attention to your match. It almost looks like you care about her.

Gordon rolled his eyes at the attempt to provoke him. If she was watching him, then he would make her work for the conversation. He projected the message string in a hologram in mid-air and relaxed against the chair cushion.

I wasn't aware you were so interested in my sex life. Of course, since the last lover you had was killed while he was

working for you . . . I suppose I can understand the preoccupation.

You haven't provided the information we require.

"Again with stating the obvious." Gordon answered out loud, looking at all the various corners of the room where he imagined micro-cameras were hidden. "I would think that would get tiring after a while, especially for a woman of your intelligence."

You're running out of time to do things your way, White.
Maybe we should attack in phases, until you learn to comply.
Jessica Rogers, food services.
Did you know that she was pregnant with her brother-in-law's baby and her mother found out?
Her mother poisoned her to get rid of it before anyone else knew.
Nearly died.
She applied for Eleusis only a few months later.
Seems as though she has all her hopes and dreams pinned
on something that was doomed to fail from the beginning.

Gordon really hated it when people tried to get to him, since it so rarely worked, and mostly just annoyed him. But going after Jessie was a different story. He was more than just annoyed and he was sure Carmina would notice. "I know very little about anything being doomed. Things happen because people make choices. You're choosing to complicate this. For everyone." He shook his head, even though he wasn't sure she was watching.

"If you begin your attack now, before we have the hardware located, then you risk compromising this entire mission and losing our path across the galaxy. If you wait for our signal to unleash hell, then you can still kill as many of the Consortium's morons as you see fit. You'll just be doing it at a time that's constructive instead of turning yourself into the latest 5 o'clock Terrorist Special."

We have substantial evidence there are more. We are investigating it now. If it proves to be true, your mission will be worthless.

"False trails and blind alleys to stub your toes in." He dismissed anything else she had to say on that subject out of hand.

"If it was easy to make, they'd have made a thousand of them by now. As it is, they were smart and they realized they had the materials to make three. If you want to try and storm Prime, be my guest. I've got no conflict with that. But the other two are here. We will find them and we will bring one or both of them back to Earth." He sighed. "It's really not a difficult conflict, unless you're acting like a toddler in a temper tantrum."

You're quick to insult my intelligence when you know that I can shoot you out of the sky without a second thought. You know how much time you have left. Don't force my hand. I'll go after your lovely lady first just so you have to watch.

Gordon actually smiled. "I'll pass on the compliment about her being lovely. She'll appreciate that." He stood up when it was clear that Carmina thought the conversation should be over, and just stood in the middle of the room in his boxers. "I am the best hope the resistance has of success, Carmina. If you choose to shoot me out of the sky, draft an apology letter to the people of Earth first for ruining their best chance at a better world."

You aren't the best.
And sometimes I wonder if you're any good at all.
There are more of you to choose from.
Get the information.

Gordon just grinned at the sign-off, and shook his head as he deleted the conversation. There was no point keeping it or trying to trace it. Carmina would emerge when and where she saw fit. If she chose to act before things had been found and secured . . . well, Gordon would have to deal with it.

"You saw most of that, I'm guessing?" He said quietly as he looked over at the bedroom.

"Some of it." Jessie replied softly, but she was avoiding his gaze as she stood there wrapped in a sheet. "I woke up when I heard you talking out loud." She'd picked the wrong time to start listening because she heard when her past was recounted to him. "I didn't know anyone else knew what happened. When I got really sick, my mother told me what she'd done. I think she was trying to clear her conscience since she thought I was dying anyway. Abortions are illegal and I'm sure she bought the poison on a black market."

"There are some things it's not possible to clear off anyone's conscience." He said quietly, though he didn't look surprised. "I'm sorry that happened to you. Nothing about it was right. Certainly not coming from the woman who gave birth to you."

"She did it because it was his baby." She didn't need to clarify who the man was, obviously. "I thought we were being careful. It wasn't like I wanted to have his baby. But it can be hard to prevent them. Even when I found some condoms, expensive as they were, he never wanted to use them."

"Well, speaking as a man who's been selfish, I can understand the objection." He ran his hands over her sides beneath the sheet. "Though that doesn't justify him overruling you. In general, what I've gathered about the people you grew up around is that they were a bunch of assholes. Your mother chief among them, in my opinion."

Jessie shrugged, since she agreed. She didn't miss her family, certainly not her mother, even though she did miss Earth. She still wasn't really able to look at Gordon as she thought about the rest of what she heard. "I don't want to die, Gordon. I really want to get to Eleusis, but I don't want to go back to Earth."

"If we do go back to Earth, it will be on our terms. Not back to the Dakotas so we can hand them a second chance to fuck with us." He lifted a hand to caress her cheek. "And there will be no dying while I can prevent it. None."

She looked briefly into his eyes before she kissed him gently. "I'm still exhausted. I'm going to go back to sleep."

He returned the kiss and nodded against her cheek. "I'm gonna get some water and see if the almighty Consortium is willing to send along some sleep drugs. I'll join you shortly."

Jessie grabbed his hand before he could get too far and she squeezed it firmly before she pulled him back into another brief kiss. "Thank you for being so understanding every time you find out more about me. I always think that you'll find something that drives you away."

"If either of us is going to be driven away by revelations about the past, it's me who'll be missing you, Jess. Not the other way around." He gave her a weak smile. "There's no way I'm ever going to hold anything in your past against you. I just hope you'll feel the same about mine as you learn more about it."

Jessie stole one more kiss so she could head back to their bed, since she was struggling to keep her eyes open. "I'm not going anywhere. I promise."

"I'm glad." He said as he watched her go, and though he stepped away to get a glass of water as he'd said, he went back to the doorway and watched her sleep for a few minutes as he drank it. He hadn't been sure when he chose her if she would actually accept him, if she would be everything that he had hoped she would be. But she was quickly turning out to be exactly that.

There were more demons in his past than she yet knew about, though. He had to wonder what she would do when she got to know them. When they got to know her. He hoped she would stay. But he wasn't joking when he told her that he wouldn't blame her for running. He would even help her do it. If he ever met someone too much like himself, he would be certain to run the other direction.

* * * * *

Carl's office wasn't hard to find, and as Tatyana entered, he was just finishing up an appointment with a man who, while not one of her own direct associates, had gotten aboard the Initiative under false pretenses to support her organization. Carl dismissed the man as soon as Tatyana showed up, and on his way out, Tatyana could see the fear in the man's eyes. Whatever Carl had on him, he was still being allowed to go, but it had been plenty sufficient to scare him. "Come in, Ms. Sery, have a seat."

Tatyana didn't appear concerned as she took the offered seat, crossing her legs at the knee. She was wearing a skirt short enough to get the attention of most, but she didn't expect Carl to pay much attention. She prided herself on knowing things that were useful to know, and the degree to which Carl seemed satisfied with his match was a very good thing to know.

"Today shouldn't take too long. As you know, I'm sure," he gave her a knowing look and a smile to go along with it, "we've been going through a sweep of everyone aboard the arm, following everything that happened at takeoff. Some of your contacts came up questionable, so I'd like to ask you some questions about them. Fairly painless."

"Whatever you need, Mr. Espinosa." She crossed her arms and leaned back slightly in her chair. "Ask away."

He hit a few buttons on the tablet to note her defensive

posture, then proceeded to bring up the file he wanted to discuss. "Sergei Kazimirov. Consortium investigations have had their eye on this guy for a while. Seems you two shared an address for about six months."

"His family and mine go back. He was having a hard time finding a place to stay, our house had room." She stated simply.

"And at the time, did you know about his involvement with the Brotherhood Incident?" Carl's tone and the look in his eyes were steady, watching her closely.

"Yes, I knew. He told me when he asked for a place to live." Tatyana watched Carl just as carefully as he watched her. She hadn't given him enough credit for his skills in investigation.

"And you were perfectly comfortable harboring a fugitive who was responsible for killing forty-seven people with poisonous gas after locking them in their office building?" Carl rattled off the details casually, without seeming affected by the incident. "Not exactly the kind of things I'd put up on a want ad when looking for a roommate."

"Who were those people? Do you know them? I didn't know them." She leaned closer to Carl after that and eyed him carefully. "Maybe they deserved it. I don't know. All I knew was that Sergei was a friend of my family and needed a place to stay."

"And when they put him in front of a firing squad last year." Carl continued, not bothered by Tatyana's proximity. She was maybe a hundred fifteen soaking wet. He could take her if she got uppity. "When they executed him for participation in terrorist activities. Do you think *he* deserved it? The people of Moscow seemed to think so. I watched the broadcast."

"It depends on who you define as a terrorist, Mr. Espinosa. But Sergei paid the price with his life. Why does it matter what I think about a dead man?"

"Because I'm not investigating a dead man. They're typically less cooperative and more difficult to interrogate. I'm investigating you." He didn't seem to be making any threats, exactly, just wanting to understand what kind of woman he was dealing with. "There are some red flags in your file that would suggest you're not safe to have aboard this station or involved with this project. It's my prerogative, at this point, to determine who is too unsafe to be allowed to continue. That would be why your opinion of a dead man matters."

"Red flags." Tatyana repeated and she just smiled at Carl in response. "I have red flags because I oppose the Consortium. I've participated in rallies and in other efforts to express my distrust and dislike of the Consortium. However, all of my participation has been peaceful, even if I have been arrested. Multiple times. Trespassing, resisting arrest, ignoring orders by a uniformed officer, to name a few. However," she leaned a little closer to him. "Don't you think all of that is too obvious? It's documented. The Consortium must already know about all of it, and they still accepted me. What do you think you are going to find when you look in obvious places, Mr. Espinosa?"

"In my experience? A well-crafted cover story." He pressed a button on his tablet and her rap sheet came up, with all the crimes she had listed picked out in bold lettering, as well as a few she hadn't. He turned around a little to look at the profile on the screen behind him. "Which to me is what this looks like. If you had come in here and immediately started calling me the tool of a fascist government bent on world domination and global atrocities, then I might have bought it. That's what the sheet makes you sound like. A protest-happy hippie with anti-establishment tendencies. But you're not." Carl said finally, staring back into her nearly-colorless eyes with his perfectly dark ones. "What I'm trying to figure out is what you actually are."

Tatyana didn't say anything immediately, since the staredown was enough to fill the space. She tapped a finger on her lips before she leaned back again. "Is it too much to ask who else you've already questioned on this kick of yours, Mr. Espinosa? All obvious suspects, clearly lying in wait to terrorize the neighborhood?"

"Yes, that would be asking too much. Though you saw Yusef on your way in, of course. Helpful guy. I think I made him nervous. Must've been my intimidating manner." He brushed away Tatyana's file and set the tablet aside on his desk, leaving nothing else between them. "Hypothetical game for you. If you were guilty of being more of a terrorist than your protestor file would paint you to be, and you were given roughly thirty seconds to make a case for why you shouldn't be immediately detained and sent to a lunar colony, how would you spend those thirty seconds?" He looked down at the time on the tablet to one side. "Clock starts now."

"You judge so quickly." She clicked her tongue and shook her head before she continued. "Let's go back to the Brotherhood incident you asked about. The only thing the news ever reported on was about those who died, and my friend, of course, as a murderer. He reportedly used a gas bomb, which was why an explosive was never considered, but people near the office reported smelling smoke." Tatyana tapped her fingers on the table, even though she knew she wouldn't be able to explain her little tale in thirty seconds.

"What was found was a *stolen*," she emphasized the word to show her obvious disbelief in the story, "canister from a nearby warehouse. The warehouse was a storage unit for a lot of companies but what was taken was a canister that belonged to J-Enterprises. That particular shipment had made it all the way from America only the day before. By the time help arrived, no one could determine what the gas had been from the bio-canister. But when Sergei was executed, it was documented that what had killed those people was the smoke of burning Oleander." She leaned forward again so that she was halfway laying on top of the desk. "Do you know what that is, Mr. Espinosa? It is a magenta flower."

"And why would a burning flower end up killing forty-some people?" He still didn't move from where he was sitting, but he wasn't checking the time on his tablet either.

"Oleander is a naturally poisonous plant, ingestion will most certainly kill you, untreated, and even the smoke can kill you if it is potent enough. But that doesn't sound like it could kill forty people, unless it is highly concentrated, correct? A few little blossoms can't kill forty people. Unless they're genetically modified to do so. The connection was dismissed, of course, J-Enterprises was not held accountable. J-Enterprises is a very large company that employs thousands of people, most of them in Japan. Among their employees, thousands, I said, they're certain to have a Botanist or two, don't you think?"

It was Carl's turn to look Tatyana over carefully, since she was better-informed than he had given her credit for prior to the meeting. She was certainly no peace-loving hippie, but he wasn't entirely sure what to make of her. "What are you suggesting, exactly? That someone inside the office killed their own people and your friend was framed?"

"I'm suggesting that you don't have the entire story." She stared at him for a moment longer and leaned back again, but when she did, she glanced once in the direction of an obvious camera before she looked back at Carl. "Maybe your match heard something more about the story. Didn't she say her parents brought her from Japan to America when she was young? Surely she has heard of J-Enterprises."

"Yes, well, I've heard of the Tooth Fairy. Doesn't mean I'm intimately familiar with their business practices." He reminded himself silently half a dozen times not to bite at the bait, or allow himself to have his suspicions turned elsewhere by a suspect, but he'd also heard too many details to her story for it to be entirely a falsehood. It was a selective rendition of the truth, at best. "I assume there are a number of other stories you feel I don't have a handle on in their entirety, right?"

"I feel as though you're targeting the wrong people. But ultimately, you're the head of security. What you do is up to you."

"I'll add Ominous Stater of the Obvious to your rap sheet. Shouldn't be too much of a sentence. Time served. Maybe a little community service." He waved at the door to dismiss her, but didn't look away from her for more than a brief glance. "If you think of more stories you'd like me to hear the rest of, feel free to drop me a line. In the meantime, I'll consider your statements. If anything needs to be done about them, you'll find out soon enough."

"I am certain I will." She got up from her chair and gave him another smile before she turned to leave, and then she paused at the doorway. "Tell Aiko hello for me."

Carl sat in his chair considering the details that Tatyana had given him for half an hour after she left, and went so far as to play back the recording of the entire interview. He did know a few things for certain. One, she was a sociopath who would need to be watched more closely. Two, she wasn't lying. Or at least, she didn't think she was.

When he found Aiko, she was in a lab looking through piles of seeds near tiny plants in early developmental stages. Even though he wasn't sneaking up on her, she noticed when he entered the lab. He was a big man, after all. "Hey." She smiled as he made his way to her. "I didn't know you were coming to see me."

"Well, I'm an unexpected kinda guy, what can I say?" He kissed her once before he started looking around the rest of the lab. "I'm not gonna screw anything up by breathing in here, right?"

"I'm breathing, aren't I?" She replied with a laugh before she pulled him back in for another kiss. "Is it lunchtime or something?

I left my communicator back in the office."

"No, I'm actually here because I need your expert opinion on something. And because I'll take any excuse I can find to hang out with you." He took a chair from the side of the room, away from the experiments themselves. "I ran into something in my interrogations that requires a botanical opinion, and you're the most gorgeous one I know."

Aiko followed him to the chair and slid into his lap easily. "You were interrogating someone and you want a botanist's opinion on something? That's incredibly strange."

"Tell me about it. Not what I expected out of my morning." He laughed and ran his hands over her waist to draw her in close. "I was interrogating someone who had a roommate connection with one of the guys involved in the Brotherhood Incident in Moscow a few years back. You remember hearing about that? First big incident with the Earth First movement? Half a dozen assholes got the firing squad for it."

"I remember." She said as her smile disappeared quickly. "My father works for J-Enterprises. All of their employees were questioned worldwide, and they even flew my father out to Moscow before the trial and execution. He said they needed his expertise on something they found at the site where the people were killed."

"Something about Oleander." He kept his voice down, since he could see the story was already familiar to her. "Or at least, that's what the woman I was questioning said. Problem is, that detail wasn't in any of the official reports. Which is why I'm wondering where she got it."

Aiko wondered who he had been questioning, but she decided to lie about what her father told her. "He didn't find anything at the site. Or if he did, he didn't tell me about it." She looked into his eyes before she continued. "Oleander is a poisonous plant, though. It looks beautiful, but it is dangerous if you do anything more than look at it."

"The kind of dangerous that could kill people if it was distilled? Or concentrated, or extracted, or whatever it is you do with plants that have a mean streak?" He didn't know much about her area of expertise, but he knew enough to know that everything she worked with could be just as deadly as anything he worked with. Moreso, sometimes.

"Yes, but it would take a lot of Oleander to do that, unless it was genetically modified. That would have been in the report, though, don't you think? And my father is a botanist. He would have been able to identify that." She looked away from him as she mentioned her father, though. "Who were you talking to?"

He hesitated before answering, but he didn't mind telling her. It was Aiko. If he couldn't trust her, the list of people he could trust on the ship was about to get a lot shorter. "Tatyana Sery. She told me to say hi from her."

Aiko felt sick, and she knew that she wasn't quick enough to hide her emotions about the woman as soon as she heard Tatyana's name. "Did she say something about me? Why would she want to say hello?"

Carl sighed as he looked back at her, wishing he wasn't quite as good at interrogating people for once. Guilt was in seven different colors all over her face, he just wasn't sure what the guilt was from.

"She mostly dropped insinuations that a botanist would know more about the story, and suggested you specifically might know more." He didn't let go of her, and his hands started moving again in the same caresses over her waist. "So the pieces of what I'm getting are this. There was a gas explosion in the office adjacent to this J-Enterprises lab. Forty-some people were killed. A ring of suspected terrorists was identified in connection with the bombing, chased for a year, then arrested, tried, and executed. But they found afterward that there was a canister of some kind of experimentally-poisonous flower missing from J-Enterprises, which fact seems to have escaped public record altogether. The insinuation, then, is that this canister and its contents is the actual cause of death for those forty-some people who died, and the Brotherhood was scapegoated." He watched her face as he ran through the explanation, leaning back in the chair. "Am I missing anything?"

"I told you, my father didn't find anything. Or if he did, I didn't know about it. I don't know about some canister that killed people." He was still caressing her waist, so that had to be a good sign, right? "Do we need to talk about this now?" She didn't look around for cameras, she didn't have to. She knew they were there. Aiko instead moved closer to kiss him before she spoke again and she whispered against his lips. "You said you would listen to me if you ever found out I was hiding something. But I can't talk here. Please."

He nodded against her kiss, and returned it warmly, just so she would know he had meant what he said. "I'll listen." He said in such a low voice that the rumble of the humidifiers in the room around them drowned out the actual sound. She could feel his voice in her chest and see his lips move, but nothing else. "But that means I need something to listen to. Just say where and when."

"Tonight. I promise. In our unit?" Aiko was surprised he was still kissing her, but she was glad he was. Her violet eyes looked into his dark ones. "I hope you don't change your mind about us."

"I hope so too." He agreed, kissing her one more time with a sigh. Their relationship was still too new for him to promise he wouldn't change his mind, no matter what, but he wished he could, just to give her that kind of reassurance. "I've got a lot more questions to ask this afternoon, so if I'm late, don't think it's because I'm avoiding anything. I'll be there when I can be."

Aiko nodded slowly though she looked incredibly sad at the same time. There had been a number of reasons why her parents had told her not to get attached to her match, not to mention that now she was going to tell Carl, he could turn her in. How would that help Kazuo at all? Aiko's gaze dropped to her feet. "I'll see you later."

* * * * *

Gordon made his way through the halls at a casual pace, but he could feel himself getting more and more irritated with every step. There were a hundred things about Tatyana that had come to annoy him over the course of their relationship. Her habit of summoning him whenever she thought it convenient was somewhere in the top twenty list. But she claimed it was something important they needed to discuss, and for all her other faults, exaggerating a situation's importance was not one of them.

Tatyana already kicked out her match when White showed up, and she smiled at him when she let him into her unit. "I have your favorite." She nodded toward the sitting area where drinks were already waiting for them. "I brought it with me."

He glared at her for that, but he wasn't going to turn down a drink, especially since the conversation with Carmina the night before was still ringing through his head. "You better not have summoned me for just a social call. You said there's been a potential breach. That's not something to celebrate."

"I was questioned today by the head of security. He's very interested in things that he should be interested in, but due to your foresight, he's matched with Aiko. So it may be no worry at all, depending on how she explains herself." Tatyana went and sat down and picked up her drink casually.

He picked up his glass, but he just held it in his hand without sipping from it after that declaration. "And why would Aiko have a need to explain herself?" He kept his voice quiet, but he didn't like the direction the conversation was going.

"Because a botanist's expertise is needed to further explain my story." She clearly didn't have any problems with enjoying her drink, and so she took another sip. "Aiko has been doing very well with him. Maybe he'll decide to listen to her and help us out. It would make things easier for us. At least she won't have been using her vagina for nothing."

He put the glass back down on the table where it had been waiting for him and walked away, because he didn't want to look at Tatyana after that comment. "You outed Aiko, to the head of security. And what's worse, if it needed a botanist, I'm guessing you outed her about the Brotherhood? In Moscow?" His voice was getting higher and louder the longer he spoke. "The same incident that first exposed our organization in the first place? The one we want security personnel to stay away from at all costs? That one?" He was glaring and nearly screaming by the time he was finished. "And you threw *Aiko* under it?"

"She'll handle it." Tatyana shrugged as she finished her drink. "I've seen them together. That man adores her. And she's still got Kazuo to worry about. She'll make it work or she'll poison him. That is what she is here for."

"She's here for her brother!" Gordon was full-on screaming by that point, though he had placed himself on the other side of the room just so he wouldn't try and throttle Tatyana. She was better in hand-to-hand combat than he was, but if he had been armed, he would have considered shooting her. "And to gather intelligence, discreetly! She's a non-combatant, and you just put her directly in harm's way. Whether to bring in her match was *her* call, *not* yours!"

"She needed some encouragement." Tatyana finally got up and approached Gordon. "We don't have anyone who can get us past the security to get where we need to be in order to get the

Twist. We need more access and you know it. She knew it was a risk coming up here, and her parents knew what we needed them for. It *is* my call. It is always my call."

Gordon stayed where he stood as she approached him, but he wasn't sure he was going to be able to keep himself from hitting her, even if she ended up killing him for it. "Now you're sounding like Carmina." He answered quietly. "Trying to replace the know-it-alls of the Consortium with the single-package Judge, Jury, and Executioner. That's not how it works, now or ever. You didn't have the right."

"Before we came up here, it was agreed that I would be the leader of this mission. I'm not trying to execute anyone, but I am trying to get things done." She stared into his eyes. "Your guilt about Aiko makes you soft about her. She's here with the same expectations as anyone else."

"No, she isn't." He disagreed, but it was just one of many aspects of their operation that he and Tatyana had never seen eye to eye on. "Some of us didn't come up here planning to give our lives for the cause. Some of us came up here because we want to *live* our lives for the cause. That involves caution, and that involves not throwing people in front of a fucking train before they're sure it's not going to run them over."

"Then you go deal with it. Expose yourself to save her." Tatyana said with a challenge in her eyes and voice. "What's done is done."

The anger continued boiling in his eyes for a deep, tense breath, before it boiled over as he hauled his hand up and backhanded her across the face. "Convenient policy, when it's something done by you."

Tatyana reached up and touched the corner of her mouth where she could taste blood. She wiped at it with her fingers before she looked down, as if appreciating the color. When her icy blue eyes looked into his, it was difficult to read the emotion there. "Feel better?"

Gordon shook his head without looking away or retreating from her, though he knew he probably should have been afraid for his life under such a look. "I'd feel better if I knew there was the slightest chance you'd actually listen to what I'm saying. Since that's never going to happen . . ." he brushed past her, took the shot glass she had poured for him, downed it, and threw the glass at the floor as he continued toward the door to her unit. "If she is compromised and gets taken into custody for what she knows, she'll be handed over to the Consortium, and they *will* break her. And all of our information will come pouring out. She's a risk that wasn't worth taking, and if your gamble ends up paying off, it'll be because her match is just that hot for her, not because there's anything smart about what you just did."

"Get out of my unit, White." She said sharply, though it wasn't obvious what she would do if he didn't.

"It's the Consortium's unit. You're just assigned to it. None of this belongs to you." He glared back at her from the door. "Or to me. Just your own life. Play with that as you like, but not with other people's." He was angry there was no way to slam a station door on his way out of it, since the gentle *whoosh* of it sliding back into place just wasn't satisfying. He pulled out his communicator as he walked and sent a quick message to Aiko, even though he hated the fact that it would be a break in pattern from their radio silence of the past two weeks. Maybe he could go back and erase it when he had time later. *Fancy an afternoon snack somewhere?*

Did you know she was going to do this? Why didn't you tell me? I care about him!!

Calm. He sent by itself first and foremost, but followed it quickly. *Not like this. Hydroponics or Ballast Control. Your choice.*

I don't want to see you.

That wasn't a choice I offered.

You can't do this to me and then want to chat afterward.

I was not involved with this. If I had been, I wouldn't be offering my help now.

I'm in hydroponics now. I'm working.

Good enough. If you get some weird error messages from your surveillance in the next ten minutes, pay no attention.

Aiko had a hard time working and not crying, but she kept the tears back as best she could. When she saw Gordon she almost burst into tears, and not because she was happy or relieved.

"That isn't going to help anyone." He pointed at her watering eyes as he closed the door behind him. "So you may as well knock it off before we even start talking. I'm aware of how little you want to do with me. Try and keep in mind that I'm on your side. What did he say?" Gordon wasn't much for lingering on the non-essential details of anything going on, preferring to get right to the details of what mattered.

"We're going to talk later when he comes back to the unit for the evening." She said softly, though she was barely able to hold her tears back. "He said he would listen to what I have to say. So he hasn't reported anything yet. That I know of." A few tears snuck down her cheeks and she wiped them away quickly. "I actually do have feelings for him, you know. This isn't just about my secrets. I could lose him too. For this. For her."

"She had the good sense to come talk to me after. So even if she doesn't have the brain to avoid the mistake, she knows who's capable of helping control the damage." He was pacing by the door, both to keep his distance from Aiko and because he was still livid at Tatyana's manipulation. "I thought it was likely you'd develop feelings for the man. Everything about him suggested you'd love him on sight."

Aiko froze at Gordon's last words and she nearly dropped the seeds in her hand. "You put us together? Did you do anything to him?" Now she was concerned that something might have happened to make Carl compromised, or if he was one of someone else's goons, it would ruin everything. "How do you know who I would love or not love? He almost died! He's been . . . I'm surprised he's not already dead between all of his injuries and all of the junk the Consortium has been pumping into him."

"All the junk?" He narrowed his eyes at her before they cleared. "Oh, you haven't figured that out yet. I thought Gold was going to work with you on that. Maybe she's been distracted with her own match. Doesn't matter." He waved it off, and actually looked like he was in a better mood. "No, I didn't do anything to him. What was done to him was done before he was even born. You need to look more closely at his genetic code. I don't have time to explain it all right now, but you'll figure it out. He's designed to run too hot, too fast, too hard, all the time. The junk they pump into him is the only reason he's still alive. It brings him down to something approaching human, which is why it probably looks like poison to you. You fuck with human biology enough and it takes its toll." He gave her a look. "Sound like anybody else you know?"

Aiko just stared at Gordon for a moment and she sighed. "You didn't answer me. Did you put him with me on purpose? Why?"

It was Gordon's turn to sigh, and he finally stopped pacing to look over at her. "Their match program, for all its faults, does a good job of pairing people up who would be good for each other. It's not perfect, and it doesn't have to be, because people aren't mathematics. They can either break a perfect match or they can make up the difference. In your case, Carl wasn't the first on your list, but he was in your top twenty. And of all the men you could have been matched with . . ." he paused, since he wasn't sure what Aiko would think, but if she already had feelings for Carl, it didn't matter if she was angry. "I thought he would be the most capable of protecting you, if things go wrong up here."

She was silent as she looked back at her work, turning completely away from Gordon as she ran her fingers over the seeds in her hand. "I worked really hard to come here. I'm not here because I'm pretending to be someone else. You know that as well as anyone. If he doesn't believe that I really have feelings for him, which I do, then I lose everything. Kazuo loses everything."

"He believes in the matching program. He's from space. He was placed with you, and everything, I mean *everything* in this guy's profile suggests that loyalty is as hard-wired into his DNA as his ridiculous healing capacity. Which is off the charts, by the way. Guy got shot once and walked himself to the infirmary." He shook his head, but went on anyway. "If he's willing to listen to you, then it's possible that Tatyana's gamble with him will pay off. You already know he won't hurt you, even if he has concerns once you've told him your story."

Aiko nodded and just stared at her work for a moment before she replied again. "I need to go back to my unit early. I can't keep talking to you. It'll be suspicious, and honestly, I still can't look at you without thinking about everything else. Please go."

Gordon nodded, needing no further explanation or request than that. "He'll take care of you. That was the most important thing to me when arranging it. No matter what else happens here, he'll protect you as much as he can." He turned back to the door and paused with his hand on the latch. "I'm sorry that Tatyana was stupid enough to put you in this position. But if there's any other way I can help, you know I will, and you know where to find me."

Aiko nodded without looking at him and when she was sure he was gone, she wiped the tears that had fallen. She needed to get back to the unit. She needed to talk to Carl.

* * * * *

True to his word, Carl was late getting home that night, but only by an hour. When he came in, she could immediately see the heaviness in him. He took his boots off by the door, just as he had been doing ever since she had done it on their first night in the unit.

"Hey." He got back up and went to join her in the living space where she was working on a holographic interface, with incredibly complicated diagrams he had no hope of understanding, so he didn't even try.

"Hi." She said softly as she looked over at him and she tried to smile, but it hurt to try, since she didn't know what was going to happen. "I made a curry. Are you hungry?"

"Yeah, I am, actually. And it smells really good. You cooked?" He hoped she didn't think he was surprised because she was actually cooking. He simply hadn't had that many meals that were freshly cooked before. Especially for him personally.

"I came hom . . . I came back early. I couldn't focus after you left, and so I thought I would come back here. I mended some of your clothing, some of your pants. I cooked. I even made a dessert, if you want it later. A chocolate souffle. Though I don't know how it will taste up here." She got up to get him a bowl of curry and brought it back to him without looking at him once.

He took the curry, but he took her hand before she could pull away. "Hey." He held her hand as he looked into her violet eyes. "I'm grateful for all this, but I told you I would listen. You didn't have to butter me up for that. Don't get me wrong, I like butter as much as the next guy, and this smells amazing. You just didn't have to do it."

"I'm not trying to butter you up. I would do things like this for you all the time, all day, if I could." She searched his eyes for a moment but she didn't keep his gaze before she sat down close to him but didn't presume to sit right next to him. When she had retrieved the curry, she disabled the security feeds so they would loop. She couldn't stand to speak with White for very long, but she had certainly taken a few of his tricks for herself.

"I didn't lie to you about who I am. Everything I've told you has been true, until today. I lied about my father and my knowledge about what happened with the Brotherhood incident. But I didn't lie to hurt you, I was trying to protect myself and my brother." She turned her attention to her hands, since it was easier to look at the lines on her hands than to look anywhere else.

"My family has been part of a rebel effort since before I was born. I'm here to gather information about the Consortium and the Initiative, but also to work on my research for Eleusis and for my brother. He's incredibly sick. We snuck him up here to see if they could cure his cancer. I still want to go to Eleusis, to do my research, to do everything I told you, and I still want to be with you."

She finally looked up again after that to look over at him. "My parents warned me not to get attached to my match, but I . . ." She took a deep breath as her voice started to shake. "I really have feelings for you. I want to be with you. But now I'm afraid you'll think this is all an act, and you'll turn me in anyway, and then I lose everything I've worked for and I'll lose you too."

He listened quietly to her entire story, and began eating the curry, since it really was good. He did look at it a little before he began, thoughts of the poisonous plants Aiko had brought with her on board running through his mind, but she was trusting him by telling him about her involvement with a rebel organization. He could trust her by eating the food she had prepared. "You're not losing me." He said with a look up at her over a spoonful of stew. "What's your relationship to Tatyana?" He couldn't give any kind of real reaction until he had all the facts.

"She's one of the leaders. She's leading our mission here with this round of acceptance into the Initiative. I don't know very much about her, except she's crazy. Crazy enough to tell the head of security that his match is actually someone that he should arrest. I had no idea . . . I wanted to tell you even after I first met you. I hate lying, but I know sometimes lying means getting things accomplished. At least that's what I believe I'm doing. Acting for the greater good."

Carl looked back up at her after that comment, sighing as he thought. "I've never been very good at the greater good. In my line of work, I've run past a lot of people who think they're doing exactly that. Working for the greater good of humanity. It's a get-out-of-legalities-free card for the conscience. I may not be a scholar of history, but I know enough to know that the vast majority of fucked-up shit that's ever been done on the planet was done in the name of something greater. Crazy is a good word for it." He sat back in his chair to watch her, without saying anything else against her. "But that doesn't mean it's wrong. What greater good are you acting for, exactly?"

"Getting humanity to Eleusis without the Consortium." She watched him eat, hoping he liked the curry even if he decided to arrest her in the end. "The Consortium has done some really terrible things in order to prepare Eleusis for whoever they see fit. And it's not us." She was slow about explaining further. "Our intelligence believes the people who died from this station were murdered. The Consortium sent all of those people to their death by destroying the arm."

That finally got a reaction from him, and he choked on the bite of curry he'd taken and actually spat out a bite before he could get a breath again. He wiped at his mouth with the back of his hand, and his eyes were wide as he looked up at her. "You think they did what?!?" He looked her over without even giving her a chance to respond. "What evidence do you have of that? That was a fucking lot of people."

"All of the leaders that were on the arm that day were slowly evacuated a few at a time starting early in the morning. None of them were killed in the incident. Communication lines were cut two hours prior, and even backup communication was disabled, due to what they called a technological malfunction that jammed the communications. However, a tech who left the arm before it fell was able to make contact with Consortium HQ twenty minutes before."

"At least half, if not more, of the Initiates had made official complaints to the Consortium only a week before the incident. They complained about being manipulated, being coerced, their work being compromised, that they were being mistreated. All of the complaints were found in long-term data storage but nowhere else. It was as if all of it had been dumped where no one would think to look. Those are only a few things that point to the incident not being an accident."

Carl couldn't continue with the stew after reports like that, and though he didn't display any more of a reaction to each of the details, he could understand how all of it could add up to a conspiracy in a hurry. "That doesn't provide motive. It was their own initiates. People who are supposed to be preparing for Eleusis. If you say they're doing some crazy things to prepare Eleusis for people they think worthy, and it's the Consortium's own hand-picked people working on it, why kill thousands of them?"

"They're picking people to make Eleusis ready, the smartest

and strongest, like I said before. The ones that will put in the effort and the know-how to make it perfect. But they also tend to be the ones who can successfully rebel against leadership. If they use and then eliminate the smartest and the strongest, then they keep the advancements and their power at the same time."

Aiko scooted just a little bit closer to him, but she still didn't touch him. "Half the people they accepted this time around are showing signs of being nearly or almost completely CV resistant. If they take our babies, they can take all of that progress, including genetic alterations, and make what they want out of Eleusis."

Carl took in all that possibility, much of which sounded like conjecture to him, and tried his best to digest it. It didn't seem like she was hedging any of her answers, at least. That went a long way toward convincing him of what she was saying. "Total count for the Initiative this time around is two thousand four hundred and ninety-two." He'd been looking at numbers for days, and some of them were burned into his brain. "Out of those, how many of you are here with your resistance? Besides you and Sery?"

"About thirty. So far." She didn't want to give him an exact number and she certainly wasn't going to give him names. She still had no idea if he was going to arrest her. "Ideally the plan is to recruit as people turn against the Initiative."

"Thirty." Carl groaned and leaned his head back against the chair cushion to ingest that information. He had run through background checks for the past week and narrowed his suspect pool down to roughly nine individuals he wasn't certain of. That meant he had missed things. Obvious and glaring things. "That was part of the plan, then?" He sat back up straight to look at her. "Recruit me? Eventually?"

"No, no." She turned toward him a little more, but she still didn't touch him. "*Their* plan is to recruit people. I told you, I'm only here for my research and my brother. I didn't have any other motive to be with you other than to be with you. I want to be with you, not to recruit you."

"But you would have, eventually." He believed her when she said she was just there for her brother, but if she was a part of something like a rebel faction, then there was no way she was going to just keep that life separate forever. His voice was still calm, but she had never actually seen Carl angry in the first place, so it was difficult to know whether his anger looked like his calm or not. "When would you have told me, if Sery hadn't thrown you to the wolves like this? I know you said you would have told me eventually, and I believe you. I just want to know what you were planning before it got taken out of your hands."

"I told you, I wanted to tell you even before we were intimate for the first time." She sighed but since she couldn't tell how he was feeling about the whole thing, she automatically felt as though he was going to leave the unit and not come back. "I would have told you soon. It was already wearing on me, not telling you the truth. But I also had to think about everyone else at risk."

"That's a lot to put at risk. I get that." She could see him thinking through the entire situation. He didn't sound angry, so if he was, he was hiding it well. He leaned forward to rest his elbows on his knees as he thought through everything, looking at the floor between his clasped hands for a while in silence.

"I've been a ward of the Consortium my whole life." He started quietly. "Since I got dropped off someplace and dumped from one orphanage to another. Even my name, I got from one of the places where I lived, not from any kind of family. Carlos Espinoza was some rich son of a bitch back in the twenty-second century who founded a place for abandoned kids, so the people working it thought it would be some kind of tribute to name me after him.

"Consortium might be a bunch of rich jackasses eating power for three squares a day, but they're the only thing I've ever known, and the only thing that makes sense to me. I never once thought they were good, or righteous, but they're the reality, so they've always been the boss. Treated me decently well, too, so I can't complain. You say they've been killing people, innocent people who didn't have it coming, then yeah, I need to think about who's signing my checks.

"I don't believe in the greater good. The greater good is always greater for some people than it is for others. Never been religious either. But I do believe in Eleusis, and I've never been able to tolerate a bully on the playground, so if that's what the Consortium is, killing their own and fucking with the system, then your club has the right idea." He held up a cautionary finger, though the look in his eyes still wasn't angry.

"Doesn't mean I need to be fitted for a team jersey just yet. But I am gonna need to know more about what your people are playing at, over time. I don't like being played. I'm not blaming you, I know you were only protecting Kazuo. But right this second, my opinion of your boss is a whole lot lower than my opinion of my boss. Sery is a certifiable psychopath, and I say that as a person who's been trained to distinguish between a sociopath and a psychopath. Not the kind of person I want calling my shots."

"I know. But I don't get much choice." Aiko said softly before she looked at the curry he had abandoned. She didn't feel any better about anything even now he knew. Now he just knew she lied to him and that he shouldn't trust her, which was not something that settled well in her stomach. But at least Kazuo still had a fighting chance, so that was something. "I didn't mean to play you. I'm sorry, Carl."

"I get the why." He said eventually, then turned to look over at her with the faintest hint of a smile on his face. "You've got people to look out for. Something you believe in. Only thing I've ever believed in is making it to the end of a work-week. Only people I've ever had are Orion and some of my friends back on the security beat. Doesn't add up to the same stakes as your end of all this. Then some computer program sticks you with the head of security. I wouldn't have told me either." He watched her carefully for a little longer, but finally reached out slowly to take her hand.

"Come here." He pulled her into his lap the same way she had been earlier that day and into a hug against his chest, wrapping his arms around her to let her know he wasn't mad and wasn't going to do anything that would harm her.

Aiko thought she had been strong the entire conversation, but she'd cried enough that day that she knew it was sheer luck that she hadn't already started crying. When he pulled her into his lap, though, and wrapped his arms around her, tears squeaked out and started running down her cheeks. "You don't think you have anything, but I'll be your something if you want me to be."

She could feel him tense up at that offer, but it was a flinch she felt from him before. He simply didn't know how to be a family to anyone else. He never had been, and he'd given hints during their conversations that he expected he never would be, a real part of a functioning family. He worked security and always took the jobs with the highest mortality rate as a general rule. He didn't expect to survive, but surviving seemed to be what he was best suited for.

His grip on her only tightened after the flinch, and he moved to kiss her neck as he held her. "You're already my something, Aiko. And I'm not going to let anything happen to you. Not by the Consortium or by your psychopath leader."

She hugged him as tightly as she could, and her fingers gripped the back of his shirt so tightly she was afraid she would rip through it. "I'm glad you're my match. I never would have felt brave enough to get to know you otherwise, especially because you're huge and I'm not and . . ." Aiko just shook her head. "I'm just happy it's you. And I'll do everything I can to make up for this somehow, I promise."

He held her until her tears stopped, then reached to wipe away the moisture from her cheeks before he moved her so he could look her in the eye with a faintly sarcastic smile. "Am I seriously that scary? I know I'm huge, but I do try to go for the whole teddy bear thing with people I don't have an interest in maiming. Apparently I'm missing the mark."

"You're pretty scary." Aiko agreed with a nod but she was able to look him in the eye long enough to reach up and run a finger across his lips. She didn't know how he managed to accept her and her explanation with so much trust, but she was grateful for it. She wanted to kiss him, but she could tell that he was still wary of her, so instead she kissed his cheek lightly. "But now I'm falling hard for you, so I'm not scared of you anymore. I'm just scared of losing you."

"I'm glad you're not scared anymore." He kept his face close to hers after the kiss, but wary or otherwise, he ran one huge hand up to her cheek and kissed her properly, both hands moving to her waist to hold her in close against him. "Just keep me in the loop from here on. Especially if anything happens that puts you anywhere even close to harm's way, I want to know about it." His grip on her waist tightened at the thought of her being in any kind of trouble, as if he could keep her out of it just by keeping her there with him. "And the next time you see your boss, tell her directly from me that she can go fuck herself."

"She probably has to already, since no one likes her enough to sleep with her." Aiko smiled before she kissed him back, since she wasn't going to pass up on a chance to keep kissing Carl. "I won't keep anything from you ever again."

He moved to the couch so that he could lie back along it, but brought her with him as he did, so she was laid out on top of him in the kisses. "You have anywhere else you need to be for the night?"

Aiko shook her head, since it wouldn't have mattered even if she was supposed to be somewhere else. She would have chosen to stay right there in Carl's arms. "No. The plants aren't in a rush to grow, so I'm perfectly fine being here. With you."

"You've got one thing right. You are perfectly fine." He kissed her again and ran his hand over her from her thigh up to the side of her chest just to illustrate his point.

Somehow he still managed to get a blush out of her every time he said things like that, but it was a rush that she loved, so she certainly didn't want him to stop. "No, *you're* perfectly fine." She kissed him heatedly and locked her hands at the back of his neck as she did, so she could kiss him until she couldn't breathe. The idea that she might lose him had clearly made her that much more passionate about having him.

"Mmmm . . ." his voice rumbled and he groaned under her kiss, sending ripples through her whole body with his voice. "If you do have other secrets," he said as his hands moved up to pull off her shirt, "tell me about them some other time. I've got a feeling make-up sex with you is gonna be the highlight of my day."

Aiko loved his assertiveness, and she was more than happy to comply. "Definitely going to be the highlight." She whimpered, since his hands were already all over her. Aiko was falling in love with Carl, and now she didn't have to worry about having her heart broken over secrets. For once, she wanted to thank Gordon, but she would never convince herself to actually do it. He'd done too much damage to make up for it now.

13

Living on a farm had made both Anna and Logan early risers by nature, and they'd both had plenty of time to get accustomed to the time difference between standard orbital time and time on Earth. A typical day would have started with one or both of them getting in the shower, getting ready for the day, getting breakfast, all a few hours before they were actually expected to be anywhere.

But there were no typical days anymore.

Logan hadn't been able to bring himself to go back to the unit he shared with Anna after the evening he'd spent with Mercury. In the morning, he got up early (and got Mercury up early in the process) and they separated to return to their own quarters.

When Anna got into the unit, there was still more than an hour and a half before their assignments for the day, and she could hear the shower running beyond the bedroom. Whoever was in there, they liked the water hot, since the entire bedroom was well steamed as she walked into it.

Anna was slow to approach the bathroom and eventually convinced herself to walk to the doorway and lean against it as she stared at the steam, but she didn't see much of anything. She was still fighting a wicked hangover and she was sore as hell, but she'd taken a shower in the other unit so she wouldn't smell like booze and sex. Her stomach twisted at the memory, both because she was about to see Logan for the first time since, and also because she'd enjoyed having sex with Orion. "I'm hoping that's you in there, Logan. Otherwise someone is seriously lost."

She could hear him flinch in the shower from the splash of the water, since he hadn't heard anyone come in, but he was still the moment after. "Yeah, it's me." His voice sounded exactly the way she felt, and she had known Logan too well for too long not to hear guilt overriding nearly everything else.

Anna stepped into the bathroom even though she wondered if she should ask permission, but asking would mean that something had changed. She wasn't going to allow that. "I hope you aren't melting in there under all this hot water." She walked up to the shower and put her hand on the glass that separated them. "I missed you."

"I missed you too." She could see the outline of him under the water, even though the steam in the room was thick. He reached up to touch the glass from his side briefly, then pushed the door aside with the water still running. He could see she looked ready for the day, so he wondered if that meant that she hadn't actually done anything with the giant the night before. He hadn't exactly been keeping tabs on her, nor she on him. "You still need to get washed up? One good thing I've been able to find out about this place so far, they never, ever run out of hot water."

Anna thought about telling him that she had already showered, but the look on his face told her he needed her to be close to him just as much as she needed him, even though the guilt felt worse when she looked into his eyes. "Yeah, I do." She lied as she pulled her shirt off and tossed it back behind her.

"Don't look at me like that." She quickly got rid of the rest of her clothes. "Don't you dare look at me with your sad eyes." Anna stepped into the steam and grabbed his hand with both of hers and brought it up to her lips and kissed his palm. "I hate seeing your sad eyes."

The tender touch from his wild wife broke his heart all over again, but he moved his fingers along the side of her neck and pulled her in against him with a lingering kiss to her cheek and a tight hug. His body was blazing hot after being under the hot water for so long, but his body shielded hers from the nearly-scalding water. "I don't like seeing yours either."

"It's only temporary." Anna reached out to lower the temperature by way of the floating hologram near the spray of the water, then curled into Logan again and kissed his skin. "You shouldn't be punishing yourself with a boiling shower. I don't love you any less today than I did yesterday, and I will never love you less than I do right now. I can only love you more."

There was an urgency in the way he was holding her, and he leaned back against the tiled wall of the shower as if he wanted to fall right through the wall and out into space along with her.

If they burned up on re-entry, at least they would be going home.

"I love you too, Anna. And you're right. It is only temporary."

He held onto her beneath the slightly-more-tolerable water for a long time before he finally stood up again and turned in the shower to have it dispense some shampoo. She could see as he did it that the selections were vastly different than they had been the day before. There was an entire array of bells and whistles that certainly hadn't been part of the unit when they first moved in.

"You should try and send something off to Ben and Cory and your dad later this morning." He turned her to lean back against him so he could wash her hair for her with one of their newly-privileged shampoos. "I sent one down to Larissa and Liam about an hour ago, asking if the honeymoon was over for him yet and if they had started henpecking him to death."

Anna nodded as he started shampooing her hair and inwardly she chastised herself for not thinking about the fact that she could probably contact her family again now. She didn't respond immediately, but she let out a slow sigh. "I'll have to do that. You'll have to let me know what Liam says, I'll be surprised if he's survived the three of them even this long."

"So will I." He continued working on her hair. He just wanted to have her close, and he wanted to feel like they could be close to each other after what had happened. Knowing it was going to happen again. "I got notice earlier that we've got access to all kinds of things now. Dietary restrictions for us both have been removed, our data and communication restrictions have been removed, and our work hours have been cut back as well. Not to mention everything else we've been given access to from inside our units. It's amazing the shit they've got on tap here." Though from the way he said 'amazing,' he clearly didn't mean it as a compliment.

Anna took a turn to get some soap and wash him up, even though she was sure he already had. She just wanted to keep touching him. "I'll have to look through it. Especially if we have no dietary restrictions. Then we should be able to get good stuff." She kissed him when the soap washed away. "This smells like you. I love the way you smell."

"I missed yours, the last week and a half or so." He ran his fingers through her hair with the ghost of a smile on his face. "Everything up here smells like it's been run over by a tanker truck full of antiseptic and rubbing alcohol. You're the only piece of home there is." He kissed her and rested his face against hers as she finished up with him. "I'm glad you came home. Another half hour under the water and they might have needed to send me to a burn unit somewhere."

"Don't do that to yourself." She emphasized, since she knew why he did it, and she didn't like it. Anna put her hands on the sides of his face and ran her fingers over his facial hair. "I'll always be your home if you'll always be mine." Anna sealed her lips to his until they both couldn't breathe. "Do we . . ." She shook her head and kept a hold of his face. "None of the other stuff matters. You matter. That's it."

He nodded his agreement with the question she wouldn't even ask, and turned his head to kiss along her palms. "Only you." He lowered his hands to run them over her a little more freely, but there was nothing insistent about the touch. They had both been with other people, possibly in hours prior, and Logan wasn't going to push for anything intimate between them with Mercury just a few hours behind in his mind, as much as he was working to section her off in her own make-believe place.

"When I saw that we had our privileges thrown wide open, I went and found something for you. If the Consortium is deciding to play with us like mice in a maze, then I'm for damn sure gonna stock up on whatever treats they decide to throw as incentive. I know it doesn't hurt them in the long run, but I can't think of a reason not to take whatever advantages they'll give us. They don't seem like the sort to respond to non-violent protests."

"I wouldn't put anything past them. They'll find new ways to poke and prod us into submission. But you found something for me?" Anna wasn't the type who thought of gifts, but she wished she was so Logan would feel as though she had been thinking of him too. She had, but she hadn't found anything to give him. She looked down at the ring she never took off, since it was one of the best things he had ever given her. "I'm sorry, babe, but nothing is going to top this gorgeous thing."

He smiled. "Any kind of gems I would've gotten you up here would've only been synthetic anyway. Doesn't feel right to get you something that wasn't pulled out of the ground." He ran his hands over her one more time to make sure the soap and shampoo were completely off her, then kissed her a final time under the water before he turned it off.

He had the decency to look just a little self-conscious when he walked out into the steamed mists that his long scalding had produced, but he didn't bother even wrapping a towel around himself as he walked through the unit, letting himself air dry.

"I had to fight with the machine for a little while to get this. I imagine there was some kind of conference going on at the other end of the controls as to whether it would be allowed or not. Eventually it came through." His voice was lighter than it had been when she came in, but still subdued. "I hope you like it."

He opened their closet and pushed back a long series of grey uniforms to reveal what looked like an incredibly out-of-place summer dress, of varying shades of blue. It looked fairly comfortable, but it was also fairly plain, and certainly didn't seem to be in line with the mischievous smile Logan gave her as he stood back to let her examine it.

Anna moved closer to him, toweling herself off as she did so, patting her hair over and over to remove the excess moisture. "You had to get special permission for a dress?" That sounded strange, even though it was a nice dress. "It's very beautiful, though, amongst all the other crap up here." Anna tossed her towel aside and went to reach for the dress, since she had to at least model it for him, but it weighed a lot more than a summer dress should weigh. "What is this thing made out of?"

That got a more genuine smile from Logan. "Look up the skirt. And believe me, that's the only time you'll hear me telling you to do that." He chuckled at the look that got from her, but he just watched as she unwrapped the rest of the present.

Once she hiked the skirt of the dress up on the hanger, it revealed two holsters hanging down from their own belt, latched to the hanger, one for either thigh. The guns the holsters held were incredibly light and thin, and matched no guns that Anna or Logan had ever seen on Earth, but they looked like the same basic functionality was present. Hold, aim, pull the trigger, not necessarily in that order. Each holster held an extra magazine of ammunition in a separate pocket, and the holsters were already adjusted to hold their guns snugly.

"They're supposed to be designed so as to be almost no-profile beneath a dress or a skirt. Obviously be a little more conspicuous with shorts or jeans. I was able to make the case to the computer that since you've been accepted as a pilot in training, you're technically a part of the air force and that should come with the right to bear personal arms. And yes, I already checked, they do fire actual bullets. The couch is still pissed at me. Not even much kick to them."

She put the dress down so she could go back and give Logan

another hug and a kiss. "I have a feeling I'm going to need them. Thank you."

He hugged her again after the kiss, the steam in the room kept their bodies from being entirely dry, but he certainly didn't mind. "What's a midwest girl without her own personal firearms, right?"

"You're damn right." She said with a soft chuckle and she held onto the hug a little bit longer. "I'm starving. Let's get something to eat. I have some weird meeting to get to this morning instead of going directly to pilot training, so I'm looking forward to that." Her sarcasm was biting, as usual, but Logan knew nothing less from his wife.

* * * * *

Orion had showered at the unit he shared with Anna prior to leaving, and was dressed in his casual clothes as he made his way back to the unit he shared with Mercury. He wished he could think of one or the other of them as simply 'home,' but he supposed that kind of tag was suspended for the time being, since he wouldn't be entirely either place until they could get away from the Consortium.

He entered cautiously, and scolded himself for it, since there was no reason for him to be walking on eggshells around Mercury. They had decided together on what needed to happen, and that was what they were doing. It was just that simple. He didn't hear or see anything immediately when he got into the unit, so he just closed and locked the door, then turned to take off his shoes.

"Hey, are you here?" He called cautiously, loud enough to be heard but not loud enough to wake her if she happened to have come home and gone to sleep. That would have made him feel even worse.

"I'm here." Mercury said as she came out from the bathroom with a brush in her hair, braiding it slowly. She gave Orion a sedated smile and nodded toward the kitchen. "I was reading over some charts for a couple new patients. It seems I have a high request for pregnancy tests, so I'll be working on those between treatment patients today. Also, I made some omelettes if you want one."

"Oh, thanks. That sounds really good, actually. Did you already eat, or were the files calling your name too loudly and they distracted you?" He went to the kitchen to check if there was still an omelet for her, since it was the kind of thing he knew she was likely to do.

"I already ate, but I'll sit with you." She finished braiding her hair and she walked up to him to give him a sideways hug while he grabbed his plate. "How did your night go? Am I allowed to ask about that?" She knew it was just diving right into a very awkward place, but Mercury wanted to know instead of letting things fester, or being left wondering all of the time.

"You can ask about anything you want." He returned the hug as he pulled her in against him, glad that she didn't seem to feel like putting him at a distance because of how they had spent their evenings. Just the fact that she could come up and touch him so easily went a long way toward easing the situation, and he was grateful. "My night was fine. We decided the best way to handle things was to sort of treat it like a friends-with-benefits situation. Though I wouldn't call it a benefit in this situation. We played video games and got incredibly drunk. Both of which generally cut down tension. Also, if you have access to some hangover medication, I think that would be the perfect accompaniment to this delicious-looking omelet."

Mercury shook her head, since she did find it a little bit amusing he and Anna had a mutual love for alcohol, since she remembered seeing Anna at the social. She did her best to ignore the jealousy she felt, even though she knew it was healthy to be jealous. Especially because they were in a forced situation that caused them to be unfaithful to their spouses.

She didn't say anything as she ordered him medication that came through almost instantly. She grabbed the pills from the delivery chute and a bottle of water. "Hydration will go a long way to help, but these will dull the ache for a few hours." She sat down next to him and swiped away the interface from her communicator. "I don't want to know details, but I'm glad that you have figured out a way to handle the situation for the both of you. This isn't our fault. We shouldn't hate ourselves for it."

He nodded, and took her hand to kiss the back of it gratefully before he took the pills. Once he kicked back the pills and sat down to eat his breakfast, he looked over at her. "What about you? I'm like you, I'm really, really not looking for details, but hopefully things weren't just a lot of glaring and being angry. I could see that happening with that guy."

"We found a way to make it work." She said simply, since she did feel a little ashamed about all of the things she had discussed with Logan, but mostly because she'd never been openly curious with Orion about those things first. "He still has a lot of anger, of course, but it wasn't directed toward me. I think it's just a means of propulsion for him, it makes him want to get things done. Everyone has different ways of motivating themselves, and he seems to use anger."

"Well, if that works for him." Orion shrugged, and moved to hold Mercury's hand while he ate, running his thumb along the back of her fingers. "In my experience, anger usually fails to motivate people right when it matters most, but that's just what I've seen. Hopefully not the situation with him."

He was quiet a little longer as he ate, but when he looked back over at her, the look in his eyes was oddly serious. "If that ever changes, the whole him not taking his anger out on you, I mean . . . you've got too much self-respect to ever let yourself take anything from anybody, so I don't have to warn you about that. Just be careful with a guy like that. I don't want to see you get hurt." The look in his eyes managed to stay serious for just a breath after that as he squeezed her hand, but then he smiled and shrugged. "Plus, I'm pretty sure he's stronger than I am, so I'd have to shoot him from a distance for laying a hand on you instead of going hand-to-hand, and that just wouldn't give me the same kind of satisfaction."

Mercury squeezed his hand and shook her head as she turned her attention to her communicator. "He won't hurt me, you don't have to worry about that." At least he wouldn't hurt her in ways that she wouldn't want, anyway. Sometimes a little pain, she discovered, was more pleasure than pain.

"He and I talked about establishing a schedule, since it seems to be the simplest way to handle something like this without it becoming awkward as to how we should spend our time. It would be temporary, of course, until either Anna or I, or both, get pregnant, or we figure out a way around the restrictions. The former seems more likely. Now that the Initiative has removed restrictions on us, it's obvious that if we go back to fighting it, everything will be even worse than it was. And threatening our families is bad enough."

"Yeah it is." That got rid of his playfulness in a hurry, and he sighed as he leaned back in the chair, putting his arm around the back of her chair. "We, um, Anna and I didn't get around to talking about ovulation schedules and whatnot. I know yours is soon, ish, but I don't know when, exactly. Do you have access to look up hers?"

"Yes, I have access." It seemed so strange and invasive to look up that kind of information about someone else, but that was her job. "I can look it up, if you think she would permit it. I don't want to go digging against her wishes. I've already invaded her life enough."

"If it's in the interest of keeping things from getting any more awkward than they already are? I don't think she would mind. If you two are on the same schedule, maybe this only has to happen a few days out of every month. I'm all for keeping it to a minimum."

"I'll check into her medical records." She glanced over at him before she looked at her communicator again. "My fertile week is actually this week. That's why Logan and I were talking about it. It's possible that we can make it happen this week and then move on."

"That would be ideal." Orion agreed, running his fingers along her back as she checked her communicator, since it was still an incredibly awkward conversation to be having, however reasonable they both tried to be about it. "Well, ideal under the circumstances, anyway."

Mercury was quiet after that and she turned toward him so that she could look into his dark eyes. "I hate feeling this way. Guilty. Ashamed. I'm trying to be strong and it's just difficult. I don't like feeling like we are leading two lives."

"I don't like it either." He pulled her in so she could lay her head on his shoulder, and pulled her long braid back over her shoulder away from her neck. "But I don't know how to feel any other way about it. I can't look at what they're pushing us to do and think of it as just doing our duty or working for the common good of Eleusis's genetic diversity or any bullshit like that. I just can't. It's coercion and duress, plain and simple."

"I know. I hate it. I just wanted to go to Eleusis and be a doctor and be with you." She sighed and closed her eyes. "I never thought it would be like this. I never thought I would hate it so much. We need to find a way out."

"We will." He promised with a kiss to her forehead. "I'm working on some things. There are opportunities to be had, it's just a matter of finding the right ones."

"I trust you." Mercury kissed his cheek and looked into his eyes again. "I love you, Orion." She kissed his lips after that, but it was gentle and warm instead of hungry and needy as some of their kisses had been before. "I need to get going, my day is packed full of patients."

"Go. Take care of new-made babies." He returned the kiss and tugged at her braid once to put a smile back on her face before she got up. "I've got some mystery meeting this morning, but I should be out by lunch."

"Send me a message when you are out and I will make time to meet you for lunch. I miss you already." She gave him another quick kiss before she got up and grabbed her communicator. "I'll be watching for your message."

He sat at the table and finished watching her get ready, then waved at her as she left. It was hard to watch, since it meant she was not only leaving him for the day but would most likely spend the night with Logan again when the workday was over. It wasn't just saying goodbye to her for the day, it was saying goodbye to her for the next who-knew-how-long. If the Consortium had figured out a way to separate them even temporarily, for no reason at all that Orion could see, then they could try to make that separation permanent. Orion still just didn't know why, or how they could avoid it.

* * * * *

He showed up to the meeting just a few minutes early, dressed in his uniform once again. He couldn't even bring himself to look around the room to see why he was there or what kind of people had been invited. He was too preoccupied with thinking about the situation with Mercury to think about anything else.

Anna skidded into the room at the last minute. She didn't even look around until she got close to the table. There was an open seat by Kaplan, and Anna eyed it for a moment before she looked around and saw Orion. Of course he would be here. It couldn't be more obviously engineered, but then Anna bounced her way to him and took the seat next to him before anyone else could. "Hey hot stuff."

Her greeting finally broke him out of his reverie, and he smiled over at her as she took the seat. "Hey. So strange meeting you here. It's like it was fated or something." He gave her a sarcastic look, but was still smiling. "You know anything about this?"

"Nope. Got a message telling me to show up here for a new, additional assignment." She gave him a reassuring smile before she bumped his shoulder with hers. "We should have brought some booze. It seems to be my coping mechanism of choice." Anna scooted her chair in but she jabbed his side playfully under the table. They were friends, after all. They'd spent the whole night fucking and playing video games. It had actually been fun, guilt aside.

"Same here." He looked around at the room and cringed a little. "I'm not sure I like where the rest of this crowd is going. Little more on the brainiac side than I generally like." He could tell most of those in the room were from orbit by the way they carried themselves. There were a few from Earth, including a Japanese man Orion recognized as the older brother of Carl's match, whose name escaped him. There was another woman he recognized from their flight up, a somewhat curvier woman who came in with her match, a nondescript stick of a man that didn't even get a second look from Orion. "Yeah, definitely not my crowd."

"Oh, give 'em a chance." Anna opened up her communicator to take notes. "How did your morning go? Mine was pretty rough. I hate seeing Logan eaten alive by guilt."

"It was the same at my place." He sighed and put an arm around the back of her chair. They were supposed to be together, after all, so there was no point acting like they weren't. "Mercury was saying, just to minimize . . . this . . . it might be a good idea for us all to know who's on what schedule and set up exactly when this is gonna make sense. There's no way not to make things awkward, but setting up something like that might help? A little? Besides, it'll give me some idea of when I need to really practice at video games so I can make sure to kick your ass."

"Clearly I'm the one who needs to practice." Anna muttered, since she didn't care about whatever schedule they established. It was whatever. "I'm fucking sore."

He smiled at that, even though he wasn't happy that she was in pain. "I would say I'm sorry about that, but I'm not. So that would be a lie."

"You should be sorry. I'm pretty sure I have a bruise on my ass." She looked over at him with a smirk as soon as the rest of the seats filled up. As much as she hated what they were being forced into, Orion was fun, and having sex with him was fun. "You are relentless."

"*I* am relentless? Me? That's hilarious, coming from you." He poked her in the shoulder as she leaned into him, and turned to face her a little more directly so only she could hear what he had to say. "I'm not the one who woke up at two in the morning and demanded to do body shots, okay? Let's not pretend I'm the only one who's completely off the rails here."

Anna smirked as she remembered it and ignored the guilt she felt for enjoying the memory of only hours ago. "Okay, I did do that. You're right." She didn't look at him again, though, since the other Kaplan, Byron, stood up to speak. "Shhh. You're distracting me." She said teasingly to Orion before she sat up straighter.

"How distracted can you be? I thought you said you were sore?" Orion teased right back before turning his attention to the other Kaplan.

"Good morning, ladies and gentlemen." Byron Kaplan, by all appearances, was the off-brand version of his brother Stephen. Both were blond, but Byron's hair faded into a kind of unenthusiastic brown, as if taking a cue from his dispassionate face. Both were tall, but Byron's shoulders were slightly hunched, and there was something of fatality in his face, even though he appeared to be the younger of the two of them. His eyes were sharper than Stephen's, though, as he looked around the room, and for all the fatigue in the rest of his posture, none of it touched his eyes. There were three dozen people in the room, and he missed nothing from any of them.

"You are all familiar with the formation of the Executive Council last week, the governing body of the Eleusis Colony that has been tasked with the legislation of the colony's guiding principles and their execution."

"By executive order J-9 of that Council, a Judiciary Board is hereby created and tasked with the oversight of legal activity. The Board is also tasked with acting as a check and balance to the powers of the Executive Council, so the Colony may be organized and administered in fairness and equity as we begin work on our new home." He looked around the room as people took in that information, and flipped to the next page of notes in front of him so that he could read off certain portions of it.

"Those of you summoned to this meeting have been recommended by your superiors as potential candidates for inclusion on this Judiciary Board, and you will act, provisionally, to establish such a board and begin to dictate its bylaws. It is suggested by the Executive Council that the Board consist of not fewer than seven but not greater than thirteen members, and the rest of those present act in an advisory capacity to those selected members until the legislative canon of Eleusis law is more thoroughly fixed."

He pushed away his notes, finally, and gave everyone around the room a small smile. "Even new planets across the galaxy are going to have paperwork that needs doing, after all. And if history teaches us anything, it's that as soon as a law is written, it's likely to be soon broken. Courts are needed to deal with such things."

"So we're supposed to pick a group of court judges from the people here?" Anna spoke up without hesitation. "Is there going to be a vote put to the rest of the Initiates once a provisional Board has been selected?" Anna knew why she was there immediately, and it wasn't because she was 'recommended by her superiors'. It was because of Logan's new position.

"That's up to us." Byron sat down, pushing his papers away as if that was the only part of the meeting he felt the need to be a part of. "The Executive Council will be ratified in a few weeks once the first draft of the Eleusis Code is completed by them, and I think it would be appropriate for our own Board to be ratified at the same time. General elections don't make much sense in a group this size, I think, with most of us still strangers to each other."

"Some of us stranger than others." A man with a thick Italian accent said from one side of the room, swiveling back and forth in his chair with a chuckle.

Byron just gave the man a brief glare before he continued. "Ratification seems the easiest way to make sure there's at least a sustaining vote behind us. Later on, when positions need to be filled, then we can start voting for individuals."

Anna looked over to the Italian man and decided to speak again. "So how do we choose from everyone here, then, as to who should be on the Board? You just said we don't know each other." She looked around the room and she could pick out a few people, mostly the people from Earth or who had been on the same shuttle. "I know maybe five people here better than the rest of you, and that's not saying much."

"Some of us have a reason for being selected." The Italian said as he stood up, looking like a strange mix of pomposity and humility, with his broad smile and his meekly clasped hands. "Agostino Capaldi. I've been working as legal counsel for Station Six's captain for seven years. I imagine there are others with similar degrees and backgrounds. I would be happy to offer my services on such a board."

"Sold to the Italian guy. Next?" Anna said as she looked around the room, clearly taking over, partially because she was feeling out of place just being there, and partially because she was pissed she was being played. Again.

"Why are you here, Mrs. Bickford?" Gordon said from where he was sitting next to his match. "Oh, I'm sorry, I remember now. Silly question, please forgive me." His voice dripped with sarcasm the entire time he was talking, but he leaned back in his chair rather than volunteering. "I, for one, am happy to act as a support to the board as it's chosen by the group. I'm no legal expert and I don't have quite the take-charge attitude that seems to be in the water over at the Bickford unit."

"I'm here because I was miraculously chosen to be here." Anna bit back with the same sarcasm but sat back in her chair, since she wasn't about to make it look like she was a lawyer or anything like it. Anna was smart, but she didn't want to be a part of a judicial board.

Jessie looked over at Gordon and remained quiet as someone else in the room spoke up, but then she whispered in his ear. "We should volunteer her. If her husband is on the Executive Council, then maybe more will get done in our favor if we have them both in leadership."

"I think so too." He whispered back, as they watched another woman who stood up to introduce herself. "Right now she doesn't seem to want it, though. We'd have to give her a reason to want to be involved."

Jessie nodded and she decided to speak after the woman from Haiti who volunteered for the Board. When Jessie spoke, she stood up, even though she was certain that people could see her. "I think Mrs. Bickford would make an excellent member of the Board. If we're functioning as a check and balance for the Executive Council, then we need someone who can act as liaison. Who better than the wife of the leader of the Executive Council?"

Anna looked at Jessie Rogers, a woman she barely knew, but recognized from the very first informational meeting that she attended. That meeting had stuck with her, obviously. "I don't think I'm really suited for that kind of position. I'm not a lawyer."

"You don't have to be a lawyer to be a fair judge." Jessie continued before she looked around, especially because most of the people in the room were clearly from Orbit and not from Earth. "I nominate Anna Bickford." Judging the temperature of the room, some were clearly lending Anna more credence on account of actually being nominated instead of simply volunteering herself.

Some of the people in the room were looking to Byron for some kind of leadership, and for the benefit of those who were, he nodded quietly and raised his hand to agree. "I'll second that nomination. Mrs. Bickford has proven herself to be both capable and prudent since coming onboard." He turned toward Anna with an approving nod.

"As acting Resource Coordinator, I've gotten more than a few reports about your actions in flight training and the several ideas which your husband has credited to you in the Executive Council. I would also add that if this is to be a judiciary board set up on a planet light years from anywhere, completely out of reach of Earth except for very intermittent contacts, a certain amount of pragmatism needs to be rooted deep in both these councils. Your husband has already shown that he has such in large quantities, and surely you would add the same principles to this judiciary."

Anna didn't look convinced, but she shrugged, knowing she would be punished for resistance in one way or another. "Yeah, sure, why not."

Gordon and Jessie both smiled at her, which made Orion nervous, but he didn't speak up to say anything as she settled back in her chair. "You know I'm gonna be calling you Your Honor later, right?" He said with a quiet smile, trying to keep the mood light between them as other people began looking around the room and holding their own quiet conversations, trying to get themselves nominated.

She looked over at him and rolled her eyes. "Don't even. There is nothing honorable about anything I did in your presence."

"I don't know. Throw a gavel in there and it'll be as honorable as you like." He grinned and looked back at the group, since some of the conversations had died off.

"I'd like to nominate Jessica Rogers." A man said across the room. He was a heavy man, but not because he was fat, clearly. He looked more like a linebacker than a lawyer, but he wore such thick glasses and dressed so conservatively that the muscle-bound image was mostly banished. His obvious lack of overconfidence helped dispel the meathead look as well.

"Sorry, hi everybody, Clark Wright-Campbell. They've got me working in food service up here, but downstairs I was an admin for local government in the Rust Belt district, northeast North America. Jessie's got a background in business administration that could come in as a useful perspective on a board like this, especially since most of you look like you've had your noses in books all your lives and never actually worked on law as it applies to the real world."

The group looked toward Jessie, which made her want to shrink down, but somehow she managed to stay still. She looked in Clark's direction and gave him a small smile. "Thanks, Clark." Jessie looked away and around at the rest of the crowd. "I would, um, be glad to take the position. I care about Eleusis just as much as all of the rest of you do."

"I'll second the nomination." Gordon said from beside her, and another small woman spoke up from the other side of the room to agree, another of Jessie's co-workers who was chronically shy. After Byron asked for any dissenting voices, as he had with Anna, no one seemed brave enough to speak up against what happened, so Jessie joined Anna on the Board. It seemed everyone else who had been appointed to the committee had been thrown in by themselves or with only one acquaintance in the bunch, which left Anna and Jessie as the only members to actually be passed in at first by common consent.

By the end of a long two and a half hour meeting, the Board had been selected, thirteen members, and the rest of the group seemed to be behind them, more or less. No one was on the Board that had been opposed, and oddly enough, there had been a few oppositions near the end of the meeting. Anna had a raging headache by the time she left, and being dehydrated from drinking the night before didn't help.

"What just happened in there?" Anna said as soon as she and Orion had walked out as other people filed out and moved on.

"I'm not a hundred percent sure, but I'm about ninety-nine percent sure you were just appointed a chief justice of an entire planet." Orion was a little incredulous at the whole thing himself, and though he had opposed his own placement on the board, he had been appointed as the primary point of contact for military judicial proceedings. "Well, for a little over two thousand people, anyway. We have to get to the planet before you're actually over an entire planet."

"Very funny." Anna covered her eyes with her hand and leaned on Orion for support, since her head was killing her. "I should go get something to eat. Or some water or something. This is too much."

"We've got drugs for hangovers up here, you know." He reached up and ran his fingers through her hair to help soothe her pounding head at least a little, then put an arm around her shoulders. "Come on, let's get you hydrated and anti-inflamed. There's a dining station around the corner from all the conference rooms."

Anna didn't even protest once he wrapped his arm around her shoulders to lead her away but she could hear people talking as they moved away. Talking about her? Judging her for bending to the Initiative? Judging her for being so open about it? Wondering about her and Logan? It hurt to consider what the hell else was going on. "Just, if you take me to a doctor, don't let it be your wife. This is weird enough."

"No doctor required. Not for a hangover, anyway." He guided her to the dining station and went to order the anti-hangover medication for her, which did bounce it off for a doctor's approval before dispensing, but he typed in a quick response for it and handed Anna water and protein bars in the meantime while they waited for the medicine. "Although, speaking of weird, the chances are fairly high that if you do get pregnant, it's gonna be Mercury doing your prenatal appointments."

"Great." She mumbled as she kept her eyes closed and drank her water first. "Maybe we can compare stories." Clearly the last thing Anna wanted was to hear Mercury describe her experience with either man, but she was bitter when she was angry and her head hurt. It was hard not to snap after the meeting they just went through. "I'm sure the last thing she wants is to see me either. Especially if I get knocked up, since it'll be your kid. Logan's kids are supposed to be mine. I'm sure she feels the same way about you."

"We're all feeling a lot of different ways right now." He agreed as he sipped from his water. "For me, any kids Mercury has are gonna be mine to help raise, no matter what. I'm sure it'll be the same with you and Logan."

"I'm not sure how I feel about having children that will be prettier than I am." She teased as she peeked at him through her fingers before she went back to attempting to massage her own temples. "Between your beautiful eyes and your skin tone, not to mention your modified genes, if a kid shows up, it's gonna be too beautiful to look at."

"Now you're making me feel a sudden need for a tiara and a sash. Maybe an evening gown and a wish for world peace while I'm at it." The medicine finally came through, and Orion took the syringe he had requested over to Anna. "Injection is faster than popping pills. I figured you'd want that headache gone as soon as possible. Which arm is your least favorite?"

Anna didn't want to think about it as she shoved up a sleeve and let him have at it. Her barbed wire was showing, but she wasn't feeling very tough. "Damn headache. I did it to myself. Next time maybe we should be a little more sober."

"Hey, the drinking is fine, just don't forget the drugs the morning after. I'm sorry I forgot to tell you about them." He was quick with the needle, but it still hurt, though she could feel it start to work only moments after. Space had the good stuff, that was for sure. "Besides, Shine always comes with a wicked punch the morning after, even with drugs. I like the buzz of it, since it feels different than other kinds of drinking, but it definitely bites you in the face for it afterward."

"No kidding." She relaxed as soon as the medication was truly in her system, and she opened her eyes and looked over at him again. "Thanks for your help. It was really killing me."

"Sure, anytime." They had settled in a fairly isolated part of the available dining space, and since their meeting had been first thing in the morning, there was almost no one else around, so it seemed a safe place for them to talk without being overheard or overtly watched. "What've they got you doing the rest of the day? Time on the simulators? Pods are down for mechanical work for the afternoon, so I've got most of the recruits in sims for the day. I imagine your schedule will be just a little different now that you're supposed to be sort of running the judicial side of things."

Anna pulled out her communicator and pulled up her schedule, and it changed before her eyes. Now she was supposed to meet with the rest of her Board without the rest of the group in an hour, and then she had an afternoon meeting with the Executive Council before she had her treatment, and then, lastly, simulation exercises. "Looks like I'm going to be in a couple of meetings before I can get into a simulator." She didn't sound excited about that, but at least she would get to see Logan. That was definitely a perk to the job, if she got to spend more time with him. "What about you?"

He had pulled out his own and looked through it with a sigh. "Since it saw that I'm nowhere official, it changed my lunch break to the next hour, same as you. Then I'm just overseeing the sims the rest of the day. Quick recap with the other pilots right before close of instruction. I should be out for dinner by six."

He set the communicator on the table between them and leaned back with a sigh. "Mercury said this week is her ovulation week, so they're going to be . . . yeah. That's where they'll be at night for the next few days. Then you said yours is in a couple more, so it kind of sounds like this is gonna be a half and half situation, the way I'm understanding it." He didn't like talking about it any more than Anna obviously did, but it was necessary if they were going to keep things practical. "If you and her are two weeks apart in cycle, then it just goes back and forth. Be a lot easier if you two were synced up, then it would only be one week out of the month, but it is what it is."

"Not much I can do about that particular bodily function, sorry." She turned her attention to the protein bar she'd ignored until that point. "If I was, then I could have been pregnant with Logan's baby before I even got on that shuttle up here." Anna sighed and took a small bite and chewed it slowly. "I like to try and make a joke out of a lot of things, but this is tough. Now all this other shit from that meeting, too. I'm not qualified for that kind of position. Those people are crazy."

"That's why you'll be good for the job." He said earnestly. "A few of them seem like they've got decent brains to work with, but aside from three or four of them, you're all from outside legal professions. You're there to make sure that things are done fairly for people, that people get compensated when things go south."

There was no one around them, and no need for anything to happen between them since she was so far away from her ovulation and technically incapable of conceiving anything at the moment, but Orion reached out anyway to take her hand across the table. "So far as you've got power in this place, I say you use it and shove it up the Initiative's ass. If you meet with the Executive Council and you decide that you've got the power to start changing the way the system works around us, then you'll be able to make this into the kind of community Eleusis ought to be in the first place."

"I don't know if I believe that anymore, though." She looked down at his hand holding hers, and she considered it for a moment but she didn't pull away. He was being a good friend and comforting her when she needed it. "I don't believe they'll abide by anything we establish if they don't want to."

Orion considered that for a while, then finally shrugged, oddly enough. "There's gonna come a point where the rest of us Initiates look more to the Board and the Council than we do to the brass. If they keep saying you've got the authority, and keep saying it and saying it, even if they don't mean it, even if they fully intend to take it away from you sometime down the road, if you say something often enough, and you act the part, then that's what you'll be. And the rest of us will follow."

Anna considered that and nodded as she squeezed his hand while the rest of the headache faded away. "That's sound logic. Thanks. I'll do my best to remember that." She leaned over to him and kissed his cheek lightly. "So, do you want to hang out tonight? I don't really want to hang around my unit alone if . . . you know, Logan is gone."

"Yeah, neither do I." He agreed with an answering squeeze to her hand. "We'll see how well you play when you've got more blood than alcohol in your veins. You'll still lose, but it'll be fun to see how good you think you are."

"Oh, challenge accepted. I'm gonna beat your sexy ass." She laughed weakly and let go of his hand. "Let's get some real food before I have to go to these stupid meetings."

14

Logan wasn't sure how to feel about the way his morning had gone. It started off simply enough, reviewing surveys of the terrain around one of the proposed landing sites and working with one of the agricultural subcommittees to evaluate its yield potential against the other dozen or so on the list.

Immediately after that meeting, though, a quick meet-up had been arranged where he met not one, but two secretaries that had been assigned to him. Logan had almost rolled his eyes when they told him, but he thought he had kept his expression impressively flat throughout.

The man and woman (whose names he had already almost purposefully forgotten) were assigned to him in his twin roles as chair of the agricultural department and chair of the Executive Council, though most people were simply calling him Governor. Both were undoubtedly a form of love letter from the Initiative brass for showing his compliance with their requirements, but he would use them nonetheless.

By the time his Executive secretary (Renata, that was her name) caught up with him around lunchtime, she handed over a few protein bars and immediately launched into a brief for the meeting he was walking into. As soon as he crunched into the first bar, he remembered how hungry he was. Maybe he could get used to having a secretary, even if the short and disproportionately-stacked Chilean woman's accent was barely intelligible and he wondered if she was some kind of plant to try and lure him away from the two women he was already supposed to be going between.

"Wait, what?" He stopped her halfway through the brief, the two of them standing in a lift on their way to whatever level Renata had selected for the next meeting. "The Consortium formed a what? Start over. From the beginning."

"A Judiciary Board was formed this morning, and you will be

meeting with them this afternoon. Whatever laws are established by the Executive Council, they will review and determine if they are legal and sound. They will also be the judges for disputes and other counsel that is necessary beyond and beside the Executive Council. Did you not read your messages? Your wife was nominated as one of the high judges on the Board."

"Like I had time to read my messages." He scoffed and shook his head, but finally processed what she had said. "Anna? Was named a judge?" That didn't fit with what he thought would be up Anna's alley. Not that she wouldn't be good at the job, she would, it just didn't sound like the kind of thing she would want to do. "Nice of them to spring this on us out of nowhere. But no, I didn't read those messages. Is there an agenda for the meeting, or what exactly are we supposed to be doing?"

"There's no agenda. The Board was just created and they will be coming straight from their first meeting together as a newly formed Board. The purpose for this meeting is to get to know each other and to start coming up with ideas about what you want to get processed as a Council and what their role is alongside you. It's an idea meeting. That's what it said, anyway."

Logan shook his head as they went down the hall toward the meeting room. "When we go in there, I want you to take a note over to Anna for me." He stopped along the way and took out the notebook he brought with him up into space, since he figured they wouldn't be big on using paper on the station if they could avoid it. He scribbled the note quickly and ripped it out of the notebook, folding it up in quarters as they walked the rest of the way to the conference room. "But wait until we're fairly well into the conversation."

Renata looked slightly confused but she nodded as she held onto the paper after he handed it to her. "Of course, Mr. Bickford. Would you like me to wait for a response from her?"

"No, I don't think that'll be necessary with this one." He handed her the note right before they headed into the room, and apparently because of his previous meetings, he was one of the last to arrive. People were still milling about the room, but it was obvious there was some tension, since every single person turned to look at him as he entered and immediately turned to look at Anna, to watch for reactions.

Logan wasn't about to play any more games than he absolutely had to on the Consortium's dime. He crossed the room at a sedate pace, saying hello to some of his other Council members on the way and greeting the other Board members he recognized, before finally getting up to Anna. "Mrs. Bickford." He said with a playful smile. "Congratulations on your new job title. Do we get health benefits with that?"

She smiled back at him since she was just happy to see Logan, no matter what the reasons. Anna wanted to pull him into a kiss since it had been a rough morning, and even though talking with Orion and eating lunch with him had helped ease some of her misgivings about the entire situation, it wasn't the same. Orion wasn't Logan, and never would be. "I would be nervous to see what they considered a benefits package." She looked into his stormy grey eyes wishing that he could read her mind. "We should talk after this meeting."

"We should. Sounds like it's been an interesting day for you." He smiled back at her without touching her, since they had to be at least a little professional in certain contexts, which he knew was what the Consortium wanted. "You'll be amazing. As always." He said quietly, as the buzz of conversation filled the room. "It'll be a good thing. One way or another."

Anna knew he could read the doubt in her eyes, but she nodded anyway and went to take a seat somewhere other than next to Logan. She wanted it to be next to Logan, but she knew what it would look like. Why was she in this position? People nominated her. Strangers. What was she thinking, accepting it?

Very quickly, other people chose to take over the conversation. Unsurprisingly, the Kaplans got things off to a start, with Stephen suggesting a number of items that would be good to clarify up front. Logan made a point of allowing each of his suggestions, but overturning one of them as a waste of time before they would actually finalize a code of laws. Koskei began to hash out a process for interactions between the two bodies, and real conversation finally got started between him and some of the other more formally-trained legal minds on Anna's team, with a few interjections from Anna and a woman whose name Logan couldn't quite remember, but who appeared to have made herself into Anna's right-hand woman.

By the time Koskei had commandeered a holographic idea board along one side of the room, Logan glanced back at Renata and gave her a nod toward Anna, to let her know that it was a good time to deliver his note. People were coming in and out all the time, and he'd only had Renata in his employ for a few hours, so no one even knew she was his yet.

When a woman approached Anna and held out a piece of paper for her, Anna looked extremely confused, since she certainly wasn't expecting a piece of paper. Who had paper up here? No one used paper up here, unless they were from Earth. Anna glanced around once quickly before she looked down and opened up the note.

Jane Parsons, Mike, and Ron. We're better than that.

Anna sighed as she remembered. Their last year of school, Jane Parsons had convinced her dad to make both the men she liked quarterbacks, to see who would come out on top. Mike and Ron had been friends since preschool, but the situation had ripped their friendship to shreds.

She read over the brief note several times before she looked up and met Logan's eyes. She shoved the note in her pocket, because she wanted to keep it. Looking at his handwriting was almost as comforting as looking at him. She gave him a warm smile when he met her gaze and a slight nod that she hoped only he would notice. They would always be on the same side, that was what mattered. The Consortium would never change the fact that they wanted to give each other the world. Literally.

* * * * *

It was early in the evening again when Logan's treatment was scheduled, since Mercury had moved him to the end of her day on purpose. She had that much freedom, at least, and she knew he probably wouldn't even notice, since he was a busy man in the first place. He probably didn't even want to see her, since he hadn't even looked at her when they parted ways that morning. For her part, she wasn't ashamed she had found a new way to enjoy herself, and she was becoming rather fond of her sexual awakening.

When Logan came in for his treatment, it seemed, at first, as though the procedure was going to be the same as it had been for the past two weeks of their stay on the station. He entered without seeming like he was in a hurry, didn't quite look at her directly as he stepped inside, and closed the door softly behind him.

"Doctor." He greeted her quietly, but the moment after, he turned and locked the door to her exam room, and stepped up to the table to present himself for her examination. "Pleasant day, I hope?"

Mercury looked over at the locked door, but went about the routine and gave him a quick physical examination. Every day she had to make sure vitals hadn't changed due to previous treatments. It was still hard to predict how people would take it from one day to another. It was a complete overhaul of their immune system, after all. "It would be a pleasant day if I had more babies to care for. Right now it's mostly treatments and various ailments."

"The babies will come along soon enough, I imagine." He let her finish with the first part of her examination, and at the point where she normally would have gone to order his treatment medication, he reached out suddenly and grabbed her by the waist of her scrubs to draw her in close. "Especially if people are enthusiastic about the process of producing them." He held her flush against him, looking down at her almost expectantly after his comment. "Last night didn't leave you with too much discomfort, I hope."

"No, I . . ." She was too stunned by his sudden movement to think, since she hadn't expected it in the slightest. He was enthusiastic about the process of making a baby with her? He certainly seemed it last night, but then this morning he seemed angry and moody, which she could understand, but it was still confusing. She wasn't exactly enthusiastic about breaking her commitment to her husband, but the sex with Logan had been phenomenal. "My muscles were a little sore, but I made time for a yoga workout this morning and that seemed to loosen them considerably."

"I'm glad to hear it." Once he had her close, his hand left its commanding hold on her waist to move up over the rest of her torso in a slow caress until it reached her face, where he traced a thumb across her lips. "After a day like the one I've had today, my intention is to relax tonight. Having you relaxed already makes it just that much easier." He leaned down into a single kiss, and his hand moved down over the side of her breasts again as he continued. "I was thinking of you earlier."

Mercury found herself melting into his kiss instantly, and she kissed him back with fervor as he kept his lips close to hers. When the kiss broke, she felt a little dazed. "You were thinking of me?" She opened her eyes slowly after the kiss, and her deep green eyes searched his grey ones. "You seemed so angry this morning when we left, I thought that I had upset you."

He shook his head quietly. "If I'm ever angry with you, you'll know it because I'll tell you. If I seem sullen or angry, and I haven't told you the cause, you may assume that you are not the reason. There are a number of games I plan to play with you, but that is not one of them." His hand continued running over her slowly, toying with her as his fingertips moved over her collarbone and her bared neck, her hair still pulled back in a braid.

"One of the other farmers talked about some of the twenty-second century attempts to terraform Mars and Venus. As soon as he mentioned Venus, I was grateful both that I was sitting down and that the table was such that no one could see me beneath it. It was a very uncomfortable second half of the meeting."

Mercury couldn't help her smirk, since she was glad she had that kind of effect on him. She reached up and ran her fingers along his beard before she kissed him again. Mercury wanted to feel what she did to him, especially if thinking about her had that kind of reaction.

"I thought about you today too." She admitted as he continued to hold her close. Mercury had been able to see Orion briefly, but he was busy with teaching and she had patients to see. "I thought about your hands, and how it feels when you touch my skin." She slid one of her hands beneath his and nearly shivered at the feeling of his calloused fingers.

He left a caress along the back of her hand as she slid it below his, before kissing her one more time. "I heard a theory once that everyone has a dominant sense regarding sexuality. Some people get turned on by nothing more than an associated smell, a certain song, someone's voice, the taste of the right wine. I'm a very visual person, myself." His touch moved up to trace the neckline exposed by her scrubs. It wasn't much, but it was the most easily accessible bare skin on her. "I could have guessed you were touch. As well you should be."

"I should be? Why is that?" Mercury was so curious to learn more, especially at the hands of an expert. Both Logan and Orion knew more about sex than she ever had.

"You're just made to be touched." His fingers went up along her throat in a light caress that tipped her chin up before tracing down her collarbone to the covered line of her cleavage. "To hold onto with both hands, every part of you." His hands moved to her backside to press her in close and take some obvious handfuls of her by way of illustration. "Just one problem, though." He reached up to tug eloquently at her braided hair.

She was all sorts of hot and bothered as he explored her body with his hands, but the simple touch tugged her back to full awareness of herself. "While I work, I usually pull it back . . ." She defended, since she didn't know what he would say. "My hair is very long and my job is often messy." The computer was dinging now to remind her that his treatment had been delivered and needed to be administered.

"I see." He didn't sound convinced, but he wasn't going to dictate what she did all the time, just when she was with him. "When you get to our unit tonight, you're to take it down, and keep it down whenever we're together for the night, unless I tell you otherwise." He nodded at the dinging computer. "Go on and grab the injection. The sooner we're finished here, the sooner we can leave. Unless you have other appointments?"

She acknowledged she should take her hair down by pulling the tie out of the braid, and letting it start to unravel and fall loose as she took the injection to him and cleaned his arm. "You're my last appointment. I moved you to the end of my day because I thought I had angered you and you would not want to see me after last night."

He let her finish with the administration of the injection and the disposal of the syringe, and watched her quietly the entire time. When she was finished and he had rolled his sleeve back down to cover the injection site, he reached out and drew her close again. This time, though, he turned her around and pulled her back against him, then reached around to the front of her pants to undo the simple tie that held them tight around her waist. Once the tie was undone, he moved his hands up to slide along her arms, placing them above and behind her head.

"You will not make assumptions regarding my emotions." His hands roamed down her body, stopping finally at the waist of her pants to pull them down just over her ass. Once it was bared to him, along with the underwear beneath, he placed a hand on one side of her ass almost gently. "If you do make assumptions, you will be punished for it, and you will come to ask me to be punished for it."

Mercury nodded slowly, though she was attempting to anticipate what he was about to do. Was he going to spank her? It really seemed like it. "I'm very sorry."

The slap to her ass came out of nowhere, and was harsh enough to sting, but mostly just surprising enough to make every nerve in her body jump in over-sensitive surprise. "Say it again, and mean it."

She couldn't help the gasp that escaped, but she did as she was told. "I'm sorry, Sir. I will do my best to make sure it never happens again."

"Better." A second spank came on the heels of the word, but his hand lingered over the stinging spot afterward, moving over her ass just to get a thorough feel of her before his hands went back to her hips and he held her back against him. "Also, from now until I no longer require daily treatments, you'll schedule them either in the late morning or early afternoon. I prefer not to go an entire day without contact. You will also, whenever you feel the urge, schedule me for physical check-ins and random treatment observations even when I don't require them by anti-CV standards." He drew her scrubs back up onto her waist and slowly tied them again blindly. "You will do this only when you can reserve an exam room that locks, and the appointment window will be scheduled long enough for me to have you at least once. Do you understand?"

"Yes, I understand." She replied breathlessly as he pulled her pants back into place, which made her extremely disappointed. "I will make sure to fulfill all of your requests. I wish I could do them all now."

"They are not requests." His hands moved up her back to her newly-freed hair, and he took a slow handful of it to pull it back so that she was resting her head against his shoulder. "They are requirements. And they will be obeyed, as time and our situation permit." His free hand moved up over her chest as he kissed her, then he let go of her hair. "How much time is left in my observation window?"

Mercury was reluctant to even look away, but she gave him an honest answer. "Eleven minutes."

He moved aside to take a seat in a chair nearby, and pulled her along with him, so that she was standing next to him as he looked up at her. His hand casually wandered down her side as he took his seat, but it soon moved between her knees, lightly flicking them apart where she stood so that his fingers could trail up her inner thighs. As his caress moved over the thin fabric of her scrubs, he looked up in her eyes to continue the conversation.

"Tell me, have you ever been so aroused you found it difficult to walk?"

She shook her head. All of the times she was aroused, she was already in the process of having sex or pleasing herself, so she had never experienced being aroused and having to wait and deal with it.

She had a feeling he was going to change that.

"Let me know when that happens." He said playfully, looking up at her to watch the look on her face as he teased her lightly. "I meant to ask you this morning when the memory was fresher, but I still want to know. Tell me your favorite part of last night. The thing you enjoyed most."

Mercury knew she should be checking his vitals again after she had administered the treatment, but she couldn't think about anything except the way that Logan was touching her. It made her heart race with every light graze. "I really enjoyed the shower this morning." The shower had been such a sensual experience, though it wasn't the first time she'd had sex in the shower. He treated her to oral after they had cleaned each other up but before intercourse, and Mercury nearly fell on her backside. "Everything about it, but most of all when you . . . when you used your mouth on me."

He smiled and actually leaned in to kiss the waistline of her scrubs, tugging the fabric down just a little to kiss her bare skin before he let the fabric slide back into place. His kisses moved down over the fabric covering her, just to remind her of what it had felt like. "I'll be sure to keep that as a reward, then. The next time, you'll be on your back. There will be no falling on your ass, but there will be no escaping, either."

Mercury could feel the heat in her skin with each teasing touch, and she found herself amazed he could do so much to her by promising things, either by reward or punishment. She was wet just by his voice and his promises, let alone his touches. "I don't want to escape you." She admitted as he ran his hands over the thin fabric of her scrubs. "Just being near you turns me on."

"I wonder what you would be like frustrated." He leaned back in the chair again, withdrawing his kisses to look up at her, but his fingers continued playing along her inner thighs. "So needy you can't even think straight. That would be a new experience for you, I'm guessing."

Mercury didn't want him to stop kissing her, especially because she was starting to *feel* needy. She stole another kiss because he didn't tell her that she couldn't kiss him, and then she responded. "I . . . have not experienced that." She didn't want to, she didn't want to be teased to the point of losing her mind, but she did at the same time.

"That's a shame." He said with a last caress, then withdrew his touch from between her legs just to sit back in the chair. "I believe you need to check my vitals again. If you can walk."

Mercury didn't want him to stop touching her, but she stepped away to get what she needed. When her hands explored him for the purposes of checking him over, he could feel how warm her touch had gotten, but she was trying not to look needy. She was flushed all over, though, and her touches were the inappropriate, lingering kind, certainly not professional.

"Your vitals look fine, except for a slightly elevated pulse." She looked into his eyes after she said that, and he could see that her eyes also betrayed how bothered she was by his attention. "Do you want me to check again, or do you want me to document the elevated number? They use the information to better prepare the treatments for future use."

"It would be unrelated information. My pulse is elevated because it's working harder to encourage my blood supply, not because of the medication." He smiled back up at her through his attempt at utilizing medical jargon. "Some other time, you should check the numbers of your male patients' pulse and blood pressure against those of other doctors in similar situations to see if yours are more elevated on average. Any heterosexual male within sight of you, let alone reach, is going to have an elevated pulse."

She smiled at that, and met his gaze again. "I don't care about what I do to them. I do care about what I do to you." Mercury ran her fingers along his arm, but that only made her situation of being needy even worse. "But perhaps it is a good thing that most of my usual patients are females or babies."

"Probably, yes." He returned the smile, and ran his hand along the side of her leg as he waited for the time to elapse. "I had a short break this afternoon." He had her moving closer to him again out of instinct. "I did some shopping. It's fascinating what kinds of things they keep in stock up here. Unless there's some kind of specialty manufacturing shop on one of the other arms of this station."

"Commerce moves quickly between stations, actually." She shivered when he ran his hand over her leg. "There are drones that can deliver things same-day usually."

"Interesting." He appeared completely relaxed in the chair as he looked up at her, running his fingers along the inner band of her scrub pants. "You'll enjoy what I found for us." It sounded partly like a command and partly like a prediction, but it was hard to tell which took precedence. "Is the observation time finished yet?"

Mercury looked back at the clock and then she looked at him again. "Two minutes." She wasn't sure what he had done to time, but it had slowed to a crawl. "I don't know if I can survive another two minutes."

"You'll have to survive longer than that. Out of this clinic and the whole walk up to our unit." He tugged at the strings he had re-tied earlier so that they were just barely hanging on, and left them that way as he stood up against her. "If you have things to get or files to finish for the day, get them and finish them. You're mine as soon as your shift ends, and I won't be denied the time that's mine."

She couldn't breathe as he stood up against her, and her whole body ached for his touch. Mercury's breasts ached the most, and she reached out for his shirt tentatively. "The door is locked. Please don't go." Mercury couldn't even think about finishing her work, especially with his broad body against hers.

He considered briefly, but nodded as his hand moved up over her torso, bypassing her breasts with only the lightest of touches. "Go finish your work. I'll wait. Be quick about it."

Mercury only nodded but she clearly felt disappointed as she backed away from him and looked up at the time. "You're good to go, Mr. Bickford." She needed to refocus herself on her tasks if she was supposed to get back to work. "I'll see you at the unit soon."

"Oh, I didn't say I was leaving." He said with a teasing smirk, then followed her over to the terminal where she had his file pulled up. He turned her around to face it as he moved in behind her, his hands coming to rest on her hips. "I said finish your work."

"How . . ." She didn't know how she was going to focus on her work with him touching and teasing her, especially because since he was standing behind her, she could feel the part of him she wanted pressed against her backside. Mercury attempted to fill in the appropriate information for his file based on the vitals she checked, but it wasn't easy.

As she finished up with his file and moved on to some of her other unfinished business from the day, he slowly pulled her hair back over her shoulders to run his fingers through it, loose and wild but still holding waves from the braid. He nudged her legs apart with one foot between hers, and made sure to keep himself flush against her as she attempted to work. His hands moved beneath her shirt casually to run his rough fingertips over her ribs just beneath her breasts, his touch brushing them slightly as he held her. "Trouble concentrating?"

Mercury felt as though if she even breathed, it would make everything that much more difficult. She looked at the same screen several times, but she remembered he told her to be quick. "Yes, as a matter-of-fact."

"Well that's a shame." His torment continued, but at that point, it moved down to her pants, tugging them down slowly so that they crept down over her hips. "You should work on handling distraction." His fingertips ran along the lines of the plain black underwear covering the most sensitive parts of her, tracing the edges to tease at her while she worked.

There were more than a few gasps that escaped her lips and many times Mercury had to re-enter information because the information she had entered didn't make any sense. "Logan," she pleaded as she got to her last file, but she couldn't even read it without one of his fingers slipping beneath her underwear and teasing her. She was amazed she wasn't getting dehydrated from how slick she was. Mercury had easily soaked through her underwear.

"Yes?" He said unapologetically, his fingers moving against her so slowly it was excruciating. There was no hurry to his touch, no push toward satisfaction, just a touch. Just possession.

"I can't . . ." She said desperately as his fingers relentlessly tortured her clit. "I can't complete . . . my work . . . like this." It was difficult enough to focus just to speak, let alone continue working when he wouldn't stop touching her.

"So you want me to stop, then." He drew his fingers away from her slowly, returning to his caresses along her thighs and hips instead of more direct teasing.

"No, I . . ." She didn't know what she wanted, and it frustrated her. Especially because he wanted her to come up with an answer. So instead of answering him, she just kept working and let him do as he liked.

He left her clit alone to roam over the rest of her body, allowing her to get at least a little of her work completed before he moved his hands up beneath her scrubs to caress along the outer curves of her breasts all the way back down to her panties. "If you remembered this every time you had to finish your documentation for the day . . ." he said against her ear, holding her a little more tightly so he could grind her back against him, "every time you stood at one of these terminals to enter information . . . that would make for some very interesting days for you, wouldn't it?"

"Interesting seems to be an appropriate word for that kind of experience, yes." She replied softly but she closed her eyes to savor his closeness and to pay closer attention to his voice in her ear. "It would be difficult to wait to see you."

"I would make it worth the wait." He promised almost in a whisper, letting his touch do the talking for him. "It would make for some difficult days for me as well, sitting through meetings all day while knowing you're just a few decks away more than ready for me."

Mercury leaned her head back into his shoulder though she kept her eyes closed as she continued to savor the feeling of his broad body. "Even when we're not scheduled to be together?"

He continued to tease her for a while as he considered his response to that. "The schedule dictates which weeks I see you during the nights. Schedule or no schedule, you'll do as you're told, or there will be consequences."

"Yes, Sir." She said dreamily as she still squirmed a little bit in front of him, as she was all sorts of achy and needy. "I need you. How much longer do I have to wait?"

"Until we get to the unit." The edge of command was in his voice as he said it, and his fingers quickened their pace to set her body on fire before they withdrew and he pulled her scrubs tenuously into position. "Leave the rest of your work. I want you as soon as I can get you."

Mercury nodded and didn't look back as they made their way across the small exam room, since she didn't want to wait any longer. She was beginning to get a little delirious with need, and she wondered if he even cared, since he had teased her with not even one ounce of hesitation. She hoped he cared about her as a person, but she could understand why he wouldn't.

This wasn't a real relationship, this was just a way to survive the Consortium. In reality, they were strangers to each other, and she didn't mean anything to him, he didn't know her. It was a little heartbreaking to remember the reality of the entire situation, so she was quiet as she followed him out of the clinic and back to the unit that was too fancy for the both of them.

The entire way back, he was similarly quiet, and even when they got to the unit on the deserted hallway, he didn't look at her as he opened the door for her and closed it behind them, locking it against intrusion.

There was a single moment, half a heartbeat's worth of hesitation between the clicking of the lock in the door and the frenzy on the man's face as he whirled himself toward her. Her back hit the wall and his lips claimed hers within the space of a blink, his hands already ripping at her scrubs to yank them down while the rest of him tried to grind into her. The same need she felt was echoed in the way he touched her, the way he tore at her shirt and her panties to throw them aside. He was well beyond teasing. He was going to have her or he was going to explode. There was no middle ground.

Mercury was shocked to be in the middle of a frenzy, since Logan seemed so calm and collected the entire time in the exam room. She could hardly think about what was happening before she was naked and he was kissing her again like he needed her breath to keep breathing. Mercury moaned with every kiss and she was desperate to feel his naked body against hers, despite the fact that everything between them was a story in their heads.

"Logan . . ." She moaned between kisses, since she was ready and dripping for him, and she desperately wanted to feel him inside of her.

The kitchen for the unit wasn't far from the entryway, and he stepped back from her only enough to throw aside whatever pointless items had been stocked on the island so he could throw Mercury onto her back on the cool surface. As soon as she was on her back, he had both her legs up on his shoulders and slid himself completely into her with a hungry growl of satisfaction. He was rock hard and hot inside her, filling her with the answer to the need he had inspired in her body. He groaned there for just a few racing heartbeats to savor the feel of her, but then laid into her with the same frenzy as she'd felt while he tore her clothes off and pressed her to the wall. If his body's language hadn't been enough, she could see the need in his eyes when he looked down at her, watching her face contort in the moans he tore from her.

"You feel so . . . good . . ." She moaned her words as he thrust hard, and she whimpered in pleasure every time he filled her completely. It was a tight fit with each thrust, but it felt incredible because he worked up every nerve ending she had, making her ready to burst into flames.

He gripped her legs tightly as he thrust inside her, wanting to watch her come apart before he allowed himself to reach the same built-up climax. He'd walked down the hall and told himself he couldn't just throw her up against any wall he pleased, take her right there in the lift the way he had wanted to. He told himself their relationship had to be contained, it had to be sectioned off from the rest of the world, in their unit, in her exam room, in the small corners of the station they could make their own. But she felt so amazing that it was going to be almost impossible to hold off his own orgasm when it came.

"I want you . . ." he forced himself to slow down, to tease her just a little bit more, but the frenzy was there behind his strokes, threatening to have instinct take over with every stroke, "I want you . . . to always want me this much. Every time you see me, every time you think about me, I want you to remember this. I want your body to beg."

Mercury was already begging as they both hovered over their orgasm. She couldn't talk any more as the need took over her mind. "Logan," she begged. "Please . . . I need to . . . Please . . ."

When her moans and gasps escalated to a fever pitch, he finally allowed himself to completely succumb to the moment and lose all restraint, slamming into her in exactly the ways he learned would tear her apart. His own climax was a foregone conclusion, but he could see hers unravel her beneath him. It was one of the most delicious things he'd ever seen, and the corner of his mind that hated what he was doing and who he was doing it with was silenced by the sight of her, if only for a little while.

Mercury felt as though she couldn't move her body after an orgasm so intense, so Logan carried her, and she was grateful again for his strength. When they both settled in the opulent couch, she finally had the opportunity to reply to him. "I'm afraid that's going to happen." She whispered into his shoulder as she curled into him. "I'm afraid I will want you this much, any time I see you. This is supposed to be a passing fantasy."

He ran his hands over her back as she pressed herself into him, and he couldn't contradict what she was saying. "Not much use in being afraid of the inevitable." He said eventually. "I could be worse for you. Come in here, demand that you get undressed, get myself off and say the hell with you, let you do as you want. But that accomplishes nothing. If anything, it reduces us to nothing more than genetic donors, and the Consortium gets what it wants. You're more than that, and so am I."

She nodded and kissed his cheek gently, and she savored the feeling of his stubble rough against her sensitive lips. "If this was going to happen no matter what, I'm glad it is with you. You've been understanding and kind, even though this is difficult for all of us. As difficult as it might be once things are said and done, I would be sad if we couldn't be friends."

"I think we're beyond being friends." He said with a tug at her hair, after which he trailed the ends over her exposed breast in a brushing caress. "But no, even when things are said and done," he poked at her stomach to get a twitch out of her, "I can't see us ever feeling less than amicable toward each other."

Mercury kissed him everywhere she could reach, since she enjoyed being more than friends at the moment. "I would be lying if I said I wasn't hoping we'll get more time than just this week. I don't want to give you up yet."

He turned to lie on his back and looked her over with a smile that was almost playful. "And here I thought I had left you satisfied."

* * * * *

After the meeting adjourned, Stephen and Maria returned to his office to find Byron there waiting with his own wife, who was speaking angrily to someone on her communicator while she paced the far side of the office. He looked up at Stephen and Maria as they came in, and set aside the tablet he'd been watching, which was showing a live feed of the conference room where the Executive/Judiciary meeting had just taken place.

Anna and Logan were still hanging around in the room, along with a few others, but Byron didn't see the need to zero in on any particular conversation for the time being. Surveillance would look things over in detail later and let them know if any red flags came up.

"You keep underestimating them." His voice was a quiet monotone, looking back and forth between them with a slight glare. "That meeting was more productive than anyone's forecasting showed it would be. Zero arguments aside from the ones you two tried to pick, and zero ill will created between sides. Zero."

"You are getting upset too easily, Byron." Maria said in a way that sounded both comforting and condescending at the same time. "Let me ask you a question. Which kind of argument is more damaging and the effects longer-lasting? An argument between strangers, or an argument between people you know, respect, and care about?" She raised an eyebrow and motioned back to the surveillance. "We need to give them time to trust each other. Eventually it will work the way we want."

"You seem to take that word as a mantra, Maria. It may *eventually* bite you in the ass." Byron said darkly as he stood up, clearly disapproving of everything that happened at the meeting. "We're here to show meaningful progress and reasonable improvement of techniques pursuant to the start of Phase Four. Not to see how long we can keep things nice and happy before they're ripped to shreds."

"I think we *have* seen improvement and progress. These people have only been here for a very short time, Byron. It hasn't even been a month yet. You have to give these things time." Maria looked over at Stephen for support, since he was being annoyingly quiet. "This Phase is supposed to take a year. We have no reason to rush things."

"They're getting restless already." Stephen chimed in more or less on cue, though his eyes never left Byron's. "Maria's idea to crossmatch a married couple has proven both divisive in terms of public opinion and effective in terms of heightening the general tension of the group. The fact that we were able to get them to comply with the cross-match so quickly and frankly so easily has other matches falling into line all over the arm. And we need them in line, for the rest of the experiment to be fully effective."

Stephen sounded legitimately hopeful, and Maria had been around him long enough to know the difference. "Some of the things this group is showing, we didn't expect to see until the next Phase or the one after that. So I'd say that's progress."

Byron just shook his head. "I don't trust your mind-games, Santos. I don't trust their effectiveness and I don't trust their reliability. Not on a long-term timetable. Show me that things will remain weak and fractious by your methods over a long period of time, with minimal involvement, and I'll be convinced. Otherwise, I'm still going to advocate more direct, systemic methods." He shared a look with his brother at that, but then turned to go. "I'll see you both tomorrow at the leadership meeting on Arm Three."

"They're choosing to spend time with someone l they didn't even want to see. They're being conditioned that if they refuse to fall in line, then they should fear the worst from us. It's working, even with the most rebellious. That's where we're supposed to be right now with this Phase. Don't push me, Byron. I know what I'm doing." Maria couldn't let him leave without some kind of last word, even if he was nearly out the door already.

Byron glared, but didn't say anything else on his way out the door, his incredibly-vocal wife walking along beside. When the door was closed and the office was theirs alone, Stephen shook his head and pressed a hand to the door panel to lock it against intrusion, just as a matter of course. "Don't mind Byron. His expectations have been too high all our lives. I don't expect it to change any time soon."

"Don't mind him? I mind threats to my projects, and he's clearly threatening to take this out of my hands. I don't take that lightly." Her tone was sharp, and uncharacteristically bothered from her usual calm. She'd yet to give in to Stephen's attempts to seduce her, but it was getting more and more difficult. Maria wanted to see how long she could hold out. "He can't condense a year-long project into a month."

"Byron's never had much talent for seeing matters through to their full conclusion. He's fond of saying that he's a sprinter, not a marathon runner."

"Clearly." She looked at the door again before she sighed and looked back at Stephen. "I think things are going well. And Logan and Anna know they are being watched, so of course they would want to make things go smoothly during their first meeting. Things will get rough." Maria had her tablet held to her chest but she lowered it so she could flip through it quickly and look over her schedule. "I have a few more individual meetings left today, so I should move along."

"No, you shouldn't." He didn't even look at his schedule,

though he knew he had several meetings as well, in preparation for their conference with the top brass the next day. "What you should do is stay here for the afternoon and get a taste of your own medicine. Might cure what ails you."

"A taste of my own medicine? What does that even mean?" She laughed, shook her head, and walked toward the door, but that meant walking toward him, since he was still standing by the door. "I'm a busy woman, Stephen. I need to go."

He put an arm across her way to block the door, and didn't look away from her. "When I met you last year, there's no way you would've ever let Byron get to you. You're wound up, you're stressed, and you're a workaholic. I actually enjoy all those things about you, but you, more than anybody I think I've ever met, are in dire need of being cut loose from the world for a while. If you turn your own psychology on yourself for a minute, you know I'm right."

"You are part of the problem." She reached out to push his arm out of the way. "You won't stop with this . . . whatever this is." Maria still hadn't figured out how she had ended up being matched with Stephen Kaplan, and it was driving her crazy that she couldn't figure out her own program. She didn't want to be played by her own system if someone had tampered with it, but she had yet to find any evidence that there had been any tampering. It was looking more and more that Stephen Kaplan was actually her best match.

When she reached up to remove his arm, he managed to snake it out of her grip and wrap it across her chest to pull her back against him in a tight hold that was surprisingly strong. "You already know what this is." He said calmly against her hair, no trace of his physical violence in his voice. "You wrote the program, you know what it does. It looks for what you need. What needs you back. And then it gives it to you. If you let it."

His insistence and forward actions felt like a jolt of desire that went straight to her core, and Maria could almost feel her pupils dilating. "I'm still not sure it hasn't been tampered. Clearly it can be tampered."

"By you. By me. By anyone who can hack the damn thing, clearly." They had some suspicions that some of the official matches had been tampered with by someone, but whoever they were, they had buried every trace of their tracks. "But you already know it hasn't been, you just don't want to admit it. You're not the only one with access to the clean backup of the program. I saw the history where you ran our names again in there. You already know it was a clean run. It wasn't just availability, it wasn't tampered. You're just too fucking stubborn to admit it when you find something for yourself."

Maria felt the heat in her face at his touches, and her pulse kicked up almost immediately. "You've been watching me?" It was hard to tell if she was offended or not, but she was definitely surprised. "You looked? You didn't believe it either?"

"I had no trouble believing it the moment it happened at the first meeting. I went in and followed your trail when you kept blowing me off, since I knew you would do your own investigation." His touch became more invasive the longer he held her.

"See, I had one of the essential ingredients in your recipe for a happy couple. I was willing to go with whoever I was paired with. The success of your matches goes up exponentially when participants express a willingness to participate, much less an actual enthusiasm to be matched with whoever the system chooses. For you, it seems like it's been just more of a curiosity, some kind of case study, when that's not how any of this works."

He leaned down until his lips were near her ear, his hands tightening their grip on her body until he was making it almost difficult for her to even draw a breath. "You have to commit to it, Doctor. Like I said, take your own medicine."

15

There was something off about Kameron that morning, and for once, it wasn't morning sickness. In fits of anger and hormonal distress, she had threatened to hurl all over Orion and Carl any time they teased her for being ten times more bitchy than she normally was. Apparently her ovaries had taken to Kazuo's efforts early. She was convinced it had happened as soon as he had convinced a woman named Melissa to join in a threesome.

That had been a *good* night.

Kazuo, however, wasn't getting any better, and it was clearly affecting Fitch in more ways than she thought possible. She cared about the guy, even if she wasn't in love with him. He was the father of the little parasite inside of her, after all.

"Fitch." Orion flicked the back of her shoulder to get her attention. "Hey, where are you wandering off to? You're drifting off center and throwing everybody off." He looked back at the rest of the ships trailing behind them, each of them piloted by one of their trainees, with an instructor riding along for support. "Come on, you're supposed to be setting an example here."

"I'm sorry." She looked back at Orion and the other ships, shaking her head. "Maybe you should take over. My head is just not here right now."

He glared at her but transferred the controls back to his console instead of hers, and righted their course. "Where is it, then? And don't say in your stomach. You've got better focus than that."

"When she wants to." Carl said from beside Orion, utilizing some of the ship's systems to monitor the immediate vicinity of the station. He had claimed there was an advantage to using a ship's systems instead of those of the station itself, because the ship was more difficult to tamper with. Orion had his doubts, but the man wanted to come along, so he came along.

"I'm surprised you're being so calm about it. I thought Aiko would be upset. Kaz had to be hospitalized this morning."

"Wait, Kaz had to be what?!?" Carl was not calm about it, and she could actually feel the ship rock just a little at the way the huge man jerked in his seat at the news. "I thought . . . Aiko thought he was getting better!"

They had been on the station nearly two months, following the direction of the Initiative, laying in and reviewing plans for the colonization of Eleusis, working to improve them at every turn, working to train new security forces and pilots and agricultural specialists, all at a breakneck pace. "He just gave a presentation to the Council last night, I was there to watch!" Kazuo and the other engineers with the project had presented their first full layout for the proposed colony, along with most of the designs for the buildings and public structures involved.

"I told him not to." She shook her head with a sigh. "He was hopped up on pain meds the whole time. He collapsed as soon as he got home, but made me swear not to call anyone. When he woke up with a fever, his vitals alerted the docs and they came and got him. They said I couldn't see him until this afternoon."

"Well why the hell are you even out on maneuvers, then?" Orion asked incredulously, though he did manage to concentrate on the flight path long enough to get them on the next lap around the station. "You could've just stayed on board."

"No, let's back up to the part where Aiko has no fucking idea." Carl interjected, having completely abandoned his work in favor of the conversation. "He said he was getting better, just last week. What happened?"

"I didn't know he was telling her that." Kameron said as she looked over at Carl, but she was starting to look like she was going to get sick again. "I thought she knew he was getting worse. His last good night was after I found out I was pregnant. It was like he kept holding out and hoping, but he hasn't gotten better. Even with her weird-ass treatments. Now they're saying it would take extremely risky and extensive surgeries to clear out all the cancer, and they would have to send for doctors from another station. This morning they told me that even with all of the surgeries, he would only have a 50% chance of survival."

"Somebody gives me a fifty-fifty shot at something, I'm gonna take it. Thought Kaz was pretty much the same way." Carl had his own way of living life, and while he didn't expect anybody else to conform to it, he always took note of those who did.

"I'm sure he will, if they actually bring in the specialists to do it. The doctors here apparently aren't able to do it. They aren't trained to deal with an aggressive cancer like this."

"Yeah, well, if he'd been up here from the start, it wouldn't have gotten as far as it has." Carl said with bitterness in his voice he had inherited from Aiko, but with which he obviously agreed. "What are they waiting on, then, if they know what he needs? Just waiting on the surgeons to be available?"

Kameron shook her head slowly and sadly. "They are waiting on approval from the Initiative to bring the specialists in. Kazuo isn't an Orbit citizen. He doesn't have any rights up here. So it's up to the *good graces* of the brass."

Orion and Carl were both quiet at that, and it was Orion's turn to have to make a quick course correction to avoid running into another one of the ships. "God help him, then, if he believes in that kind of thing."

"He's supposed to get better so he can help me raise this thing that's making me so sick." She knew she looked much sadder than they expected, but she and Kazuo had become good friends. "I'm not parent material. He is."

"Hopefully they take all that into account when they decide what to do." Carl's tone was attempting, and failing, to be optimistic. "I mean, he was accepted into the program. That means they've got a responsibility to him. To all of us."

Fitch let out a humorless laugh. "Cuz they've been so understanding and compassionate so far. Orion is still hooking up with the shortie. That's not cuz he wants to."

Orion did his best to keep his expression neutral, but he knew he would fail if he tried, so he focused on flying instead. One of the fliers behind them was Anna, flying solo for the first time because she was the most advanced in the class. "If they accepted him, then he has value to them. If nothing else, I hope they'll want to protect their investment. I think that's about the most any of us can hope for from the Initiative at this point."

"I hope you're right. We'll find out for sure once we get back and I get to see him." Orion was right, she should have stayed behind in the first place.

"I'm telling Aiko." Carl typed out a message on his terminal. "That's not me asking permission, that's me just letting you know. She's his sister, and she's been thinking for weeks that he's getting better. She needs to know."

Kameron nodded as she rubbed her hands over her face. "I really didn't know he was lying to her. I thought they were super close or some shit like that. He loves his sister. But he's kind of a pessimistic dude. Maybe he thought it would be better to lie to her. Especially because she was getting closer to you. Girl loves you. Maybe he wanted her to focus on you and not him."

"Him before anyone else in the world." Carl said darkly, then sighed as he sent off the message. "She loses him, her world falls apart. Seriously."

"I hate to be the real downer in the room," Orion said quietly, "but the world has already fallen apart, for all of us. All we're trying to do right now is put it back together some kind of way that makes sense."

"I'm not in love with the guy, but I care about him too." She looked over at Orion again. "Do you think Anna can do something to help him?"

"If it involves resources beyond the ones we have . . ." Orion shook his head. "I mean, yeah, she can probably lean on Logan to make sure he pushes the doctors we already have to do all they can, but if it's something beyond their abilities, then it's beyond their jurisdiction."

"Mercury can't pull in any favors either? She knows a lot of doctors. Do you think she could reach out to any of them? I'm all about bypassing the brass." Kameron glanced around as if she expected them to punish her for even saying such a thing.

"I'll ask her. See what she can do." Orion said quieter, since things with Mercury were . . . strange, to say the least. "I know she's got a couple friends who are oncologists, so I'll see if she can get them to fly in, at least send them his scans to see what they think."

"Thank you." Kameron felt a little bit better about that, but she still knew it was a long shot. All of it was a long shot for Kaz. "How, uh, how is all of that going with you and Mercury and the shortie?"

Orion sent out a message calling for an end to maneuvers for the afternoon, since he knew Carl was going to want to get to Aiko as quickly as possible and Kam needed to be with her match, no matter what the doctors said. "It's . . . going. Mostly we all seem to get along by not talking about it. Mercury's gotten more distant during times she's spent a week with the guy, but this past week has been pretty good for us."

Of course, that meant Mercury was going to be leaving him in just another day and a half, but Orion was trying not to think about it. "We just need to find a way . . . well, like you said, Kam. We all need to find a way around the brass."

Kameron sighed as they turned around to head back toward the station, glad that she was going to get to check on Kazuo. "I'm sorry things aren't going well. It sucks when you have to spend time with someone you don't want to be with. I thought Anna was cooler than that."`

"Things are going as well as they can, I think. It's not her fault." His voice sounded tired as he said so, since he really was tired of reminding himself all the time that it wasn't his fault. "It just sucks. Once we hit lift-off and start on our way to Eleusis, I don't think any of us care what the brass would have to say about it, we're doing things our way and on our time, with who we please."

"That's at least ten months from now. My kid will be here before we even blast off for Eleusis." Kameron said as she glanced down at herself before she looked at Carl and Orion, but then she looked at Orion again. "I bet that's got to suck, though, having a kid with someone and then not being a part of their life. I mean, clearly Anna's kid is going to grow up knowing that Logan isn't his or her dad. You and Logan don't look anything alike."

"Yeah, there's not gonna be a whole lot of getting around that." He twisted the wrong way on purpose, then the right way again, just to see who was paying attention and who was just trying to copy his lead behind him. "That's one conversation all of us have managed to have on all sides, what we'll do once we get to Eleusis. It was decided that whatever happens, we're gonna need to stay pretty close. Kids being every fucking which way and all."

"Maybe you'll dodge it, right? I mean, some people try over and over and never actually get lucky. Maybe it'll be a non-issue and then you'll get to Eleusis and get back to normal." She shrugged and held onto her straps a little tighter since he was changing directions all over the place. "Dude, take it easy. I'm gonna get sick again if you don't."

"I apologize. I forgot for ten seconds that I was transporting an invalid. Thank you for reminding me." He glared over at her with a ghost of a smirk, but the comment got a full laugh from Carl.

"Kam, I swear, if you were straight, you two would've gotten matched. Then one of you would've killed the other within a year."

"Obviously I would have killed him first. No way would Orion beat me. Even though a tiny parasite is giving me a run for my money, so . . ." She shook her head and ran her hands over her face again. "You two are fucking lucky with your lack of ability to get knocked up. I never thought I would actually be in this position, and I'm kind of glad that I wasn't well-warned. If someone told me I would hate it this much, I totally would have avoided it."

"And the fun is *just* beginning." Orion's smile was beginning to come back, since Fitch complaining about something made the world seem normal again. "Wait till you have to evict that thing. I've seen childbirth. It's not for the faint of heart."

"Shut up." She said sharply, looking around for something to throw at him, though it would do little good since they were flying. Throwing something would mean it would just float away from her. "Keep your comments to yourself."

The rest of the trip into the station and the docking went fairly smoothly, with only one of the trainees needing extra help. They were far from professional pilots, but Orion had high hopes. They had learned very quickly that the name of the game was to learn quickly or bow out. They were down to only half a dozen active trainees, but Orion was sure they would all pass muster eventually.

He got out of the ship and watched as Carl and Kam floated away toward the lifts, but he caught Anna before she was able to run away with the rest of the trainees. "Hey, float with me for a minute. I'm headed down to get showered off for the afternoon, I've been stuck in a ship with a vomiting woman most of the day. Where are you headed?"

"Fitch having a hard time?" Anna stayed at his side as they slowly made their way further in. Anna looked back at the ships and just smiled, since she had an amazing time flying by herself. "I'm not sure where I'm going yet, I haven't powered on my communicator."

"You could say she is, yeah." He smiled at her obvious good mood, since he was glad to see somebody happy, especially someone he cared about. "I didn't realize you could be sainted for suffering through morning sickness, but she's got the martyr act nailed. I almost felt sorry for her today. Then she threw up on me, so that pretty much killed what little sympathy she had going for her."

Anna wrinkled her nose and shook her head. "I hope it isn't like that for me. I'd like to get one of those pregnancies where I tell people I feel the best I've ever felt and I'm glowing and all that shit." She laughed at the idea and she looked up at him. "Getting puked on must have really ruined your morning. You barely cracked a smile. We had a good morning! We got to fly!"

His smile brightened just a little bit more and he nodded as they reached the lift, taking one of the smaller ones for themselves. "Any day you get to fly is a good one, you're right. Unless you're flying because someone's chasing you. Then things get complicated." He sighed once they got into the lift and braced himself against one wall in preparation for the onset of some kind of gravity. "Have you met the Tanaka siblings? Carl and Fitch's matches?"

"A couple of times, yeah, but only briefly. I mean, whenever we've gone out for drinks with everyone, she's always with Carl, right? Never drinks? Super quiet?"

"Never drinks because she really wants to get pregnant. Super paranoid about alcohol's effect, et cetera. And yeah, super shy. I've barely had two conversations with her." He shook his head, since it wasn't Aiko he wanted to talk about. "Her brother's got about eight different kinds of late-stage cancer. Been fighting it for years, apparently. They hospitalized him today for observation and treatment, but apparently the only doctors who could do anything meaningful aren't on this station. And the brass is twiddling their thumbs."

That chased Anna's good mood away in a hurry. "What? They can't fuck with people's lives like that. I mean, it's bad enough what they are doing with matches and all that shit, but if he's dying, then he should get shipped off to a station where they can help him, for fuck's sake."

"I doubt he would want to be shipped off anywhere. He and his sister might as well be twins, they're tight like that." He hated to see anyone in such a position, especially someone who had been forced to live on Earth their entire lives and then got to orbit, only to be killed by something that was completely preventable with the right care.

"I was wondering if there's something you or Logan could do to help him. If you know of any way either the Board or the Council could force the brass to call in the resources to help the guy. I don't know anything about the case, but if it's possible, it seems to me like it should happen."

"I can try, but that's not really my job around here, you know? They didn't give me the power to push for situations like that." She sighed and thought about it for a moment before she said anything else. "I'll talk to Logan to see if he thinks we can do anything. Or if he can do anything. It's worth a shot."

"Thank you." He gave her a grateful smile and leaned in to kiss her on the cheek once as the lift descended. It was a perfectly chaste gesture, even a friendly one, since she had seen that Orion was just as friendly to all his friends, but the touch was still a complicated one. "The guy is just a friend of a friend, but I think if we've learned anything these past couple months, it's that we've all gotta have each other's backs, since obviously no one else will."

"No kidding." Anna's smile returned after the kiss to her cheek, and she chuckled a little as she looked away from him. "What was that? Are we kissing cheeks now?"

"Just wanted to say thank you, that's all." He shrugged. "And I've kissed just about every other part of you, why should the cheek be weird?"

Anna laughed again. "I don't know. It's not weird. It's cute." She looked away from him though, and her smile faded again in increments. "You know what is weird, though? It's been two months of living up here, and most of it I've spent with you. That's not a bad thing, it's just weird." She glanced at his arm before she spoke again. "I feel closer to you than I do Logan anymore. It's rough."

He nodded without looking at her directly. "Mercury and I are the same way. We still have good times sometimes when we're together. We went out flying the other day, just took a pod and did some Earth-watching, that was fun. But for the most part . . . she's somewhere else. And not just when she's actually in a different place, she's just thinking about other things."

"I thought I knew everything about him, and I thought he would talk to me about this stuff. But I don't, and he doesn't." She reached out for Orion's hand and she held it firmly before she looked up at him again. "Maybe things will be able to go back to normal one day, but it gets less and less likely every day."

"Did either of us even get a chance to find out what normal looked like?" He asked as he squeezed her hand, holding her closer as the spun gravity of the station took hold on them both.

"I mean, I look at couples like my parents and it seems like they've been together since before the Crisis. They had their newlywed days, which is how three of us got here so damn fast one after the other, then they've had twenty-some years just to stare at each other and settle in. We both got what, a few weeks? A few really complicated, really crazy weeks? And then this. I don't even know what a normal marriage would be like. With anyone."

"Obviously I don't either." She was glad he squeezed her hand, and even though she knew she probably shouldn't, Anna yanked him in closer so she could kiss his lips. They were still somewhat floating, so it was easier to yank him around. Anna kept kissing him as she held onto his face with both hands. "At least when I'm with you, I don't feel like your mind is a hundred worlds away and I can't reach you."

He shook his head after the kisses, and didn't pull away. There was no point in trying to only be affectionate with Anna when the calendar said he should be. Friendships didn't run on schedules, and neither did any other feelings. "No, my mind tends to stay more or less where I put it. And it's generally wherever I happen to be at the time. I try to be simple like that."

"There's nothing wrong with that." Anna kissed him once more, but she didn't want to push it to a point where he told her to stop, so she pulled back. "I get worried about a lot of things." She ran her fingers across his face slowly. "I worry that he'll miss her, and I worry that you *won't* miss me."

That pushed away what was left of his smile, but he didn't let go of her once she pulled away. "I think all of us have gotten to the point where we do a lot of missing, no matter who we're with." He shook his head. "I hate that that's what's happened, but I hate it without hating you or Mercury in the process. It just is what it is."

"Yeah." Anna knew she was out of her league with both Orion and Logan, which often made her wonder if it would come down to both of them fighting over the redheaded goddess while she got left behind. "Well, hey, you still get time with Mercury. It's not time for her to go with Logan yet. So there you go."

"Yeah. There I go." He sounded more resigned than excited as he said so, but he let go of her anyway, as the lift finally got to their deck. "Anyway, let me know what Logan says. I'll be up in the hospital wing if you need me."

"Yeah. Sure. I'll let you know." Anna moved out of the lift

first, but she didn't look at him again. It sucked to want, especially because she wanted Orion and she wanted Logan for very different reasons. "See ya, Orion."

Orion stayed just outside the lift for a while to watch her go, then finally sighed and headed in another direction toward the hospital. He would be able to stop in and talk to Mercury on the way, but he found himself looking back the direction Anna had gone nearly the entire way to the hospital wing.

It felt like he was trying to fly a ship to two different destinations at once. Eventually it would tear apart in the process. But he wasn't going to allow himself to think that far ahead. One step at a time.

* * * * *

Carl strode through the halls next to Aiko, both of them trying not to run as they advanced toward the hospital wing. "If anyone so much as mentions the words 'visiting hours', I promise to feed them their own vocal cords." He was worried about Kazuo right along with Aiko, since they hadn't gotten any updates about his condition, from Fitch or anyone else.

Aiko wasn't really able to think or talk as they walked. As soon as she got to the threshold, though, she stopped dead in her tracks. "What if they won't do it? What if he's dying and I can't do anything about it?"

"You can always do something about it." Carl said quietly, pulling her off to one side after she stopped. "You can be there for him through it. More than most people get on their way out of this world. Everyone dies eventually, there's no stopping that. All that matters is that he knows you're with him, that people care about him. I know that's all I'm gonna care about when I check out one of these days."

Aiko looked into his dark eyes and felt like crying, but she was afraid to cry. It would feel like she had given up. "We came here for him." She put her hand over her face as her eyes burned. "What if I didn't have you? Without Kazuo and you . . . I would be alone."

"Well, you'd have your plants. You talk to them like they can hear you, so you wouldn't be completely alone." He smiled faintly and pulled her into a brief kiss in the hopes of keeping the tears from her eyes. "Come on, let's go see what he's up to."

Kameron was sitting by Kaz's bed when they heard the overhead system tell them another visitor had arrived. Kameron took Kaz's hand and glanced back toward the door. "That's probably your sister."

He just groaned, looking truly weak and at the end of his rope. She had seen him that way several times, but before, he had always bounced back. This time, not only did he look like he was at the end, he just looked more tired than anything else. "You should tell her to come back tomorrow. I didn't even shower this morning."

"She doesn't care about that. I'm the one who's been sleeping with you and I think you smell fine." Kameron squeezed his hand gently before she kissed his cheek and looked back as soon as the door opened. "Seems like she was in a rush to see you."

Kazuo turned his head toward the door, but Aiko managed to get into the room and most of the way to the bed before he could complete even that simple motion. "Sis." He managed, closing his eyes in a very long blink, just to keep her from seeing too much of the pain in his eyes. "You really . . . should've called ahead. I'm very popular in here. So many appointments . . ."

"That's not funny." She immediately took Kameron's place next to his bed as soon as the pilot got up and moved away. Aiko was definitely crying now. "You lied to me. You said you were getting better."

"At chess." He said in feigned exasperation that came out as honest exhaustion. "I said I was getting better at chess. You never did listen to me." However exhausted he was, there was resolution in his eyes that wasn't going to just give in or change because he was dying. "I've had episodes like this before. Usually it takes about a day for the medications to run their course and then I'm back on my feet again. Still waiting for Byron to render his decision."

"He's the one it's with now?" Carl asked from across the room, already pulling out his communicator.

"Who I knew had it last, yeah." Kazuo said without even turning to look at Carl, since he didn't really have the strength to be turning himself every which way.

Carl just held up his communicator so Aiko could see what he was doing, then slipped out of the room. He was head of security. He was going to have some words with Byron Kaplan.

Kameron watched Carl leave the room and followed quickly after him, since she felt like she was invading the brother/sister moment in Kaz's room. "Hey, wait up. I'm going with you."

Carl stalked down the hallway in silence for a long while before they got to the lifts and keyed in the floor for the brass offices.

"He's not going to do it." Carl said once the lift doors were closed. "I've been working with Byron for two months now, he's not going to authorize anything out of line for Kaz. The man's own wife was having a crisis with her family the week after we got here and he wouldn't let her leave the station to deal with it. Said it was against Initiative protocols."

"So what are you going to do?" She asked curiously, since she'd been trying to think of ways to get Kaz the help he needed, but she didn't know how to make it work. "I thought about busting him out of here in a cargo hold and stealing a ship and taking it to Seven. But I don't know if he would make the trip without all the shit they have him hooked up to."

"I don't know if he would either. My bet would be no." He ran his hand over his newly-buzzed head in irritation. "We'll have to find a way to convince him it's in his own best interests. That's the only language I imagine a man like Byron will listen to."

"And how do we do that?" Kameron looked at Carl like he was crazy. "Kaz is fucking brilliant, we all know that, but even the most brilliant are replaceable. I know for sure that I'm replaceable. You are too. Byron doesn't care about us."

"No, he doesn't. But he does care about the Initiative. He cares about success, and he cares about control. If we show him that by losing Kazuo, he begins to lose control, then maybe he'll listen."

Kameron looked confused. "How are we going to show him that he'll lose control if we lose Kaz? Kaz isn't exactly a leader of anything."

"Still makes him look bad." The lift stopped and they headed down the hall toward the administration offices. There was no one in the hallway except a pair of guards near the front door. They took a single look at Carl and went back to their conversation. The head of security didn't warrant a second look from them, apparently.

Kameron, however, was either confrontational enough or stupid enough to say something as they approached. "Hey, we want to talk to one of your bosses. I'm assuming that means we go through you, unless you're just gonna let us waltz on through."

The man looked up from the conversation, amused, and when

he spoke, it was with a thick accent, though it was intelligible. "What exactly do you want and with which of our bosses? All of them have something better to be doing than talking to you, so your reason had better be world-shattering."

"Byron Kaplan." She looked not at all amused, certain that pregnant or not, she could still kick some ass if it was necessary. "My business with him doesn't include you, so what I want is none of your business."

"Oh, you're one of those." The man chuckled, but he did move toward the hallway that led back toward the other offices. "Should I at least give him the name of someone asking for him, or should I just describe you to him? Short, bitchy brunette who thinks the station revolves around her."

"Sure, if you think that's the best description you can do, go for it." Kameron crossed her arms, mostly to keep from punching the guy in his smarmy face.

It only took a few moments for the man to come back down the hallway and wave them along, though he still had the same smug smile on his face. Byron's office wasn't hard to find, and he was sitting behind his desk as they entered, working on some kind of report without looking up at them.

"Please have a seat." His chronically-flat voice filled only a corner of the room, and his eyes didn't quite focus even on the things he was working on. "I'll be with you in a moment."

Fitch looked back at Carl and went to stand behind the chair instead of sitting down, since she didn't want to be caught off guard. If she was going to get angry, she didn't want to be sitting. "Take your time. It's not going to change what we have to say."

He did take a few more minutes to complete whatever he was working on, but he eventually closed the program and set it aside before turning to face the two of them. "What is it you need?"

"What you need, not what we need." Carl started in, now in one of the seats and looking much more at ease than Fitch, though that wasn't hard. "You need to authorize doctors from Seven, cancer specialists, to come here to treat Kazuo Tanaka."

"Yes, I received that request soon after the beginning of the project. It seems Mr. Tanaka came up here under false pretenses with regards to his health." Byron didn't sound angry, but it didn't sound like he was sympathetic, either. "He's been undergoing alternative treatment ever since, though I did get a report earlier today that he seems to have taken a turn. Why do you say this is something that I need rather than something you need?"

"He's the best engineer you have here, and you know it. The report and presentation he just gave only days ago is a revolutionary idea about how to best build our infrastructure on Eleusis, and we need him once we get there to implement it." Fitch knew how to sound a lot smarter than she really was, but it helped that she'd been listening to Kaz for two months about his ideas for Eleusis.

"Yes, I attended that presentation. It was quite remarkable, some of the strides he's made in material efficiency and manufacturing replication." Byron's words were complimentary, but his tone wasn't. He looked back and forth between Fitch and Carl as if he was trying to figure out which of them was less boring. "You're incorrect about the implementation, though. His designs are the property of the Initiative, and will be implemented with or without his presence. Which is fortunate, since he's unlikely to survive until the departure date, let alone the full journey to Eleusis."

Fitch tightened her hold on the chair she was standing behind as she stared Byron down. "He could survive if you bring in the right specialists to attend to his needs. And if you don't, you'll regret the loss of his contribution. You *do* need him there."

"We don't, in point of fact." Byron's voice was always cold, but it seemed especially so just from his lack of reaction to the obvious anger in her voice.

"No one, no ten, no hundred people are essential to the success of the Eleusis colonization. To imagine that's the case is vanity of the highest order. Mr. Tanaka was born, as I understand the research done on him, with a genetic weakness in combating the Crisis Virus. Therefore, in spite of his young age, he has succumbed to cancer, a regrettable but entirely known side effect of the rampant development of CV in humans."

"Frankly, Ms. Fitch, had you not already been pregnant at the time we learned of the extent of Mr. Tanaka's condition, you would have been rematched with someone who could provide a better genetic contribution to your future. As it is, you are likely to watch your child grow sick and die an agonizing death in twenty years because of its father's defects."

Kameron didn't know what to say immediately, but she just felt angry. "But he can be fixed. Anyone can be fixed up here. So why aren't you?"

"Because the primary concern of a functioning society is not what *can* happen, Ms. Fitch, but what *should* happen." Byron's voice was just as tired and apathetic as always, but for once, there was nothing detached about the look in his eyes. There was an incisive, poisonous quality to them, as if anyone who looked in them for too long would feel the effects for days to come.

"Your misguided impulse to storm in here and demand that I authorize the necessary treatments for Mr. Tanaka comes from affection for him, which I take as a sign of a successful match. This is only natural, and to be forgiven. But the larger priorities of the Initiative will always take precedence over individual concerns. Such it is here as it is in any organization in history, including the military hierarchy of which you've so long been a part. Mr. Tanaka is an engineering genius, and he will be missed. But more than his genius, he is a liability and a strain on resources that Eleusis will simply not be prepared to support. We will not, now or ever, place the success of this project in jeopardy because of individual concerns."

"You're sentencing a man to death." Carl said quietly, having taken in about as much of the man's condescension as he could stomach. "You're deciding to allow him to die when you have the power to save him. He can't go to Eleusis? Fine. I doubt he'd mind. Send him off to Seven, kick him out of the Initiative, fix him up and put him to work on Station Maintenance. You know how valuable he'd be as a part of that team."

"Mr. Tanaka is not a citizen of the Orbital Consortium." Byron answered in clipped syllables. "Nor is the Consortium willing to offer him citizenship and additional medical resources. I have already applied to that route of possibility and found his proposal to be rejected."

Kameron didn't believe the asshole in front of her had done anything to help Kaz's situation, and she certainly didn't believe he had applied for anything on Kazuo's behalf. There wasn't even a flicker of compassion in the man's eyes. "You're full of shit." She shook her head as she glared at him. "If it was your brother or your life on the line, you'd make damn sure someone was taking care of business, and your brother sure as hell isn't a fucking engineering genius."

"That is true, my brother's talents have always been in leadership and organization. He has very little talent for engineering or mathematics." His tone remained just as flat as ever, and he hardly even moved in his chair as he looked back and forth between the two of them. "If Mr. Tanaka's condition is deteriorating, then the answer of the Consortium board is upheld. He will be made comfortable and his dignity maintained as well as our resources on this station are able. There will be no further measures taken to involve outside resources."

"You let him die, you send a very clear message." Carl said with a warning behind his voice. As large and boisterous as the man typically was, Fitch had never seen him so quiet. It was unsettling. "The minute he dies and the rest of the colonists find out that you or the rest of the brass could have saved him, every one of them realizes that you're the enemy, because any one of us could be next. Hallway could fall through, potentially cripple someone, and then what, we'll be left paralyzed for our whole lives, when we could just be shipped off for a week and made whole? You let Kazuo die and every single other person realizes that they're expendable, and you'll have a very different kind of population on your hands."

"Good." Byron said just as quietly. "If the current colonists believe, for whatever reason, that they are any more special or valued than any other lives in the world, then they are wrong. It's best they were disabused of that notion as quickly and thoroughly as possible."

The chair creaked a little bit with the amount of strain that Kameron was putting on it with her grip, and all she could imagine was taking the damn thing and breaking it over the bastard's head. "You're about to fuck with a population that's half Earth-born. They just finished their treatments. They have all the hope in the world for a full life past thirty-five. If you make them believe that you would take it away in an instant, they'll turn against you like a fucking rabid animal. You can't do that to people."

Byron looked bored as he stared back up at her, but he did at least make eye contact for once. "Ms. Fitch, the world hardly requires my assistance to take people's lives from them or to snatch hope away from people's hearts. I did not cause Mr. Tanaka's advanced condition, nor have I somehow pre-populated the many dangers I am sure you will face on Eleusis. You are correct in assuming that I care not at all who people blame for the conditions under which they grew up, and even less who they blame for the repercussions of their own choices."

"I did not encourage Mr. Tanaka to commit fraud and apply

for this strenuous program when he was not in the best of health. Nor did I force anyone in this Initiative to apply and leave behind the Earth. Hope is its own manacle and chain, and I do not hold the key. People will die before the end of this project. If you want to blame me for that, I am comfortable with that blame, since it is as meaningless as your attempts to prevent Mr. Tanaka's death."

Kameron stared for a moment and started laughing. "My god, you have somehow actually managed to remove yourself from feeling any guilt at doing nothing. You have made it perfectly okay to fuck with people as much as you want by saying they signed up for it. Wow." She started to turn away but she looked back at him again. "I don't believe in much, but I believe in people getting what they deserve. It'll be a good day when you get yours."

"If people got what they deserve in this world, Ms. Fitch, I would have died years ago." He sounded unimpressed as he nodded back to her. "And so would you. And you . . ." he said as he looked over at Carl with the slightest hint of a smirk on his face. It was the one and only time he had displayed any emotion in the time either Kam or Carl had seen him there on Nine, and it was able to shut even Carl up. "You would have died in infancy." He waved them both off and turned back to his terminal. "Please convey my best wishes for a miraculous recovery to Mr. Tanaka. I sincerely hope he recovers with the resources available here. His talents and his contribution are appreciated."

Kam wondered if there was actual smoke coming from her nostrils. "You're the closest I've ever come to a real snake." She didn't even wait for Carl as she bolted out of the office, and she sincerely hoped she didn't see the guard again or someone was going to get hurt.

Carl followed her out of the room and down to the lift silently, then punched the number for the hospital deck as soon as they were inside. "Kaz is a tough bastard." He knew firsthand that much was true, he just hoped it was true enough to help Kaz. "Knowing him, he's gonna outlive the rest of us and make bad jokes about it at our funerals."

"You better be right." She leaned back against one wall of the lift as she rubbed at her face almost violently. "I seriously want to fuck some shit up right now." Fitch said as she clenched and unclenched her hands repeatedly after she rubbed her face. "I wanted to beat that fucker's face in."

Carl was strangely pensive as they rode, thinking back over the conversation as he paced against one side of the car. He wasn't capable of sitting still. "He bothers me." He said as if he was surprised by the observation.

"Only *now* he bothers you?" She said in surprise as she looked over at Carl again. "I haven't known Orion as long as you have, and you and I haven't worked together that often yet since you're more security and I'm more about hopping ships, but since when does anyone with that much power not get 'bothersome'?"

"That's why he bothers me. He's the wrong kind of asshole." Carl looked at the door of the lift as if it was going to open on the answers he was looking for, but nothing seemed forthcoming. "Not giving a shit about other people's lives, sure, I get it. Administration attracts psychopaths. But the one thing assholes with power always want is to keep their asshole power. I talked about people turning against him and he didn't even bat an eye. That makes no fucking sense." He shook his head, since it was too confusing for him to wrap his brain around it. "It's like if the whole station turned on him and went all mob-mentality tomorrow, he wouldn't even lose sleep. That doesn't fit."

"Seemed to me like he wanted it." She looked away from him and down at herself, but what he said about her baby was freaking her out more than she wanted to admit. Was she really going to watch her baby die long before it should? "Sounds like he wants everyone to tear this place to pieces."

"And after all the smoke they've been blowing up our asses for two months about making Eleusis the most amazing thing humanity ever did since it discovered sex . . . that makes no sense." He nodded back toward the ceiling. "Why would he be on the admin staff if he just wants to watch the whole thing burn?"

"Hell if I know." Kameron shrugged, since she wasn't one to over-analyze a person. If someone was a shitty person, then they just were. If they were a good person, then they just were. She didn't go looking for motivation. "That's just what it seems like."

Carl shook his head again, but as the lift opened to let them out on the hospital deck, his communicator beeped harshly from his pocket, demanding his attention every few seconds until he managed to get it out and silence it with a quizzical expression. "Something weird at navigation. Notifying me on protocols." He tucked his communicator back in his pocket and turned back toward the lift. "Tell Aiko I had to go respond to this, but keep me updated about Kaz. I'll be down as soon as I get an all-clear."

"No, I'm going with you." She followed him whether he liked it or not. "Aiko and Kaz could use more time together before they get shitty news like that, and I'm in the way there. I can help you with whatever the problem is."

"Good. You also speak Navigation." He looked at his communicator again and tossed it to her. "What do you make of that? It's gibberish to me."

His communicator had a message in a bright red frame pulsing on the screen to get the attention of anyone who was actually watching for it. *Unidentified Xeno-Class object in intrastational range, alteration in trajectory detected, no natural gravitational causation noted. Intercept probability increase of ninety-seven percent. Long-range scans inconclusive, cross-checking current databases for matching configurations.*

"Something is coming at us. Fast." She went through his communicator to get in contact with Orion, though she figured he had gotten the message as well. "We're going to have to get out there and blow it up or it will hit the station."

"I thought that was all automated? Blowing up little chunks of space debris before they can hit the station and put holes in people's windows?" He was looking at the numbers on the lift and wishing there was a way he could tell them to go faster, but technology didn't generally listen to him when he yelled at it.

"You wouldn't have gotten a notice if it was some random piece of space junk." A reply from Orion popped onto his communicator saying he would meet them at the dock. Once she saw that, she tossed Carl the device. "It would have been caught and destroyed long before it even got close. But that message said the trajectory was altered, and not by a change in gravity. That means someone is coming at us on purpose."

Carl took in that information as he watched the numbers rise slowly, then pulled up an equally-red and equally-glaring system in his communicator. "All security teams, ready station one, drill negative. All active and reserve, station one. Potential inbound. Arm and stand by." The order was conveyed through the communicator and Carl sighed as he put it away. "Just what I wanted today. Somebody to shoot at."

"Don't sound sad about that." Fitch said as she felt anxious but actually a little bit excited. It meant that she could do something with all the anger inside of her, since she couldn't attack Byron Kaplan. "If I can take this out on someone who deserves it, I'll feel a whole lot better."

"You and me both." Carl's hand went to the two guns he wore along one thigh at all times, not sure which one he was itching to draw more, since they were very different weapons. "Who in the damn world is stupid enough to try and just barrel into one of the big Stations? Is anyone seriously that suicidal?"

"After what happened to all the ships just trying to get up here in the first place, I'm surprised it's been two months before any other shit happened. Obviously people don't like us very much. It seems like someone wants to do some damage, no matter what the cost." Fitch grabbed her own gun and ran out of the lift to get onto a ship so they could possibly get off the station and do something about whatever was flying at them.

What she didn't expect to find, however, was that they were locked out of the shuttle. No one could get into it, and Orion was already trying furiously to override whatever was stopping them. "What's going on? Who locked us out?"

"We don't know yet." Orion had stepped back to allow others to work on overriding the systems, but for the time being, Orion and the rest of the pilots were gathered in the near-zero gravity of the dock with nothing more to do than twiddle their thumbs.

"All ships and pods were docked as of twenty minutes ago when the lock came through. All we've got to deal with whoever's out there is the station systems, and all those are locked down. If they're sending a battering ram through, this whole place could get blown apart and there's not a damn thing we can do about it."

"They're slowing down, sir." Pablo said from one of the control panels nearby, where he and half a dozen others were watching the telemetry on the unidentified object coming toward them. "Standard docking procedure, from the looks of it. Cargo Lock Three." He pointed off to the largest open space in the dock, where large cargo ships could come up and unload the bulk of their haul at once, with wide, gaping airlocks designed to interface with the freight ships.

"Great." Fitch said as she looked over at Cargo Three, and she shook her head when she looked back and forth between Orion and Carl. "I hope you're ready for this. Firing a gun in near-zero is about the worst thing in the world, but I have a feeling that's going to be necessary."

"It's not the worst thing. So long as you make sure your bullets find their way into a body." Carl said as he pulled out his gun and checked it over. It had been a while since he had fired one, but it certainly wasn't a skill he had permitted to get dusty. "They start bouncing around up here and pretty much anything could happen." He looked over at Orion once his gun had received his approval, and holstered it again with a sigh. "Gutierrez! What's the ETA on our UFO?"

"Six minutes!" Pablo shouted back from the navigational control side of the docks, sounding fairly worried.

Carl looked over at Orion and shrugged. "You're the senior officer here. Time to put that promotion to work. What's our play?"

Orion glared at his friend but his mind was already thinking ahead. "Fitch, you're one of our better shots. Take half a dozen and find perches around the dock with cover. I want to get as much shielding from ricochets as possible. Carl, grab another half-dozen and find whatever riot-style protection you can, I want you and some goons up close and personal once the first volleys are over. The rest of us will be barricaded down here in the columns front and center to give them somebody to shoot at."

"Once whoever's on there gets in and gets locked, they're likely to come out swinging. If that happens, snipers give them a dozen heartbeats to get in here and get comfortable before you start picking them off at the door. Goons, a dozen after that. Depending on how many we're dealing with, we'll put them in a grinder between the three of us and go home to have a nice dinner later tonight. Steaks on me for anybody who's left in good enough condition to chew it."

"I'll just be glad to get someone to shoot at. Too bad we can't get Kaplan down here." Kameron grumbled and looked away from her friends and started moving to pick people to follow her. "Don't die, you two. See you on the other side of this."

* * * * *

Many decks out from the dock, Gordon was walking with Jessie through the gallery, looking down on a night-side Earth. He chuckled at her question and shook his head. "No, it wasn't anything that glamorous, unfortunately. Though that's a good story, I'll have to remember to use that one sometime. No, I was mostly a shut-in when I was a kid, and I discovered some technology tutorials very early on. Once I got started, I never went back. Just picked things up as I got tossed around from place to place."

"You just seem to know so much." Jessie said with a bit of awe in her voice as she walked next to him, holding his hand. Jessie knew she was holding the hand of a dangerous man, though she never could get it out of him how dangerous he actually was. "I'm jealous."

He gave her a playful glare for saying so. "I know a lot about very specific things, and almost nothing about the majority of everything else. For example, I know you grew up on a vineyard, but the extent of my wine knowledge is telling a red from a white. And I've had maybe three varieties of each. That's the extent of my wine knowledge."

"Well, if we ever get to Eleusis and start a vineyard with native grapes, I'll do my best to educate you." She smiled at him and kissed his cheek before she looked out again, but just as something caught her eye, both their communicators beeped at the same time with a warning to return to their unit.

Gordon turned with her to head back toward the lift, but he was pulling out his own interface to run an inquiry. "Something's happened." All the lightheartedness had gone out of his tone, and he walked more quickly with every step. "They just barely got done telling us yesterday that things were fine and moving quickly, they're not gonna monkey-wrench it now before they've had a chance to work . . ." he trailed off into mutterings he clearly thought were speech, but ended up being nothing but gibberish as he searched through the station database to find out what had triggered the alert.

"Shit." He stopped for a moment and his jaw tightened as he looked at the hologram in front of him. "Unknown vessel inbound, no classification. That has to be Carmina. The odds of there being two people in the world as stupid as she is would be incalculable." He took off running once he knew what was happening, and he didn't show any signs of slowing down, even in the lower gravity. "How are you with a gun?"

"A gun?!?" Jessie clearly wasn't expecting that kind of question. "I've used a shotgun . . . but not at people!"

"I might need you working on something else, then." He ran up one hallway to what looked like one of a thousand different supply cabinets, and took out the data core he always wore around his neck. Placing it up against the locked panel cued the device into activity, with a holographic projection in the air of the process it was quickly engaging in to unlock the panel, but it was over almost before Jessie had a chance to even see what he was doing.

The lock on the panel clicked, and there was a small armory behind it, with half a dozen guns and several racks of ammunition. He grabbed one and handed it to her before he took one for himself. "Don't let any of the brass see you have that. If we get to the other side of this, we're gonna have to put it back where we found it. But you are not getting caught unarmed by Carmina if I have anything to say about it."

He shut and locked the panel, then headed off down the hall again, stowing his stolen gun under his shirt in the band of his pants at the small of his back. "She's here for the Twist, that's all she cares about. But she'll have to shoot her way in and get through all the security personnel to get to the brass. Then she'll try and torture them to get the location of it, and by then they'll have moved it. Which is what she's not thinking of. So we need to stop her at the shooting-her-way-in phase of things."

"Do you really think she would come here herself?" Jessie was clearly not in a great frame of mind, but she was attempting to stay as calm as possible. On her family's vineyard, all she had ever had to worry about was unruly young people trying to steal wine. Mostly that meant just sending a few warning shots in the air to scare people off. This was way beyond her experience or understanding.

"Oh yeah. She'll definitely come herself." Gordon's absolute certainty in the answer was far from comforting. "She didn't have that many people with her when she broke away, and if my intelligence is right, now she has even fewer. She's not gonna risk this mission on other people the same way I wasn't about to risk this kind of operation just on Tatyana and the others. You want something done right . . ." he shrugged and finally pulled them into a lift, where they could relax briefly.

He pulled out his data core and looked at an updated report, then swore half a dozen times. "She's coming for the dock. She clearly has no idea where she's going, or she'd board literally anywhere else." He rolled his eyes and dismissed the hologram, then met Jessie's eyes and quickly handed her the core. "I'm going to the dock. Most of the others will probably think along the same lines and join me there, but I want you rounding up the others. Hyacinth will get you to each of their units and help make sure they're armed. She's good like that. A ship Carmina's size, we're gonna need as many as we can get."

Jessie nodded before she looked down at the core in her hand. "Okay. I'll get to everyone as fast as I can. I promise." She looked sad as she looked into his eyes before she reached out to touch his face lightly. It looked like she wanted to say something, but she stopped herself from saying anything more. He needed her to act, not get mushy, so that's what she would do.

"And don't get shot." He turned his face to kiss her palm as she touched his face, then reached out to pull her in by her shirt until she was flush against him. Once he was holding her, he sighed into her hair. "Don't worry about all this. Carmina has a lot of people, and she's very smart, but she's not as smart as she thinks she is. She hasn't thought this through, and she won't win. We'll be alright."

Jessie dipped her head down so she could kiss the side of his neck and close her eyes for a moment as he held onto her. "Don't get shot either." She said softly against his neck, as calmly as she could, though her heart was pounding with fear. "I don't want to know what it's like without you around."

"Pretty boring, I expect." His hands moved over her sides as he leaned down to kiss her own neck. "And I love you too, Jessie." He rested his cheek against hers as he held her, wishing there was something else he could say or do to keep her a little farther from harm's way.

She turned her head so she could kiss his lips, since she knew the lift was almost to the destination, and she didn't want him to go. Jessie kissed him so hard it made her heart ache. "I swear, as long as you don't die, I'll do whatever you want me to do. I'll wait for you naked all the time in our unit. Whatever you want."

That brought a very relaxed smile to Gordon's lips, and he reached up between them to caress her face as the lift stopped, all urgency forgotten, if only for a moment. "If any man ever had more of a reason to live than that, I would be fucking shocked." He kissed her with urgency and heat, then patted her hand with the data core still in it as his expression grew a little more serious. "If things go completely to shit and something's happened to me, take this and whoever else you can grab that you trust, take a pod and get back to Earth as fast as you fucking can."

Jessie nodded and bit down on her lip to stop herself from kissing him again as soon as the lift opened. She had a feeling, though, even if he escaped unscathed, it wouldn't be the last time she was worried for his life. "I love you." She finally said out loud, since it had been hard for her to even admit the words to herself. "Don't worry about me. Go kick some ass."

Gordon gave her a last look before he turned and ran off in the direction that would take him the rest of the way to the docks, taking his communicator from his pocket as he went. "Send a message. Open the circuit between me and the contact listed as Unknown Sender." He paused to wait for the communicator to chime and indicate a successful contact, then sighed before he continued. "Last chance to back out of this without blood, Carmina. Some of it yours."

It was only seconds before a message came back through. *Most of it yours.*

Gordon shook his head and got to the last lift to get to the docks and checked the gun against the small of his back just to make sure it was still there and ready for use. "Blood is blood. Mine or yours makes no difference. What matters is our success or failure, and all you're doing by this action is making it harder for us to succeed. We have people inside security now, and my systems are working through the station's security protocols to get to what we're looking for. Shooting your way into this is not going to solve anything."

"It's going to change everything, though." Carmina replied immediately, and cut off her communicator before she turned her attention to the docking ship. "White is still trying to keep us out of this." The crew of the shuttle was small, but well-armored and well-prepared. "Remember, we're not here for the Twist, even though they will think we are. We're here for information so we can get the Twist. Shoot at everyone and anyone. I don't care who it is, if they aren't us, they're in the way. I'm going after White's unit. He's not sharing everything he's got."

Her crew already knew the plan, and they had all chosen to be on board with, but most of them had solemn looks on their faces.

"How much time do you think you'll need?" One man said, with an unintelligibly-thick Spanish accent. Most of those around the cabin were preparing their guns for the docking and the shooting that would follow. Most of them were heavily armored. He, on the other hand, was busy checking more than a dozen knives stashed around his person.

"At least twenty-five minutes. I have the shortest path to his unit, but that's without anyone getting in my way, which isn't likely." Carmina glanced at the man as the docking gear engaged and the pressure changed as they were locked in. "Keep them blind." She yelled back to a couple of people swiping through holograms and inputting information wildly. They were armored, but not weaponized, so their job was to keep the brass in the dark as long as possible and to keep as much locked down on the station as possible. "Let's go, people!"

The Spaniard with the knives got up beside her in the moment before the doors opened, then pulled the visor of his helmet down to cover his eyes. "See you on the other side, Carmina." He drew two of his knives and as soon as the door was open, he was the first one out.

He drew fire from a dozen different sources through the open space of the dock, but all their shots did was draw attention to the shooters. The Spaniard himself was covered in bulletproof armor, and launched himself at one target after another, aiming for them with his knives and doing as much damage as he could. They needed chaos if Carmina was going to get to her target. The world depended on the chaos they could create.

When the intruders came in blazing, Fitch was ready. She didn't even pay attention to Carl or Orion, she just went after the enemy, guns blazing. Someone had to die.

Orion wasn't surprised by Fitch's ferocity, but he knew Carl was, and he spared a moment in the middle of the shooting gallery that followed to grin at his friend. She was a fighter and a half and he had always respected her for that. If she wanted to kill some people, she came to the right place.

He was, however, surprised by the amount of people he saw flying out of the attacking ship, pouring into the dock with weapons spraying, even though some of their own people were getting into the line of fire. There were dozens of them, and Orion only managed to pick off three or four before some of them were too close for him to be using guns anymore. Bullets were already ricocheting like mad around the dock and picking off some of those who had chosen to abandon their cover, some of them on his side, some of them on the other.

And a knife? What madman brought a knife to a gunfight? One of the knives came at him and sliced across his calf. It didn't get much through the leg of his uniform, but it still hurt. He whirled around and landed a backhand on the man's jaw and sent him spinning, but the man's reflexes were impressive, and Orion had his hands full.

Fitch was an agile woman, and she managed to get in several shots before she got shot in the arm, complicating her ability to shoot back. Being wounded wouldn't matter if they were all dead, though, so she had to keep shooting. A bullet grazed the side of her neck, but she barely allowed herself to feel it before returning fire to put down the one who'd put it there. Bullets rang off the cover all around her, catching the side of her shirt as she returned fire, reminding her again of the life inside her.

That life wouldn't live if they didn't repel the attack. Nothing else mattered but the fight, until the fight could be finished.

Carl pushed himself back from the main line of defense to try and follow whatever strategy the attackers came in with. When he saw they were heading for the arm that housed the rest of the Initiative, he dove toward the lift to cut off the ones making their way directly toward the only people he really cared about. Instead of firing at them, he went for them physically, throwing his entire weight at two of the women who had managed to skip past the rest of the front-line fighters.

Carmina noticed the large man barreling at them and immediately turned her gun on him. She fired half a dozen times before she threw herself against a wall, changing her direction before the giant could get to her. She needed to get to White's room.

Carl didn't have any way of stopping himself once he was shot, but he had managed to deflect the bullets to make sure they only hit his legs and the side of his shoulder. He knew the second it hit his shoulder that he was going to be feeling it for a long time, but that didn't matter. He had things to do, and those things involved killing the people who just shot him.

He landed against one of the men who'd been with Carmina. All it took was a quick jerk of his arms to snap the man's neck, and a push-off with his legs to follow the woman in charge. He did that, however, before he remembered he had just been shot in the same leg he was using to kick off. The move failed spectacularly, and he ended up tumbling end over end in mid-air while trying to fire at the woman in a mad spin.

Carmina felt it like fire when a bullet embedded into her shoulder, but she ignored it as she pressed on. She made it past the rest and didn't look back. She knew where she needed to go.

None of her other people managed to follow and she got into

the lift before Carl could reach her. He swore and slammed into the lift doors, but then turned and shot back at the approaching group of the woman's fighters still trying to kill him. At the moment, they were doing a better job of killing him than he was of killing them.

Orion managed to pick off a few more before the initial barrage of bullets began to slow down in their ricochets. He popped up through the door of the pod he had been hiding in and grabbed a knife that had lodged itself in one of the pipes nearby. It was the only weapon he had at hand, but it would have to do.

Anna was somewhere in the mess, Carl, so was Fitch, so were half a dozen other people he cared about, but he couldn't follow anyone in the chaos. All he could do was identify the ones who had invaded the station. None of them seemed to be trying too hard to get farther into the station, which he thought was strange, but he was too worried about staying alive to do much wondering about why.

* * * * *

It was disappointingly easy to get into Gordon's room. What Carmina didn't expect, though, was to see a woman standing there with a gun pointed at her.

"He gave you a gun. Interesting." She didn't bother shutting the door behind her as she strutted inside, sizing the woman up. "He really does care about you."

Jessie trembled as she kept the gun pointed at the woman who had busted into her unit, but she didn't back down or lower the gun. "You're the person who keeps sending the threats. He's not here. You won't find anything you want here."

Carmina just smiled. "You are here. That's pretty valuable, if you ask me. You are important to White and I need him to know that I'm serious about what I say when he doesn't cooperate with me."

"Gordon knows more than you think about your threats. Nothing you say to me will matter. It's bigger than whatever you have to say." Jessie put a little more pressure on the trigger of the gun.

"If nothing I say matters, then maybe *doing* something will matter more." Carmina stared down the gun before she looked the woman in the eye. "You can't do it. And you know it. What a shame."

* * * * *

The attack seemed to last days, as people hunkered down in their quarters to wait for some kind of word. Gordon went from one hall to the next trying to figure out what kind of game Carmina's people were playing. They weren't going for one of the other arms where he thought the Twist was housed, which made no sense to him at all. They weren't really coming down toward the main population centers of the Initiative either, or headed for the brass offices.

So far as he could tell, they had fought the Initiative security to a standstill in the dock and pushed outliers only a few decks beyond, without appearing to be pushing any farther. Gordon was heading down from one deck to the next trying to get a fix on Carmina herself when he finally found her, jumping up from one level of utility maintenance to another with something clutched in one hand.

He shot without even thinking, aiming for her legs as she glided from one level to the next, then braced himself behind a bulkhead to watch whether she was being accompanied and guarded by anyone. When no other answering shots came, he sighed and watched her spin through the near-zero gravity. "Good to see you again, Violet. You've lost weight."

"How kind of you to notice." Carmina's leg burned from the bullet lodged against her shin. "I was wondering when you would find me."

"Well, wonder no longer." He kept the gun trained on her, but remained behind the bulkhead. "What are you here for, Carmina? The Twist isn't on this arm. You knew that coming in here. Was all this just to kill some of the brass?"

"I'm here for information." She replied simply as she continued to bleed, but apparently she didn't care. "I got what I needed already, thank you for your diligence in your research. I only wish you would have given me more information when I asked."

"Give me a reason." He tightened his grip on his gun. "Give me one reason why I shouldn't take the open shot and kill you right now. We worked together long enough that you've earned one shot at staying alive."

"The longer you stay here and chat with me, the less likely it is that your girlfriend is going to survive." The ice of her face was unrelenting. "Tick tock, White."

His eyes widened, and he started firing. He wasn't a sharpshooter, but what he lacked in accuracy, he made up for in quantity. If she had hurt Jessie, she needed to die, and she needed to do it quickly so he could find out what the hell she had done.

Carmina managed to shoot him in turn, but not before he managed to land a few more on her. She didn't know how many more bullet wounds she could take before it impacted her mental capacity. She dropped the data core she had taken, but she'd already uploaded information she needed and corrupted it while his girlfriend lay whimpering on the floor.

"Today isn't your day to kill me." She replied before she leapt toward a reliable exit. Her crew would be waiting for her. "Maybe next time."

Gordon couldn't do anything more than float down to the closest floor and groan at the pain of the impact. She'd gotten him in the right side of his chest and probably punctured at least one of his lungs, but it wasn't the worst he'd ever felt. His only regret was that he had run out of bullets.

He saw his data core on the floor a few meters away and swore while he made his way over to it. If she had that, then she hadn't been bluffing about how long Jessie had to live. He needed to get to her, and fast. He pulled his communicator out of his pocket and breathed a sigh of gratitude that it still worked. He found Mercury's name quickly, and called her, though he knew she was probably up to her eyeballs in patients at the moment.

Mercury was already working on patching up an injured officer, but she kept her communicator out so if she heard anything from Orion, she would be able to get in contact with him. She knew he was in the line of fire. She wasn't expecting a call from Gordon White. "Doctor Finnegan here." She answered brusquely, since she didn't have time for any nonsense.

"Jessie is hurt." He groaned in pain, since he could barely keep himself conscious. "Probably in our unit, it was broken into. I'm guessing gunshot wounds. Please. You're closer than I am."

Mercury continued to work on the patient in front of her. "I'm already working on bullet wounds and you're trying to pull me away on a guess?"

"I just shot the woman who rubbed it in my face that she shot

Jessie. Bullet wounds. At least send someone for first . . ." He groaned again and sucked in a breath in pain. "Just send somebody to check. Please."

"I'll lock onto both your locations and get someone to you both. Sit tight, Mr. White. Don't die on me." Mercury ended the communication so she could dispatch some help, but she finished up with her patient to go check on Jessie herself. When she was leaving the clinic more people were coming in, but she didn't pause. Instead, she followed the communicator to Jessie's unit and tried to contact Logan on the way.

Logan was clearly running from the sound in her ear as she got in touch with him, but he answered quickly. There was gunfire in the background, but it sounded like it was at a distance. "Are you alright?"

"Yes, I wanted to make sure you were alright. Anna and Orion, I haven't heard from them . . ." She was panicking but she was hiding it the best she could. "The unit I'm going to apparently has a gunshot victim. I'm a little afraid I'm going to run into an active shooter."

"Anna got a bullet in the side, but she's already been triaged. She's pissed she got hit so early and got out of it. I haven't heard anything about Orion." He groaned again and held the communicator away from his face to yell an order at someone to get back to checking the surveillance systems, then returned to the conversation. "What deck are you going to check out? They've pulled back from everything outside five, as far as we can tell. Seems like they're trying to get back on board their ship."

"Five." She looked at the map she was following and closed her eyes for just a moment before she moved even faster. "Be careful, alright? I don't want anything to happen to you." She didn't want anyone else to get hurt, certainly not Logan or Orion.

"Do what you need to do. I'm on three. I'll come down to you." He closed the connection and ran down the stairs as quickly as he could, checking all directions as he did. There were two more invaders he had to deal with on the way, but he'd had years of practice hunting in the backwoods of his district to improve his aim.

His communicator led him directly to Mercury and he was glad to see the halls were clear immediately around her. That didn't stop him from checking every angle of the hallway around her before he got close, and he certainly didn't lower his gun. "Lead the way. I haven't had to shoot anybody for a deck and a half."

Mercury was glad to see him as soon as he appeared, and the flood of relief was evident in her eyes. She moved closer to him and gave him a quick kiss on the cheek before she moved quickly again toward Jessie and Gordon's unit. "I'm glad you're here."

"And I'm glad you're alright." He returned the kiss, but hurried after her, scanning every which way quickly as he did. "These maniacs came out of nowhere. There's been no communication from the brass, nothing whatsoever to say what they even fucking want."

"I'm sure the brass are just as confused as the rest of us." Mercury was losing faith in their leadership by the day.

When they arrived at the unit, Mercury could already see bloody footprints, and when she stepped inside, it was not easy to see Jessie in a puddle of her own blood. She was pinned to the floor with knives through her hands, and there were various cuts and bullet wounds throughout her limbs. One deep gash in her cheek. "My god. Help me get the knives out."

Logan closed the door behind them and rushed through the unit first to make sure there was no one lying in wait, then grabbed an armful of towels from the bathroom as he finished his check on his way back to Jessie. He worked as quickly as he could to get the knives out, but it was like something out of a horror film.

"I'm not a doctor, but I don't see anything major cut or shot. Torso looks completely undamaged." He pulled the knives out of Jessie's hands, glad for her sake that she was unconscious, and bandaged them with the towels as tightly as he could. "Whatever this was, it was for the pain. Which makes it personal."

"So someone took all this effort just to torture this woman? That seems incredibly extreme." Mercury helped Logan bandage the wounds, but she was more concerned about blood loss. "She's going to need a transfusion. We need to get her back to the clinic."

Logan nodded as he worked, and eventually wiped some of the blood from his hands on yet another towel before he handed his gun over to Mercury, since obviously she wasn't going to be the one to carry Jessie. "I assume you've never used one of these before?" He only waited for her to take the gun from his fingers before he reached down to heft Jessie into both arms. She would need every second they could give her.

"No, I haven't." She followed after Logan out of the unit. "But I will manage, we just need to get her to the clinic before she dies in your arms. I'll figure out the gun."

* * * * *

Up on the dock, Orion watched helplessly as Carl drifted past him, blood dripping from his clothes to form spiraling patterns in the air. More than a dozen other bodies were floating through the dock in the same fashion, presenting themselves either as target practice or morbid obstacles to getting a clean shot at the enemy. Orion had been hit by too many shots to even focus on who was left, but as he saw another shape rush past him toward the enemy vessel, he lifted his remaining arm and fired. He had no idea whether he hit anything or not, and the person's shouts were lost in the chaos of strange silence around him.

He absently saw two more figures climb into the enemy ship, but his arm wouldn't respond to his brain's command to fire at them. Had he been shot again? He wouldn't have been surprised. Bullets were still ricocheting every which way, so it was entirely possible. The hatch closed behind the last two figures, and Orion wished he could breathe a sigh of relief. Anything approaching a sigh hurt too much, though, and wouldn't have been worth the effort. It was all he could do just to breathe.

He pulled one of his arms up near his face, and managed to tighten his grip enough to activate his communicator, though he had no idea if anyone was still even alive to answer him. "Fitch." He groaned through the pain. "Report."

There was a long stretch of silence. Fitch never answered.

The next thing he heard was a message from the brass saying that the enemy threat had been neutralized and everyone was to stay in their unit until everything was clear. Just as Orion was starting to black out, there was a familiar face that appeared above him in a haze of red.

Mercury had a hard time holding back tears as she looked down at Orion, but as soon as Jessie had been left in someone else's care, she was adamant about going to look for him. Her fingers were gentle as she caressed his face before she turned her attention to quick-patching his wounds. "I'm not going to let you die, do you hear me, Orion?"

He nodded, or at least he thought he nodded, but he was completely limp in her hands, floating without anything to stop him between the guiding columns of the dock. "Good. That's good. Wouldn't want . . . to die . . . without permission. Looks bad . . . on a resume . . ."

Even when he was dying, he was joking. Mercury didn't know if she should laugh or cry, but she did know it probably wouldn't be the last time she saw him so close to death, not the way things were going.

16

Anna was released from medical supervision the day after the attack, but most weren't so lucky. She checked on Orion a few times before she was sent home, but she limited her attempted visits for fear of running into Mercury, and he was unconscious every time she tried.

After release, she went back to her unit per her instructions, but Logan wasn't there. Anna wondered if he was avoiding her or hanging around to see Mercury, but she tried not to think about it. It would only add more pain to an already rough situation.

It was much later in the afternoon when Logan came home, closing the door slowly behind him before she could hear him slump back against it in exhaustion. He didn't even see her at first, since his eyes were half-closed and he was clearly so tired he didn't even look around his own unit.

Eventually, he opened his eyes and saw her lying on the couch nearby. He gave her a fatigued smile, then managed to cross the room toward her. It looked more like he was just falling artfully in her direction rather than walking, from the way he stumbled with nearly every step, but he eventually made it over to her and fell next to the couch before resting his head against her hip.

"I went to check on you this morning, but you were still out of it. Then when I went back this afternoon, they said you'd been discharged."

"Are you alright?" She asked as she ran her fingers through his hair. There was still jealousy in her thoughts as she looked at him, but he looked genuinely exhausted. Maybe he hadn't been with Mercury after all. "I was worried about you. I . . . wondered if you were with her."

He shook his head beneath her touch, but he didn't seem surprised by the question. "I was in the area yesterday during the last part of the attack and ran security for her while she cleaned up some of the wounded. I didn't see her again until the Council meeting this morning. And that was just by hologram. Since the brass isn't doing shit about the attack, we figured it was on us. She's been in the clinic most of the day monitoring the wounded and taking shifts on the code team."

He reached up to take one of her hands gently, sighing against her side. "A hundred and twenty-six wounded. Sixty-eight already pronounced dead. And counting." He squeezed his eyes tightly shut as if he could block out the numbers. "Nothing is worth that. I don't care what they were after, nothing is worth slaughtering innocent people who are just trying to hide in their units."

Anna agreed as she closed her eyes as well. "I heard that the attackers tapped into our network. No one can figure out what they were looking for or what they took." She opened her eyes eventually to look at him again, but the fatigue was clearly shared between them.

"They want to interrogate Jessica Rogers and Gordon White. The network tap came through their unit and her injuries look like torture. Like someone was trying to get something from her." She knew he knew what Jessie looked like, and Logan was the reason she was still alive, so Anna was told. "You saved her life. She almost bled out."

"Gordon called Mercury and said one of the attackers was taunting him, telling him she was going to die if he didn't hurry up. We were closer." He shook his head against her waist and kept his eyes shut.

"The shit these people do to each other up here . . . The shit they've all done to themselves . . . They've convinced themselves the world has to be a certain way, and it doesn't. Jessie got strapped down with a pair of knives like a low-G crucifixion. And with the way her legs were shot to hell, who knows if she'll walk again."

"But the brass is right, if only about this. It had to be personal. And my guess is it's personal against Gordon. He's a shady fucker, but unless he's got a side hobby of molesting people, there's no reasonable explanation for somebody being hated that much."

"Then maybe he's someone we need to get to know." Anna massaged his temples slowly, hoping to ease even a tiny piece of the day's anxiety. "It's getting worse, being up here. Things are getting tough." She didn't have to explain what she meant. "I'm scared . . . I . . . I miss you. I worry about you. Us. Especially with this kind of shit."

"I miss you too." He reached up to lift the bottom edge of her shirt just so he could kiss her bare skin directly. He didn't push for anything more, though, since she had been injured and he hadn't slept in nearly forty-eight hours. "I thought at first that we could just get past it, ignore it while we're together. But I also know you're with him just about all the time when you're not with me. I've stopped going up to the bar at the dock because I know the chances are good that you two are gonna be up there at Nav control. Which is what you're tasked with doing, I get it. I just . . ."

He sighed against her skin and went back to resting her forehead against her. "I just feel like we hardly got the chance to even be with each other before somebody put a gun to our heads and turned all four of us into somebody else."

Anna was quiet because she hated the fact she felt dirty and guilty for the time she spent with Orion, even though she actually liked spending time with him. But she wasn't in love with him. Was she? No. She loved Logan. "And I'm afraid that every time you're with her that you'll never want to come back to me. There *is* something different, something has changed. But I don't know what it is."

"How I feel about you hasn't changed." He said without moving away. "I love you. Nothing they do or force us to do can change that."

"So I won't lose you?" She ran her fingers through his hair again and tugged slightly, as if she was going to possess him by holding into his hair. "You're still mine?"

He paused briefly without answering, then gave a grunt of effort as he pushed himself up to his feet. Instead of walking away, he put a knee on the couch beside her hip and leaned down to rest his forehead against hers. He had been busy the past two days, that much was obvious from the scent of him, but the scent was all Logan.

"I'm still yours." He sighed the promise, his hands pressing into the cushion on either side of her to hold himself up and keep from aggravating her injuries. "I'll always be yours. That's what I want and what I promised. That hasn't changed."

Anna put her hands on his face and she was surprised when her eyes burned with tears and those tears fell down her cheeks. "I love you so much. I am always yours. Orion and I are friends, but I am in love with *you*."

Logan remained perched over her for as long as he could, but he finally kissed her and slumped slowly onto the edge of the couch cushions. "I need a bath and about a week of sleep. Join me for both?"

Anna nodded and followed him off of the couch when he finally got up to make his way for a relaxing bath. Before she walked into the bathroom, though, she glanced over to where she had left her communicator and didn't see any new messages. Whenever Orion woke up, she hoped he would think to send her something to let her know that it was okay to visit him.

* * * * *

Whenever Mercury had the chance, she was sitting next to Orion's bed, checking over his monitor to make sure he received the best care possible. She was exhausted from the near-endless stream of victims, but she wanted to be there when he woke up. His injuries themselves weren't life-threatening, but his blood loss had been, for a while.

It was late in the afternoon a day and a half after the attack that Orion finally began to show signs of coming around, and he did so with a jerk that nearly tore the IV out of his arm, though he groaned the moment afterward.

"Ugh . . . I knew I should've invested in that new mattress . . . this bed is for shit." His eyes were still closed and he couldn't feel anyone actually holding onto him or leaning on him, but he knew he was in the clinic just from the infernal beeping. He winced without even opening his eyes, and when he tried, he immediately closed them again. "Anybody there?"

"I'm here." Mercury replied as she sat down next to him. She had momentarily gotten up to check on her other patients through her communicator. As soon as he pulled his IV out, she was there, fixing it. "Are you feeling alright? Do you need more pain medication?"

He shook his head cautiously and tried to open his eyes again and stopped immediately. "I want to stay awake a little longer before I hit too much more on the meds. If you're giving me the option, I assume that's a good sign. Can you turn down the lights a little?"

"Sure." Mercury went to the holographic interface and dimmed the lights as low as they would go before she returned to his side. "You lost a lot of blood and you suffered a concussion and seven bullet wounds, but none to vital organs. The blood loss was most concerning, but you'll get better, day by day."

"No wonder my head feels like a busted gearbox." He grunted under his breath, just to keep from really making noise about his level of pain. At least he was able to open his eyes a little once she turned down the lights. He didn't move his body but she could see him flexing his fingers and toes, just to make sure they all still worked. He looked her up and down without moving his head. "What about you?"

"Me? I'm fine, I wasn't in the line of fire." She reached for his hand and held it in both of hers gingerly, as though she thought he might break. "I've been working like crazy, but I didn't get riddled with bullets." Mercury brought his hand to her lips and kissed his skin gently. "Anna was discharged earlier. She had a gunshot wound to the side and a dislocated shoulder, but otherwise she's alright."

She could feel him tense a little in pain as he nodded, since one of the bullets had gone through his shoulder and it hurt to move his neck. "Thank you. I'm glad to hear that." He squeezed her hand, gingerly at first and then a little more forcefully when he realized it didn't hurt too much to move his hand. "What about Logan?"

"I haven't seen him much. The last I heard from him he was going home to get a shower and some sleep, he's been extremely busy trying to get information on what happened, who was involved, and why. He wasn't harmed, though." She squeezed his hand a little bit more once she knew his hand was fine.

"I hate seeing you like this, but it could be a lot worse. Carl is . . . well, he's alive, but that's not saying much. He shouldn't be, with his injuries. Fitch is in a medically-induced coma as well. I've been monitoring her baby, she had a severe head wound and multiple gunshots, but it doesn't look like she'll have any lasting brain damage. We'll have to see how she responds when she wakes up."

A wound through his side made the sigh that escaped him painful, and he cut it short. "Carl won't take long to pull through. When he does, try not to ask too many questions or publish anything about him. You'll get shut down. He's a freak, but ever since he started working security in our teens, they've done their best to keep just how freakish he is under wraps."

He pulled her in closer with his good hand, and ran his fingers over the side of her face. "I'm so glad you're alright. When I passed out, I didn't know what the world was gonna look like when I woke up, if I did at all. I'm glad it looks like you."

"I've been here as often as I could be. I wanted to be here when you woke up." Mercury leaned in and kissed his lips gently before she pulled back to look into his dark eyes. "I was so scared that I was going to lose you. Body after body came in, and I was afraid you were going to be one of the dead ones. There's over sixty dead, Orion."

He closed his eyes again at that number, since it hurt worse than any of his injuries. "What about the people who attacked us? I hope we gave better than we got. What the hell did they want?"

Mercury shook her head. "Logan said something about an information breach, but I didn't get much more than that. I don't really know. I haven't had time to ask to know more, there are over a hundred people injured here and we don't have the doctors or staff to keep up. I've only had a couple of hours of sleep in over two days."

"Sounds like you could use a quick medically-induced coma yourself." He attempted a smile, squeezing her hand again. "Don't run yourself ragged. You can't save people the way you do if you can't see straight."

"They trained us on Seven how to work situations like this in case of times of crisis. I'm alright." Mercury kissed his forehead and sat up straighter. "Is there anything I can get for you?"

"No, I think I'm alright. I might need some pain meds in a little while, since this whole being conscious thing doesn't seem to be working out for me." He ran his thumb along the back of her hand as he held it, searching her eyes for anything beyond the medical professionalism he knew she had to maintain. "I love you." He said finally, giving her a small smile. "All I could think of every time I got shot was that it's been a while since I had a chance to tell you that."

Mercury responded by kissing his lips gently again before her green eyes focused on his eyes again. "I love you too." She sighed before she said anything else, but her hand held his firmly. "I miss you. I miss laughing with you, being us."

"That makes two of us." He looked up as if trying to look at the bandage he could feel along one side of his skull. "The concussion is not gonna do some kind of personality-alteration shit to me or anything, right? Because if something's gonna kill my sense of humor, then I need to make sure I'm as funny as possible with the time I've got left."

"No, a concussion won't do anything like that." She ran her thumb along his bottom lip and pressed her lips against his again afterward. "Don't scare me like that. I don't like wondering if you're dead or alive."

"Well good. More things we agree on. I didn't enjoy wondering that about myself either." He smiled under her lips, attempting to move as little as possible so as not to have to feel the pain of his multiple injuries. "Normally I just stick to flying. I'm better at shooting people if my ship is doing most of the work for me. Hand to hand has always been Carl's department, and I prefer it that way."

She still didn't like knowing that it was probably only a matter of time before Orion was in the thick of it again. "We need to get away from here." Mercury whispered against his lips before she stole another kiss. "This was not what I trained for, this is not what I dedicated my life toward. I'm scared we're going to end up dead if we don't get away."

He gave her a long look as she lingered with her lips near his, and nodded without flinching for once. "I've been looking into supply ships. Switching out. Getting enough distance to get to Earth. All four of us."

Mercury certainly wouldn't want to leave Logan behind, but it made her feel a little strange that he was thinking about the future in the context of the four of them instead of the two of them. She nodded and went to kiss him again when she heard her communicator going off.

She looked over and saw a scrolling message from Anna, wondering if Orion was awake and how he was doing. She almost felt like Anna was always interfering, but she tried not to think about it that way. "Anna is worried about you too. She's been checking on you since she woke up."

"Well, she probably wants to make sure I'm actually and truly dead. I'm a mean son of a bitch when I get into instruction mode." His weak smile told her he knew it wasn't like that at all, but he didn't push it too far. "I've been looking into it just because I know it's . . . possible . . . that one or the other of you might be pregnant before I can find an open window. They don't deserve to be here any more than we do."

Mercury agreed but it was clear there was a lot more behind her eyes she wasn't saying. "Things will undoubtedly get worse after this attack. With so many more people dead . . . they'll push us more. Push babies more. I don't know what their motive is about that, but it has to be on their minds. Maybe if Anna and I can get the schedules down perfectly, we can make it happen faster."

He didn't look happy about that, but he didn't disagree with her either, since he knew she was right. "We're getting off this station. Maybe not this week, considering I don't think I could pilot a toaster right now, but we're getting off." He had resolution in his eyes she'd seen from him only a few times when he was being fully serious. It had been there when he had married her, it had been there when he told her he loved her after they had been cross-matched with the Bickfords, and it was there in his promise to get them away from Nine. "I'll find a way. No matter what roadblocks they throw at us."

She kissed him one more time, her lips tasting his breath, his emotion, and revealing her own before she grabbed his communicator instead of her own. "Do you think you can respond to her? Or would you like me to?"

"I can answer her. You need to get some rest. I've got one working hand." He flexed his hand and then caressed her face before she got too far away. "How long before you expect I'll be back on my feet? I feel like something shot me in the foot. Did I get a toe shot off?"

"You have all of your toes." She replied with a small laugh. "Your feet are fine. You're probably just achy from the blood loss and being stuck in bed." Mercury stole one more smoldering kiss, and another heaving breath before she knew she needed to back off. Apparently she had figured out how to be more aggressive in her kissing.

He moaned under the touch unashamedly, though he realized a little late that he didn't actually know if they were alone in the room. "Well, I'm gonna stay stuck for a little longer. You go save some lives and be amazing. Don't worry about me."

"Call me if you need anything, alright?" She ran her fingers along his cheek and started to get up slowly. "Anything. I'll be here."

"Anything?" He said with an obviously-scandalous grin back up at her. "I might be pretty heavy on that call button if you give me a window that wide."

Mercury smirked and shook her head just a little bit. "Is there something of that nature that you want right now? I'll let you look, but you can't touch. You're not healed enough for touching."

"All the more reason for me to heal quickly. You said I lost a lot of blood, so if I get even a glimpse, I'm pretty sure of how I'd be making use of whatever blood I've got left. Better wait until I can actually get my hands on you again." He managed to wink at her with another up-and-down look, just glad to see her smiling. "I'll try and be patient until you certify me healthy enough to get you back into a shower where I like you."

Her cheeks flushed but it felt normal and it certainly made her smile. Orion always made her smile. "I'll be glad to reward you for all that healing as soon as I can." Mercury watched him a little bit longer before she made her way to the door. "I love you." She emphasized before she put her hand on the door. "I'll be back to check on you as soon as I can."

17

When Fitch came to, there were a number of things she might have been expecting. Some kind of afterlife would have made perfect sense, given her last memories before blacking out, but the strange sensations around her certainly didn't feel like an afterlife.

She might have expected to wake up in a hospital bed, even, but that didn't seem to be the case either. Instead, she could immediately feel that she was still mostly-weightless, so somewhere near the center of a station, but she was also completely naked.

Not only that, she was also lying on something fairly hard, and she was wet. The moment after she began to return to consciousness and her mind made all such discoveries, she felt something warm drip against her shoulder and felt the sponge move down gingerly to avoid one of her injuries.

When the sponge withdrew and she opened her eyes, she could see Kazuo kneeling next to her, wringing it out with one hand while his other arm rested in a sling pinned tight against his chest. Not exactly the way she might have expected to wake up, especially considering the last time she had seen him.

Kameron was glad for the dim lighting when she fully opened her eyes, and she was glad the first thing she saw was Kazuo, since he was the last thing she'd thought about. It was strange to realize he was that important to her, since she figured her last thoughts would be about some beautiful, naked woman. "Am I hallucinating right now?"

He jumped when she spoke, since he hadn't noticed her waking up, but he smiled weakly, bringing the newly-soaped sponge back over to continue her bath. "I don't know. Are there pink elephants or leprechauns involved? Then you might be hallucinating. If you're just talking about the bath and the being alive part, then no, that's all real."

"Didn't mean to scare you." She replied after he jumped, but she was glad to see him, even if it was a hallucination. "I'm kinda surprised about the alive part. I thought for sure I'd be seeing you on the other side, sitting on fluffy clouds."

"Please. Neither of us are fluffy clouds people." He glared at her with a smile and continued the bath along her shoulder and neck. "You got shot to hell, that's for sure, and you took a hell of a crack to the head, but nothing life-threatening. And the baby is alright." He gave her a weak smile and glanced down at her stomach, where there was a small monitor taped to her side. "They're keeping a close eye on it, but the doc said none of the trauma should affect the kid."

"That's good." She didn't look down at her stomach, even though she was happy her baby wasn't harmed. "I wasn't really thinking about the baby when I went into that. I didn't care." She admitted even though it might be hurtful to him to hear that she had momentarily not cared about their baby. "I was so angry after talking to that bastard Kaplan that I wanted to kill anything I could." Kameron didn't know if he was even aware she had gone to plead his case, but he mattered to her.

Kazuo's smile wilted at that comment, but he nodded anyway, since he could understand that impulse. "I take it he's not too interested in taking extraordinary measures in my case."

"No. I'm sorry." Now that she could see him, the pain of knowing for sure that he was going to die tore through her chest. "Fuck. You can't die. You're supposed to be the good parent. This kid has no hope if it's just me. It'll die of sugar overdose or some shit."

That made Kazuo smile in spite of the morbid conversation, and he continued on with her bath as if nothing was happening, lifting her arm to set it on the edge of the tub so he could reach her side. "I've known I was terminal since I was ten. Knowing I'm gonna die isn't really news to me. I'm not even sure I'd be a good parent, all things considered. I'm a workaholic, and let's face it, the kid would grow up with the most twisted sense of humor in the universe. Probably best if that doesn't get passed on too directly."

She shook her head slowly, though it ached to move. Every muscle in her screamed. "No, it's not best." Kam grabbed his hand with the sponge in it, but she winced. "I was fucking dying and I was thinking about you. Not some naked chick under a waterfall, though that sounds incredible. I was thinking about you. You matter to me. It's not better if you're dead. It's worse."

He held her hand after she grabbed his and leaned into the tub to kiss her once, though it wasn't something they had done much of in their strange relationship. There was no heat behind the kiss, none of the fire he had seen when they'd had their threesome weeks before, but he cared about Kameron, and it showed in his kiss.

"I was unconscious for most of the fight." He sat back on his knees beside the tub. "When I woke up, the emergency lights were still on and it was a while before anyone could explain to me what was going on. But as soon as they told me there was fighting, I knew you'd be in the middle of it. I just hoped I would see you again."

Kameron looked him over as best she could in the tub and in her position before she just closed her eyes. She didn't have the physical strength to kiss him back, and he'd moved back too far to pull him close. "I didn't go in hoping to die, but by the end, I thought for sure I would. Everything about this place is fucked up. The brass. The training. People dying for no fucking reason. What is this kid going to come into? A life of fear and no dad? I had a dad. This kid needs their dad. *Two* moms and a dad."

That made him laugh, but she could hear how difficult it was for him to laugh, since he couldn't take a full breath. "*Three* moms and a dad, thank you very much. If you deserve a hot blonde somewhere, you'd better make sure she's got a sister who likes skinny guys."

He continued with the bath once she laid her head back against the wall of the tub. "The kid is gonna come into Eleusis, if I have anything to say about it. It's gonna grow up under a sky that isn't trying to kill everyone beneath it. That's all that matters. Get off this station and get to a place where people actually stand a chance."

She didn't try to resist him bathing her. It felt good to be clean, and she couldn't have resisted even if she wanted to. "Three moms and a dad, then." Kameron agreed and closed her eyes. "Did you want to give me a bath just to see me naked? I'm sure I look like swiss cheese right now."

"I wanted to give you a bath because you were a fucking mess." He coughed a short laugh. "There's so many casualties, the medical staff doesn't exactly have time for sponge-baths up in the clinic right now, so once they pronounced you unlikely-to-die, I asked to bring you back here to see you the rest of the way. I've been hospitalized enough times myself that I can change an IV and check stitches. Which means I'm your nurse until you're back on your feet."

He shrugged once she opened her eyes to look at him again. "But now that you're mostly cleaned up, you should realize you're a lot hotter than swiss cheese. I've never once looked at cheese or any other food product and wished I was healthy enough to fuck it."

Kameron laughed and winced again, but her smile lingered, so apparently she didn't care about the pain. "Well, aren't we just a pair." She felt lucky to have Kazuo on her side, since he was probably the person she cared about most on the whole station, even though Carl and Orion were pretty important to her too. "Once moving doesn't feel so painful, we'll work something out. A dying man deserves to have as much sex as he wants."

That made him laugh again, but it was fairly appropriate as conversations went, since her chest was one of the last parts of her that he needed to clean. Rather than using the sponge, he squeezed out some of the soapy water high on her collarbone and let it stream down over her, then leaned in to do the actual washing with his bare hand. She hadn't suffered any injuries on her torso aside from a graze to her side, but he figured he should be thorough.

"I'll have to check with Melissa and see what her status is these days. She was more into you than her own match, I'm pretty sure, but she also seemed to like my dick more than you do. I'm glad you don't seem to completely hate it, but if we can run with the best of both worlds, I'd rather see you happy with whatever time I've got left."

Kameron continued to smile, since she had thoroughly enjoyed the way things worked between the three of them. "You might be the only man in the world capable of winning my love. Who would have thought that was possible."

"Not me, that's for sure." He ran his hands freely over her breasts for a while longer than was strictly necessary to get her clean, but then eventually leaned in and kissed her again, just because he wanted to. "I love you too, Kam." He grinned against her lips and kissed her again, his hand lingering along her chest just to reassure himself that her heart was steady, or would be, in time.

* * * * *

Even in medically induced sleep, Jessie still had nightmares. She hadn't stood much of a chance against Carmina, and once she didn't have a weapon anymore, Carmina made it a game to torture her. Not only physically, but apparently the woman had read up on her, since she knew all the worst things to tell her.

Jessie not only had nightmares about being attacked again, about being cut open with knives as Carmina had promised, but also about being attacked by Gordon, being abandoned by him. Carmina had not skimped on the details of what Gordon had done before Jessie had met the man. Her imagination had run with it the longer they kept her under, and when she finally woke, the immediate smell of medical cleanliness made her think she was a prisoner, with Carmina or Gordon waiting to cut out her insides.

Jessie screamed involuntarily, and tried to move. Moving was a terrible idea. Everything hurt.

"It's alright, it's alright." Gordon's voice was there immediately, plucked out of her nightmares and placed right at her bedside. "Don't try to move too much, baby. You've got one arm and one leg in casts. Take it slow, you're safe. You're alright."

Hearing his voice didn't calm her, it just made her feel even more afraid and confused at the same time, and she looked panicked as she stared at him. *He killed a man by systematically removing his organs after paralyzing him. The man was awake the entire time.* That was what Carmina had told her. Was it true? Why would he do that to someone? Was he capable of that?

"Don't . . . I . . ."

"Shhh . . . she's gone. You're alright." He continued, and she could feel his touch on her non-casted arm, soft and loving as it had always been. "There's been a lot of damage to your arms and legs. You've been asleep for two days while they finished the surgeries on you. There's still some wait-and-see with your hands, but for the rest, the doctors say you'll be back to full mobility soon."

Jessie tried to wiggle her arm away so he wouldn't touch her. Was he going to hurt her? She both wanted to be left alone and wanted to curl into him at the same time. "You're not going to hurt me?" She rasped her words, since she had been intubated for her surgeries until that morning.

She could hear his confusion in the pause that followed, and his grip tightened on her arm slightly, still without being harsh. "I would never hurt you, Jessie. That's the last thing in the universe I want."

"She took the core." Jessie figured he probably knew that she had lost it, maybe he wanted her to, she didn't know. "She connected it to the network. She showed me images." He could see that she was about to cry. "She told me I was one of your toys that you weren't bored of yet."

The look on Gordon's face hardened, but his touch on her arm softened as his hand moved slowly up to her shoulder, one of the few places on her arm that hadn't been abused. "You've never been a toy to me, Jess."

As she came fully awake, she could tell they were alone in a clinic observation room with the door closed, the lights dimmed almost to sleep level. "I'll answer any questions you have about any images she showed you, if you want to hear the answers. But I've never once wanted to hurt you. I never will."

Jessie shook her head slowly. "I don't know why you would do that to someone. I don't want to know." Her stomach twisted as she thought about what she saw, and what she was told.

"How do I know?" Her voice trembled as her eyes burned with tears. She remembered screaming from the pain until she couldn't scream anymore, especially when her hands had been flayed open. "How do I know you won't hurt me? Why didn't you tell me? Why did they come after me? They didn't hurt you." She could see that he was more or less unscathed. "How do I know what's real with you? How do I know how you really feel?"

"You knew before she got here." He said quietly, sounding more sad than angry or upset. There was certainly no blame in his eyes and his touch didn't move from her shoulder. "I didn't tell you because there are a thousand things you don't know. And the things she told you about, judging by the history in our unit, aren't a tenth of what I've done."

He took a deep breath and looked down at her arms and legs, riddled with bandages and braces just because she had been the most important person to him on the station. "Carmina was always very interested in that particular story. Before I met you at the liftoff site to come up here, I drove directly from an air transit hub on the shore of the Great Lakes. I'd been working there for the past six months, picking up information for our work and following leads on human trafficking the Consortium was running through there. Mostly young children, but a few young teenagers. Not too young for some."

The hard look in his eyes was back, but there was no apology to go along with it. There never had been, she realized. "The day before I left to meet you, all twenty-seven workers with that airlift station mysteriously disappeared. They've been missing ever since. Last I checked, the authorities haven't recovered a single body. If I had to bet on it, I'd imagine it'll be summer before they do, at this point."

He looked down at her again, and slowly removed his touch from her shoulder. "I'm not sorry for the things I've done. I've always known what I was doing and chosen to do it. I don't work by accident or fleeting emotion. But that includes you. I chose to be with you. You're the only person in this world that I want to be with. Honestly, you're the one person in the world I would never harm, even to get what I want. Everyone else is secondary and expendable, at least to me. You can believe that or not. That's your choice. But no matter what you choose, it won't change the way I feel about you."

Tears burned as they trailed down her cheeks, but it still didn't change the conflict she felt. "I love you, but I'm scared of you." She replied in her rough, airy rasp. "I'm scared of what might happen. She told me if she ever saw me again, she'd kill me. I'm not the person you need, I couldn't shoot her. I can't defend myself or anyone else. She was right. I'm not strong enough for any of this. I don't deserve to go to Eleusis."

Gordon paused for a long time to consider all of that, but then eventually moved his hand slowly up over her shoulder to the unmarked side of her face, caressing her cheek with the back of his fingers even as he felt her shake in fear of him. The look in her eyes was the one he had been hoping never to see there, but he had known it was only a matter of time. Anyone who knew anything about him would be afraid of him, or at least wary.

"You, of everyone here on this god-forsaken station, deserve Eleusis. You deserve the house we talked about. Porch facing south toward the coast and a bedroom with a west window to watch the sunsets. I've never heard of an inability to kill as a disqualifier for deserving a life of peace." He ran his fingers along her temple, moving slowly so that she wouldn't feel like he was threatening her.

"I love you, Jessie. Now, even more than before, you know

that's not something that comes easily for a monster like me. I did my best to kill Carmina on her way back to her ship, but I don't know if I managed or not. All she got the chance to do was hit my leg a few times. When I see her again, I plan to take a year killing her for every bullet she put through you. I can be very patient that way." He took in a deep breath, and Jessie actually saw a tear forming in his eye, though he showed no other signs of crying. "I made a mistake in assuming what she would be coming for. I should never have left you alone, and I won't again unless you want me to. I'm sorry."

"I don't want to be alone." She meant it in so many ways, but ultimately, she felt too frightened to be alone, even though she was still frightened of him. "But I don't want to die either. I want to be happy. I've never been happy until I was with you. Now I don't know what to think."

In spite of everything else, Gordon smiled slightly at that comment, and his caress continued along her cheek. "I'm glad you've been happy. I'm normally very good at being able to tell what people are thinking or feeling, but I've never been much good at identifying when someone is really happy. Too much of the world is too good at faking it."

He wanted to kiss her, wanted to hold her, wanted to take her out of the clinic and keep her safe in their unit in case Carmina found something in the information she had taken and decided to come back for more, but he kept his distance. She was afraid of him, and that wasn't something he was going to encourage.

"I'll do whatever you want me to do. I'll stay, I'll go, I'll go back to the unit, cook dinner and start from the beginning. Everything I am, everything I've done, you can have it all. You always could. Just say the word, and whatever you want, it's done."

"I . . ." She didn't know what to say, but she knew she didn't want him to go. Afraid or not, she was still in love with him. Some of her fears were that he wouldn't want her. Her mind was all over the place. "I want you to stay. Just . . . tell me something good. Half my nightmares are you cutting me open or telling me that you want someone better and stronger than me. Tell me something good to hold onto."

He thought about it for a moment, but the smile that crossed his lips was profoundly sad. His fingertips traced the side of her face as she watched him. "Ever since I was ten years old, I've slept with either a knife or a gun within arm's reach. No matter where

I was. I've had to use both, more than once, and the knife I had to use twice on the person I was sleeping next to. Here on the station, with you, is the first time I've ever slept without it. You're the first person I've felt safe with. No one else will ever be that first for me."

A few more tears slipped down her cheeks but it wasn't because it made her happy to hear that, it made her sad that even though he wasn't afraid of her, she was still afraid of him. She just nodded, but she couldn't even wipe away her own tears, her hands and her arms were too badly injured. "I'm glad you feel safe with me. I wanted . . . want you to trust me."

He reached up to wipe away the tears for her, since he knew her hands couldn't. "There's no one I trust more. In this world or any other." He turned the gesture into a caress and moved his thumb across her lips without moving away. "What can I get for you? I can talk to the doctors to see if they have anything to keep you from dreaming. You need some real rest after what you've been through."

Jessie nodded again slowly. "I don't want to dream anymore. It hurts."

"Then you won't." He promised, as another tear of his own fell. "They want to keep you sedated for a couple more days, so that your treatment can get under way. But I'm not leaving. I'll be here when you wake up. I promise."

She looked into his eyes after his promise and wondered if he really meant it. If he would really be there when she woke up, or if he would change his mind. She hoped he meant it and, at the same time, she was scared he did. "Okay."

When one of the doctors came and administered the sedation, Gordon finally began to relax a little, though he didn't move away from the bed where Jessie rested. She was in terrible shape, more thoroughly injured than he knew the drugs allowed her to really feel while she was awake.

"And you're absolutely certain that this sedation will keep her from dreaming while she's out?" Gordon snapped at the woman who came in. He was partly irritated because neither Mercury nor Blue, the doctor he preferred to work with, had been available, but the dozen doctors the Initiative had on hand were all over-worked at the moment, and he could only be pushy so far without drawing undue attention to himself.

"Yes." The doctor replied with her own irritation. "We have a new chemist on staff, since we've had to use more natural methods in this time of emergency. And the leadership thinks that we should use medications that are based on Eleusis vegetation since we will be living there soon enough. If you would like to speak with the chemist, I can retrieve her for you."

"Make me an appointment some day next week. I do want to talk to her about whatever we're dealing with." He knew he was being officious, but Brits bothered him just on principle, and the condescending doctor was no different. "I'm sure you have other patients that require your attention. Go on and do your work. If something changes, believe me, you'll hear me shouting about it."

"I have no doubt." The doctor checked over Jessie's vitals once more before she grabbed her tablet and moved out of the room. "If you truly wish to make an appointment with the chemist, you will need to contact Ms. Tanaka yourself."

Gordon nearly rolled his eyes, but he contained himself, if only barely. "Once upon a time, service was a word that meant something." He didn't even look at the woman as she headed out of the room, but he did pull out his communicator. Encrypting a message on his own private network took longer than he would have liked, and would take longer until he could reconfigure and re-secure his data core again, but utilizing it in its present state wasn't an option.

Need to talk about casualties and implications of theft. In Jessie's room. Find me when you're able. He had no need or desire to rush into the conversations ahead of him, and certainly no intention of leaving the room while Jessie was in such terrible condition. The rest of his colleagues could come to him to discuss what needed to happen going forward.

It wasn't long after he sent his message that there was a knock on Jessie's door, and when he went to greet the person on the other side, Tatyana was standing there. "I was glad to find out that you didn't die in all of this. Most of our friends remained unharmed, actually."

He let Tatyana into the room and closed the door before he answered. "That's because most of our friends know how most of Carmina's friends think and could fight accordingly. I know about two of my own unit who are still on the fence in critical condition, but two question marks out of a dozen is something I can live with."

Tatyana looked past him at his match and shook her head. "I

heard about her too. Will she be alright?"

"Eventually." He answered without looking at her, heading back to the seat he had claimed for the past two days. "No major organ damage, but she'll need some fairly extensive physical therapy once her wounds have mostly patched up. They tell me they won't know an exact timeline until she gets up and starts moving, but they estimate about a month before she's back to herself again."

Tatyana didn't say anything immediately and she stared at Jessica. "I'm surprised that Carmina went to all that effort to harm her. Clearly she was trying to send a message. I'm sorry that it had to happen to someone who isn't really involved in all of this."

"She's as involved as either of us." He countered without looking away from Jessie. "Carmina targeted her because she knew it was her one shot at getting to me. I think she wanted to impair my judgment. Time will tell if she's succeeded, but if not, she's as close as she'll ever get."

He sighed and finally tore his eyes away from Jessie. "What's worse, at least for us right now, is that Carmina got to Hyacinth. Uploaded the data and wiped it clean. I'm sure she left a few nasty bugs for me to deal with too, but everything I've managed to gather so far is Carmina's now."

"How did she get it? She didn't get to you, so . . . you left it behind?" Tatyana's expression was unreadable, but clearly she wasn't happy about the fact that their valuable information had been lost due to his misjudgement.

"I thought she would target me. So yes, I left it with Jessie when I went to confront Carmina." Gordon had never been a fan of people who attempted to hide their own mistakes, and he wasn't about to try and hide his own. "And now, because she believes she can walk in, take what she wants, and leave again with minimal loss of life on the side of her own people, she'll believe she can do that in the future as well."

"And even if we manage to get a Twist off of here, we won't know a damn thing about it." She let out a low growl of a sigh, running a hand through her bright blonde hair. "I imagine Carmina will send you a message to gloat about her victory. Let me know when that happens. Until then, we'll keep a closer eye on your unit, and we'll get you a new core with the accessibility the last one had and all of our updated information. Minus whatever was lost, of course."

"I have the needful components in my lab. I've already started rebuilding the main systems as much as I can from here." His fingers tightened into a fist when he thought about Carmina sending a message to gloat, but he consciously relaxed them one by one. "I've already been informed that the brass intends to question both me and Jessie with regard to why she was targeted so specifically. I have some ideas on sidesteps, I just wanted you to be aware."

"If I were you, I'd let her do most of the talking when it comes to an interrogation. She knows the least, and she was honestly targeted without cause. Well, we know the cause. But she's innocent to any involvement, other than sleeping with you." She looked him up and down and then looked at her modified communicator. "The brass is going to make significant changes after this. Everyone will be monitored closely. Watch your step. And hers, since I know she's going to be jumpy after this."

"Jumpy is one way to put it." He looked back at Jessie but she hadn't moved, which he knew was for the best. "If they decide to execute me, you're the best chance we have up here of getting a Twist disengaged and transported to Earth. From there, well," he looked back over at Tatyana with a sigh, since there were some subjects that he truly preferred to stay away from, "I assume you know who you can go to for help in recovering my work."

She just nodded at first. "I have some ideas, certainly." Tatyana was always careful in what she said, so when she spoke, there were often pauses. "They won't execute you. Especially not now, not with all the people dead and with so much uncertainty about the attack. If anything, they'll lock you away. If that happens, we won't leave you behind."

"Yes you will." There was no anger in his tone as he said it, but there wasn't any doubt either. "You'll get the Twist and get to Earth and I'll deal with whatever cage they put me in. You of all people know that a rescue attempt would be a waste of resources if the goal is in sight. And if the goal isn't in sight, then you might as well leave me in the cage anyway, since that's all this planet ultimately is to begin with."

Tatyana looked at him for a moment and shook her head, though there was a small smile on her lips. "I'm not *completely* heartless, you know. Sometimes a rescue attempt is worth the effort, if the person is valuable enough to keep. What would you have us do with your match if you were locked away and she's clearly a liability? She knows too much already to be left behind, and she isn't enough of an asset to put her to work. She's your problem, so in order to protect ourselves, you have to be around to take care of your problems."

"You underestimate her abilities." His tone quieted in ways he knew Tatyana would recognize as a warning. "But then again, so does she, so I suppose that error can be forgiven on your part."

She didn't agree with his assessment of the woman that he had chosen for his match, but she didn't get a chance to say so before all of their communicators went off at once with a station-wide message. Tatyana opened her communicator first and requested the message be read out loud.

Initiates of Station Nine,

As all of you know, we have again suffered a great loss. Friends, lovers, and comrades were lost in the attack. We have taken great care in deciding how the Initiative should proceed, especially because the attacks were acts of terror in an attempt to stop humankind from making it to Eleusis. We cannot stop moving toward our righteous cause, and therefore, with heavy hearts, we must press on.

First and foremost, we want to inform all of you that we have been able to move up our launch date for Eleusis. The exact date has yet to be determined, but this is joyous news for all, since it means we can reach our destination sooner. This also means that everyone will be expected to work harder, longer, and more fervently toward preparations for Eleusis. We expect no less.

Secondly, for those of you now left unmatched, the program will be run again so that everyone has a match when the time comes to leave for Eleusis. We would heavily encourage that everyone still matched and soon to be re-matched would again focus your efforts on building the future of Eleusis. Those who succeed in the procreative process will be vastly rewarded for your efforts toward the success of this Initiative.

Thirdly, as a measure of safety, there will be an increase in security personnel as well as in-station monitoring. Vitals will be carefully monitored to alert medical staff if you are in physical distress. If an attack happens again, we want to protect all of you. The only way to ensure your safety is to keep everyone and everywhere under close monitoring. There will also be some systematic questioning in place, just to ensure that everyone on the station belongs here. Some of the new security personnel will come from Consortium resources, and they will arrive within the next week. Along with them, we will be bringing in a new wave of Initiates, though discreetly. Due to the losses we faced at launch and now more than a hundred more lives lost, a new wave is necessary.

Please do your utmost to welcome our new initiates and security personnel, as we are all working toward a better future. Should you have any concerns or questions, please feel free to seek out your community leaders.

All the best,
Vice Director Gehrig

Gordon sighed when the message finished, shaking his head as he rested his forehead on one hand. "We should have killed Carmina when we had the chance. Not a mistake I intend to make again." He ingested everything that had been relayed in the message and finally looked back at Tatyana. "I don't suppose you were lucky enough to have your previous match killed in the fighting? I'm all for having a useful dog around the house once in a while, but I've seen convincing wax sculptures with more life to them. It might be advantageous if you or a few of us were rematched with some of the new wave."

"He did die, actually." Tatyana said without any remorse or sadness in her voice, since she hadn't been happy with him anyway. "I found out this morning that his injuries were not such that he could recover. They took him off life support." She put her communicator away. "I'll have to look over the list of new arrivals. I'm not going to be matched with someone intolerable this time."

"I should have access to do my usual tampering within the next few days. I'll get you the list and my recommendations, see what can be done." He looked over the message again. "They're all going to be Consortium plants. Like the Kaplans and that one couple in hydroponics that everyone's lost their minds over. A few might be legitimate, but my money is on the majority of them being insiders, just biding time and guiding developments in the direction the Consortium wants."

"I can handle it. I have no problem fucking the enemy." She smiled as though the challenge excited her, then got up to leave, since they had enough to deal with without looking too suspicious together. "If you have any other reason to reach out, you know how to get a hold of me."

"There's one more thing." He said quietly before she got to the door. "Camina inadvertently gave us a piece of information that I don't think she intended us to have. Or at least, in her taunting messages prior to the attack, she seemed to enjoy rubbing my face in the fact that we didn't have it." He kept his voice down, though if they were under surveillance he couldn't block, there wasn't much he could do about it by that point.

"The Twist is on Arm Two. I checked all the lift logs during the time of the attack. There were whole parties of Consortium goons who went to the dock and didn't engage with Carmina's people at all. They just crossed the space to the lifts for the second arm. The only reason I can think of for the brass to send them to a supposedly abandoned arm of the station is if it actually contains what they need most to guard."

Tatyana raised an eyebrow and nodded. "Then we'll have to learn as much as we can about Arm Two. But we need fresh blood. People who aren't going to be watched as heavily as you or I. I assume we can find people willing to join our cause."

"We weren't supposed to be actively recruiting until later in the process." He tried not to let it sound too much like a complaint. "Have your people start pushing whatever prospects they have under way. I'll begin with mine. I doubt I'll have much trouble getting them on board. If the Initiative is moving faster than we thought they would, then we have to be faster than they thought we would be too."

"Exactly. We don't have time to waste. Never did." She opened the door after looking over at Jessie once more. "I hope for your sake she ends up alright. You seem to care deeply about her." When her eyes looked up at his again, she gave him a slight nod. "Keep me updated on your progress."

"Of course. You're in charge." He knew she would catch the irony in his tone as he said it, but there was nothing else for them to discuss. They had suffered losses, Carmina was in possession of data Gordon knew she wouldn't be able to utilize, and they were only half a step closer to getting their hands on what humanity needed. He told himself over and over again that he should be happy about that half-step, but he couldn't be. Not with Jessie lying unconscious in a bed next to him.

They had to get to Eleusis. The Consortium needed to be dethroned. Humanity needed a chance. Jessie deserved peace. Gordon had no illusions about any of those things. He knew what he deserved. All he wanted was to be a part of helping the rest of the world get there, whether he ever saw it himself or not.

He moved to stand beside the bed and put his hand lightly on top of Jessie's, covered with thick bandages. "You'll get there." He promised quietly. "I won't stop until you do."

18

Two months had passed since the attack, and while Carl had completely healed in only a week and a half, it had taken most people longer. Most of the seriously injured who survived had only returned to their matches and their units after a month of care or more.

As soon as Carl was able to be back in the unit with Aiko, he seemed to have more of a lust for life, and for her, which had resulted in some news she hadn't shared with him yet. She didn't want to share it with him until she knew what was going on with him.

It helped that he seemed impossible to kill (since she wanted him very much alive and very much with her), but she still needed to understand what she was dealing with.

Every day since his return to their unit, she took the glass he drank his maintenance medication from. Every day she analyzed it, and it wasn't long before she understood what they were giving him, though it was a different regimen of medication each day of the week, even if he didn't know it.

Figuring out what he was taking, though, was the easy part. Figuring out why took much longer.

Aiko wasn't about to lose someone else important to her, and Kazuo was sicker by the day. It was a miracle he was still alive, but his impending death only made her work harder. If Aiko and Carl were going to somehow find freedom from the Consortium and the Initiative, she had to figure out what was going on with his body and how to maintain it if they didn't have access to the Consortium's daily cocktail. Otherwise he was essentially a slave to them just to stay alive, and he didn't even know it.

It wasn't uncommon for Aiko to come home from her lab to find Carl already at home. He had attempted to cook once and failed miserably, but there were two or three dishes he had learned to prepare to her liking through sheer persistence. She caught the scent of freshly-cooked rice and vegetables as soon as she came through the door and saw their table was already set with several small dishes, all covered and set in small warmers to keep them fresh. Carl himself was apparently having yet another high-intensity day, and though she could hear him, actually finding him in the unit proved more difficult than it should have been.

Eventually, she looked up at the ceiling around a corner of the unit, and found him doing what looked like inverted push-ups against the far side of a room separator in their living space. There were handles bolted into the ceiling for grips, and his feet were braced against the wall above the door frame leading into their bedroom. He had harsh music playing, which explained why she had been able to sneak up on him without being noticed.

Carl's muscles weren't waiting for the beat of the music, his arms pumping him up against the ceiling tiles quickly. As usual, while at home, he was wearing a pair of shorts and nothing else, and the entirety of him was covered in a sheen of sweat from his exertion, his eyes fixed on the tiles above his face.

"Is this show for me?" She said loudly over the music, but she stayed back far enough to be out of his way if he dropped down. "Because this is incredibly impressive to watch. I could eat and watch this all day."

He flinched when she spoke but he didn't drop from the ceiling, he just turned to look at her over his shoulder with a smile. "I've been meaning to put these in for a while, but the system wouldn't hand them over. Then I came home and we've got a bunch of vegetables in the fridge and the bars I asked for in the delivery chute." He shrugged, which only made the muscles in his shoulders bunch up impressively, then swung himself down to the floor with an impact that felt like it should have thrown the station off its orbit. He dusted off his hands and leaned down to kiss her once to welcome her home. "I had some time after dinner so I figured I'd test them out."

Her smile faltered when he said things had been delivered unexpectedly, and she realized that during her systematic health screening they must have discovered her pregnancy with the blood draw. She'd kept it a secret for as long as she could, hoping that they wouldn't test for something like that unless she asked for it. Clearly she should have known better. Now they were being 'rewarded'. "It all smells great. You didn't have to do all of this for me."

"Well, like I said, I got home a little early, so I figured I'd give the kitchen another shot." He looked her over with a smile and kissed her before he nodded toward the bedroom. "I'm gonna go shower off real quick, but go ahead and get started. I'll only be a minute."

Aiko opened her mouth to say something but then nodded and let him go. "Sure. I'll wait for you, though." She smiled and stepped back so that he could go.

He was quick, as he'd said, and he came back with a different pair of shorts on, still toweling off his arms before he tossed the towel into a laundry chute. The entire unit had taken on a unique blend of scents that had become home over the months. The aroma of her lethal, ever-blooming flowers from the bedroom, the scent of dinner waiting on the table, of Carl's own workout from a few minutes before, and the earthy soap that steamed out of the shower.

He sighed once he was more or less dry, and shook out his arms, still clearly ready for another workout, which they always seemed to be. "Sorry about that. Tried to hurry up. How was the lab?"

"Busy. But not with work." She responded vaguely as she sat next to the table, on the floor. Carl had shortened their table so they could sit on the ground. Aiko kissed him as soon as he sat down next to her, and without any explanation, she moved to sit in his lap. "I have a lot to tell you."

He was surprised she wasn't digging into the food, but he sat back to make plenty of room in his lap, and his arms quickly encircled her. "Well, I like the way the story's starting, so I already look forward to the rest." He brushed his lips over hers as his hands moved over her back, as if to re-claim her every time he had the chance. "I'm listening."

"So it starts with a confession." She admitted with a reassuring kiss to quell his worries. "I've been taking your cups to analyze what you drink every day for your medication. You knew I was going to look into it, though." Aiko was glad to feel his arms around her, and she snuggled against his rock-solid chest.

"Figuring out the medications they were giving you was easy. Figuring out why has been extremely difficult, but I felt like I really needed to know. I've ransacked your medical files, but there are pieces missing. On purpose." She leaned back so she could meet his gaze. "Specifically, the genome listed in your medical file has pieces missing. Luckily, I live with you, so I was able to examine a direct sample and fill in the gaps. What I found were some markers that are . . . I'm getting ahead of things, I'm sorry."

She paused again to kiss him one more time, running a hand over his face to hold his attention. "You told me once that your parents abandoned you to grow up in foster care. From what I've found, that's not what your history says. You weren't abandoned by your parents. You don't have any. I mean, biologically, of course the pieces of you came from somewhere, but the redacted pieces of your genetic code were markers used for identification in scientific trials. You were made. In a lab, raised in an artificial womb."

The smile on his face persisted all the way through her crack about her hacking skills, but the smile evaporated when she talked about his parents. Or the lack thereof. "I was . . . how did you . . . that doesn't make any sense." He was confused, but he certainly wasn't letting go, or doubting her. The months since they had been matched had been a long road of building trust between them, and if Aiko had told him space itself was actually filled with tiny dragons, Carl would have believed her.

"Why would somebody grow a . . . well, an artificial person," it was the most appropriate term he could come up with, if no one had ever actually given birth to him and he had been designed rather than just created, "and then abandon them?"

"They didn't, exactly. They left you in an orphanage, according to the file that your social worker left, to track you and to keep you detached. The only continuity in your life was the support given by the Consortium." She grabbed her communicator and pulled up a copy of a report and brought it up so he could read it in the air.

"The Consortium wanted you to grow up feeling as though you could always depend on them, and only them. So, eventually, when job offers came, it was a no-brainer for you to join their armed forces." Aiko hadn't liked the information she found, but it still hadn't answered many of her questions. At first. "It still didn't make sense, though. Why? Why would they do that? Why would they make babies, raise them in that way just to make them loyal?"

She swiped through the hologram and brought up a few reports at once. "So I went back to the beginning. I looked at the medications they give you. Immunosuppressants. That doesn't make sense either, why suppress your immune system? Then I looked at the lab that made you and tried to figure out who they were. They don't exist anymore, or if they do, they're some other entity now. But they started out as a CV research company."

She pulled up the company history next so he could see it. "They were taken over by the Consortium before you were created. Since I saw they worked on CV research, I checked your medical records again. You don't have CV, of course, you've lived up here your whole life. But I compared your blood samples with others that I could find with Dr. Finnegan's research. You can't get CV. It's impossible."

From the look on his face he was clearly drowning in information, but he looked over the holograms she had shown him, especially the ones concerning his own design. "Everyone gets CV. I've been down planetside dozens of times. Had to get the shot afterward just like everybody else. Why wouldn't I get it if everybody else gets it? Especially if they've been apparently suppressing my immune system this whole time. I should've died of a damn cold by now if that was the case. I never get sick."

"They're only suppressing it by a certain amount. Your immune system still works, but they're preventing it from *overworking*. The best I can figure, which isn't perfect, is that somehow they made you not only CV-immune, but in doing so, they took different genetic aspects and attempted to make the perfect human. Except of course that never happens, since there's no such thing."

She followed up quickly, though she wasn't trying to make it sound like a criticism or a jab. "And they messed up. You're perfect in some ways. You're nearly impossible to kill, but that's only if you're taking all the crap they give you every day. If you skipped out on your medication for even a week, your own body would basically start to self-destruct. Your temperature would skyrocket, your brain would boil, your insides would try to heal things that don't need to heal, which would turn into instant aggressive cancer. I am almost certain that they didn't do any of that on purpose, but it ended up working in their favor, because you can't leave their assistance. You need them to survive, and in turn, they've been treating you and using you as one of the best fighters they could ever want on their payroll."

He could see the logic in what she was saying to him, and he appreciated the way she had broken out the list of ingredients she had found in his daily cocktails, labeling them in ways he would understand to explain their function. The smile was long gone from his face, and he eventually nodded as he looked through some of the documents.

"So they made themselves a slave. An enthusiastic slave." He had always known he was stronger than most, faster to heal than most, but he had blamed it on just having good luck in his genetics, not an actual design behind them. "A slave with . . . looks like nineteen different fathers and twenty-two mothers. Damn. That's a lot of Christmases to go to." He didn't smile as he attempted the joke, and his fingers finally moved down to the report she had managed to dig up detailing his successful maturation in the artificial womb. Some of the other experiments hadn't been so lucky as to survive until their 'birth,' such as it was. "Subject 76. Maybe I should change my name."

She frowned, since she knew it was a lot to take in, but she hadn't gotten to the good part yet. "I still need to find a way to talk to Mercury about it, since she's a doctor and I'm not, and she'll understand it better than I do." Aiko pressed her forehead to his and she kissed him passionately, even if he wasn't in a kissing mood.

"The reason why I did all this, though, is twofold. Once I could figure out why they give you certain things and what they do, then I can figure out how to make something that will work the same way on your body but without destroying it. I can give you things that will do the same things, and you don't have to depend on the Consortium. You don't have to be trapped by them and worry that you're going to be dead if you manage to get away."

She brought up another image, which appeared to be the recipe for everything she would need to put together to give him a treatment without using any resources from the Consortium. "You can have the document, just in case . . . well, if you change your mind about us. I won't trap you the way they have. You're a free man."

He looked over her plan and felt his head swimming due to how complicated it looked. Eventually, he turned back to look at her, and hugged her against him tightly as he kissed her in response. "I've got no interest in being away from you. If I'm free, then it's with you. Anything else is just another kind of trapped, since it would mean something's keeping me from getting back to where I want to be."

Aiko quietly kissed along his neck as he held her close and she closed her eyes before she said anything else. She was worried about what his reaction might be to the rest of what she had to say. "The first reason was that I wanted to help you. The second reason is because I need to know what might happen with my body or a baby that would have some of your genetic code. Good thing I figured a lot of it out. I'm going to need it for the next nine months or so."

First, he just nodded, but then she could feel him freeze as he realized what she was saying. "You're gonna . . . wha?" He pulled back to look her in the eye, then looked down as if he could see what she was talking about with some kind of x-ray vision. "Seriously?" All the energy that had drained from his face during their conversation had returned in a heartbeat, and his hands held her by the waist so tightly it was almost painful.

She nodded and smiled as soon as she felt his energy return, since she hated being the reason he would be upset about anything. "All the stuff they dumped on us confirms it, but I've known for a little while. Seriously." Aiko confirmed and then waited until his eyes met her violet ones again. "Is that okay?"

"That's the best news I've ever gotten in my life." He reassured her with a growing smile and a kiss that was hungry for every part of her at once. She could feel him remind himself that she wasn't unbreakable and he held back from holding too tight, but he still held her against him in an iron grip even after the kiss had broken.

"Wait." He said as he pulled back again, looking her up and down almost frantically. "So it's not gonna hurt you? Me being a freak and the baby being at least half-freak? And all the modifications and the changes and the immuno-bullshit?"

"I don't think so." She placed a hand gently on his cheek. "I checked my blood to see if I could see any changes, and all I could see was a slight increase in white blood cells, but nothing dangerous. I'll take all of this to Mercury and see what she thinks. Even if she's worried, I'll take some of my own creations if I have to. I'll dilute the formula I've made for you if necessary and see what it does. I'm not worried or afraid for the baby, now that I know what to expect." She kissed him again several times. "Do you want to know what it is?"

Anxiety and enthusiasm were vying for control on his face, but as he considered whether he did or not, he laid back on the floor mat and brought her with him so that she was laid against his torso. "I don't know. I think . . . Yeah. If you know, then I want to know. I want to be together on things. It's just one in there, right? I'd be worried about you if it was multiples. You don't have a whole lot of room before you would explode." His hands couldn't quite fit completely around her waist, but between how petite she was and how large he was, it wasn't far off.

"You're right, I might explode if it was more than one. But there is only one." She wiggled against him as he held her on top of him so she could reach his lips again. "It's a boy."

He smiled quietly, and rested his head back against the floor with a sigh. "I'm gonna have a tiny lookalike running around." He shook his head and laughed, bouncing her on top of him as his hands wandered absently over her sides and up over her shoulders. "That's pretty fucking terrifying. To the rest of the world, I mean. One me is bad enough." He looked back up at her and kissed her again deeply. "And he's alright? I mean, from whatever check up has already been done on him, genetics-wise and everything?"

"I think so." Aiko ran her hand along his cheek again. "I haven't had an official checkup. I didn't go in to get tested, but when they ran my blood yesterday, they must have found out and rewarded us by giving us some things we wanted. I'll make an appointment to see Mercury so she can run more extensive tests."

"If you want me to go with you on anything, just tell me. I'll be there." He moved to lay her on her back beside him, and kissed his way down over her neck and breasts to get down to her stomach, where he deposited the last of his kisses just below her belly button. "You'd better behave for your mother, boy. Otherwise you're gonna catch hell when you get out here."

He kissed along her waist again before he worked his way back up over her body to her lips, hovering over her the entire time so that she wouldn't have to bear his entire weight all at once. "Are you alright? I mean, with this? I know it's what we're supposed to be doing, but I honestly couldn't give less of a shit about that. Only person whose opinion I care about when it comes to having a kid is yours."

"I love you." She said with the weight of the world in her words, since she meant it so deeply it was almost difficult to say. "I'll be happy if I can have one thing." Aiko looked into his eyes again as he hovered over her. "I want to marry you."

That condition got a broad smile and he reached up to caress her face as he nodded. "I want to marry you too, Aiko." His smile dimmed slightly as he thought about it, though, but he kissed her to reassure her. "I don't want to keep Espinoza, though. I'd rather drop it and take Tanaka. That way, at least the kid gets something real, not some bullshit a researcher thought up in a lab somewhere."

"We can do that." Aiko put both her hands on his face and pulled him into another kiss that had her head spinning by the time her lips actually separated from his again. "Maybe we can come back to the food later." She said breathily as she ran her fingers down over his bare chest. "What do you think?"

He parted from her far enough to pull her shirt up over her head and toss it aside, then leaned down to kiss his way up the slope of her breasts. "What food?"

A moan involuntarily escaped her lips as his kisses teased her sensitive skin. Only a little more than four months together and he knew far more about pleasing her than any other previous lover she'd ever had. "No food. Just you. That's all I want."

One of his huge hands moved up to cup her breast as his lips took hers, and rather than hover above her, he slid to the floor beside her so that his hand could wander all over her body. He could feel in every muscle just how tense she had been coming into the discussion, and he could understand why. She had simultaneously taken away what little past he'd thought he had and placed a future in front of him that was better than he had ever expected for himself. It was a lot to put on a person, but he wanted her to know that as long as he still had her, nothing else mattered. His parents could have been deranged killers from some Mars colony and he wouldn't have cared, so long as Aiko still loved him.

"I love you, Aiko." He said between kisses, his hand moved down between her legs as he looked her in the eye. "This kid might be starting from a fairly crazy place, but I'm gonna make sure he, and you, have a good life ahead. The long and happy kind."

His wandering hands made it difficult for her to think or respond, but she tried to nod to acknowledge what he said. "All of us together." She finally responded, though it was followed by another moan. "A big family. Our family. On Eleusis."

"A big family, huh?" He grinned as he teased her, reaching along her waist to casually shove her pants down over her hips out of his way so that he could get to her the way he wanted, one of his large fingers sliding through her silken core. "I like the sound of that. Means I'm gonna be making them with you for a long, long while."

"As if . . . I would ever want to stop." Aiko and Carl had learned to adjust to each other, since there were definitely some roadblocks in size, but they made it work. Aiko was just as interested in pleasing him as he was in pleasing her. "I bet your super body means that you'll never need medication for your manhood."

That had him laughing again, but it didn't impact the way he touched her. She needed to be all kinds of ready for him in order for things to work, but he had gone into the relationship as a singularly patient man. That hadn't changed in the months since. "Is this you being a dirty, horny old woman a few decades in advance? I think I'd be okay with that. Who knows, if I'm that fucked up genetically, maybe I'll just live forever and you'll have to find the formula for eternal life. Just so I can keep you."

"I'll find a way." She had closed her eyes already, since it was easier to focus on what she was feeling with her eyes closed, and she was never disappointed. "I only want to die if you're going to come with me. If not, I'm staying here with you."

"Good." He kissed down her neck and felt her gasping for breath as his fingers worked to turn her inside out, encouraging her to chase after the tension, stroke by stroke of his fingers. He had to shift the way he was lying because of the hardness in his shorts, but he was focused on Aiko first and foremost. "Only place we're going is Eleusis, and the only place on Eleusis I care about is a huge bed, with you, in a soundproof room with a door that locks."

"Mmmmm." Aiko couldn't verbally respond. All she could do was writhe underneath his touch. Every stroke of his fingers left her panting and slicker by the second. "I like hearing what you want." She said quietly, because she couldn't produce more than a whisper. "I always . . . Want to know . . . What your fantasies are."

"You." He answered as she rocked herself against his hand. "You are my fantasies. Every single one of them is you, shaking and satisfied on my watch. Every single one."

Aiko let out a needy whimper when his hand slowed just to tease her. She didn't want him to ease up, she wanted him to keep going. Her clit, her core, she was aching for more. "I'm your fantasy?"

All he did was smile that she was even questioning it, but he settled in against her with one arm around her shoulders, encircling her completely with his body as he teased her. "I had a dream the other night." His voice was so low that it rumbled through the tiled floor beneath her back and seemed to form walls of its own around them to close them in their own world.

"We were living in this luxury suite I stayed in once when I got hired to guard some bureaucrats on Forty-Seven. Big, private, billionaire-style pad, the whole place. I came into the bedroom and you were sleeping in this huge bed with silk sheets, wearing just those stretch pants you like and a flimsy top. All I had to do was slip in bed and kiss along your neck and you were already cumming for me. So you want to talk about fantasies, you're living full time in my brain, baby. Conscious and otherwise."

"I do like it . . . when you kiss my neck." She whimpered as she edged closer to climax, her body aching for him to continue. Aiko could feel the tension bubbling in her veins, her breaths quick and needy. "I like everything . . . you do to me. Your mouth. Your lips. So strong and sexy."

His pace against her increased as she invited it, and his kisses moved to her neck just to bring the dream a little closer to reality. "There's nothing I don't want from you." Aiko could feel the hardness of him easily through his shorts, and the truth there. Her clothes were in disarray, since he hadn't seen the point of removing them altogether, he just wanted to touch her. He kept her knees locked together and intensified everything that he was doing to her between her legs by how little room she had to move. "You're the most beautiful thing I've ever seen. Everything about the way you feel, the way you move, your voice, everything about you just makes me want you more. If you weren't already mine, I'd be fighting like hell to have you, and I'll fight like hell to keep you no matter what."

"Did you think . . . like that . . . when you met me on Earth?" Aiko was known for being a bit of a talker, even during sex, but she liked hearing what he was thinking about. Telling her his thoughts and talking dirty to her was a turn-on.

"The second I saw you, I hoped you weren't in data support." He said with a chuckle. "Because then you would've seen my porn search history and realized you were exactly what I'd been fantasizing about since I was old enough not to get caught."

"It would have been fun to catch you." She admitted and moaned louder, since she was *so close*. His fingertip grazed up and down and circled in a maddening pattern. "I'll replace your porn." She moaned again. "With pictures of me."

"You are so much better than anything I ever saw before you." His kisses moved down from her neck over her breasts, and as he slipped a second finger inside her, his pace turned relentless since he could feel how much her body was begging for release. "Come for me, Wife. That's the picture I want."

Wife. He called her his wife. Aiko felt a warm rush of emotion in her chest, but it was quickly overshadowed by fiery need, and only moments later she was crying out as an orgasm ripped through her body and flooded her brain. "Oh, Carl . . ." She managed to moan, but not much else.

His fingers rode her straight through the orgasm, each wave of pleasure more delicious and satisfying than the last. His fingertips circled her clit just once before he withdrew them from her, drawing a squeak from her that made him grin, but it was just another way for him to make love to her, teasing her body up to the point where it could take no more. "That's one image I'm happy to have locked in memory."

19

Ever since the attack, Mercury felt like she was stuck in some kind of limbo. Her work had increased with the injured, but also with the women who conceived in the Initiative within the last four months. There was an influx of women asking to be tested, with the recent incentives becoming sufficient to motivate a larger number of people. Clearly it was working.

It took Orion about a month to fully heal, and she had been by his side as often as she could manage, which meant not devoting much time to Logan. But when she was with Logan, it was incredible. She loved every moment spent with him, and it confused her even more because she knew he was only with her because they were trying to get pregnant. They were intimate when the time was right and they didn't really speak much otherwise. They both were trying to maintain their relationships with their spouses, but it was getting more and more difficult for Mercury to stick to the schedule. She *wanted* to spend more time with Logan, even though she was also happy spending time with Orion.

The night before, she and Orion had both been so tired from the day's activities to do much more than sit and watch television, but it had been nice just to be together so casually in the middle of everything else that was going on. He was awake before her, as always, and he was already out of the bedroom by the time she actually got up and went to get showered.

By the time she was out of the shower, though, she caught the scent of pancakes and strawberries from the bedroom. When she stepped out, there was a tray with breakfast spread on it sitting on the bed, Orion half-dressed off to one side smiling at her. "Good morning, Beautiful."

"You made me breakfast?" She replied with a small smile as she finished braiding her hair while she walked toward the bed. Mercury was wrapped tightly in a fluffy robe (which had been awarded to her for being with Logan, but she liked it too much to leave it one place or another) as she went to sit on the edge of the bed. "This smells delicious."

"You can thank Aiko for the actual fruit. The strawberries are a hybrid one of her other botanical friends developed for Eleusis." He didn't get up, looking her up and down in her robe with a contented sigh before he caught her by the belt to bring her in closer, still warm from the shower. "One day of the year that everybody ought to get something special, if you ask me. Happy birthday."

He could see the flicker of confusion which made it clear she hadn't even realized what day it was. "You remembered." She beamed and pulled him into a searing kiss, grateful for his attention to detail and his eagerness to make her feel special.

"Of course I remembered. It's you." He returned the kiss, and held her by the front of her robe. "Go on, get to it. They don't stay hot very long." He didn't move off the bed, but there was plenty of room for her between him and the tray, and he acted as a backrest for her in the process. "Barring anything too crazy, do you think you'll be out more or less normal time tonight?"

Mercury nodded as she meticulously cut up her pancakes, and when she took a bite, she was careful about it. Even on her own, she monitored her food intake. "I should be out at a normal time, I think. I really hope nothing crazy happens. We've had quite enough."

"Damn right we have." He agreed as he put one arm around her waist, the other reaching up to rub at her neck beneath her braid as she ate. "I got permission to take out one of the shuttles tonight and get some away-time, just the two of us. We're not permitted to jump over to Prime for a vacation or anything like that, but I thought it would be good to just get off the station for a while, given how hectic everything's been lately."

She didn't reply right away, since she was surprised anyone would be permitted to leave, especially the two of them together. They could run away. Was the Initiative playing some kind of game, letting her and Orion get away for a while? Mercury ate another bite before she finally replied. "You don't have any plans?" Anna's fertile week was coming up soon, and she didn't know when he would want to go be with her.

"Not today." He said sadly, but as he spoke quietly against her ear, it became obvious that he had taken the question differently than she had intended it. "The only stations close enough to be even a possibility tonight are Prime and Nineteen. Prime is big enough to get lost in, but it's also too well monitored to give us any chance of doing anything ourselves from there. And Nineteen isn't much more than a supply depot and hydroponics farm. They'd find us within hours. Believe me, I ran a lot of scenarios."

"We can't leave them behind anyway." She whispered before she took another bite, but she didn't want to think about why she didn't want to leave without Logan. "I was asking if you have any plans with Anna."

"Oh, no, not for a couple more days." He said just as dubiously, and kissed the back of her neck. "Do you want some coffee to go with the pancakes?"

Mercury shook her head and took another bite as she leaned back firmly against his chest. She hated the conflict she felt, or even the comparisons that sometimes ran through her mind, but she couldn't help it. "Do you want some? I don't like to eat by myself if I can help it."

"Sure." He reached over her and pulled the tray closer, grabbed her fork and a bite of her pancakes to pop into his mouth over her shoulder. It left his arm over her chest to hold her against him, which he didn't mind a bit. "Not bad. That strawberry packs a punch. Clearly the chef is a man of incredible talents."

"Clearly." She responded with a laugh, even though she really did think Orion was a man of incredible talents. Mercury took a couple more bites before she said anything else. "So do I get a present?" Her green eyes sparkled with her teasing tone, though she didn't really think it was fair to ask, considering she hadn't even remembered her own birthday.

"Of course you do. What kind of birthday would it be without presents?" Her teasing tone brought a grin back and he just watched her smile for a paused moment before he kissed her and slid away. "I couldn't find any wrapping paper, so it's not particularly well-presented. Sorry about that."

He went to their shared closet and started moving his half-dozen uniforms on their hangers, taking small boxes out of each one, since they were the only hiding place he had been able to come up with. Eventually he had a thin plastic bag of small boxes in one hand, and he reached up along the wall of the closet to dislodge a large panel, where he had hidden the last piece of her present. "I didn't think it was right that they wouldn't give you any extra space to bring along some of your supplies when we left

Seven. So I wanted you to have some here."

The larger panel that he brought over to her was a bound case with a few dozen large sheets of canvas inside, and the small boxes in the bag he handed her contained brushes of various shapes and sizes and some small paint containers. Not nearly as much as she'd had in her own unit on Seven, but enough to get started, certainly. "I hope they're actually good. I tried to find another artist to ask their opinion of what I was trying to get, but as far as I can find, you're the only real painter in the whole Initiative."

As soon as he handed her the art supplies Mercury was stunned into silence. She hadn't really expected a gift and had started to forget that she loved to paint since their world flipped upside down. Mercury ran her fingers over the canvas as she opened up the case and she smiled with tear-filled emerald eyes at Orion. "Thank you. I could use some time to get away and paint."

She set the canvas aside and dug through a small table on her side of the bed. Mercury pulled out a small pad of paper and held it out. There were light pencil drawings of various things inside, but at least half of them were of Orion with different expressions, always when he didn't know that she was looking at him. "I started this after we met." She handed it over so he could flip through and peruse. Mercury had also drawn Logan a few times too, but those pieces of paper would never be found in her shared unit with Orion.

"These are amazing. I didn't know you worked with pencils too." He laid on the edge of the bed with his head in her lap so he could look through the drawings. He laughed at one, and shook his head. "Does my forehead actually do that? That's embarrassing." He traced a crinkle she had drawn on the paper and then checked it against his forehead before he laughed again. "Yeah, that's a thing. Guess I'm just turning into an old man. These are beautiful."

"I had to learn to draw before I could really learn to paint. At least that was what I told myself." A perfect feeling of warmth spread through her chest as he smiled, and she ran her fingers along his forehead. "You're not even close to an old man. Old men don't look like you. They would kill to look like you."

"Old-man-me might look like me someday. Grey the hair a little, give me that distinguished old-man goatee, a couple wrinkles around the eyes. That way maybe there'll be ninety-six-year-old men in the nursing home killing to look like me. That could be fun." He chuckled and kissed the inside of her wrist as she touched the lines in his face. "Meanwhile, women of every age in every part of the world would kill to look like you. Ninety-four-year-old you is gonna come visit me in the nursing home, younger woman that you are, and half a dozen men will die of heart failure from hard-ons they can no longer sustain."

"But you won't be one of those men. Even at ninety-six, I can't imagine your equipment having any sort of failure." She leaned down to kiss him upside down, and even upside down his lips made her whimper. "You have amazing equipment. Age-proof. That is my medical opinion."

"I like your medical opinion." He smirked and reached to tug her braid to bring her down into another kiss. "Though if I keep growing at this rate for the next . . . seventy-two years, we're both gonna be in trouble. Because I'm gonna be about four meters tall with a half-meter cock. I don't think that would work out well."

"You won't keep growing." She replied with a reassuring giggle before she met his warm lips with her soft ones. "Maybe a few more centimeters one way or another, but you'll stop soon."

"You don't know that. It could happen." He sat up once he reached the end of the sketchbook, and looked over the final sketch with a smile. "These are beautiful, Mercury. I hope you never stop." He closed it and handed it back to her reverently. "I know things have been insane, but insanity never stopped any other great artist from pursuing their art."

"I'm not a great artist. A good doctor, but not really a great artist." She took her sketchbook and set it aside, since looking at the real version of Orion was far better than looking at sketches. "I'll have to paint you something now that you gave me such a great gift. Any requests?"

"I'll have to think about that. I've never had a personal artist before. Could be fun." He sat behind her again so she could finish her breakfast, but he stole another bite of pancake before he let her get back to it. "What else do you want for your birthday? You've got a whole . . . sixteen hours and change left. Could get pretty wild."

"How wild?" She asked half teasingly, but also with curiosity. "If we don't go into work, are we going to get into trouble?"

"We might. That could be fun, actually." He grinned against her neck as he kissed down her shoulder, peeling back her robe one bit at a time. His trailing touches left lines of heat down her skin that made Mercury shiver with anticipation. "Just to see how creative they get about double-talking their way into trying to break us up. Somebody might have an emergency case of the didn't-exist-before-itis that's going around, and there could be some routine question of flight plan mechanics that somehow only I can answer."

"Don't tempt them." She said immediately with an edge of worry, but she was too distracted by his sly attempt to get her robe off of her to worry that much. "Are you trying to be sneaky?"

"Sneaky? No. I'm never sneaky. I don't have much talent for sneaky." He continued his kisses, though, pulling the fabric slowly down over her shoulder and just coincidentally trailing his lips along the exposed skin.

"Now you're just being sarcastic." She snickered and then, because it was fun, she pulled her robe back up over her shoulder. "You're going to have to be bolder if you want this robe off of me."

"Oooh, hard to get." His heated laugh brushed against her skin and he returned his kisses to her neck. His free hand, denied the robe, moved down over her side to her leg, which wasn't fully covered by the robe, and rested along her thigh as she sat there on the bed with him. His fingers hooked the bottom edge of the robe easily and drew it up along the inside of her thigh as his lips moved up behind her ear. "How much bolder are we talking, exactly?"

"Incredibly bold." Mercury murmured as a jolt of electricity ran down her spine from his expert teasing along her thigh. More and more Mercury felt like she was two people living two lives and it was difficult to try to balance her identity with each man, but she was trying.

"Incredibly. Hm. I wonder what incredibly bold would look like." His tone was pure curiosity, but his fingers took their time moving up her leg, beckoning her knees just apart in the process. "Maybe bold enough to make you incredibly late to work just because I can't convince myself to let you get out of this bed right now. 'I'm sorry, boss,'" his voice jumped a few octaves, even though Mercury's normal speaking voice wasn't that high, "I was late because I was . . . in a compromised position."

"You make me sound so polite." Mercury's legs parted as far as he wanted them to go. She wasn't feeling at all polite. "It's my birthday. Doesn't that mean if I want to take my time having fun with my husband, I get to do that?"

"In my rulebook? Absolutely. Your birthday, you do whatever you want. Including me. Please, including me." His fingers finally reached their destination between her legs, and his touch was, per her request, bolder than usual, moving in a caressing demand against the most sensitive, now soaking, parts of her.

Mercury wasn't expecting that kind of boldness, and she gasped sharply at first. "Definitely including you." She leaned into him as he explored her. She found her guilt about the situation with Logan often gave her a reason to avoid Orion, but she didn't actually *want* to avoid him. She just didn't want to feel guilty. In that moment, though, she almost felt normal again. Almost. "You're my husband."

"Damn right." He put his arm around her chest as she leaned back against him and slowly laid them both down on the bed so her back was against him. He moved one of his arms beneath her head as a pillow with his hand cupping her breast, the other wreaking havoc between her legs. She wasn't a small woman, but Orion was one of the few men on the station who could envelop her so completely and make her his, setting her entire body at rest against him while he set her nerves on fire with every stroke of the finger. "Maybe I'll just call in sick later myself. If only I knew a doctor somewhere who could write me a note for the day and get me out of things."

"I'll . . . write you . . . ten notes, if you want." She loved the way he completely enclosed her. It made her feel as though she fit in better with the world around her. She fit with Orion, and it felt amazing to fit. It felt incredible to feel smaller, feel feminine in his embrace. Mercury moaned softly as his hand teased her breast through the robe, but she wanted to feel his hand on her skin, so she opened the robe and exposed herself completely. The rest of the world would have to wait.

"That's more like it." He moved his hand away only long enough to pull the knot of her belt loose and remove the robe completely. His fingers savored her porcelain skin and then returned to the silk between her legs. They moved quickly and passionately but as he kissed her neck and newly-exposed shoulder, she could feel that he recognized the same thing she did. Times together were rare, and it made him want her even more, it made the urgency of the encounter even more intense.

Mercury squirmed in pleasure on top of him but her mind was still stuck on wanting to give instead of take. She wanted to make him happy. Had her personality somehow been altered by Logan that she would always want to do things that way? "I miss you so much. I miss your hands. Your lips. I even miss the way we look together." They were a striking couple in many ways, and she liked that. Mercury liked the way her fair skin was against his darker skin, or her shocking red hair contrasting his dark eyes. They were meant to catch attention together, and she liked that. She loved being with him and she loved it when people noticed them together.

"Especially naked, but I could be biased." He let her roll onto her back so he could kiss her, the deep bronze of his body moving over her pale skin like a warm eclipse. "I miss finding out new things about you. New things you like, things you want. I miss the way you taste." His tongue danced with hers in the kiss that followed, his entire body pressed against hers so that she could feel the growing hardness through his shorts, aching for her the same as the day they met.

Stars, he could kiss. Mercury had forgotten all about his talent for kissing, and she felt another stab of guilt that she hadn't thought about it recently. Mercury's tongue explored his as their kiss sent fireworks through her body. As she felt his hardness against her, all she wanted was to feel him inside her, to feel his cock fill her, own her. She slid a hand without hesitation into his shorts to stroke him. "I think I miss this the most."

"Oh, I see." He managed to say after a gasp of pleasure as her deft fingers wrapped around him. "I see how it is. I'm just a piece of meat to you." He wiggled comically against the bed to work his way out of his shorts without taking his hands off her, but eventually he was exposed and still kissed her breathless. "I'm strangely comfortable with that right now, but I'll have to remember to be offended later. That part of me has missed you too much to care right now."

"Don't say something like that." She whispered against his lips between kisses. "You mean so much to me, you're not a piece of meat." Mercury's kisses became silken fire as she tried to prove her words, all clothes forgotten and their bodies pressed skin-to-skin. He was all heat, sharp lines, and sinewy muscle. Every ridge of his body complemented every curve of her own. "I love you."

His eyes shimmered with heat, fathomless dark that captivated her as he returned her kiss, returning her intensity as if to make up for making light of things. "I love you too, Mercury." He met her eyes and rocked his hips against her hand, his need and emotions evident there. "You're the first person in this universe for me, and I'm never gonna have enough of you. Even if I do end up as that ninety-six year old giant in the nursing home with the hottest senior citizen wife in the galaxy."

"I hope that's how we end up." Mercury stroked him several times, slowly, confidently, as he looked into her eyes. She enjoyed every second of teasing his velvet, hard cock in her hands. "We just . . . need to survive this."

"What, breakfast?" He teased again, but he moved his fingers away from her dripping heat to move himself between her legs instead, kissing her all the while as she stroked him. "I don't . . . know. Death by incredible orgasm is pretty high on my list of ways I'd prefer to make my . . . exit. Dear god, woman, your hands . . ."

Mercury had learned a lot in the last four months, but those were details Orion wouldn't want to know. She focused on every stroke. Harder. Faster. "I'm glad you think so. It feels like . . . it has been years." She knew that wasn't true, but the most recent sex between them seemed like obligation, and Mercury wasn't proud of it. This was different. This was the real Orion and Mercury. "I like to please you."

"You should be loving life, then." He moaned against her lips, thrusting involuntarily into both her hands as she stroked him. He wanted her, wanted to be inside her and feel like she was his again, if only for a while, and the desperation was evident. "All the other bullshit aside, you're my wife. I don't need anything else in the world but that, and I'm all manner of pleased."

"You make it sound so simple." Nothing was simple. She used to believe that life was simple, that the rules made everything easy, but the "rules" of the Initiative made things complicated. "I want it to be simple." Mercury hooked a leg around his waist to keep him close. "I want you, and I want things the way they were."

"Mmm . . ." he moaned and rocked back slightly to put himself out of reach before he moved to put her shoulders back on a pillow. He laid his lean body against her, his hardness pressed against her slick folds as he kissed her. "I believe this is the way things were." He chuckled as he ran his hands up over her body. "Our first time together." He clarified in another kiss, as he began to slide himself inside.

Mercury trembled as he slid in, and she savored his slow pace. "Except then . . . I didn't know how wonderful it would be." She gasped softly and wrapped her leg around his waist to encourage him further, since it didn't feel right unless he was completely inside of her. "Now you've made me needy."

"Have I?" He whispered shakily, burying himself inside her heat as he kissed along her shoulder. A growl of contentment escaped him as he moved at an easy pace inside her, taking his time because it made everything that much more delicious. "And what . . . do you need . . . exactly?"

Mercury wrapped her arms around his neck and kissed him senseless before she broke the kiss with a gasp as he increased speed. "I need *you*." Mercury's fingertips massaged at the base of his skull as she held onto him. She felt conflicting emotions, but she was glad for one thing. Mercury didn't ever worry about what Orion was thinking about because he was very open about what was on his mind. She didn't wonder if he was thinking about Anna while she occasionally had to push aside thoughts of Logan. "We . . . fit perfectly."

"Fuckin' right we do." He moaned against her kisses and caressed her face as he drew more moans from her. He drove Mercury wildest when things moved slowly between them, gradually, and he wanted to take her far, far away from everything else around them. He wanted her all to himself again, he wanted to feel her come apart for him and only him. "You've got me." He promised with a frantic kiss.

Mercury was surprised by how much it meant to hear him say that he was hers, and her eyes burned with tears that she couldn't fight as he increased his pace. The tension inside of her continued to build and her pulse thudded loudly. She wished that it was her fertile week and she could spend it with Orion, because she wanted *their* family. She wanted to have *his* children, despite her emotions otherwise when she wasn't with him. "I love you."

They were lost in each other for a long time beyond that shared declaration, and they twisted and writhed inside their own world there on the bed as the heat built between them. Every time he was about to hit his own climax, he redoubled his efforts with her and changed their position so that he could please her. Every time he could feel her close to her own, she fought back and turned the tables on him, leaving them both grinning and gasping in the constant dance between them.

It was easily the best he'd ever had, with Mercury or anybody else and when she finally overcame him, pressing her hips down onto him as she rode him on his back, it was all he could do to hold her desperately against him. "I'm going . . ." He couldn't speak beyond that, clinging to her and the scent and softness that was so uniquely her. She was all he had never even known he wanted, and she was his.

He had to believe that she was his.

As soon as she knew he couldn't hold off any longer, she didn't hold back and she tumbled into blissful oblivion right after him. The angle she had on top of him made it even better, and her whole body shook as she tilted her head back in enjoyment. Sex with the right people was the best thing in the world, and Mercury felt connected to Orion in a way she wouldn't trade for the world. There were no barriers between them, and no reason for barriers. He knew her. More than that, she loved him. The only complicated thing was that she didn't realize it was possible to truly love more than one person at once, but she ignored that as she enjoyed the perfect moment.

Orion was never shy about letting her know his enjoyment, and it was a long while before he managed to quiet down. His hands roamed over her back and shoulders as she rested on top of him. "This," he eventually said breathlessly, kissing up her neck to her lips, "this right here is what I live for." He was huffing for breath and their bodies were slick with sweat, but he wouldn't have traded it for the world. "This moment right here with you is the only place I want to spend my day."

He ignored the fact that Mercury's cuddling reminded him a little of Anna's, and pushed aside thoughts of all the ways that Anna curled into him after she'd been satisfied, shaking herself against him to tease every last shock of his orgasm out of him. Mercury was more calm and relaxed rather than playful, but he loved her, and he loved having her there. It wasn't a moment for comparisons.

"Mmm." Mercury replied in response at first, still too relaxed to think or do much else. Mercury kissed along his skin and her hands wandered, so she could re-memorize everything about him. Thankfully, he and Logan felt very different, and there was no mistaking their bodies as her fingers trailed over Orion. "Happy birthday to both of us, then."

He chuckled and smiled before another blistering kiss. "I look forward to ending your birthday the same way it's gotten started. Now I just have to figure out how to make pancakes in zero gravity."

* * * * *

Most of Mercury's birthday went by without any major incidents. A few of her co-workers wished her a happy birthday, including Barry, who brought cookies into the clinic that Erebi made. Two more women came in with positive pregnancy tests, though only one of them was actually happy about it. The majority of her appointments were women who asked about pregnancy symptoms to make sure they weren't outside the norm. It was just one sign that the world was moving a little closer to the one Mercury was accustomed to; reassuring pregnant women, conducting checkups, running blood tests, preparing them to bring the life they had created into the world. The world started to feel almost normal again when her communicator beeped in her pocket, with the specified tone designated for Logan.

Mercury finished her chart before she looked at the communicator, since Logan was a distraction in her life and she didn't want to get something wrong on someone's medical record. She took a deep breath before she pulled it out of her pocket. She briefly thought about her still-braided hair, since it was one of those things she knew she would never forget with Logan. A braid was fine when she was with Orion, it would never be permitted by Logan otherwise.

I got my shoulder cut open a few minutes ago. I need you to do some stitching.

It was a short and curt message, but Mercury was getting used to those kinds of messages from Logan, so she logged out of her programs and tidied up her OB exam room. If one of her patients came looking for her, it would alert her communicator directly. Mercury replied quickly, even though a cut that required stitches wouldn't be life-threatening. Not to mention he could have asked another doctor to assist, but she knew he didn't trust any of the others. *I'm here.*

It was only a few minutes before he showed up in the main area of the clinic looking for her. His shirt was halfway-on and she could see that the half hanging down had been doused in blood. He'd had enough foresight to press a small towel against the injury and was holding it with his free hand as he walked, ignoring the receptionist at the clinic to go directly with Mercury.

"One of the shelving units in hydroponics came loose. The endcap hit me on the way down." He winced a little as he pulled the towel away to let her examine it, but the bleeding had begun to slow, at least. The gash went from just below the edge of his collarbone down over one side of his chest, and was much rougher and uglier at the top than the clean slice at the bottom where the rack had trailed away from him.

"Alright. It looks like it didn't get too deep into muscle." She led him back into a small exam room that sometimes doubled as emergency triage. After the last attack, they weren't going to be left unprepared. She first applied a gel that would numb the area, and she could have applied a bonding agent instead of doing stitches, but she knew he preferred the thread. The fewer orbital chemicals in his body the better, she'd heard him say.

He seemed cranky when he came in the room, but when he saw her come at him with the stitches, he actually smiled slightly. "I'm glad you're as good with a needle and thread as you are with everything else. What did I steal you away from?"

"Charting. I haven't had a patient for about an hour." She tested to make sure he was numb enough before she started stitching without giving him any warning. Clearly he could see what she was doing, and she didn't want to sound so much like a doctor all of the time. Even though it was hard for her not to, usually. "Hopefully someone is taking care of whatever you were working on, I don't want you to move this shoulder too much after this."

"I've had worse than this. That one healed up in about three days. Cut my leg open jumping rocks in the stream about six years ago." He let her work for a while in silence, but then moved his stool to get a little closer to the table she was sitting on so she wouldn't have to lean so far. He rested his hands on her legs as she worked, wincing once in a while as the numbing began to wear off in places. He didn't mind. He'd been stitched without numbing before, so any anesthetic was a bonus.

"The rest of the agricultural board can probably deal with what I was working on without getting themselves killed. I'll sling the arm for a couple days." He looked up at her with a look that was somewhere between a wince of pain and a smirk. "Just means I'll have to get other people to do things for me in the meantime. Shouldn't be hard."

Mercury gave him a small smile in return. "You're good at

getting things done, and especially at encouraging people to help out. I'm not worried that you'll be able to follow a doctor's . . . *suggestion.*" Mercury was just as precise with her stitching as she was with most things in her life, and she was sure that his scar would heal in a neat line. "If you want, I can prescribe you a few pain pills. Though a couple of drinks from the bar would work just as well. It's up to you."

"If I'm given the choice between narcotics and alcohol, I will always choose alcohol." His smile widened a little, and his touch along the side of her legs turned more to a caress as he waited for her to finish. "I read some interesting articles about pain relief back on Earth. I had a bitch of a toothache that I didn't feel like seeing the doctor about, so I did my own reading. Had a couple places recommend that sexual excitement has the same effect as prescription-strength painkillers when it comes to brain chemistry."

"That's probably accurate. At least for a short amount of time. Painkillers are designed to last much longer, though. And sexual excitement tends to lead to action, which isn't necessarily best for the patient." She babbled on but didn't look up once from her task, since she was dedicated to doing it as perfectly as she could manage. "It would probably be effective for tooth pain. Teeth aren't usually moving parts unless someone is taking them out."

"I'll remember that next time I have a toothache." He smiled brighter and sat up straighter so she could get to the bottom of the gash, wiping away the excess blood from beneath it as she worked. "I meant to stop by earlier during lunch, but I got caught up with a legal review session."

"Oh?" She looked up at him once, briefly, before she looked down at her work again. Mercury wasn't surprised he had a meeting, but she was surprised that he would want to see her. It was an off-week, so it was his time with his wife, and she knew he cherished spending time with Anna. She respected that, of course, and she enjoyed spending time with Orion. It didn't mean she didn't think about Logan, but she understood the boundaries everyone agreed upon and she abided by them. Things had been strange and fluid at first, but now they had a schedule and they stuck to it.

"I wanted to come by and give you your present." He said with a smirk, though it was interrupted by a wince as she tugged on one of the stitches to get it closed. "Don't tell me you thought I would forget."

At first she didn't know what he was talking about until she remembered for the second time that day that it was her birthday. He had commented on it once when they were looking over each other's files. "Oh, you're talking about my birthday." She laughed, but she was obviously uncomfortable about it. "I didn't know you would remember. And I didn't expect a present. That's very thoughtful of you."

"It's something you mentioned wanting a couple months ago." The gash on his chest was long, but she was making short work of it with her stitches, which he appreciated. "Well, it's along the lines of something you mentioned. We'll see if you enjoy it or not."

"Alright. I'm nearly finished." She focused on his wound and cleaned it carefully afterward before she covered it with gauze. "I'll take them out in a couple of days."

"Unless I get to them first." He grinned as he stood up, testing his arm to see about his range of motion and assess his pain level. "Used to piss off my district doctor down below. I've never had a doctor take out my stitches." Apparently satisfied with his arm, he looked down at her and reached up to take her chin in his hand, using his good arm to humor her. "Thank you. Feels better already."

She couldn't suppress the chill of excitement as soon as he touched her, but she gave him a nod. "I'm glad that I could help. Try not to let that happen too often or else I might think you're doing it on purpose just to come here."

"I get myself torn up plenty, but not generally on purpose." He leaned down to kiss her once, then reached down into a pocket of his pants to pull out a small box. It was in dark packaging with three pink slashes around a corner, meaning it was privately manufactured rather than station-issued. "Happy birthday. But you only get half the present. The other half, I keep."

Mercury looked at the box in her hand carefully. The feeling of his kiss was still tingling on her lips because it felt so forbidden. They weren't supposed to be together right now. She opened the box slowly, since she had no idea what could be inside.

The inside of the small box was lined in tissue paper, but what was lying on the paper was difficult to identify at first, since it looked like nothing more than a strip of fabric in a haphazard pile. When she pulled it out, though, the end of it was heavier than the rest, and once it was untangled, she could see it was a very skimpy set of underwear, with something slightly more weighted in the part of it would press against her clit. As she took it out and examined it, Logan put both his hands in his pockets and tapped something, which made the underwear vibrate briefly in her hands. "Like I said, I keep the other half."

Mercury's cheeks flushed immediately but it was only partly because she was scandalized. Mostly she flushed at the idea of her pleasure literally being at his beck and call. "It will be fun to try." She said as politely as she could manage. They still had a couple of days before they would be spending time together.

"It will be fun." He smirked at the flush in her cheeks and looked her up and down once as he hesitated, though only for a moment. "I'll come in here some day, find a reason to be in the clinic, talk to one of the other doctors, maybe, or just come by to see you for a while in the afternoon, and I'll turn them on when you're with another patient. Maybe when you're charting."

"It might not be a good idea if I'm performing an examination or administering something. Or sewing someone up, for example." Mercury teased as she motioned toward his chest before she looked back at the underwear. "I'm glad I got to see you, even though I'm not happy you were hurt. Sometimes I struggle with the boundaries and schedules. I enjoy spending time with you."

"You aren't the only one." He agreed, though it was a bit of a change to actually be talking about their relationship openly. "The others," he was only going to be open up to a certain point, since he couldn't mention their spouses by name, "spend quite a lot of time together. Always have, it seems like. It's difficult sometimes to feel where the boundaries were supposed to be."

"They're friends. They have a lot in common, and he's her teacher." Mercury shrugged one shoulder as though it didn't bother her, but it did. It bothered her she had to think about Orion spending so much time with Anna and it bothered her she had limited time with Logan. "We're on one committee together, but we don't have much else in common. Even if we did, it doesn't matter. Ann . . . She's your best friend. You don't need to worry about her, and you and I . . . well, this isn't real."

"Not real?" All trace of teasing or game-playing was gone and he took half a step closer to her, leaving only inches between them. "I thought I warned you never to lie to me."

"I'm not lying to you, Logan." Mercury looked up into his

depthless greys and ignored the impulse to loosen her hair just because he was there. "You don't know me and you don't want to. We built this entire structure so we could indulge the Initiative and move on. Isn't that true?"

There was a slight flicker of hesitation again, but the living wall of muscle in front of her didn't back down. "No, it isn't. And you knew that before you asked. I do know you." He may have hesitated, but there was no flicker of uncertainty in his stormy eyes as they looked down into hers. "And I intend to know more."

Mercury felt confused as she stared, since she still didn't understand if he was just trying to push whatever game they were playing or if he really meant that he wanted something real with her. Anna and Orion were friends. Really good friends, as far as she could tell. But she and Logan were . . . nothing. Not friends. Not even really acquaintances, they were just two people doing what they were told to do because they were afraid for their own families.

That was what she told herself.

Mercury had developed real emotions toward Logan, and she was afraid she was falling for him, but she was falling for a part that he was playing. An act. "We don't know each other very well. This is an act. A game. It works for what we need, and that's all that matters. Sex feels good, but this doesn't make you happy. If it did, you would smile more."

There was always something churning behind the storm in Logan's eyes. Thoughts that felt like they were just out of reach, written in a language that seemed like it should be understandable, but slipped away at the last moment. He considered what she was saying in silence, but then caressed along her jaw with his fingertips.

"Every person I've met has a different kind of happy. Not everyone is smiles and jokes and hysterical laughter. For some people, happy is what you feel at the end of the day when you've worked hard and you can go home and do what you want with who you want." His fingers moved over her neck, but kept her face tilted up toward him. "You know things about me that nobody else ever has. And I know you in ways I know no one else ever has. That's not a question, it's a fact."

The tiniest hint of a smile twisted in his expression as he looked at her, something that anyone more than a whisper away from his face could have missed. "Now. Tell me again that you're just acting whenever you're with me. Lie again, and see what happens."

"I didn't say that *I* was acting." Mercury admitted softly, since she really hadn't specified, and it was because she hadn't wanted to admit that she wasn't acting when she felt like he was. "This wasn't supposed to matter. I didn't want to allow myself to think I matter to you, not the way she does. That's as it should be. This is temporary."

There was another pause from Logan, but it didn't seem like he was hesitating that time, only thinking through the weight of something that seemed to be settling in on him. "Is it?" He seemed content to leave that as a rhetorical question, and his fingertips moved back over her neck to brush along her shoulder, grazing the edge of the braid that was still holding her hair. "You matter to me. Whether you are supposed to or not is irrelevant. What we're *supposed* to do has become more and more irrelevant ever since we set foot on this station. What matters is what we want, all of us. We want Eleusis, we want peace, and we want to go to sleep satisfied at night. I want those things for you, and I will fight like hell to make sure you get them. That's not a game to me. Not some act that I turn on and off when it's convenient. It's what I want."

Mercury turned her face toward his hand, like a cat searching for more attention at its master's hand. "I think about you all the time, even though I know I shouldn't. I want to see you more often, even though I shouldn't." She took a deep breath before she moved closer to him by a fraction. "I'm falling for you. And that's the truth."

She felt a slight tremor in his fingers as she admitted her truth, but he didn't move away from her or remove his touch when she nuzzled her cheek against his hand. "Much of my day, every day, is spent with you in my mind." Logan said quietly, letting his fingers move down from her cheek to the neckline of her scrubs. "Tell me about some of these thoughts you're having about me on the days we aren't together."

Was this really happening? He didn't stop touching her, and he said that he thought about her every day. She thought about him every day. They shouldn't be admitting these things to each other, much less indulging them, but she didn't stop. That morning before she stepped out to a surprise breakfast that Orion had made for her, she'd stepped into the shower and thought about Logan. Maybe she shouldn't have, but she did.

"I had a dream about you last night, and when I woke up, I didn't want to stop thinking about you." Mercury tentatively touched her fingertips to his bare torso and then down his abs. He was just so gorgeous, nevermind that she just stitched him up. "So I went into the shower alone. I got lost in the steam and hot water. I closed my eyes and thought about your hands on me. I touched myself until I orgasmed. Twice."

Her story and her touch had drawn a small smile from him, which was the most he typically ever had on his face around her, even at his happiest, but he didn't pull away from her or try and tease her as Orion might have. He was a very different man than her husband, and his wandering touch along the neckline of her scrubs proved it. "And how often has that happened to you recently?" He asked nonchalantly, his other hand moving to the waist of her scrubs to toy with the tie that was keeping them in place.

Mercury felt a little embarrassed admitting it, but she answered anyway. "At least once a day. Usually more." She was speaking just above a whisper, even though they were alone in the exam room. "Definitely more when I don't get to see you."

"Good." He said right away, smiling a little wider as he thought about it. "If I had my way at all times, I'd be making you come half a dozen times a day, every day. Just to see how much you can take and how much more you want from me." His fingers tugged at the tie of her scrubs until it came loose, but he didn't make any other motion to remove them. "From now on, when you do, I want you to remember that I want you doing that. I don't want a day to go by where you don't picture my face when you come at least twice."

"Mhm." She nodded so he knew she understood, but she was clearly distracted, since she wondered what his intentions were with untying her scrubs. Technically she was still supposed to be working. "Twice. I understand."

"At least twice." He corrected, then moved his hand down to shove her pants to the floor around her feet, without looking away from her eyes, darkened now to a forest green with desire. His fingers moved to the underwear and his expression turned into a slight scold. "It seems you're wearing the wrong underwear. How careless of you. Fix that."

Mercury nodded in compliance even though she didn't know

what to change into, until she realized she was still holding the gifted underwear in her hand. She slid the others down and the new ones on, and then gently kicked her scrubs aside so they wouldn't get in the way. Before he could scold her about her hair, though, she reached back and pulled the tie out of her braid and hoped that it would fall free on its own.

He nodded his approval as she pulled her hair free and stepped in close against her after she had the 'correct' underwear on. "Don't wait next time." His possessive hand moved to her waist, which was barely covered at all by the slip of fabric he'd given her. His touch moved over her waist to her backside before he drew it away and smacked her ass, hard enough to sting but not quite hard enough to hurt. "So long as you're mine, when you see me, the hair comes down."

"I will remember." She felt tortured by his proximity, but he didn't touch her again after smacking her backside. Mercury wanted so much more. She was *desperate* for more. "I want you so much." She whispered her confession as she stepped closer to him and tentatively touched him again. "I ache."

"Just the way I like you." His hand found her backside again, and he pressed her flush against him, but his other hand had disappeared into his pocket. The rest of her body started paying attention quickly when the small vibrator embedded in her panties sprang to life at his touch.

Mercury gasped first and moaned softly as her grip on his arm tightened, just in case her knees gave way. She was careful of his wound but it was hard to think otherwise. "You . . . you said you think about me." She inquired, though it was hard to talk. "Do you . . . touch yourself too?"

He left the panties at a slow vibration but took her free hand and led it to his groin, where she could feel that the conversation had definitely had the same effect on him. "Our unit isn't too far from our offices." He knew she knew, but the obvious deserved to be stated from time to time. "Recently I've been going back there for lunch, especially if I've been with agricultural meetings all morning. Get a meal, get a good long shower of my own . . . that happens more days than not."

"I love that you think about me." She rasped as she held firmly to his manhood, desperate to stroke it, lick it, anything to please him. "I wish I was there with you."

"Two days and you will be." He reminded her and increased

the pace of the vibration in her panties. "You'll get there immediately at the end of your shift and leave your clothes by the door. I want to come in and catch you in our bed, already thinking about what I'm going to do to you. Because I'm going to be impatient when I get there. We'll have a week together and I'm not going to let any of it go to waste."

Mercury didn't acknowledge what he told her, she just pressed closer and kissed him, moaning between kisses because of the vibrating panties. For so long she had avoided showing too much affection because she was afraid of him knowing she had real feelings, but now she wanted to indulge her feelings. "Two days is so far away." She pleaded as her orgasm built. "I want you now. *Please.*"

He relished the pleading tone in her voice as the pace of the vibrator intensified at his command, but out of nowhere, as her moans began to escalate, he switched it off entirely leaving her core with only the aching memory of its intensity. He moved to one side of the room and quickly undid his pants, sliding them to the floor before he sat back in a chair, slouching so that the hardness of him was fully exposed to her. "Take off your clothes, Venus." He commanded as he sat down. "And come get me."

Mercury was quick to comply, nearly tearing off the rest of her clothes before tossing them aside with no care to where they landed. Everything about her was aching with need and she eagerly stroked his velvety skin over his erection as soon as he commanded her. Her core was slick with anticipation, but it didn't take much where Logan was concerned. Mercury didn't even ask permission to climb onto his lap, nor did she ask permission to slide down on top of him, and utter pleasure escaped her lips in a hushed cry as he filled her completely.

It was the kind of order he had given her half a hundred times before, but always in their unit, after he had teased her to the point of frantic need. The high from it, the ability to talk to another person and be obeyed with Mercury's kind of enthusiasm, was a rush he couldn't bring himself to hate. It didn't matter if it was the first time or the hundredth, having that kind of control was intoxicating, and he couldn't get enough of her.

She attacked him with a vengeance after all the teasing, and though he opened his mouth a few times to tell her to slow down, to delay their satisfaction, he couldn't bring himself to actually utter the words. He wanted her too much, wanted everything about her too much. His hands went to her waist so that he could position her on top of him however he wanted, but she had been riding him for four months. She knew exactly what he liked, what worked for him, and more importantly, she knew what her own body liked. He smacked her ass a few more times just for the jerk in her hips it produced, but the most he could do was rest his head back against the wall behind him. "Oh, fuck, that's good . . ."

She loved seeing him like this, clearly pleased and with his guard down. Mercury's body didn't stop moving, but instead of attempting to make it look and feel impersonal, she took the initiative to kiss him. Kissing and sex on top of feeling as though she could be open about the emotions was a high she couldn't anticipate. Mercury didn't just want Logan's body, she wanted *him*. It created even more conflict, wanting two men, but it wasn't any less true.

After she moaned against his lips, her body trembled with the tension of her impending orgasm. "I'm yours, Logan." It was also rare for her to say his name, but she loved the sound of it. At that moment she couldn't think of anything or anyone else and she only wanted him. She was Venus, and Venus belonged to Logan.

Her Logan had never been one to hold back, but the way he touched her, the way he moved his hand up to her neck to hold her against him, it was possessive. He gripped her as she rode him, looking up in her eyes to see her own pleasure there. "And I'm yours." He managed to growl between moans, the chair he sat on set to rocking beneath her attention. "Harder, baby. Come and get it."

He didn't have to ask her twice, and Mercury was riding him so hard her whole body was flushed and shaking from the exertion, but she was clearly enjoying herself. Probably too loudly, since they were still in the clinic and she wasn't exactly being quiet. Due to privacy protocols, she knew that there were some measures of the walls being somewhat soundproof, but she was testing the limits of those measures. Mercury climaxed in a haze of pleasure that blinded her and flooded her body, but she kept moving hard on top of him.

Logan held himself off as long as he could just to watch her unravel while he savored the wild abandon in her as her hair fell free of her braid. She held so much back all the time, held herself perfectly with practiced posture, professional detachment, she was almost cold in every other aspect of her life. But she was white-hot as she rocked herself against him, as she ground her hips into him. Another two days and he would have her all to himself again, at least for a week. She wasn't his that day, or at least she shouldn't have been, but she was. Every bit of her belonged to him, especially as she clung to him, crying out his name every time she came. It wasn't long before she drew his orgasm from him, and he was lost in the blind, blazing pleasure that shot down his spine like fire.

Coming down off the high Logan gave her was slow, and Mercury enjoyed savoring him as long as she could, especially since she wasn't supposed to have him at all that day. Mercury tasted his lips several times between heaving breaths, then pressed her slick forehead to his. "Are you alright?" She could see the gauze over his injury on his shoulder and it was pink from blood coming through. "You're bleeding."

That actually made him laugh and he shook his head. "I'm fine. You're more than worth shedding blood for." His strong hands kneaded over her hips and backside before working their way up her back. "Besides, if something goes wrong with my stitches, all it means is that I'll be back tomorrow for you to sew me up again."

Addicted. She was addicted. Mercury couldn't stop touching him and her lips couldn't stop kissing him. "I wish I could see you every day." She admitted in a whisper against his shoulder. "I've been holding my feelings back for so long that I'm overwhelmed by them. And you."

"If you saw me every day, you'd be begging for mercy in a matter of weeks. And I wouldn't give it to you." He promised with a threatening kiss, his lips dominating hers. "But I know what you mean about holding back. I've been holding a lot of things back, from a lot of people." He ran his hands up over her chest, sending aftershocks of sensation through every nerve in her body still ringing from endorphins. "I thought, for a while, that holding back was the way to get through all of this. But I've got a feeling I'm going to be doing less and less of that from now on."

"I'm glad." She responded out of reflex before she sealed her lips to his, and from the heat behind her kiss he felt her *need* for him. "I should look at your stitches again. I hope none of them ripped through."

"Go get something for us to wash up first. I've made a mess out of you." He returned the heat by marking her lips with his again, and he growled by the end. "You'd better move. Stay on a little while longer and I'll break you all over again."

"That sounds less like a threat than I'm sure you intended." Mercury liked his growls, so she tempted fate and his patience by kissing him once more before she did as commanded. "Thank you for my wonderful birthday present."

"I'm glad you like it. I plan to get a lot of use out of it." He leaned back in the chair to relax, then glanced down at the dressing over his cut with a shrug before she returned and took the gauze off to examine the stitches. None of them had come loose, but the cut had still bled in a few places due to the rough sex.

Mercury took a warm, wet towel to his skin to get him cleaned up. She started with his groin and then used a new, sterile towel to clean and check his wound. "It doesn't look too bad. I'll get a little medication for it."

He got up once he was more or less cleaned up and got his pants back up around his waist with a quiet sigh of regret that he had to get dressed in the first place. "It's going to be a long two days."

Mercury watched him as he dressed then went up to him, still naked, and applied the medication over his stitches and applied fresh gauze. "It doesn't have to be." She responded with too much hope in her voice. "I think you should come back tomorrow so I can check the stitches. I don't want you to get an infection." She was serious about checking on him, but clearly had other motives as well. It was difficult to be completely serious when she was taking care of his injury with her breasts out between them.

"No, I suppose we wouldn't want that." He smiled, running his hands over her breasts as she tended to his chest. "I'll be here."

She whimpered as he ran his hands over her breasts, her nipples aching for his attention again. "I love the way you touch me." Mercury confessed, and she didn't want him to go, but she knew he needed to. "I wish you could stay longer."

"Maybe tomorrow I will." He moved his hand down from her breast along her side, until eventually, he took her hand. Everything else in the world, they had done to each other, touched each other every which way, except for something as simple as that. "I'll see you then."

Mercury nodded as she squeezed his hand but she eventually let go, since he wasn't really hers to keep. She didn't want to see him walk out, though, so she grabbed her clothes and turned away so that she could get dressed and he could leave. She would see him again in a day. It would never be enough.

20

That night it was late when Logan got home, but Anna had been able to verify that he was, in fact, working on a late report with a few members of the engineering board. Kazuo had had one of his good days and wanted to take advantage of it, so the rest of the meeting had stayed for as long as the man had strength.

She heard him come in, and he even put an arm around her as they slept, but by the time she woke up in the morning, he was gone again.

Their lunch that day was put aside as well, since one of the Initiative members had broken the arm of another that morning on purpose. The council had never established legal parameters for assault between the colonists, and it had taken a special session to get things settled. The man's trial took place over lunch, which put Anna and Logan in the same room, just not to socialize. The man was sentenced by Anna and her colleagues in accordance with what they thought was fair, and everyone was exhausted by the end of the day.

Anna was still, somehow, home before Logan, even though she had to meet with her colleagues after the sentencing. She knew she was supposed to be with Orion for a week starting the next day, but she felt short-changed. He didn't seem to be in a hurry to spend time with her on their last night together for a week.

She felt a little crazy, angrier than usual, and wanting to cry at the same time. It was probably just hormones.

Anna packed a few things in a bag in preparation for the upcoming week and sat down to read a little to clear her mind. Next she knew, she was waking up to the sound of Logan's boots through the doorway. When she looked at her communicator, she realized it was late.

Orion was never this flaky.

"You decided to come home from work after all?"

Logan hadn't expected her to be home when he got there, but

he put his bag down before he set about getting rid of his coat. "I brought work home with me, actually. Permutations of interpersonal criminality. Should make for a fantastic few days of work, all thanks to Mr. Geller's temper." He took off his boots off by the door and tossed them into a corner rather than lining them up. Being exact about things like that didn't matter. Not when so much else was going wrong with the world.

Anna walked over and lined his boots for him and looked over at him again. "I have hardly seen you at all. I doubt you would have noticed if I wasn't home yesterday or today."

"I would've noticed." He didn't even look at her directly. At least not at first. When he did, she could see the same fatigue in his eyes that she fought, though he didn't look away. "You were great today. I know you said when they first put you on the Judiciary they made a mistake, but they didn't. And it shows."

"I don't care about that." She stared at him for a moment and moved closer to him. As soon as she was close enough to touch him, she attempted to take off his shirt so she could check his cut. "How are you feeling?"

He accommodated getting rid of his shirt, and tossed it across the back of a chair nearby. "It's fine. It was sore yesterday and this morning, but after the Council adjourned, I went and grabbed a couple shots of Shine up at the dock before I came back down here. Better than letting any more Orbital medication near me." He looked down at the line of stitches where his skin had started to close over and return to normal. "It's not as bad as the time I got shredded on my way out of the oak tree, and even those were better in a few days. I don't think this is gonna be any different."

"I was concerned then and I'm concerned now." Anna ran her finger gingerly over his stitches and looked up into his stormy eyes. "You didn't say who looked at it for you."

"I got Mercury to stitch it up." He admitted flatly. "Patel has barely looked at me since before launch, Barry was with a patient, and I knew Mercury was on maternity visits that day. She had some time to do sutures. She checked over it yesterday too, and gave me an antibiotic for an infection near the top. It's gone now."

"You went in and had them checked? Doc would be impressed." He never kept follow-up appointments. Not before Mercury, at least. Did he really go out of concern for an infection? Or did he go to see *her*? "You don't usually care about that."

"Well, back home, following up on stitches meant an hour and a half in the car and listening to a lecture. Here it's four decks up and ten minutes when I don't have to listen to idiots taking up my time." He shook his head and looked down at it with a shrug. "But no, it's alright. What about you? You were moving in your sleep last night, holding your arm. The bullets from the boarding incident still bothering you?"

"Sometimes. They said it damaged muscle, so it goes numb and hurts sometimes." Anna stared at his bared chest before her eyes finally flicked. It was much easier to read her bright eyes than his stormy grey ones, and a shirtless Logan always scrambled her brain. "You could have told me you were going to the bar. I would have gone for drinks with you."

"I thought you were still caught up with meetings. I would've liked that." She had known him long enough to tell when he was lying, and he wasn't, but he was still distanced. "It won't be the last of the drinking I do tonight, that's for sure."

"Let me get changed, we can go back to the dock and drink and dance, then. There's always good music and a good crowd." She looked down at her worn t-shirt and cutoff shorts. "I'll get dressed up and everything."

"And watch them take what else from us?" He asked with an exhaustion that had nothing to do with how he felt physically. "I know you've been lying about getting updates from home. Just like you know I have. I haven't gotten anything in two weeks. From anyone. Last I heard was Larissa . . ." he clipped off his comment, since he knew Anna knew. It had been a deep-snow winter for the midwest district, and it had isolated his family even more than usual. Larissa had been sick for three weeks when communications went silent, with very limited access to anything resembling medical attention. He'd never been informed as to whether she recovered or not.

"She's strong. She's doing fine, I'm sure of it." Anna tried to reassure him the best she could. "I've been lying because I know it's my fault. I'm not fucking pregnant. I'm starting to believe I never will be. If I was, they would let us talk to them. But that doesn't change the fact that we can be together tonight, Logan. Come on."

She was nearly begging, but it didn't look like it mattered. "I'm not going to see you for a week except on lunches. Just go out with me."

Logan didn't answer that right away, but eventually he shook his head. "It's not your fault. But going out tonight won't change anything." He started to walk past her toward the bedroom, but he did brush her on the way.

"Logan." She reached out and grabbed his arm forcefully as he brushed past her, because she wasn't going to let him just push her away. "You do not get to walk away like this. I'm your wife, for fuck's sake. Or does that not matter anymore either?"

"Of course that matters!" He actually shouted back at her, with the first real energy she had seen in days. His voice was still raised as he continued, but he didn't shout anymore. "You matter more to me than any other person in the world, and every chance I get to show it to you, they take something else away. From me, from you, from both of us."

He sighed, trying to calm himself down, though he had limited success. "Seven times, in the past four months. Seven times, I've had some kind of plan laid out to get off this hunk of junk and back home. Seven times, it's gotten cut off at the knees. So then what? We wait this out, keep spending less and less time with each other until finally we go to Eleusis and find out the Consortium will take that too?"

Some of the Initiates that came after the attack rose quickly in the ranks, thanks to Consortium support and the good graces of the commanders. Very few among the original initiates missed the writing on the wall where they were concerned.

"And live like slaves the rest of our lives. That's the future I'm staring down every day, and the more we try to stay with each other, the harder the fuckers are going to try to push us apart." Logan had always been the type to bottle up everything, but when it came pouring out, it was a monsoon.

Anna took it in stride, since she knew Logan well enough to know she had prodded him on purpose to get a response. Any response. "It's not her turn. It's my turn. I don't care about what they do to me if that means I lose you in the process, Logan." She was usually the emotional one, but apparently she was good at staying calm when someone else was losing their mind. "Our marriage won't fucking survive this if we think we can just ignore it and hope it is still there someday. That's not how it works. If you push me away and spend all of your time working or with her, then I lose you. There's no way I won't if you do that."

"Then you're gonna have to teach me how to be selfish." He shot back without moving away, desperately trying to put his own temper back in the bottle, but it was too late for that. It was too late for a lot of things. "Because that's not something I know how to do. Hold onto you when holding on means they could be at your dad's house right now putting poison in your brother's morning coffee. When they could be trimming your dad's lifespan by a few more months just to push your buttons. Teach me how to be *that* selfish; to choose holding onto you even if it means they destroy everything else that you love, all the while making sure you know that I'm the reason why."

"I have never blamed you for their fuckery, Logan." Anna kept a firm hold on his muscular arm, but even if he pulled away, she would go after him. "The truth is, they could have already killed our families and we wouldn't know. We have no control over what they do or don't do. The only thing we can control is this. Us." Anna slid her hand down his arm to take ahold of his hand and she held it so tightly it hurt. "Fuck, Logan, we left them all behind and everything we knew for *us*. We want a better life for them too, that was a factor, but all of this was for us. A lifetime together, knowing that we might never see them again. Now what?"

"Now what?" His voice was softer as he asked that question, and he sighed, squeezing her hand back. "Let me show you. This is what." He pulled her with him across the room to where the main viewscreen was taking up most of a wall, and woke the display with a gesture.

He quickly jumped into his files, which she could see looked a lot like hers; lots of correspondence about trifles, a few decent business-type emails back and forth, and loads of information that both of them were expected to review but neither of them fully understood. He sifted through the jumble quickly, and got to one labeled "Beta Site."

It contained, first and foremost, a hologram of Eleusis, but instead of just the main landing site that they had all been surveying and mapping, there was a second site identified. All the way on the other side of the planet. "This came through three days ago. No one outside the Council has seen it, or is supposed to, since it hasn't been put to a vote yet. The proposal is that a portion of the colonists be sent to the secondary site, in order to maximize research capabilities and provide greater probability of success in colonization."

"It all sounds great on paper, and Kaplan has nearly bought enough votes to overrule me. One or two more and he'll have what he needs to do it." He zoomed in on the secondary site, and immediately, Anna could see that it resembled their home. Rolling plains with little to no definition in the topography, ample water supply, more than enough rainfall, no noted harshness in weather conditions, ideal growing conditions, and year-round, no less. "The agricultural teams would be housed here, primarily. Me included. Leaving the main station and the main colony of Eleusis back at the primary site. Where you and Orion would be assigned."

"So you're trying to get away from me or you're trying to prevent it from happening? You didn't say how you wanted to vote, only that Kaplan is opposing you." God, was he trying to dump her right here and now, before they even had a chance to try to escape and go home or get to Eleusis on their own terms? "It kind of sounds like you already gave up on us. I mean, I almost don't blame you. I'm sure Mercury would be a perfect wife."

"Of course I'm fucking opposed to it!" He was back to shouting, his usually-calm baritone booming through the unit until the walls nearly shook. "This isn't what I wanted! This isn't what any of us wanted! But that's my whole point." He took a few quick breaths as his voice came back to more or less normal levels.

"Everything we try. Every time we think we've got this tiny slice of power, this inch of wiggle room, it evaporates. Every single time." He gestured in resignation at the screen, as if the deal was already done and sealed. "I'm trying to see the end, Anna. I want to see it. I want to see the end where you and I are sitting on that porch, watching the sun rise over another planet as we drink whatever passes for coffee on Eleusis. I want to see that. But no matter how hard I go looking for it, I can't find it. Tell me where it is. Tell me how we get there, and I'm with you. How do we fight a system that has every single kind of power and control over what we do every day?"

"I don't have an answer." She responded brokenly as she just stared, but she felt shattered that he was willing to give up. "I just know that giving up isn't the answer." Anna looked at him in silence after that, but she had to look away as her eyes burned with tears. She hated crying, but she especially hated crying in front of Logan. Anna fiddled with her wedding ring on her hand and she stared down at it through blurry vision. "But I can't make you do anything or force you to keep fighting. And I'm tired of wondering. I'm tired of feeling pushed aside and avoided."

Logan didn't move away as she looked down, but he didn't move closer to her either. He felt like someone had put his entire soul in a meat grinder and they were taking their time turning the crank. "We chose wrong." He eventually said, his voice barely above a whisper. "We've both known that for a while, I think, but that's one thought that just won't leave me alone. Because there's no way that I would've done other than I did, every step of the way to get on that shuttle. But ever since that seatbelt got locked, it's been their game."

He left that to sink heavily into the air between them, but finally stepped up closer, putting one hand on the side of her face to hold her against him, his lips down by her ear. It looked as though he was just holding her to console her, but he spoke once his face was hidden by her hair, in a whisper so quiet she could barely hear it herself. "I've got one gamble left, and it's the last one I ever wanted to take. But I'm out of other options. I need them to think they've broken us. That's the only time they ever ease up. On anybody."

The tears that she thought she could hold back slid down her face anyway, because she knew that if he was giving in to them, even for 'appearances', it wouldn't mean good things for her. One of her father's sayings came into her mind, one about playing with fire and getting burned. Logan thought he knew the game he was playing, but that meant getting closer to Mercury and further from her.

"We chose wrong before. Are you really willing to risk choosing wrong again?" Her heart hurt. Everything hurt. "I already feel broken."

He didn't care what appearances would look like for them there in the unit, if anyone was indeed watching them. He put his arms around Anna and held her tightly as she cried. There was no way he was ever going to allow something like that to happen without doing something about it. "You said it yourself." He whispered again. "The only wrong choice at this point is not to fight. I don't take a chance, they win. I take a chance, maybe they still win, but at least there's a chance. It's the only way I've got left that I can see."

"What do you want me to say?" She finally looked up at him even as he kept his arms around her, and tears continued down her cheeks. "You're asking too much, Logan."

He reached up to wipe away some of the tears, though a part

of him was surprised that she would even let him. "All I care about in this world is building a future with you. Anything that makes that impossible or hinders that from happening is something I consider hostile. Right now, we just need time." He couldn't say much more about the chance that he was planning to take, especially since he wasn't sure if Anna would be a fan of the gamble when she eventually learned of it.

"And if that fails too . . . then if you ask me, we should order all the food and booze they'll let us stockpile in this unit, jerry-rig some weapons, barricade the door, hole up in here and wait to die. If I had to pick my way to go, it'd be that one. Next to you and still shooting. Still fighting."

Anna turned into him and buried her face into his shoulder as she wrapped her arms around him. She was scared of everything, but mostly she was constantly scared of losing him for good. One way or another, it didn't matter, all that mattered was if she lost him, she was losing the most important person in the world to her. "I want a future with you. I've wanted that for as long as I can remember wanting anything. All of this is killing me, and I'm scared I'm going to lose you for good, either to death or a tall redhead."

She could almost feel his heated glare down at her for that comment, but his grip on her didn't loosen in the slightest. "I promised you until death do us part. That's the only one of those two options that's ever going to split us up completely."

Anna looked into his endless grey eyes, even as he glared at her. "You've never been worried? Not once?" She didn't think she was giving him anything to worry about, not like he was giving her plenty of reason to worry. Anna and Orion were friends, and while she cared about him deeply, she did her utmost not to entertain the L-word in relation to Orion. Friends. Lovers. But not IN love. Logan's relationship with Mercury was so different than hers that she couldn't help but wonder what Mercury was offering him that Anna couldn't. She didn't know anything about their relationship. "You stay away from me as though it's going to help. All the while I'm wondering why her pussy is more magical than mine. It's not fair."

"Nothing about her is more magical than you." He snapped quickly, looking her over once. "And yes, I worry. I married my best friend a couple weeks before we got onto this station, and my best friend happens to be matched up with a guy who she's quickly become best friends with. So yeah, you could say I'm worried."

"He's not my best friend. You're my best friend." Anna grabbed Logan's face and pulled him into a searing kiss, because she didn't care who was watching. "Orion and I are friends. That's it." She and Orion had a lot in common, more than she and Logan did, but Logan was her best friend. Her future. "I love you."

"I love you too, Anna." He breathed against her lips after the kiss, and he didn't pull away since it felt like it had been too long since he'd been anywhere near her. "No matter where, no matter when, no matter what. I love you."

Anna kissed him and felt the heat in her bones, her marrow, and her hands gripped his shoulders so hard her knuckles turned white. "I'm not letting you go. I'm keeping you right here. No drinks. No food. No nothing except my kisses, so you better be hungry for those."

Logan almost wanted to cry at the feeling of Anna holding onto him. What he wouldn't have done to feel her touch him that same way five years before. How many times had he lain in bed at night and fantasized about what it would be like to finally tell her how he felt, tell her that he loved her, to have her bring his dreams to life and say she loved him too? How long had he been waiting for that kind of paradise? Too long. Always too long. "As a rule, I'm known for my appetite. Especially where you're concerned."

Anna jumped up and wrapped her legs around his waist and moaned as his hands went to her ass. She kissed him a few more times before she leaned and whispered into his ear. "The first time I saw you naked, it was an accident. But I dreamt about it again and again. I remember waking up wet and wanton because I would dream about everything I wanted to do with you. We're meant to be together."

He walked them into the bedroom, kissing her senseless as they went before his lips moved down onto her neck. He knew he would leave a mark on her, since she hickey-ed easily, but he didn't feel bad about that. "I've been having wet dreams about you since I was twelve. The first time I ever actually got a good look at you was one time when you took a shower at my place, then took your time toweling yourself off in front of the sink instead of staying in the stall. The door was open a crack, and I came over to try and take a leak, but there you were on the other side of the door. I watched, and I'm pretty sure I jerked off at least five times in the twenty-four hours following."

"That's fucking hot." She murmured as she tilted her head and he branded her skin with his lips. Anna didn't care if he wrote his name in hickies, since she wanted his mark. "Though I'm sure I didn't have much going on at that age."

"Oh no, the seeing you naked was after your tits came in." He laid her back on their bed, reaching down to tug off her shoes and throw them away. "They seemed pretty new to you too at the time, since you couldn't stop touching them. Like you had just taken them out of the box or something." He kissed his way down over the fabric of her shirt to the inner curve of one of her breasts. "Definitely wished you'd outsource that job to me at the time, but I had no problem settling for the memory. You just looked so cocky and ambitious. I loved it."

"They're great tits, don't you think?" She didn't hesitate to pull off her shirt once he lifted his face off the fabric and she cupped one of her own breasts through her bra. "It took too long for me to get them, but I appreciate them." She unclasped her bra and tossed it aside as well. "Did you ever hear that I pierced my nipples once?"

"No, I never did, but I wondered that the first time I actually got a good close look at these babies." He leaned down and licked her nipple and sucked briefly but strongly at her peak to entice it to attention. "Just the barbells through? You've got the dots on either side."

She had a difficult time responding as he sucked on her nipple. The heat of his mouth and tongue had her squirming. "Yeah . . . just the barbells. Fuck, babe." Anna felt tingles that shot straight to her core. "I . . . I was fucking drunk . . . they didn't last."

"Not enough fun when people play with them to compensate for the healing?" He chuckled against her skin before he popped from one breast to the next, melting her brain with his tongue. "I've got no trouble picturing you doing that. Especially if someone dared you or some shit."

"They made my nipples ultra sensitive and most men are dumbasses about it." She groaned as he continued to worship her tits with his mouth. Logan definitely wasn't a dumbass when it came to the female body. "Someone dared me."

He actually chuckled again, though it wasn't the free and open laughter she knew. "I figured as much." He sighed against her chest at the taste of her, the simplicity of being with her, against all of the complications. "They were always sensitive to begin with.

I heard once from somebody that you were the only woman they'd ever seen cum from just these alone. I didn't believe it at the time, but ever since . . . well, seeing is believing."

"I'm an odd one." She agreed as she ran her hands through his hair. Anna loved feeling him so close, especially his beard against her skin. "I like talking about how things were. It reminds me that home is still out there. Every time I think about home, you're there with me. There's no part of my past that doesn't have you." Anna raked her hands down his back slowly, as far down as she could reach. "Even when we were little. And you thought I was annoying and icky. You told me girls couldn't play baseball. Or climb trees. Or ride bikes. Anything to keep me away when you were around your buddies. When it was just us, you didn't seem to care."

"I was a kid." His hands moved over every part of her, eventually unclasping her pants and moved them off her hips. "I still thought how many friends you had actually mattered. At the time I still thought that entire crowd was my friends, not just hanging out with me because that meant they could eat free at the estate."

"It was good food." She teased, since she hadn't been his friend just for the food. Once her pants were off, he could see that she was wearing a thin scrap of lace fabric. Anna was all about being sexy whatever way she could manage. "We're probably going to have all girls and every last one of them is going to want to play baseball just to spite you."

"That'd be fine with me." He ran his hands over the tiny excuse for underwear, but he didn't remove it. It was too fun to tease her with it. "They'd have the right mother to teach them how. You were always better at baseball than I was. Even if I could still always kick your ass in football."

"That's because you fucking tackled me to the ground just to laugh at me." She both glared and groaned, since he was still torturing her with his fingers. "Just like you were obsessed with drowning me whenever we're swimming."

"I didn't drown you except the once. And you came back from the dead, so I don't know what you're complaining about." He backed away from her on the bed to stand beside it to shove his remaining clothes to the floor. He looked down at her for a while and ran his hands over her legs to enjoy her smooth skin, and the familiarity of her body beneath his fingers. "And you got back at me. You might not have killed me or broken anything, but my ribs were sore for weeks."

"I'm going to make sure you are sore all over again, Logan Bickford." She crawled up to him as soon as he was naked, and she quickly found his cock with her hands. "I love your cock." Anna stroked him until she got a groan from him. "I want you to fuck me hard, babe."

He stayed at the edge of the bed to let her stroke him as she pleased, but he reached down past her hands to tear away her panties. The sound of ripping fabric filled her veins with need. His fingers moved against her to feel her slick center nearly begging for his cock. "Then you'll be the one who walks away sore. If you can still walk."

Anna was always up for anything, including wild and rough sex. "You promise?"

He ran his hands down her legs again, then grabbed her by the waist to pull her quickly to the edge of the bed. It was about to be her fertile week. By every standard the Consortium had given them, they should have been avoiding each other. But Logan didn't want to avoid her, that day or any other. He could feel a conflict in him as thoughts of Mercury rose up to challenge what he wanted with Anna, but everything with Mercury felt like it was happening in a different world. Every time he was with Anna, he was back on Earth, back in the world that made sense. He wanted to hold onto that. He wanted to hold onto something he shouldn't have to feel conflicted about wanting.

He jerked her toward him so that she was close enough to wrap her legs around his waist and feel the head of his dick tease her begging slit. "I promise."

Everything was frantic after that, and Anna loved it. He plunged into her, and she cried out in pleasure the second he filled her completely. His hands were as rough as his kisses had been, and he'd left plenty of hickies on her neck already and one on the inside of her breast. He was everywhere, and she loved the frenzy. "Logan . . ." She kept saying his name over and over, worshipping him with her words and her body.

Having her there on the edge of the bed, she was completely at his mercy, and he took every advantage of it that he wanted. He wasn't gentle about it, as she had requested, and he knew he would leave bruises on her hips and on her ass where he grabbed her. If it had her moaning louder and louder, he didn't care. Her pleasure was all he cared about, and he knew exactly how his wife liked to be touched. The whole time, though, he had her on her back looking up at him. He wanted to see the look on her face, wanted to see it in her eyes when she rocked against him. It was the only thing that made sense anymore in his world.

It didn't take long for Anna to reach climax the way that Logan handled her, and when she did, her eyes sizzled with pleasure as she stared into his steel greys. Anna cried out loudly when she came, followed by a lot of fucks and other swears, a language of love every bit as rough as the rest of her.

After she did, Logan pressed himself into her and leaned down on the bed to lay his entire weight against her. One hand supported him on the bed and the other moved up to grip her breast. He savored the sound of her moans as she continued to shake beneath him, her muscles spasming in the aftershocks, but he wasn't finished. Not by a long shot. "Nothing compares to you, Anna." He said as he drew back and slammed into her again. "Nothing."

Even as she came down from her orgasm, every time he slammed into her, she cried out in pleasure. "You . . . are my world." She replied with a moan, since she was in a haze of pleasure. "I never thought I would have you. I'm not letting you go."

"Good." He managed to growl as his pace picked up again, the angle between them and everything else about the moment different than it had been moments before. He was a big man, and everything about him was rough, but his roughness turned tender as he kissed her, driving himself into her with moans and growls of abandon. It was like the first time she'd had him, he lost himself inside her until nothing else in the world mattered or existed. His moans escalated against her neck and his arms tightened around her as he clung to her like the last thing in the world.

"I love you." She said between moans. He was going to wring her dry of orgasms. "I love you more than anything or anyone." Her whole body gripped tight, her legs, her arms, her hands. He had to know how much he meant to her. He had to know she would do anything and everything for him. Their future was in the balance, and she would do anything.

When his climax finally came, everything about him froze. He ground his hips into hers with a gasping moan, and every muscle in his body locked around hers, gripping her tight. Everything else was darkness and chaos, but the two of them there on that bed, wrapped up in each other, that was warm. That was the extent of what mattered to either of them. "I love you." He moaned, while her body drank his dry.

Anna collapsed when he did but their bodies stayed tangled as they laid together. She wasn't thinking about anyone or anything other than Logan and the tiny little hope they would make a baby together instead of her and Orion. She didn't know if that would happen and she didn't know what they would do to her if they found out she defied their system, but she wanted a baby with Logan before they joined the Initiative. Being away from Earth didn't change what she wanted, and she wanted a family with Logan. "That . . . was incredible."

He nodded against her shoulder, but couldn't move or speak aside from that. He didn't want to move, didn't want to leave her. Leaving her would mean she was going to see Orion and he was going to go back to Mercury. It meant he would lose his hold on the world as he thought he knew it all over again, and go back to the world the Consortium had made and the version of himself the Consortium had molded.

Anna stayed there with him as long as she could without saying anything, since the night was still theirs. She didn't have to go to Orion until midnight. Her fingers memorized every contour of his solid chest, every muscle, every scar, savoring each touch. "With my eyes closed I can pretend we're still back home. In your house. In our bed."

He kept his own eyes closed and kissed her neck, the taste of her skin on his lips. "With the rest of the house off to bed in their own wings. The heat keeps trying to kick on but it's still cold because it can't heat the whole fucking house at once."

"I always thought that was funny. Whenever we all were at your house in the winter it ended up being *this* close to an orgy just because everyone was trying to keep warm."

"I wonder if the person who built the place did that on purpose." He chuckled breathlessly and finally moved, rolling toward the pillows and taking her with him. "I know they made it so it could hold a dozen families, host the craziest parties in the district. I wouldn't be surprised if they did the heating thing on purpose."

"Well, your brother is a quarter of the way there." She curled into his side happily before she started kissing along his perfect, muscular arms. "How many do you want to have?"

"Families? Just the one, thank you." He rolled his eyes and scratched along her back as she curled into him, his eyes still closed as they played their game of fantasy.

"I mean children, silly." She said with a laugh and teasingly scraped her teeth along his skin. He smelled like his woodsy soap, sex, and all man. "I'm just curious what kind of damage I should expect for my vagina."

"Pretty severe, I'd bet. I want to get as many out of you as I can. Two at a time, if possible. I imagine that would leave a mark, but I want as many little versions of you running around the world as possible."

"Two at a time? How much room do you think I have in here?" Anna giggled and crawled back on top of him, since she liked being on top of him, against him, whatever she could get. "That's a lot of babies. You better be helping me with diapers."

"Only the piss ones. The shit ones are all yours. I ain't touching that. Plus, come on, I'm gonna be too busy working. I'm gonna need you to stay home. Pregnant and in the kitchen. The barefoot part is optional."

She laughed harder and it made her feel light. For once. "Then I need cooking lessons. Otherwise you're gonna starve to death." Anna's lips sought his velvet lips several more times. "I'll give you ten. That's it."

"Oh come on. Let's go for round numbers and make it an even dozen. Four boys, eight girls. Though I suppose I should have a conversation with my own boys about that." He moved his hips a little against her to illustrate his point, then moved his hands to roam over her pert backside. He didn't have to open his eyes to see her with his touch.

"Eight girls? Are you insane? Do you realize what kind of hormones you're going to have to deal with?" She enjoyed feeling his hips buck against her, just as she enjoyed feeling everything about him. "If you were smart, you'd discuss a team of all boys. Get them out in the fields, working hard, building up everything. Let other people have the girls." She smiled and nipped at his bottom lip with her teeth. "I'd be a terrible girl mom."

"You'll be an amazing mom. Boys, girls, however they pop. You'll be amazing." He returned the kiss, and a nip to her own lip, then reached up to massage her neck. "But yeah, maybe we'll just go with all boys. Fewer shotguns I'll have to keep around for future boyfriends. God, the number of men who came sniffing around Larissa that I really wanted to shoot . . . I don't think I'd be able to stop myself if it was my own daughter."

"You have to know that your sister is a catch. She's pretty, she's an amazing cook, she's shy but she's loyal and sweet. I'm not surprised there were so many."

That finally managed to chase the smile away from Logan's face, and his voice, all over again, as his thoughts turned back to the place where the conversation had started. "I want to believe she's alright. That I'll see her again, her and whatever kids she has with your brother while we're gone. I don't know when that'll be, or how, anymore. I just hope I see them again."

"We will." She said sincerely, though she wasn't sure how she sounded so confident. "I'm sure Liam will already have us beat by the time he gets back. Triplets with three wives is already nine kids right there." Anna kissed him again in an attempt to distract him from his worries. "No getting sad. Not right now."

Logan nodded and kissed her again as he settled back into the pillows. "Not right now."

* * * * *

They attacked each other one more time before they spent a few more hours reminiscing, and Anna fell asleep to the sound of Logan's voice.

When she woke up, though, he was gone.

Anna didn't have to wonder where, she could see by the clock that it was already a few hours past midnight, and that their week with the others had officially started. She also knew that Logan didn't want to take more risks than necessary, and he probably left so they wouldn't get in trouble for being together.

It still hurt.

Anna sent him a quick message to let him know that she missed him and that she loved him, but then she laid back against the pillows and let a few silent tears fall. Another half hour passed before she picked up her communicator again, and there was no reply from Logan, nothing from anyone.

She sighed heavily before she tapped on Orion's name.

Did you get ditched too, or am I the only one?

Orion's reply came through quickly, but she could tell from four months of communicating with the man that he had been mostly asleep while typing it.

I didthe ditcing. Been here snc middle night. Didnt wnna watch her leeve. I'm coming over.

Anna got up and took a slow, hot shower, so she could finish crying and so she wouldn't smell like sex when she went to see Orion. That would make things a hell of a lot more awkward. Anna even took the time to dry her hair before she piled it up on top of her head, got dressed, and headed out.

When she made it to the unit she shared with Orion, she tiptoed in, left her bag and shoes by the door, and found Orion asleep again. Without any warning, Anna climbed onto the bed and curled into him from behind. It made her want to cry again, but Orion was always nice to cuddle next to, regardless.

Orion startled when she curled into him, and turned his head toward her to look at her with his eyes half-open. "Hey." He put his head back on the pillow, but reached behind with his long arm to hold her tight against him by her ass. "I was wondering if that was an actual message or if you popped into the dream I had about taking a spacewalk to go get ice cream. Guess not."

"You have weird dreams." She mumbled into his back as he held her. "You should be worried about that." Anna kept her eyes closed in the darkness since she didn't want to start crying again. Things just felt different now, and she wasn't sure why she was so emotional about it. She really was worried that Logan was going to do something extreme and something would happen again. Orion didn't want her, he wanted Mercury, yet here they were - together again.

"Oh, that's not the half of it." He yawned with a laugh, as he looked at her over his shoulder. "I had this one long, detailed dream when I was maybe thirteen or fourteen, started with me sliding down a bannister on a stairway that went from Three all the way down to the southern coast of the Caliphate, except I had to keep stopping every few steps because there were bands playing and I needed to buy their music. They wouldn't sell it on Earth, so I had to get it on the stairs on the rebs way down. Then, just as I got through the atmosphere, there was a hang glider going right past the stairs with nothing actually driving it, just this bright blue t-shirt. And that was just the first few minutes." He smiled and turned around to face her. "If I was gonna be worried about crazy, I would've started a long time ago. Now I just go along with the crazy. Works out better that way."

"You should probably be evaluated for that." She mumbled softly, but she buried her face into his arm once he turned so he wouldn't ask her questions about her red, puffy face. The last thing she needed was for him to make fun of her for crying. She wasn't typically a crier.

"Please. I'd be willing to bet a fair wad of cash that you could out-crazy me any day or night, conscious or unconscious." He started massaging her back as she buried her face. He didn't need to ask why she was upset. They'd spent the majority of their time on Station Nine together. He knew what she was feeling without her needing to spell it out for him. "Come on, you know you've had some bat-shit crazy dreams. Let's hear it."

"I'm not about to admit that I'm as crazy as you are." She felt even more emotional when she thought about her own crazy dreams, because it just further proved that her crazy was like Orion's crazy. Everyone had weird dreams, but only certain people would really get a kick out of it and share it with other people, and she knew he was doing it to make her laugh and lighten the mood. Logan didn't do that. She was the one always trying to make *him* laugh. "If you want to prove I'm crazy, you'll just have to do it another way."

"Fine. I'll just start keeping a record of all the crazy shit you say when you're asleep and prove it from there." He shrugged, bouncing her head on his arm as his massage continued. "What was it the other night . . . you were completely stone asleep, but then you just like, twitched your leg this weird way like you were trying to kick somebody. I didn't understand the first thing you said, since you woke me up with the kick, but then you said something like 'put it back, that doesn't go there!' I just turned over and laughed myself silly."

That almost made her smile, but she wasn't smiling when she finally lifted her head to look into Orion's night-dark eyes. Logan didn't make comments about what she did when she was asleep. He used to, even when they were just friends. Logan had changed so much in a short time. "I'm scared." She admitted eventually. "I just . . . I'm sorry, I'm just not in a laughing mood."

"I noticed." Orion brushed some stray hair out of her face as he finally looked her in the eye. "Because let's face it, I'm hilarious. So if you're not laughing, you really must not be in the mood at all."

"You *are* hilarious." Anna confirmed with the smallest of

smirks, but it was gone as quickly as it came. "And it would be easier to make jokes and laugh and pretend like shit isn't falling apart."

Orion nodded and his smile dimmed. "But jokes won't stop them from falling apart anyway. Just makes the falling apart seem a little farther away." He didn't pull away, but he wasn't exactly pushing anything either. He just held her. "I took Mercury out for her birthday the other night. Had the whole thing prepared, all set up, we had a great morning, a really great night. Then we got into the unit after we got back and the first thing she started doing once we're home is put together her overnight bag." He shook his head and shrugged again. "I didn't even say anything. Not much to even say. No matter how much she's with me when she's with me, when she's not with me she's not."

Anna thought about how good things had been with Logan only hours before, but then he'd left without even so much as a goodbye. Not a kiss. Not an 'I love you'. Not a touch. Maybe he thought it was easier that way, but not for her. "They're so different. They're different than we are. They . . . even he's different. He's changed." Had she changed? Probably. But she didn't feel like she had. If she had, it could not have been that much. Not like Logan. "He says things, and I want to believe him, but I have a hard time."

Orion agreed, and his large hand rested along her waist. "It was supposed to be temporary. For all of us. I'm not sure how temporary it can be anymore. No matter what happens."

"The other thing that scares me is that sometimes I wonder if you're a better match for me than he is, even though Logan and I weren't matched, obviously." Anna looked away from Orion's eyes after that, since she hadn't wanted to admit it. "Not that it matters." She recovered quickly, since she wasn't going to leave her husband and he wasn't going to leave his wife. Clearly. Right? She'd just told Logan hours before that they would fight to the end. He said he would fight. And then he left her in the middle of the night. Talk about hot and cold. "I care about you a lot. But we're mostly just friends." After previously admitting that she was falling for him, they still avoided any heavy talk. Usually.

He didn't look her in the eye either and purposefully rolled onto his back to relax against the pillows, drawing her with him so she could use his bare chest as a pillow instead of his arm. "Mercury said the same kind of thing to me just a couple weeks after we started doing this. How did she put it? She said she could see why the program had matched us the way it had, and she could see the logic behind the match as it was redone. She didn't elaborate on what she meant by any of that, and I didn't ask her to. But I'm pretty sure she thinks that Logan is a better match for her than I am." He sighed and stroked Anna's hair as she laid against him. "And it's not hard for me to see all the ways you're a better match for me than Mercury. Eyes half-closed and I could still see it."

"What do we do with that?" She rested against his chest easily but she closed her eyes again, since it was easier. "I mean, if we escaped tomorrow, I don't know if Logan would actually be able to end things with Mercury." Anna hesitated, but then continued. "Some fucking lingerie company sent me a customer satisfaction survey, since I'm Mrs. Bickford. Too bad Mr. Bickford hasn't given me any lingerie. Those 'smart computers' can be really fucking stupid sometimes."

Orion sighed, but he didn't look surprised. "I hate finding out about shit like that sideways. I . . . yeah, I try not to even look on her side of the closet anymore. I saw some stuff she had packed away that I didn't really want to see. That's not . . . that's not the way any of this was supposed to go. Hiding things from each other, sneaking around about it. We were supposed to trust each other. All of us."

"Which is probably why it's happening this way. If we trust each other, we're dangerous." Anna huffed against Orion's chest and rested her hand on his abs, which meant she was absently running her fingers across his skin. "I think I've been honest with you and Logan." Anna chewed on her bottom lip before she added something else. "Except about one thing."

He hadn't stopped touching either, but he did move his head to one side to raise his eyebrows and look down at her as she said that. "What one thing is that?"

"I told Logan today that you and I are just friends because he was worried. I didn't want him to worry like I do. He said you and I are *best* friends." It wasn't untrue, and though she had denied it, she knew Logan well enough that he wouldn't dismiss it just because she denied it. "Since almost the beginning, you've been my best friend here." Anna felt wrong saying it out loud, but it was true. She was closer to Orion than Logan, but it wasn't entirely her fault. She stuck to the plan, she thought being friends would just keep things simple, and it had. Kind of.

Except Logan had been pulling away from her as she became better friends with Orion. Now there was a rift between her and Logan and nothing but closeness between her and Orion. The last several hours were evidence of that, if nothing else. She and Logan felt close because they had spent the entire time reminiscing. They had talked about the future a few times, kids, but only in that dreamy way that teenagers talk about their future. Not something real and solid. "I know I've said before that I was falling in love with you, but I'm pretty sure I'm *in* love with you, Orion. And that makes this shit really fucking complicated. Which is why I lied."

She could see him process that for a while, but without even saying anything else, he put his hands on her sides and pulled her farther up on him so he could kiss her. It wasn't some kind of deep, lingering, passionate touch, just a gentle caress of his lips on hers, and his arms wrapped around her.

"Mercury doesn't ask, and I haven't asked her. I don't think I want to hear her answer. I also know she wouldn't want to hear mine, because I love you too, Anna." He kissed her again, and rested his head on the pillow with a defeated sigh. "But you're right, that does make this shit incredibly fucking complicated. Sometimes I wonder if that's what they wanted this whole time, to see if they're capable of forcing people to fall in love with each other. But nobody put a gun to my heart and forced me. You're amazing, and whenever I'm around you, I feel lucky to get the chance. You've been my best friend here too. Especially since my previous best friend is busy with his match and all his own drama, you know how it goes. So congratulations, you got that job."

"I like the job. You're fun. And funny." Anna's kisses were as featherlight as his, flirting, tempting, but also tentative. "I like being your best friend, so Carl can't have it back. Anyway, you said he went and got Aiko all knocked up. He's got other things to worry about."

"Yeah he does." He agreed with a chuckle, his hands moving down to her hips as she moved on top of him. "You're better company than he is anyway. And, having seen both of you naked, I can honestly say that I vastly, *vastly* prefer you." He moved to kiss along her shoulder, which was one of the few parts of her that was exposed at the moment. She wasn't even in pajamas, but Orion figured she'd had a lot on her mind and pajamas weren't a priority.

"You better. Otherwise you are the best actor I know." Anna appreciated his kisses, though, and she tilted her head to encourage him to kiss her some more until she realized that Logan had probably covered her in hickies. At least it was dim lighting. "I'm sorry if, um . . . well, I bruise easily."

"Don't apologize." He kept his kisses to the parts of her that hadn't already been covered by Logan, but mostly it was his hands that did the exploring. His long fingers massaged into her back and moved down over her backside to grip her against him as he sighed. She could almost hear his thoughts, and the realization only drove home what she had been talking about herself earlier. He didn't like sleeping alone, and she could tell that he was glad she was there, no matter the rest of their circumstances. "You forget to pack your pajamas?"

"They're in my bag. My mind was somewhere else when I got out of the shower, and I'd spent the whole shower crying, so I didn't even think." At least she wasn't in some hidden lingerie that wasn't meant for her. Anna relaxed by degrees as his hands continued to unkink her muscles, his hands commanding her body to relax. "What do you think it would have been like, if we had been matched without all the other stuff? What if I came here single and you were single and we were matched? Do you think we would have been happy together?"

"Oh, absolutely not." He said lightly, and didn't take his hands off her curves. "No, not a chance. We'd have taken one look at each other and started fighting. Wouldn't have stopped all the way to Eleusis. I'm just nice to you because our lives are otherwise completely fucked up." His hands slid beneath her shirt to massage against her skin directly, and he chuckled as he kissed her again. "I mean, seriously, what kind of crazy person prefers a shotgun to an automatic weapon? I don't care if it is just a video game, you can't tell me that the spray from a shotgun actually makes up the difference of having automatic refiring. If we had been matched, the second I found that out about you, I would've been complaining to somebody to get me a replacement. I'm still not sure how I put up with you."

Anna rolled her eyes so hard they almost fell out. "You are ridiculous. You're right, I wouldn't have lasted. You're too opinionated and you don't listen. Have you actually killed anything with a shotgun? It is *incredibly* effective, thank you very much. Just wait until we actually get somewhere where we have to shoot our dinner, and you'll see who comes out on top."

Orion laughed at her sass, the sound rumbling through her directly from his chest to hers. "I look forward to that. For now, though, we don't have to shoot our dinner, but you still do plenty of coming on top. Some on the bottom, but it seems easier for you on top."

"That's because you have a monstrous cock I have to wrangle, and it's easier on top." She replied with a smirk before she grazed her lips against his. "That was a serious question before, you know."

"What? That was a serious answer. Our firearm preference discrepancies would be a problem." He returned the kiss fervently, his fingers kneading her muscles as he held her. "We would've been happy. I think we would've fought a fair bit, sure, but I expect to do that anyway. I think we would've gotten here, found out a little more about what was going on, then made a break for it in one of the pods. Just to see how far we could get."

"I wish we could do that now." Anna followed that up quickly. "I mean all four of us." She sat up to take off her shirt, since a massage would feel much better while naked. Anna tossed it aside and devoured his lips again. "I have another serious question for you. Prepare yourself so you don't get overloaded." She smirked and paused just to be dramatic, but she did have another serious question. "So if I do get knocked up before we get off this station, do you want to be involved? I mean, past the point of conception?" She didn't like the idea that he wouldn't know his kid, especially because she loved him. The kid wouldn't be meaningless. Orion mattered to her.

"I assume you mean more than just cuddling afterward." He said dryly, but he continued quickly so he could forestall getting smacked. "Of course I'm gonna want to be involved. It's my kid. Or will be. I'll want to be involved. As much as you want me to be, anyway."

"I want them to know their dad. Two dads are better than no dad. You and Logan both, I want you to love the kid." She ran her fingers over his lips before she tasted his lips again. "I don't want to stop seeing you if it happens this week. Do you?"

Orion shook his head, looking serious for once. "I know I should want to stop seeing you, but I don't. I like this too much." He ran his hand over her side and her chest to her neck as he kissed her. "I like being with you too much. Kicking your ass at video games, waking up next to you, sleeping with you, just hanging out with you anywhere. I like all of it too much to stop. Any of it."

"That was mostly sweet." She laughed, even though she agreed with what he said. Anna knew she should want to stop too, and it would be easier to stop if she hadn't admitted that she actually loved the big brute. "And mostly true, except the kicking my ass part. You can't like that, cuz it's not true." She covered his lips with her hand then grinned since he couldn't contradict her with his mouth covered. "I should want to stop seeing you too. Should is such a tricky thing." Anna kept her hand over his mouth and then she ducked down to kiss along his chest. "You're just so fucking gorgeous. And fun. You make me smile. I need that, and I need *you* in this shithole."

"Mmhm. Mmmhmhm." He mumbled beneath her hand, but it sounded like he was agreeing with her at least. One of his hands moved to caress the side of her face as she kissed him, glad just to have her close with so much going on.

Anna finally lifted her hand from his mouth as she sat up near his waist. She was still wearing her pants, but she was down to her bra. "What was that? Sounded like you said I'm a better shot than you are."

"I said keep telling yourself that." He latched both his hands on her backside and sat up beneath her, leaning in to kiss the bared curve of her breasts above her bra.

She frowned at him, even though it was mean to do that when he kissed her breast. "Come on, you know I am." Anna grabbed his face to force him to look at her, but she just kissed him roughly. "Do I really talk in my sleep like that? I don't remember hearing that I kick people."

"You have kicked me at least half a dozen times while we've been sleeping together." He accused with a laugh, then tossed her off his lap to flail on the bed beside him so he could strip her down. "You've also elbowed me in the face twice. That's why I always try and sleep spooning behind you. Not because I'm always trying to fuck you in the middle of the night, though that's usually true, that's just where I'm safest from your nocturnal wrath. And yes, you talk in your sleep. But usually only when you're incredibly tired."

"Hopefully I haven't given up any secrets while I'm asleep." She wiggled out of her pants as he tugged. He really was gorgeous, she wasn't teasing about that. "Or said the wrong name? God, that has been one of my biggest fears, um, forever."

"I've done that three times." He laughed as he tossed her pants to the floor, then proceeded to assault her legs with his mouth in the same mix of forceful and playful that Orion embodied in most of his life. "Twice it ended really badly, the third time she thought it was hot and wanted to see pictures of the girl whose name I said. Weird girl. Strange self-esteem issues. But no, I don't think you've yelled the wrong name. My dick apparently stands out enough that you can differentiate it without thinking too much."

Anna nodded as she looked toward said dick, though he was still wearing boxers. "Probably the biggest one I've ever seen. I can't account for the times when I was too drunk to measure accurately, so that's why I say probably." She met his dark eyes. "I'm sorry I'm not quite tall enough to make it work smoothly." They definitely had fun together, but she knew that she wasn't Mercury. She wasn't a tall, curvy woman who fit better with both Orion *and* Logan. "I try my best."

"Hey, don't apologize." He kissed his way back up to her chest and then laid down beside her on the bed. "You work just fine. I've been a freak all my life, I'm used to it. You . . ." he shook his head and laughed nervously as he turned toward her and kissed her once. "I'm not blowing smoke or anything else up your ass when I tell you that you're the single most talented fucker I've ever been with. Fucker in the very literal sense, I mean. I've had women string me along pussy-whipped before. Like, they just do it that well. I paid a girl's rent once. For six months. Yes, I was younger and stupider than I like to think I am now, but seriously, she was incredible. If you had come at single-me with some of the shit you can do with this tiny body of yours, you could've talked me into financing your own fucking Station. Don't ever apologize for something you're as good at as you are at sex. You blow my fucking mind."

"Would single-you have even looked twice at me?" She laughed, though she appreciated the compliment, since she'd worked hard at being close to sex goddess status. "You said you dated models."

"That was just the circles I ran in, not because I went looking for them. Usually they came looking for me." He shrugged and snapped her bra playfully against her back before he unhooked it and pulled it away from her. "It's gotta work the same way on

Earth. People get together and swap talk about what they've put in every single orifice, like you crazy people always do, you start comparing notes, somebody throws out a number, somebody else gets curious, comes looking. I never lacked for a date if I was in the mood to go out, that was for sure."

Anna watched as her bra flew across the room and fell to the floor out of his hands. "Usually when women wanted to know who to find, they asked me. Either that or they hated me for sleeping with their ex, their current, or their hopeful." Anna looked mildly guilty and then she just shrugged. "I didn't ever sleep with someone who was actually with someone at the time. Not knowingly. But when the one you want is taken, everyone else doesn't seem so bad. I did avoid some. Not many."

He shrugged right back, since her past didn't matter to him. It was no worse or better than his own. Honestly, it was one of the reasons why he got along with her so well. They had both decided sometime very early on in their prescribed relationship not to judge each other. "My point is, I would've noticed you." His kisses teased and tugged at her lips, then started down her neck and chest. His hand grazed along her side to extend her arm above her head, and he laced his fingers with hers as he splayed her out beneath him. "You're different from them, though. You'd have made me want to stick around and go the distance with somebody. For once."

Anna could easily get lost in his dark eyes, and she let the depths take her as she wondered what it would have been like if she would have met Orion a year earlier. She would have fallen for Orion, married him, and never looked back. It was hard to realize that someone who wasn't Logan could have made her happy.

For the time being, though, Logan had ditched her after whispering how much he loved her. "I don't want to feel conflicted. So right now I'm going to pretend that really happened. That I caught you, Orion Al-Jabbar, and I'm not letting go." In reality, he belonged to someone else, but right now she just wanted to pretend that nothing painful existed. She was doing a lot of pretending anymore.

"That you caught me? That you *caught* me?" He smirked as his lips teased her nipples in their descent. "Well that's not very specific. Am I a fish or a communicable disease? I'm confused." His lips moved down to the waistline of her panties and continued moving south without giving her a chance to respond. "Either way, go on and keep me, baby. I'm not going anywhere."

Anna hadn't realized he was going south with a purpose. "I . . . I'm pretending that I caught you with my sexuality. You couldn't resist me."

"You're right, I absolutely couldn't." His lips continued over her panties, his tongue flicking against her thighs as he reached up to tug her underwear away. "I imagine you walking up to me in a club, with a real drink in your hand, not some bullshit fruity margarita. You hand me the drink and tell me I'm gonna dance with you. From there, as soon as I saw this ass in motion, I'd be all over you."

"That is incredibly realistic. I don't drink the fruity shit unless I'm already so bombed I can't tell." Anna whimpered as his heated breath tortured her. "And I *would* be that bossy. You seriously know me so well."

"Then at some point in the night," his fingers touched her before his tongue did, sliding inside her slowly and gently to start teasing her, "we'd be flirting and you'd make some kind of claim about getting me addicted to you in one try. I'd be incredibly turned on and pretending like I wasn't. Then you'd actually take that shot and I'd have exactly no defense against you. Ever again."

Anna moaned in response as his finger slid inside of her. He had excellent fingers, long and knowledgeable. "We need to go to the dock and act this out. Please."

"Right now?" He kissed a little closer to her aching clit, where she was soaking with need for him.

There was a pause and she shook her head. "Not now. Tomorrow?" She didn't know if she could keep it together if he stopped, but it would be really fun to act out meeting him for the first time. Later.

"It's a date. A *first* date." He finally began to attack her directly, his fingers still inside her working magic that spoke of just as much experience with women as Anna had had with men. The way he saw it, Anna was in dire need of some cheering up, and he knew of no more surefire way than multiple orgasms.

With that kind of attack, Anna was completely defenseless, her whole body a gasping, whimpering mess as he continued relentlessly. He knew how to destroy her, and she was alright with him having that power over her. The scent of his skin, sharp and crisp, and his body hovering over her, it all overwhelmed her.

"Best . . . boyfriend . . . ever."

Eventually, he had completely exhausted her with his fingers and his tongue. He looked smug as he pulled away to allow her to roll onto her side and recover from his assault. He moved up on the bed to lie behind her, one arm tucked under her head and the other roaming her torso. "How's that massage? Still feeling tense at all?"

"Not even a little bit." She replied dreamily, since she was a puddle of endorphins still attempting to recover from his mouth. She had experience with recreational drug usage on Earth and she was starting to think that Orion was her space version of weed. Full relaxation. "What about you?"

"What about me? I'm the masseuse this evening, not the masseussed." He rubbed at her shoulders almost comically, but every touch was an extension of the caresses he'd been using on her body.

"So you don't want any action at all? That's weird." She tried to turn toward him but she gave up and rested her head against his arm again. "I was kind of hoping I could pay you for your attention with my vagina."

"I didn't say I wasn't interested." He pulled her back so her backside was flush against him, but he was still wearing his boxers. "I'm always happy to take payment via vagina. It's actually one of my favorite kinds of currency." He kissed the back of her shoulder, and even though his tone was joking, everything about his touch was intimate. He held onto her with care and ran his hands over her insatiably. Everything about him wanted her, every breath against her skin and every move of his body was focused on her and her alone.

Anna wiggled her backside against his groin before she turned over to face him. Her boobs looked bigger all mashed together and she liked that. Anna's lips explored his face and landed on his lips where she could taste the tang of herself in his lips. She didn't care, his lips were what she wanted. She slid her hand down his side and then tugged his boxers off slowly.

"I love you." She said tentatively, since she knew it was trouble to keep repeating it, but she wanted to have intimate moments with Orion. All joking aside.

"I love you too." He moved to get out of his boxers, and gave a brief groan of relief once they were gone. When he slept with Anna, he almost always slept naked, a habit he thoroughly enjoyed.

"I hope I can show it enough, now and, well, until whenever I get the chance. I'm not big on mixed signals or uncertainty. I love you, and I want you to know it every way I can get it across."

"Me too." She slid her hand up and down the length of him slowly before she kissed down his neck to his chest and then back up again. "Just being around you excites me, I never know what to expect, and I know you're just as adventurous as I am."

That made him grin. "I do tend to be up for anything. I like to think of myself as a hard man to shock. Though a few girls have taken a pretty fair stab at being shocking."

"We need more public hookups." She teased before she stroked him a little harder until he groaned in pleasure. "I love your cock. Seriously. It is fucking awesome." Anna looked down at his perfect manhood and then she started stroking him all over again. "I dream about this penis. Really and truly."

"Just the penis? Disembodied? That's unfortunate." He groaned as she stroked him, and separated his knees so that the fulness of him hung free for her to do with as she pleased. "I dream about these." He leaned in to kiss her nipples once to get them back to attention for him. "I had one the other night where I fucked you straight through your flight license exam. You were pissed but you were coming the whole time. So I figure it was a wash."

"Not a disembodied penis. Don't make it scary." She scolded him even while she was stroking him, so she doubted he was paying much attention. "Can that actually happen? Can you fuck me while I take an exam?"

"If I'm the ride-along instructor? Yes, I absolutely can. But I'm a little worried about how much faith you put in my fucking abilities if you think you could pass a test while riding me."

"Don't look at it that way." She stopped stroking him long enough to climb on top of him and sit down on top of his abs, but not before her backside grazed his erection. "You have trained me so well I can do it in my sleep. Hence also while fucking. That's the better way to think about it."

"Uh huh." He didn't seem convinced, but the sight of her on top of him was too good to argue about anything. "We can do that. Strap both of us into the same seat for your final shuttle test, see how well you perform under pressure." His hands reached up to apply pressure to her breasts at the appropriate moment, and as his hands raked down over her again, his thumb went south to toy with her. He looked up in her eyes and smiled. "You pass the test like that and I'll be suitably impressed."

"Oh, I can pass. Just you wait. You'll never be able to fly again without thinking about getting fucked in your seat or against a console." She giggled but it was hard to laugh again as his fingers slipped inside her. Anna went back to rubbing her backside against his cock before she moved so she was hovering over him, then slowly lowered herself down on top of him, inch by inch. "You know I love challenging you."

"I do." He groaned as she took him, but as she did, he took his hands off her and put them behind his head, letting her have all the control to do with him as she liked. "This week . . . we'll go more public. I've got some ideas we haven't tried yet."

"Hell yes." She moaned loudly as more of him pushed inside of her. "I'm always . . . up for whatever kinky ideas you might have." Anna smiled, but it twisted into something more as he started to move in response to her hips. They really did work well together.

"Maintenance tunnel. Sector six." He managed to say in between moans, the muscles of his chest and arms flexing as he stretched languidly, enjoying everything she was doing to him. "Very good chance of people working on the ballast conduits right around the corner from us."

Anna didn't want to be watched, but she didn't mind being heard, since she knew that people would find it both shocking and probably arousing. It was being heard but not getting caught that was the real turn-on for her. "I'm surprised . . . that you're into it."

"You shouldn't be." He moved his hands back to her chest to draw her down to him again, rocking into her as deeply as her body would accommodate. "I like having a reputation, remember? You scream and people are gonna know who's making you do it."

As soon as she was close enough she kissed him again, tasting his skin as her lips trailed down his neck. "They sure will." She nipped at his neck with her teeth while her hips continued their magic, since she always knew what she was doing. "But no one better come looking for you afterward."

"Only you, looking for more, I hope." His hands dug into her back as she rode him, but he was groaning with every little movement she made on top of him. The woman was a machine. "Good *god*, that's incredible."

Anna worked harder and faster after hearing his praise, since his compliments made her more eager. His pleasure and cursing made her feel like a goddess. Anna sat up straighter so she could quicken her pace. The feeling of him filling her to the brim was intoxicating. "You're perfect." She wistfully moaned as she ran her hands down his chest before she gripped his shoulders. He was flawless. It was unreal.

Orion did his best to turn the tables on her whenever they were in bed, but as tired as they were, he was content to lie back and let her have her way with him. As Anna was a talented lover, it wasn't long before his moans escalated to the rhythm of her hips, and the grip of his hands on her waist turned frantic. "Oh, fuck . . . you gonna . . . mmm . . . you gonna come with me, baby?"

"Fuck yeah." She growled and leaned back to change the angle so he would hit her in the right spot, and their moans escalated together, but she still orgasmed first. She had her hands behind her body to grip to his legs, which was a testament to her flexibility, but her hips didn't stop.

With Anna at that angle she had the leverage to hit him hard, and when he finally climaxed, his hands clenched her waist to encourage her as she rode him straight through it. If their unit was anything but soundproof, he surely would have woken their neighbors, but as it was, his moans just echoed in their own walls as he spent himself.

His entire body was twitching afterward and he struggled to catch his breath, and his head rested back on the pillow as he panted and hauled her close. "Ho . . . kay." He finally managed to say between gasping breaths. "I'm dead. I think you just fucked me straight to heaven."

Anna grinned proudly and she curled into him as she always did once she carefully slid off of him. Anna was all sorts of a sweaty mess, but she didn't care. The feeling of Orion's arm around her was enough to keep her warm and comfortable, even naked. "That's . . . what I like . . . to hear." She kissed his cheek and then closed her eyes. She was so tired. "I'm sleeping in tomorrow. Fuck everything else."

"No no, fuck *me*. Ignore everything else. I thought we had that cleared up." He said sleepily as he turned to kiss her cheek once before he reached to pull a thin sheet over them. It was all he ever slept with and always claimed he didn't need anything else, especially when sleeping with someone else in the bed with him. "Sweet dreams, baby."

Anna hugged him as tightly as she could manage before she said anything. "Mmm. I love you." And she was out like a light.

21

There weren't many places on the station where Logan felt like he could really find decent solitude, even in the middle of designated 'night' hours. There was always someone coming down a hallway doing night-shift maintenance, always someone moving to get a midnight snack or a late night drink. It was funny to Logan that the station even tried to simulate things like day or night in the first place, since they still did a full circuit of Earth every forty-five minutes regardless of what "time" it was. There were constant sunrises and sunsets to be had for those who wanted to sit around and watch for them. So often that no one ever watched them in space. It was sad, from Logan's point of view, but he was guilty of the same complacency.

That midnight was different, at least for him. He left Anna still sleeping, since he didn't want to disturb her after everything they'd talked through. They spent most of the night reminiscing until they both fell asleep halfway-wrapped in their own dream-world of the past and the way they had both envisioned their future. If she was still in that world, he certainly wasn't going to wake her up just to say goodbye on his way to see another woman.

He didn't go to Mercury directly, though. After everything with Anna, he couldn't bring himself to go directly from one unit to the other, even in the middle of the night.

Instead, he wandered the halls for a while, heading in no particular direction but slowly making his way toward the luxurious levels where his unit with Mercury was located. When he got to the right deck, he still didn't actually go to his unit. His mind was moving in too many circles to go through another door. Instead, he walked the long gallery, marvelling at the massive expanse of glass that stood between him and oblivion. It seemed paper-thin, even though he knew it was actually several meters thick and perfectly safe. The apparent fragility of it suited his mood.

He found a corner of the gallery that folded out on itself, one of several places he imagined had been designed with the rich and fancy in mind. A pocket of space that, while still technically public, was private in practice, since no one could easily see into the pocket once he was in it. The fold made the rest of the universe outside the glass seem that much heavier and dangerous, while at the same time helped him to forget that he was standing on a space station at all. In the middle of the glass fold it was like he was just hanging on oblivion's doorstep, watching the world spin and unable to do anything but spin right along with it. More elements of the place that suited his mood.

He retrieved a comfortable chair from the gallery and pulled it into the fold, just to sit and enjoy the absence for a while. He watched the Earth far below, watched the sun set on one side and rise on the other, watched the moon spin. It was all such chaos at first glance, such carefully-maintained order on further thought. He wasn't sure which was the more apt descriptor of his own life.

Mercury had gone up to Logan's unit once Orion left, but when Logan didn't show up and his communicator was off, she worried. She stayed awake and read some research while she waited, answered messages from her patients, but he still didn't come. Soon enough she was too worried to wait, so she wrapped herself up tight in one of his robes and went wandering, hoping that she would find him. She once felt as though the station was a safe place, but she hadn't felt that way for some time. Anything could have happened to Logan, and she hated the thought that he was hurt or dying. After the last attack, she knew it wasn't impossible.

The gallery wasn't the first place anyone would go looking, even in the middle of the night, and when her wandering finally led her back to it, the grand hall appeared empty. The bar was quiet, no one at any of the tables, certainly not at two o'clock in the morning. As she was about to leave the gallery and head back, there was a sound from an offshoot of the gallery, a man cleared his throat. It wasn't purposeful, just a casual cough, and the sound was greatly distorted. It could have been Logan, even though she still didn't actually see anyone down the branching hallway.

Mercury walked toward the sound but she watched carefully, since she didn't want to get jumped. She pulled Logan's robe tighter over herself, since she was wearing a revealing nightgown underneath. Everything she wore around Logan was some kind of revealing, unless she was in scrubs. She liked it, but it made a situation like this one more than a little nerve-wracking. "Hello? Is someone there?"

There was a pause before anyone answered, but when he did, it was clearly Logan. "In here." His voice echoed confusingly through the gallery branch, but when she passed a few other pockets in the glass that were empty and then saw the very back corner of a chair pulled into another, a closer look showed her Logan sitting back in the chair and staring out into space. He had a button-down shirt pulled over his shoulders, but it was hanging open over his chest and abs. The shorts he wore were some that she'd seen him wear when he felt like being comfortable. A pair of well-worn sandals were on the floor in front of the chair.

"I didn't mean to worry you." The cut of the glass pocket surrounding him gave his voice a strange resonance. "Just went to walk for a while."

"Oh, I see. I was worried when I didn't hear from you." She watched him for a moment but didn't get any closer once she could see him, since he didn't turn around. "I'm glad you're alright. I didn't mean to interrupt."

"You aren't interrupting anything." He still didn't turn toward her immediately, but when he didn't hear her moving, he turned his head slightly in her direction. "Come here."

Mercury hesitated a little because she really felt like she was intruding on his personal space and time, but ultimately, doing what he commanded was more important. She walked slowly up to the side of the chair and stood there next to him. "I can go back to the unit. It's just after everything that has happened, I was concerned you were injured. Or worse."

"I should have let you know that I would be late. That's understandable." He hadn't looked at her at first, but when she was there next to him, he looked her over, and leaned his head back to look up into her eyes. She could see his eyes flick to her hair quickly, but it had been out of her usual braid for some time, the memory of it remaining in some of the curls around her shoulders. "Drop the robe."

A cold panic went through Mercury at the very idea, since they were in a public place, even though it was private enough. She looked back over her shoulder before she looked at him again, and she knew he could see the conflict in her eyes. "I'm . . . I'm wearing a nightgown." She hoped that was enough to indicate she was wearing something she would never wear in public.

Logan's eyebrows went up just slightly but that was his only outward reaction to her statement. "And?"

Mercury played with the robe between her fingers, visibly uncomfortable as she slowly untied the belt. "We're not in our unit. What if someone sees me?" The robe parted slightly when she finished untying the belt, and he could see she was wearing a black nightgown that wasn't sheer, but it was satin and short enough in both directions to show her long legs, barely cover her backside, and cut low in the front that he could see a sliver of her ample cleavage.

"I heard you walking a minute ago, even barefoot, and you were the first person I'd heard for more than half an hour." His voice was slightly impatient as he answered, but he had thought it through before giving her the order. "You know better than to think I've ever had any intention of embarrassing you. Or that I have any intention of sharing the sight of you with anyone else."

"I'm sorry." She chewed on her bottom lip, since she should have known that he wouldn't embarrass her. "You're right, I do know better. I wasn't thinking." Clearly she was still nervous, though, as she pushed the robe off and let it fall to the floor.

Once the robe was on the floor, Logan moved his hand from the arm of the chair and ran it over her side to take in the feel of the fabric and of Mercury beneath it. His fingers brushed casually over the side of her breasts and her hip and his fingertips trailed over her ass before he nodded to the end of the fold in front of him, facing down on the night side of the Earth. "Stand by the glass, and tell me what you see."

She wondered if he was testing her over something she didn't know about, but she walked over and stood by the glass as instructed, placing a single hand against the glass when she did. "I see our neighboring station, quite a distance away. A few shuttles." She looked past those things, though, and noticed the stars next, and her fingers traced designs on the glass over a few constellations she could see. "A few constellations."

He enjoyed the view of her for a while, her black nightie blending her in with the darkness of space, as if the universe itself had an incredible ass just within his reach. He got up from the chair slowly and stepped up behind her to put his hands on her hips. His rough touch slid over the smooth fabric that barely covered her, and he looked over her shoulder at the same stars and constellations.

"What about down there?" He nodded down to the Earth in the distance, a few light clusters occasionally showing night-time activity over most of Africa, since it was the most densely-populated place remaining in the world, after all.

Mercury never thought much about Earth. During her entire life, Earth was just a thing that she could see out her window, just like the stars and the moon and the sun. Earth was never relevant to her life, even though she studied the people down there and about their babies all the time. The first time she'd ever been there was to pick up the Initiates, and even then, it had been only a few hours on solid ground.

"It's beautiful to look at." She admitted as she turned her attention to Earth exclusively. "It was incredible to feel the wind and to see landscape when I went down there. But I don't know what to think when I look at it. It mostly just makes me think about my research."

He nodded against her hair as he held her, clearly not surprised by that answer. "We grew up on the ground thinking people in Orbit must either hate us or pity us. Short lives, limited resources, low population density, almost always orphans before we're fully grown. We also grew up on the ground either hating or pitying people in Orbit. Rigidly restricted lifestyles, never knowing what it's like to get lost somewhere no one can find you, every move you make monitored by somebody somewhere."

He sighed as he looked down at the world, since South America was starting to come into view, and the farthest edge of the northern horizon was still south of his home. "Then I get up here and it turns out that everybody is wrong about everybody else. I certainly never expected you up here." He moved his hands to put her arms above her head, letting her lock them around his neck as his hands wandered over her entire torso. The movement lifted the nightie up off her ass as well, but clearly he didn't mind. "I thought I'd come up here and the lot of you would be some kind of skinny, malnourished, alien-looking creatures. I certainly wasn't expecting a goddess."

Mercury shivered at the feeling of his hands wandering up and down her body, and her fingers grazed his skin as her hands locked behind his neck. It was strange feeling so exposed, but with Logan pressed against her, she was starting to forget her surroundings. "My parents have always been judgmental of people from Earth, even though my father helped many of them assimilate once they decided to come up here. I didn't know I would meet someone like you either." She gasped softly when his fingertips grazed her chest. "Not that I know many people, but you're still very different from anyone I've ever known. And it's wonderful. I want to learn more about you every time I see you. And I wish I could see your home. The way you describe it makes it sound incredible."

"My home wasn't exactly standard as Earth accommodations go." He enjoyed the way she gasped every time he touched her, but more than that, he just enjoyed having her exposed against the universe, even if he knew the coatings and protective materials on the outside of the glass would prevent anyone actually seeing in from the outside.

"There are millions of people down there. Not the billions we used to be or the trillions that most people back then thought we would be by this point, but still millions. Millions of people who don't understand what's going on here. Maybe they never will. Maybe they'll never want to. But we're still working for them anyway." He sighed as he looked out, but his touch turned a little rougher as he held her against him, a little tighter, more possessive. He pressed her against the glass as he leaned into her, and enjoyed the feel of her nipples going taut against the cold glass. "I need to hear from someone that it's worth it. That the future is worth it. No matter what it costs."

Mercury wanted to turn to face him, but she knew he had turned her away for a reason. Maybe he didn't want to look at her, maybe he just wanted to look at Earth and think about home, she rarely knew what was going on in his mind. He didn't like to let people in, or at least not her. Not very often.

"The future is always worth it, Logan. It's the only thing everyone has in common. Somewhere, whether or not people want to think about the future or if they care, every single one of us makes some kind of difference." Mercury turned her attention back to Earth, since she couldn't look at Logan. "We're not married. We don't have a future as lovers, certainly not if we get away from here somehow. But maybe, if we make it happen, we can have a beautiful baby together, and then when you look at that baby you'll know why the future is so important. I see it every time I help babies come into the universe. I wonder what they'll do, what they'll see and experience. The future matters."

Her comments had him conflicted all over again, but even

when she said they didn't have a future as lovers, it didn't stop his hands from roaming over her as they pleased. As he pressed her against the glass, she could feel that her proximity, scantily-clad as she was, had produced a tangible effect on him, as always, and he breathed heavily as he took her breasts in his huge hands. "Maybe that's why I can't see it, then." He said breathily. "I can't see a future without you in it anymore. I can't see a life where your hair is up and you're busy about something else and I don't want to throw you down wherever we are and have you to myself. I'm not sure that's even possible anymore."

Mercury moaned softly as his hands teased her breasts through the thin fabric, certainly no barrier to his touch. She loosened her hands from behind his neck and touched his hand and twisted his wedding ring around his finger. "We don't belong to each other." It pained her to remind him, because it felt like they belonged *with* each other. Especially in moments like the present.

He didn't move his hand away as she reminded him, but afterward, he did move his hand up to the neckline of her nightie. He pulled it down slightly, as it was barely holding onto her ample breasts, and went to place his hand directly over her heart as he leaned down to kiss her neck.

"That's a lie." He said quietly. "No matter where we go, or what happens from here, you're always going to be mine. And I'm always going to be yours."

Mercury trembled in excitement feeling his lips on her neck and his hand on her skin. She didn't know how she would ever be able to resist him in the future either, but somehow they would have to figure it out. "I wish that were true." She gasped softly, her thoughts swimming, her own reminder sounding false under Logan's insistence. "If it was, I wouldn't have to stop myself from wanting to kiss you every time I see you. Or holding your hand. That's not our reality."

Whether it was their reality or not, it clearly didn't stop Logan from touching her the way he wanted there against the glass. "Reality is what we make it." His touch moved back to her hips and teased her by lifting the nightie so he could run his hands over her bare hips.

"If we break free of the Consortium, get to Eleusis on our own terms, with our own people, then life has a chance to be what we decide to make it. Our own choices." He sighed against her hair, since what he was saying wasn't even something he had admitted out loud before.

"If all the strings on all of us were cut, all of us left to our own devices, our own free choice, no one pressing buttons or forcing occasions, no past life commitments, the four of us set adrift to choose what we choose . . . I don't know if she or I would be completely convinced that we would make the same choice again. And I have to think you and him are the same way."

She didn't respond right away, but not because she didn't know what to say, it was just harder to speak when his hands and body were all over hers. "I don't think I would." Mercury admitted, even though it pained her to do so. Mercury loved Orion, but if pressed to make a choice . . . "I feel as though you and I have a connection that I can't really explain. It's so much more than physical. I love Orion, but I love you too. Maybe a little more."

"Maybe." He agreed with another kiss to her neck. "I asked you what you see when you look out there." He said without looking, though he watched her eyes as she looked for herself. "And you see what there is. I appreciate that about you. What I see is the impossible. A billion trillion objects all circling each other in ridiculously improbable configurations. But it exists anyway. It has to be dealt with anyway. No matter how impossible it seems."

"But you don't have to do it alone. Impossible or not, I will support you however I can. I'm a doctor, I'm smart and resourceful. I can help you." Mercury leaned back into him even more. "I don't want to have to tiptoe around you in public. I want to support you."

He nodded against her impossibly beautiful crimson hair, and instead of continuing to fondle every piece of her, he locked his arms around her waist. "You will. I just hope the gamble I have in mind pays off."

"Gamble?" She attempted to turn around slowly, glad he let her so she could finally look into his eyes again. "What gamble?"

"I'll tell you in the morning." He leaned down to kiss her once and nodded back toward their unit. "Put the robe back on in case someone's out for a late-night walk."

Mercury bent down so he could see her bare backside, since she was learning how to be sexy. At least for Logan's tastes. She grabbed the robe and stood up slowly to put it on. "I trust you. Completely."

"Good." He watched her closely, since she was watching him watching her, and he smiled at the way she moved. He knew it was just for him, and he enjoyed every minute of it. "Let's get home. There's a lot of night between now and the morning, and it's my intention to have you under me for most of it."

22

Jessie was quiet the month and a half after being released from her hospital stay. She was released earlier than anyone thought she would be, but she attended therapy daily for her hands, which still weren't back to normal functionality. Maybe they never would be again. Jessie wondered, often, if she would ever get back to the person she was before the attack. It didn't feel like she ever would. She still had nightmares, and the nightmares were the reason she was awake far earlier than she should have been. She had gotten good at not waking Gordon when she got out of bed.

She sat at the kitchen table, piecing together a puzzle he had given her, when her communicator beeped. Jessie read over the medical report, accustomed to getting a daily report of her therapy notes. They took a blood draw every three days just to watch her, which felt more invasive than anything else. In some ways she thought that they were treating her like a criminal for being attacked, but there was nothing she could do about it. She was involved with Gordon, and because of his 'rebel' status, she had been attacked. It looked suspicious. She couldn't blame everyone for thinking she was suspicious. She *was* suspicious.

Her medical report for the day included a note from the physician, uncharacteristic for her records. Everything was typically automatic and sterile, even her therapy. It just made the note look that much more out of place.

Ms. Rogers,

Your therapy is progressing well. Recent scans have indicated that some of our early diagnostics may have been unnecessarily pessimistic regarding your future range of motion. There are some techniques we've come up with that we're very hopeful about in terms of your hands.

Aside from that, there are a couple things that came up on your most recent blood draw that we'd like to talk to you about, if you have some free time today to come by the clinic. Nothing negative, I promise, just some items of conversation to be aware of. Let me know when you're coming in and I'll clear a block for you.

Talk to you soon. -- Barry Woods

Jessie read over it again just to make sure she was reading it right, but it didn't help the uneasy feeling in her stomach. What were they going to question her about now? Even though the message said it was nothing negative, she didn't believe anything anymore. Anyone could be lying at any moment, no matter what they 'promised'.

I will be there as soon as the clinic opens for the day.
-Jessica Rogers

Gordon was still asleep as she got dressed. They had been distant the previous day because he had been working with Tatyana on some kind of operation they were planning over the next few days. Only when she was finished with her morning routine did she see the note pinned inside the door to their unit, the only place Gordon had known for certain she would see it in the morning before she left.

Inside the folded letter, there was a small purple flower no larger than her thumbnail, the stem still green. The note itself was short, but Gordon had never been one for long speeches or declarations.

I hope today is a good one for you, baby. I miss you. I'll see you tonight.

Jessie looked over at Gordon as he slept, and there was a tiny smile on her lips, but she didn't read the letter again. She folded it up and put it down on her side of the bed, but she put the flower behind her ear into her hair.

She thought about leaving him a note but Jessie still struggled with her thoughts and feelings. The pain she endured daily was because of her connection to him. He hadn't hurt her, but he was the only one she could blame. It was hard. Maybe she could try to talk with him later that day.

The clinic was fairly busy most hours of the day or night, since there was such limited staff for so many people, but as promised, when she went to check in, the receptionist sent her straight back to Dr. Woods' office. She'd seen Barry a few times for her physical therapy. The small, unassuming man had always been pleasant to her, but she had never had occasion to meet his wife. When she got to his office, though, it was obvious that they had just been finishing up breakfast together in his office and she was on her way out.

"Yes, I'm doing lunch, and yes, I am fully capable of making pasta, thank you very much. I recognize that the last time was more rubber than pasta, but I've learned from my mistakes, I promise." He leaned down to kiss the even-smaller woman who was apparently his wife, with a smile on his face that hid no secrets, no tortured past, no complicated relationships, just a doctor who liked working with kids. "Twelve thirty good for you?"

Erebi nodded and kissed him one more time before she stood up and gave her husband a warm hug. "Twelve thirty is fine. I'll see you then." She smiled and ran her fingers along his cheek before she turned to see the silhouette of someone standing outside of his office. "Looks like you already have someone waiting, my love."

"Oh, that must be Ms. Rogers." He wiped at his mouth and went to pull the door open for her. He gave Jessie a broad, genuine smile when he saw her. "Ms. Rogers. You're up early. Do you two know each other?" He looked back and forth between her and his wife, who was as much the inverse of Jessie as it was possible for another woman to be. Short, skinny, dark-skinned, with a trace of an accent that marked her as anything but American and sharp features that marked her as beautiful without even trying. "Erebi, Jessie, Jessie, my dear and long-suffering wife Erebi."

"He's not making a joke. His pasta can make you suffer." Erebi teased as she took Jessie's outstretched hand, though she was careful with the woman's hands. She knew what had happened. Everyone did. "Nice to meet you, Ms. Rogers."

"Likewise." Jessie gave the small woman a polite smile, but she was quiet and closed. Her new normal. "I'm sorry for the interruption."

"No no, you're not interrupting, you're right on time, come on in." He held the door for her and waved again at Erebi. "See you for lunch, love. No suffering included." He gave Erebi a playful glare as she left, then stepped back into his office. "Have a seat, Ms. Rogers. I didn't expect you in immediately, you're quick. Let me grab your file."

"I was awake. Have been for a while." She sat in the seat his wife had vacated. They were a ridiculously happy couple. It was a little disgusting.

"I wanted to talk to you briefly about some of the bloodwork results we got back yesterday." He pulled up a hologram of her file off the side of the room so his desk wouldn't be between them. There wasn't much she hadn't seen before, just a few different level markers she didn't recognize. "Just so you know, we're going to be making some alterations to a couple of your medications. Most of them you'll be off within the next few weeks by current progressions, but all the same, we're going to be changing things up just a little. Due to some other considerations."

He smiled over at her and enlarged part of the hologram, which highlighted an entry titled Human Chorionic Gonadotropin, with a level of 35 beside it, whatever that meant. "Once this number comes up past the teens, there isn't generally much doubt as to its indication. We expect it to continue to rise steadily from here, with all other indications. There's nothing else in your biology that we've seen to inhibit it. You are pregnant, Ms. Rogers."

Jessie's gaze snapped from the hologram over to the doctor, her face shocked into stillness. She and Gordon had only slept together a few times since she had been released, which was a significant decrease from nearly every day before the attack. "Are you sure?"

"Quite sure, yes. We tested all three samples we took from you yesterday and checked them twice. We don't mess around when it comes to pregnancy around here." He gave her another reassuring smile, but left the information up on the screen. "There are some things to go over in terms of prenatal care, but I know this can be a lot to take in, especially if it's your first. We can talk about the medical side of things later on after you've had some time to yourself and with your match. I just didn't want you to be confused when your medications were changed later. And this is the kind of thing that's usually best to know as early as possible."

"Right." She looked at the hologram again and then down at herself and her hands, which still didn't work right. How in the world was she going to take care of a baby? She could grip things better in her right than her left, but it was still painful. He said in his message they had ideas about making it better, but there were never any guarantees. Jessie had been so out of it that she hadn't even considered that her period was late. "Do I tell him, or does my match get some kind of notification about this?"

Barry's smile fell a little. "Our policy has been that you are the one who is pregnant, Ms. Rogers, not your match. It's your decision when or whether to inform him. We try not to step on any more toes than necessary."

"I'll tell him." She didn't look up at him again. "He's usually very busy. I'll find a time to let him know." She realized she was repeating herself, but she was still surprised she was pregnant in the first place. "I wasn't expecting this. Intimacy has been rare since I was discharged."

"Well, we've actually seen a lot of strange cases when it comes to pregnancy these past two months. Some of the obstetricians are working on research specific to the effect of trauma on fertility rates. It hasn't really been what we expected either." He closed the hologram and set aside her file, and leaned on the desk to talk to her with a smile.

"I don't know Gordon very well, but my wife works with him pretty often. The stories she's told me about him usually run along the lines of him being incredibly closed off and withdrawn, but with a strangely fervent disposition to help when he's asked, even if he still doesn't talk much. He's a weird one for sure, but he seems devoted to whatever he decides is important to him. Kids are important to people. I'm sure he'll be happy about it."

"I hope you're right, Doctor." She sighed and attempted to open and close her hands, but it still wasn't right and still hurt. "Do you think I'll be ready to come off my medication? Will the medication hurt the baby?"

"Yes and no. Yes, you'll be ready, and no, I met with some of the other doctors this morning to do a quick med review, and there's nothing in anything you've been taking that should have any side effects on your baby at this stage of development. We're switching a few of them as a precaution, but that's not because we have evidence of harm, we just have better evidence that the other ones won't, if that makes sense."

He motioned down to her hands before he reached out to do a quick test on both, and he didn't seem surprised by the different points at which she winced or still felt stiff. "As for the other therapies that I mentioned, there are some studies that have just recently concluded about ligament range of motion that we'd like to try, to restore full range for you. They'll be more effective on the left than the right, since your right should be back to full capacity in another month or so on its own. The more extensive damage on the left has us being a little more creative."

She nodded and remained quiet for a moment before she looked up again. "Do I still have to have a psych evaluation by Dr. Santos?" Jessie hesitated, since she obviously didn't want to admit to the next point. "I'm still having nightmares." She knew she didn't have to admit it for them to find out, since they could easily monitor her sleep as they could anything else.

That part clearly wasn't Barry's area of expertise, but he was one of the primary doctors on her case, so he was familiar with all the aspects of it going forward. "She recommended a final one to follow up, but it wasn't a physician order, so no, it's not a requirement. But if you feel like it would help you to talk to someone about them, I know she'd be glad to help."

Jessie was relieved that she wouldn't have to go back into another interrogation posed as an evaluation, and nodded again. "I'll keep that in mind. Thank you." She knew he probably didn't have any reason to keep her, so she scooted her chair back slightly. "Is that all that you wanted to talk about?"

"Yes, that's all I had, unless there's something more I can do for you this morning." He stood up along with her, the smile still mostly present on his face, even if she hadn't exactly been leaping in the air with joy at news of her pregnancy.

She gave him a tentative smile and held out her hand to shake his. Jessie was determined to use her hands whenever necessary, even if it was still painful. "Thank you for meeting with me so early in your day. Have a good day, Doctor."

"You too, Ms. Rogers. Give my best and my congratulations to your match whenever you speak to him." He gave her a genuine smile and was careful with her hand, then held the door for her on her way out of his office.

Jessie spent the rest of her day doing the things she was assigned to do, even though she still felt strange that she wasn't helping with food prep anymore. She was allowed to leave early as a perk of her 'condition', and she was even given two days off so that she could relax and celebrate her addition to come.

She didn't know if she felt like celebrating. Gordon would probably be happy, but they were still on shaky terms most of the time, and she didn't know how things would go. Eventually he would find what he needed and they would leave, but Jessie still wasn't sure that staying with him was what she wanted. She loved him, but she was still afraid of him. She still didn't trust him. And by extension, he probably didn't trust her either.

When she returned home early, though, Gordon was already in their unit, oddly enough. He stood in their living room in the middle of holograms that covered almost the entire room, but it wasn't the first time she had seen him engrossed in his coding work. Just from the look of things around him, though, he wasn't doing his usual station maintenance. He was constructing something, fitting pieces back together that had angry red edges and didn't want to play with each other, so he stopped between each one to try to fix the edges until they fit. Whatever he was doing, it looked tedious, to say the least.

He didn't see her until the door actually clicked shut, and he gestured a few of his coding blocks out of the way to smile over at her. She could see his eyes flick to the flower in her hair, and his smile widened just a little more. "Hey. Welcome home. How was the monitoring?"

"It was alright." She said cautiously, since she wasn't expecting him to be home. "I didn't think I would see you until late. If then, even. You're . . . here?"

"I'm here." He nodded back, and tossed a few more gestures into his machinations, which froze them all exactly where they were, at which point he stepped out of them to get closer to her. "I got some good news earlier that meant I had some work to do. It's news you should enjoy hearing about too, all things considered."

He gestured across the room at the kitchen, where there was a bottle of wine sitting out on ice. "It's nothing like the quality where you're from, I'm sure, but it's that kind of day, I thought a glass would be a pretty appropriate means of celebrating."

Jessie walked over to the wine, but she just stood next to it instead of pouring any. "What are we celebrating?" She didn't even look at the wine, she just stared at him, as she often did. Either she looked confused or scared, rarely did she look happy, but she was trying. Day by day.

"A couple things." He was confused as to why she wasn't pouring, but he tried not to push her when it came to things she didn't seem to want to do. "First and foremost, we know where Carmina is. Or at least, we did as of about ten this morning."

He walked over to the kitchen but didn't reach for a glass if she wasn't having one. He was more interested in talking to her than drinking. "She tried to access some of the files she stole from us during the raid this morning. I'm surprised it's taken her this long, but it was probably just the first time she fucked up trying. She tripped one of my security measures and her location lit up like a Christmas tree. One of our squads planetside hit her at a safehouse she had set up just outside Beirut an hour later. They encountered some resistance, but no one was ready for them. Carmina herself wasn't found in the remains, but a sizable chunk of those who left our movement with her were. Which means she's down a whole lot of resources, and whatever data she hasn't already gotten out of the stash she stole has fried itself."

"That *is* cause for celebration." She grabbed a glass and poured it, but she slid it toward Gordon. "I hope it wasn't a trap to lure the rebels somehow. It seems strange she would trip up now."

He took the glass she had poured for him, but didn't sip from it, since it didn't look like she was drinking, which confused him, but he still didn't say anything about it. "I think so too. I like to think she just eventually got so pissed off with all the coding booby traps I left on that thing that she pushed the wrong button out of frustration, but I don't know that for sure. Best they could tell, Carmina got away in a ground vehicle, so some of our teams are still trying to hunt her down. I hope to have even better news soon, but she's been slippery before." He finally took a sip, but then set the glass down. "Are you alright? You don't look as happy as I kind of hoped you would."

"I don't believe it will be that easy to be rid of her, but it is good news." She knew she was distracted, but what she said was true. She still expected to be attacked again, even if it wasn't Carmina herself. "You said a couple of things. What's the other thing?"

"We found it." He said simply, still smiling in spite of her momentary ambivalence. "What we're looking for. We've got it localized to a specific sector on Arm Two. And it was your idea that finally did it. Find a non-residential sector with cameras that can be tapped and do a body count."

She had suggested that if they tracked the movement of people in various sectors of the arm, they could eventually distinguish patterns, especially if a person went into a sector and didn't come out again or appear again elsewhere in the arm for a few hours or days. It had taken a lot of surveillance-watching and a lot of number crunching, but eventually they had managed to isolate the area, all without putting a single person in danger on an arm where they weren't supposed to be or overstepping Gordon's technological reach.

Jessie smiled a little bit brighter. She was glad her idea hadn't been useless. "I'm glad. What's the next step, then?" She turned away from him and left the wine behind to get a bottle of water instead.

"Security review and bail-out plan." He said with less of a smile. "Since it's not on a system I can access without being tracked, we're going to have some of our own people install covert surveillance so we can watch security patterns and assess how best to extract it. Some of the rest of us are working on contingencies, like you and Clark were a while back. Naturally, most of Tatyana's goons want to go in shooting and hope for the best, but I managed to talk them down. Enough people have been hurt by all this already, no sense expanding that number. But once we've figured out how to get off this station and back to Earth safely, things are going to move fast."

She took in the information and took a deep breath before she sipped on her water for a while. Jessie was still thinking about her news from that morning, and she wondered when she should even tell him. "You should find a way to talk to Anna Bickford and Orion Al-Jabbar. They're some of the most talented fliers and two people on this station with some of the biggest motivation to get out of here."

He quirked an eyebrow at that, and living with the man for four months had taught her that it was the only way anyone would ever know they had surprised him. "They're also some of the most deeply in the spotlight. Not to mention, Al-Jabbar is military. You think they'd be willing to help? Most recent rumor I've heard is that all four of them are knuckling under pretty hard. Especially if the rumors I heard about the ballast maintenance shafts this morning are true."

"Anna is still wearing her wedding ring. If she's still wearing her ring and she's knocking boots with Orion, then she's conflicted. I'm sure they've had two tons of pressure put on them to buckle. Which means they're being forced, even if they're enjoying it in one way. The match system works. That's part of the problem." She shrugged, since if he didn't think her idea was worth trying, they would find someone else to help. "It looks like the four of them are getting fucked over worse than most. I think that would make them listen."

The quirk in his eyebrow went away as he listened to her. "You should talk to them." He said after another sip of his wine. "You know Anna through the Judiciary, she'd listen to you. So would Orion, I'm sure. If they're as conflicted about everything as you say, they'll talk to their spouses and bring them along too. It would be good to have Logan on our side, maybe help to have some people look the other way when it's needful."

"Sure. I'll talk to Anna. Anyway, Carl is on our side, right? That will go a long way to convincing Orion." Jessie took another sip of water and she finally looked him in the eye. She stared into his eyes for a moment, but then she ended up looking away quickly. "The doctor wanted to see me this morning. He's adjusting my medication, and I don't have to see Santos about the nightmares if I don't want to."

"That's good." His hopeful tone sounded glad that she was talking to him. "Adjusting them down, up, sideways? It seems like you just got settled into the ones you already have."

"Down. Out of precaution." She gripped the bottle of water a little bit more before she continued. She really couldn't look at him. "For the baby."

He froze, but a few breaths later he finally managed to respond. "For the . . ." all the other data in the world, he could ingest and process as quickly as he pleased, but the news there was a baby on the way appeared to be more than his brain could take in all at one swallow. "The baby?" He crossed the distance between them in the kitchen slowly and hoped she wouldn't pull away. "They're sure?"

"I asked the doctor that. He said they checked my blood sample three times, so he's sure." When he was close enough to touch her, she finally looked up again. "I almost didn't believe him, because you and I haven't . . . well, it's been rare. But I'm late. And I'm usually not. I just wasn't paying attention."

"Well, there's been some other things on our minds." Some of his usual sarcastic edge came back, but the look on his face was still cautious as he stood by her. He decided it was no time to be completely cautious about anything, though, and he reached up to caress the side of her face, his fingers brushing the end of the flower stem in her hair. "I think it's the best thing I've heard all year. But you don't seem that happy about it."

The best thing he'd heard all year? That was not what she was expecting to hear from Gordon, though she didn't know what she expected anymore. "I guess I thought when I got pregnant that I wouldn't be worried about the baby's future. Or scared of their father." She didn't pull away from his touch, but she didn't return it either. "How do I know Carmina's people won't show up here again and carve this baby out of me just to prove something to you?" It was a graphic image, but her nightmares had done a number on the thoughts that ran through her head.

"Because they would have to carve through me to get to you." He said almost lightly, but he didn't look away from her eyes. "Not that I've ever been renowned for my fighting skills, but after carving through me, doing anything to you would be a little after-the-fact if Carmina was trying to get under my skin. And I will die before I let anything else happen to you." He glanced down and poked at her stomach once lightly. "Or her. Or him, them, whichever the case may be."

She wasn't expecting his touch again, so she flinched a little, but she still didn't move away. Jessie desperately wanted to believe him, that he would protect her, but she didn't know if it was true. "If it was between me and the Twist, would you still protect me?"

His smile disappeared entirely, not because of the answer he wanted to give her, but because she'd needed to ask it at all. "In the years to come, my own organization will have opportunities to either steal one of the three Twists in operation currently or discover the specific resources we would need to create another one of our own. The technology was created once, it can and will be done again if it has to be."

He looked her up and down again and withdrew his touch from her face, since obviously it wasn't welcome, and he didn't want to stay anywhere he wasn't welcome. "Trite as the saying might be, it isn't wrong. In all of human history, there has never been and will never again be another you. I may be a cold asshole and capable of doing terrible things, but I still recognize that. That's not even a contest."

Jessie's eyes softened even though she was conflicted about him withdrawing his touch. She just stared into his eyes a little bit longer. "I'm still so scared. But I also miss you, and I miss the way things were. I want to be happy about this. I want a family. I don't want to be a single mom somewhere because I'm scared to let you back in. I want to be happy."

She could see the sympathy in his eyes as he nodded. Gordon was the only person who really knew about her pulling away from him, but he had never once looked at her or spoken to her as if he thought her pulling away wasn't justified. He knew better than anyone else just how justified it was. "I hope you will be. I miss the way things were too."

He still didn't move in to touch her, since he didn't want to push anything she didn't want. "When I first approached you, back on Earth, when I changed the match program to connect us, the biggest question I had was how to tell you about my track record and still somehow convince you that I try to be a decent person. Or at the very least, that I'm only a danger to those who deserve it. That's how I thought of myself. But obviously that's not true. I'm a danger to people who are important to me. Who might actually care about me. I just haven't typically needed to worry about that category of people."

"There are maybe ten people in my entire life who have cared whether I lived or died, and at least five of those are dead already. I thought I could tell you that there was more about me you didn't know, tell you a little at a time, and then by the time you learned everything that was to learn, you would already have seen me trying to be a good person long enough to believe it's possible. If I hadn't, and you had been matched with someone else, this wouldn't have happened. I don't know if I've ever said that I'm sorry for that. But for that aspect of it, I am. I never once wanted to put you in harm's way."

Jessie still wasn't quick to respond, but she reached out slowly to take his hand without flinching or wincing. She stepped up a little closer and let out a slow breath as though she had been holding it in for weeks. "You've never been angry or impatient with me through all of this. Thank you. I know I'm not a pleasant person to be around anymore. But I don't want to be like this."

"You've got a lot of reasons to be angry." He held her hand gently, since he didn't want to hurt her, but he did tug her closer. "I know what that's like better than most. I'm the last person who's ever going to fault you for it."

When he tugged her in close she allowed him to do so, and she kissed his cheek lightly. "I'm going to get so fat. What if you don't want me anymore?"

The sarcasm that came naturally to him came back full force as he lowered his chin to glare at her. "Four months of living with me and you still don't know how insatiable I am with you yet? Don't make me up my game. You'll never make it into work."

She kissed his cheek again and looked toward the couch. "Will you sit with me? I have something else to show you."

"Sure." He waited for her to lead the way then sat with her, gesturing once when they got into the living room to brush his work aside. He left it up so she could see he wasn't trying to hide anything from her, but it was all mostly a jumble of numbers and code.

She sat down next to him on the couch and leaned into him as she pulled out her communicator. Jessie held it out so that he could see it. "We get the next two days off, for starters. But I asked the doctor to send me the genetic code when they were finished examining it. I wanted to know what the baby is." She looked down at the unopened message and then looked over at him again. "But I didn't want to open it without you."

He smiled at her thoughtfulness, and put his arm around her. "Don't be surprised if the doctors go a little apeshit about the kid's genetic code over the next few weeks as they analyze it. I've got some disclosures to give you when we've got some spare time. Nothing inherently bad or that'll hurt the kid, don't worry." He leaned in to kiss her cheek and nodded at the communicator. "Let's see it."

Jessie wasn't sure how to respond, but she smiled at him anyway before she tapped open the message. They read over the report, and there was a lot that Jessie didn't understand. Some things were tagged as abnormal, but the gist of the report seemed to show that everything was healthy. "Do you understand any of this?"

"Most of it." He reached over to flip through it while she held the communicator itself, and he actually chuckled as he went past some of the bits and pieces of data, most of it gibberish. "Relevant bit is the twenty-third chromosome right now. Though the sixth and the third are also highlights of mine. I've always hated how my sixteenth chromosome looks in pictures, and it looks like the kid is getting most of that. Sorry about that, baby." He scrolled through to the last chromosome, and looked through most of the gibberish of it twice just to make sure he was reading it right. "Two X chromosomes. Looks like it's a girl." He smiled and leaned over to kiss her cheek, his hand rubbing at her shoulder a little as he did.

"Really?" She looked over at him with tears in her eyes that she didn't realize would crop up. "A girl?"

"Looks that way, yeah." He smiled at the tears in her eyes and kissed her cheek again. "Do you want to see her? There's some imaging code I found a few years back that'll present a fairly close image. It predicted my brothers pretty well when I went to go looking for them."

Jessie thought for a moment and shook her head. "I'll see her when she gets here. It will be fun to wonder what she looks like and who she looks like." She looked at the report again and down at her unchanged stomach. "I don't know why they are pushing all of us to make these babies, but I don't want to lose her."

"We won't." He promised as his free hand moved down to her stomach. He rested his head against hers briefly with a sigh. "They're pushing us because of this." He tapped her stomach, then moved his hand back to her communicator and scrolled quickly through the code until he got to the sixth chromosome and a particular sequence of genes within it. It was a needle in a haystack, but apparently it was a needle that Gordon was intimately familiar with and adept at finding.

He scanned through it quickly, nodding every so often as he obviously recognized something, and then sighed again before he went on with his explanation. "I knew there wasn't much possibility that she wouldn't, but it's worth checking all the same. She has the immunity markers. That's what the Consortium wants. Part of what they want, anyway. They want to see how their breeding programs stack up and what kind of results they get. If their program's attempts at producing the right immunities are successful."

"Immunity markers? They're breeding us like animals?" Jessie found that particularly offensive, but thankfully she had wanted a baby anyway, so she couldn't be that upset.

"Not exactly like animals. But pretty close, yes." He scrolled a little more through their daughter's genome with more sighs, but he eventually chuckled. "Good, at least she won't be completely pale like her dad." He shook his head and dismissed the hologram.

"The Consortium is running a dozen or so different experiments on us all at the same time. Everyone's looking for just one thing that the Consortium wants, and they're not gonna find it. Because there's a lot of things they want all at once. They're running probabilities on producing offspring with the right immunity marker, offspring without, they're running psychological experiments, even sexual behavior experiments.

Behavioral modification by way of chemical inducement, hormone tampering, stress testing, you name it, they're working on it. We're a petri dish and a rat maze for a few hundred Consortium eggheads right now."

"Except they don't ever plan on rewarding us, do they?" She sighed and looked down at her stomach again. "We have to get back to Earth. Away from all of this. We can't have a normal family here. Ever."

"No, we can't." He squeezed her shoulder so she was tighter against him. "We'll get there. With any luck, you'll be on Earth for most of your second and third trimester. Give birth in a place with decent gravity. Let her be born on Earth, not in this damn tin can."

Jessie slowly turned toward him and kissed his lips. There was hesitation but once the kiss began it only deepened. She loved him. That had never stopped. Her fear had never stopped either, though, and that was the problem. But she had to decide how she was going to deal with it; like a quiet little mouse or like someone who wanted to take back her life. The second was definitely what she wanted.

He kept his distance as she wanted ever since the attack, but every time she had shown any interest in being with him, at having any kind of intimacy at all, he had been right there to answer her with a vengeance. The kiss he returned was no different and as it deepened, he plucked the communicator out of her hand and tossed it on the cushions nearby before he wrapped her in both arms to kiss her breathless. She was going to be the mother of his child. It wasn't something he thought he would ever have in his kind of life, but it was something he wanted more than almost anything else.

She was surprised by how urgently he responded to her kiss, and she was more surprised by herself. She was *glad* about his eagerness. Jessie loved being wrapped in his arms even before the attack, but now it felt like he was not only holding her, but protecting her. At least she hoped he would. She knew she had to make a decision to either trust him or not. Going back and forth on it wasn't doing anyone any good, certainly not herself. The hope for a family and being with a man who loved her was worth the risk that he might be lying, because she truly had nothing to lose except that hope for a better future.

"I'm still scared." She admitted between breathless kisses and she pressed her forehead to his. "But I would rather choose to believe that you love me and you won't hurt me than to live the way I have lived for the last two months. Our daughter deserves better than fear. So . . . I'm choosing to trust you."

He caressed her cheek again and nodded against her forehead. "Everything in my power to protect you, to make you happy, I'm going to do. Everything I can do to provide a happy life for our daughter, I'm going to do. That's never going to change." He took a deep breath after that, since there was a 'but' lingering at the end of what he was saying. "There may be times when you find out that I've done the kinds of things Carmina started telling you about, and there will, I'm sure, be times when I'm ruthless, and even cruel by some measures. But it will never be towards you or our family. I'll never claim to be anything but a monster, but I'm also a monster who can aim. I'll never hurt you. Either of you."

Jessie nodded in acknowledgement, since she knew from the beginning there was a lot that Gordon was hiding, even his own name, though she knew what it was now and she hadn't at the beginning. "It wasn't necessarily what you did that scared me, though I didn't realize you were capable of those things. It was more about believing that you could or would do it to me."

"Never happen." He reassured as he kissed her again, pulling her into a tight hug just to keep her close. "I am capable . . . of some terrible things. I'm capable of much worse than I've actually done. But all I want to be capable of is making you happy."

"No one has ever wanted to do that for me." Jessie kissed his neck as he held her. "It was easier to believe that you wanted to hurt me than to be with me." She admitted softly. "I love you. I didn't stop, even if it was hard."

"I love you too, Jess." He ran his hands over her back as he sighed against her hair, and his fingers dug into her with the fervor of how much he wanted to hold onto her. "We're going to get the Twist, get off this station, get to Earth, and make a life for our daughter. Nothing is going to stop me from doing that."

Never before had Jessie cared for anyone calling her Jess, but it felt right that Gordon called her Jess when no one else did. It also felt strange that Jessie wanted to get back to Earth now when she desperately wanted to leave it before. Eleusis was all she wanted before, and now, now that she had someone important to her and a family on the way, she just wanted to get to a place where she could have that instead. "Okay. Let's make it happen."

23

It was amazing how fast and how slow two and a half weeks could go. Time with Orion moved quickly, filled with laughs and easy hours. Time with Logan was quiet and tense, stretching out in a painful reminder of how easy it had once been. He talked about his gamble but he didn't explain what it was, only that it had been delayed.

When Anna was back with Orion during Mercury's fertile week and the world seemed like a brighter and happier place again, she had to go in for routine bloodwork. With Mercury. It was an awkward twenty minutes of poking needles and Mercury asking questions before Anna could run out of the clinic.

Late that day, after Mercury had finished up at the clinic, she headed back to her unit to meet Logan for what she hoped would be a relaxing evening. She was used to the several messages she received every hour, since as an obstetrician, there were endless questions and concerns. She always kept an eye out for lab results, however, since problems were always best treated immediately. The labs she got back from that day, though, were not a problem. They were an answer.

Anna was pregnant.

"That isn't your good-news face." Logan's voice came at her sideways from down a corridor, apparently headed the same direction she was, from the cautious smile on his face. He was dressed in the coat that had become his signature piece of clothing over the past few months, and he carried a cloth bag in one hand. She could see Renata disappearing the other direction down the same corridor, apparently recently dismissed by Logan to go off and do whatever it was he constantly had his secretary doing on his behalf.

Mercury was reading over the labs carefully before she was startled by Logan's voice and dropped her communicator in front of their unit. "I received a lab report back. It had some unexpected news on it."

"Oh. Well, with that kind of face, unexpected should mean somebody's dying or losing a limb or some such. I'm sorry to hear about that." He picked up her communicator for her and handed it back, then put his palm on the plate outside their door and nodded her inside, already giving casual orders as he always did. "Are you done for the day or does unexpected news mean you've got more to go back and do?"

"I can send a message to the patient to have her contact me so she and I can meet at her convenience." Mercury went inside and looked over at Logan before she looked toward their bathroom. Bathrooms were notoriously a place of privacy, even on Nine. "Can I show you something? In there?"

He looked her up and down with a playful grin, obviously in a good mood, but then he nodded more seriously, since she didn't seem to be returning his good humor. "Sure. After you."

Mercury hurried into the bathroom and closed the door after Logan, but she turned on the shower just in case. She knew she was being paranoid, leadership could have already accessed Anna's results, but she wasn't going to take any more of a risk. She didn't know what might happen to Anna if the Initiative knew.

"These are Anna's lab results." She held out her communicator for him. "She's pregnant with twins."

"She's . . ." all trace of a playful attitude fled as he looked at the results, but the only part of the report that made any sense to him was the number of fetuses. "They know all this from a blood test? Everything about the babies?"

"Blood tests have become very advanced over the years. They could once do DNA testing with the mother's blood past ten weeks, but now DNA can be tested as soon as the Hcg levels are high enough to show a positive pregnancy result. A little blood goes a long way." Mercury pointed at different data points, but apparently she was struggling to explain them, for once.

"The concerning thing is not that there are twins. Or that she's pregnant." She sighed as she highlighted a few points as she looked over the report. "Look at this. Baby A, conceived first, has markers for grey eyes." She looked up at him, and then she continued. "Baby B will have dark eyes. Anna's eyes are neither grey, nor particularly dark. So those markers must be inherited from the father." She moved to another point. "Baby A and Baby B have different blood types. Baby B's blood type is consistent with his father. Baby A doesn't match either Anna or Orion exactly, nor a combination of the two."

Logan finally understood what she was saying, and the shock on his face slowly subsided into recognition. "You're saying they're not just fraternal." He knew what she was saying, but he had to say it out loud to make it real, even if he said it very quietly. "That one is Orion's. And the other isn't."

Mercury nodded as she looked up into the grey eyes that apparently had been passed to Baby A. "She seems to take after her father. At least in some ways."

Logan sighed, and leaned his head into his hand as he processed the entirety of what she was saying. Mercury had seen a lot of first-time fathers in her day, given the news of a new pregnancy to a lot of couples in a lot of situations. The look in Logan's eyes wasn't the look of a man who was being told for the first time that he was going to be a father. But he would have mentioned any other children in his past, surely. "What about the markers Santos was going on about when we first got here? Any indication of those in her genome?"

"Not in the girl, actually. Yes in the boy." She watched him carefully, since she really didn't know what to expect from Logan as far as his emotions went. Was he happy? Angry? Sad? "I haven't sent this to Anna, I . . . no one can find out about this. I don't know what they'll do."

"The results are already in the system. How can they not find out about this now?" He was suddenly partly in panic mode as well, since he hadn't immediately considered that aspect of the news. If they had wanted so badly for him and Anna *not* to produce a child together, then the fact that they *had* probably wouldn't sit well with the brass.

"I'll report tampering with the sample. Re-run a test, and then actually input the data myself instead of letting it be computer-run."

"And if they find out that you did that?" He wasn't going to let her risk herself if there was too much exposure. "This is hardly the last time they're going to take blood or run tests on a pregnant woman. You'd have to end up falsifying every single thing they do."

"I'll re-run a few of the others and say it was a glitch in the testing machine. They do break. No one would think anything of it." Mercury didn't seem concerned that she might get caught, she was more concerned about Anna. "I have to tell Anna. She deserves to know. Orion . . ." She looked up at Logan again. He was going to be a father. Orion too. Apparently they hadn't needed her after all. "They need to know. You do. Even if you don't look happy about it. I thought you wanted this? You came here hoping for this."

"I came here thinking a lot of things." Wheels were still spinning behind his eyes as the information settled. "And a lot of things have changed in the meantime. I want to be happy about it. But it's too complicated for something that's supposed to be as simple as happy should feel."

"It's not that complicated. You are going to be a father. Anna is your wife, and you are having babies together." She closed up her communicator and went to turn off the shower. The whole room had fogged with steam. "This is a good thing."

"I hope it will be. Eventually." He reached out to touch Mercury's arm and pulled her into a gentle kiss, even as distracted as he was. "Let me know what she says. I'm going to make dinner with some of the vegetables I brought back from hydroponics."

She watched him move away from her, but she moved in front of him just in time to prevent the door from closing. She wedged herself between him and the door. When he looked into her eyes, she put her hand up to his cheek. "You get lost in there so easily." Mercury ran her fingers along his temple and pulled him into another kiss. "I don't want you to be sad about this."

He was a little surprised she was being so forceful about it, but he didn't try to push past her. "It's just a new life, started someplace I would never want it to grow up. And if the Consortium is going to try and kill us before we leave for Eleusis, if all this is just a game to them . . . it's more to lose for us. The stakes are higher. And they know it. They know we'll care more, act accordingly. And that's what they want. I hate giving them what they want."

"We'll care more to get out of here, too." She wrapped her arms around his neck and hugged him tightly with her eyes closed. Both of the men in her life had a permanent tie to Anna now, and while she was jealous of the thought of Anna having Orion's child in the beginning, she was now also jealous of Anna taking what was supposed to be hers. "I hoped I would be the one to have your baby." Mercury admitted softly against his cheek. "Anna does a great job of making me jealous without even trying."

He shook his head against her shoulder and ran his hands over her as she held him. "Don't be. You'll have triplets out of me soon enough."

Mercury laughed softly and continued to hold onto him. "I don't like losing you. Not to Anna or your work, or even to your mind. I like you here with me."

"You don't lose me to those things." Every time he was around her, he was always free and casual with the way he touched her. It was something he'd had to pay particular attention to whenever they were out in public. In private, his hands weren't shy about roaming over her, even in moments when they weren't about to get into anything intimate. Once he let her go, his hands moved up over her breasts before he took her face in his hands to kiss her. "I'm still yours. Just misplaced for a little while. I do my best to keep it to a minimum."

* * * * *

While Mercury hadn't intended to seduce Logan in the bathroom, it seemed to relax both of them, and she was never sad about the time they spent wrapped up in each other. Mercury didn't stop kissing him for a long time even after her heart rate slowed, and she remained next to him on the tile floor, since they hadn't made it out of the steam. "I think you are trying to make me sore on purpose." She mused, since she certainly wasn't going to complain about being sore.

"Not really. Sore would mean I shouldn't do that to you again later tonight. Which I intend to. You seem to enjoy it that much more when things get rough." He looked over at her almost lazily and yanked her in for a kiss as she laid mostly-bare beside him. He'd kept her shirt around her elbows and wrists for part of it just to tie her up for a while, but she had been released afterward.

Mercury ran her hand across his chest once she could get it free from his binding. "I like it that you touch me all the time. It makes me feel wanted." She kissed his cheek gently and then his lips again. "Will you tell me something else about you?" Mercury had made it a game recently to find out whatever he would tell her, and he seemed freer to talk when he was relaxed.

He nodded contentedly and laid flat on the floor as he moved his hand slowly over her back. "You can have two questions."

"What were you like as a young boy?" She asked curiously,

since she wanted to picture what he was like before she knew him.

"I was . . . exactly like my twin brother Liam still is." He grunted a laugh, echoing off the tile. "I was impetuous, and a little crazy. I ran pretty wild. But we all did. My parents would send us out of the house to go running through the fields and woods and all they told us was 'Don't die, be back by sundown.' That was it. So we were all over the place. There isn't much to see in the midwest district when it comes to natural landmarks or whatnot, but what there was, we saw it all."

Mercury smiled as she thought about a young Logan on the loose. "That sounds like fun. I wish I could have had a chance to run wild. Even when my friends got together on Station Seven we would play board games or study. I'm sure there was wildness to be had, but I didn't participate." Mercury turned onto her side to face him a little bit more.

"I always thought if I ever went to Earth, I wanted to try two things. One, to learn how to ride a bike, and two, swim in an ocean. Or a lake or something." Mercury kissed along his jaw and ran her fingers over his beard. "I also always wondered what a real, fresh picked apple tastes like. Or meat that hasn't been processed beyond recognition. The fresh things here are alright, but I imagine they're not like they are on Earth."

"No, they're not." He had to laugh, since the difference was so clear it still bothered him after four and a half months in space. "Nothing tastes right up here. Water, maybe, but I don't even trust that." He looked her up and down with a growing smile.

"I'll have to show you all those things when we get to Eleusis. There'll be apples there, if Ms. Tanaka has anything to say about it. And oceans and lakes. Bicycles might be a little while, but they're worth having around, so we'll get to those eventually. As for the meat, there's not much that makes you feel closer to nature than going out with your own weapon, killing your dinner, gathering the herbs to cook it in the wild, then cooking the whole mess that night and enjoying it out in the open under the stars. You get to disconnect from everything and everyone else in the world and just live for yourself. Even just for a day. Liam and I had a friend when we were twelve who took us out for a summer and taught us all kinds of crazy shit about the outdoors. I don't know how much you'll enjoy that part, but the rest you'll like."

"I think I would like it. I would like to spend time with you underneath the stars." She nipped at his lip with her teeth before she kissed him gently in contrast. "Especially if you laugh like that all of the time." Mercury was grinning as soon as she heard it, since it was so rare to get a laugh out of him. "Second question . . . what is a tradition you have? A family tradition or a birthday tradition or . . . anything."

"Hm. Traditions . . ." He laid back and thought for a moment, but he dragged her closer at the same time. Naked as they both were, any contact between them was intimate, but he was always moving her where he wanted her, whether they were actively engaged in having sex or not. There was nothing about his touch on her that wasn't some kind of sexual anymore. That was just his nature.

He spun her so that she could lie on her back on top of him, stretched out along his chest with her red hair spilling over his shoulder. It left every piece of her open to his lazy caresses, and he took every advantage of it that the position afforded him. "Well, my father's name was actually James Bickford the Fifth. Until me, the family went in a straight line from one James to the next. Liam and I had an older brother who died in infancy from a fall and some respiratory problems he developed afterward. He was the sixth. So if I ever have a boy, he'd be the seventh. Or if Liam does, I guess. Though I'm pretty sure I called dibs on that a few years ago."

"Dibs, huh?" She hoped she already had his son on its way to conception inside of her, but she wouldn't know for some time. Anna had his daughter. Maybe she could have his son. "That's a good way to remember family, passing on a name like that. I'm sorry you didn't get a chance to know him. My parents never had any more children after I was born, though they would have been afforded the permission if they wanted. They said they got everything they wanted or needed with me." She shrugged. "It would have been fun to have a friend."

"Siblings are good. Twin siblings are a mixed blessing." He chuckled as his hands moved over her thighs, spreading them wide just because he could before his hands massaged over the rest of her torso. "He was at least as much trouble as he was worth, sometimes more. I'm sure I was just as bad. But I've never had many complaints about Larissa. You'll like her a lot, actually."

"I can't wait to meet them both." She didn't know if she ever would, if she would see Earth or if his siblings would see Eleusis, but she wanted to meet them. "Your brother seems incredibly entertaining. And your sister sounds quite sweet."

"Entertaining is one word for him." He sighed as he thought about his siblings, since thinking about them meant thinking about Earth, and the life he had left behind there. The life that seemed to be fading all the time. "Maybe I'll get to meet your parents someday too. They sound like interesting people. Especially the whole boss/secretary relationship they started with." He chuckled beneath her, and the sound rumbled through her directly.

"They would really like you." It was the truth, and she knew it. They hadn't cared for Orion or her decision to marry him, but they would like Logan. He was a determined man who knew what he was doing and always seemed to have a plan. Much more their preference. "They are interesting people. I miss them very much." She wondered what her father must think by now, since she hadn't been able to send a message out for over a month. "Especially my father. We were quite close. And yes, their relationship is funny. He swears an Irishman just can't resist an Irish woman, and so that's why the match program wouldn't match them with anyone else other than each other."

"That's not Irishmen, that's all men." He moved to kiss her neck as it was exposed to him, and laced his fingers with hers. "One of these nights, I'm going to find the filthiest romance novel ever written and have you sit naked on the end of the bed while you read it to me. That voice of yours is as perfect as the rest of you."

Mercury laughed at that image, and shook with her laughter on top of him, since it seemed both so scandalous and silly at the same time. "You want me to read filthy romance novels to you?"

His attempt at an impression of an Irish accent was awful, and he knew it, but he tried anyway. "Might be me only chance to find out how that mouth o' yours wraps around some o' the filthier words in the language. Sure and you're not gonna go 'round sayin' shite like 'what the feck are you doing here' and, well, pretty much anything involving the F word." He liked her proper, since it was just a part of who she was, but that didn't mean he wasn't ever going to give her grief for it.

His attempt at an Irish accent made her laugh even harder, and she put her hands to her face to cover it even though he couldn't see her, since she was on top of him. "I can curse." She eventually said between giggles. "If I want to." Though he was right, she usually shied away from the filthier words, even when she was angry or upset. It was improper, according to her parents and all of her educators on Seven. Language was meant to be used correctly and properly and precisely. That didn't include curse words. "If you want me to."

"We'll find a book someday." Her laugh wasn't something he had heard that often lately, and he kissed her shoulder again as if to savor it by touch. "Otherwise, I'm not going to ask you to change or start up with cursing. I love you as you are. The only change I'm ever going to tell you to make is from one costume to another if I suddenly decide I want a maid instead of a cheerleader."

"I can do that." She turned slightly to look down at him, but eventually she turned over completely on top of him and smiled brighter as soon as she met his eyes. "I love learning more about you."

"You'll know everything there is to know from now on." He groaned as she moved against him since he never needed much time to get hard again, and it had never taken much for Mercury to turn him on to begin with. "And I'll know everything there is to know about you. Every bit of you."

"Whatever you want to know." Her lips sealed the promise of honesty against his decadent lips. "I'll tell you anything."

He held her for another moment without saying anything, but his smile faded slightly. "Tell me you'll stay with me. No matter what happens."

Mercury searched his steel eyes for a moment, since she wasn't sure if he was being serious about it, or if he just wanted her to be willing to do whatever he said. Did he really want her to stay with him? "I will." She started to say, her emerald eyes still searching his for the truth behind them. "As long as I don't have to share you. No matter what else happens." It wasn't exactly the answer he had asked for, but it was as close as she would concede.

He nodded and kissed her without saying anything else by way of explanation. "Fuck me again, Venus. Then we'll go deliver some news to the rest of the world."

* * * * *

Anna hadn't expected a request from Mercury to meet so late at night but Anna figured that Mercury was a bit of a weird one anyway, so she shouldn't be surprised that her doctor had unconventional practices. Like calling patients in to review labs at random hours.

After meeting with Mercury, though, Anna felt more sick than anything else, and it didn't have anything to do with the babies inside of her.

She honestly didn't really believe it was possible to have twins that were only half siblings, but she understood clearly how it had happened. Still, it felt more like a strike of bad luck than it felt like a miracle.

Secondly, Mercury had mentioned that she shared the results with Logan first, which her doctor had apologized for, but the realization twisted in Anna's gut as she walked back toward her shared unit with Orion.

Logan knew, he knew before she did, and yet he wasn't there when she got the news. He didn't even try to tell her the news himself, he didn't . . . he hadn't been involved at all. What did that mean?

Anna paused in her walk back toward the unit to send Logan a message, but she was quick and short about it.

Unexpected surprise. How do you feel about it?

She left out all details just in case, since Mercury mentioned that she would have to falsify Anna's official report just to keep Anna and Logan out of trouble. Anna wanted to feel grateful, but she didn't. It meant that she *owed* something to Mercury, and all the while it already felt like Mercury had stolen her husband and Anna couldn't do a damn thing about it.

When she stepped into the unit she wondered if Orion went back to sleep, but instead he was there waiting for her. He was clearly anxious about the random message and what it meant for all of them. Probably because Mercury hadn't informed him either, which was just another stab to the heart. Mercury hadn't taken the time to give any information to her actual husband, but instead she told Logan before everyone else. It said a lot about what was going on, and it just made Anna feel even more conflicted.

While Anna was gone, Orion had actually worked, which was unusual for the time they typically spent together in their unit. She could see a hologram of the station in the middle of their living space with a few dozen flight paths highlighted around it. He made adjustments across the room to run different scenarios for her flight training class, but he looked over at her immediately when she came in. "Well, you're still walking, but you look a little paler than usual. What was that all about?"

"Well, first, it's always awkward as hell to see her. I mean, she's way too familiar with places that I'm familiar with *and* she's had to examine me in places that I didn't ever want her to see." Anna grumbled as she went to the couch and plopped down unceremoniously. "She got my lab results back." She stared at him quietly, almost savoring the moment before the plunge into certain chaos, before she covered her eyes with her hands. "Apparently I'm such a talented sex goddess that I got knocked up by you *and* Logan. Mazel Tov."

"You . . ." Anna had had the entire visit in Mercury's office to ingest that information, but she had laid it on him all at once, and none of it had been what he was expecting. "Okay, I need you to say that one more time, just to make sure I didn't just hallucinate or something."

Anna didn't look thrilled when she sat up and uncovered her eyes. Honestly, she wished Orion would just walk over and sit with her, but she didn't figure he would want to. "I'm pregnant with twins." Anna replied in a tone that was calmer, but sounded much more fragile. "The girl is apparently Logan's, and the boy is yours."

His expression was one of pure shock as he ingested that information, but then he shook it off again and blinked a few times. "That's . . ." He shook his head again and headed over to the couch. Orion sank down onto the cushions next to her and wrapped one arm around her shoulders to pull her in close. "That's awesome, baby. Incredibly weird and really, really rare, I imagine, but that is awesome."

Anna turned in against Orion's chest and started crying without warning. It was what all her emotions demanded from her. Tears. "She fucking told him first. She told him and he still wasn't there with me. He hasn't responded to me. He made me sit through that alone when he already knew. She just sat there and jabbered on and on about the DNA and all that fucking bullshit and he wasn't there. My fucking husband." A part of her knew it was messed up that she was crying in another man's embrace, but Orion was her best friend now. Logan had apparently dropped the job. Loving them both was complicated business.

Orion held to her closely as she cried, and didn't say anything as she let out the emotions. He did his best during the entire ordeal not to bad-mouth Logan in any way, but the man's lack of action was something he wasn't sure if he could keep from criticizing. "I don't really know him that well, but as broody as the guy is, he probably hasn't even finished processing it himself. I know it's not what anybody could have been expecting."

"What the fuck does that matter?" She cried into his chest. "I *just found out. You* just found out, *you're* here with me!" Anna held tighter to Orion and crawled into his lap so she could be wrapped up in his embrace. "This was all some fucking grand plan and instead of being with me, he makes me deal with Mercury alone. I mean, why didn't she fucking tell you? Why didn't she call both of us there? Don't you deserve to know along with me? You could have held my hand, but maybe she didn't want to see that shit. They both are being so fucking selfish."

"If," he started off slowly, "if she had called him in to be around for the news, maybe she was thinking it could have been monitored. She probably doesn't want it to look like one of them is his and one is mine. But shit, that's on the report already, isn't it?" His mind was finally catching up to where they were, and he was clearly scared on her behalf. "If they know that one of them is his . . ."

"She's falsifying the report. Saying some shit about the machine messing up, and she's gonna do it with some others too." Anna wasn't entirely convinced the Initiative and the Consortium didn't already know, but clearly Logan and Mercury thought she was too stupid to argue with them. Mercury and Logan had everything under control. "Or maybe he just doesn't give a shit. You know what it looks like when a husband goes to a prenatal appointment? A supportive husband. There's nothing fucking suspicious about that."

"It also . . ." he shook his head and shut his mouth. "You're right. That's what it looks like. I'm not gonna make excuses for him. Or for her. They should've done it differently. But that doesn't change the fact that this is good news. We're gonna have a kid. That's a life. That overrules a lot of bad mixed in."

Anna nodded against his shoulder for a moment before she looked up at him with puffy eyes. "A little boy is all yours. I assume he'll want his sister to hang around too, though." She said with a halfhearted laugh before she stared into his endlessly dark eyes. "Are you really happy about it? Or are you just faking for my benefit?"

"You know better than to think I have to fake anything for

you." He gave her a joking glare and drew her in to kiss her cheek. "I'm really happy about it."

"At least I haven't gotten sick." She mumbled, though she knew that her pregnancy had probably been discovered before her body even knew to start reacting to it, so she was definitely being grateful for something that would probably happen anyway. Modern science. It was a little too modern.

Anna stayed curled up in his lap and held onto his shirt as she attempted to not freak out all over again. "Just don't let me go." Anna pleaded, since the last thing she wanted was to be alone. "I don't . . . I can't be alone. I don't want to do this alone."

"I'm not going anywhere." He rubbed her back as he held her. "Now or for the rest of you and these kids' lives. We knew we were gonna be getting into forever the second they told us we were supposed to have kids together. That's how far we're in this."

Anna covered her face with her hands again. "Someone else promised me something similar, and I haven't heard from him." She kept to her silence, unbroken by any beeps of notification from her communicator. Normally she couldn't get the thing to shut up, but it was even worse in its silence. "Let's just go to sleep. At least we get the next couple days off now."

"Oh, that's right, we do. Well, that is definitely a perk." He sighed against her neck and kissed her cheek again. "Alright, then. Time to go get naked and get some sleep. In case no one told you, pregnant women are incredibly sexy."

Anna actually laughed at that. "Uh huh. Says the man who can get any woman he wants, including goddesses. Have you actually ever seen any pregnant women? If so, have you really thought, 'Man, I would love to fuck that one'?"

"So what if I have? Come on." He got up from the couch and picked her up with him, carrying her in his arms as he made his way to the bedroom.

"Wait a minute. No, no, no, you can't just brush that aside. I saw that look!" She grabbed his chin since he was carrying her to force him to look her in the eye. "You *do* have a thing for pregnant women! Oh my god! I am unlocking the dirty secrets of Orion Al-Jabbar right now. That's a twisty one, Giant."

"Yeah, yeah, that's what they tell me." He smiled at the accusation and set her down on the bed. "There was a name for it that I heard a while ago, I forget it now. Some kind of -philia. I don't know if it's actually supposed to be diagnosable, but if it is,

I've got it."

Anna started laughing again and broke into giggles before she grabbed onto him and pulled him down into the bed with her. Being distracted by Orion was ten times better than being angry at Logan. "So the more pregnant-looking I get . . ."

"Yup, that's about how the math on that shakes out." He took his time stripping off his clothing before he joined her in the bed. "The more pregnant you get, the less you're gonna get away from me."

"I can't promise I'll be anything to look at when I'm hugely pregnant." She wasn't about to promise him she would gladly give in to him whenever he wanted, since she knew it wouldn't last. There was no reason to think it would. She was the first one down, the first one to get knocked up, and technically there was no more reason for them to see each other if he didn't want to see her. The deed was done.

"You'll get more time with Mercury now. Maybe things will go back the way you wa . . . the way they were supposed to be. There's no reason to worry about a fertile week if I'm already pregnant. That's three out of four weeks I won't be kicking you in your sleep."

He shook his head. "We talked a long time ago about the fact that neither of us have any intention of stopping this. And I can't say for sure if Mercury will either. I don't know what's going to happen. Neither of us do. But this . . ." He looked down at her and poked her in the stomach. "I know what's going to happen with this. I'm going to be around. That's what."

"I'm glad. I want you to be." She said simply as she took the hand that poked her and kissed his palm before she let go so that she could undress. "Let's go to sleep."

24

Kazuo's world felt like it had been on a roller coaster for days, but it might have been longer than that, he wasn't really sure. One moment he would look to his right and Aiko was there, then he would blink and there would be no one. Then Kam. Then both of them with hallucinations of everybody else he'd ever seen somehow all packed into the same room.

When he opened his eyes again, he saw the vague shape of Aiko next to him and tried to reach out, but he wasn't sure what actually happened.

"It's in my brain now, isn't it?" He asked without fully opening his eyes.

Aiko turned toward her brother as soon as she heard him talking, even though it was hard to hear him at all. She reached out for his hand and held it gently as she moved in closer to him. "Yes, it is." She looked down at her hand holding his and shook her head. He was never supposed to look so frail. "I'm glad you're awake. Kameron has been worried that you wouldn't wake up again."

He nodded, or at least he tried to nod. "Pretty soon now, I'm not going to." He couldn't open his eyes fully, and he wasn't really sure why. But it didn't matter. They felt so heavy. He could see Aiko well enough, though. "I guess you get this one last chance to yell at me for sleeping in."

Aiko tried to laugh but it turned into a sob. "You are supposed to teach my kid how to do all sorts of things to get him into trouble. You can't go."

"I left . . ." he paused to take a deep breath, but it took a few minutes. "I left a how-to manual. It's in my files. They're keyed to you and Fitch."

She squeezed his hand a little bit more. "Always one step ahead." Aiko was always crying around her brother and that day was no exception. She didn't know if she would ever see him awake again, and she was glad for another chance. He was truly on his deathbed. "Let me get Kameron, okay? She really wants to see you. Don't go back to sleep."

"I'll try not to. No promises." He shook his head and tried to nod toward the door, to indicate she could go get Kameron.

Aiko hurried out as best she could, and even though she wasn't that far along, he could see a small baby bump on her tiny frame. Whatever big baby Carl had put inside of her was going to be obvious about taking up space, clearly.

Kameron came rushing into the room as soon as Aiko said Kaz was awake, and she immediately went to his side and smiled at him, though he looked terrible. She was used to it, but it was still shitty. "Hey, you. You're awake. I was wondering how many days you could go without sex. The fact that you're awake means I won't be losing too much money, right?" Clearly she was teasing, but she couldn't help herself. Humor was her coping mechanism. One of many things it turned out she and Kaz had in common.

"No, that's one bet you would win." He managed to reply, though his eyes remained mostly closed. "If only late-stage terminal cancer of nearly every organ didn't also cause a complete loss of sexual function. I've complained about that, but management doesn't seem to be listening." He tried his best to shrug and only managed a slight movement of his shoulder.

"Damn cancer." She said softly as she bit back tears. "I know I shouldn't stay here too long, Aiko needs to be the one who is here with you. I'm just the girl you knocked up." Kameron laughed again but it made the tears in her eyes burn even more. "I just wanted to see you so badly. Talk to you."

"I missed you too." He tried to squeeze her hand, and smiled up at her as well as he could. "Time . . . has been weird. Guess that happens when something is living in your brain without paying rent. It feels like it's been years since I talked to you. She should be grown up by now. Riding a bike down an Eleusis hillside. Streamers on the handlebars, those are very important."

"She will. I'll make sure there are streamers." He was turning into a blur in her vision, but she wasn't dying, she was just fighting her damndest not to cry. Kameron brought his hand to her lips and started to cry anyway. "I fucking love you, you know. She does too."

"Really thought that was the other way around." He smiled and managed to open his eyes just a little wider, but only briefly.

"I love you too, Kam. You might be the biggest bitch I ever had the pleasure of knowing, and you'd better make sure she inherits every gram of it. I don't want her . . ."

He had to stop to catch his breath again, and it looked like he might go into some kind of an attack, but he fought it off as best he could. "I don't want her . . . taking shit from anyone she doesn't have to. Certain . . . not the . . . Consor . . ." he did devolve into a coughing fit and it was a long time before he could breathe regularly, though they could still hear a slight wheeze in his breath.

Kameron moved closer so he wouldn't have to talk loudly, and she laid there next to his side to comfort him until he could breathe evenly. She knew Aiko was standing by the door watching, hoping her brother wouldn't die, but they all knew he was only hanging on by threads. Kameron rested her head against his bony shoulder and kissed his cheek gently. "She won't take shit from anyone." She finally confirmed before she moved to kiss his lips gently. "I promise. I promise she'll know you. I'm so sorry that I couldn't do a fucking thing to help you, I'm sorry that . . . well, it was pretty fucked up that you got put with me in the first place. I wish things were different for you. You deserve to live, to go to Eleusis."

"No. That's a mistake." He barely whispered. "What people deserve . . . doesn't change things. Only what they do changes anything. Cancer didn't interview me before I caught it. Unless it erased that bit. I wouldn't be surprised." His eyes opened wide for a moment in some kind of system alarm, but they closed again afterward as his whole body squirmed, leaving him breathing hard with his eyes back to half-closed.

"You . . . are going to be amazing, Kam. I'm grateful for that." He lifted a finger to let her know he wasn't done talking, just having trouble getting air. "I . . . d . . . de . . . designed a . . . a house. For you. Lots of . . . space. You always said . . . that you were . . . tired of being crammed in all the time. Aiko can . . . find it."

Kam nodded against his shoulder, still crying, but she didn't care anymore. A young, brilliant man was dying and while he might have been saved, he was robbed of everything. A future. His dignity, even. Because someone couldn't be bothered to give a damn. "Thank you." She didn't want to think about the future when he was dying in front of her. Kameron put his hand on her stomach and then kissed his jawline a few times.

"Before Aiko kicks me off the bed, I need your help with one thing. I need you to help me pick a name for her. I'm shit with all the girly crap, you know that. If you leave it up to me, she'll be named Morgan or Blake or something like that."

He managed to smile. "Those wouldn't be too bad." He breathed heavily for a while and his eyes were closed, so it was difficult to tell whether he was awake and thinking or asleep and about to die.

"Kasumi." He said finally, moving his face a little to kiss her cheek. "People argue over the best meaning for it. I always read it as mist. Something beautiful that isn't around for very long. To remind her where she came from."

Kameron nodded yet again, even though he wasn't looking at her. "Kasumi. It's beautiful." She was nearly sobbing, but she was staying as close to him as she could. "I don't know . . . if you believe in an afterlife or whatever. But if you do, stay close to us, okay?"

"Okay. Unless the afterlife has a beach. Then I might step away and go . . . tanning . . . once in a while." He did his best to grip her hand, and she saw a tear slip from his own eye. "Be happy, Kam. Be happy, take care of our daughter, and kick as much ass as possible. Not necessarily in that order. Please not all at once."

"I'll try not to do it all at once. Even though kicking ass makes me happy." She pressed her face to the side of his and took in a deep breath of his scent before she kissed him one last time. "I love you. I really, really do." Kameron had to pull herself away since she knew she was stealing vital time, and Aiko needed to be with her brother. It wasn't fair, none of it was fair, but the Consortium was a big fucking asshole in a life that was unfair enough without their help.

Kazuo was out of it for a while after the brief conversation, but he awoke later with a gasp of pain and a surprisingly strong clench of his hand around Aiko's.

He vaguely heard a nurse on his other side asking him what hurt, what was wrong, but he couldn't even answer. Not because he couldn't talk, but because he didn't know what to say.

Everything hurt. Everything just felt wrong, but that wasn't exactly a medical diagnosis.

"I'm fine." He tried to say as glibly as possible. He tried to open his eyes and give the nurse a sarcastic look, but nothing responded to his commands. "What, like you've . . . never been tickled by an invisible ghost before?"

"Very funny." Aiko responded for him, then nodded toward the nurse who took the hint and stepped back. Aiko was the one who got up and went to grab a syringe to put into his IV. "This will help with the pain. No one is supposed to get a dosage like this of this stuff, but you're dying anyway. I doubt you're too worried about chronic liver damage." She finished putting the meds into his IV and sat down next to him again. "I hate seeing you in pain."

"You won't have to for much longer." He said without any trace of a joke in his tone for once. "Have you . . ." he sighed as some of the medication she gave him began to take effect, and when he spoke again it was clearer, though he still couldn't quite open his eyes. "Have you been able to talk to Mom and Dad at all?"

"No, not really. Once I got pregnant they were allowing some of my messages to go through, but I only got a few photos from Mom and Dad. Nothing else. They're really buckling down on everything up here."

Kazuo nodded weakly. "Tell them I died in a kickboxing accident or something. Or no, better yet, tell them I just spontaneously combusted somewhere and immediately turned to ash. Dad always liked the really weird medical cases."

"How about I tell them you married this crazy woman and ran off with her to live a happy life?" She said softly as she held his hand tighter. "That's what they want to hear. You acting wild for once."

"Hey, that's a good one too. I like it." He managed to force his eyes open as the drugs took effect, and he nodded across the room to where Kameron stood. "Tell 'em I ran off with this gorgeous brunette who couldn't get enough of me. We'll send a postcard when we've colonized Pluto."

"You know, they might actually believe it once I send them pictures of Kameron and your baby." She smiled as she glanced over at Kameron, who, completely out of her character, was crying while Carl held an arm around her shoulders. "I didn't think it would work out so well between you two. But I'm happy it did."

"Yeah, I don't think anybody could've called that." He smiled again and rested his head back against his pillow. "Carl." He said quietly.

"Yeah, man, right over here." Carl didn't move away from

Kameron, since he wasn't going to get between Kazuo and Aiko.

"Anything happens to my sister, I haunt you the rest of my afterlife." Kazuo said without even looking at the much-larger man. "And not the funny kind of haunting where I just close a door every once in a while, either. I'm talking full-on poltergeist shit."

"I believe you." Carl smiled in spite of the situation, since he had always liked Kazuo. The man's sense of humor was about as morbid as they came. "Anything happens to her, means it already happened to me. And nothing's getting through me, brother. Unlike some people I could mention, things have a hard time killing me."

That got a broad smile from Kazuo and he attempted to laugh, though it only came out as a cough. "Take care of that one, sis. He'll take care of you. Not that you need it."

"I think I need him more than I realize." Aiko met Carl's eyes for a moment before she looked back at her brother and she leaned down to hug him as tightly as she could without hurting him. "I need you too." She admitted, but her voice cracked when she did. "Kaplan is going to pay for this, Kaz." She whispered against her brother's cheek.

He managed to open his eyes a little more and shook his head almost imperceptibly before he sighed, since he didn't have time or energy to try and talk her out of it. "Don't get caught." He settled on saying, slurring his words a little. "Plenty of people have it coming. Don't get caught up in helping karma catch up to them. You've got more important things to do with your life."

"This is an important thing to do with my life. We came up here for you. To get you help. And he fucking . . ." Aiko never cursed, but apparently Carl and Kameron had rubbed off on her recently. At least in the moment, as her heart was breaking and her best friend was dying in front of her. "I have to do it. For you. For me. He deserves it."

Kazuo didn't fight her after that and just nodded against her cheek. "I'll bet he's terrible at dying. It's a real art form, I'm finding. You've gotta nail it on the first try or else it's just embarrassing." He took in a sharp breath, and she could hear a tiny whimper in him as he held off whatever was happening to him, but he turned to speak directly in her ear.

"You need . . . to know . . . Mom and Dad . . . didn't want you to worry." He blinked a few times and tried to focus, but it was becoming more and more difficult. "Before . . . launch . . ."

"Before launch?" She didn't understand what he was trying to say, but she knew it was important if he was struggling so much to say it. "What about the launch?" Aiko leaned back to look into his eyes, but they were closed, so she just leaned back down to press her face to his. Was he already dead? She felt cold, sick. As though she was falling apart. "Kaz . . ."

He took a few labored breaths and shuddered again, but it was hard to tell if it was some kind of twitch or if he was trying to shake himself awake. "Get off the station." He managed to get out, though it was still just in a whisper. "Before launch. Or all . . . like before." He shook his head, but it wasn't doing much good. He opened his eyes, but they were unfocused and unseeing as they darted around in front of him. "No matter . . . what it takes, get off before. Anywhere else. Be anywhere else."

Aiko felt a terrible sense of dread when she heard her brother say that, but she just nodded against his cheek and held tightly to him. "I will. I'll do whatever it takes." Including getting involved with someone she swore never to acknowledge again. Apparently she was going to need him for a few reasons. "I love you, Kazuo."

"I love you too, Aiko." He took in another deep breath as he tried in vain to hold onto her, but his breathing became more labored with every passing moment.

"I wish . . ." he whispered in the middle of a gasp, and she could feel a tear falling from her brother's eye and hitting her own cheek. "I wish . . . I could've . . . seen . . ."

His mouth moved, but no more words came out, and she could feel him slowly lose the struggle to breathe. He lost consciousness first, going limp beneath her as his body struggled automatically to take in any air whatsoever, but no matter how much air he did take in, it wasn't enough. His shoulders rose and fell with the deep breaths he was taking, but one by one, they turned more ragged, until his chest stopped moving altogether, and the lights on the machines surrounding him went still.

It was a nightmare. It wasn't real. Her mind wouldn't accept it. Aiko was sobbing into her brother's still chest, most of her mind waiting for it to struggle to move again, to breathe, just one more breath. It was real. Too real. They had risked everything to save his life and he died anyway. Aiko's sobs were loud and painful and she kept calling her brother's name, hoping he would wake up again. But he didn't. He wouldn't, ever again.

The sound of the doctor stepping into the room seemed like it was happening a world away. Even the stated time of death echoed in nothing. Eventually she felt Carl move to the side of the bed to be near her, though he didn't make any move to separate her from her brother's body.

When she turned her head to look at Carl, she realized he was alone, and Kameron had disappeared. It made her mourn even more on her brother's behalf, since he would never get to see or hold his baby. She reached out for Carl but mostly collapsed into him.

"They won't even send him home." She whimpered as Carl gathered her into his arms. "It'll take too many resources to send him home. They're just going to burn him up and never look back."

He picked her up once she curled into him, and held her against his chest easily with one huge arm under her back and the other under her knees. "I actually got Orion working on something for him. He's better at a couple things than I am." He stood up and took a few steps away from the bed to allow some of the nurses to unhook Kazuo from all his machines and cover him.

"I got Vance to sign off on a void burial for him. I know you probably don't do many of those down on the ground." His voice was sedated but he was still trying to keep her with him, trying to talk her through it. They had known it was coming, it was just a matter of when. "Sometimes, if people can figure it out and get a crew to help, they'll put themselves in a capsule that can be jettisoned or shot from a station. Sometimes they want to end up back on Earth, sometimes different planets. Orion worked out a path that should get Kaz to Eleusis. In, you know, a few thousand years."

"At least he'll get there." She buried her face into Carl's chest and gripped him as tightly as she could. Her knuckles hurt from holding too tightly to everything around her, but she didn't care. The pain felt necessary. It was nothing next to the pain inside her chest. "I'm here because of him. He was supposed to live."

"I know he was." He agreed, holding her tightly as they moved away and out of the small clinic room. "It's not right. It'll never be right, no matter what happens from here."

Aiko couldn't talk the rest of the way back to their unit. She felt numb, but she also felt angry. Irrationally angry. When he laid her down on their bed, she looked toward the giant window they had been afforded because of her position, studying her plants against their backdrop of dark space.

"I need my communicator. Do you know where it is?" She had been out of her mind since Kazuo was re-admitted to intensive care, and she wasn't even aware of how much time had passed.

"Yeah, I've got it." He let his hand rest on her shoulder for another minute before he moved away to get it out of a bag he'd been carrying around ever since Kazuo had gone back in. She vaguely remembered him producing protein bars and bottles of water now and then, prompting her to eat whenever Kazuo was resting. "Here." He handed it to her and sat down on the bed next to her to take off her shoes for her so that she could rest a little more comfortably in the bed.

Aiko took the communicator, but she watched him as he helped her out of her shoes. For some reason the action prompted her to start crying again. "I'm sorry that I've . . . that you've had to help me so much. But thank you."

He shook his head and tossed the shoes aside so he could put them by the door later. "I can't imagine what it's like. And I'm not just saying that, I really can't imagine. If Orion died, yeah, that would be about as close as it's ever gonna get for me. I know there's not much I can do, but what I can, I'm gonna do." He moved closer to her, just to hold her until she stopped crying, at least temporarily. "I'm gonna go make some dinner. You need some decent food."

Aiko nodded and thanked him a few more times before she was alone in their bed, and the world felt even heavier in his absence. It was sitting on her shoulders. Her brother was dead. She couldn't do anything to save him anymore.

Aiko wiped at the fresh tears sharply before she actually brought the communicator to her face so that she could call someone instead of sending a message. The contact she chose was labeled simply.

White.

The line rang a few times before he picked up, but she could hear the ambient noise of what sounded like a cafeteria around him when he did. The line was silent at first, but she heard Gordon sigh before she heard anything else.

"I just saw." He knew he wouldn't need to explain what it was he had seen, or how. Especially not to someone who had known him as long as she had. "I'm so sorry, Aiko."

"I don't need your apologies." She said in a sharp reply, though there was no anger in her voice. Not for him. "I need your help."

There was a long pause on the other end, since that was clearly the last thing he had expected to hear from her. "It's yours. What can I do?"

"Kazuo might not be dead if someone had fucking cared." She flinched a little at herself cursing, but it was getting easier. "Someone specific said he wasn't important enough to save. And that person needs to pay for what he took."

That brought on an even longer pause, and she had known 'Gordon' long enough to know most of what he was probably thinking. Images from the past came swimming up to mingle with the present, images of different dead bodies, none of them her brother.

"I understand. Ideally, I'll need about twenty-four hours to identify and guarantee a workable window. What other helpers do I need to account for? Just you, or will she want in on it as well?"

"I'm not telling anyone else. Just you. You can get me in and I can do the rest. If you're there, you can keep watch." Aiko looked toward her window again and closed her eyes. "It'll get messy if anyone else is involved."

"True." He agreed, still clearly surprised about the entire thing. "Well, in that case, it's . . . two in the afternoon right now," mention of the time brought back a haunting echo of a doctor's voice so recently declaring Kazuo's time of death, as if the pronouncement was stuck in her hearing for later processing, "it'll probably be easiest to arrange a late-night window. Can you be ready by one-thirty?"

"Yes. I can be ready whenever you think it's possible." She had been ready as soon as she found out that some high-and-mighty bastard could make the decision about her brother's life without even trying to help. "There's something that he said to me before . . . there's just something he said that you should know. Or maybe you already do, I don't know."

"I know a lot of things, but I don't recall ever claiming to know everything. So it could go either way." He kept his tone even, cautious, exactly the way he'd been every time they had spoken for a very long time.

"It's about what happened before . . . and our launch."

"Ah." She could hear the understanding in Gordon's tone, and that told her more than she really wanted to know. "Yes, that falls into the category of things I know. Though it surprises me that he knew it. Your parents, I expect. They always were better informed than they ever let anyone know. But yes, my information matches that . . . expectation."

"Then we need to work together to do something about that." Aiko had avoided helping Gordon in any way, but now she had made a promise to Kazuo, and she certainly had no desire to die in the first place. "I intend to see Eleusis."

"I intend for you to do that too." His tone sounded slightly more relaxed, as it had been in the first days of their acquaintance. Before she had really known him. "It was never my intention to leave you or your brother here in that eventuality. Never intended to leave anyone here, honestly. Well, those who deserve to be left, of course." He sighed, and she could see him working through things behind his eyes without even looking at him. "First things first. When tonight's business is concluded, we'll talk further about next steps."

"Alright." She said softly, since she could hear Carl cooking not far from her, and while she didn't want to leave him out of it, she knew it was best. Just this once. "You know where to find me if you need to update me."

* * * * *

Carl stayed awake to make sure she was asleep, even if she wasn't actually asleep by the time he was apparently convinced and went to lie down beside her. He had always been a heavy sleeper once he really got settled, since his body needed to overcompensate for its overactivity by going into something more closely resembling a coma than normal sleep.

He didn't make a sound as she got up to leave, and even when she opened the door and slipped out, there was no sound of surprise from the bedroom.

The hallway outside her room was quiet, but she had been out during the 'night' before, and it had always been lit enough for basic visibility. The hallway at the moment, though, was almost pitch-dark, with only running lights along one side of the ceiling to provide dim illumination. After the night-lights of her unit, it was blinding for a few minutes before her eyes began to adjust.

476

Gordon's voice came from somewhere unseen to her left before the adjustment could be completed. "You have everything you need?"

Aiko gasped and turned to face Gordon with an unseen glare on her exhausted face. She was sure she looked like hell. Between losing sleep over Kazuo and not taking care of herself *and* being pregnant, she probably looked near death. She rested one hand on a small pouch at her side as she nodded. "I have what I need."

"Alright then." He led the way up the corridor, keeping his hands in his pockets.

It was a long, silent walk to their destination, and whenever they approached a hallway where there were lights to be had, Gordon would take out a data core she'd never seen him without, and pop its dim holograms into the air in front of him. A few flicks of the fingers and the lights would be out. They never once had to break stride or stop their progress, and when they got to the lift, one was waiting and open to take them up to the higher levels of the station.

Only when the lift began to rise did Gordon say anything. "Will what you brought leave any aftereffects that need to be explained?" He doubted it, but if he was helping on something, it was always best to cover his bases.

She shook her head as she kept a hand on her pouch. "One is for temporary paralysis, the other will shut down the organs while he's still awake." Aiko knew it sounded cruel, and she intended it to be. Between what they had done to Carl all of his life and sentencing her brother to death, Aiko thought someone ought to suffer for them both. "They'll metabolize fully before their cascade is even finished. The Consortium's post-mortem policies don't test for any traces they would leave. Everything is synthetic up here. No one is supposed to die by exposure to exotic, deadly plants."

"I expected as much." He gave her a nod that was actually respectful, though he wasn't looking at her directly. "Just a precaution on my part." They rose a few more floors, and Gordon checked his data core again, looking at a small map projection.

"His match is sleeping in her own unit tonight, as usual, and his other company was released only about fifteen minutes ago. Vital signs from inside his unit indicate he's the only presence and he's already unconscious, but I warn you not to be surprised or curious if we get out on his floor and you hear someone crying.

They're given instructions not to speak to anyone and just to board the shuttle waiting for them once they've gone and gotten themselves cleaned up, but it sometimes takes them a while afterward to muster up the will to move that far."

"What kind of . . . disgusting piece of trash . . ." she shook her head as she looked down at her pouch, not bothering to finish the question. She had many of her own creations stored inside, all of which served various purposes. They were things she had tested and tested hundreds of times, tweaked a thousand times, and while they would never be perfect, they were independent of the Consortium and anyone else. "Is it someone we can help?"

"Not without getting caught." He said coldly, even though he knew she would probably hate him even more for that kind of pragmatism. "She's expected on the shuttle, and if she doesn't show, the suspicion snowballs. Unless you've got something in there that can effectively and efficiently erase the last four hours of her life from her memory, there's not much we can do to help her."

"I do have something for memory loss, but it usually goes further than four hours." She didn't want to get caught, but she didn't like leaving victims alone without help either. "I should have killed him sooner. He and his brother both. They're disgusting."

"They're also high-profile." He said quietly, not warning her, just discussing the situation. "Not in the grand scheme of things, they're really just no more than a pack of well-trained dogs, all in all. But their master will notice when one of them goes missing. Your methods resemble natural causes, even if that cause is sudden and unexplained organ failure. For one person, one death, that is enough to call that strange, but no more. Any more than just one person and the Consortium would know their boys are vulnerable to assassination. They need to believe they're safe in order to be in real danger."

"Well, maybe I need to find out what Dr. Santos has been prescribing recently and pin the other one on her." Aiko shook her head as the lift finally neared the destination. "All it took was for them to kill my best friend, and look, I'm no better than you are."

"You'll always be better than I am." He said it without regret or judgment or even a hint of mockery in his voice, but he still wouldn't look at her. "It took this instance to push you to this point. I just needed someone to ask me if I would, hypothetically, and I was off to the races, as it were."

The lift stopped, and Gordon's voice dropped once the doors opened on the dark hallway. The glass of the gallery admitted a great deal of light into the hallway, but they kept to the shaded side, away from the brightness of the moon outside the windows.

Somewhere in the dark, far away in the gallery itself, someone was deep in a kind of moaning cry. The emptiness of the place distorted the sound, but it was high-pitched and keening, though it was just as obvious that the owner of the voice was trying to be quiet.

Gordon continued as if he couldn't hear it. "You've never, to my knowledge, done anything without firmly believing that it was the right thing to do. Including the severing of our friendship. Most people just never quite make the moral leap to understand there really are times in which killing another person is the right thing to do."

Aiko tried to ignore the crying, but it was difficult. She didn't want to know what would cause someone to cry like that, since she'd just spent days crying a soul-wrenching sob over the inevitable loss of her brother and best friend.

"Do you know what he does to them?" She wished she hadn't asked as soon as it came out of her mouth, but it would give her even more justification for what she was about to do.

"I have a vague concept, yes." Gordon looked back at her and shook his head, but he answered the question anyway. He had lost enough of Aiko's trust. If she was actually asking him for information, he wasn't going to keep anything from her. She had proven she could be trusted with anything long since.

"From the movement and vitals scanners we've managed to tap, it always involves a single person, and some compound that achieves the same effect as what you've said you're carrying. There is a long period of zero physical activity, during which the subject's anxiety escalates slowly to dangerous levels. Subjects have stroked out before. There was one just last week, actually. This period of anxiety is followed by somewhere around an hour of physical activity, involving a great deal of pain for the subject. Afterward, by all indications, first aid is performed on the subject during a quieting period in which anxiety levels continue to spike intermittently, after which the subject is released. This pattern has been repeated two nights per week, without deviation, ever since our arrival on the station. The victims never recur."

"He really does think people are just toys." Aiko gripped her pouch and started moving faster toward the unit, though she remained in the shadows the whole time. "He's about to find out what it's like to be toyed with."

Once they got close to the door, Gordon turned to stop her, with a hand extended that didn't quite touch her shoulder. He was looking at her for once, and his dark eyes were even darker in the near-void he had created for them in the hallway.

"I know you're angry, and I don't pretend to understand the kind of anger you're feeling. I've never loved any of my brothers the way you love yours. You have every right to that anger, and everything you're about to do with it. But my goal here on this station is to save lives. Not just ours. Everyone's, everywhere. If you get carried away with this, or do anything that will compromise that, I need you to understand that I will stop you."

He took a slow breath after that declaration, since he didn't want to fight her, or even contradict her, but he knew he might have to. "I need to know that you trust me enough to let me do that. That you will listen to me, if only for the next few minutes. I don't have to remind you how well I understand what you're about to do."

"I will listen to you, but I'm not going to do anything outrageous. I'm going to paralyze the bastard, let him know that I'm the reason why he's going to die, and then kill him. I'm not going to dance on his entrails. I just want him to die."

"That's wise. Entrails get very slippery. Especially on these tiles." He looked down at the floor beneath them, then took out two pairs of gloves from his own pocket and handed one set over to Aiko. Another few gestures with the data core and the handprint panel beside Kaplan's door turned a faint green, allowing Gordon to open the door, slowly and soundlessly.

The inside of the man's unit was incredibly disappointing. There was almost nothing personal to be seen anywhere, and the only sign that anything had ever been anything but immaculate was a couch that was slightly ajar across the living space. The unit was large, but empty, and felt more empty for being so large, even larger for being empty.

The bedroom door was open, since there was very rarely any reason to close it in such intimate quarters. The bedroom also seemed like it was the tamest and most boring of places at first glance. Byron Kaplan was sleeping under a single thin sheet in the middle of the huge bed, but beyond him, there were a number of blood spatters, some small, some larger, some looking like it had been sprayed rather than soaked into the fabric. There was more on the tile floor around the bed, and Gordon pointed to some of them, making sure she was careful not to step on them as they approached.

Aiko could only look at the blood long enough to avoid it, and she tried not to imagine what happened to his poor victims, even though it would fuel her hatred for him. How could he sleep peacefully, with blood all around him, as if it was the only satisfactory decoration for his disgusting home? She pulled out a syringe from her pouch, ready at Gordon's signal.

Gordon looked back at the door once to make sure he could see the faint red light that meant it was secure, then went to pick up a spare blanket from the other side of the room. He refolded it into a long strip, and then painstakingly tied one end to the leg of the bed on one side and pulled it mid-air across Byron's body to wrap it around one of his arms so that he could hold the other end. It would leave no bruises on the man and no signs of a struggle. He pointed to the sheet where Byron's leg was visible through the thin sheet, to an artery. He tugged on the blanket to be sure of it, then nodded to her, letting her know he was ready.

Aiko looked at Gordon once and at Kaplan's leg before she took a deep breath and raised her arm. She knew it would hurt. She wanted it to hurt. She wanted him to wake up in pain.

The needle came down, stabbing his leg soundlessly. She injected the paralytic as quickly as she could before he could jerk his leg away. It was a double dose. She had to be sure that even if he got away from her before she could inject it all that he would still be paralyzed and unable to attack her. By the time he tried, his legs would already be useless.

His reflexes were good, but as he came awake with a grunt of pain, Gordon came down with the blanket and locked the man against the bed. Kaplan struggled and rocked the bed as he yelled wordlessly, but he was too confounded by the blanket and confused by the rude awakening to do anything effectively. After only a few seconds the immediate rush of his heart rate had dispersed the paralytic through his entire system, and he began to settle down.

"You . . ." He heaved out a question as he tried to push himself up, but his arm betrayed him and flopped to the covers. When he fell back, it was as if he had never even gotten up, except that he was staring at Gordon and Aiko from his pillow. "You . . . what are you . . ." he lingered on the look Aiko was giving him, and understanding settled into place along with the paralytic.

"Ah. That's right." His words slurred a little, but he was still clear enough to be understood, even if the rest of his body wasn't really responding. "He died today. I'd already forgotten."

"Yes, well, you remember *now*, don't you? I'm sure you believed you had no cause to worry when you signed his death warrant. Now you do."

"I don't recall signing anything. In fact, I believe it was the absence of my signature which caused such anger rather than its presence." He couldn't move any of the muscles in his body, but Aiko could still see one of his fingers moving sluggishly as he tried and failed, testing the limits of his paralysis. "I expect you're here to murder me, Ms. Tanaka."

"I am." She looked him up and down and shook her head. "I don't have the mind or the tolerance to flay you open or take you apart limb by limb. So I suppose I should just get on with it."

"Probably best." Byron said with a bored look on his face. His eyes flicked around to the blood on the sheets and on the floor around the bed, and Aiko could see a small smile on his lips. "She'll probably be blamed. But that's obviously not your concern."

"I'll make sure no one is blamed. I mean, how can anyone be blamed for multiple organ failure with no trace of a drug?" Aiko opened her pouch again and pulled out a different syringe before she stowed the first, used one. "I thought you would care about your life a little more. It doesn't matter, though. No amount of begging would matter. You not hurting anyone else. That's what matters."

"Begging isn't really my strong suit." Byron just closed his eyes and sighed at the sight of the syringe. "You've planned ahead. That's for the best. Have you decided how you're going to dispose of my body, or will it look that much like natural causes?"

"Why do you care?" She asked suspiciously, since she didn't know what he was getting at. "You'll be dead."

"Well, it's the last real curiosity in life. What's going to happen after death. Soul, body, research, all the moving parts go somewhere. Just wondering where." He looked over at Gordon as

Aiko hesitated with the syringe. "I do wish I could notify someone about you, though. We've suspected you for a long time, but there were at least three others we were trying to pin down before we moved. That would have been satisfying."

"You've had too much satisfaction." Aiko didn't care to chat it up with the bastard, especially since the longer she waited, the more she would put it off. Aiko tapped the syringe and stepped up to Byron's side again before she lifted up his limp arm. No one would go looking for an injection site in his armpit.

"He might have died anyway. I know that. But you were supposed to help him. You refused. Not because you couldn't, but because you wanted to send a message about compliance." She didn't give him any sort of chance to talk his way out of it by giving her some kind of sob story before she jabbed in the syringe. He was a terrible person. Willing to abuse innocent women, willing to be a party to mass murder. He didn't deserve to live. "Five minutes until it circulates. At least an hour of suffering before you die of complete organ failure. Even if someone finds you before you die, they'll have no antidote to fix you."

"It's good to be certain of things." He said without opening his eyes, even though he still could. "Are you going to stay and watch? You'll want to be certain I'm dead. That your revenge is complete, your brother is at rest, all that."

"I'm not like you." Aiko said as she looked at Byron before she looked over at Gordon, and looked away from both of them. "I don't take twisted pleasure in watching people suffer."

"It's not always about taking pleasure in it." Byron said with a brief attempt to move his shoulder that only resulted in a mild spasm. "It's just the way the world is. And killing me won't make it better. It'll just let you tell yourself that for a while."

"You won't get to destroy anyone else. I call that a better world." Aiko turned toward Gordon and whispered into his ear. "Can we go?"

"Almost." Gordon was still eyeing the man, and he checked a few displays on his data core before he proceeded, since he wanted to make absolutely sure they weren't observed. "Look at me, Mr. Kaplan."

Byron did actually open his eyes at that, looking mildly curious, but he couldn't move his head even to turn and look at Gordon.

"Arm Two." Gordon said quietly. "Sector twenty-nine. Rooms 9F and 10C."

For the first time that Aiko had ever seen from Byron, his eyes flared, and his entire body twitched, as his brain sent frantic signals to muscles that weren't capable of responding. "You can't." Byron slurred in an attempt at a shout that came out more as a moan, some drool beginning to fall from the corner of his mouth. "You don't know . . . you can't . . ."

"We can." Gordon said as he stepped back from the bed. "And we will."

Byron was frantic on the bed, but all he could do was rumple the sheets as he laid in them. Whatever he was trying to say was coming out gibberish, and the look on Gordon's face said most of what she needed to know. He didn't look happy, or victorious, but she knew Gordon, and both of those emotions were right beneath the surface. "Killing someone is one thing. Revenge is usually better if it destroys the whole person, not just the body."

"I don't care about that. As long as he's gone." She barely glanced at Byron once and she shook her head and looked away. Lab trials had been enough to tell her what the rest of Byron Kaplan's life would look like. "I don't want to watch."

He walked out with her and locked everything up behind them. "I'll monitor him on the room machines. It won't take long."

Aiko walked out ahead of Gordon before she allowed herself to look up again. The crying in the hall was gone. "Hopefully the gap between time of death and the woman's appearance on the ship will protect her."

"Don't worry too much about her. They . . . she's more or less beyond suspicion." He kept walking, but spoke quietly. "He has them shipped in from an orphanage on Prime. Same one he and his brother were in as kids. Not exactly people of means. Or the know-how to produce organ failure and get away with it."

Aiko felt sick at knowing that particular detail and she just kept walking. "One less terrible person in the universe. That's something. Even though Kaz is still gone."

"That part doesn't change. If it could, I would help with that too. I always liked Kazuo, even if he did die still hating me. But yes, it is one less terrible person in the universe. And that's not nothing."

She felt wobbly and tired with the deed done, and Kaz was still dead. It wasn't as though she thought killing Byron Kaplan would bring her brother back to life, but the anger that had sustained her after Kazuo stopped breathing was gone. The debilitating pain was starting to seep back into her bones. "I need to get back. I don't feel well."

"If you need to stop somewhere and throw up, now is the time to say so. It would be best to do it downstairs, but I'll understand if you can't wait that long." He nodded off in the direction of a bathroom as they neared the lift, but the look on his face was sympathetic, which wasn't something anyone was accustomed to seeing from Gordon. "First time is always the worst."

Aiko decided to go into the bathroom even if she thought she could handle it, and it turned out to be a good decision on her part. The dinner Carl had so thoughtfully made for her came up and much more, but she was already so malnourished that it ended up being worse than she knew it should have been.

She had a hard time even standing when she couldn't throw up anymore, and she stumbled out to Gordon after too long in the bathroom. "I feel really dizzy. I think . . ." She shook her head to clear it, but ended up throwing off her entire sense of balance in the process. "I need to get back. Carl will . . . worry."

He went to help her stand, but then ended up mostly carrying her the rest of the way to the lift. There was no one around to share it with, which was good, since he had to slump to the floor of the lift with her as it got into motion. "You're going to be alright. I've been where you are, and I know how it feels. You'll be alright."

"Nothing feels alright." She mumbled as she sat on the floor of the lift and tears came anew, sliding down her face silently. "I'm up here without Kazuo, I'm going to have a baby, Kameron is going to have Kazuo's baby and he's not even . . . I just want to go back to St. Louis."

"I know." He reached into one of the pockets of the pants he was wearing and pulled out a handkerchief that he used to dry her tears, then put it back in his pocket. "You know why I'm here. You know what I'm looking for. It's in the rooms I mentioned to Kaplan. We're going to get it, and we're going to go home. And you, and Kameron, and Carl, are all coming with us."

Aiko nodded slowly, since she was glad that at least he cared about her enough not to leave her behind. She supposed he had always cared about her. She had been the one to end their friendship, after all, not him. "I . . . I want to help." She whispered. "Somehow."

"We'll talk once you've rested. And kept some food down. I'll be glad to have your help." He lifted her face a little to look her in the eye, just to make sure that she wasn't so down that she needed a doctor before he got her back to her unit. "We'll get home."

"I hope you're right." Aiko looked into his eyes as he lifted her face. "This doesn't mean we're friends again." She said adamantly, even though she was depending on him at the moment just to get back to her unit. He could leave her behind and she couldn't do a thing about it. "But we're still on the same side."

He let go of her face and moved away from her as the lift descended, giving them both more feeling of weight than the upper levels generated. "You may not consider me a friend anymore, but that opinion is one-sided."

Aiko looked down at the pouch at her side before she looked over at him again. "I never wanted to kill you. That amazes me a little. Never thought about it once. Even though I usually can't stand to even look at you."

"Yes, well, you've seen me without my shirt on. Most who've had that experience don't care to repeat it." The biting tone of his sense of humor, completely unchanged after so long, bit a little too deeply at the moment, since it was just a reminder of Kazuo. He and her brother had become fast friends based on that particular shared quality of theirs. "And you knew at the time that it was the right thing to do. You may not have approved of my methods, you still probably don't. I've never blamed you for that. But you knew I was right to do what I did."

"No, I still don't know if it was right." She shook her head slowly. "But we were close friends. It's hard to hate someone you care about." Aiko wanted the lift to hurry, since she was too tired and too broken to want to continue to talk about such heavy things. "You helped me now and you didn't have to. I'm grateful for that at least."

"I told you once that I would help you any way I could." He stood up as the lift approached their destination, and reached out to help her to her feet as well, even though she had to lean on him to walk. "You really think I care about you so little that something as trivial as you hating me would change that?"

"I don't know what goes on in your head. I never have."

She continued to lean on him all the way back to her unit, except when she opened the door, Carl was standing at the other side looking panicked. When he saw Gordon, he looked angry.

"Carl, I can explain."

He could see that she was barely standing on her own, so the first thing he did was reach out and hold onto her with one arm. It was half practical and half just relief that she was back and more or less in one piece.

But as he held her, he reached out through the doorway and grabbed Gordon by the shirt and dragged him through the door. He resisted, but couldn't quite break the giant's grip, and when the door closed, Carl took him off his feet with a hand to his throat and slammed him against the door.

"What the *fuck* do you think you're doing?" Carl roared at Gordon as the smaller man struggled to get air.

"Don't hurt him!" Aiko said as she watched Gordon struggle to breathe. She had once wondered if it would make her happy to see him put in his place, but it seemed she didn't actually want to see that happen. "He was helping me."

Carl looked back and forth between the two of them a few times as Gordon continued to choke and gasp for breath. Eventually he put the smaller man down, though he didn't take his hand away from his throat. Gordon could at least breathe, but Carl wasn't letting him go anywhere until he had an explanation. "Helping you with what? You were exhausted. You should be asleep."

Aiko was already slumped to the floor again, since Carl's attention had been diverted. Apparently she was still so exhausted she couldn't stand anymore. "He helped me kill Byron Kaplan." She responded matter-of-factly, even though she didn't know how Carl would take it. Maybe he wouldn't want her anymore if he knew she was capable of murder and being somewhat cavalier about it. She hoped that wasn't the case.

He looked back and forth between her and Gordon and finally let the smaller man go. Gordon slumped back against the door with his hands at his throat, still gasping for air, but he was recovering slowly as he looked down at Aiko. "Would it have killed you to leave a note?" He croaked, then started coughing, though it didn't seem like there had been any permanent damage done.

Her attention was focused on Carl, since he hadn't said anything, even after Gordon's comment. "If he knew where I went, he would have come after me. I didn't want to get anyone else I care about into a situation like that. I needed to do it as much on my own as I could."

Carl obviously wasn't happy with that answer, but Gordon didn't seem too surprised. Carl gave her a hurt look and shoved Gordon out of the way to open the door again. "Get out."

Gordon nodded and coughed again before he looked up at Carl. "Apology accepted. No hard feelings." He gave him a sarcastic glare then gave Aiko one last look before he turned to leave. "Take care of her. She threw up a few minutes ago, so she needs food and water and sleep. In roughly that order." He turned and headed down the hall in the darkness, still rubbing at his throat.

"I'm sorry." Aiko said as she looked up at Carl as he remained by the door and she was still on the floor, but apparently the tears had returned. She was surprised she could cry anymore, and she knew it wasn't a good sign for her or the baby that her whole body was aching. "I only asked for his help because he's one of a few people that can get through the entire station undetected. I had to do it. For . . ."

"I get why you did it. I just thought you would wait until you could walk on your own first." He scooped her up to carry her the rest of the way into their bedroom. Again. She hadn't even gotten changed from the clothes she'd been wearing in Kazuo's room the past few days, so he went to get a bottle of water for her and started undressing her. "I would have stayed put if you had asked. I can't promise I would've been happy about it, but I would've stayed put."

"I would have wanted you with me." She admitted as he started undressing her. He ran a hand over her tiny bump, as he always did, and it made her eyes burn even more. "I'm not . . . it was . . . I couldn't stay. I didn't want to watch. I just wanted him dead."

"That part I understand." He got her shirt off and motioned to the water again to prompt her to drink. If she'd been throwing up, she didn't need to get dehydrated. "Last week, I was sitting with Kaz for a while. You were running down to the garden to get some things together for him. We thought he'd sleep through a while longer, but he woke up and we were talking about some things."

He finished with her shirt and pulled a blanket up around her, settling her in to keep her warm. "We were thinking about what's going to happen from here on, with the rest of the project. And we realized there's really only one way this ends for everyone, if everything we think we know about the Consortium is true. Either they're going to try and kill us, or a bunch of us are going to get together and try to kill them."

He grabbed a cloth from their bathroom and ran it under hot water, then brought it back to help wash her face and neck. "Ever since that conversation, I've been looking forward to using it as an excuse to get at Kaplan. But the sooner the better, if you ask me."

Aiko closed her eyes as he ran the warm cloth over her skin. "They are planning to kill us. That's what Kazuo told me at the end." She opened her eyes halfway to watch him. "I think they're pushing pregnancies because they want to take the babies and then kill us after."

Carl shook his head at just how twisted that idea was, but he wouldn't put it past the Consortium. "After what you told me about my meds, I don't think anything can surprise me anymore." He kept up the massaging cloth until she looked a little more relaxed, then set it aside on their nightstand and sat beside her on the bed.

"I wanted to believe, for a while, that it was just the Initiative that was psychotic. Leaders had somehow gone rogue, started going all mad scientist on people. Then I heard Vance talking to Alpert on his communicator a few weeks ago." The board of directors of the Consortium was almost never heard from directly, but the chair of the board was still a well-known name, both on Earth and in Orbit. Dominic Alpert had been chair for over a decade, and his word was law, at least in space. "I couldn't hear Alpert's half of the conversation, but they sounded like old friends, and Vance sounded like he was getting all the approval he could've asked for. It goes all the way to the top. Which never bodes well for the people at the bottom."

"We have to get out. Get down to Earth. It's the only way to make sure we don't die. Going to Eleusis would be a gamble at this point, since we don't know what's there. We need to get out, Carl." She looked at him again and reached out to touch his hand. "I want to have a future with you."

"I want that with you too." He squeezed her hand once, then leaned down to kiss her cheek. "Next time you go to kill somebody, just promise you'll take me with you. Okay?"

"I promise." She reached out weakly and ran her fingers along his cheek. "I'm not going anywhere without you. You and Will are my whole life now."

That got a subdued smile from him, and he ran his hand down over the blanket to rest it over her bump. "We'll make sure it's a good one. Get some rest. I've already told them I won't be in tomorrow, we're going to stay home and get you back on your feet."

Aiko nodded, but that was all she could do before she closed her eyes and fell asleep. Trying to do anything else was more than she could handle.

25

The chamber that was designated as the official meeting place of the Executive Council went silent as Stephen Kaplan came in, all eyes turning to him in a spectrum of faces from sympathy to fear. He had proven himself to be unpredictable in terms of the measures he would support, the kind of persona he exhibited every day with the rest of the Council, and even in his personal relationships. No one was certain, as he walked silently through the room to take his seat, what was going through his mind.

His brother had died, for no good reason that anyone could identify, in the middle of the night. Logan thought the man should've taken some comfort in the fact that Byron had apparently died peacefully in his sleep, but dead was dead.

No one else spoke as Stephen got to his seat, so Logan decided it was his job to do what no one else would do. "We were all informed a few minutes ago of what happened with Byron, Stephen." He said gently. "I know you two were close. You had been through a lot together. Session can wait, if you need some time."

Stephen shook his head and sat back numbly in his seat, his eyes scanning the rest of the Council before settling on Logan and Mercury. "I'm fine. He's in autopsy now, and that won't be finished before the session is. Let's get on with it."

Mercury watched Stephen carefully and looked around the room before she let herself look at Logan again. She still didn't know what Logan's gamble was. It was a secret even to her, but she did trust him. Mercury gave him a slight nod of encouragement so he would remember that she was on his side regardless.

Logan returned the nod and pushed himself to his feet, since it had become tradition for him as the head of the Council, to begin and end sessions with whatever business he thought most appropriate, or just to get things started formally. "Getting on with it, then. Session this morning is convened as a general session of the Executive Council, all members expected in attendance or represented by proxy. Is such attendance achieved?"

Koskei answered from his seat by the door, where he had appropriated a desk for himself and gotten comfortable as the council secretary. "It is achieved, representation is sufficient."

"Good, then listen closely." Logan said with a quiet smile, which had the same effect on the room it always did. If Logan was smiling, it meant he was confident about something. Or at least, that was what the Council had learned from the show he constantly put on for their benefit.

"I bring a motion before the general Council for adoption into Eleusis law. You are all receiving copies of the particulars." He pressed a button on his communicator which made the file he'd been working on for weeks available to everyone immediately. "You are all free to review the legalese to your hearts' content, but you all know me well enough to know I don't have much patience for parliamentary or legislative tricks. I want a law passed, the law says one thing, and I want us voting on it based on that one thing. So here is what this law says."

He looked over at Kaplan, since he felt a bit bad that he was bringing the motion on the day after his brother died and he fully expected Kaplan and Santos to fight tooth and nail to see that his motion was not carried.

Let them try.

"It says that once Eleusis law takes over this Initiative following our launch, all matches and enforcement of those matches will become null and void. All previously-existing marital conditions, in fact, formed by any sovereign authority on Earth or in Orbit, will become null and void." He looked around the room, since that had raised nearly every eyebrow in attendance.

"This law will require all those who wish to either continue in their present marital or matched arrangements to present themselves to an officiator, appointed by the Judicial Board, to solemnize their arrangement, whatever form it may take. The document you have in front of you accounts for marital unions of all types and degrees currently in common practice on Earth or in Orbit, with provision for review of other formally recognized interpersonal arrangements as citizens may wish to consider. Such arrangements, if solemnized by Eleusis-appointed officials, will be legal and binding following launch." He looked around and put his hands in his pockets, meeting many sets of widened eyes across the table. "The motion is now open for comment from other members of the Council."

"So the decision must be made before launch and then will be made binding once we're on Eleusis? Or are you expecting everyone to rush to the Board after we land, just to get married?" A woman said with a raised eyebrow as she looked across at him. "Why present this now when you're saying it won't matter until we get there? Why not present it there?"

"As it stands, when we move from here onto the ship and launch for Eleusis, a great many things are going to change all at once. Legal proceedings, hierarchies, accountability, it's going to be a difficult transition as it is. All those other laws, all those other methods for living our life on Eleusis, are going to be small. Everyday mistakes that can be corrected as we go. But the laws governing who we spend our life with, how we shape our families, those are not small choices. They're foundations of our lives, and if everyone here can make that choice for themselves, it will be a step toward stability in the world ahead of us. This law states that the freedom to choose how to shape our families is ours."

There was a lot of talking amongst the people of the Council, but Maria looked across the table to Stephen, even though he seemed to forget she was even there. She could understand that. His brother was dead. But she couldn't figure out what Logan was trying to get out of the legislation. It wouldn't change life on Nine. "Why not take it a step further, Mr. Bickford? If it's so important, why not challenge the Initiative's authority and pass it to become effective before launch?"

"The authority of the Initiative and this Council are two separate and non-conflicting entities, Dr. Santos." Logan managed a slight tone of shock without being anywhere near as sarcastic as Mercury knew he could be. "The boundaries of that authority, on both parts, is something that was established in the very first session of this Council, and they are not a matter I intend to dispute. The Initiative has jurisdiction here on this station, and when we depart, the authority of this Council will be paramount. The law has been written with that in mind. I am proposing that couples be permitted to choose each other and decide on the circumstances of their future in the same way that this entire body has been selected, pursuant to future needs."

"Choose now, marry later. Interesting." Maria replied and

glanced over at Mercury before she looked back at Logan. She knew Logan and Mercury were getting along quite well, so she smirked. "I'm sure your wife will be happy to have you back, if this passes." She didn't even look over at Mercury, but she could almost feel the woman stiffen in her seat.

"I imagine there are a number of wives and husbands who will be happy to have their spouses back to themselves alone. And a number who will be happy to be away from their matches." Logan kept tight control on his tone. He had clearly expected something from Santos about the motion. "The program has proven effective in many cases, and those cases are free to choose a relationship that lasts. But what will end is prescribed intimacy between those who have not chosen that involvement for themselves."

"And the population of Eleusis doesn't matter to you? The diversity of the program? We have had great results, and more people matched are showing satisfaction than before they were matched. They are happier." She looked between him and Mercury again. "Would you disagree? Would you say that the program is not effective?"

"So you would suggest that statistical happiness should drive our legislation? Excellent. Something we agree on." Logan reached down and hit another button on his communicator, and a number of graphs popped up on holograms around the room.

"This is an aggregate study of marital satisfaction over the last ten years, gathered from both urban and rural areas all over the Earth. None of them were matched. Sixty-four percent satisfied. Twenty-two percent highly satisfied. Six percent dissatisfied, eight percent highly dissatisfied. Before you ask, yes, satisfaction is a very broad category. Stick with me. It gets better."

He switched to another set of graphs that looked very similar. "Fifty-eight percent satisfied, twenty-nine percent highly satisfied. Thirteen percent highly dissatisfied. The only difference between matched couples and personally-chosen couples is that there are more at both ends of the spectrum. More highly satisfied and more highly dissatisfied. So yes, I would agree that the program is effective." He turned back to Maria with a nod. "Almost exactly as effective as personal freedom to choose."

Mercury didn't look at Logan or Maria, she just looked around at the people. "The people in this program have been chosen from all over the world. Genetic diversity is not an issue. Whoever people choose to be with or not to be with, there will not be an issue of diversity. Also, Eleusis will be populated by more people over time, after we have arrived. People who, I assume," she looked over at Stephen briefly before she continued, "will be chosen in a similar fashion, furthering the options for anyone already on Eleusis. We will be fine with the babies already made, as well as the diversity that will be available."

"The requirements for diversity have been stringently researched prior to the beginning of this Initiative." Stephen interjected in frustration. "And just because you eyeball it and you say everything looks fine, that should be made policy?"

"Dr. Finnegan is an expert in her field, which includes both reproductive medicine and genetic profiling. As such, I guarantee her eyeball guess is plenty." Logan tossed the comment at Stephen dismissively. "And she makes an excellent point. If it only takes a year to reach Eleusis, and the travel is successful, then once the world is established, as many people as possible could come to participate in the colonization."

He glanced over at Maria and tilted his head to the side. "Which begs the question of why such stringent genetic diversity enforcement was necessary in this Initiative in the first place, but as I said, it's not my place to challenge the authority or the decisions of the Initiative. My concern is policy on Eleusis going forward."

Maria stared at Logan for a moment before she responded. "It will be another long process to vet people for the next round of Initiates to Eleusis. They all have to be screened, medically treated, and trained for their jobs, just the same as this Initiative. It could be years before the next wave can get there after you. There's a process, limited resources, there is so much more that goes into it that none of you ever see. You're oversimplifying a very complicated process."

"Right. You mean I'm indulging in the same kind of over-simplification that you and the rest of the recruiters used on the Earth-born to convince them to enlist? Does this sound familiar?" He had to look through his communicator for a moment, but then he finally pulled up the clip he was looking for, from his own initiation session.

Diego hadn't been included on the Executive Council, but many of those present still knew him as one of Stephen's closest friends. His image popped up between the seats, mid-lecture. *If all progresses well with the setup on Eleusis itself,* the image of Diego said with a smile, *the Second Wave will arrive two years after that, then two years after that, and so on until we can ramp up transport hopefully around the fifth or sixth wave to bring more people on larger transports.*

Logan stopped the playback there, and dismissed the image of Diego with a look over at Maria. "Now, was he misinformed, or was that false advertising on the part of the Consortium?"

"He was acting on information and knowledge at that time. Since that clip, we have been attacked twice and there have been other issues that the Consortium has handled down on Earth. None of us knew there would be this kind of resistance to the cause. That means slower processes, more security, so on and so forth. Don't try to make this into something it isn't, Mr. Bickford." Maria said as she narrowed her eyes at him, but then she shook her head. "If you want to marry your match, you should go about things the old fashioned way and divorce your wife. It's distasteful for you to use this Council for your own personal agenda."

"Whatever taste this law leaves in your mouth is none of my concern, Dr. Santos. But I am glad that the vehemence with which you're attempting to sidestep this legal action is now public record for everyone in this Initiative to review." He actually smiled at her when he said that, and shook his head as he turned back to the rest of the group, most of whom were sitting and watching the argument, keeping their own opinions to themselves.

"She brings up an interesting point, though, which I'm grateful to her for mentioning, all things considered. I have that option." He shrugged as he looked around at everyone else present. "It is possible, under current legal context, for me, for anyone who came to this Initiative previously married, to pursue a divorce and remarriage within the present laws. Or is it?" He glanced back at Maria, appearing confused, though he clearly wasn't.

"I've heard reports, though of course these are all anecdotal, of people who came to this Initiative in a marital relationship with someone of a non-heterosexual nature, who have been forced away from their spouses. Not just for procreation, no, you can say all you want that they were warned about that kind of involvement before they signed on, we all understand that for the time being. But I mean forced away, even beyond the point of impregnating or being impregnated by the person who was prescribed to them."

He looked around the room instead of continuing to look at

Maria and invite a response. "Oh, will you look at that? Not a single surprised face in the room. Fascinating. Maybe the anecdotes I've heard aren't the only ones." He sighed and looked a little more serious as he continued. "This law is a promise to all future citizens of Eleusis that those anecdotes will end. That they will not be the norm for the new world we are trying to build."

Mercury watched as people considered it, and she was glad they didn't hear from Maria every two seconds after that. People overall weren't happy with the idea of there being another shuffle, but some people were desperate for another shot with someone else. Others just wanted all of the marriages, matches, and so on to be just dissolved indefinitely so that people could change partners whenever they wanted to. Some people made interesting points about marriages being legal and taking unnecessary time from the Judicial Board, but overall, after an hour of discussion, people seemed generally in favor of Logan's proposal.

"I want to thank you all," Logan said when the discussion seemed to wind down, "for the concerns raised, the amendments proposed, and the general manner of this discussion. It's my hope that all actions regarding our people will proceed in this way going forward, with meaningful contributions and rational legislation being created. I rule the discussion on the current matter closed and call for all votes from the members of the Council present and otherwise represented."

Of course Kaplan and Santos were against, and a few followed them immediately with a raise of the left hand. Mercury was concerned even after she raised her right hand in support of Logan, but she hoped that his proposal would pass and then move on to the Judicial Board.

When Koskei tallied the votes and added his own support to the measure, it passed with over a two thirds majority. With the final number stamped on the screen, Logan sighed and nodded from where he'd stood for most of the discussion. "The motion is passed and is hereby recommended for review by the Judicial Board." He took his seat slowly, and made a point of not even looking over at Kaplan and Santos. "The floor is now open for other business."

Mercury couldn't really focus for the rest of the meeting, but fortunately it seemed like everyone else felt the same way. No one wanted to extend the meeting much longer after that. Once the meeting was adjourned Mercury packed up her things slowly, since she didn't know if Logan would feel celebratory or moody on account of his motion actually passing. She could see both ways.

He was just as slow about packing up his notes, and he quickly dismissed Renata with orders to make certain the motion was brought before the Judiciary as soon as feasible. He and Mercury were the last two left in the room, and he heard Koskei lock the doors behind him as he left. Logan had to smile at how much of a friend the man had become over the course of working together.

"I'm sorry I didn't warn you." He finally said when they were alone. "I haven't spoken to anyone about this since I had the idea. Even the entire text of the law I drew up on a standalone tablet."

"You don't need to apologize. You have your reasons." She slung her bag over her shoulder before she looked up at him. "You've worked hard to ensure that no one will be able to come between you and Anna. And a lot of people will be happy about the freedom they will have because of this."

"It's the people I'm interested in." He looked her over with a sigh and then shook his head. "When this passes the Judiciary, there will be a rush of marriages. Some of the more obvious ones first, then other people will start matching themselves up along different lines than the ones the Initiative set for them. And when they're disobedient to their matching, they'll be more prone to disobey in other ways." He turned around to lean back against the table where he'd sat, then reached out to hook one side of her shirt and pull her in closer to him. "Things will change, and not in ways the Initiative is gonna be happy about."

"But I thought the whole point was that it isn't actually effective until after we leave?" She understood there would be a rush of marriages, but they wouldn't actually mean much of anything until they made it to Eleusis. Except as a means of rebellion, as Logan had mentioned. "It'll turn into a dating game up here. All the while, the Initiative will still be pushing the matches they made because their word is still law here."

"Which means everyone who's lived the past four months taking it for granted that they're locked into their matched relationship will wake up and realize they don't have to do what they're told. That the Consortium won't always have that kind of control over us." He still had a hand on her shirt, and he pulled her in for a quick kiss. "It'll be chaos. But it will get people in motion."

Mercury kissed him slowly and ran a few fingers across his beard. He was irresistible. "I don't want to lose you. I don't want to lose this."

"We won't." He kissed her again and actually tightened his hold on her shirt. "This is going to be crazy for all of us. But we'll get through it."

Mercury kissed him harder, and he could tell she was feeling worried and needy. "I want to be your wife." She said between kisses, since she wanted to say it out loud. It was a confession that could change her entire life. "I don't want you to pick her. As selfish as it is."

He nodded his agreement and returned the kisses. "There's going to be a lot of selfishness going around pretty soon. And I'm going to be doing plenty of it myself." He knew that wasn't a commitment either way, but his kisses lacked nothing for heat. "I love you. I'll see you later tonight."

"I love you too." Mercury said as she let go, since he was leaving whether she wanted it or not. She didn't want him to go find Anna. He would pick Anna. Mercury opened her mouth to say something, but she didn't. She would see him later. That had to be enough.

26

Orion was leaning back in his chair when Anna came in, looking through his communicator at new messages. He grinned up at her and tossed his communicator on the table, looking pleased with himself. "I heard a rumor this morning that you're gonna enjoy."

"Oh yeah? Is it a big, juicy one?" She replied suggestively as she sat on the table next to his plate in front of him. She swiped some incredibly fake bacon off his plate, trying not to wrinkle her nose as she ate it. Eating for three was a valid excuse for food thievery, in her estimation.

As she got settled, he took her knees and spread them until she had one foot on either side of him. He then leaned in and lifted up her shirt to place a kiss on her stomach before he sat back and continued with his meal. "Carl told me he had to phase out not one, not two, but three different complaints about people hearing loud moaning in sector Q-6. They all apparently thought something had gone wrong with the soundproofing between their unit and their neighbor."

Anna giggled and kissed him a few times between bites of his meal. "That makes me feel like such a dirty girl." She stole another bite of his food and chewed quickly before she kissed his cheek. "What sector should we defile next?"

"I'm thinking hydroponics." He picked up his drink and shot back the colored liquid inside. It was more like flavored water than juice. "Aiko would probably kill us, but what she doesn't know shouldn't haunt her nightmares for too long. I want to get you out in the open somewhere."

"Up against a giant Eleusis tree? You gonna leave marks on my backside and brag about it?" Anna beamed and teased him with nibbles along his face and neck while he attempted to eat. "Does Carl know it was us?"

"After the first report, no. After getting three reports? Yeah, he knew it was us. Already called me up and reamed me about it. I laughed my ass off." He pushed her face aside once to get a bite and then let her resume what she was doing. "He told me to keep it to places that won't get as many complaints. So I'm thinking we need to find a way to get into one of the cafeterias without getting caught."

"We'll work our way up to it." She grabbed his face for a moment and looked into his dark eyes. "Thank you for helping me forget about all of that shit from last night. I love you."

"One of my many talents in life. Being completely oblivious to serious things and helping other people be similarly oblivious." He reached up to brush her hair back. "I'm just glad you were open to being distracted." He looked down at his communicator and sighed, spinning it so she could read the summons they had both received for a Judicial Board session. "Yay, more distractions."

Anna pouted, since she had been doing a great job of ignoring any outside contact until that moment. "Can we find some way to skip it? We're supposed to be released from duty due to my *delicate condition.*"

"It's a special session. I doubt they would've sent us the invite if we could get out of it, but I'll send Rogers a message and see if we can skip it. Or have her delegate for you, if not." He picked up his communicator and started typing.

While Anna waited to see what answer Orion could come up with, she checked to see if she had heard from Logan. Apparently he wanted to meet with her, but she was supposed to tell him when. She didn't even know what she would say to him, she was still so angry. Instead of answering right away, she waited to hear from Orion if they could skip their meeting or not.

When a reply finally chimed through, Orion sighed theatrically and leaned his head over the back of the chair in overdramatic exasperation. "She said she's already a delegate for Intombe, and that's only because he's sick. Looks like we do actually have to be there."

Anna pouted and slid into his lap carefully off the table while he had his head tipped back. "That sucks. I was really looking forward to exploring hydroponics."

"You and me both." He ran his hands over her ass once it was in his lap before he even looked up. "I guess this means I have to get dressed sometime today. That's unfortunate."

"That is *so* unfortunate. Your cock should not be caged up like that. It's too perfect." Anna kissed him several more times. "I want to stay here with you. I'm happy here. Out there is nothing but a shit storm."

"I used to think there were good places out there." He got a little more serious than normal when she put it that way, and he kissed her neck again. "There still are. We'll find them sometime, once we get out of here. The galactic tour of sex. I look forward to that."

Anna wrapped her arms as far around his body as she could, but she was a lot shorter than he was, even though he was thin. She pressed her cheek against his warm chest and closed her eyes. "Logan wants to meet with me, I guess after the Board meeting. It has to be about something they passed this morning, otherwise it wouldn't be an emergency meeting." She gripped Orion's body tighter. "I don't know what to say to him now."

"I don't know either, but I know there's gonna be a lot of four-letter words involved. Also, knowing you, probably a good bit of screaming." His voice was sympathetic, but she knew him well enough to hear the anger underneath it. "Whatever he says, either he was being stupid or being purposefully stupid. Purposefully stupid would be only slightly better than accidentally stupid, depending on the purpose. Either way, stupid is stupid."

"No kidding." She muttered against Orion's skin, and she sighed before she opened her eyes again. Once her eyes were open, her arms loosened so that she could run her fingers along the ridges of his abs. "At least you love our baby. I can't do this shit alone."

"Babies." He corrected gently, with a nod down at her stomach. "Anything related to that vagina, I'm fond of."

That made her smile even more. "You'd claim them both?" Technically he had to, since no one could know that one of the babies was Logan's, but Logan didn't seem to want it anyway.

"Of course I would. I mean, one's gonna be more likely to raise questions when I drop them off at daycare, but yeah, I would absolutely claim them both. What's yours is mine, what's mine is also mine, you know the drill."

Anna finally looked up at him again after he said that. "People only say that when they're married." She blinked a few times as she looked into his endlessly dark eyes. For someone so playful, the depths of his eyes still managed to keep the secrets of his thoughts. "At least that's how it goes on Earth. I'm not great at figuring out how things usually go up here."

"Well, for me . . ." he cut himself off, since he didn't really have anything else that he could say about that particular phrase, and certainly not just a glib comeback to play it off. "I've only had two people I've felt like I could say that about, and the other one . . . hasn't been returning my calls for a while now, metaphorically speaking. I'm new at this, but it's how I feel."

She kissed him gently before she said anything else. "I would be lucky to be your wife. But I don't want to be your second choice. It sucks to be someone's backup." She ran her thumb across his cheek and kissed him once more. "Before we really talk about something like that, that kind of commitment, we should talk to Logan and Mercury. I don't know if Logan even wants to talk to me anymore, other than some kind of business, but we shouldn't just jump to conclusions. If we're going to be together, we should choose each other. Not just end up together."

He was quiet for a long time after she said that, and he leaned his head back on his chair again as she held herself to him. "I thought about it a few nights ago. How I wished it didn't feel like they made the choice for us."

"But it does." She couldn't stop touching him, even though she knew it wouldn't make any difference about what she was saying. "But is that untrue? I mean, they jumped into it before we did. We have been doing the 'friends with benefits' thing almost this whole time. Not to mention, I'm a mouse compared to Mercury. A dangerous mouse, maybe, but comparatively speaking, you had a fucking giant, perfect cake before. I'm not a cake. I'm an overdone cookie at best."

He looked up just to glare at her, and shook his head before he leaned back again. "You know, every time you say something like that, you're trying to draw a comparison between the two of you like it was a competition from the day you were born. It's not. That's not the way it works. You're you. She's her. There's no runway, no prize podium, no judging booth. It's you and me in this room. Until you bring her in."

Anna sighed as she turned to start to get off of his lap. "She's your wife, of course there's judging going on. I mean, you and I weren't supposed to end up together. We were put together, and we had to get drunk in order to make it happen. I'm always going to wonder what would have happened if the match program had given you both of us at once, and what you would have chosen. Not to mention my own former fucking best friend has basically cut off my existence in preference of her. Months. He's known her for mere months. And still, he goes running after her. You're telling me it's not a competition? Then why do I always feel like I'm a consolation prize?"

He looked at her again and kissed her thoroughly after a question like that. "Probably because you don't believe either of us when we tell you otherwise. I tell you that I love you, and it seems like all you hear is the rest of this fucked up situation echoing that yes, I love her too. Just like you love Logan. Probably not as much as you love Logan, honestly. You've had a lot more time to love him than I've had to love her."

Anna had loved Logan almost her whole life, but that was part of what scared her. "I know. And even after spending a lifetime loving him, he still doesn't love me the same way back." She pressed her forehead to Orion's and then she spoke softly. "I want a love that is going to last. I fucked around forever, and sure, I learned a lot, but I didn't get anything else out of it. Just heartache. I don't want that shit anymore. I want a real marriage. Dedication. Eyes for one person, lovey-dovey shit. I want that."

"Lovey-dovey shit. I love it when you talk romantic." He smiled and kissed her again, then reached up to caress her cheek. "I want that too. And you should never feel like you come in second when it comes to somebody looking for that. I want . . . something that I can feel. Not just something that makes sense on paper and looks good on a computer."

Her mind tripped over all of the things she had already thought about. If she had met Orion only a month before, if she met him before a piece of a space station fell onto Earth, she would have snapped him up and married him. She wouldn't have waited, she wouldn't have questioned anything, she wouldn't have wasted any more of her life pining over Logan, since a lot of her life was spent pining with no return.

When she and Logan got together, the world changed for her. He meant everything to her, and she didn't think that could or would ever change. But clearly it had. She didn't know how, she didn't know what she did wrong for him to just cut her off, but every day, every hour, he was farther away from her.

"I want that too." She finally admitted softly against his lips. "If I had known you before, I would have found a way to keep you no matter what it took. Even if I had to manipulate you to get you to marry me. I would have never let you get away."

"Oh. Well, that's clearly true love right there. When a woman is willing to manipulate you into a lifelong commitment, then it must be written in the stars." He chuckled and kissed her again. "You wouldn't have had to manipulate me. If I had met you before and we had started up together, I never would have wanted it to end. No one I ever dated on my own time made the world feel like it was a good place for making long-term plans. You do."

"Then maybe we should start making long-term plans. I've already got a couple of kids for you." She teased quietly before she kissed him again. Anna meant what she said about them talking to Logan and Mercury, but it was difficult even thinking about that.

What hurt even more was that after finding out about the babies and after hearing nothing from Logan, she didn't even feel right wearing her ring anymore. She had taken it off the night before, the moment she realized that Logan wasn't going to show up to be with her. If things were really over, then she needed to give the ring back to him. "I love you."

Even with their discussion of feeling like a second choice, Orion couldn't help feeling a twinge of that when she said so. But that feeling didn't make the fact that they loved each other any less true either. "I love you too, Anna." He kissed her until she bent backward over the table in front of him, then kept on kissing right over her uniform with a sigh. "I'd also love to keep you here and break another dining room table, but it looks like I need to get dressed so we can go be judgy."

She groaned as he teased her with his kisses over her uniform. "You're mean." She was always so aware of him, especially when he was naked, even though she was fully clothed. "Fine, go." Anna had a hard time convincing herself to back off, but she knew he was right. They needed to get moving to whatever emergency was waiting for them.

Since Orion was only an auxiliary member of the Judiciary, he tended to act more as a support for Anna than as an actual member of the board itself. As such, he also dressed as though he was attending a casual get-together with friends rather than some kind of official function, and that day was no different. He ignored the usual looks that he got from some of the more serious members of the Board for not taking the place more seriously than he did, with his old t-shirt and casual pants. He was only concerned about what Anna thought of him, not the rest of the hypocrites that mostly made up the Board.

"Well, everybody looks nervous." He took his seat behind Anna, leaning in to speak over her shoulder. "Which means there are at least rumors about what we're here for, and they're nerve-inducing. I love a good nerve-inducing meeting in the afternoon."

Anna wanted to laugh, but everyone who was whispering kept stealing furtive glances at her. It did not make her feel confident about whatever she was about to hear. She powered on her tablet and logged into her portal so she could pull up the agenda for the meeting, but it only took a few glances over the agenda and the attached document for her to understand why everyone was talking about her. It was something about a marriage bill, and it was proposed by Logan.

Orion was still leaning over her shoulder as she scanned through the highlights of the bill, but he felt a little sick the longer he read it. Especially when he got to the end and saw that Mercury had voted in favor of it already.

It was . . . he understood what it would do, what it would mean for the people of the Initiative, but more specifically what it would mean for the four of them.

And the two of them had been together on proposing and passing it.

"That's . . ." he searched for any kind of joke that he could try to make, but nothing came to mind. His wife had voted to dissolve their marriage without even once talking to him about it.

Anna's first impulse was to throw her tablet across the room and watch it shatter against the wall before she got up and stormed out, but instead she sat there calmly. Dangerously calm.

"Let's worry about what it means later." She glanced back at Orion as her fingers gripped the tablet so tightly it creaked slightly under the pressure. "Let's just get through this meeting so I can go break something." Anna added softly, since she couldn't even go get trashed after this. She was good and knocked up now, which meant booze could no longer be a coping mechanism. How nice for her.

The meeting progressed with those leading the session walking over eggshells with every word they said. Rather than go into too many arguments about the proposed bill right up front, footage of the Executive Council's proceedings was shown in selected clips, from Logan's initial description of the bill's effects to his later argument with Maria about its impact. The room was quiet as the footage concluded, with a few people clearing their throats nervously and looking anywhere in the room but at Anna.

"Well, this is quite the turn." Gordon spoke up from one side of the room beside Jessie, and stood up with his hands in his pockets to address everyone, Anna included. "Normally we're all over every piece of legislation the Council gives us trying to nitpick every inconsistency and flaw to show how it contradicts our vision for Eleusis, but I think maybe, just maybe, we finally have our first piece of legislation that no one here will feel the need to fight about."

Several people in the room were looking at him like he had gone insane, but he continued anyway, looking at Anna directly. "It's not my intention to read into the personal agendas of various individuals on either the Council or this Board, but I do want to offer my two cents and say that this move makes sense for everyone in this Initiative. It makes sense that everyone should be given the freedom from our previously-prescribed matches so that we can marry and make plans as we like. Not everyone lucked out in the matching quite like I did. But let's treat this bill as what it is, a legal precedent to set for Eleusis, rather than some kind of personal agenda. I don't believe that was its purpose." He gave Anna a slightly sympathetic look before he sat back down to concede the floor to someone else.

Anna didn't say a word after Gordon's small speech, and no one else who spoke had any comments against it. It seemed like people were unanimously in favor of stripping power from the Consortium and the Initiative and keeping it among the people who were actually going to Eleusis. Anna wasn't surprised when Orion stayed quiet, but she didn't say anything until there was a lull in the conversation.

People wanted it passed. Gordon wasn't the only one who felt that there was no personal agenda, but if there wasn't, Logan would have told her. He would have warned her, talked to her about it, not avoided her and her unborn children like the plague. Santos' comments from the clips just kept repeating themselves in her head, if Logan wanted to divorce her, he should do it the old fashioned way. Apparently he wanted to dodge any kind of legal proceedings dissolving a marriage that was a joke anyway. As if she really could have actually married Logan and it would work. Fine. If this was what Logan wanted, he could have it.

"Let's vote, then. Those in favor?" Anna was the first to raise her hand, which she knew shocked people, but her expression remained unreadable and cold.

Everyone else in the room was more cautious about raising their hands, but the vote came back overwhelmingly in the majority. Even those who had initially raised their hands to oppose decided instead to simply abstain, and soon Gordon had decided it was time to say something, just to break the tension of Anna's serial-killer expression.

"The act passes judicial review by clear numbers, and is enacted into the code of Eleusis. It will be published to all Initiative members today following entry into the code, and officials will be identified at our next session to take action on the impending love-fest ahead of us. I see no further reason for this emergency session to be prolonged, and move that it be dismissed, seeing as some of us were busy with other things today."

Anna picked up her things as though it was the end of any other meeting, but not before she sent off a message through her communicator. When she looked up again, Orion was standing there next to her, attempting to ignore the rest of the chamber talking about them. "I really wish we could go to the dock."

Orion thought that was a fairly random desire, considering everything else that had happened, but it wasn't the craziest idea. They had spent a lot of time there, after all. "In the mood for some zero-gravity distraction?"

"That and booze." Anna said as she looked up at him, but then she got up and immediately hugged herself to him, just to hide her face. She didn't care what people saw. Usually they were conservative about what they showed in their relationship, but if Logan was going to vote to divorce her and not even tell her, she was in a mood to say fuck it to everything else.

"Really makes you wonder about medical science, honestly." His tone was light, as always, just because he wanted to distract her from what was going on as much as possible. "We can keep over a hundred occupied stations in the air, some of them with hundreds of thousands of occupants, we've got colonies on Mars, we're about to jet halfway across the galaxy to start a new civilization on a brand new world, and yet they somehow can't figure out how to let pregnant women get trashed. I think the scientific community needs to get its priorities straight."

She could feel that his shirt was getting wet from her crying into his chest. "Can we go home?"

"You mean where we probably should've been permitted to stay, all things considered?" He kissed her hair. "Yeah, we can go home. Couple more people emptying out, then we can get back to things making sense."

They stayed locked together until they were halfway back to their unit and a message came through, on Orion's communicator this time. Anna was ignoring hers. It was from Mercury.

Can we talk tonight?

Orion hesitated as he looked at the message for a while. He wanted to respond with anger, since being around Anna was contagious, but whatever sins Anna could lay at Logan's feet, things weren't the same between him and Mercury. The expectations between them had been different from the very beginning. *You mean because Logan is meeting with Anna anyway? Sure, that's fine. Back at our unit?*

That's fine. I'll make dinner. Mercury sighed as she sent the message, looking up at Logan. They'd only just been notified that the bill had passed, but Anna's hateful communication had sent a message to the both of them ahead of whatever official message came after. "He's angry too."

"Well, you at least can tell him you were surprised this morning, if you want." He had gone to visit her at the clinic for one of his usual visits and hadn't even been questioned by the secretaries. They were accustomed to his visits, and accustomed to him doing as he pleased while he was there. "I have no such excuse."

"What she said was inappropriate. You haven't had a chance to explain. Doesn't she have any faith in you?" Mercury was irritated on Logan's behalf, since she knew he was a better man than Anna was painting him to be.

"If she did, I think it's been gone for a while now." He said sadly, since he and Mercury spent more time talking about their marriages than he did with the woman he was actually married to. "She's got her reasons to be angry at me, and she doesn't have much reason to think I did this for any reasons besides the obvious."

He stood beside the exam table in the room with his hands tucked into the pockets of his coat and sighed as he looked Mercury over. "She can be angry. I wouldn't be surprised if the two of them have already appointed someone else from the Board and gotten married. I hope they would do us the courtesy of talking to us first, but I doubt Anna intends to do anything courteous around me for a very long time."

"She wanted you to be there last night when I talked to her. She just kept asking me where you were, if you were going to talk to her. I apologized for not telling her first, but she cared more about you not being there." Mercury said softly before she looked up at him again. "She's your wife and the mother of your child. She still needs you."

"Anna's never needed anyone." He shook his head with a chuckle at that idea, since Anna was easily one of the most independent people he'd ever known in his life.

"It's going to be a long night, no matter what happens with them. But I've had Renata listening in on what's been happening all over the rest of this place." He had looked conflicted all day long, for one reason or another, and Mercury could see the same conflict in his expression when he mentioned Renata's eavesdropping. "People are losing their minds, kind of like we talked about. Consortium is doing its best to run damage control through the new batch of Initiates, but all it's doing is making people suspicious of the new batch. Friendships are going crazy, there have been co-workers who actually started fighting in the Engineering lab. People packing their bags and moving units all day long, even before it passed the Judiciary. It's chaos out there."

"Just what you hoped for." She went up to him and pulled him into a kiss unprompted. No permission asked. "I should finish up here. I told Orion I would make a meal, so I need to get back to my unit."

Logan nodded, but held onto her after she mentioned Orion, since the thought of her going back and spending an evening with her husband was hardly what he wanted to imagine. "I don't know how long my conversation with Anna is going to take, but I'll see you back at our unit sometime tonight. If you get there before me, go on and go to sleep."

"Go to sleep without you?" She didn't like the idea of going to bed alone, especially since they were both going into uncomfortable conversations that were bound to hurt. "I don't sleep well alone anymore."

"Then go to bed thinking about me." His hand moved down over her scrubs to slide between her legs, though he never broke eye contact. "And if you come home and I'm already in bed, then come and get me. You have my permission to wake me up, provided you are creative about your method of doing so."

The smallest smile tugged at the corner of her mouth, as he kept touching her, since she ached for him to touch her as often as he pleased. "I hope I am getting better with my creativity." Mercury leaned in for another kiss as his hand continued to explore her body. "I love it that you always want more."

"You think someday I'm going to reach some kind of threshold of being with you and suddenly require nothing else?" He smiled a little wider at that thought, since it was just that insane. "There are several things about me that you should never underestimate. The lengths to which I'm willing to go for the people who matter to me, and the degree to which I want you. Among other things."

"You really think there's no limit? That you'll never get sick of touching me or being near me?" She thought it was physically impossible for someone to not eventually be satisfied with one thing or another, no matter how sexually insatiable he seemed to be. "I want you to want me. Always. I just don't know if it is possible that you always will. Especially when I get old. I'm already older than you are."

"Yes, but if your research into Earth-born physiology is right, I'm going to live longer." He teased with even more of a smile. "We're both going to get old. Sixty years from now, we'll be going to bed with decades of memories behind us of the things we've managed to do to each other. I've spoken to a few older people since we've come aboard, and one of them told me that the best consolation he has at his age isn't Eleusis, it's remembering how good his life has been. And that's something you and I can absolutely have when we reach that age."

Mercury traced the edge of his smile with her fingertip as though she was memorizing it through touch. "If you go talk to Anna and you change your mind, I won't be angry with you. I just want you to know that. I love you, I want to be with you. But I also love you enough to realize that this is complicated, and you loved her first. She loved you first. You came here together to *be* together. That means something, and I respect that."

He searched her eyes for a long time and reached up to run his thumb along the perfect ridge of her eyebrows. Everything about her was inhumanly perfect, down to the tiniest detail of her features, and every time he looked at her, he couldn't help but see the work of art that she truly was. But more than that, she understood things without being told that continued to shock him. She was capable of doing things that no one else he'd ever met was capable of doing. "I could say the same thing about you and him. You came here with that purpose too. It wasn't my intention when you and I started this that we would end up breaking that."

"I know it wasn't. You're a good man, with the best intentions." She turned her head so she could catch the inside of his hand and kiss it tenderly. He had big, strong hands that she enjoyed feeling all over her body, and she didn't want to lose them or him. "I would have a happy life with Orion, but I think I would have a happier life with you. Either way, neither choice is bad." She moved to capture his lips once more.

"I better go." She repeated softly when the kiss broke, but she was having a hard time moving away from him, especially if it was some kind of twisted goodbye. She would still see him that night, but it could mean that when she did, it was only going to be temporary.

Logan nodded, but still didn't release her and he let his caress linger along the cheek, as if the slight contact was the string by which she was tethered to him. The feeling of obedience in her entire body, the look in her eyes that she would do whatever he asked, just because he asked it, was like a drug he couldn't bring himself to set aside. After a captured breath, he finally withdrew the tiny, lingering touch. "Go. I'll see you tonight."

Mercury didn't think she could go unless he told her to, and she let out a tiny sigh caught in her lungs when he told her to go. It was still difficult to leave, her whole body screamed at her not to go, but she did. She left her clinic and she didn't look back at Logan and she headed toward the unit she shared with Orion.

In her heart, she was fairly certain of the choice she would make, but she knew she needed to talk to Orion and explain. Mercury wanted to be with Logan. She wanted to marry him. She had no idea if, in the end, he would choose her too.

27

At the time she had appointed, Orion stepped through the door, punctual as ever. He had told her once that it was a habit of being in the military, and not one that he imagined he would ever be rid of. "Smells good." He said from the doorway, and gave her a slight smile as he bent down to take off his shoes.

"I thought I would try something new." Mercury said as she turned and looked at him at the doorway. It was a strange feeling to be happy and sad to see someone at the same time. Orion was always sweet, funny, kind, supportive . . . there was nothing about him that she didn't enjoy. He had never hurt her or gave her any reason not to want to be with him, but obviously this was far more complicated than something like that. "It's curry. I hope you like it. The spices alone pack quite a punch."

"Curry doesn't scare me. Been a while since I had it." He set his shoes aside and went to stand on the far side of the kitchen counter from her, looking over everything. "What can I help with?"

"Will you set the table? I haven't gotten around to that yet, I'm sorry." She had the dishes and silverware out to set up the table, but she hadn't placed everything yet. Mercury was an organized woman in just about every aspect of her life, and apparently making dinner was no exception.

He set the table, even though it wasn't much just for two people. Still, when she brought their plates of curry over to the table, the napkin for her place setting was folded into the shape of a crane. He saw her face when she saw it, and shrugged when she looked up at him. "I warned you once that all my long hours spent mid-flight just coasting through space had yielded an abundance of freaking weird skills. One more off the list."

"It's a fun skill to have." Mercury said with a smile before she sat down with her plate after putting his in front of him. It was still steaming hot, but she dipped a spoon into it and moved it around with the rice to try and cool it down. "Thanks for coming. I know you probably didn't want to, and that you're angry with me."

"I'm . . . just turned around." He shook his head as he played with his food the same way she was playing with hers. One of the things they found they had in common early on - a low tolerance for hot temperatures. "And I know you well enough to know you wouldn't ask to talk unless you had something in mind to say. I'm really not sure what to say from my end first, so it's probably for the best if you start and I can chime in with some of the highlights of the past . . . two months or so from my end."

Mercury played with her food a little bit more and chewed on her bottom lip carefully as she thought about exactly what she wanted to say. "I'll start with today. I did not know Logan's plan or anything about his proposal, but I do know after all that's happened, he didn't propose it to put aside his wife and marry me. He did it to act in opposition to the Consortium and the Initiative. And it worked."

She didn't have to be a trained interrogator to see the shock on Orion's face at that, and he sat there with his mouth open for a while as he processed that information. Slowly, understanding filled the confusion behind his eyes, and he gave a small nod. "Yeah, I guess it did, if that's what he was going for. It's been mayhem today. Carl and Aiko are already lined up to get married, of course. Barry and Erebi are still solid, I saw her on the way out of the meeting earlier. But Fitch was telling me about some of the other pilots and some of the shit they're getting in the middle of now, it's all hell out there when it comes to relationships."

"The dust will settle with relationships and people will be with people they want to be with, and they'll realize that they want more. They will not want to be pushed around by the Initiative anymore, and they'll push back. It's what we need in order to break the Initiative. There are more of us than there are of them, and they need to realize that we have the upper hand. Otherwise they'll continue to threaten and restrict us in order to control us."

Mercury picked up her bottle of water and took a sip. "Logan wanted to talk with Anna about it, but if she knew, her reaction wouldn't have been genuine. I know that has to be why he didn't talk to her. He said he wanted to, but never told me why he didn't. There have been too many people that have not taken some things seriously because of Anna and Logan's opposing positions. This turns the focus back to the real enemy."

Orion was back to being dumbstruck at that conjecture on her part, but it wasn't understanding that took over his features as he processed it, it was disgust. "And that's the kind of man you really want to share everything with? The kind of man who would manipulate and torment his own wife when she needs him most just for the sake of manipulating public perception?"

"He wouldn't do it if it wasn't life or death." Mercury frowned. "He's doing it to help us get out of here, away to somewhere safe. I think hurting someone's feelings is something they can recover from, while being treated like a laboratory rat until the mad scientist is done with you is worse."

Orion shook his head and looked down at his food without focusing on anything that was in front of him. "I don't know if this is the kind of thing a person can recover from. It's certainly not the kind of thing Anna is going to forgive any time soon." He reached up to rub at his eyes before he looked back at her. "So is that the whole plan, then? Shake things up and make people mad about the Consortium again? Or is there more to it? Because marrying you, me marrying Anna, would seem a little bit counter-message at this point, considering it's the Consortium that put us together with them in the first place."

"That's not . . ." Mercury sighed again. "There's no . . . Logan and I haven't been plotting to break up our marriages with you and Anna to be together. I've been happy with you, and he was happy with her. I don't think any of us thought that we would have intimate feelings for anyone other than the people we chose. You tell me how you feel. Anna is the mother of your child, you can't tell me that doesn't mean something to you. I know you care deeply about her. And I know you have to realize she's an incredible match for you."

"I do care about her." He agreed, still without looking at her. "And I understand what you said early on, about the possibility they are better matches for us than we are for each other." He stirred the curry again, enjoying the aroma even without tasting any of it yet. "But even going by the shitstorm that Logan stirred up today, it's not about better or worse, or genetic compatibility or whatever other bullshit tags get put on by the brass. It's about choice. It's about looking someone in the eye and saying this life is *ours* now. Not just yours or mine, but ours. And then sticking to that for life."

"Tell me what's going through your mind, then. What do you want? Do you still want to be with me?" Mercury didn't know why he would, other than out of loyalty, because she felt like a different person now. She didn't think she could go back to the type of relationship she had with Orion, but he didn't know about the kind of relationship she had with Logan. "Do we hold off on making a decision until we absolutely have to? What is the right thing to do?"

"That depends." His voice took on an almost fatalistic tone, the likes of which she had never heard from him, as far as memory served. "Whose 'right' are you talking about? Because the right thing to do is gonna change based on who you mean. What's right for us? What's right for all four of us? What's right for our children? For the Initiative? The entire fucking human race?"

He closed his eyes and visibly pulled himself back from the roll he'd put himself on. "Logan is a leader. He has to think about the big picture, and if today is any indication, he's playing about six moves ahead of where he should be. That's sure to piss off some of the brass, and you better believe they're gonna retaliate. I just don't know how. What's right for humanity, the entire scope of human history right now, is for us to survive, get to Eleusis, and really make it what it should be. Keep it safe from the Consortium. Everything that gets us there is good, and everything that doesn't is just in the way."

"So then we can work together to make it happen, all four of us." Mercury drank more water, but still didn't take a bite of her own meal. "Don't tell me what the right thing to do is, then. Tell me what you want."

He shook his head and finally scooped up a bite of the curry. "What I want isn't possible, so there's no point dwelling on it." He lifted the bite to his mouth and then put it back down with another sigh. "What I want is a time machine, to go back to the moment you and I both realized we couldn't trust the Consortium and chose to ignore that feeling."

"A lot of people here want that." She finally took a bite, eyes and tone downcast. "That's no way to live a life, though. Wondering and wishing for something that doesn't exist and won't exist." Mercury looked up at him again. "I've changed. You've changed. They've changed." She reached out to put a hand on top of his. "I still love you, Orion. That hasn't changed. I just don't think I can go back to the way things were."

He looked at her again when she put it that way, and though he squeezed her hand, she could tell that was all he was going to do after that kind of statement. "You were happy the way things were. I hope happiness isn't something you've completely taken off the menu."

"Of course not. I still want to be happy. I still want you to be happy." Mercury held onto his hand and just stared down at it, since his hand was still so large, which was something she often forgot about. He was just a large man. "It's different. I can't explain."

That raised a look of suspicion from him, though he squeezed her hand anyway. "Can't? You managed to explain the current status of all CV research to me in under half an hour, and there's something in the world that you can't explain?"

Well, she *could* explain it, but it would also mean admitting to a lot of things she didn't think Orion would want to know. Even though she should have been more open with him about her need for sexual exploration from the very beginning. "I can explain. But I don't think you want to know why or how my relationship with Logan works. Do you want to explain to me the inner workings of your relationship with Anna?"

Orion hesitated at that question, and sat back a little in his chair with a nod. "Fair point. I guess I'm just not used to you talking around something instead of directly through it. It's not like you. But then again, like you said, we've all changed." He was still holding her hand, and he squeezed again before he finally took a bite of the curry. "Still never had anything that you've made that wasn't delicious. That's one thing that hasn't changed, at least."

Mercury smiled weakly and continued to hold his hand while she took a few bites of the food. She glanced at his hand a few times and shook her head slowly. "You still make me smile. You're good at that." She looked up into his dark eyes, and she remembered instantly how incredible she'd always thought they were. So captivating.

"You said you agree we've all changed. Tell me how you have changed. I've seen you and Anna together, you're always laughing." He had always been a happy person, but when she would see him with Anna in passing, it was like they just fit. Mercury always felt out of place with his friends and his environment, even though she loved him for their differences. "You share a lot of interests."

"True, we do. And she's turning into a hell of a pilot, for which I honestly can't take all that much credit. Not that that stops me." He shrugged and gave another weak smile, but he really was proud of Anna for what she had accomplished in just a few months. "I don't know, I think . . . I just can't honestly say that I understood it before. I never had a reason to try. Earth was its own problem and we had our own issues to deal with up here and let everybody sort out their own bullshit. But when you learn how connected all the different problems are . . . things get a little more serious. I don't feel like I have the luxury of not caring about the rest of the human race anymore. It's been a switch for me. Going from not caring about much past the control panel in front of me to actually looking down at the world and seeing something that matters."

"Me too." She agreed, thinking back to the night that Logan asked her to look out the window and tell him what she saw. There was a lot more there, and it made her cheeks burn a little to think about him touching her again, but she tried to focus on the moment.

"I study CV. I met people, families, from Earth all the time growing up. But it was still so distant from me. They're more vibrant, don't you think? The people from Earth. They have such a complex understanding of the universe, because Earth is so complicated. It's not like life up here. It makes them so interesting and unique."

"It makes them a lot of things." He took a few bites in silence. "Things are gonna get a hell of a lot worse from here. Especially with Logan kicking up dust with every move he makes. They're not gonna just let it happen." He gave a short, humorless laugh as he looked down at his curry. "That's another thing that's changed, I guess. Before, 'them' meant people from Earth. Now 'them' means the Consortium. The people you and I have worked for all our lives."

"Neither of us knew how corrupt they are. Some of them, anyway." Mercury refused to believe the entire Consortium was corrupt, especially because her father was a leader and a part of the Consortium too. "It's too big to believe the entire thing is corrupt."

She chewed on her bottom lip again and gripped his hand tighter. "More than anything else, we need to get away from here. None of the relationship issues matter if we're all just going to die because we can't figure out a way to work together. There is even more to think about now, with Anna and the babies." She looked at him and waited for him to look at her again. "I still love you. I hope you know that. I love him too, though. There isn't a right answer to this, or a wrong answer. There's just what we want."

"I've been telling myself that a lot too." He squeezed her hand in return and attempted another smile. "It makes it easier. Sometimes."

Mercury still couldn't tell what he wanted, and apparently he wasn't going to come out and say it, so she didn't know what to do. She wasn't going to push him. "We don't have to make a decision now." She thought that they would, but there was no reason to, really. They had time. "I don't know what you want. Time machines don't exist."

"No, they don't." He took the last bite of his plate as he left that to hang in the air, then got up slowly from the table and moved over to stand beside her, leaning back slightly on the table. "And by the time they're invented someday, no one will want to use them anymore. I hope." He looked down into her beautiful forest green eyes and he couldn't help but reach out to caress along the side of her face.

"I want you to be happy. If I could define what it means to love somebody, that's the definition I would give it. Wanting another person's happiness so much you're willing to devote your life to that cause. I wanted to do that for you, and I still will, no matter what you need or when. But I'm glad that Logan seems to make you happy. I hope that never changes, and that I can do the same for Anna."

"As uncomfortable as this makes me feel, maybe we should all four try to get together and talk." The logical thing was to put things out in the open so that it didn't turn into a he-said, she-said, or the blame game. "I don't know what Logan wants, he's difficult to understand sometimes. Do you know what Anna wants?" Mercury knew that she wanted to be with Logan, but she still loved Orion. Logan made more sense to her, but she was used to choosing the logical choice. That didn't always make it the correct one.

"I don't think having all four of us in the same place is going to help things much." Orion heard everything Anna had ever said about Mercury while they were together running through his mind all at once, and quickly pushed aside any thought of having both women in the same place while he was around. "But no, I can't honestly say that I do." He shook his head and let his touch fall away from her face, since she clearly wasn't interested in him being close to her for the time being. "Those two love each other like their lives were designed for it. It's different, and it's not something I even pretend to understand. You don't get as angry with someone as she is with him right now unless you love that person right down to the soul."

"Do you think you could love her like that? Or me?" She had a hard time understanding it too, since she had never loved someone quite like that before. Not the way he described. "I don't understand it either. Even as much as I love you, as much as I love Logan, it has only been months. I don't understand a lifetime of loving someone like that."

"Neither do I. But I hope I do someday." He smiled down at her, since however else she had changed, she was still wide-eyed and curious about everything in the world. He had always loved that about her. "I think our marriage is a good beginning for something like that. Something you and I could look back on decades from now, under an Eleusis sky, and tell our kids 'yup, first sight, I knew it. No doubts. Sure, we were matched, but the second I saw her, I was sold.' And then you of course would get to give me grief over making out with the bartender on my way to our matching just because I was so nervous about the whole thing, and we can laugh about how long ago it was and how amazing the next few weeks were together just getting to know each other . . ." He smiled as he thought back over it, since it had been an idyllic time in his life, that was for sure. "It was a good beginning. I can't imagine a better one."

Mercury smiled after he said that, since it was a good beginning. A better beginning than being forced with someone that she didn't want to be with and who didn't want to be with her. But the intensity she felt with Logan . . . it was incredible. She didn't think she could live without that either. Orion was good at making her feel conflicted. It was an easier choice when she spent her time with Logan, but as soon as she talked to Orion, it became harder. "Maybe we need a little more time to decide. Anna is better for you than I'll ever be."

"I don't know. She's a little more of an alcoholic than you are. I haven't drunk this much since I graduated from flight school." He chuckled as he played it off, but the look in his eyes was serious as he looked down at his wife. "Your parents would like Logan better. Can't dispute that."

"I know they would. But I'm not looking to make a decision based on what my parents want." She stared into his eyes for a moment and she moved closer to him without saying anything and just kissed him. There was emotion there, there was passion, but it didn't burn as hot as what she felt with Logan. Maybe it was her fault. Maybe it would, if she told him the truth about what kind of relationship she wanted and needed. Could Orion be like that? She had a hard time imagining her jokester husband being anything like the domineering personality she needed and wanted.

When the kiss broke, she didn't look into his eyes, she just held her forehead against his. "When you kiss her, do you feel more than this? Or less?"

His arms moved around her of their own accord, and he couldn't deny that it felt good to hold her. Like coming home, in some ways, even if they hadn't been home to each other for very long. "It's different. And for once, that's not actually me evading a question, it's just the truth." He scratched up along her back to make her shiver the way he knew she always did, and smiled at the familiarity of the motion. "It's a different kind of relationship, just because she's a very different woman. Same as I'm sure the two of them are different with each other than they are with us. It feels different because we're all different people with different . . . counterparts."

Mercury wrapped her arms around him and kissed him again, just because she could, but then she sighed. "I didn't know enough about myself. I still don't in some ways. I don't feel like the woman you met is the same person I am now. I still don't know nearly enough about a lot of things." She kissed him again and held tighter to him. "I wouldn't want you to feel as though you needed to change who you are to be who I need."

That got a very thoughtful look from him as he pulled back after the kiss, but whatever he was considering behind his dark eyes, he didn't share it immediately. "That's . . . good." His hands moved down to her hips, moving over her scrubs as he pushed down a hundred different joking responses to a comment like that, since he could tell she was being completely serious. "You look pretty similar, to me. I never had any interest in you being anyone else on my account." He shrugged. "I mean, aside from the occasional naughty nursemaid outfit, but, you know, all things in moderation."

Moderation. She wasn't looking for something like what she had with Logan in moderation. Mercury's eyebrow raised slightly and she opened her mouth to speak about his offhand comment, but she didn't. It was just further evidence that he wouldn't understand. "I don't look different, but I am. I want different things."

"Different things that . . ." he began, but then cut himself off. "And you get them with him, whatever these things are."

She nodded slowly and closed her eyes, because she didn't want to see his hurt or judgemental expression, if it was there. "I don't think you want to know."

"If you don't think I do, then I'm pretty sure I don't." With that kind of mystery hanging between them, it felt a little strange even to hold her, but he still didn't want to let go. He loosened his grip just enough to reach up between them and tilt her face back up toward his until she opened her eyes again. "It sounds like you were right in the beginning of all this, about him being a good match for you. If there's something you need, I love you enough to be glad you're getting it. Won't keep me from wishing for that time machine, but still."

Her green eyes searched his dark ones quietly as she considered that, before she just kissed him again. "A lot of things would probably be different with a time machine." Mercury put her hand on the side of his face and separated herself from him a bit more. "Let's finish our meal. Watch some television together. I ordered your favorite ice cream."

Orion wasn't entirely in the mood for ice cream after that kind of conversation, but he nodded anyway and went back to his side of the table. He knew he shouldn't try to figure out what Mercury meant by getting something else from Logan, but he couldn't help it. He'd spent most of his life being curious by nature, and it was a habit he knew was likely to get him killed someday. As soon as he knew there was something he didn't know, all he wanted was to know it. But it wasn't his business. Mercury had made that very clear. And if there was something else that he wouldn't be able to supply . . . he had no idea what it would be.

What he did know, as he sat back down at the table, was exactly how Anna had felt for the past few months as she slowly lost her husband. He had never been particularly jealous of Logan, exactly, even if he had been possessive of Mercury in the beginning. He never once felt as though Logan could do something for her that he couldn't, be a better man somehow for her. He had never once felt like he was in a competition with the rest of the world in some way that he couldn't win, except against Carl, and the two of them had always made it a point never to cross each other when it came to women. Feeling inadequate was new for him, and it wasn't a feeling that was going to go away lightly.

* * * * *

Anna felt strange in her own unit, and she hated that she felt strange. She hated when she looked at the pictures taped to the walls that they felt like a different life, that she felt like a different person, and the life that she had lived before felt like a lie.

Instead of sitting still and seething, though, she spent time cleaning until the tips of her fingers were bleeding from the exertion, though she didn't feel it. She was sweating, she was on her knees scrubbing, but it didn't help her anger. It wouldn't go away.

Anna couldn't think it through, she couldn't find a single logical explanation why Logan had distanced himself from her, why he wouldn't respond to her, or why he would propose a bill to divorce her and not even warn her. She didn't know how she had gone from being on his team, being his partner, to being a bystander. She had supported him as often and as completely as she could, she had tried to keep in constant contact with him, but he was the one who limited everything and she had no explanation. No explanation except one. He didn't *want* to talk to her. He didn't *want* to warn her. He didn't *want* to celebrate their baby. He didn't want *her*. That was the only thing that made sense.

The world that seemed so distant in the pictures all over the walls felt even more distant when the man she'd shared that world with finally came through the door. She had been with him when his sister and her brother gave him the coat he wore. It was just another piece of their life that felt like it should have tied them closer together and failed. He took the coat off and hung it up near the door, then kicked off his shoes and turned to face her.

He didn't look repentant, he didn't look apologetic, but he didn't look cruel or triumphant, either. He just looked like the man she'd gotten accustomed to watching videos of on the Executive Council feeds. Cold, authoritative, with an undercurrent of confidence that had always been covered or pushed aside for their friendship prior to coming into space. "If you want to scream at me before I start talking, I'll understand."

"Don't talk to me like that." She snapped, since just the fact that he would indulge her anger before it was 'his turn' to talk made her feel like he was treating her like a child. "Don't tell me what you'll allow like I'm some kind of child that needs to get a temper tantrum out of the way. I was your partner before you decided to *dismiss* me."

Anna glared at him from where she knelt on the pristine floor before she went back to cleaning. Erasing whatever evidence there was that they had even existed in the room together. "What you're looking for is on the table. Your freedom." Anna said bitingly, since she'd left her wedding ring on the table. It was nicer than throwing it at him like she wanted to do.

He looked at the table and did his best to deflect the knife he felt slicing through his chest. He had known, when he began, what he was doing, what it was likely to do to them, to Anna, but it was a risk he had chosen to take. "I didn't come here for that." He stepped past the table to get a little closer to her, down on the floor scrubbing at things like some kind of slave. "I came to talk to you."

Anna just gave a short, humorless snort when he said that, but she did stop scrubbing and tossed the brush into the bucket nearby. She ignored her still-bleeding fingers as she sat down on the floor and against the wall. She had no interest in getting any closer to him. "*Now* you want to talk to me. Now. Not before, when I tried to meet with you to spend time with you. Not before when I found out I was fucking pregnant and one of them is your baby. Not before, when I didn't know a damn thing about your fucking proposal and you blindsided me. What the hell could you possibly have to say to me right now, Logan Bickford?"

"That I'm sorry." He said simply, without going into any more explanation about what he was sorry for just yet. "And that it's working. That what I did, I did so you and me, and our daughter, can have a chance. Together. Even though I know that's the last thing it felt like."

"So, what, that's what a marriage is now? One person makes all the decisions and the other person is just supposed to sit back and wait it out?" Anna just stared up at him, clearly still furious, even though he said that he was sorry. He didn't look sorry. He didn't act sorry. Especially when he followed it up with the self-assuring statement that what he did was working. "I fucking needed you. Over and over and over. And you fucking left me to deal with shit on my own. We haven't done a damn thing together for months. It's been me supporting you by halfway guessing what the fuck is going on, and you not even bothering to look back to see if I'm still managing to stick with you. People who love each other don't do that. They don't hope that someone is still there when the fucking smoke settles. They hang onto them."

"Even when hanging onto the other person gets both of them killed?" His voice was less calm than his usual infuriating self, but his confidence hadn't gone away. "Because those are the stakes right now, and it took me a long time to figure that out. Yes, I fucking left you to deal with shit on your own. I haven't been here. I haven't been with you." She knew him well enough to hear pain in his voice when he said so, but it was pain without an apology.

"But I can't stand here and say I should have been. If you and me had just dug our heels in as soon as we got here, we'd be dead, and most likely, so would our families, if they're not already. We'd have been together and we'd have been dead. There are a lot of days when I wonder if that would've been preferable, but it's not the choice we made. Either of us, together or apart."

"You know, sometimes there are ways to make things happen that aren't just your way. You could have found a way to warn me, even if we never saw each other. You could have found ways to let me know that whatever you did, it was for the best, but you didn't." Anna finally got up off the floor in a rapid, fluid motion, but it was only because she wanted to get the fuck away from him. "Silence. You gave me silence. You know what? I never would have done that to you."

"I know." He said quietly, though she was still yelling at him. "I gave you silence because we needed the brass to believe what was happening. I needed them to look at us, see a couple that's lost hope, and move on to other problems. Like the problems they've got after today. That's exactly what happened, and I lied to you to get there." He admitted, still without sounding like it was an apology.

"Everything I've done, everything we're doing here, is to get away from them. We've both said that from the start. That we need to get away from them and get somewhere they can't keep fucking with our lives like chew toys. But anything that could get you hurt, that could get our baby hurt, is not a chance I'm willing to take. Not until we can see a way out."

"Are you listening to me at all? I said there are other ways." She wasn't yelling now, but she was still hurt, clearly. "You're not the only one that has power to fuck with the brass. If you would fucking talk to me, you would know, but you won't. And if lying to me now is how you want to accomplish shit, then how do I know you won't do it again? And again? Even if we get away, even if we're back on Earth?"

Clearly the damage done ran deep, since Anna was clinging onto the pain that she felt. "You sure did a great job at accomplishing what you wanted to accomplish. You wanted a couple that lost hope? You got it. And props to you, you even managed to swipe a trophy wife all at the same time. She seems a lot more compliant than I am."

"This isn't about Mercury." It was Logan's turn to start sounding angry, since he had intentionally kept her just as much in the dark as he had Anna. "She didn't know about it either until I proposed it in Council. No one did. If anyone had known, it would've been you, but I know that doesn't mean shit to you right now. Throw it in my face if you want, it's the truth."

"This isn't about Mercury? None of it is about Mercury?" She wanted to laugh at that, since she knew that was another lie. Anna crossed her arms and continued to stare him down. "If I said 'fuck all of this, we can get off now, let's go.' Would you? Would you leave with me? Leave now or die trying to save everyone else."

"Yes." He said bluntly, though he doubted it was the answer she was expecting to hear from him. "If you were sitting in a shuttle that magically couldn't be tracked, with a course set for someplace the Consortium would never find our families, I would be on board. I would probably have nightmares about all the people we left behind for the rest of my life and the guilt over thousands of people being still prisoners of the brass might eventually make me an alcoholic and kill me, but I would leave. I'm a big enough coward that if the chance to run came, I would take it." He stayed beside the dining room table away from her, and sighed when he was done speaking. "So if you've got a magic getaway car for us, now's the time to say so. Otherwise, there's still a shit-ton of work to be done."

"I don't have a getaway car." She shook her head and refused to look at him again, since she didn't really believe him anyway.

Anna didn't think he would leave with her, mostly because she knew he was incredibly in love with Mercury. "I can fly the shit out of most shuttles, but I can't get the clearance to get away unnoticed." Anna moved to sit on the couch to get away from him.

"What's the point of coming clean now, then?" She eventually asked in a tone that sounded more broken than anything else. "You can't go back on what you already started. They'll know. So, conveniently, you have to go back to Mercury." Anna forced herself to look at him again, though it was painful. She couldn't believe, after spending nearly her whole life wishing to be Logan's wife, that it would end up looking like this. "I hope you're not planning on inviting me to the goddamn ceremony."

"I'm not marrying Mercury." He said quietly. He wasn't mad about all the barbs she was throwing at him. He had expected them. Most of them, anyway. Anna had always been more creative about being hurtful than anyone gave her credit for. In his experience, she had spent so much time being a people-pleaser that it was incredibly easy to forget how adept she was at doing precisely the opposite when the situation called for it. He had just never been on the receiving end of it before.

"The point of all this wasn't to gain some kind of freedom, or get away from you. The point of this was to remind the rest of the people around us that they can live their own lives their own way. If some of the shit my secretary's already told me about is true, things have already turned crazy all over this arm of the station. A lot of couples fighting, obviously, that much was sort of inevitable. But a lot of people moving their things from one unit to another, moving in with the people they want to be with instead of who they've been stuck with. Some of the new batch has started trying to mess with people going against matching orders, and things have already gotten violent between them. Things are turning ugly a lot faster than the brass expected, and it's not just going to blow over this time."

"Okay, so you've clearly accomplished your goal." She snipped, since that was apparently obvious. "What now, Mr. President? What do you want now?"

He knew she had only asked the question to be mocking, but he answered it anyway, after a long pause to let her know she had made her point. "I was approached a long while ago by Gehrig, who wanted me to sign off on a security review of everyone on board. Carl started on it a long time ago, but never returned any results. The point was to look for rebels who had managed to sneak into the Initiative." He knew she wouldn't particularly care about any of that, so he continued without stopping. "When things keep getting worse and people start getting angrier, at some point, those rebels will come out of the woodwork. They'll want to take credit for what's happened. When they do show themselves, I plan to get all the information out of them that I can, and get everyone in this Initiative to safety who can be trusted not to inform the Consortium."

"I don't think their plan is to come out of the woodwork." She said slowly, since she had more information, but she didn't know what to tell Logan now. He had lied to her, he'd taken everything into his own hands, did he even want to know what she knew? "It seems more like they want to destroy the woodwork. But not before innocent people are out of the way." Anna replied softly, but she was looking down at her hands. They were starting to hurt now that her anger was deflating.

"Jessie Rogers has approached me and met with me a couple of times. I don't have a lot of information yet, but there's a plan in action. I intend to find out more and be a part of that plan. You would know about it already if you hadn't ignored me for just about a solid fucking month and a half."

That gave him more pause than she had seen from him in the rest of the conversation, and she knew Logan well enough to see when he was brushing self-doubt aside just to move ahead. He'd been doing it most of his life, usually in conversations with her. "I can get on board with destroying the woodwork, as long as part of the goal is to avoid getting innocent people caught up in it."

He didn't move any closer to her, since even if she sounded less angry, that wasn't necessarily a good sign. "All I want is to get off this station and get back to where we can have a home away from the Consortium. If anybody knows how to do that, it would have to be the people who managed to sneak on here without the Consortium knowing about them."

"Apparently there are quite a few of them." Jessie mentioned a couple of people that Anna could trust, but she didn't know if she should start listing names for Logan. She hated that, even temporarily, she felt like she couldn't trust him. He had already lied and manipulated her to make something believable. She couldn't put it past him to do it again. "Orion and I are going to help them with getting some more intel. I'm not sure what yet, but if they give me a job to do, I'm going to do it."

It was Logan's turn to narrow his eyes a little at that, his tone turning slightly sharper. "So that's how you turn things around on me? By going and risking your life for somebody you barely know without me even knowing? That's how you get back at me?"

"I'm not trying to get back at you, Logan. It was supposed to be you. It was supposed to be you and me, working together with the rebels. After she talked to me, I wanted to talk to you. I scheduled three fucking lunches in a row with you, and you cancelled on me every single time." Anna looked up from her hands as soon as his tone went sharp, even though her hands were really starting to throb. "You blew me off. So I told Orion everything and we decided to do it together. It's not my fault you decided to leave me out. You pushed me away, so I couldn't even tell you anything."

Logan quieted again at that, since he really hadn't given her any opportunity to talk to him, and he was certainly in no position to blame her for a lack of communication. "Whatever they're sending you after, be careful. And don't trust them, not that you need me to tell you that. As far as I'm concerned, they're the lesser of two evils when you stick them next to the Consortium, but that doesn't make them the good guys. They're just the only ticket out of here that seems likely at this point aside from a body bag."

"Maybe they are the good guys. Hell if I know anymore." She let out a heavy sigh and covered her face with her injured hands. "I want so badly to hate you. But I can't convince myself to do it. It's easier to hate you. But instead I'm scared to trust you. Instead, I feel doubt and fear and worry. When I found out about the babies, I wanted to be happy about it. It was something we wanted, and I had to deal with it alone. I mean, she's not even Orion's baby and he wants her more than you do."

He couldn't bring himself to respond to the reality of that at first, since he knew that was what it seemed like, from the way he'd behaved even just the past few days. "I wish she hadn't told me." He said eventually. "That I could have heard about it from you instead. Even if it was right now, when you still want to hate me." He moved to lean back against the wall near the opposite end of the couch from her. "I was thinking of Jeanine Lynnette. For our mothers. Make sure they both get their granddaughter just in case the rest of the kids are boys."

His last statement stunned her into silence, since he was talking about 'the rest of the kids' like they were going to go on with their life anyway. She truly didn't know if she believed he really wanted to stay married to her. "Lynnette is a prettier first name." Anna whispered and moved down the couch so she could see him better. "The rest of the kids?"

He wasn't smiling when he looked back at her, but he wasn't scowling either. "Well, you're never the type to stop something once you've started. The twins aren't going to be it for you, at least not if I have anything to say about it."

"I do want a big family." Anna looked at him as he stared at her, and she realized it was the first time they were looking eye to eye in a long time. "Fuck, Logan, I can't tell if you mean it. I can't tell if you really want that with me or if you're just saying that. I know you're not the cruel type, but I can't read you anymore."

"I've always wanted that with you." He said quietly, since they both knew it was more complicated than just what *they* wanted anymore. "Being up here has changed so much, gotten us all twisted around and shuffled . . . when all this started, we said that this, here, between us, was supposed to be the thing we could always come back to. The thing that would never change, no matter what." He sighed, not looking angry or cocky or condescending anymore. "But it's changed anyway. You love him. You're happy with him. It's not just something the Consortium shoved us into anymore. Either of us."

"I do love him." Anna admitted without looking ashamed, even though she felt like her relationship with Orion was still vastly different than Logan's with Mercury. Anna finally got up and moved so that she was sitting in front of Logan on the floor. "But I'm not his choice. I know he wants to be with Mercury. The question is, do *you* want to be with Mercury?"

"It's not that simple a question." He didn't move away from her, but he didn't try to get closer either. "Things with me and Mercury are . . . different. I've been a lot of things the past few months that I've never been before, and I haven't figured out yet whether that's a good thing or not."

"So talk to me for crying out loud. We used to talk about anything and everything. Before Mel died. After. You'll tell Mercury stuff and you won't tell me? I'm the most fucked up, mentally unstable person you know. I'm also a big girl. I can handle it." Anna sighed as she looked at him. "We all can't keep dancing in this nowhere land, it doesn't work. You can't love two people who also love two people. It tears people apart."

She moved close enough to put a hand on his leg. "I fucking watched you with other girls for most of my life. It was terrible, but I handled it. So if you don't want to be with me, then just say it. If you do, then we can't keep . . . it's not fair to anyone." She didn't think she could actually handle seeing Logan with Mercury, not after being his wife, but she would tell him anything to keep him in some capacity, even as only a friend.

"Nothing about this situation has been fair to anyone from the beginning." He agreed, but he didn't respond to the rest of her questions for a long while. "Did you ever cross paths or . . . exboyfriends with Denise Howard? She lived up in one of the communes near the Waste, used to come down to see Liam once in a while?"

"Probably ex-boyfriends, since a few of the men I knew were from near the Waste." Anna was confused why he was talking about someone random they knew from Earth. "I remember her. Liam introduced me to her a few times."

"Mostly I knew her because she actually batted around the idea of hosting a competition at her house after her parents died a couple years ago. She wanted to challenge you." He almost smiled at that mention, since he did think it was funny in retrospect. "I think Liam convinced her not to, and probably told her that she would lose, which I doubt she really wanted to hear." He shook his head. "She wasn't his type. She was . . . I think the euphemism is 'bossy,' but from what he told me, there was a lot of leather and handcuffs involved whenever he visited her place, and she was never the one wearing the cuffs."

Anna raised an eyebrow, though she looked a little impressed, since she didn't know the woman was that kind of feminine power enthusiast. "Huh. Never would have pegged her for the dominatrix type. That's kinky." She still didn't know why Logan was mentioning the woman, except maybe he was trying to remind her that she used to be a woman of many men. "I never would have . . . it wasn't like that. I wasn't trying to conquer men or reach some kind of number for shits and giggles. I was trying to learn. Every man likes to be blown differently, ridden differently, touched, kissed, it was all just to learn."

"No, I never thought you were like that. And neither Liam nor I have ever been big on being submissive." He shook his head, since he still clearly didn't want to come down and actually talk about the kind of relationship he had with Mercury, even though he could see that Anna did need to know. "I never understood, really, why somebody would want to get invested in something like that, except for maybe the occasional mix-it-up run through the bedroom. Everybody likes a good set of handcuffs every once in a while, but what I didn't realize at the time was that it's not really about that. It's about control, and being controlled. And finding . . . a kind of escape in that, on one side of it or the other."

Anna was still trying to figure out why he was stuck on this Denise chick and why anything was relevant . . . until she remembered that he said he didn't like to be submissive and finding escape.

Well, fuck.

As soon as Anna realized what he was saying, she met his steel grey eyes again. "Oh." She just watched his eyes for a moment and finally looked away. She was finding out all sorts of freaky sex details about the men in her life, apparently. "So that's why you don't want . . . cuz I'm not as submissive as she is? I didn't know that was a thing of yours. You didn't say anything . . ." Anna was completely different from Mercury. She could be submissive if she wanted to be, but that wasn't something that came naturally to her.

"There's never going to be a world in which I don't want you." He followed quickly, since that wasn't the case at all. "And I didn't know it was a thing of mine either, until we got here. It was supposed to be a way for both of us to distance things from reality. Separate it from everything else going on here on the station, from our original relationships with you and Orion. Make it something completely different that has nothing to do with the rest of who we are." He took a slow breath and let it out slowly. "But it does. It turned into more than just some kind of distancing game. For both of us. I didn't know, before coming up here. You would have known."

Anna moved again so she was sitting with her hip against his, but she was facing the wall while his back was against it. Her hands looked pretty red and covered in dry blood, but she didn't care that they hurt. She did it to herself, after all. "Logan, I could write a fucking encyclopedia on kink. I don't fucking care what you need or want, I can be it. I promise. It's not something to be ashamed of." Anna didn't know how to be exactly the woman he needed, if he was saying that he needed someone like Mercury, but she loved him. She would do whatever she could to try to be what he needed if he still wanted her.

"I don't want you to be that. I want you to be you." He finally reached out to put an arm around her waist tentatively. It didn't seem like she would pull away, but he wouldn't have been surprised if she did. "I've never wanted to be that with you. I like you wild. Always have."

"What's the point of being me if that means you want to be with her?" Anna knew that she sounded ridiculous saying that, but they had left everything behind for each other. They wanted nothing more than a long life together. That was the whole point. "I didn't fucking come up here to lose you. I came here to keep you."

"Same reason I came up here." He agreed without answering her question. "I don't want to lose you either. I don't want to lose the life we wanted. I want it back. I want Eleusis, I want us, and I want things to be simple. I just don't know how to have that anymore. You're pregnant, and I imagine Mercury won't be far behind you, especially given the quantity of fertility medication she discovered they're pumping into our systems through our food. All of us are tied up together in one big, jacked-up family now."

"I know that." He was barely holding onto her, and she wanted him to tell her a lot of things that he just wouldn't say. "But even though we have to be together as a family, that doesn't mean that you and Orion share wives. I can't live that way. I'm sick and tired of feeling like I'm chasing both of you because she's got your attention and his. If you both want to fucking fight over her, then do it. But leave me out of it. I'm not going to bounce back and forth and build my family on the random sperm of the weekend. I need someone who is mine. Only mine."

"I don't want to live that way either." He pulled her in a little tighter at the mention of being shared between him and Orion, since he didn't want to think about that. "Right now, I wanted to talk to you about all of us not declaring anything for the time being, especially if you and Orion are going to be working with Jessie and the rebels. We need the brass focused on the rest of the chaos with the rest of the colonists and ignoring us until we can get a solid escape plan together and get the hell out of here. Then once we get back to Earth, or on our way to Eleusis, I don't really care which at this point, we can go back to the way things should be. The way we wanted things to be in the first place."

"Really?" She looked all too hopeful when he said that things could go back to how they were. Anna thought about Orion, she thought about how happy she was with him and that she loved him, but he wanted Mercury. Orion felt like a better fit for her in several ways, but Logan was her husband. And she loved him too. She wanted a life with Logan. She didn't want to be someone's second choice, but at this point, she still felt like both Orion and Logan's second choice. "That's really what you want? To be with me?"

"That's always been what I want." He said finally, since it felt too good not to say so. "It's just more complicated now. I don't know what to do with the rest of what I've turned into up here. I don't want to be . . . defined by that. But when I'm acting on the Council or . . . other times, I am. That's why I want to get away. From everything. All I want is us."

Anna reached up and ran her hand along his beard, since it reminded her of what being close to him felt like, and she missed kissing him and the feel of his beard on her skin. "I want us too." She finally replied as she ran her thumb across his bottom lip. "I want to see you hold our babies, smiling. I miss your fucking amazing smile."

That statement was enough to bring his smile back to his face, but it was only a ghost of its former self. He had always been brooding by nature, but the look on his face was haunted after everything they had put themselves through just to avoid the Consortium's games. "We'll find a way."

Anna moved to sit in Logan's lap, even though he didn't invite her to do so. She rested her head on his shoulder and she closed her eyes, since she knew she was going to start to cry. "Are you really happy about the babies?" She just wanted him to want her babies, and to want her too.

"Of course I am." He put his arms around her, holding her gently, compared to some of the ferocity he had shown with her before. It was like his arms were giving her the out in case she wanted to take it, rather than locking her down with or without her consent. "I'm not . . . giddy about the fact that they're gonna be half and half, but I'm happy about them. I look forward to meeting them. Watching you be a mom. You're going to be amazing."

"*You're* going to be amazing. Especially with a little girl." She smiled weakly and hugged him tighter. "Hug me right, you asshole. After all this shit, you should know I'm not made of glass."

At that invitation, he hugged her against him until it was actually difficult to breathe, and she could feel his fingers digging into her sides as his arms squeezed her in a vise-grip. His beard scratched along her neck as he kissed her, and he took a deep breath to convince his senses that he really was holding her. "I love you, Anna. Everything I've done and everything I do, I'm doing to try and get us home. Whatever home ends up looking like after all is said and done up here."

Even if the hug was a little painful, she hugged him back as tightly as she could. Tears trickled down her face and her voice cracked with emotion. "I love you too, Logan. Just fucking include me when you're trying to change the world. We're partners. Even when things go to shit."

He held her for a long time and let her tears fall as the desperation in both of them came to a calmer place. He didn't let go of her, but when he eventually moved to kiss her lips, his hands moved down to her sides and he nodded to the table. "Go put your ring back on."

Anna smiled and kissed him again before she slid off of his lap to get her ring. She looked at it when she picked it up and hoped that this would be the last time she wondered if she should wear it or not. She slid it back on her finger and made a few silly poses to model it back on her hand. Her face was still red and puffy from crying, but she was smiling at him. It was rare for anyone to see Anna cry, but Logan had definitely seen it before. Especially when her mom died. He had been there for her, every moment. "There, it's back in place."

Her posing did get a smile from him, and he got up slowly, without taking his eyes off her. "Where it should be." He pulled her into another kiss and finally reached up to wipe his thumbs beneath her eyes. "I think we need to get you cleaned up. The unit looks immaculate, but you're a mess."

Anna looked down at herself and she nodded, but when she took a few steps back, she was holding onto his arm with a grip that said she wasn't going to let go. "You're coming with me, right?"

He nodded and advanced along with her as she moved toward the bathroom. "Yes, I'm coming with you." He slowed her down as they moved, though, and he reached out to take hold of her shirt and yanked it off over her head and threw it to the floor without even looking at it. "But this isn't." He pushed her a few more steps and her bra followed, but he kept backing her toward the bathroom. He reached up to cup her face in one hand, then reached back to take hold of the hair tie that was holding her brown hair back in a ponytail. He slid it free, and tossed it down as well and watched her the whole time as her hair fell loose around her shoulders. "Neither is this."

She smiled at him as he removed her clothing, even her hair tie, since she didn't care and certainly didn't need him to ask permission, not when she wanted him and everything that went with it. There was a little part of her that felt exposed, like it was new for them again, even though it really hadn't been that long since they had touched each other. The twins were only just conceived. However, it had been a long time since they had been so open with each other, exposed and vulnerable.

Anna whimpered as he ran his hands possessively over her skin, his fingers lingering on her tattoos here and there. "I still want to get more ink." She said between kisses. "There are so many things that should be here. You." She said as she ran her hand down his chest, and she tugged off his shirt as well. "I want you here with all of the things that matter to me. Permanently."

"There's a girl I've heard who's doing them for people here, even though they try to get her in trouble every time she does. Unsanitary, against guidelines, et cetera." He pushed her back against the door frame leading into their bedroom to kiss along her neck as his hands undid her pants and shoved them down over her hips. "She does good work, just don't let her tattoo anything kinky. She'd enjoy the view of you more than she'd enjoy getting a look at me."

She and Logan had their fair share of rough sex, but this felt different, and while Anna found it strange, she didn't dislike it. Anna stepped out of her pants and stepped back up to him again, her hands deftly working at his belt while she pressed against him in her skimpy underwear. "You know I don't care for tits. Just a good, stiff cock." Anna grazed one hand over his groin and moaned against his now-bare chest. "I can't believe . . . I thought I lost you." She replied almost reverently against his skin, as though she was touching something sacred.

Once they were both standing mostly-bare in the doorway, he leaned her head back and kissed her with the same reverence in his touch, though he was still pressed against her just to savor the heat of her skin against his. "Whatever happens from here, Anna, whatever else goes on here on this station or anywhere else in the world, I will always belong to you. That's just a fact of my existence."

That brought tears to her eyes, and Anna cried a little as she kissed him harder. "I've loved you longer than I've loved anyone, except my family." Anna paused to just look up into his grey eyes. "You've always been a part of me." She ran a hand down his side and then tucked her fingers in the waist of his boxers. "I love you so much that it hurts when I feel like I've lost you. I need you. Maybe you don't think I do, but I do."

"You've got me." His stone-grey eyes sealed the promise as they looked down into hers, and the touch of his hand as it raked up her chest to hold onto her was exactly the touch of the violently-possessive Logan she had married not even half a year prior. "For better or for worse." He added with the tiniest of smiles.

28

Carl was hesitant when he received his assignment that morning, but he knew he should have been grateful. He and several of the others from his team and Orion's had been assigned to cargo duty in the dock, and Aiko had been reassigned to help coordinate along with him. There were reports of a large number of couples being reassigned to work together, apparently as a kind of reward. Except the only couples who had been assigned to share work were the ones who had been matched in the first place and had quickly decided to solidify that match through Eleusis-legal marriage.

Carl spent part of the morning trying to wrap his head around whatever game the brass were playing, then got bored and gave up. He and Aiko were committed to each other and each other alone. That was enough for him.

"See, this is why it's a good thing I met you down where there's gravity." He chuckled toward Aiko as she moved a massive pallet of supplies out of the back of the cargo shuttle and tossed it at him easily. "If I met you up here, I would've thought you were some kind of superwoman and gotten intimidated."

"Who says I'm not?" She smiled quietly, flexing shyly after throwing the pallet around in near-zero gravity. Aiko hadn't felt great due to her pregnancy, and she still cried often because she missed her brother, but she was trying to get back into some kind of routine. She was trying to keep living. Aiko was ever more grateful for Gordon's manipulation, since she loved Carl and she was glad she wasn't being punished for being with the man that she loved. "I think I'm pretty super. You weren't complaining last night."

"Different kind of super. And no, you'll never hear me complaining about that." He winked at her and caught the pallet, redirecting it toward Orion much farther down the line toward the lifts. "Pretty sure for that kind of super, you don't get a cape and tights." He reconsidered as he caught the next pallet and then shrugged. "Okay, maybe some tights."

"Whatever makes you happy, husband." Aiko beamed at him and kept moving things along, though she quieted her voice after looking around at the rest of the crew. Most of the people around her weren't in the kind of mood that she was.

Fitch came in late, but that was routine for her anymore. She had been having the worst morning sickness, and Aiko felt bad for complaining whenever Kameron was around. The dark circles under Kameron's eyes said a lot about her recent sleep, or the lack thereof.

"Sorry I'm late." Kameron said as she joined the line to help. "Between the baby and hearing all the shit in the residential hall all night, I managed to actually fucking break the speaker for my alarm. Most satisfying thing I've done in ages."

"Wow. That's impressive. Even I haven't done that yet." Carl laughed and tossed her a pallet purely out of mischief. "How's the baby girl? Still giving you hell?"

"Depends on what you define as hell. If every scent known to man makes you vomit, every food except bread and cheese, and if you have to pee every thirty minutes means you're in hell, then yes. I am in hell." Kameron glanced down at her stomach, though there really wasn't much physical evidence of anything. She was further along than almost all the pregnant women on the station, but apparently she had a long torso. The baby was growing upwards instead of out, so she didn't show much.

Kameron glanced around to see who else was working. "Did you hear about the shit that went down with Pablo? His husband slept on the fucking floor outside of Pablo's unit until I heard him talking in his sleep last night. I let him into my unit so he could sleep on the couch. The fucking Initiative locked him out, and when Pablo tried to open the fucking door, it wouldn't open until this morning. I don't get it. Pablo knocked up his match. What more could they care about?"

Carl gave her a dark look and continued tossing down supplies, though they were down to smaller boxes and shipping containers that were easier to move. "That strikes me as an excellent question, mostly because there's exactly no reasonable answer for it." He looked back at Aiko too, since they had had a similar conversation just the day before about some of the same things. "So, if you remove reasonable answers, all you're left with, however unreasonable, must be the truth."

Kameron shook her head and kept her voice down. "That Melissa chick contacted me after shit went crazy. She said she wasn't looking for a wedding but she was looking for a girlfriend." She looked up from her work, but she didn't have a look of excitement. "I told her to stay with her match."

Carl sighed and looked back at Kameron long enough that he missed the next box and got hit in the shoulder. He managed to recover in time to catch it, and he tossed it at her with a grunt of faked pain. "They haven't messed with you for messing with her before this. They wouldn't mess with you now when they've got everything else to deal with, I don't think. Unless you run off and start putting out vows."

"Before it was with Kaz. Now it's different. I'm not going to go looking for a man, but I'm also not going to go looking for trouble, either. If she leaves her match and comes to be with me, they might punish us both for it. They haven't re-assigned me to anyone, and I'm staying out of it until they do. I can't risk my baby girl for a kinky set of tits. No fucking way. I don't trust anything anymore." She shook her head and kept working, even though she always looked tired. "The people who leave their match are catching all sorts of hell. I'm not getting mixed up in that."

Carl caught the next pallet, which was the last for the time being, so he took it out under his arm to wait for the ship to move on and the next one to take its place. "If the place gets too crazy, just come crash on our couch for a while. Not like you're gonna get in trouble for shacking up with a couple that followed protocols. But if you throw up on any of our shit, I will not be excited about it."

Kameron considered the idea, but she was too worried she might actually throw up on something. She had a severe problem with throwing up recently. Clearly. "I don't think I can promise that. It would be nice to be in a unit with other people, though. Living alone is depressing."

She ached for Kazuo's company as she had every second since he died, but she didn't talk about it. She wasn't his wife, she wasn't his girlfriend, she wasn't anything, really. A friend who he fucked because the Initiative said so, and now she was the mother of his baby. But still, she didn't feel like she had any right to openly mourn him. Kameron hadn't known him for long. His sister deserved to mourn him. Not her.

Kameron looked down the line and saw Orion working, but neither Anna nor Mercury were anywhere in sight. Probably because he hadn't actually picked one to keep. "I think I'm going to go help Orion."

"He might need more help than you can offer right this second." Carl said with an offhanded laugh, but there was no humor in it. "I haven't seen him this cranky since he got beat in the Eleusis Course contest. He's not having the time of his life. But you're welcome to try and help." He took the case she was holding and pushed himself off in the direction of Aiko, expecting her to catch him mid-air, which she did. "Just keep the offer in mind. You're family. Couch is yours if you need it."

"Even if I vomit too much?" Kameron asked as she angled herself to make it over to Orion as quickly and efficiently as possible. She hoped she angled right, she was getting off on too many things recently. "Cuz if you could be super understanding about the hell I mentioned, I would be glad to crash on your couch. You two better not be super noisy, though. Sex noises are cruel to the celibate."

"We'll hang a tie." He shot back at her, since there was no way he was restraining himself with Aiko, even for the sake of a friend.

Carl hadn't exaggerated about Orion's mood. As she floated down toward him, she caught him in full drill-sergeant mode, which was something she hadn't seen from him since the two of them were in flight school together. "Look, I'm aware this isn't our normal duty shift, but even your normal duties involve *reading* from time to time. This one stays in Nav Control, which means it doesn't go to the lifts! Right there!" He took the box out of the man's hands and whistled loudly to get the attention of one of the cargo handlers up near Nav Control, then sent the box spinning through the air to its correct destination. "Read, *then* throw. Next!"

"Yikes. And I thought *I* was having a bad morning." Fitch managed to catch a wall hook and stopped before she made any sort of mess. "Carl was right, you are in a *mood*. It can't be that time of the month, I thought our cycles were synched."

"Maybe they are, but I do humanity the courtesy of taking medication for it." He didn't even look over at her as she got closer, just moved on to another box and tossed it toward the lift while making sure his team was still working in the right place. "What are you doing on duty? I thought you were on medical leave this week?"

Kameron was supposed to be resting because of dehydration, but the medication she had been prescribed did nothing for boredom, though it had helped with morning sickness somewhat. "Mercury fixed me up for now. I'm supposed to go back to the clinic after I'm done here so they can check on me. Sitting in that unit alone is fucking depressing. Especially because Kazuo was the one who decorated the place. It's lonely."

The look on Orion's face was still cranky, but he narrowed his eyes at her as he grabbed the next box. "You never had a problem living alone before. You were rooming alone on Three forever."

"Yeah, well, now I'm fucking pregnant so I'm a tangled web of emotions. Shit happens." She replied quickly before she narrowed her eyes back at him to poke him even more. "Talk to me. What's your deal?"

"Just been a long week, that's all." One of the other pilots came up and took the box he reached out to grab, but Orion actually looked angry that the guy threw it in the right direction for sorting and distribution, so he just hung back with Kameron and gritted his teeth. "Kind of a lot going on."

"Everyone has a lot going on." She went up to Orion's side and grabbed his arm for a moment. "Let's sit back for a short break. I'm supposed to be on medical leave, so you can say you were looking out for me." Kameron pulled him back slightly, hoping he wouldn't resist. She was worried since he was so angry, Orion never got this angry. "Shit has been raining down on us for months. What pushed you to this point?"

He was still snarling as she pulled him back, but he wasn't growling at her, exactly. Just clearly pissed at the world. "Normally I have an umbrella for the raining shit. Well, two, if you want to get technical."

"Fancy umbrella." She looked over at him, though he was avoiding her gaze. "Talk. Spill the feelings." Kameron let go of his arm as soon as she was sure he wasn't going to dart away. "Is it Anna? I heard she got sick yesterday at a lunch when she met with Logan. There were all sorts of rumors that she got food poisoning for meeting with him."

"Yeah. She did." The look on his face got even darker at the mention of Anna. "She's been under the weather since that lunch and she canceled her lunch for today because she can't keep anything down."

Kameron was quiet for a moment after that, but she looked in

Aiko's direction. "Maybe Aiko can give her something. We can go visit her. Hell, you should be with her instead of being here. Use my medical leave or something. I'm sure she'd rather have you around cracking jokes than being miserable in bed."

"She doesn't want me around." He said grumpily. "She wants to be alone, because she knows the Initiative poisoned her for spending time with Logan."

"Well, you're not Logan. You're her best friend. Sometimes she's wrong about what she wants. Or she's probably lying." Kameron looked at the work around her and then looked back at her friend. "We should definitely go see her. I'll go with you."

"She seemed pretty certain about what she wanted." Orion sighed and didn't make any move to approach the lifts. "I get her wanting to be alone. It's just one more thing in this whole shit-pile that's pushing everyone toward something they didn't originally choose. Everything that happens takes it one step further from what we all wanted." He took a bundle of empty packing fiber and balled it up tighter before he randomly threw it at the back of one of his subordinates' heads. "Meanwhile, Mercury hasn't left the unit she shared with Logan, even when it isn't their scheduled week. And I don't imagine she's going to."

"She's probably just as afraid to step out of line, especially because she knows there are a ton of women depending on her to take care of them now." Kameron knew *she* didn't want her doctor to get sick, and she knew the Initiative would do it, too, if they wanted to.

Fitch looked away for a moment and thought about what she was talking about with Carl, and she struggled to say what she was thinking. It was unusual for that to happen with her. "This might be the worst idea in the world, but if it will help you, then maybe it would be worth it. You shouldn't have to avoid a woman you love because of the Initiative. I'm *alone* because of the Initiative. Kaz is dead." Kameron didn't need a reminder about Kaz, but it was good in one way to remember that the enemy was still lurking about, waiting to attack them at any opportunity.

"I just told Carl that I am not getting into any kind of mess with Melissa. And I'm still not. But maybe she can help you."

"Melissa? Your . . . blonde, threesome-loving tattoo-artist admirer?" That was far enough out in left field for Orion to stop his scowling and look over at her. "How would she help, exactly?"

"Well, you could have a threesome, of course!" She said

sarcastically before she glared at Orion. "You told me that you wanted more ink done, and you said Anna did too. So let's have a feel-better party and invite Melissa and Anna can tell her what she wants. Maybe getting new ink will distract her from feeling shitty. If she's just laying in bed anyway, that's perfect. Being pregnant and getting tattooed isn't usually recommended but with the shit we have going on…"

Orion actually thought about that for a while, and it did seem to pull him out of his mood at least a little. "That's not a bad idea. What kind of duty is she on today?"

"Hell if I know. I've been ignoring her sexts since before Kaz died. She's relentless, though." Kameron pulled out her communicator and pulled up Melissa's contact, though she hesitated. She didn't want to give the woman any ideas, but in the back of her mind, she did want an excuse to see Melissa. She was lonely. "Let me see what she's up to."

Personal tattoo emergency, think you can bust out of your daily chores and meet me somewhere?

It wasn't long before she got a text back. It never took long with Melissa. *For you, hotness? I'll bust out of more than my chores. Tell me where, I'll bring the gun and the art.*

"God, she better not bust out of anything in front of me. These baby hormones are terrible." Kameron knew that Orion hadn't read the text, but she was sure he could catch on to what she was talking about. "Let's go check on Anna now. I'll have Melissa meet us. We'll say you had to escort me home."

Look up Orion Al-Jabbar. Meet at his unit. His girlfriend needs some tattoo therapy.

Oh, that's cheating. You said personal! Fine, be that way. I'll meet you at his unit. Give me an hour to play hookie and get my stuff.

It is *personal. He's one of my best friends. I owe you one.* "Okay." Kameron said before she looked up. This was going to be a bad idea. Play with fire . . . "She's gonna get her stuff and meet us there."

Orion looked skeptical, but they finished clearing the second cargo ship of the morning, and the other two weren't due for another few hours. He sighed in frustration that there wasn't even a legitimate way of getting around going with Kameron and finally pushed himself toward the lifts.

"I haven't gotten a new tattoo in four years." He said more to himself than to her. "And the last one was at least done in a decent parlor back on Three. You sure this chick is good?"

Fitch just glared at him again. "Would I subject you to a terrible artist? I would have to live with that kind of hell forever, you bitching at me all the time because you got fucked up ink. Like I want to deal with that for the rest of my career. Yes, she's great." She lifted up her shirt and showed some Kanji on her side. "Kaz picked it out after our first go-round with Melissa."

"Oh, of course." Orion put out a hand to grip the side of her pants so he could hold her steady and get a look at the details. It was beautiful work, with clean lines and delicate curves, like it had just been painted onto her skin with a calligraphy brush. "That clearly says 'for a good time call,' that's perfect for you."

Kameron smacked his hand after that, since it did not say that. Or, at least, she hoped it didn't. It was supposed to say 'Live happy, live loud', or something similar. She had depended on Kazuo's expert Japanese to not lead her astray. "Stop being a dick. Come on, let's go. If we don't get there first, Anna is going to be so confused."

"You mean sexually? Because I really don't think we need to throw a third ring into this circus." The lift doors closed, and Orion calmed down a little as they descended, turning more downtrodden than cranky. "I'm sorry I'm being a dick. Contrary to popular opinion, I can actually hear myself. I'm just tired of sitting around waiting for Bickford to make up his mind so I can move on with my life as the runner-up."

She definitely wasn't expecting to hear that come out of Orion's mouth, especially because she knew his extensive dating history. The man was never a runner-up, and sometimes she had been jealous of all the female attention he got. She never got what he did. "Why are you waiting on him to get what you want? Who cares what he does? Pick for yourself, for crying out loud. You have two of the sexiest women in the world in front of you and you're whining because you want someone else to pick first. Let him suffer for being an indecisive asshole."

"Right, sure, I didn't think of that." He glared at her again, but then just stared at the numbers as they approached the residential level for his shared unit with Anna. "I'm sure the guy is suffering plenty, and I can never hate him for more than a few minutes at a time because I know what a shit-show this is. But Mercury doesn't even come home anymore, and every time Anna does, her head's not with me, it's with him. She says she's waiting for . . . I don't even fucking know anymore." He shook his head and calmed down a little more, incapable of remaining angry for too long, especially once he was finally forced to talk about it. "I made up my mind a long while ago. I thought everybody else had too, but apparently not."

"First of all, don't assume you know where her head is. That gets me into a fuckton of trouble every time I do that, and I still haven't learned my lesson." Kameron shook her head and sighed loudly. "Secondly, when you made up your mind about Anna," she put Anna's name out there because she wanted him to pick Anna. Anna was ten times more fun than Mercury, and if the rumors about public noise were true, then Kameron liked her even more. Mercury was hot, but she was definitely not the best woman for Orion. "Did you tell her, 'hey, we should be together forever because we fucking have a great time and we're awesome together'? Or are you still 'friends with benefits' because no one wants to talk shit out?"

Orion was accustomed to Kameron being the most likely of all his friends not to pay attention to filters when it came to talking through difficult issues, but Station Nine had brought her to a whole new level of directness. "She's still married and head over heels in love with her husband. Who she's known just about her entire life. Mercury might have decided she's going to commit completely to the new match and made herself available to bust their marriage into smithereens, but that still means something to me. If I respect Anna, I respect what's important to her. Which Logan still obviously is."

"And yet he's kind of been an asshole to her anyway, right?" Kameron clearly wasn't a fan of Logan either, but that was mostly because she thought he was a cold and unfeeling leader, and she especially had a problem with people that had a superiority complex. At least one Kaplan ended up dead, so maybe there was good fucking karma somewhere.

"The only way to live anymore is by doing things that make you happy. Regardless of rules or laws or expectations. Is Anna happily married? Sure as hell doesn't look like it. And now that Mercury has jumped ship, Anna is just going to keep getting hurt. Maybe she's just hanging on for the same reason you're giving her space. For the same reason you're still wearing your wedding ring. Because you made a commitment. But clearly the other two people don't care about that shit, so why should you? Don't you just want to be happy? Don't you want Anna to be happy?"

"You've known me forever. When have I not wanted somebody to be happy?" He snapped back at her. "And don't say the dorm martial in our fourth year. That guy was a piece of shit and he deserved what he got. To this day, every time somebody on a show or in a clinic mentions a laxative, I get this fond grin on my face." Even his instinctive attempt to joke his way out of every situation didn't work on himself, though, and he leaned back against the lift wall to shake his head.

"Wanting everybody to be happy doesn't make it reality. You're right, though. You know that, I know that. Doesn't make being right any easier." He paused when the lift stopped, and walked out with her beside him, heading down the hall toward his unit. "I hope your blonde is as good as you think she is. I've kept these arms blank for a reason, and she'd better not fuck them up."

"I told you, she won't." Kameron backed off on the conversation as soon as he said she was right but that it didn't make it easier. At least he knew she was right and that he should do something about it. The rest was up to him. Once they got to the unit, Kameron looked up at Orion expectantly, and he hesitantly opened the door, which bothered her. It was his own unit, for crying out loud.

As soon as Anna heard the door open, she looked over at the clock beside the bed and buried her face back into her pillow. Apparently Orion was home early. At least she wasn't feeling like death, but she didn't want to be too grateful, since Mercury was the reason why she was able to hold down fluids. Life was a bitch sometimes. Instead of saying anything, she just responded to hearing Orion enter the unit with a groan.

"Make yourself at home." He said mostly to let Anna know that he hadn't come home by himself. "There's some fruit left over from what Aiko handed us a few days ago, help yourself." He headed over to the bedroom and paused in the doorway. "You don't typically groan that way if you're asleep, so I'm gonna assume you're conscious. Anything I can get for you?"

Anna lifted her head up from the pillow for just a moment to turn her head so she could look at him, and she just blinked in silence a few times before she said anything. "You're back early." She croaked, since her throat was still raw. "Did something bad happen?"

"No, everything's fine. We got done with the first couple ships and I didn't feel like running crates all over the station, so I handed it off. Kam's in the kitchen, she's out of heavy lifting duty too. One of her friends is on the way. We're just gonna hang out for the afternoon, but we'll stick to the living room and leave you here to die. I mean rest." He finished with an attempt at a smile.

She gave him the smallest smile, but she found it a little strange that Orion was having some kind of party instead of working, since he never did anything like that. Certainly not in the middle of the day. Kameron and a friend? "Okay. Are you sure you're okay?"

"Yeah, everything's . . . well, as fine as it was when I left a few hours ago, anyway." He shrugged and managed to muster more of a smile. "Just yell if you need anything. I won't be far away." He pulled the door closed just as a knock came to the door to his unit.

Instead of going to answer it, Orion went to one of the couches in his living space and pulled a tablet off one of his side tables to start doing a search. "You gonna get that?" He glanced up at Kameron, since Melissa was her friend, after all.

"It's your unit." She mumbled, but she got up anyway, since she did want to see Melissa. She just didn't *want* to want to see her. It wasn't as though she didn't want to spend time with the woman. Hell, she'd keep her naked in the bed as often as she could if it didn't mean that they would suffer for it.

She reluctantly opened the door and she had to stop herself from openly ogling Melissa as she stood there. "Hey. You're here early."

"I come quickly. Especially when you tell me to." Melissa smiled at her as she stepped through the door and Kameron closed it behind her, but she didn't reach out to touch Fitch until the door was closed and they were clearly out of public view.

She leaned in to give Kameron a quick kiss with a hand on her waist, but it was a fairly chaste touch compared to some of the ones they'd shared before. Melissa Svendssen was slightly taller than Kameron, her hair a lighter blonde than the more darker-haired Kam, and every bit as curvy as Kameron's wildest dreams had imagined a woman should be. Scandinavia had lost something when she accepted a position with the Initiative, namely her bright blue eyes and perfect features, which were only accented by the ink with which she had adorned her body over the years. Her pale blonde hair was dyed pink at the tips, falling down her back and over her shoulders to just past her full breasts.

She wore as little as she could get away with in public at all times, so the tight tank top and short jean shorts she was wearing were hardly a surprise, but it was still striking to see her and all of her ink exposed. Her accent was fairly thick, but it only made her seem more tantalizing with every syllable that dropped from her lips.

"I missed you. And you do owe me for teasing like this. I thought you were finally going to let me go to work on you again." She hefted the case of supplies that she carried in her other hand with a dramatic sigh, but the following smile was a forgiving one. "How is my baby?"

It was a rare occasion to see Kameron out of sorts, but she was rendered speechless upon seeing Melissa again. God, the woman was fucking gorgeous. Once Kaz had been admitted permanently to the hospital, Kameron had stayed away from Melissa. She'd been avoiding her ever since, and now she felt like a starving woman by the buffet. A hormonal, starving woman by the buffet.

"Your baby?" She was temporarily confused, but then she looked down at herself and a small laugh escaped her lips. It was definitely as much Melissa's as Kaz', if they were going by time spent attempting to conceive. Only Melissa couldn't actually donate any of her gorgeous genetic material. "She's pretty good. I think. She beats me up all the time, makes me sick, you know, typical baby shit." Kameron didn't acknowledge the owing Melissa part, mostly because she knew she would be in trouble if she thought about how Melissa would want her to pay up.

Melissa chuckled at that, then crouched down to put her face near Kameron's stomach. She was wearing heeled sandals that made her even taller than she already was, but having her mouth so close to Kameron's waist (again) stirred up interesting memories. "You in there. Be good to your mother. I said so." She leaned in and kissed Kam's stomach through her shirt, then stood up slowly and looked around the room. "So, you must be the friend in need of some ink?"

Orion watched the entire exchange with a barely suppressed laugh behind his lips, since it was too much fun to watch Kameron flustered. He got up when she spoke to him and left the tablet on the low table next to the couch. "Orion Al-Jabbar, pleased to meet you. I've heard . . . probably more than I should have about you."

"And I've heard plenty about you." She took Orion's hand with a broad smile, craning her neck to look up at him the way nearly everyone did. "And if you've heard plenty about me from this beauty over here, then it's a fair exchange. I've heard lots about you making your girlfriend scream your name in the maintenance hallways, so should we say that makes us even?"

Orion actually gave a genuine smile at that, and shrugged. "Our reputations precede us. I can live with that."

"Everyone knows I can't keep my mouth shut. I had to brag and the truth took fire by itself." Kameron shrugged as she glanced at Melissa again, but the glance turned into another once-over before she forced herself to look back at Orion. "I mean, am I right or am I fucking right? Look at her. Fucking gorgeous."

"The mop is in the closet for when you start getting drool on my floor." Orion winked over at Kameron, then nodded toward the couch. "I found some artwork that is close to what I'm looking for, if you want to get started."

"Mmm. Starter art. Tattoo foreplay. Gimme." Melissa followed Orion over to the living area but made sure Kameron wasn't far away as they looked through designs Orion found.

Anna had fallen to sleep again fairly quickly after Orion closed the door to their room, but as soon as she heard some loud laughing and a weird buzzing sound, she dragged herself out of bed. She needed some water anyway. Anna certainly didn't look like she was going to win any beauty competitions with her hair piled on her head and her worn pajamas, but she didn't care. Her shirt was almost see-through, but she wasn't thinking about that when she stepped out to find out what was going on.

"Babe?" She asked as she stepped out, especially when she saw two women hovering over his arm, one who she thought she recognized as Fitch, but the other one was definitely new. "Did I miss something?"

"Hey, you're awake." For Orion's part, he was laying back along the couch with his shirt off as the women examined him. That might have been concerning, if it had been any other pair of women involved, but the two of them seemed much more intent on touching each other every chance they got than touching her match.

Once that thought had a chance to process through her sleepy brain, she wondered why he had his shirt off. The answer was readily available as Melissa moved slightly in her work to show the source of the buzzing as a tattoo gun. Something was taking shape on Orion's left bicep, though her bleary-eyed self couldn't really make out what it was from across the room. "Sorry if we bothered you, we were trying to keep it down."

"It's okay." Anna slowly made her way toward the small group, but she walked to Orion's other side, opposite the two touchy-feely women. Kameron's hand was about half an inch above the other woman's ass, and apparently the woman was okay with it. "You're . . . getting a tattoo?" Okay, was she in some whacked up pregnancy dream? "I didn't know . . . that was an option."

"It's not. Officially. I'm a bad, bad, disobedient person." He gave Anna as much of a smile as he could muster, since as soon as she had gotten up, his anxiety over their relationship had returned to replace the lightheartedness the women had instilled in him over the course of the tattoo. "But Kazuo went looking for somebody to come play with Fitch, and Fitch was kind enough to inform me that her friend is a tattoo artist. And a fucking good one, too, from the look of things so far."

"If you like this, you should see some of the art my match has been getting this whole time." Melissa said as she licked her lips. "The male body is definitely a distant second choice for me, but his is still gorgeous. And fun to draw on. Permanently. Hold still, I need to finish this branch." She smacked Orion's shoulder to get him to stop moving, and got back to work.

Orion just grinned over at her, since she was so bossy he could tell why Kameron was into her, but then he looked back up at Anna, since she was close enough to get a good look at the tattoo.

Part of it, Anna recognized immediately, since it was a selection of barbed wire that looked like an exact replica of the ink she had around her own left arm, just with slightly longer and sharper lines to it. Just above the vicious points was a stylized word in Arabic that seemed to almost flow into the barbed wire beneath it. Underneath, Melissa was working on outlining two circles descending his arm in the same kind of thorny design, so that it looked like the entire pattern was an outgrowth of the wire he had clearly stolen from Anna in the first place.

Anna smiled as she looked over at the barbed wire, but she didn't say anything immediately. She wanted to reach out and touch it, but obviously that would have been a terrible idea. "What does it say?"

He was glad to see her smiling about it, and he rested his head back against the pillow behind him to look up at her. "*Ameera.*" He said with a grin, since he hadn't exactly been giving her Arabic lessons in between their video game sessions and flight simulator training. "Princess."

"Princess?" Anna thought that was a strange thing to put on his arm, but not every tattoo had to make sense to her. It was still beautiful artwork, though, and she couldn't pull her gaze away from it. "It looks gorgeous. I can't let you leave." Anna said before she looked up at the artist, who she still hadn't officially been introduced. "I have a lot of ink I want, and if I'm going to die of food poisoning, then I want to look good at the funeral."

The smile on Orion's face lasted right up until she started talking to Melissa, then evaporated slowly before he turned away from Anna and looked back at the ink that was nearly finished. "Well, I've got her for the rest of the afternoon, as far as I know. You got other plans besides sneaking out of duty to come be artistic?"

Melissa shrugged. "I have to go back to my unit and fuck my match at some point tonight, but that can wait until later. Ovulating in three days. Four months and my ovaries apparently just don't want to put out. It's like they don't even belong to me."

Clearly Kameron wasn't a fan of the idea of Melissa going back to her match, but it wasn't her place to say anything. She was just jealous. Her hand dropped away, along with her smile, and both she and Orion looked unhappy. "They can be fickle." She eventually responded.

Anna noticed Orion wasn't smiling anymore, but she wasn't sure why, even though most of her attention was on the art being created. "It looks like mine. The wire." She moved closer to him and put her hands on his free arm, even though she knew her hands felt a bit cold and clammy. "Did you pick that because you like mine?"

Orion looked up at her for a moment and opened his mouth to respond, but Melissa beat him to it, without looking up from her work. "I had to sneak in and get a good look at yours while you were sleeping. It's good work, whoever did it. Leaves things open, keeps everything contained in one strip, I like it." She seemed completely oblivious to the expression on Orion's face or anything else about the conversation as she wiped away the excess from Orion's skin and dipped her gun for some more ink.

"I'll have to get another look at your shoulder in about . . ."

she glanced up at Anna's stomach and apparently did some quick math, "seven or eight months, just so I can match the font whenever those two decide to come out, come back and fill these birthdays in. Don't worry, that part I'll do for free. Kam's on the hook for the bill as it is." She grinned over at Kameron and went back to work, continuing to ignore anything else going on around her.

Anna looked over at Kameron who just shrugged, but was acting more withdrawn after Melissa said she would have to go, and Anna looked down at Orion again. "Will you help me decide on something in Arabic? It's gorgeous." She squeezed his hand weakly. "Is the Princess part for Lynnette? I have "Prince" on my back." She clarified for Melissa's benefit, though she wondered how deeply she was sleeping and how much of her the artist had peeped.

Kameron was annoyed enough by her jealousy over Melissa with someone else that she was a little too irritable for her own good. She gave Orion two seconds to explain, but he hesitated too long. "No, it's for you."

Orion glanced over at Kameron with a brief glare, but just looked away afterward, clearly not denying what she'd said.

Anna didn't really know what to say to that, since she wasn't expecting him to get a tattoo for her. They weren't married, and she was sure he was just biding his time until Mercury got knocked up so he could get back to his life. "Wow, I, um. I didn't know . . . that you intended to do that." He loved her and she loved him, but she didn't think he would do something like this. "It's beautiful. Thank you." She wanted to ask him what he was going to get for Mercury, or what he thought Mercury would think about his permanent tribute to her, but she didn't.

Orion nodded without looking back up at her at first, then when he did, he looked at her arm instead, where she had the matching wire. "I've had it in mind for a while, just didn't realize we had a decent artist on board with us. Figured this was as good an opportunity as any to get it done."

She leaned down and kissed his cheek gently, grateful in the moment she had remembered to brush her teeth. Anna squeezed his hand again, tightly, but then she found herself whispering into his ear. "You are more confusing than you give yourself credit for."

He shook his head after that and leaned his head back to look up in her eyes, whispering back. "I may be confusing, but I'm not confused."

Anna just stared into his dark eyes for a moment, since she was sure she wasn't understanding what she thought he was saying. "You're not? You're not waiting to go back to what you had before?" This probably wasn't a good place to talk about whatever they were going to talk about, but she couldn't stop herself. "Getting a tattoo is a huge thing for me. You know that. All of mine have so much meaning behind them, and if that's for me . . ."

"The last tattoo I got was the one on my back for Ahmed." He said to interrupt her. His voice was partly hurt because she needed it spelled out for her, but the look in his eyes was intense in other ways as well. "The only others I have are for my god and my unit. As clubs go, it's a fairly small one, and it's not one I add to on a whim or by accident. So no. I've got no interest in waiting." He finally looked away from her, and glanced down at the artwork again as Melissa worked on one of the last barbs of the second circle. "I get that that's not where you are. I even get why. But it's where I am."

"I didn't think you wanted that with me." She said softly as she watched his tattoo. "I thought you were waiting." Anna felt painfully conflicted, not because she couldn't choose between Orion and Logan, but because she knew what she would choose. "I thought you both were."

Despite her reconciliation with Logan, after the food poisoning incident, he hadn't spoken a word to her. She didn't imagine he would, so at this point either they would never speak again if the Initiative succeeded in killing them, or she wouldn't be able to talk to him until they had escaped. Regardless of the outcome, she'd felt hurt all over again, as well as scared. If she had gotten sick enough, the Initiative could have killed her slowly. They still might.

"Right. I'm waiting for her." Orion nodded sarcastically. "Seems like that's what the last few months have been about, both for you and for me. You waiting on him and me waiting on her. Maybe that's the way the brass wants us. Maybe that's why Mercury hasn't gotten pregnant. If they can give you food poisoning, they can sure as hell keep her from getting knocked up until they're done playing their games. Doesn't matter. Mercury didn't choose to have Logan's babies over my babies, she's chosen

Logan over me. And I'm not even mad about it for my own sake."

He knew he was rambling and spilling more personal details than he had really wanted to, especially in front of a relative stranger like Melissa, but he couldn't stop himself. "All I know is that she's happy with him some kind of way that I don't provide. And good for her, finding it. She was right from the beginning of this whole clusterfuck."

He finally glanced back up at Anna again in the middle of the tirade, but he didn't stop, even if his eye contact was still spotty. "I'm not making up my mind because somebody else made up theirs. I love her, and always will, but I've got no reason to hedge about my priorities or what I want. What I want is you, and our son, and all the crazy that you and me together are gonna get into for as long as you can tolerate me. It's not even a difficult decision. Only agony that's come out of that kind of choice is how much this needle stings right now."

"Sorry not sorry." Melissa said with a quiet smile, since she had done her best to keep herself and her tattoo gun quiet for the duration of the speech. "We might be able to get across the galaxy in a single trip, but needles still hurt. Just the realities of the universe, I'm afraid."

Kameron was grinning even though she knew she shouldn't be, but she felt pretty proud of the fact she actually got Orion to talk. She never would have expected it would be in front of her, but it was good to see. He needed to say what was said.

Anna couldn't say that it wasn't a difficult decision, because it was. Logan was the man of her dreams, the man she had always wanted. They wanted a family together, they wanted a future together. Especially now, though, she was starting to believe that he was never meant to be anything more than the man of her dreams. Otherwise she would have been able to keep him. But every time she thought they were on the same page, they weren't.

"I love him too." The last deep discussion she had with Logan kept replaying in her mind, and Anna felt pain in her chest as she thought about making a decision. Especially if Orion didn't know the truth about Mercury and Logan. Maybe if he knew the truth, he would understand Mercury's distance. If he didn't know and then he found out later, would he regret choosing her? "It's not that you can't give her what she needs. It's just that she's probably afraid to tell you."

Kameron watched as Melissa finally released Orion's arm once she had completed the piece. Almost instantly, Anna was in Orion's lap, but she was careful not to bump his arm. Kameron wanted to know what Anna was talking about, but she looked over at Melissa as soon as she finished putting ointment on the ink. "You need a break. Let's go raid his fridge."

"Great idea." Melissa said as she scooted back quickly. The lovers had apparently decided to have a moment. "I mean, I'm up for watching as much as the next girl, but I don't think that's what they were going for. Out of my way." She slapped Kameron's ass hard enough to make her jump out of the way of the fridge, then bent over more than absolutely necessary once she had it open. "If they've got chocolate syrup in here, it's gonna be a long break."

Kameron tried not to audibly whimper as she watched Melissa's tight shorts rise up when she bent over. Heaven help her if the woman wasn't wearing any underwear. "No syrup." She eventually mumbled without being able to pull her gaze away. "We can't hook up. Or even make out. Tit . . . it's too dangerous."

Orion didn't try to move away from Anna or get up from the couch, he just pulled her down to lie against him once she'd gotten settled. "We talked about it back when you had your last big fight with Logan. She said she would explain if I wanted her to, and I said I didn't. Whatever it is, I don't want to know. It's their business, not mine. If she had wanted me to know, she would've told me outright and not given me the option. Doesn't matter."

Anna took a deep breath as she laid her head on Orion's shoulder, and she closed her eyes. "The last time Logan and I talked, we talked about wanting to get away. We talked about wanting to be together, no matter what. We talked about our future family. And the whole time, I knew something would happen again." Anna leaned her head closer to tuck it underneath his chin.

"I don't know how to move past the fact that he was the man I always wanted and could never have. I don't know how to reconcile that with the fact that if I had met you on Earth, I would have married you and never looked back or wondered anything else. I don't want you to wonder any more than I want to wonder."

He wasn't sure how to answer that at first, so he just ran his hand over her back. "All four of us got here and immediately suffered our love lives being put in a blender. I don't think there's ever gonna be a time when we're not wondering what would've happened. Or wishing we had a time machine. Not necessarily so we can change what we've got, but just to go back and avoid the whole damn thing in the first place. You're gonna wonder. I'm gonna wonder. Wonder wonder wonder, won't do shit. What matters are the answers we give, not the questions we ask."

"You won't regret being with me?" Anna and Mercury were absolutely nothing alike, and while she knew she was asking the same things several times, she needed to feel two hundred percent sure she wasn't fucking shit up. "Even though we told each other from the beginning that we were just in it for the fun?"

"We told each other in the beginning that we would keep things fun. Keep things a distraction from the rest of the shit going on here." He looked her over and reached up to push some stray hair out of her face. "You've known for a long while that you're more than that for me. We do have a lot of fun, and we have a happy life, when it's just us on our own terms. I want to keep that. I want life to be like that, not just the little corner of life that we've been telling ourselves we can keep on the side while we agonize over all the rest."

"I want that too." Anna agreed as he held her close with one arm after he had brushed some of the hair out of her face. She felt terrible for wanting to hold onto Logan before, for pushing so hard for something she knew that he wanted, but also he wasn't fully able to commit to. Logan had changed, but she knew that he was holding onto pieces of himself that she knew. She just didn't know who would come out in the end, the Logan she knew, or the man she had seen so often recently. "I love you. I really want . . ."

For the first time in a long time, there was a loud chiming noise that filled the unit, and Anna, as well as everyone else, stopped moving and talking to hear the warning message.

Emergency Alert. Please return to your assigned unit immediately. This is not a drill. Military personnel, stand by for further instructions.

29

Kameron looked back at Orion with Anna on his lap, and she looked both suspicious and concerned. The last attack was random, but shit had been completely unpredictable recently. She had her hand on Melissa's side, but that was as far as she had allowed, despite Melissa's attempt to get handsy before the alert.

Once Orion started to get up, Kameron looked back at Melissa again. "Let's get you back to your unit. Or you can stay in mine, if you want. I actually have a gun, and I can keep you safe. I'm not so sure about your dopey match, as *gorgeous* as he is." Kameron clearly had some jealousy issues, especially when she didn't want to share.

Melissa rolled her eyes, but went with Kameron anyway, since everyone was in motion very quickly. "Oh, come on. The guy *is* gorgeous. That's not me getting excited to get on his dick again, that's just a fact. He's gorgeous. And he might not be too bright, but he's worth saving. Which means we go get your gun and then you come back to my place."

"Fine." Kameron snipped as she looked at Orion and Anna, who were up and moving. "You gonna be okay here?" Kameron paused at his door and met his eyes.

"Yeah, we'll be alright." Orion was busy getting a uniform back on, but he was wincing as he pulled it over his arm, since he wasn't even supposed to have anything over it besides a dressing, which they hadn't had time to do. "Keep your head down. If bullets start flying, it could be from the brass, so know who you're shooting at before you start. Be safe."

"You too. Keep in contact. I may see you if they call me up." She looked over at Anna and back at Orion. "Keep her safe too." Kameron stepped out of the unit and held Melissa's hand, since she didn't want to get separated from her if shit was about to go down.

"I really did want to see you again." She admitted to the

beautiful blonde next to her, since she was always honest, but more so if she was possibly going to die. "I want to do a lot of things with you again. Even be your girlfriend, if you want that. I just . . . don't want to see you get poisoned by a fucked up system just because you were with me."

"Yeah, I saw the princess." Melissa glanced back as they jogged through the hall. They had left her tattoo materials in Orion's unit, which she thought was a shame, but she was running anyway. "I don't want that either. And I don't want you hurt." She turned a corner and got yanked behind Fitch when she stopped, leaning awkwardly against her back briefly before starting off at a run again. "Do you really think we're gonna get out of here? Completely out of here?"

"I'm going to try my damndest to make it happen. So yeah, I do. I promised Kaz that this baby girl would have a full and happy life. I don't break promises." She glanced back at Melissa briefly before she continued toward her unit. Fortunately it wasn't that far from Orion's, even though Orion's was a private unit and Fitch was in a residential hall, so she had neighbors all around and a much smaller living space. "I get serious too fast. My last girlfriend told me that repeatedly. I can't really help it."

"Says the girl who hasn't let me touch her for weeks." She gave Fitch an accusatory look and slapped her ass as they got into Kameron's room. "Chronic problem, getting too serious too fast. Though the real problem, from my perspective, is not getting serious enough. That's usually my problem."

Kameron didn't respond before they got to her unit. Once she scanned her hand to get inside, she pulled Melissa in right behind her, since she didn't want her lingering in the hallway by herself. "I kept my distance because you seemed like you only wanted a good time. I enjoy a good time, but I have more to think about now. I know you said you wanted a girlfriend, but you sent the message with a fucking winky-face. I can't take that shit seriously."

She opened her small closet and pulled out two guns, one of which had secretly belonged to Kaz, since she stole one for him. She could wear them both. Kameron quickly grabbed both holsters and pulled off her shirt so that she could position the guns against the sides of her chest. She didn't want it to be obvious if she was going to truly have to fight someone. "I have a kid on the way. One who is probably going to be taking care of *me*, since I'm that messed up, but still. I'm not looking for a perpetual flirt."

Melissa stayed by the door, openly ogling Kameron as she took her shirt off and got herself prepared. "I had . . . a family back on Earth. A bunch of little brothers and sisters, half or full, cousins, the whole deal. I was the one mostly taking care of them. Since I was twelve. Next oldest under me was seven at the time." She shrugged, trying not to look as guilty as she felt. "I was relieved when I got accepted up here. Soon as I got here, it was the party I'd never been able to have. If we go back down, I don't know what kind of life I'm gonna have. Do I go back? Do I stay away and let the men I set my sisters up with handle things? These are questions I try not to ask. So I flirt instead. It's easier."

Kameron stopped once she heard the conflict and concern in Melissa's voice, and she turned toward her to look her in the eye. Melissa was only a short distance away from her, so she reached out to touch her cheek tenderly. Kameron was capable of tenderness, in the right moment with the right person. "If you don't want to go back, you don't have to. You can have whatever life you want to have. I'm sure if you still want to live like life is a party, you can do that. No one is going to say no to flirting with you, or sleeping with you. Men, women, or both."

Melissa shook her head against Kameron's touch, and smiled the short distance down to her. "I've had my share of both. Both is what's getting a lot of people on this station into trouble this past week. I don't want both. I want you." She leaned down and kissed Kameron again, a longer, lingering touch in spite of the repeated beeps from the emergency system urging people to follow instructions. "Once we get away from all this, I mean. I don't want you poisoned either."

After being kissed by Melissa it was hard for Kameron to get her head back into things. It felt like it had been far too long since she had properly been kissed. It seemed so much more intimate with just the two of them. Kameron pulled Melissa into another kiss, but Kam's responding kiss was blazing hot with need. "I want you too. You have no fucking idea."

"I'm pretty sure I do." She grinned and copped a feel, but then backed up toward the door, dragging Kameron along. "You, my dear, are not built for celibacy. Certainly not while pregnant. I can't even imagine. After this, you are in for a time like you haven't had in months, I promise you that."

Kameron was afraid to even entertain the idea, but she

desperately wanted to. "I need to grab my shirt before I go back out there." She said with a laugh as she broke away from Melissa to pick up her shirt off the floor. She looked at Melissa up against the door, and pulled on her shirt before she kissed the woman again, pressed against the door. "Definitely not built for celibacy." She said quickly before she bunched up Melissa's shirt in her hand, but she knew they needed to move. Her hormones were frying her brain, though. With her other hand she put it against the panel to open the door, but instead of letting them out, it turned red.

Melissa turned around and stared at the door. "What the hell? This isn't my unit. You're military, you're supposed to be . . . out shooting people, I thought?"

"You would think." Kameron let go of Melissa and pulled her communicator out of her back pocket. Other than the annoying overhead message, Kam hadn't gotten any further instructions. When she tried the door again, it wouldn't budge. Melissa's communicator was still asking her to return to her unit, but the damn door wouldn't move.

When Kameron asked for clarification by way of orders, she didn't get an immediate reply. When she did, it was loud in her unit.

Kameron Fitch. By order of the Initiative, you are now under lockdown for the safety of the Initiative and pending investigation. Do not attempt to escape. Should you make any such attempt, you will be considered a fugitive of the law.

"What the fuck? Pending investigation? This is bullshit!" Kameron tried to access anything else on her communicator, but the message was locked, and she had no access to anything or anyone else. Not a single friend. Not a single email, nothing.

"I'm locked out." Melissa said with a shiver to her voice as she tried the same things on her own communicator, looking back and forth between the communicator and the door as if it would help to keep looking at it. "Why did they . . . what is . . ." It was clear she had never been in a life and death situation before.

"Hey, it's okay." Kameron said as she grabbed Melissa's chin to force the woman to look at her. "There's no one in here with us, and we have food and what we need. Let's just move away from the door so we can watch in case anyone tries to come in here and start shit."

"O . . . okay." Melissa moved as Kameron told her to, and together they hunkered down behind the counter in the kitchen, once they had gathered some extra ammunition from Kameron's bedroom for her guns. "You think . . . I mean, you're not a fugitive. You're not a criminal. What would they be investigating you for? And they have to know I'm here. They didn't say anything about me being under investigation too."

"I don't know. They'll make up anything anymore." Kameron sat down on the floor next to Melissa and wrapped her arm around her shoulders to keep her close. She couldn't help but turn her head and bury her nose into Melissa's hair. "I've been talking a lot of shit about the Initiative. About getting away. They probably think I'm going to try and bomb the place or something."

Melissa visibly calmed once Kam pulled her close, and kissed the side of Kameron's neck just because she was close enough to do so. "Are you?"

"You think I'm going to blow this place up?" Kameron was worried that someone she cared about thought she was capable of being a thoughtless murderer. "I only shoot at people who deserve it, Liss. Not . . . I'm not . . ."

"I was doing some ink for one of the new batch guys the other day." She said a little sheepishly, since she had done her best to keep the fact that she was a tattoo artist a secret among her own friends. "He wouldn't tell me how he found out that I did ink, but he said he'd make things miserable for me if I didn't do a piece for him." She shrugged, obviously not that bothered by being used in whatever way people felt like using her. It was something she seemed well and truly accustomed to, on a number of levels.

"Anyway, he was talking about how everyone should just spread out over the whole station instead of just staying on this arm, all bunched up against each other. He said the whole place is deserted except for this arm and some maintenance personnel on a couple others. That means no bystanders."

She was whispering by the time she was finished, obviously not enthusiastic about the idea herself, but Kam had been the one who mentioned it. "If we get the people off who are . . . trapped in their units right now and scared for their lives because the Initiative is just . . . fucking with us, then there are worse things that could happen than blowing up the rest."

"I don't really have the power or resources to make that happen, but . . ." Kameron was whispering now too. "Orion knows some people, apparently. He's one of my best friends. He'll know what to do." Kameron held Melissa even closer to her and ran a hand down her back. "Why didn't you tell me about that fucker who forced you to ink him? I would have took him out at the fucking knees. No one should force you to do anything."

"It's not the first time." She shook her head and gave Kameron a quick kiss. "I knew what I was getting into, coming up here to space. No one has a choice what they do up here. Only the illusion of a choice. You've been military since you could handle a gun. You take orders. Even the non-military orbitals take orders and get in line. You're taught up here that you do that or terrible things happen, so it never surprises you. I had friends on Earth who told me about what it was like, and I chose it anyway. I just . . . didn't realize how far they would go."

"No one did." Kameron kissed Melissa in return until she realized maybe that was what they wanted. They wanted her to break orders. To take a person that wasn't her match so they could punish her for it. "They probably trapped us here so they could punish us for it later. I'm not your match."

Melissa considered that for a minute and just slumped back in the corner of the kitchen cabinets, pulling Kameron with her. "If they locked us in here to have us break the rules, then they're manipulating people just so they can punish them. How can anyone win with that?" She pulled Kameron in closely for another kiss. "And why even fight in a no-win situation?"

"They never wanted anything good for anyone except themselves." Kameron moaned under the kiss and she couldn't help but respond with a hungry kiss as a hand wandered to Melissa's breast. She wanted her so much, it was painful. Kameron knew she shouldn't. She knew she needed to abstain, for her baby's sake. But it was so hard . . .

There was a loud bang outside the door, which made both of them flinch, but there were no sounds to follow. No explanation, no further noises, no screaming. Just a lingering silence that seemed to go on forever before there was another thud, but farther away. "That doesn't sound good."

"Come on, let's move into the bedroom. If they're going to start blowing shit up, we need to be further away." She got up quickly and she pulled Melissa up after her. Kameron had no idea what was happening, but she was scared. They had to get out. Somehow.

* * * * *

Gordon listened to the security message again for what seemed like the hundredth time, and rolled his eyes before he continued working. It had been three hours since the lockdown began, and he had long since ceased to be freaked out by the constant noises outside in the hallway. If he had to put money on it, he imagined there were a dozen or so of the new batch of Initiates just running around with metal pipes banging on people's walls.

Pathetic, really.

He was lying across the bed with his head in Jessie's lap, working on a hologram display that was hanging in the air above his head. "They're up to eighty-seven percent of units locked down. Seven percent of us are from the new batch, so I'm guessing the highest we're gonna get is about ninety. It's a little impressive, actually. I thought it would take them longer to get everybody wrapped up like this."

"You don't seem very worried, but they can still do a lot of damage. They poisoned Anna." Jessie ran her fingers through his hair. Maybe the noise didn't bother him, but it made her flinch every so often. "They could gas us all right now if they wanted to."

"Which means they don't want to." He said calmly, then gave her the same look he'd been giving her for hours, which was to calm down. "If they wanted to kill us all, they've had every opportunity to do it. What they want is to play with us. Not kill us. Not yet, anyway." He switched over to a different view of the arm, which showed him the presence of several of the brass in their offices and private units. "They've got their lackeys out cleaning up stragglers and making noise while they all sit back and just . . . what, have a cigarette?"

"What is the point of bringing us up here? If they don't want to send us to Eleusis and they just want to research something, what is it? What is it they are trying to even accomplish? How does this help Eleusis, even if we aren't the ones going there?" Jessie was trying to make sense of senseless things and it was driving her crazier and crazier. "Why force us to be with other people, to make babies, if they just want to kill us? Are they going to trap us like animals and take our babies? I mean, what the hell is the end goal?"

Gordon shook his head, and turned back to look at Jessie with a sigh. "They're interested in a lot of things. Babies are one of them." He pushed himself up to sit beside her, and shoved the rest of the holograms out of the way so he could sit back next to her.

"Mostly, from what I've seen watching them these past few months, they want to run tests on behavior, test for responses to chemical prompts. All the hormones they've been pumping into the food, for example. Reason why a lot of people have been completely insatiable up here until they get pregnant." He pulled her in for a kiss and grinned afterward, even as a loud bang sounded in the hall. "They stopped pumping them into ours a week after you got knocked up, so this past couple months, the only excuse I can give for wanting you as much as I do is that I'm just a horny bastard."

She was worried as soon as he mentioned hormones, but she looked immediately relieved once he said that he was just horny. "I'm glad, then. I want you to want me." It was still a slow process of mental recovery for her, but she and Gordon were in a much better place than they had been. "I will die before they take our baby, though." Jessie put a hand on her stomach, even though there wasn't much there to touch. "How are we going to get out of here? How are we going to get in touch with anyone else?"

"Really? You're asking me that question? Do you know nothing about me after four months?" He still sounded light-hearted as he asked, then pulled his holographic interface a little closer and dug through it for a moment. A few seconds later, he gestured toward their front door, which was visible through the open door of their bedroom. A flick of the interface and the panel next to the door turned from red to the usual pale white glow that indicated it wasn't locked. Another flick put it back to red. He smiled over at her afterward and shrugged. "Technology is control. Control the technology and we control their control."

Jessie remained as close to him as possible as she rested her chin on his shoulder. "We should wait until they're not watching everyone so closely. I don't know how long that's going to take, but I don't want to be another target."

"Neither do I." He leaned down and kissed her head, putting one arm around her shoulders to hold her. "If they're initiating a lockdown like this, then they're not going to let up until they've gotten what they want. Considering what they want is going to take . . . at least eight more months to start producing results, that could be a while. They wanted to test behavioral patterns the way they've been doing for the past few months, but recent developments have rendered them unable to do that. So now they just lock down all the rats so they're all in tidy little cages."

"They did it to themselves." She said softly. "Can we get ahold of Anna and Orion still? They were going to investigate the Twist before she got sick."

"I was going to give her another day to recover before we actually sent her out. You think she'd be up for it?" He moved through his programming until he got to Anna and Orion's unit. The scans showed both of them inside, alone, with their vitals within acceptable ranges. More details were available for both of them, but Gordon wasn't particularly interested. "She's not running a fever anymore, at least. That's progress."

"Maybe one more day wouldn't hurt." She hoped they were alright, that Anna was alright. Jessie wasn't exactly friends with anyone other than Gordon, but she wanted friends. Even if she was a bitch. Hopefully some people eventually wouldn't mind how bitchy she was. "She's pregnant too. I sympathize with her just a little bit more than I otherwise would."

"She say anything about yours? You and your complete lack of any adverse pregnancy symptoms?" He chuckled and turned her so she could lean back against him as he started to massage her shoulders.

"She said it was probably because she was unfortunate enough to get knocked up with twins." Jessie shrugged, but she was becoming more and more relaxed as he worked on her shoulders. "I'm lucky, that's all."

Gordon laughed and kept working, since if they were going to be stuck in their unit, he wasn't going to spend the time keeping his hands off her. "I like you lucky. We're gonna make sure to keep you that way."

He pulled her hair back and moved it over to one side of her shoulders as she relaxed into him, then pulled his hologram closer again with one hand. "Most of the brass has been awake watching the show most of the day. They'll let things run in isolation tonight just to scare people, keep them in suspense, maybe even in the dark. I wouldn't put it past them. We can get Anna and Orion in motion later at night when they've got everything on blackout. They won't be looking for any movement, which means when I keep them from seeing everything, they won't be surprised."

"Do you think she'll stay with Orion?" Jessie eventually asked, since she knew it had no relevance to their plan, but she was still curious.

"I have no idea." He laughed again and shook his head behind her. "There are pools all over the station over how things are gonna pan out. I haven't put any money on anything yet, considering the fact that we plan on getting out of here, but if I had to . . ." he shrugged. "I would say they'll probably end up staying together. Logan and Mercury are a drug addiction that neither of them will ever go into rehab for, and Orion and Anna have too much fun for their own good most of the time. Neither of those things is something a sane person walks away from by choice."

"Interesting rationale." She leaned back into him as he continued massaging. "If I had ended up with one of the men I was supposed to be matched with, do you think I would have stayed? Would you have stayed with whoever you were supposed to have?"

"Would I have stayed with somebody I didn't choose? No. I came up here to steal the Twist and get home. And to be with you. Not to give myself blindly away to a stranger." He leaned down to kiss her neck. "As for the other men you were matched with, you know a couple of them. Pablo was one of them, the man who slept on the floor the other night because the Initiative locked him out of his husband's room."

"They were going to put me with a gay man?" She remembered vaguely he had shown her her possible matches before, but she didn't remember them now. She hadn't wanted him to show them to her then, so none of their faces stuck with her. "These tits don't work on gay men. That's not even fair. They are the only thing I have going for me."

"You have a lot of things going for you. The tits don't hurt, but they're far from your only virtue." He moved his hands down over her shoulders to get a good grasp on said virtues, then returned to his massage. "Any of them would have been lucky to have you with them. And any of them would've fallen in love with you. It's not hard."

"Not a gay man. That would have ended in heartbreak." Jessie sighed and turned her head so she could kiss his cheek. "It will be strange to go back to Earth, but I already miss it. This station is terrible. I want to feel the breeze again. The sun, maybe. As long as you're with me."

"Now you're getting knee-deep in my fantasies." He moved to lay her on her back on the bed and kissed her as he got comfortable. "House with a private balcony somewhere, you under the sun and the breeze. Oh, and if I didn't mention clothes, you can take that to have been a purposeful omission."

Jessie smiled and pulled him into another kiss. "Lockdown isn't terrible at all. It means that I get you all to myself and we don't have to work." She ran her fingers along the side of his face as she attempted to memorize everything about him, just in case something bad happened. "You should tell me more about your fantasies."

"Should I?" He smiled and kissed farther down her neck to her chest. "You've hit most of them already, actually. I had never done much in the shower, so there was plenty of that. I've got a few outdoor ones that we'll be sure to hit when we get back on the ground. Only thing missing is some good zero-gravity sex, but we may or may not have time to get around to that in what we've got left up here."

"Who says?" Jessie ran her fingers through his hair, and then tugged his head up off her chest with a little bit of effort. "You have the power to shut down this entire place, if you want to. It's artificially on the whole station anyway. Why not just turn it off?"

He looked at her like it was a joke at first. "Sure, it's artificial, but it's based on the station rotation. If we turn off the rotational maintenance thrusters . . ." his face got a little more serious as he thought about it, and he actually laughed a moment later. "If we turn those off, every system on the station goes haywire all at once. That'll be chaos."

"We have flashlights. As long as the oxygen doesn't go off. That would be bad." She pulled him into another kiss. She had seen his expression start scheming and she wanted to keep his attention on her instead of his plots. "I want to satisfy your fantasies. We'll be going back to Earth and we'll miss our chance."

He smiled under the kiss and moaned a little at the way she was holding onto him. "We'll do exactly that. Right before we leave this place. I want to be nailing you on the living room couch when the world turns upside down and the rest of the Consortium loses its mind trying to figure out why."

Jessie slid her hand down his pants so she could stroke him a couple of times. "We're not going to do it now?" She was disappointed, since she wanted to please him and she definitely wanted to feel pleased with herself. "That's sad." Jessie pulled her hand back out slowly. "We're locked in here."

"Not for long." He reassured her with a grin, and ripped at the buttons on the front of her flimsy shirt. There wasn't much point getting dressed if they weren't going to be leaving the unit. "If they succeed tonight, we could leave as early as tomorrow. I know I'm ready for that, what about you?"

"I'm ready for anything. I trust you. You'll keep me safe. Our baby too." Jessie shivered once he exposed her by pulling away the shirt. Apparently she had decided a bra wasn't necessary and her nipples puckered at being exposed. "You said you were going to wait another day. They might need the extra time to recover. Either way, it means we're going home soon. Anything is better than this place."

"*Most* things are better than this place." He smiled as he pulled away a little to kiss her lips again. "There are *some* worse things, though. We're just not gonna go anywhere near any of those."

Jessie looked into his eyes between kisses and she ran her fingers along the side of his face. "As long as I don't have to go back to my family, I don't care where we go. My family hates me. Granted, they're not trying to kill me, but they hate me. And my sister would probably try to sleep with you just to get revenge on me, if she found out about me."

"I've seen pictures of your sister. She doesn't interest me."

She opened her mouth to remind him that her sister was gorgeous even if she was a raging bitch, but she decided not to say anything about it. "You make it sound like no one could steal you away."

"What am I, a wallet? A wad of cash? No, no one could steal me away. Stealing me would imply I don't have a choice, and I do. I chose you." He resumed his kisses along her chest with worshipful sighs at the softness of her.

Jessie moaned softly as he kissed down her chest, she loved feeling his lips on her skin. She loved having him close. "I love you so much." She pulled him up so that she could kiss his lips and then whisper directly into his ear. "Jason. I love you, Jason."

It had been a very rare occurrence for her to call him by his real name, but it never failed to get a reaction out of him. His kisses got more intense, his touch on her got heavier, and he started ripping at her pants the same way he had ripped at her shirt. He might not have been on hormones supplied by the Initiative, but that clearly wasn't stopping him from being crazy for her.

* * * * *

Almost immediately after Kameron and Melissa left, Anna thought for sure Orion would receive further instruction to rush out and save someone. He was far ahead of her in military status, even though she could handle herself with a gun.

When they didn't hear anything, Anna got even more nervous. She was scared. Scared enough to want to run and do something, but the moment they tried to leave, they were denied. They couldn't get out. At all. "We're trapped?"

Orion looked just as confused as she was, and he tried the door himself after her handprint was denied, only to have the same response. "What the hell . . ." He tried to do a manual override on the door by way of the handle embedded in the frame above it, but even though the override handle moved, it did exactly nothing to loosen the door. "What is . . . Computer, what is this? Why can't we leave?"

Security protocols in place. Please remain in your unit until further instructions are received.

"Yeah, like I've got a fucking choice? The door is barred!"

Security protocols in place. Please remain . . .

"I heard you the first time, shut the hell up." Orion glared at the door and Anna could see his hand lingering near his gun, but he didn't actually draw it. He knew it would do no good. "Why would they lock us in? That makes no damn sense. If we're under attack, we need to be able to move, go report for defense. Not . . . sit around here and do nothing."

"Is there some way to tell if we are actually under attack?" Anna went through her communicator, and fortunately, she was able to contact other people. At the moment. She sent a message to Logan to see if he could tell her anything, but she didn't know if he would respond.

It took a few minutes for Logan to answer, but the messages came short and clipped when he finally did. *Just got back to our unit when the message came through. Tried to leave, can't. Banging in the hallways. No one's reporting in. Where are you?*

Never left the unit after I got sick. At least he was responding, that

570

meant he wasn't dead. She definitely didn't want him to be dead. *We're both stuck too. Even the override won't work.*

Tried it here too. No response from anyone except you. I don't know what's happening.

They want us to be trapped. Anna sent off the message and she received another emergency notification on her communicator, which just made her want to turn it off. She didn't even believe there was an emergency at this point. "Logan says they're trapped too. We aren't the only ones."

"Then everybody is being locked down." He was still clearly worried at first as he said so, but he looked at the door again and looked more curious than anything. "Or just . . . the problematic ones? If it's an attack, I should be out there. You should be out there. Kicking ass. Not sitting in here. Logan should be out there dealing with people."

"He's the one that started all of this, and I voted to support it. The Initiative hates us right now." Anna sighed and groaned a little, since she was feeling nauseous again. "I need a drink and some meds. I hate this."

Orion went immediately into their kitchen and punched in the requisition for the medicine Anna had been taking for the past two days to combat the food poisoning, but all he got in response was an angry-sounding beep from the machine. "What the . . . this was dispensed just four hours ago. Come on, send it through."

Anna looked back at him and went to sit down so she wouldn't throw up. "Why isn't it working? Why won't it give you any medication?" Was the Initiative truly trying to kill her? Or torture her, in the very least?

Orion leaned on the counter, looking like he wanted to maim something. "Well, you did say they hate us right now. I guess you were right." He looked over at her in concern and sighed. "Have you got anything left from earlier? What kind of food do we have stashed?"

"I might have some medication left over in the bedroom. We have a ton of food, though. I made a big order before I got sick, since we were going to cook together." Anna glanced over at the refrigeration block, and she hoped for a moment it was still running, she wouldn't put it past the Initiative to ruin their food just to make them starve.

"This is so fucked up. And I didn't even get my tattoos." She whined as she followed him slowly into the bedroom and sat down on the edge of the bed on her side. "I thought I was coming up here to live, not to die."

"Living is exactly what we're gonna do." Orion said as he joined her in the bedroom, walking over to her side of the bed to sit next to her. "If they wanted us dead, they could have pulled the air and been done with it. But clearly they don't. Which means they're not done with us yet. There's still gonna be time to get out of here."

Anna leaned into Orion and put aside her communicator as soon as he sat down next to her. She closed her eyes when he wrapped his arms around her, and she snuggled in close to him. "I'm glad you're here. It would have fucking sucked to be trapped in here alone. You've been sweet to take care of me."

"Well, I have ulterior motives. I want you to live. I'm selfish like that."

"I want you to live too." Anna sat there listening to his steady heartbeat as he held her against his chest. "How is your arm?"

"It hurts. But it wasn't that solid a tattoo, I've had worse. It'll be fine by tomorrow." He sighed and tried to think of any other way to make light of the situation, but it was a dire one. There weren't many ways around that. "She left her stuff. I could still do you if you wanted some ink. No promises on how good it would be, though."

"It's alright. I can wait longer. I want it to be a surprise, anyway." Anna looked over at his arm, but his new tattoo was covered up by his shirt. She tugged at the bottom of his shirt to try and convince him to take it off. "Can I see it again?"

He hesitated, but only because he had just gotten the shirt on. Even so, it didn't seem like they were going anywhere fast. "Yeah, of course. It belongs to you anyway." He pulled his shirt off over his head, and was careful of the new tattoo.

"I really do love it." Anna said softly as she looked it over, since it was beautiful, even if it was also simple. "Thank you for getting it for me. I already love staring at you, this gives me even more of an excuse."

He smiled as she took it in, and leaned in to kiss her forehead. "You're not a temporary thing for me. We might have said before we would be, or we planned to be, but you're not. You're part of my life, and I like you that way."

"I like you in my life too, Orion." Anna ran her hands over his bare skin, since she couldn't ever stop herself when he was bare-chested in front of her. Anna traced her fingers over the previous ink he had so she wouldn't irritate a fresh wound.

She was quiet for a long time, holding onto Orion as if he was her only lifeline left. "I hope you get to meet my family. I don't know what all this shit is going to boil down to, but I hope you do. Someday, maybe. It feels like so long since I've seen them last, but it's only been a little less than half a year. It feels like a lifetime."

"Feels that way for me too." He laid back on the bed and brought her with him. "I was used to hanging out with Khadijah every other day. Called my parents every couple weeks when I remembered. I haven't heard anything I trust from any of them for at least two months. They don't even know they're gonna be grandparents again yet, I'm betting."

"None of my family knows, I didn't even try to send a message. It would not have gone through anyway." She was especially sad about missing out on updated information about her family, but she tried not to spend too much time thinking about it. "Did you think about what we should name him?"

He gave a noncommittal shrug as another round of banging echoed outside their door, this time more violent. It subsided within a few bangs and Orion shook his head again. "I don't know. My parents gave me my name because my father had a great-uncle he was fond of named Orion, and he died the year I was born. They named me in his memory. I don't have any dying great-uncles that I'm aware of, so that kind of screws me out of that."

He looked incredibly depressed about that for just long enough to let the sarcasm settle in before going on. "It should be something that goes with Lynnette, though. Not, like, Lynnette and . . . Wakizashi or Ibrahim or something like that. They're twins, it should be obvious that they're a package deal, whatever it is."

"People back home usually have some kind of theme. Like with my family, my parents just started at the beginning of the alphabet and worked their way as far as they could. Logan and his siblings are Ls, except for the older brother he had that died as a baby." She wasn't dwelling on Logan, though. She was focused on Orion. "I totally thought you were named after the constellation because you live up here in space."

"My great-great-uncle's generation were all constellations. It was a fad that went around at the time on their station. Happens every now and then up here, so you're not wrong. I've also known people who do actually start at Mercury and get all the way through all the planets, but that was because they got clearance to adopt a bunch of orphans. They went for a second round and had to go past Pluto and Persephone all the way back to Luna and Ceres. People do it all the time."

"So maybe we can name him after a constellation, then. An L constellation to go with Lynnette?" She just couldn't stop touching him, and she moved so she could kiss him before he could respond.

"Well, we could name him Libra, but he's not gonna be born in the right month, I don't think. Pretty sure those are October. I don't think he'd appreciate Lyra either. Or Lupus. It's never Lupus."

"Leo sounds pretty badass. You know, a lion and everything." Anna leaned back so she could look up into his eyes. "What do you think?"

"Leo does sound badass." He smiled at her, and reached over to caress her neck, since he wasn't sure how she was feeling and wasn't sure whether they should actually start anything while people were banging down the hallways outside. "I like it."

Since she managed to find leftover medication, Anna was feeling okay enough to slide into Orion's lap, facing him. She took both hands and put them on his face so she could keep his gaze. "I love you. I don't know what they're going to do to us, but I want you to know that I choose you. I want to be with you. You make me so happy, even though you drive me crazy sometimes. I want to have ten babies with you and have a family with you."

She remembered the conversation she had with Logan about the future, and she remembered it was hard for her to have it. It was pulling at strings that weren't really there. It was wanting to hold onto something that kept them close to home. But now she wasn't thinking about any of that. She was thinking about Orion and a bright future with him, if they could get away.

He kissed her as she said so and rolled with her on the bed to fold her against him. "I love you too. I can supply the ten babies, that's not a problem at all. There's plenty of constellations to get to after Leo."

"I think we should do that." She held onto him as tightly as she could and buried her face into his bare chest. It felt so good to just be with him, to not feel so twisted up and conflicted. She knew when she saw Logan again she would feel twisted up and guilty, but she was wondering if Logan would thank her. He was happier with Mercury. At least, that's what she believed and that was what she was going to tell herself. "We should sign up for the official marriage thing. I don't want to give them any ideas I would dare be matched with someone else again. You're it for me. Once you find a cock like yours, you keep it." She teased, in spite of everything.

The fact that she was capable of cracking a joke like that made Orion smile, and he kissed her deeply. "It's all yours, baby. Right now, as a matter of fact. Cock before sign-up. The cock needs you right now a whole lot more than the paperwork does."

"You are so needy." She tore off his clothes, since it was easier to finish getting him undressed. He was halfway there already. Anna would love to have said cock in her mouth, but considering her currently-sensitive gag reflex, she didn't want to ruin the moment. "I hope you are always needy for me."

"The day I say no, please put a tag on my toe and burn my body." He groaned under the way she tore at him, loving the expert touch of her hands and the heat of her body against him. "Because I'll have died or gone so stupid as to no longer have a reason to live."

Anna giggled, but she was quick to get undressed. "I love feeling your muscles against my body. Everything about you is so unbelievably sexy. You know that, right? It's like I'm drawn to you."

"I'm glad you like what you see." He pulled her down onto her back on the bed and leaned over her to kiss her thoroughly before he drew back to let a free hand explore her body. "I like what I see, what I feel. I love these." He leaned down to tease her nipples with his tongue, then pulled away with a self-assured grin once he teased a moan from her. "I love the fact that you can kick ass with an ass as fine as yours, that you keep on coming back for more every time. The fact that everything is a challenge you're determined to kick the shit out of."

Anna couldn't respond as he teased her nipples with his tongue, especially because they were far more sensitive than she was used to. In a good way. "I bet . . . people wonder how we make it work." He was still a giant and she was a shorter woman than Mercury. It had to look strange, but she couldn't care less even though she wondered how they made it work half the time too.

That made him laugh, and he laid down next to her on the bed and pulled her into him so her back was against his chest, giving him the freedom to explore every part of her with his hands as her backside came back flush with his abs. It was exactly where he wanted her, and on account of the size difference she was talking about, it was the easiest position for both of them. "We have our ways. But I can tell you, nobody's wondering about you and me. Carl and Aiko took that cake and ate it a long fucking time ago."

"You're right." She moaned as his large hands devoured her body. It was definitely a new way to battle nausea, since her body was so distracted by wanting and need that she couldn't think about much else. "Do you . . . do you think Melissa would tattoo . . . some rings for us?"

He had one arm under her head to be her pillow, but he took his left hand off her for long enough to examine it as if it had to undergo inspection before it could take ink. He took hers as well, to look over the same space. She had not worn her wedding ring for the past couple days since she'd gotten sick, but the indentation was still there. "Yeah, I think she would."

"I still want a real one. But a permanent one will do." Anna knitted her fingers with his after he was done examining her hand. "I'm sorry for hurting you. For being so unsure for so long. I . . . I never wanted to hurt you. I promise. I just thought for the longest time that you were waiting for Mercury."

She felt him nod against the back of her shoulder as he curled up against her a little more. She could feel the effect she had on him clearly by the way they were positioned, and as soon as the heat of him touched her, his kisses against her skin and the grip of his hands on her turned into an inferno. "Do I look like a guy who's waiting for anybody?"

Anna growled as soon as she could feel him teasing her entrance, and as he started to slide inside of her, she moaned softly. "Thank god you aren't waiting. Cuz I'm incredibly impatient." She whimpered as he pushed further inside of her, slowly, since it was a delicious slowness. "Fuck. I love your cock."

She could feel him smile against her neck as he kissed everywhere he could reach, rocking her against him to keep her completely at his mercy. "I love that dirty mouth of yours." He captured her completely in a rough caress, moving one long-fingered hand down between her legs to tease her mercilessly as he rocked inside her. "And everything you do with it."

"Mmmmm." She agreed with everything he said, since she would say anything to keep him doing exactly what he was doing. "For the rest . . . of our lives. This mouth . . . will do whatever you fucking want."

It was easy to lose himself in Anna. Easy to lose all awareness of the world around them, the situation they were in, the heavy feeling of something waiting to harm them somewhere else that lingered over everything and everyone aboard the station. She made it easy to ignore, to focus completely on her to the exclusion of all else.

Every once in a while, more banging would sound in the hallway outside, threatening to distract them from each other, but if anything, it only redoubled Orion's desire to drive her insane with pleasure just to keep their minds off everything else. Every time the sound came from outside, Orion just drove himself into her harder or deeper, his hands grasping her so tight it was like he was daring her to get away, even if neither of them wanted to. It was their life. Their world. It was going to be dangerous, it was going to be difficult, but it was theirs. That was all he needed or wanted.

Anna was sure she was going to be bruised when Orion was done with her, but she couldn't find it in her to care. He was fucking her so hard that all she could think about was how it felt to be owned and possessed by him in the rawness of the moment, and before she even knew to prepare, she was blindsided by a powerful orgasm that had her crying out in pleasure, her whole body shaking.

When Orion reached his own, the world seemed to stop, and he clutched her against him so tight she could feel his heartbeat slamming against her spine. They were both slick with sweat and shaking as they struggled for breath, but his arms refused to let her go. The banging outside in the hall no longer succeeded in bothering either of them, and it was all he could do to move his face slightly and kiss her shoulder.

"You," he began breathlessly, his voice just above a whisper, "are perfect."

She moaned again, enjoying the feel of his hold, like she was the last person in the world that mattered to him. "So are you." Anna said between gasps, since she was recovering very slowly, though she was enjoying every ripple of pleasure. "Husband."

30

Not knowing had put Logan into something between rage and apathy. The absolute silence in the unit immediately following the lockdown had put him so much on edge that he had taken to pacing the huge windows of their unit like a wild cat penned up in a zoo. He paced for the better part of an hour, then, oddly, went to sleep, with instructions to wake him up if anything whatsoever happened.

When he woke up on his own a few hours later, he seemed angry that nothing had come along to merit a wake-up.

He could see the time ticking by on a wall panel, pressing them close to midnight, even though the Earth below them was lit by daylight. No ships were coming or going, so far as Logan could see, and nothing about the rest of the station's appearance led him to believe that anything whatsoever was actually wrong. It was infuriating, and his patience had long since departed. The sleep he'd gotten had done exactly nothing for his temper.

"Here, drink this." Mercury slid a glass flask that still looked too orbital to be anything close to Earth-made, but she was trying to be a calm, supportive presence even when it seemed like Logan wanted to blow up the entire station. "I brought some of it with me from Seven. I have a small collection of alcohol that was given to me as gifts by proud fathers of new babies. I thought I could at least use it for cleaning purposes in an emergency, but you need it more than the plans I had for it. This one is as close to whiskey as we make up here."

He looked over at her as she offered the flask, and uncapped it to take a sip. It was strong stuff, he would give it that, but there was always something missing when it came to space-made food or alcohol. Shine had been the only exception, and that was just because it was so quintessentially unearthly to begin with. "It's not bad, actually. Thank you." He took another sip and handed it back to her, so that she could try it if she wanted or put it back if she didn't.

"I've never been fond of silence." He growled through a sigh. It was contrary to his own demeanor for the past few hours, but Logan was aware of the contradiction. "You would think I would be good at it, living a hundred kilometers from anywhere back on Earth, but even there, something was going on. Liam or Larissa coming and going, a phone going off constantly, schoolwork that needed to be done, farm equipment grumbling somewhere, even just the wind. This is just . . . nothing."

They had been under radio silence ever since his first conversation with Anna, and he had no way of knowing what was happening anywhere else. They could have been the last two people alive on the station, abandoned in the black, and they would never know.

"I wish there was something I could do to get us out." Mercury looked around, but she had taken the lockdown much differently. Apparently her patients could still contact her at least, and she still had her research. She had taken it as a forced time to sit down and study, and so she wasn't as angry about it, even if she was worried about what it might mean. "You could help me go through research, if that doesn't sound completely boring. It's the only thing I can do here that feels worthwhile and constructive."

It was the first thing that sounded at all like a solution to him, and he agreed that it would get his mind off the current situation. Even Mercury's patients clearly had their communications monitored in some way, since they were all locked down as well, but Logan couldn't get any other details out of them about the rest of the station. Everyone seemed just as clueless as he was.

He turned away from the window and headed down into the living area with her, toward the terminal she set up. "Your research is always more important than just about anything else I can think of that's going on up here." He went to her chair and drew her into his lap so he could watch what she was doing. "Where are you?"

Mercury was glad to be back in his lap again, but she was happier that he was willing to sit with her and help, even if it wasn't his area. "I'm looking for genetic markers. I pulled up patterns from the previous research where babies were born CV-immune. Since I have the power to do it here, I had genetic maps created for everyone I've run blood tests for. It's the majority of the Initiative." She smiled just a little, since she knew that she had gotten away with something.

"I figured it would be interesting to compare our first wave with the research of centuries. It would be nice if we could figure out a way to protect Eleusis from that kind of devastation." She pulled up an unnamed map and started pointing to certain flags that told her the person was not CV-immune, but was a carrier for potential CV-immunity.

He watched her work for a while with his hands on her waist, touching her idly as he always did. She was working, but she was working within the rules he had established for their home, in nothing but the bathrobe he permitted her while she was in the unit. It made it easy to touch her as he pleased, though he tried to keep it from being too distracting.

"That doesn't make much sense, according to your own scans. Or maybe I just don't know enough about it." He leaned in a little bit past her, and shook his head. "The part of the genome that controls immunity and immune response characteristics is nowhere near those. The rest of that area looks like the genes are concerned with toxin processing. Is that just different genes being found in different places that do the same thing? Immune on more than one chromosome?"

Mercury shook her head slowly, but only because she was uncertain. "Every geneticist I've ever been able to work with says that the body interprets CV as a neurological toxin, and you can see that here, there are flags by the toxin processors. That tells me that they are not immune. If you look at the other part of the map, where the immune response is, there are no flags. That's why it looks like this person is a carrier for immunity, but is not immune. Their body has the same toxin-response in the presence of CV, but the actual virus doesn't alter the immune response of the genome. This person most likely died of cancer. Most people do, who have CV. Their immune system works incredibly well, but the toxin response alters the body's immune response. It messes things up monumentally. That's why it is so brutal."

Logan just looked even more confused after that explanation, but he wasn't a doctor. He hadn't really expected to fully understand when he'd asked. "Is CV the only virus the body interprets as a neurotoxin? I've never heard of that before. Usually a virus is a virus. White blood cells, bone marrow overdrive, antibodies, all the usual immune system response."

"Usually a virus is a virus, you're right. That's one of the biggest mysteries of CV, why it behaves the way it does, independently from anything else any doctors have ever seen before. That's why there's no cure. It behaves so differently." Mercury leaned forward and pulled up another genetic map. "This one is yours."

Logan's eyebrows went up a little and he looked at it intently, though it wasn't likely he was going to understand much of what he saw. The entire code was represented in some kind of standard notation that Mercury could obviously navigate, but he wasn't likely to have much success.

"I look complicated." He saw her check for the immune status previously, though, so he managed to find at least one set of those flags, and gave a 'hmph' at the information that was displayed. "So by this, it looks like I carry some of the traits for dealing with the toxin, but no actual immunity markers."

Mercury nodded and she looked his over carefully before she pulled up another. "Here's mine. I never thought to look at my own before, but I think that's because I knew I'm genetically altered. My parents went to a certified family planner, like most people do, but they had the pull to choose just about everything about me. Including something like near-immunity. As close as anyone has been able to get. If I'm ever exposed, it will kill me slower than most."

Logan was fascinated by what he was seeing, especially since her record was more annotated than most. Because she had been more or less designed by hand, the different genetic markers that had been intentionally altered were flagged, for research purposes. It was a fairly large percentage of her genome, or at least it seemed that way to Logan.

"So this is what you really look like naked." He smiled at the idea and looked through some of the markers that had been intentionally changed at her conception. "That's . . . really strange. It looks like they turned up your neurotoxin processing, same as mine, but they actually turned your immune system . . . down. Didn't they? Am I reading that wrong?"

"No, that's right. My immune system isn't as good as yours. But I think that's what delays the effects of CV. My weaker immune system, while still great, won't go into overdrive right away in the presence of CV."

Logan was more confused by what he saw and something about it felt wrong, but he knew Mercury shared that feeling, even though neither of them knew exactly why. "With the rest of the cases you've surveyed, you said before you couldn't find a pattern or a precise means of saying 'yes, this is it, this is the way to become completely immune to CV.' Is that still true with everything you've gotten up here from the Initiative?"

"Ever since I've gotten here, I've had little time to do research or to even go through everything I have. It's been expecting mothers and any other medical emergency that pops up." She stared at her own map and sighed. "It's no wonder I haven't gotten pregnant. Stress can play a huge factor in preventing a wanted pregnancy."

"You've been busy, that's an understatement." They all were going a little crazy, but Logan knew that was what the Initiative wanted. Keep them busy, keep them focused on the issues that didn't matter so they would eventually fold on the ones that did.

"Computer. Take the displayed information and ignore neurotoxin processing factors. Show us the strength of genetic immune factors alone compared against a life expectancy due to CV." He had an idea forming, but it sounded crazy even in his own mind, so he wasn't sure how it would actually display in the data.

Mercury watched as the display changed, and even though he was still touching her, she seemed more or less oblivious to it as she watched the information process and change. She kept up both of their genetic maps so that she could look them over at the same time once the information was processed. "Looks like I would live to fifty-five. You would live to thirty-seven. Approximately."

"That's just the two of us, though. Everybody else . . ." He looked over the rest of the data that was cycling through, and there wasn't much of a trend aside from a few outliers. "Most of those with more moderate immune systems like yours live longer, but that still only pushes it to maybe forty-five in some places. And there's some in here with ridiculously high immune systems that only live to thirty-four." He could see why most people completely gave up with CV research. "Which doesn't make any sense. The better the disease response, you would think the longer the life expectancy."

He swiped away the results when his head started to hurt, and he had a different question in mind. "Computer, now ignore immune system response completely and display strength of neurotoxin response alone compared against CV-exposed life expectancy." It took the system a moment to spin through the huge amounts of data Mercury had uncovered, but as it populated the display, Logan sat back and watched.

It was a much more direct correlation, and that gave him a sense of anxiety like a pit in his stomach as he watched it grow more and more well-defined the more data was added to it.

Mercury started to feel sick as well, since it looked like the more toxin response, the stronger the strain of CV, the shorter the life. "That doesn't really make any sense. CV is everywhere down there, there can't be stronger concentrations in some places than others, can there? Unless there's something *creating* the CV, but no research has found any links to plants or animals." She shook her head and as she started swiping through the information, an error appeared in a bright red hologram.

Data corrupted. Error 43721.

Logan narrowed his eyes at the error, but he didn't try to help her dismiss it or retrieve the data. "Processing power sufficient to calculate orbital adjustments and maintain the ballast systems of this entire station, keep us spinning, keep us out of the way of every other object hurtling through the black up here, and the system errors out on a spreadsheet?" He didn't even sound surprised as he commented on the absurdity of it. "Not likely."

When Mercury tried to pull the information back it wouldn't load, and she sighed as she looked at the images attempting to load. Her mind was still busy trying to think about what could create CV instead of CV being a spontaneously existing virus, but her concentration was shattered when she heard yelling in the hallway outside of the unit. "Maybe we should take a break right now. I still have a backup drive that I can look into later."

He agreed quickly and got up when the yelling continued. He didn't have much by way of weapons in the unit with them, but he had acquired a gun early on in his tenure as the head of the Executive Council. He went to retrieve it and stayed with Mercury near the door to the bedroom, watching the door to their unit until the yelling and banging outside moved down the hall.

It was maddening not to know any details of what was happening, but no single word or name came through the walls, only noise. "Eventually," he said into the silence that followed, both of them still waiting to see if anything else would come of the disturbance, "they're going to have to have some kind of play.

Whether that's to try and kill us or try to just reassure us to death the way they have been doing, I have no idea."

"None of my patients have been harmed, at least it's not showing any change in their health when I ask for a scan." She went to get a bottle of water for herself, drinking it slowly before she brought one to Logan. Just as she handed off the water to him, she received a message. Instead of reading it privately, she asked the computer to put it up on the wall.

Dr. Mercury Finnegan,

This is a courtesy message to let you know the Consortium has received information about the recent dissolution of your marriage. Official notes have been received, and your personal information will be updated within forty-eight hours.

Mercury didn't understand why she was getting a notification from the Consortium. "What does the Consortium have to do with anything? Their laws are different than ours. The dissolution doesn't even go into effect until we go to Eleusis, but regardless . . . I didn't file for an official divorce with the Consortium."

Logan was holding his own communicator as she spoke, and he looked up at her and gave his own message the same instruction.

Mr. Logan Bickford,

This is a courtesy message to let you know the Consortium has received information about the recent dissolution of your marriage. Official notes have been received, and your personal information will be updated within forty-eight hours.

He looked through his communicator for a moment afterward until he pulled up Anna's name, and her file displayed in a hologram so Mercury could see it. At first, nothing looked different, but soon the system updated itself with current information. "Anna Al-Jabbar."

"Wait, what?" Mercury said as she stared at the information and moved closer to Logan. "That can't be right. They would have told us, right? I mean, I thought the plan was to do nothing right now . . ."

"It was." Logan stared at the image, and felt something . . . fold in on him, like a house falling in on itself just as the last needed support beam was supposed to fall into place. "That was the plan. Do nothing, let things continue . . ." he shook his head and finally turned away from the image, since he didn't want to look at it any longer. "It's either fake and the Consortium is trying to manipulate us with it, which I doubt, since we'd be able to find out about it later, or it's real. Which means they've decided the plan isn't for them."

Mercury looked at her own message a little longer, but she swiped it away carefully and looked down at her hands. "I'm sorry." She said softly, since she knew he felt differently about it than she did. She felt relieved, a little. Mercury loved Orion, but clearly he knew a life together wasn't what she wanted. Maybe he hadn't wanted it either. It was hard to know. "I'm sorry that she decided to change her mind about the plan. Orion seemed to understand what I wanted was different than what he wanted or could provide, but I know it was different for you and Anna."

Logan didn't answer at first, and although there was no further sound of disturbance from outside in the hall, he didn't put away the gun he had picked up as he crossed the room. "It is different." He agreed, looking out the massive windows again at the rest of the universe. He clenched his fists a few times, and tapped the gun against his leg, but eventually he just placed the gun down on a table beside the window.

"I thought I would feel different when I lost her. There was a moment, the first time. Looking back on it, I knew I had lost her, I just didn't know how. Maybe it's different because with Anna, I know how." He shook his head and looked out at the moon, which was as bright as a pale sun out their windows. "I thought I would be . . . sad."

That definitely wasn't the response she was expecting to hear from Logan, since she thought she was about to watch a man break down in front of her eyes. Slowly she walked up behind him and stood just behind him as he stared out the window. "You're not sad? I thought she was the woman you waited your whole life for?"

He shook his head, though he didn't turn around to look at her. "If I had waited my whole life for her, I wouldn't have let myself get married the first time." There was a distance to his stare that had nothing to do with the infinity of the universe in front of him, but he eventually shook his head. "She wouldn't have made that choice now if she wasn't sure about it. The only reason for it would be if she knew he could make her happier."

Mercury reached tentatively to touch the back of his arm for a moment, but her hand dropped away after that. He hadn't chosen her, but she wondered if he would have. If he wanted to. He was forever impossible to read. "I want you, Logan. I wanted to make that choice. Even though our plan was to not make a choice."

He still didn't turn around right away after her declaration, but eventually he put his back to the window to face her and pulled her into a kiss as he stood against the black of space. "I love you, Mercury. I would have chosen to be with you, when the time came for it. Anna is happier with Orion, and you . . ." His hands moved over her body in ways that were incapable of being anything but sexual, no matter what kind of situation they found themselves in or what mood. When his eyes met hers, the storm in them was raging, but they were absolutely focused on her. "You understand me better than I think anyone ever has. Even myself, sometimes. I want you, I want this that we have together."

Mercury felt her eyes burning with tears, happy tears, as she held tightly to him and kissed him harder. "I love you too." She replied against his lips before she kissed him again. "I want a family together, and a future. I'll be yours." Mercury felt the hot tears slide down her cheeks, but she couldn't be embarrassed about it. She was happy and overcome with the reality in front of her. "Only yours."

He held her for a long time to let her tears subside, his huge arms wrapped around her back to crush her against him. She wasn't a small woman, but she still fit perfectly against him, the warmth and softness of her nestled against him in all the right ways. Life felt easier with Mercury. Simpler, in some ways, but infinitely more deliciously complicated in others. His head swam with the scent of her, and every single time he touched her, he wanted more. When her tears quieted and the moment between them turned calm, he turned his face to kiss her neck and whisper in her ear.

"Picture the home we're going to have." He said quietly, walking her backward toward the bed. "Tell me what you see."

Mercury closed her eyes, since he was walking her backward and if she trusted him to do that, she trusted him to lead her with her eyes closed. "I imagine a house with a large kitchen and paintings and photography on the walls. We can see other houses in the distance, but we're more or less on our own in the middle of the grassy plains of Eleusis." She shivered as his beard continued to tickle along her skin as he kissed her everywhere except her mouth. "Lots of rooms for lots of children." She opened her eyes and she looked into his stormy eyes. "If you want them too."

"I expect them." He said flatly, in the same tone that accompanied all of his expectations of her. "However many come our way, I want them all." They got to the bed and he pushed her back lightly to sit on it in front of him, but remained standing to look down in her eyes. "I want them to grow up knowing better than to come near Mom and Dad's room when the door is locked. I want them running wild all over the countryside and claiming estates on Eleusis that even their great-grandchildren will have space enough to expand on. I want kids who grow up telling everyone they date that they want a relationship as strong as their mom and dad's."

"I want that too." She stared up into his grey eyes and her hands gripped the edge of the bed as she got lost in his gaze. "I'm still working on the children. I thought the first would be inside of me already."

"So did I." He brushed her hair back over her shoulders to get a better look at her face, and left rough caresses over her cheeks and neck. "It hasn't been for lack of trying. They'll come soon."

"They?" She said with a smirk as she reached up to caress his face, since she wanted to touch him as much as he touched her. "How many are you planning to put in there?"

"I was thinking twins to start." He leaned down over her to lay her back on the bed, and put a single knee up beside her as he began untying her robe. "If you handle those easily enough, we'll try triplets later on." He undid the knot holding her bathrobe in place but left the fabric covering her as his hand moved up to cup her breasts through it, teasing her with long, lingering caresses. "Production of children takes time, and I want as many little pieces of you in the world as possible."

Mercury smiled brighter because it really meant that he cherished her. Wanting her was one thing. She wanted him to not only want her physically, but to want everything about her. His touch showed her clearly the physical nature of their relationship was already solid. "Red hair, accent, and all?"

"I'm not even going to talk the whole time they're growing up. Want to make sure the accent is solid before I start giving them a drawl." He finally smiled at that possibility and leaned down to kiss her warmly as his hands roamed over her. She was his, and every chance he got, he made sure she and her body knew it.

"I like your drawl." She said after a whimper, but he was teasing her by not exposing her skin, only touching her through the fabric. "I love everything about you, Logan Bickford." Mercury arched her body slightly with every touch, since she was feeling needy. "You still haven't asked me to read dirty words out loud to you yet."

That widened his grin, and he leaned over her to kiss along her collarbone. "There's a few things I want you doing right now. Reading isn't one of them."

Mercury's voice was breathy as he kissed along her collarbone, his beard scratching along her skin, which made her body feel even more electric with desire. "What do you want me to do, Sir?"

He moved his kisses up to her lips briefly, but ran his hand up her arm to weave his fingers through hers. "This hand is mine." He said between kisses. "It works for me now, not for you." He pulled her hand down and held it as he guided her palm over her body, moving down over her breasts to the soft fabric barely managing to cover the heat between her thighs. He aligned his fingers with hers and parted the fabric deftly before setting her fingers to slow, steady work.

"Close your eyes and imagine that house. That field on Eleusis we're gonna make our own. The darker sky, the darker sun. I want you to think of this when we get there. I want you to think that this is where you're going to fuck your husband for the rest of your life."

Mercury moaned loudly, not only from his control over her hand, but also because he had called himself her husband. They probably didn't talk about a lot of things the way couples should, but she hoped that they would talk more now, that he would feel more free with her than before. "I think about you all the time." She finally spoke, but she was squirming beneath his commanding touch, since her fingers were driving her crazy. "There's no way that will change on Eleusis."

He kept the pace of her own touch slow just so he could watch the world crumble in her eyes, but it had been too stressful a day and there was too much uncertainty in him to allow for too much teasing on his part. Still, he would hold off as long as he could. That was part of the fun of their game, for both of them. Even if the game had become their entire lives.

"I might permit you a little more freedom as my wife. If I'm feeling generous." He wove his own fingers against hers as she stroked her core, mingling their touches until it was difficult for her body to tell which of them was doing what. "A wife should be free to touch her husband more often than just when he gives her permission. Whenever you want me, from now on, you have permission to come and let me know you want me elsewhere."

"I'm already addicted to you . . . this might become a problem." Mercury's moans were louder as she felt his fingers working her, and it wouldn't be long before he had pushed her over the edge. All of his touching had more than prepared her. Also, sitting in a thin robe made her aware of every surface against her skin when she sat down or moved about the unit, which always had her feeling sensitive. "Like now. I want you now."

"I couldn't tell." He grinned against the next kiss he gave her, and slowed the movements of her hand torturously just to keep her squirming. "You have me." He promised, reaching down between them to push down the shorts he wore, exposing the entirety of himself in the process. "You have me from now until you can't even walk. I'm yours."

Mercury was exposed and needy, and she couldn't help but think back to what things were like for her only a year ago. She never would have imagined herself in such a position, certainly, never would have imagined such a relationship, but she knew it was because she hadn't had the slightest concept of what she could have.

Mercury looked up at Logan as he teased her heated core with the tip of his rigid cock, and she felt love along with everything else. "I love you, Logan." She said between gasps, because she didn't ever want to miss the chance to say it to him. No matter what the moment.

He laid her bare as the words lived between them in the kisses they shared, and only once she was free of the robe did he look back in her eyes. "I love you too, Mercury."

When he took her, it was different. The entire world was different, and the warmth between them had expanded to envelop them completely. They had been with each other hundreds of times, in all manner of ways, but that moment turned purely sensual, purely ecstatic, as they fully enjoyed each other without limits, without doubts, without second-guesses, for the first time.

They were no longer a distraction to each other, no longer something on the side or something temporary. She was his in every way he could have her, and he was hers, in every way he could be had. It made everything about them different, everything about the way they felt the world around them.

* * * *

Maria watched the vitals in Logan's unit and smirked as she looked back at Stephen. "I told you they would crack. Both of them." She plopped down into a comfy chair in her own unit, drinking celebratory wine while everyone else was locked away in their units. "The taste of sweet success."

Stephen shook his head, since things hadn't evolved quite as he had expected. "I really thought Bickford would crack first. I'm impressed." He looked over the marital status declarations again and took a sip of his own wine before he looked over at Maria. "So this proves what, exactly, aside from your capacity for manipulation? Plug me full of pheromones and put me in a room with a woman that gorgeous, I'm likely to fall in love too."

"She *is* incredibly gorgeous." Maria commented almost longingly before answering his question. "It proves that we can push people to adapt, if we select the right people. This is a man who was once nearly suicidal down on Earth. A man who was picked up out of that depression by his best friend, who he then married and then *left* without looking back. He'd be a fucking good leader if he wasn't so violent."

Maria just tsked and sighed. "The point of it was adaptability for most of them, given the amount of push and the end goal of Eleusis remaining as the light at the end of the tunnel. Even Mercury has changed exponentially. We need that in our doctors too."

"And you expect to be able to globalize these results?" He paced, which he knew annoyed her, but it certainly didn't stop him. He walked behind her chair with his wine in one hand and the other trailing absently along her shoulders and neck in a casual touch. "Dealing with a couple thousand people in an environment that you completely control is one thing. Taking something like this global is a very different proposition."

"Not if we have control over that world in the first place. No one gets to Eleusis unless we allow it. That means we can handpick everyone we want to bring to further colonize the place. We need workers, but we need workers who will adapt no matter what. We also need babies, babies that are born in safe situations that we can take and raise. I explained this to you. This is the ideal situation, especially now. Now that they're all trapped, and by their own doing."

"Controlling entry is one thing, I'm talking about when they get there." He snapped back, since he knew she hated having to explain things twice. "If they're malleable and changeable here in prep, they might adapt in ways you don't want once they arrive on Eleusis. Every revolution in history was begun by citizens who were once obedient. Eleusis is a big place. What's to stop some of them from deciding they want to run away from the homestead and try things on their own?"

"With what materials? They have only a fraction of knowledge of the kinds of plants and animals on Eleusis, the beasts especially. They would die if they ran off on their own. More than half of our current test subjects were raised in a station where every desire was one tap away. Even the doctors deal with mostly routine medical procedures, not an arm being ripped off by a giant Eleusis beast. They will depend on the people who know the most."

"Until they've lived there for a few years and acquired some of this knowledge for themselves. You're thinking individuals and batches. I'm thinking about the long-term." He went to stand by the footstool of the massive chair she had plopped herself into, and put one bare foot up onto it to look down on her. "Molding people into what we want them to be, pounding them until they're as flexible as we want them, is a wonderful thing, and impressive. But too much longer under these kinds of constraints and people are going to start breaking. Even if they're happy most of the time. We need something to keep them on the hook."

"Let's show them more of Eleusis, then." She looked up at him from her chair. He was attractive, but sometimes she hated how attracted she was to him. He was an asshole most of the time, even if he was smart and they worked well together. Maria also had a twinge of feelings for him. "We have permission to do so."

"What do you have in mind?" He didn't get any closer to her, pretending to enjoy his wine without being affected by her, but the truth was that he could never quite get enough of her. He knew perfectly well what kinds of addictions he was prone to, and Maria satisfied nearly every one of them. He just had to be careful never to let her know exactly how satisfied he was with her. That would only end badly.

"Let's give them more detailed photos of Eleusis, send out new samples of some of the vegetation. We can blame the quarantine on that, we can say that we don't know how they'll physically react, and we have to keep any allergic potential separated from the rest of the group." Maria kept her eyes fixed on his, mostly. She looked down a few times. "Do you enjoy hovering over me like this?"

"Sometimes." He said without apology. The way she was lying back on the chair with her feet tucked up against her left her in one of the most passive positions possible. "You already know I enjoy you when you're vulnerable. Even if you like to think that isn't the case as often as it is."

Maria rolled her eyes and stretched one of her legs to push back on him with her bare foot. "I'm not vulnerable. We're discussing options and future tactical moves with our current wave of citizens. Mercury was the vulnerable one. Did you see the spike of norepinephrine when she was waiting to see how Logan would respond to the news about Anna? She thought he was going to drop her, or at least be furious about Anna. I am not like that."

"If you were, you'd be boring." He leaned against her foot as she pushed at him, and took her ankle in one hand to remove it from his chest before he pressed a little closer to her. "The only thing I've ever known you to be afraid of is yourself, and even then, only when you're feeling very, very introspective."

Maria raised an eyebrow as he pushed closer to her. "I'm learning not to be afraid of myself. If I was, we wouldn't have so many toys to play with." She motioned toward different vital screens floating in the air around their unit. "What's our next move, then? Other than giving them something more to look toward. Who is our next in-depth study? You know, for us?"

"Giving them more of Eleusis to hang onto will keep them in line for a while, I think. Just to be safe and explain some of the chaos, we'll have to take about thirty to forty of them and either relocate them or toss them out an airlock. Call them casualties of incautious dealings with foreign substances, et cetera. Encourage a healthy fear of the unknown."

He put his wine down on the table next to her chair and took the leg he had removed and wrapped it around one side of his waist as he leaned in closer to her. "That and the remaining structural projects should keep everyone on the hook until we get closer to the end of some of the important pregnancies."

He put a hand on the back of the chair above her as he looked down into her eyes, leaving one hand to wander over her as he saw fit. They were celebrating, after all. "As for us, we should take one of the people we plan to get rid of for our next trials. See if we can keep this round of study from being fatal."

She grabbed onto his hand and stopped it, because she knew he liked it when she resisted. "I don't want one of them. I want someone else. I want someone important to play with. They're all going to be dead soon anyway."

"Someone important?" He pushed against her hand anyway, and he was stronger than she was, after all, but he didn't force his touch on her too quickly. They were each other's plaything first and foremost, after all. "That would create some chaos in the ranks, no matter who we chose, but that could be fun too."

He took the hand she'd resisted with and moved it against her will to the flimsy shorts he wore. She was a psychiatrist, and he knew how much she enjoyed knowing the effect she had on him, manipulation or otherwise. "If we wait until after we lift the lockdown, we can take one that I've been meaning to go after for a very, very long time. When I got here, I intended to have her all to myself for a while, but it seems like she's important when it comes to producing some babies for our trials. So we'll have to wait until after she's been knocked up."

"I suppose I can wait. For you." She said the last with a smirk as she wrapped her hand around the length of him firmly and stroked him once through his shorts before she tried to pull her hand away. "You can't tempt me. No means no."

"Only when I say it does." He caught her wrist again, a little painfully, and put her hand back where she had just begun to tease him. "We're celebrating, and I intend to celebrate for the rest of the night and into the morning. Nobody else out there is going anywhere."

"You intend to celebrate, do you?" She stroked him a few more times through his shorts. "What if I just tease you and leave you like that? Wanting and needing and with a stiff, painful cock?"

"You won't be leaving anything." He promised confidently, since he knew her better than that, and she knew him better than to think that was possible. "The mood I'm in, I would break both your legs if you tried to run."

"One of my legs is already around your waist. You don't need to break it. I have nice legs." Maria moved her hand to yank his shorts down so she could tease his bare cock. "I didn't know you were in a mood. Other than to celebrate." Maria ran her hand up and down his length roughly to get a groan out of him. "Are you already thinking about what you are going to do?"

"Only to you." His hand finally moved down to take hold of the flimsy shirt she was wearing, and he bunched a fistful of it tightly to arch her back toward him. "One toy at a time, unless it's the one we're sharing." He looked over at the side of their room, where there was a collection of bottles and instruments, all a part of the work they did together. "One of these days, we'll have it down to a point where you can try it without lingering side effects. I'm looking forward to that."

Maria licked her lips and looked at his as he held her close by her shirt. "Should we try again now?"

Stephen grinned, and nodded toward the bottled liquid. "You should. You've got more of a tolerance for it than I do. Go with a single milligram this time. Two had you laid out for a day and a half last time. And even though I know *you* enjoyed that, I'm a selfish bastard, and I want you to myself."

"You are selfish." She moved away from him once he mentioned the dosage, even though she had to pry his fingers off of her shirt. Maria went to the collection of bottles and pulled a dropper out of one to place a single drop on her tongue before she looked back at him. "But we have that in common."

31

It was an entire day and more that Anna and Orion remained on lockdown before they heard anything from anyone else, other than the loud noises on the outside, which eventually subsided. They weren't expecting to hear from anyone other than some kind of leadership, but just as they finished their dinner, Anna saw a request for video communication from Gordon White. "I guess I should put clothes on before I answer that, right?"

"Yes, please." Orion said sarcastically from the other side of the couch, where he also ate naked. They had no reason to put on clothes, after all. They had no need to put any barriers between them. "Those tits are mine, and nobody else is allowed even a peek, let alone a video conference."

Anna smirked and went to grab a shirt off the floor quickly. She pulled it over her head and hastily pulled on her underwear but decided to go pants-less. Gordon would only see her upper-body anyway. When she answered she knew she looked crazy, but she didn't care. Sex hair had never been on any list of items for which she was willing to apologize.

"Well, lookie here. The one person who can get through an all-out lockdown is Mr. White."

"Yes, well, you did miss the memo I sent out to the universe that I sit on the pantheon of Gods of Technology. I was so sure I included you on that message. How forgetful of me." Gordon rolled his eyes at her but kept walking. He appeared to be strolling down a corridor, even though it was supposed to be the middle of the night. Jessie was walking beside him, smiling at Anna and her sex-hair in the hologram.

"I saw the change of marital status for you and Orion in the station registry. Mazel tov. I'm going to do you and your husband both a favor and not ask any more questions about it. Are the two of you relatively well-rested and ready to get to work?"

"Well-rested?" She laughed and glanced over at Orion before

she shrugged. "Probably not the most well-rested. But I'm pretty damn sore, so a break to get out and work might be a good idea. My husband is hung like a horse." She knew Gordon didn't give a shit, but she wanted to brag. And she had to get used to referring to Orion as her husband. It was still so very new.

"I'm sure I needed that information." Gordon's tone was dry enough that the eye-roll was implied. "Fortunately, men like your husband and myself have the advantage of having been tampered with genetically in the process of our conception. Such tampering generally brings along with it some enhanced capacities for size and endurance on both our parts. Fathers, such as they are, are typically charitable enough in the design stages of their son's life to want him to have a bigger dick than they did."

"If we could, however, move past your husband's equine cock for a moment, Jessie and I will be arriving shortly with presents, so put some pants on. Dark shades of grey are best for the kind of work I have in mind for you, but low sound trumps low visibility."

"Moving past the cock, then. Temporarily." Anna looked at the hologram of Gordon and stood up a little straighter, even though she was conscious not to expose her lady-parts. "Grey pants. Got it. See you soon, I guess. We are ready for whatever you have to throw at us."

"I'm glad you think so." Gordon said with a knowing smile as the hologram winked out.

Orion shook his head but was already in motion, grabbing clothes out of their closet. He tossed her a pair of uniform pants that would conceal her well enough and pulled on a pair of the same for himself. "Why is it every time I talk to that guy, I feel like I'm choosing the lesser of two evils rather than working for the greater good?"

"We probably are. But he's the only one who has something solid to get us off this godforsaken station. Logan has his own plan, but fuck if I know anything about it." Clearly she was still angry about Logan throwing her to the wolves, but she didn't regret her decision. Orion was her husband. That was the end of it. "So we go with White. Doing nothing is a guaranteed death sentence for us, our babies, and everyone else."

"I know the argument. Still doesn't mean I have to be happy about it." He finished suiting up and pulled on his boots. "The lesser of two evils is usually done with people once they've served their purpose. I just don't want to do whatever it is he needs us to do and get left out in the cold. The cold here means the cold, dark vacuum of space-y nothingness."

"We're not going to be left anywhere." Anna finished getting dressed. "Leo and Lynnette are going to come into some kind of world, Earth or Eleusis, and they're going to live a long life. Because of us."

"If for no other reason than that their mother is just that much of a badass." He smiled down at her, obviously still nervous, but less so with her there next to him.

As she looked him over, though, moving uncomfortably inside the same uniform she had seen him wear nearly every day for four months, it was increasingly obvious that he wasn't uncomfortable with whatever they were actually going to be asked to do, just with the fact that for the first time in his life he was becoming a rebel against the only authority he had ever served.

"Have I ever told you that you look good in uniform?" He rested a hand along her neck as he leaned down to kiss her, wanting anything to take away the uneasiness he felt.

"Mmmmm." She responded as she continued kissing him while both of her hands held his face down to hers. When the kiss broke, she kept his face close. "I'll keep the uniform just for you, big guy." Anna whispered and kissed him once more before she leaned back just enough to look into his depthless eyes. "We're doing the right thing. Even if it doesn't feel that way. They've just conditioned you to make you feel like this is wrong. It's not."

Orion nodded, his hands resting on her waist. "I get that. Still gonna take me a while to get my . . ." he was cut off by a click from the doorway as their door unlocked and he reflexively pulled her behind him, just in case whoever was coming in wasn't friendly.

Thankfully, the door opened to admit Gordon and Jessie, each of them carrying a sturdy-looking case. He held the door open for Jessie so she could get inside, then closed and locked it behind them, even though Orion knew the man shouldn't have had the print permissions to do so. He really hadn't been kidding about his technological godhood. "Glad to see you were speedy about getting dressed. The night is young, but it's not getting any younger."

Anna glanced at Jessie who gave her a nod, before she looked at Gordon again. "Whatever this is, you better not be sending us into a trap. Because if I get out alive from a trap, I'm coming after you first. We're in this to survive, and you're a sketchy kind of guy. Though I'm sure you know that."

"Sketchy is one of the nicer things I've been called, so thank you for that." He laid his case on the couch next to Jessie's once she set hers down, and opened both to let Anna and Orion get a look at the contents.

The cases were lined with what looked like small camera modules and data cores, along with a pair of sleek guns that weren't of any kind that Anna had ever used. "I'm not sending you into a trap unless you count a place that's going to be high-surveillance and heavy guards a trap. There's a room I need you to get into on Arm Two. Once you're inside, plant cameras where they won't be found, set the bugs on every server you can find, and try not to get yourselves killed."

He took a deep breath as he looked back and forth between them. "There's no easy way to say this, so I'm glad you're both standing up. The Consortium has what's called a Twist. They have three of them. Two of them are here on this station. They fold space between here and Eleusis. It's not a year-long trip, it's instantaneous. I need you to confirm which rooms the two they have are in, and plant the bugs to confirm guard routes and surveillance. You have . . ." he made a show of looking at his wrist, even though it was bare, "exactly thirty seconds to freak the fuck out, then you're gonna need to get to work."

Anna couldn't even respond, since that was a hell of a lot of information to take in all at once. She was trying not to let herself freak out, but all of a sudden she was supposed to dodge armed guards and use guns she'd never used, and what the fuck did he say about bending space? "You know that sounds like a load of bullshit, right?"

"You live on a space station. Four hundred meters from here, you're practically weightless. How do you think your life story would've sounded to someone from about five hundred years ago?" There was no trace on Gordon's face of evidence that he was lying in any way, and he picked up the sleek gun, cocked it once with a lever along the side, and handed it to her by the grip.

"Energy pistol. Packs a hell of a burn, try not to point it at glass unless you want it to explode." He was looking over the equipment as he allowed the two of them to process what he'd told them, more than a little distracted himself.

"One of the Twists should be rather large, maybe ten meters across and four to five high. It'll be surrounded by a metal and composite frame, and the room will probably be hot. It utilizes a tremendous amount of power. If it's active, you'll hear a loud humming that feels like somebody's playing music on high volume. If it's idle, the open space will be braced with silicate bars in a lattice pattern like you're looking through a honeycomb."

All that detail just made Orion more suspicious, and he hung back even after he took his own pistol. "That's an awful lot of details about something you need other people to go find. You know all this how?"

Gordon worked in the case for another moment before answering the question, and didn't look up at anyone when he did. "Because my brother designed it."

He handed a few more small camera units to Anna and waited for her and Orion to get their gear stowed before he closed the case and looked back up at the two of them. "I'll send directions to your communicators. Use your earpieces and keep an open line, I'll be on the wire with you the whole time."

Jessie looked at Orion and Anna and took a deep breath. "Look, the only way we can get to Eleusis is if we get one of those things and bust the hell out of this place. It sounds dangerous, but being here is just as deadly as doing something about it. Right now, we're all definitely going to die. If we get the Twist, we might not die. So as risky as it sounds, at least it's not certain death."

Orion was still reeling from the information that Eleusis wasn't light years away anymore, but right around the corner. Even so, he secured the bugs they'd been given in a few of his pockets and checked the feel of the gun in one of the holsters of his uniform.

"Well, when you put it like that, it all just seems so simple." He glared at Gordon when the man finally looked up again and retrieved his communicator from a nearby table, fitting the earpiece for it in place so that it would be comfortable and secure. "When this is all over, I've got a bone to pick with your brother. He beat me out of that competition."

"You're welcome to take it up with him as you like." Gordon headed back toward the door. "When you see him, tell him I've been looking for him to see whether he's alive or dead. Haven't known for a few years now."

Both Anna and Jessie looked over at Gordon, clearly thinking along the same lines. The man had secrets, and both women knew the secrets were probably far too many. Anna finished loading herself up with all the illegal tech that she could carry, and she looked up at Orion with a sigh. "Well, are you ready? You can worry about your former competition later. He's not as hot as you are, anyway. Guaranteed."

That made Orion smile, but if the joke was funny or true, Gordon didn't react either way. "Jessie and I are gonna head back to our unit before the hall monitors catch us up and out of bed at such an indecent time of night. Head for the Deck 17 maintenance conduit linkup and find a place to hide near the hatch until I can get you access." He looked back and forth between them before they went out into the hallway with a sigh. "Thank you. Don't get shot. See you in a couple of hours."

Once Gordon and Jessie were gone, Anna took Orion's hand and held it firmly, even though his hand entirely enveloped hers easily. "Come on. It's a good thing you're freakishly tall, and I'm still skinny enough to be flexible. Otherwise he'd have to do this dangerous shit himself."

"He doesn't seem like the type." It was strange to be walking through halls they normally navigated without fear and suddenly have the feeling that they were doing something incredibly wrong, but Orion knew no one would exactly be out roaming the halls looking for them. The brass still thought everyone was under lockdown, so there was certainly no reason to be monitoring passageways too closely.

Still, he checked around corners and up stairwells twice as they made their way down to the deck where Gordon had directed them. "Saying goes, there's two kinds of people. Officers and grunts. You and me do our fair share of grunting. Types like White typically don't get their own hands dirty, they just get off on telling other people what kind of dirt to get into."

"I'm not a grunt." She countered with a shake of the head, since she didn't like the idea of someone else always being in charge of her life. "I just don't mind getting my hands dirty to save my own ass. Yours too." Anna gave him a smirk as she glanced over at said ass. "Looks good, babe."

That got him smiling again as they turned the last corner, and the light next to the hatch they were looking for was already green. Gordon worked fast. "Speaking of asses, up you go, baby." He got over to the corner of the stairwell and let her ahead of him to hoist her up by her hips until she could reach the hatch and yank it open. They had been in a similar position only a few hours earlier with her ass in his face, but he much preferred the version of the maneuver that didn't involve clothes.

Anna felt her heart in her throat as soon as they had the hatch open and she was staring up at the ventilation into the darkness of the hole. She easily pulled herself up into it from the height Orion held her up, but she still hesitated before she was in completely. Anna sat there in the vent for a moment before she peeked down at Orion. "Come on up." She said softly. "These vents are amazingly clean." If she pretended like everything wasn't terrifying, maybe it wouldn't be.

"They should be." He jumped up and pulled himself in, closing the hatch behind him. It was a much tighter fit for him than it had been for her, but he was going to be crawling most of the way anyway. "Only things that ever come through here most of the time are the service drones that keep them swept. They're not really meant for humans except under emergency conditions."

He started down the conduit at her side, though it was slow going for them. The trip between arms was going to take most of the night by itself. "Place is roomier than my first apartment, though, gotta give it that."

"Where did you live, a coffin?" She hoped it was a joke, but she put nothing past the peculiarities of orbital life. "I thought the bedroom I had back home was small. I lived in the attic, since it was the only private place in the whole house. I couldn't have boys up there, though." She added with a half-hearted laugh. "Too many snuck in, but my dad would always know. Most of them hit their heads on the ceiling. It left a mark." Anna shrugged. "Boys have reflex reactions when your tongue goes a little crazy."

"Sadist. You probably chose the location for exactly that reason." They reached a part of the conduit where it became easier for him to pull himself along a pipe running above them than to continue to crawl along the edge of the vent, so he flipped himself upside down and made better progress. "Your poor downstairs siblings. Bet they got pretty tired of their ceiling getting thumped."

"Maybe I chose that location for multiple reasons, but I will say that my excuse was privacy." She looked up at him pulling himself along a pipe and shook her head as she kept crawling. "Half my siblings were too young to understand anything and were fast asleep before I brought anyone home. The rest of them learned to sleep with a radio on if I went somewhere after dinner." Anna looked away from him as she thought about her siblings, and it felt like years since she had heard from them last. "I miss them so much."

Orion felt bad, briefly, that he didn't feel the same kinds of pangs for his family as she did for hers. Khadi he missed, but that was just because she had run away from their parents and spent most of her adolescence and brief adult life bumming around on Three with him. She was the only one of his family he really knew all that well.

"You'll see them again soon, especially if this actually works." He paused when a jet of air sounded nearby but continued cautiously, pointing to a space just ahead of Anna and below her hands on the floor. "If you want to say hi to the abyss, now's your chance."

Some of the drones that cleaned the passage had collected at a catch-point and were depositing the miniscule amounts of dust and debris that accumulated in the ventilation system. The debris was being condensed systematically into packets and ejected through a very tiny airlock into open space, where Anna could see through a visor-sized window that they were being quickly vaporized by the station's own micro-defenses.

Every time she had looked through the family telescope as a child at some of the stations, it always seemed like they were a constant lightning storm of tiny strikes, appearing to short-circuit themselves. Instead, they were a constant dance of automated violence in the name of self-protection. "I'm sure they'll all be pissed that you haven't written in a while. Should be interesting to hear what they have to say about all the shit that's gone down up here."

"If they're still alright." She stared out the small window as she paused for a moment but kept going once she knew it was okay to proceed. "I don't know what fucked up shit the Consortium could have done by now. And they live on a farm that's relatively secluded. Even if they disappeared, I don't know how many people would go looking." She shook her head. "I want you to meet them. But even if we make it down to Earth, I don't think it would be safe to contact our families. The Consortium would expect us to reach out to them."

"There's still gotta be ways of making sure they're alright.

Even if we can't reach out to them directly." He swung back down from the pipe when it ended and groaned at the discovery that the conduit was still too narrow for them to crouch and move. "And I'm sure they're just as worried about you as you are about them."

"Well, they'll definitely be in for a surprise if I ever get the chance to take you home." Anna said as she looked over at him again. "Can I crawl underneath you when you crawl? Are you tall enough for that?" She was trying to give him more room, but it wasn't like she was able to expand the space.

"You get under me like that, I'm gonna forget we're here to work, doesn't matter how tight the space is." He smiled at her and stopped in the conduit for just a moment to pull her into a kiss. They were working, but that didn't mean he could keep his hands off her for very long. "I'm alright, just a few more bulkheads. We're coming up on the other side past this service module."

Anna smiled at him after the kiss, and at the idea of distracting him from danger by being underneath him. "Hopefully it wouldn't be the last time I get to be underneath you."

"I thought you were sore?" He grinned back at her and groaned as they reached a maintenance hub on the far end of the conduit where he could pull himself out of the narrow opening and actually stand completely upright, though the space was still limited.

"I am. But the possibility of dying makes me want to ignore that fact." Anna jumped down after him, but from the limited space, they were pressed together anyway. She took advantage of it by holding onto him for a moment. "I'm scared, babe."

He could see the exit hatch not far away, but he stayed with her in the near-darkness of the maintenance lights and ran his hands over her back. "If there's one thing I've learned about you these past months, Anna, it's that there's nothing you can't do. I mean that both as dirty as possible and in the more profound, pep-talk kind of way that's hopefully more helpful right this second. All we need to do is get in here and get eyes on what White is after. It's the middle of the night. We keep eyes open in the back of our heads, we'll be fine. Don't start getting nervous about every noise if it's not helping you focus."

Anna pressed her head to his chest for a moment and sighed as she heard his heartbeat. It was a slow, steady rhythm that had helped her fall asleep too many times to count. Orion was a constant, even when the waters were rough. "Get in there. Focus.

We can do this."

* * * * *

Gordon watched the surveillance feeds that he disabled for Anna and Orion's benefit, as he worked quickly across the entirety of his display all at once. In spite of the frenzy of activity, he didn't look stressed, only focused. Disabling the cameras and replacing them with dummy feeds was so simple he could have done it half-asleep, and he was being kept well-caffeinated by Jessie nearby. Their two covert agents seemed to be having a relatively easy time of things, but they had a long way to go to reach the sector where Gordon believed the Twist was housed.

"His name was Charles." He said abruptly. "I'm sorry I haven't talked more about him. Or the rest of my brothers. They don't come up much in conversation, and I usually try not to think about them, as a rule. It wasn't something I was trying to keep secret from you."

"So many things are a secret, though. Even if you say that you aren't keeping me in the dark on purpose." Jessie sat next to him and watched. "You don't talk about them very much, but obviously they still mean something to you. You don't talk about anything very much, and when you do, it's always veiled conversation. Never the entire truth in even one sentence."

He adjusted a few of the surveillance cameras along the route that Orion and Anna were taking, and gave them the all-clear before he settled back to watch with a sigh. "Most of the time, I don't talk about things that are true because I'm not a fan of them. It's easier to say nothing." He took her hand briefly, since Orion and Anna were proceeding cautiously and it would hopefully be a while before he was needed again.

"I grew up in a lab until I was six. My brothers and I were part of a project for genetic alterations that aren't on your typical genetic manipulation menu, even up here. I ran away from the lab and got caught by the Consortium. They found the rest of the lab and the rest of my brothers because of me. There are six of us still alive, that I know of. If everything goes to plan, you'll meet at least one of them." He took a deep breath, unaccustomed to actually unburdening himself, even if it still wasn't with the full truth all at once.

"I got away from the Consortium when I was ten and left the

rest of them behind, the ones that hadn't already escaped themselves. I spent a few years looking for the older ones who escaped before me, but I couldn't find them. I wandered on my own on the fringes until I was sixteen. I met a woman who took me in. Gave me my first home, even if it wasn't what most people would call decent. Her name was Hyacinth."

It was a lot to take in at once, but Jessie was listening carefully. She knew it wasn't often that Gordon . . . Jason . . . was actually forthcoming about the details of his life. "I'm glad you were smart enough to keep yourself away from them. That you *are* smart enough, I mean. We never would have met otherwise." She said with a small smile. "Hyacinth, huh? Like your data core?"

He nodded, but still wasn't quite looking at her. "She was . . . a good friend to me. She taught me a lot. I've been told that my opinion of her is what they used to call Stockholm Syndrome, considering the fact that I was sixteen at the time and she was thirty, but I still can't bring myself to think badly of her."

"I met her in St. Louis, trying to get away from New York and make my own way. Went home with her to the northern Dakota region. She never had children, never had a husband, an only child of a couple of recluses. Kept her own few acres out in the middle of nowhere, grew her own food, went down to St. Louis only when she really needed to do some resupplying. It was a good place to be off the grid. She died just before I turned nineteen."

"I guess I'm glad that she was good to you and kept you safe." Jessie knew that older people with younger adults wasn't unheard of, but a thirty year old woman with a sixteen year old was . . . well, wrong. Jessie typically kept her interests to those her age, though her brother-in-law had been several years older than both her and her sister. "I'm older than you are."

He actually smiled and turned to give her a look, but the meaning behind it was far from clear. "Anyway, after she died, I stayed there for a few months, using some of the skills she let me develop for technology while I was there. Tracked down my brothers, the ones that had gotten away, and went to find them. I met up with the rest of the resistance. I've been with them, more or less, ever since."

"Did you actually like being with someone who was twice your age? I mean, she could have been your mother." Clearly Jessie was stuck on the idea of the woman being so much older than he was, though teens behaving like adults wasn't that uncommon on

Earth. Life expectancies of forty to fifty years did that to the world. "It would have been better for you to stay in St. Louis. That was closer to me."

"I was a little young for touring vineyards." He laughed again, and shook his head. "I didn't know any different. Not until later. I never saw people together in the lab. Just the researchers and the surgeons. I saw people together out in the rest of the world, but I didn't really understand it. Not until her. I didn't know it was weird. Or how wrong it was. I just knew she wanted to teach me, and it was . . . fine with me to be taught."

"I guess you wouldn't have known, huh?" Jessie turned her attention to the screen again and just stared at it without saying anything. "My family didn't like me, but only when it was clear that I was a disappointment. At least I had a stable family, though. A place to call home. Reliable food, education. I'm sorry you didn't have that."

His smile disappeared slowly at that comment, and shook his head afterward. "I don't want you to feel sorry for me. That's part of why I don't talk about it. I've been my brothers' project for years. I can't stand the look in their eyes every time they see me. Even Tatyana felt sorry for me, and I'm not sure I've ever seen her feel sorry for another living person. I don't want that."

Jessie turned just enough to kiss him on his cheek. "When people care about someone else, they feel pain on their behalf. I love you. It makes me feel all sorts of emotions, including ones that make me wish you didn't have to live on the run when you were a kid. It doesn't mean that I am going to treat you any differently. I like learning more about you. No one actually wants to be in love with a mystery. That's too dangerous."

He turned to kiss her and rested his face against hers afterward. "We're all in love with a mystery. That's what's so dangerous about loving someone in the first place. Someday I'll think I know everything about you and you'll know everything about me, but we'll still surprise each other. I'll just try to make them smaller surprises as time goes on." He turned back to watch Anna and Orion, and made a few adjustments in the surveillance on their behalf, smiling as he did. "I've still got a few pretty big ones up my sleeve, though, don't worry. Can't let you get too bored with me just yet."

"Bored? You knocked me up. I can't get bored from now on. This little girl won't let that happen, I'm sure." Jessie stole another kiss before she let him move away from her. "But I'll take whatever I can as long as you're still with me."

"I'm interested in going nowhere else." He smiled as he glanced down at her stomach with a faraway look in his eyes. Being a parent was an entirely foreign concept to him, since he hadn't had parents of his own. He just hoped he could keep their daughter safe. "Hold position, you two. There's movement one corridor away from you. Doesn't seem to be inbound, but hold and wait for my mark."

Anna and Orion stopped moving and Jessie watched carefully as Gordon monitored the screen. She held her breath until he gave them the clear to start moving again. "Do you think that they'll be able to do this? Without getting caught? None of us are exactly trained for this, no matter how much we want to be involved."

"Orion is." Gordon watched them move. "His training is mostly theoretical, of course, but he's been drilled enough to have the right instincts. As for Anna, she grew up sneaking into and out of other people's houses. She knows how not to get caught when she doesn't want to be. But there's only so far a person *can* be trained for this. No one's ever invaded a space station before. Not for a century, since the last of the pirate syndicates was taken down. People aren't trained for station assaults anymore. Which is why they did so terribly a couple months ago."

"How do you know what you know?" Jessie asked when she looked at him again. "You said you were up here before. How did you get up here? Why were you here?"

His expression grew more serious and he nodded up once to indicate the rest of the station around them. "This is where they brought me. When I was six. This is where I stayed, until the Consortium decided I would be more useful down on the ground, as bait for my brothers. I was on Arm Four. Where they are now."

He indicated the screen in front of him. "I know those maintenance tunnels because I crawled through them trying to escape more than once. I know those labs, those corridors. They've done a little remodeling for the Twist power generators, but not much." He pointed at the screen where Anna and Orion hid themselves for a moment to make sure the coast was clear. "I hid right there, in that same alcove, once when I was eight. It's the closest I ever got to reaching the lifts that would take me to the dock. I thought if I could somehow get up there, I would magically be able to get away. Didn't work that way."

"Do you know who your parents are? I mean, the people who you came from. You came from someone, right? You had to, somewhere down the line."

Gordon shook his head, and switched over a last set of surveillance equipment to his feed, his eyes still on Anna and Orion as they moved through the hostile corridors. "I don't have any. That was actually part of the thesis of the researchers who created us. They believed that prior genetic research and manipulation, people similar to Carl and Mercury and even our boy Orion over there, were all flawed because they began with natural materials and then just changed bits and pieces."

"My brothers and I are as fully synthetic as it is possible to create. They took a fertilized egg, stilled it, and carved out anything that had been there before until the DNA was completely rewritten according to their own designs. I don't fully understand how that process worked, and there's not too much in this world I have trouble wrapping my head around. So yes, technically that egg and sperm came from somebody at some point, but I've got no idea who it was. They just needed living materials so it could be rewritten as somebody else."

"Sounds like someone with a god complex." She replied as she stared at Orion. "Though I don't think I would have been bothered too much if someone had fiddled with my DNA and turned me into Mercury. She's flawless. And a genius."

"Being inhumanly tall might have become irksome after a while, but it could have been fun." He smirked as he commented on her staring at Orion. "I've never been angry at the people who created me. Besides, they're all dead now, so there's no one left to be mad at. I wish they had done a better job of hiding their creations."

He shrugged and leaned back from his console for a moment, since Anna and Orion were in the clear for the time being. "People who meddle with things too much traditionally reap consequences they didn't intend. Such it is with me and my brothers and so it will be with all of this for me one day, I expect." He looked over at her, and pulled her into a quiet kiss. "I'm glad no one meddled with you. I love you as you are, for who you are, not in spite of what you aren't."

"I'm glad someone does." Jessie wasn't great at taking compliments, and she didn't imagine she ever would be. Their relationship had been all over the place and sometimes she still had nightmares. Nightmares that he would leave her, nightmares that he would hurt her. It was a mess in her head. "Well, no one did anything to our baby. She's cooking like she should be. Unaltered."

"She just won't have much to inherit from me by way of grandparents." He reached down to touch Jessie's stomach for a moment, though she wasn't showing yet by any means. "I just hope she'll grow up in a better world than we did."

"Growing up without grandparents isn't unusual for Earth. My mother will probably be dead soon, if she's not already. My father is long gone. That's just how things are, but you're right, I hope they're not always that way." Jessie rested her hand on top of his as he touched her stomach and she leaned over and kissed his cheek. "You're capable of being very sweet and tender, you know. I don't think anyone else knows that about you."

"Let's keep it that way." He said with a smile, and a caress along her stomach as if their daughter could somehow feel him close by and understand he was there for her. "I have a reputation to maintain. If word got out that I was capable of being cuddly, it would be disastrous."

"Alright, I'll keep it a secret." She blocked his view for just a moment so she could kiss him properly, and then she let him work. They had to get out alive in order for their daughter to have a future at all, and that was a task all by itself. "What if they get in there and someone tries to use it? Are they going to get sucked in or something?"

"I have no idea." He said with a shrug and a wider smile. "One of many risks we're taking with them going in there at all. I know what's supposed to happen, I know what it's supposed to look like, but as to what the Consortium has actually made of it?" He shook his head. "No idea whatsoever."

"Great. Hopefully we won't be suffering the wrath of Logan Bickford if Anna gets thrown through space to Eleusis and he never has a chance to say goodbye. Even if I'm not sure he cares that much anymore." She shrugged and watched more intently. "How close are they?"

"Right around the corner." Gordon's look turned just as intense, watching the layout of the station up ahead with several blank spaces in his display for the rooms he could not yet see.

Orion had long since gotten tired of looking over his shoulder. He was too tall to properly enjoy sneaking around. "Final corridor clear." He whispered so Gordon would pick it up on his end, then took a few steps out into the open hallway. The doors that were outlined as their goal on his communicator were set back in a double-braced vestibule just off the hallway, with a few sets of their own cameras. "Are those the ones you can't touch?"

"Those are the ones." Gordon's voice came through their earpieces and he sounded more relaxed than anyone had a right to be at the moment. "I can scramble things for a few seconds so you can get the bugs in place. Just work fast. Close proximity to the cameras is all I need. Doesn't have to be pretty. Fifteen-second burst commencing in five, four, three . . ."

Adrenaline took over as soon as Anna had to act, and Orion was quick about hoisting her up onto his shoulders so she could get a couple of bugs in place as close as they could to the cameras without getting spotted or actually touching the things. Anna nearly fell off of Orion's back after getting a couple bugs in place, but she was rather *bendy,* as Orion had called her once, and she righted herself quickly enough, with her heart still racing. "Fuck." She whispered as she clung to Orion's head for stability.

They had crouched down in a corner as far out of sight of the bugs as they could get, and aside from heaving breaths, Orion was trying his best to stay still. "White?"

"Stay still, I'm working through their system." Gordon's voice came back coldly through the earpieces. "The cameras work on a different kind of network than I expected, it's an externally-housed . . . got it. A few more seconds to get back to a secured bit of feed . . ."

Gordon talked to himself as he worked, narrating his own efforts on their behalf, until he finally let out a sigh. "Alright, I've got them. Nobody inside the chambers right now, but . . . man, it's beautiful. Go on inside and take a look."

"Go inside." Anna was frightened as Orion lowered her off of his shoulders, and she clung to him as they moved forward. They were in for some real shit now, that was for damn sure. "Come on, let's get in before someone sees us."

Orion hesitated at the inner door, but he heard a series of locks click open at Gordon's command, and he spared a glare at the cameras for the man's showing off before he stepped inside.

The chamber that opened up in front of them as soon as the doors parted was larger than most on the station. Stairs descended in broad ranks from the door, down to a well like an amphitheater, at the base of which was the Twist itself, exactly as Gordon had described it.

The machinery surrounding it was more complicated than Orion had expected, and the machine itself was larger than Gordon had said it would be, standing easily three times Orion's height and five times that in width, like a broad gaping mouth waiting to open on the other side of the universe. It was the first tangible proof Orion had seen of what Jessie told Anna, and it locked the world into a skewed kind of order that a small piece of Orion had hoped wasn't real.

Anna stepped in first and stared at the Twist as though she was seeing a hallucination. "I didn't know if it would be fucking real." She looked around before she took too many steps, since she was suspicious of being watched or caught. They were there to bug the surveillance, after all. "I can't fathom the idea that the right person pushes a button and we could be on Eleusis."

Orion wasn't often speechless, but all he could do was nod as he walked beside her, still taking in the sight of the Twist in all its glory. The room would have made no sense if he hadn't known what he was looking at, since there was clearly a ramp that led into thin air in the middle of the structure and then cut off as if sliced by god's machete. Between the double doors and the Twist itself at the far end, there were half a dozen ranks of large observation barriers set with windows in them so that those hiding behind the barriers could watch the Twist itself without being impacted by . . . whatever was on the other side. Orion could hardly even speculate, but he didn't imagine cross-galactic travel was easy, or without turbulence.

"I'm out of a job." Orion said numbly, but squeezed Anna's hand afterward.

Anna kept a tight hold on his hand as they dared to move closer, but she also tried to wait for further instructions from the one who was watching them and probably laughing because they looked like kids who had discovered the world's best theme park. "You'll never be out of a job. I'm sure it's a hell of a lot cheaper to fly people places than to build a beast like this."

She's right about that. Gordon's voice chimed in their ears. *See that lattice-work in the center of the opening? If you had even a kilogram of that stuff for sale to the Consortium, you'd never work another day in your life, and neither would your great-grandchildren. The difficulty in producing that particular material is the reason there's only three of these things.*

She startled a little to hear Gordon's voice in her ear, even though she expected further instruction. "What are we supposed to do next?" Anna asked in a whisper as she looked around, hoping and praying that no one would pop in on them. "You gave us a shit ton of these bugs."

Yes, well, I actually expected better security. Never underestimate the power of complacency. Gordon's voice was snarky as ever, and he actually chuckled once in what sounded like real giddiness before he continued. *Any equipment you can get your hands on, bug it. I need at least four around the far edges of the Twist itself, though take care not to place any inside the actual event horizon. I need to get telemetry on its operations to replace some intel that was stolen from me a while back. Bug the cameras, and especially bug the switchboard there at your nine o'clock. That looks to be the main control hub for it on this side.*

"What do you mean, on this side?" Orion was already in motion, trying to get as many bugs placed as possible before they had to beat a hasty getaway from the room.

Well, it's a door, Captain. They typically have knobs on both sides. Wouldn't be much of a door, otherwise.

"Huh." Anna moved to get a closer look at the switchboard. Anything that had knobs, buttons, or anything operational on it was always interesting to Anna. Her technological and mechanical curiosity was as useful as it was dangerous. Too many times she'd pressed a button she shouldn't have, just to see what the hell would happen. The impulse to press buttons was still there as she stared at the switchboard, but she didn't touch anything except to bug it. "Too bad we can't just nab it now. I'd like to see how this thing works."

Speaking of nabbing things, you two need to move on and check about five other rooms. This one is too big for us to cart out of here when we leave, not that I wouldn't love to try. We need to find the smaller secondary one they've got in use here. That's the one we'll need to . . .

Gordon's voice cut off, and he made a few confused-sounding noises for a few moments, talking to himself under his breath as he reviewed some of the new information he was getting through the control panel bug. *Axial differentiation . . . what is . . . oh, fucking hell, get behind something! Both of you! Now! As in right now!*

"Get behind something?" Anna looked around and grabbed onto Orion's hand, since he was the first to get moving when told to do so. Orion dragged her behind him since his long legs moved a lot faster than her own. They barely made it behind one of the observation barriers before they heard loud electrical snapping behind them and the whole room jumped at least fifteen degrees in temperature.

The machinery beside them roared to life at the same time the rest of the room did, but the heat came in waves from the Twist itself and was blocked somewhat by the many ranks of barriers on either side of the room. As Orion looked up between the machinery and the nearest barrier beside them, he couldn't take his eyes away from what he was seeing. His mind said it had to be an illusion, just a holographic image coming to life in front of him like one of the hologames he and Anna spent so much of their time playing.

The Twist was glowing, from end to end, with waves and whirlpools of light forming in Orion's vision too quickly for him to follow. The room continued getting hotter and hotter until he was worried the two of them would be incinerated where they huddled against each other, but eventually, the storm of the machinery seemed to reach its apex, in a single note.

Orion knew as soon as he heard the sound that he had no way to adequately describe it. It was so loud it was painful, but the volume of it was only secondarily painful to the beauty of it. The harmonies of the machine tore through every auditory sense he had, for a moment that lasted a lifetime before it abruptly vanished. It felt like there was a hole in Orion's heart where the sound had torn its way through, but the room was filled with the white noise of ventilation shafts roaring to life in the next moment, and Orion had a chance to blink the dazzling lights clear of his eyes.

Even when he opened them again, the room was much brighter than it had been, but for a very different reason.

"Oh my god." Anna said louder than she realized, but fortunately, they were still alone. At least temporarily. She was clutching to Orion's side as she stared through the gaping hole of the Twist, and part of her wanted to get up and run toward it just to make sure it was real.

They were looking at a piece of unfamiliar but beautiful landscape. They gazed at mountains in the distance, lush, green fields with flowers of a thousand colors, all too far below their vantage point to pick out details. It was so idyllic that Anna really couldn't believe her eyes. "It's real. It's fucking real."

There was no question in Orion's mind that what they were

seeing was half the galaxy away. The place was beautiful in an untouched, unbroken kind of way that Orion had never seen before on Earth or in Orbit. They could . . . smell . . . the new world. Fresh air, strange pollen and a slight sting of salt that spoke of a nearby ocean.

It had to be close to midday where the other side of the Twist was located, with the sun blazing directly down on the fields and mountains through a cloudless sky. The sun itself was barely visible through the upper edge of the twist, a slightly dimmer light in the sky instead of the Earth's own golden Sol. The world seemed just that much stranger for the different quality of light shining down on it, but the beauty of it took away the breath Orion hadn't realized he was holding.

"It is real." He felt the last of his skepticism die inside him, his doubts washed out of him by the brilliant sunlight pouring into the room from another world. "It's all . . . just . . ."

Get down. Technicians on their way up the ramp from the other side, some others about to cross through. Gordon's voice was filled with the same kind of awe theirs was, but he was trying hard to be present and cautious in the moment.

Anna crouched lower and closer into Orion's side, but she didn't tear her gaze away from what she saw. She was afraid of what or who was coming through, but she was too fascinated to do anything but stare. "It's so beautiful. And raw. Untouched. We could build a house anywhere we wanted there." She whispered into his ear as she clung to him.

"You might have to help me out with that. I've never lived in a house before." He whispered back as they watched.

A few technicians in maintenance suits came up to the edges of the Twist, bringing large banded cables with them. They attached the cables on the Eleusis side of the opening to a similar set on the Station side, and Orion could hear a thrum of power coursing through the circuits on both ends as energy and information traveled between the two places. It was a dance of efficiency and precision, but there were more distracting things to look at than a bunch of cables.

"Those mountains look like they could be fun. Build a house up on the ridge, right there where it flattens out on the shoulder. Have a good view of this entire valley and whatever's on the other side."

She looked toward the spot he mentioned and smiled a little

bit wider before she kissed along his neck. Anna was terrified, sure, but her imagination won out over fear. It usually did, which was part of her problem with danger. "A good view of everything else, but keep a private view for ourselves." Anna kissed his cheek as one hand gripped the side of his uniform. "We could walk around naked up there all the time, if we were the only ones up there."

"Place certainly feels warm enough." He agreed without missing a beat. He moved a little in their hiding place so that he was crouching behind her, almost completely enveloping her against him as they watched the work unfolding in front of them. "Though even if it was a little cold, I doubt I'd mind." One of his hands moved around the front of her to cup her breast through the uniform she wore, and even if they were in danger, they were still in it very much together.

"We'll have to make that a goal, baby." He said more seriously once his cheek pressed against hers to watch the proceedings. "On the other side of all this, whatever happens, when we get to Eleusis, we're gonna find this valley, we're gonna find that mountain, find a good spot for our house, and then I'm going to fuck you beneath that weird-ass sky until we make that dimmer-switch sun blush red."

Even though there wasn't much that made Anna blush, there was something about his sincerity, something about the idea of being so intimate in a new, untouched place that actually made her cheeks flush with heat. "More than a goal. A promise."

"I'm going to hold you to that." He moved to kiss her neck, then turned his attention back to the Twist field in front of them, since something new was coming up the walkway on the far side toward them.

Vance's voice was audible before the man himself came in sight, since the walkway clearly curved away and down along the slope where it was perched on Eleusis. "It's not as though we didn't know this was coming." He said with a laugh, as he and Gehrig finally came in sight, walking side by side. "As soon as things accelerated ahead of expectations, we knew we were going to get the termination order early. I'd like a little more time with this group, and I know Maria would, but we'll just have to make the most out of what we have left. Orders are orders."

Gehrig shook her head as she paused to look at the Twist and kept walking forward, bracing herself for the strange, and sometimes painful, electric sensation that came with walking through without the proper device to offset the charge. "I think we can get a few more months, two, at the very least, before we'll have to eliminate this wave. I think this time, though, the plan is to launch them and have a shuttle malfunction. We obviously cannot have another station malfunction. That was far too pricey and too attention-grabbing. Shuttles malfunction much more often. And Earth can have their little celebration of watching the damn thing take off toward Eleusis."

"I agree. The arm was effective for its purpose, but the next . . . should be less theatrical. The waiting list for the second wave is endless as it is, and I doubt many of those will be deterred by a shuttle accident if they weren't deterred by the arm's malfunction."

They both braced themselves as they came up to the horizon of the device itself, then pushed themselves through with a few forced steps, their fists clenched at their sides at the shock. With nothing more than a few steps, though, they had passed through the narrow field separating the two spaces and back onto the platform within the station. "Talk with Maria and Stephen about the new timetables, so they know what they have to work with. I'll get in touch with the Committee and give them my report."

"I'll talk to them, though I'm sure they won't be happy about it. They had some big plans that they were hoping to accomplish with this wave, but it was Maria's ambition that got us a wave this unruly and rebellious." She shook her head and shook out her arms to get rid of the tingling before she looked back at Eleusis through the Twist. "Sometimes I wish we could just stay there. Life is so much easier there. Simpler."

"We will. Eventually." Vance had almost a wistful look on his face as he joined her in looking back, taking in the sight of it as he too-rarely remembered to do for its own sake. "I almost didn't take this assignment because I didn't want to leave. Though of course, that's not how it works, I understand that. We just have to make sure the same mistakes that have been made here aren't permitted to happen there. As we've been told by the Committee, we've been given paradise. It falls to us not to make a mess of it."

Gehrig sighed and looked back at Vance before she nodded. "I'll talk to everyone else in charge, you report to the Committee, and we'll move on from there." Gehrig kept walking for a moment before she paused again, the Twist still open and alive behind them. "The Committee will want to know our plans for the conceived children. I think it is probably best to remove the mothers and put them in quarantine just before the rest are sent off toward Eleusis, don't you? Until the babies are born, of course."

"Work with Stephen and Maria on procedures for that. I don't want any of their usual seat-of-the-pants games with that particular piece of things. They need to be reminded that this project is not their personal playground. There is too much at stake to risk that particular branch of the research. The way things are right now, if the mothers were removed, people would resist. Violently. If it can be done otherwise, fine. Otherwise we'll have to move to mass sedation." Vance's tone sounded actually concerned as he spoke, but not for human life, only for the ideas and the research they were pursuing. It was enough to send a chill down Orion's spine at the complete disregard for humanity in both people.

Anna felt nauseous as she watched the two go their separate ways. She looked down at herself, and even though she couldn't see any difference in her body, she knew there were two babies in there depending on her to keep them safe. She felt like crying and going into a fury at the same time, for the same reason.

"We have to get away from here." She finally whispered when the coast was clear. "I'm not some incubator they're just going to cut open and throw away."

"No, you're not." Orion growled beside her, though it was still in a whisper. They couldn't see much of the Twist from where they were hidden, but it was clear that no one else was coming through after Vance and Gehrig.

Eventually, the maintenance technicians came through again and unhooked the cables that had connected Eleusis to Station Nine, then stepped back to clear the platform. When they were back far enough, Orion had to duck down and hold tight to Anna as the Twist appeared to fold in on itself. The world on the other side of the opening seemed to fracture and twist in mirrors and convolutions of the room where Anna and Orion huddled, until both vanished completely, leaving all the machinery in the room to whine as it powered down. The gate had been open no more than a few minutes, but in those few minutes, the universe had been a much smaller place.

We're going to get out of here long before any of that happens. Gordon's voice came through their earpieces, reminding them that they had a job to do, and he had been listening in on the entire thing. *So long as we get what we came for. Stay where you are for a few minutes. I'm having to do double work on the exterior monitoring systems. Give me a minute.*

Anna didn't say anything more about Eleusis or her babies after that, but she did continue to hold tightly to Orion as they waited for further instruction.

It felt like much too long before he responded with anything more than absent-minded mumbles, but he eventually breathed a sigh and cleared his throat. *Alright, I still need bugs on the device itself. No other inquiries inbound and according to the rest of these readings, the device requires at least an hour to reset and rebuild the charge for transport. Not surprising, since just that last walk took more power than most metropolitan centers on Earth use in a month.*

Bug the frame on both sides and also hit those information conduits somewhere that won't be noticeable. Those will be useful. Then all we need to do is find the secondary portal and you two can head home the way you came.

"Great." She replied with less enthusiasm, even though seeing Eleusis had been incredible, hearing they were supposed to be dead in a matter of months had pretty well ruined whatever excitement she felt.

Planting the rest of the bugs was hair-raising, to say the least. Much of the equipment was still hot from the gateway process, but Orion managed to find some spaces that Gordon said were acceptable for bug placement, and they finished with the room in a matter of minutes. He still had to stop at the top of the amphitheater steps to look back at the maw of the gate with a sigh. "Press a button and jump across the universe. Really makes me wish we could. Right now, no warning. Press a button, run through, run for the hills and come what may. And no, White, I'm not talking to you."

Anna looked up at Orion and looked back at the Twist for a moment as she considered it, really and truly. "I would do it with you. If I knew how to work that thing. I would." She looked back at Orion again and then yanked him down to her level for a passionate kiss. "Even though I would feel guilty about leaving the other two behind, though they have their own plan, it seems like. They haven't exactly been inclusive about their schemes to bust us out of here."

"I'm pretty sure that's because they don't really have one."

Orion added darkly, but he returned the kiss anyway. "I guess this is just one more thing I'm gonna have to learn how to fly eventually. Let's go find the baby one for now and get the hell out of here."

Getting to the other Twist was almost too easy, and planting the bugs moved smoothly, which made Anna feel even more uneasy as she climbed to place one up by the secondary Twist itself. "Shouldn't there be some fucking alarms or something like that?" She looked around, but the room was eerily quiet. "I mean, I know White is listening and that he's disabling cameras and shit, but this feels too easy."

"If I were them, I'd be watching the places people usually move." Orion climbed down from his own side of the second frame. It was a great deal smaller than the first, located only a few rooms away, to draw from the same power source. It stood just a meter taller than Orion, and was just barely wide enough for him to have stretched out his arms to grasp both sides.

Still, it was impressive, and it felt like even more of an invasion of reality somehow, something so small standing against every truth either of them thought they knew about the universe. "I'd have the maintenance hatches locked down, sure, but I wouldn't be paying most of my attention to them. So if there's a little code that looks out of whack about the locks on a maintenance shaft, that's gonna ring a lot fewer bells than a hijacked lift tube."

"Still. It just doesn't feel right. You would think they would have stuff like this under more surveillance, like armed guards. I would." Anna jumped down into a crouch and sighed as she looked over at Orion again. "Hey, White. Are you still listening?"

After getting yelled at earlier, I thought it best to keep my peace. Wouldn't want to upset you. But yes, I'm still listening.

"Figured. So when the big guy and I get out of here and back to our unit, can you meet us there?" Anna looked over at Orion when she said it, mostly because he didn't know about what she brought with her into orbit. Even Logan didn't know, but since she'd almost died for it, she figured it was worth hauling around. Especially after the way her family was questioned when the piece of the space station crashed into Earth. "I have something you need to see."

While I'm flattered by the offer, Mrs. Al-Jabbar, my own wife has pretty much everything I need to see right here, thank you very much.

"Very funny." She snipped back at him, since knowing Jessie,

Anna was truly not Gordon's type. Not that she was offering in the first place. "Jessie has better assets up top than I do anyway. That's not what I meant."

Whatever it is you need to show me, then, I'll be there to review. I certainly owe you two a favor or twenty for tonight's services rendered. Besides, I need the rest of my bugs back. Gordon's voice trailed off into his usual self-narrating dribble of vowels and nouns for a while before he spoke clearly again. *The path on your communicators is clear back to the maintenance shaft. I think you've gotten everything we needed here. I'm scanning the premises for guards now. Move quietly and try not to attract any trouble.*

Anna nodded, even though he wasn't really able to see her unless he had cameras on her, but she grabbed Orion's hand as soon as they were given the all-clear. "Come on. I know you don't know what I'm going to show him, but that's only because I don't really know what it is either. Logan doesn't know about it either. No one does. Not until now, anyway."

"Woman of mystery, huh?" Orion teased as they headed through the halls at a quiet jog. He wasn't looking forward to getting back into the maintenance shaft, but it was better than . . .

Stop and take a left. Now. Gordon's voice was on the edge of panic, and didn't leave any room for argument or discussion.

Orion squeezed Anna's hand tighter and darted into the short corridor to the left of them, which was not a part of the route. "What's going . . ."

And quiet, unless the idea of getting killed is exciting to you for some reason. White said just as frantically. *Down the corridor and take a right, then find someplace to not be seen. Four guards patrolling right behind you.*

They ran as fast and as quietly as they possibly could before they found someplace to hide, but still, they were close enough to hear the guards' voices echoing down the corridor. The place was too quiet for them to not hear the raucous guards. Anna folded into Orion, since hiding was easier that way.

"I heard they're going to lift the lockdown for some of the rats." A woman's voice said as it slowly got closer to Anna and Orion's location. "I wonder if we get to pick some for ourselves once they start getting rid of them. Just like Kaplan's brother before he went off and died."

"Nah, they don't like you that much." One of the others answered, with a general laugh from the others as they shoved each other around. "Once Santos gets her shit to work, though, there's gonna be plenty for all of us."

"Our own personal Wicked Witch. I knew I liked her the second I signed on here." Another answered, with more laughter. "So long as you can give her a reason to hand one over to you, I don't see why they wouldn't. Get a videotape for her to study and she'll let you do pretty much whatever you want with whoever's convenient."

"Doesn't bother me. I've been on camera before. I ain't shy."

Another woman spoke up, apparently feeling as though she needed to be the voice of reason. "You can't tamper with research just for the hell of it." She said coldly. "And the doctor isn't just going to hand out vials to anybody. None of you could handle that stuff. I should know, I was in one of the early trials myself. I volunteered. That shit is *not* to be fucked with."

"I don't know, I thought it sounded like fun. Wait, was that the day you came home and had to take the rest of the week off?" Far from being open to listening to reason, the comment put the rest of the guards into another fit of laughter.

"I still can't fucking remember half of that week." She bit back, even though the others were laughing. "It's addictive. Had to have an IV flush and a sedative the next day. It's no joke."

"I still live by the 'try anything once' mentality. Sign me up. Especially for some shit like that." The general laughter continued past the recess where Anna and Orion were hiding, but just when it seemed they could get past without incident, one of the guards that Anna could see stopped where he was walking. "Hey, Control, any other active bodies in this sector besides us?"

Negative, Harlow. What are you seeing?

"Probably nothing, just getting some weird noise on the scanner when I try to patch into the rest of the overhead systems. See if there's a glitch on the cameras, will you? I was registering six bodies on thermals a minute ago and now I'm back to just the four of us."

Roger that, Harlow, we'll get on diagnostics. For now, split and get eyes on the panels for the local equipment.

Anna trembled a little as she kept her face buried into Orion's chest, but she listened for Gordon's next instruction. All she could repeat in her head over and over was some kind of plea with the universe they wouldn't be discovered. They would be killed for sure if someone found them, or worse, turned into true lab rats.

She didn't even want to think about whatever the hell those guards were talking about at the disposal of Maria Santos. The woman was fucked up in all the ways that mattered.

The party of four guards split into two pairs and headed off in different directions, not at all in a hurry or perturbed by the possible disturbance. They continued laughing and joking as they walked, and it wasn't long before their voices faded into nothing more than echoes.

Get your shit together and be ready to move in about fifteen seconds. Gordon said in a low voice, even if it was only in their ears. *You're gonna head down the corridor until you join back up with the main drag you came up earlier. Once you get there and the door is closed behind you, haul ass back to the maintenance shaft. I've got a solid hold on the cameras and sensors in the main hallway, and they're not good enough to know I'm there. They're not looking for you, they're looking for technical issues. Run.*

Orion broke off in a quiet run with Anna at his side, though they still stopped at every corner to make sure they wouldn't be casually observed by anyone out of doors. He couldn't even say anything, to Anna or to Gordon, for fear of being overheard. He had never particularly believed too fervently in the god his parents worshipped, but it felt like a pretty good time to start.

Anna's heart pounded the entire way back to the maintenance shaft, and even when they managed to get back inside, she was afraid to talk or move until they were given an all clear that they weren't spotted or followed. She remained still against Orion and closed her eyes as she attempted to gain control of her breathing again. "Fuck."

"Yeah." Orion agreed, breathing heavily right against her as they caught their breath. The space was cramped and awkward for both of them, but the concealment felt too good to be bothered by it. "That's about as close to getting captured and tortured as I think I ever want to get."

"No kidding." She panted as she tried to convince herself that she was safe, even though there was no way in hell she was any safer now, only she wasn't being pursued right now. "First they want to send us off on a defunct ship to our death, then they want to drug us and torture us? What the actual fuck?"

I'm sorry to intrude, but are either of you really surprised at this point? Gordon's voice had retaken its usual condescension. *I mean, you, Captain, I can understand, but Anna? You watched an entire arm of this station fall from the sky with thousands of people dead on board. You've watched them tear apart your marriage to satisfy their own curiosities, and you're really surprised that they would satisfy whatever vagaries with you they like? That's all they've been doing with any of us since we set foot on this station.*

"It wasn't supposed to be this way." Orion jumped in defensively, though he didn't loosen his grip on Anna. "And the rest of us don't go around expecting the world to be a fucked-up place wherever we look."

Clearly you need to get out more, then.

"Stop being an asshole." Anna said as she contemplated ripping the earpiece out of her ear. "Stop. If I thought the world was that fucking shitty, then I wouldn't have even volunteered my life just now for your cause. I still have some fucking faith in humanity, or else I would have found a way to kill myself by now. A universe without hope isn't worth living in. And you must have some fucking hope too, or else you wouldn't have wasted your time knocking up your girlfriend."

I have faith in specific people. Humanity as a whole is a mob. It's never been more or less than the entire spectrum. It's shit and gold, depending on who you're talking to. I'm not going to try and romanticize a world that isn't worth the poetry.

But when it comes to the Consortium, if you're going to fight this war with me, with the rest of us, then you both need to decide you're going to understand what you're dealing with and call it what it is. It will destroy everything you've ever found beautiful, and you will become a number in someone's research journal, nothing more.

Start crawling. It's a long way home.

Anna took the earpiece out of her ear after that and felt like chucking it down the shaft, but she just looked at Orion instead. "He's lucky I'm not in the same room with him right now, I'd punch his fucking face." She squeezed her hand tightly around the earpiece and took a bug out of her pocket and stuck it randomly on the side of the maintenance shaft. "Get that fucking bug back yourself if it's so valuable. What an ass."

32

There were no further comments from Gordon as they crawled along the maintenance shaft, but Orion did stop her a few times when he received instructions to do so, waiting for one or another hatch to be opened or a monitor to be decommissioned.

"The world is worth it." Orion finally said after what seemed like an eternity of crawling along the same piping, the same grating, dangling in space with only a few feet of steel and glass between them and a quick, agonizing demise. "The entire world might not be, but that doesn't mean the world itself isn't. I joined the force originally because I wanted to serve people. I believe they're worth serving. Worth saving. Just a question of what from. And no, White, that wasn't an invitation to you."

He looked back at Anna as they went, pausing to let her get ahead of him. "Just wanted you to know I'm with you on this. Whatever kind of shit people live in the world, I'm not gonna let the Kaplans and Marias and Vances convince me the world isn't worth fighting for."

"The whole reason I came up here is because I wanted a better world. A better life. Not just for me, either." She looked back at Orion once he let her pass, and she kept moving, slowly. "I still want that. I refuse to believe that the entire universe is against a better life."

Idealists. Gordon said with a sigh, even though only Orion could actually hear him. *You're the kind who get people killed. Hopefully you know that, so it's less of a shock later.*

"Shut up, White." Orion growled as he crawled, and Gordon, for once, complied.

Exiting the maintenance shaft wasn't quite the relief Orion had thought it would be, but they didn't have far to go to get back to their unit. When they arrived and the door was locked and sealed behind them, only then did Orion allow himself to breathe a deep and exhausted sigh of relief, as he pinned Anna between himself and the wall to keep her close. "I like to think I have a pretty broad definition of the word 'fun.' That did not qualify."

Anna wrapped her arms around his slender middle and held onto him without saying anything after that, since he was right. It wasn't fun. It wasn't easy. They almost died, more than once. Her arms and knees ached from crawling and climbing and jumping and more crawling and she just wanted to be held for once without being tough. "At least we survived. For now, anyway."

"I'm comfortable with 'for now.' So long as it's with you." Orion said with a final sigh and a kiss to the side of her head. "Shower. I am in need of a shower. And as much as I love you, so are you. White, take your time getting down here, we need to decompress."

Anna and Orion took their time showering, mostly to hold onto each other and touch each other to remind themselves that they were as safe as they could be together. After the shower they curled up together on the couch, Anna in Orion's lap as he wrapped his arms around her and held her close. It was a tender moment, and Anna was grateful for it, especially because she was exhausted in every way she could be. Pregnancy was bad enough, fighting for her life on top of it was even worse.

Orion was tempted to fall asleep, but he was still too wired from the entire ordeal to allow himself to relax. All he wanted to do was lie back and hold onto Anna. "So what is it that you've got stashed away to show White? I wasn't aware you had any secrets left for me to discover."

"I don't really know what kind of secrets it holds, but I know it has to be valuable." Anna reluctantly slid off of his lap and went digging into her things, even though there wasn't much to dig through in the first place.

Anna pulled out a well-hidden tablet she stuffed between photos and personal clothing items. She'd put it into a case and no one had questioned her for bringing a tablet along with her, even if it was strange that she brought one with a shattered faceplate.

She brought it over to Orion and held it out for him to see. "I hadn't seen one of this particular make, but when Logan and I went to the wreckage from the station piece that fell . . ." She looked down at the tablet and her shattered reflection in dark glass. "Logan went inside the house to check on our neighbors, the house was badly damaged. I went behind the house to see if anyone could have survived falling from space and through the atmosphere. No one did. It was horrific."

She shook her head, since she knew she'd told the story before, but it was still difficult to relive in her mind. "There was an old man that I could get to. His body was trapped in netting, and it looked like he did it to try and save himself, but he had this clutched in his arms like it was the most important thing in the world to him. I sliced open my arm trying to get to it." She held out her arm to show him the faint scar, a pale line all the way down her arm. "Then the authorities came and questioned my family and I like we were criminals, and I knew they were looking for something. Maybe to see if we took anything like this. It could be nothing. But it could be something."

Orion looked it over gingerly, since it looked like the thing was barely held together. "It's station-issued. Scientific, though, not personal. Aiko uses these all the time, got 'em all over her unit and lab. Maybe your guy was one of the researchers on the arm that came down."

"Maybe so, I don't know." She looked at Orion, and his face was enough to help her focus on the moment and not the horrible things etched in her memory. "Hopefully it's not completely damaged to the point that someone can't tap into it. There has to be a reason why a dying man would hold onto it."

"If I'm plummeting toward a planet and burning to a crisp on atmospheric entry, I'm sure as hell not clutching a tablet to keep me company on the way down. Knowing me, if I was past the point of no return, I'd just close my eyes and . . . well, I'd think of you. Hope that you're safe." They'd been forced to contemplate the possibility of their own demise fairly recently, and it was still clearly fresh in Orion's mind.

Anna took the tablet out of his hand and set it aside so that she could hold onto his large hands with hers. She squeezed his hands for a moment and slid back into his lap, straddling his legs as she took his face in her hands. "You really must love me if you're spending your dying thoughts on me."

"I guess I must." He agreed, turning to kiss her wrists before pulling her down into a proper kiss. "They would probably be dirty thoughts, even if I'm dying, but still, love is definitely the overall theme. There's no one I would want farther away in a situation like that."

"We're not going to plummet to Earth, and you're not going

to die. I won't let you." Anna kissed him harder and kept her lips close to his afterward. "I need you. If you're going to die, then we'll die old and together."

"I'm gonna be bald. I'm just telling you that right now. I've got maybe ten years of hair left, and then it's gone. My dad's got just about nothing left up here. I hope you're okay with that." He put a hand up on his close-cropped hair, which showed no signs of receding or falling out, but she had seen pictures of his family, and he wasn't lying.

Anna ran a hand along his close-cropped hair and smiled as she looked into his dark eyes. "You know, I really don't care. I never thought I would live to be old. I don't care what you'll look like, or what I'll look like. If we live to be old, that will be something amazing all in itself."

There was a knock at their door before Orion could answer that, and he sighed, since White wasn't really someone he wanted to see at four o'clock in the morning. Still, it was better to get their visiting finished before the world was supposed to be awake. "We'll work on the growing old part. Though I have a feeling that our new rebel friend won't have that chance if he does too much more mouthing off around you."

"You're not fucking kidding." Anna got off of his lap again and moved to sit down next to him, since there was no point in going to try and open the door. They were still on lockdown as far as she knew. "It's LOCKED!" She yelled, knowing that Gordon would probably hear her voice, in the very least.

A few seconds passed, but then the panel beside the door dinged, and Gordon walked through with a smile at Anna's sarcasm. "I mostly just wanted to make sure the two of you were clothed before I came in. I didn't figure you would be screaming if you weren't. At least not at me." He shrugged and stepped in past their dining area with a bag slung across his chest and his usual data core in his hand. "You said you had something you wanted me to see?"

"My nudity is only for Orion, thank you." She stretched over Orion to get the tablet on the other side of him before she got up from the couch to hand it over to Gordon. "The long story short is that I found this in the wreckage from when the arm of the station crashed. An old man had it, was clinging to it as if it was the difference between life and death, but he died anyway. No one knew I had it, no one questioned me about a broken tablet. I figured I could find someone who might be able to get into it up here, so I brought it with me. I didn't want my family to be responsible for stolen tech."

She could tell from the moment she mentioned the fallen arm of the station that she had Gordon's undivided attention, and he advanced on her quickly once she was finished describing where she'd gotten it, with a hand outstretched and a gleam in his eyes. "May I?"

"I sure as hell can't do anything about it." Anna put the broken tablet into Gordon's hands and looked into his eyes. "I'm not sure what it has on it, but I do know that the Consortium knew they lost something. They questioned my family about it afterward."

Gordon turned the tablet over a few times in his hands, then moved across the room to the port for their own personal tablets to charge against the wall. He worked quickly, using his data core and attaching it to their room's interface to take over everything about their unit in no more than a few heartbeats.

Once he was sure that his own equipment was in charge, he made some quick repairs to the physical interface port on the broken tablet and attached it to the wall unit.

"The arm that fell to Earth was mainly cleared prior to falling. The only personnel who remained were Eleusis researchers and some maintenance crewmen, or so the story goes. Maintenance isn't going to be holding onto a research tablet and only a few of the researchers who were included in the death count were what could be considered old, even by Earth standards. Most of the older generation thinks that Eleusis is a waste of time and resources, and we should all just be focused on . . . there. Got you."

He cut himself off mid-stream as some graphics came up on his data core's holograms, showing the present state of the broken device, viable memory against corrupted data or fractured programming. His fingers worked like they were weaving magic through the interface, instructing his device to stitch together the various data inconsistencies from the damage of the crash to recreate a full image of the tablet's contents from the remains. Even for him and for his software, it was not a quick process.

"Off the record," he continued as he worked, his eyes darting through the interface followed by his hands, though he spoke without being bothered by the split concentration, "the Consortium sent about two hundred people down to the crash site afterward, ostensibly for salvage and cleanup crews, but actually verifying the dead and destroying what little was shown to have survived the crash. This tablet was . . . yup, catalogued to the geological team surveying Eleusis for tectonic stability and composition, assigned to . . ." he stopped, and gulped as he read one line of code over and over again as if to verify that he wasn't seeing things.

Orion let the man's shocked silence linger for a while, but then leaned a little closer on the couch where he was still sitting. "You know that's not a complete sentence, right?"

Gordon just shook his head. "It was registered to someone I respected. That's all." His voice sounded more profoundly sad than Orion had given the asshole credit for being capable of. He went back to work quickly, restoring the data pathways and connections with a deftness that left Orion mostly confused but impressed. He had never seen a fish in water, but he imagined Gordon came close.

Anna watched Gordon closely, as if she was going to learn his skills by watching him once, but she couldn't help her fascination. He was good at what he did, hacking into things he shouldn't, but she still thought he was a huge asshole. Her eyes darted between everything that appeared, but she didn't really understand much of what she saw. "So is there anything useful there for us?"

"I have to get it all back in one piece before I can figure out if it's useful or not." Gordon said as he worked, sighing deeply once in a while for no apparent reason. The barriers Anna could see in the visual representation of the code fell one by one or were bridged by Gordon's programming. Entire spaces came up with code that made almost no sense, but Gordon's fingers flew through the hologram to patch it until it ran smoothly again.

"This has . . . you don't even know what's in here." Gordon said absently as he worked. "The tablet was patched into the main servers of the research team. It's got echoes of most of the main body of research in here, blueprints, technical schematics, rosters, readings from Eleusis deposits . . . most of the files actually housed locally are video logs. He always did like to record his findings himself and let the system do the transcribing." He broke off into mumbling to himself in Russian for a while, but Anna could see the tablet's virtually-represented circuitry getting closer and closer to being whole.

His face darkened as he neared the end, and he sighed again.

"The most recent file is a video entry. It's time-stamped to the arm's fall." He spared a moment to glance over at Anna and Orion. "You may not want to watch this. And believe it or not, I don't intend that in a patronizing sense. I can't imagine either of you get any particular satisfaction from watching people die."

"I saw what he looked like after he was already dead." Anna said sadly as she looked over at Gordon, though he was right. She didn't want to watch a video of someone dying, but she also wanted to know what she had risked her life for when she went after and kept the tablet. "I almost bled to death because I went after this thing. I want to know what he had to say."

Gordon nodded and finished his work quickly, forming a patched but complete virtual version of the tablet's contents in mid-air before he began to access it virtually as if it were intact. He stepped back to allow the hologram to expand over most of the wall of the room, and navigated quickly through several menus that were listed in the Cyrillic alphabet rather than English. Still, the listings were straightforward enough, and he navigated to the video entries, most of which involved cover images showing a white-haired man sitting comfortably in a lab with glasses partway down his nose. The last cover image was one Anna recognized, since it was a still image of the man's panicked face in the pod where she had found him.

As soon as Gordon selected the video and it began to play, the recording was chaos. Light and shadow played over and over again across the lens of the tablet's camera before the man got it somewhat stabilized, obviously dragging it with him along a corridor while in free-fall. There was screaming everywhere, both in pain and in panic, and the man was taking deep, moaning, panicked breaths as he scrambled. Soon he reached an emergency panel and forced his way into the escape pod, but he lingered in the hatch before climbing in. He turned and looked around half a dozen times, clearly already crying desperate tears, then forced himself into the pod and slammed the door shut behind him.

He secured himself quickly and clutched the tablet close as he initiated the emergency breakaway. Only when the pod gained some distance from the rest of the station did the chaotic motion of the world surrounding the tablet cease, leaving the man's sobbing as the only sound left. One corner of the camera looked out through the glass of the pod at the station falling away. The pod was attempting to regain orbit, which allowed the arm something of a head start as it began to enter the atmosphere.

Warning . . . the pod's automated system chimed in, *unable to maintain orbit. Switching to atmospheric entry parameters . . . Please ensure that all occupants are* . . . the voice droned on about safety procedures, but the man started talking and drowned out the voice, grumbling through sobs in a thick Russian accent.

"I don't know where everybody is." Gordon began translating solemnly, his voice flat as he allowed the man on the screen to supply the tearful emotion behind his words. The white-haired scientist was thrown from one end of the pod to the other, bloodying his forehead and leaving an audible crack as one shoulder hit, but he kept talking anyway, and Gordon kept translating.

"Everyone was supposed to be in the conference chamber for some kind of meeting, I don't know what happened. I don't know what happened." The man wedged himself into place in the seat, but Anna knew from training in those same pods that he had belted himself in wrong, and the restraints clearly hadn't helped him much in the crash.

All he could do was scream as the pod's systems warned him of an unrecoverable angle for atmospheric entry, insufficient power to recover either altitude or correct entry velocity. "My god, my god, it looks like . . ." Gordon's voice was still flat as he translated, and the man turned the tablet to take in everything he was seeing. Flames were beginning to lick along the edges of the falling arm, along with other detritus from the explosion that had torn it loose. It was an ocean of bits and pieces, some of them human bodies, floating in a descending inferno.

"I don't know how to fly this thing." Gordon went on when the man finally started to get hold of himself. "I'm going to die. I'm going to . . ." he devolved into weeping for a while, and he turned the camera to look down at the world that was coming up at him quickly. He was over the Rockies, it looked like, from what she could see by his trembling camerawork.

"I don't want to die. I don't want to die. It was supposed to be tomorrow. One more day . . . just one more day and we would all have been . . . so far from here . . ." The man's voice was getting calmer and yet more frantic at the same time as fire engulfed the outside of the pod. They were protected from all kinds of heat and cold variances, so the man wouldn't feel any of it, but being encased in fire still had an effect on the mind.

"I wanted to make a difference." Gordon's voice betrayed an edge of bitterness that the man's voice didn't have, but clearly he was getting angrier the longer he watched. "I could have. I could have helped. They've killed us all. Everyone . . . Sasha, Alexander, Tiya . . . they're all . . ." he devolved into sobbing as the camera shook, but fire was the only thing visible on the screen. "I love you . . . I love you all . . . I'll see you again. It will be over soon. We'll be together again soon. I don't understand. I don't . . ."

The world got closer, and as they entered the atmosphere, Anna could see the man's pod getting closer to other pieces of debris, all of them bouncing off each other and breaking up inside the massive trail of fire behind what had to be the main arm of the station, pulling them all into its wake. The man was screaming and crying, but Anna could identify one word in the chaos even before Gordon translated it for her.

"I wanted to go to Eleusis. They told us we would be the first . . . we'll never . . . they never . . . I'll never see Eleusis." After that, all Anna could see was a single frame of the man's face before he tucked the tablet between his body and the webbing where she had found it, and everything went black.

"Dear god." Anna said softly, and she didn't even try to wipe away the tears that fell down her cheeks, since she had wanted to save the man before she even saw anything about him, and it felt worse to watch him die knowing that he was already dead. She turned toward Orion and refused to look toward the screen again, even though it was black. "Fucking bastards. What the hell is wrong with these people?"

"They're efficient." Gordon said coldly as he returned to looking through some of the other data on the tablet, setting the man's videos aside completely, since he had no desire to look at the dead man any more than Anna or Orion. "That's what's wrong with them. The most efficient way to move forward with any undertaking is to control the flow of information about it as narrowly as possible and give those involved in doing the work as much motivation as humanly possible to complete their task. So far, by that standard, they've been doing very well."

"That man just died screaming." Orion said in awe from the couch, his jaw hanging open as he stared at Gordon, who sounded like he was giving a lecture, as usual. "Along with thousands of other people. You call that efficiency? That's mass murder!"

"Mass murder is one of many things known to have been

incredibly efficient in the past." Gordon said without even looking back at Orion. "With a single admittedly-expensive and complicated move, the Consortium removed the purely-academic engines that came up with many of the solutions we'll require on Eleusis to thrive and grow, thereby keeping the ideas without having to continue tolerating the people who came up with them, who might be inclined to insurrection or ownership of those ideas."

"Now, they have us, another batch of a little over two thousand people being led through the theoretical implementation of some of those ideas so that they can test them out and improve upon them, before they do the same to us. With their perfected solutions and the pity of the entire world that they've managed to turn against the big, bad terrorists, they have a conduit for all the control over Eleusis they want, all the while having not lost more than a few of their own foot soldiers in the fight against those rebels. It's efficiency, nothing more or less."

He finally glanced back at Orion and Anna before returning his eyes to his work. "It's also evil, but evil does have more of a reputation for efficiency in its activities than nobility and righteousness, you have to admit."

"Well, screw efficiency, then." Anna replied sharply. "I'm all for mass chaos if it means these fuckers die for what they've done. Someone has to pay for that, and it sure as hell isn't going to be me. Or my family."

That made Gordon smile when he looked back at her, and in the wake of what they had just watched, his smile was more than a little chilling. "I knew I was going to like you the moment we met, Mrs. Al-Jabbar. But don't worry, it won't hurt my feelings if the feeling isn't mutual."

He unhooked the shattered tablet and tossed it back to her, since obviously he had gotten everything he needed. "In case you find yourself in need of a paperweight. I would recommend wiping that down as thoroughly as you can with every cleaning solution available to you and then tossing it in a public trash compaction unit for destruction. It will take some time before I can completely thank you for what you did in retrieving it. The data on that device is going to help us more than I can explain right now."

"Then I'm glad I kept it." Anna looked down at the mangled piece of tech and sighed. "Just remember that you owe me, then.

And don't leave us behind or out of the loop. I'm not going to die in some fucking space shuttle plummeting to Earth. I'm going to die old. Either on Eleusis or Earth, I'm really not picky at this point."

"Best not to be, when you're a rebel against the powers that be." Gordon said with another smile. "I do pay my debts. You won't be left out. Just stay alive until you can be of use again. I expect we'll need the two of you to help us fly out of here." He looked past her to Orion, but he knew Anna had been learning to be a pilot as well in the months since they had been on the station. "In the meantime, be thinking about ways to steal as many ships and pods as possible as quickly as possible when the time comes. More than two thousand people to get off this tin can is going to take just about everything we've got."

"It'll be easier if they actually let us out." She wandered back over to Orion and easily curled into his side. Now that her anger settled to a simmer, exhaustion was creeping back in. "I don't think I can handle any more shit right now, though. This all seems like a never-ending nightmare."

"All nightmares end." Gordon had a sad smile on his face as he took down his data core's interface and tucked it back into his shirt. "One way or another." He turned and gathered up the remaining bug devices, then started for the door to let himself out. "I have another visit to make before the morning breaks. Do the two of you need anything else for now? Aside from about twenty hours' direct sleep?"

"Can you hack into the food programming and send some chocolate? I would love some chocolate." Anna said sleepily, especially as soon as Orion put an arm around her and held her close. "Also can you tell us if Fitch is okay? She was here with her friend right before we all got locked up."

"I haven't checked in on her, but I will. No promises on the chocolate, but I'll see what I can do." He nodded to them both and sighed before he opened the door. "Get some sleep. It's going to be a long rebellion." He gave them a sarcastic smile and slipped out as if it was just another normal day on a space station.

* * * * *

Tatyana was sound asleep on the couch when she heard the door to her unit unlock, and while she thought it meant that the

635

lockdown was over, she heard a soft knock on the door afterward. She sat up slowly and reached for her gun, but she didn't go to open the door. She wasn't going to greet someone if it meant giving them any kind of upper hand. "Enter." She kept her hand on her gun as she waited. A few of her guards were snoring nearby, but she didn't want to alert them just yet.

The door clicked open at her invitation, and Gordon shook his head at her sleeping guards. "Are they drunk, or just heavy sleepers?" He asked in Russian, nodding toward the sleeping figures as he approached.

"Both. Once they realized they were trapped in here with me instead of their matches, they kept themselves entertained with my vodka." She crossed her arms as she stared intently at Gordon. She slept in skimpy clothing, which was why she had banned the fumbling fools to her room and told them to stay there and sleep it off. Once they remembered she had a gun, they listened quickly. Gordon, though, she didn't mind having around in skimpy clothing.

"I'm not sure 'entertaining' is the first word that comes to mind where your vodka is concerned, but it's in the top ten." He took the bag off his shoulder and set it down on a chair nearby with a sigh as his smile quickly disappeared. He wasn't there on a happy errand, after all.

"First and foremost, Commander," he said formally, since she'd made it so clear that she was in charge of their operations on the station, "I'm here to report that the operation with the Al-Jabbars was successful. They proved themselves uniquely qualified for the mission and had none of the one-upmanship our own goons have displayed a little too often. Both Twists were located, the large and the smaller, in exactly the rooms our intelligence indicated. The rooms are bugged and telemetry is flowing as we speak. I'll be spending most of the next few days mainlining caffeine and pouring through analysis of the information as quickly as I can."

She nodded and was clearly pleased to hear that, since she hadn't been completely confident with his selection of people for the task. "I'm glad they accomplished what was necessary. I had my doubts, as you know." Tatyana touched his arm and motioned toward the couch where she had been sleeping. "Let's sit down. I want to look over what they accomplished."

He went with her to the couch and set his data core up on the low table in front of it so that the hologram had plenty of room to spread out through the room. Just a few moments later, he had accessed surveillance on both rooms housing the Twist machinery, though neither was active at the moment. He then took her back through the footage he had managed to tap into while Orion and Anna were in the room, and played back the conversation between Vance and Gehrig, with the real-time vision of Eleusis in the background behind them.

"I imagined more trees, but the vegetation local to the Twist seems more low grass rather than forests. It'll make an assault on the compound more difficult, but certainly not impossible."

Tatyana looked at the image of Eleusis through the Twist and she reached out to enlarge the clip and the image. "My father used to try to describe it to us in his messages. But then he would say, 'It's so beautiful, you wouldn't believe me if I could explain it.'" There was a sad smile on her lips as she let go of the hologram and it shrunk back to its original size. "He was so close."

Gordon nodded solemnly and let the image linger in the moments between Vance and Gehrig leaving the room and the Twist's shutdown. He didn't want to let go of the image any more than she did. "There's something else you need to see, that Anna retrieved. Not from the Twist rooms, but while she was on Earth." He couldn't look at her and he took his time navigating over to the data files for the tablet. "And I'm not showing you this as a subordinate. Just as someone who cares."

"Someone who cares about what? Me?" She wasn't sure he did care about her anymore, though it was hard to tell what or who he cared about, unless it was the woman having his baby. "I didn't think you cared about me anymore."

"I am capable of disagreeing with you in fundamental ways and still caring about you as a person, Tatyana. My emotional range is complicated like that." He gave a sedated smile but it vanished quickly as he reached the files. "Anna and Logan were the first responders to the crash site, carrying away Earth-dwelling survivors. Anna also went searching among the escape pods that fell around the station to try and find anyone who could have made it safely to the ground. She didn't find anyone, but she did find a man with white hair, clutching a shattered tablet to his chest inside the pod." As soon as he selected the tablet information and the directories displayed in Cyrillic, he doubted she would need more explanation.

Tatyana went still and it felt like ice had been poured down her back as she looked at the display. She couldn't tear her eyes away, for fear she would miss something. "She saw him? She . . . this is his? They said there was nothing left." Of course, Tatyana knew it was a lie, the Consortium would cover up everything, but she had yet to find anything that was left behind or missed by the Consortium.

"This is his." He nodded, and pulled up the section of video entries. "He made a recording on the way . . . after the arm had been ejected from the station. I managed to salvage just about everything that was on the tablet except for some of the geological survey results, but I can probably find those in our current systems to supplement the data. All of his entries, his notes, his messages, his logs, are here."

Tatyana looked at the files that contained the videos, and the last one, the most recent, kept her attention. The one he said must have been on the way down. She moved closer to Gordon so she could access his information herself, and she reached out to grab the video file. She pushed the hologram up to make it bigger, and his frantic expression made her stomach twist. Tatyana didn't want to watch it. She didn't want to watch her father frantic, scared, in pain . . . ultimately, she didn't want to watch him die. But she had to.

Tatyana didn't say anything before she started the clip, but immediately she wished she hadn't. The sound of his voice thrilled her, but the fear in his voice, the clear danger, it made her both furious and frightened. They were supposed to reunite on Eleusis. They were supposed to be together in a brand new world with a new life, free of sickness and heartache. They had cured his cancer so that he could work on the Eleusis project. They had given him and their family hope again, only to dash it by killing him in the end. The Consortium had changed her by killing her father, but she would use it to bring them down.

"He was so close." She said a few times, since he was a rebel himself despite working for the Consortium, a rebel trying to get the right people on Eleusis. He had died for it.

Gordon had only met the man once, right before he had left for the first wave of the Initiative, but he had respected him. He had certainly never wanted to see him end in such a terrified way. "He was close. And now we're a few steps closer. We'll make it there."

"Vance made that call, you know. I saw his signature on the order. It was supposed to be destroyed, of course, but it was there. I saw it." She swiped away the video angrily, and there was a single tear sliding down her cheek. Tatyana was broken because of what happened, but not helpless. "I'm going to kill that bastard myself."

"If I can ever pin him down, I'll be sure you get that chance. On that, we agree completely." He closed the data file once she swiped away the video, and in just a few gestures, she could see he had copied all of the data to her own core. It had been her father's, after all, it was her inheritance. "So long as I still have your word that if the time comes and the opportunity presents itself, you'll do the same for me where Gehrig is concerned."

"I'll tie her up and keep her gagged until you get there." She promised and finally wiped at the tear on her cheek. "Thank you. For bringing this to me."

"I'm sorry that I had to." He leaned forward to retrieve his data core, then looked back at her again once it was tucked beneath his shirt. "We have our confirmation, soon I'll make sure we have the information we need to achieve our goals. It won't be long now."

* * * * *

Mercury couldn't remember many times when she'd slept deeply, mostly because she always had something on her mind that kept her from sleeping soundly. There was still a lot on her mind when she opened her eyes; she still had patients that needed her and her personal life was still complicated, but it wasn't a mess. It felt right, even if it was complicated.

She turned onto her side and looked over for Logan, but he wasn't there. She ran her fingers through her messy hair and sat up, but she didn't hear anything in the unit. She assumed the doors were still locked, but they could have been let out by now. She had no idea.

"Logan?" She asked loudly, hoping he would hear her.

"Out here." His voice came from the kitchen. When he opened their bedroom door a moment later, the scent of coffee came with him. He had showered and was more dressed than they had been for most of the week they had been locked in the unit with each other, loose boxers hanging on his hips that did nothing to disguise what she knew was underneath. They also hadn't had coffee the whole week, since there hadn't exactly been a need to hurry. She could tell everything about his mood by the way he moved. He was relaxed, unhurried, confident, as close to peace as Logan was capable of in recent circumstances.

He went to her side of the bed to offer her a mug of coffee and sat beside her with his own as she rubbed at her eyes. "It sounded like you were having a good dream when I got up. You were moaning the same way you did the other day when I woke you up. Tell me about it."

Mercury's pale cheeks flushed crimson when he said she was moaning in her sleep, since she was embarrassed by her body behaving in ways that she didn't expect. "I, um . . ." She took the mug of coffee and gulped down the hot liquid as she attempted to recall her dream. It was already fading from her mind, the longer she was awake.

"You kept touching and teasing me but you wouldn't let me finish." It wasn't uncommon for Logan to torture her in the best of ways, and her subconscious was acutely aware of it. "You were teasing me and you would tell me that we needed to get some sleep, and you would roll over and stop. Only to tease me again and again." Her pulse kicked up just a little from both the coffee and the dream, but mostly from her dream. It had done a number on her already, even in her sleep.

"It sounds like your subconscious thinks I'm capable of some truly black-hearted cruelty." He reached out with one hand to run his fingers through her hair, which already looked as though she was ready for a photo-shoot just ten seconds after waking up. "I'm not sure whether to be flattered by that or concerned."

Mercury definitely liked the feeling of his hand in her hair and slid herself closer to him as she held her mug of coffee with both hands. "It was a good kind of cruel." She smiled as she looked over at him with her dark green eyes. "Or, at least, my body seems to think so."

"Good." He approved, especially as his hand slid down her neck to draw the blanket away from her. She had never once been permitted to sleep in clothes unless they were for the express purpose of allowing her to strip them off for him in the morning, and that week past, they had been bare at all times. That morning was no exception, and his hand found nothing but her pale skin as he pulled the blanket away.

He leaned in to kiss her once, his lips hot and bitter from the black coffee in his mug. "Someday, I'll be so deep in your subconscious that all you'll need to do is think my name, imagine being beneath me just for an instant, and it'll turn you needy like this." He put his coffee down on the table beside her as he leaned into her, as his hand moved between her legs to satisfy what the dream had started. "That's the way I want you, and the way I plan to have you."

"You are relentless." She responded breathily, and she was quick to put aside her coffee as well. Mercury kissed along his neck and his shoulder as he leaned into her, wherever she could reach, her lips tasted his skin. There was something quite amazing about feeling in love with someone and having them as yours, since Logan was finally hers. "Does it make you happy . . . to see me like this?"

"Yes, it does." He held her in close as she kissed him, but there was nothing teasing or cruel about his touch. He meant to finish the job her dream started, and he knew everything there was to know about how she liked to be handled. "I'm a great fan of paradox, I've learned recently. Or perhaps only when it comes to you. I want you unbound by anyone or anything, but bound to me unbreakably. I want you thoroughly satisfied at all times, but impossible to satiate. I want you regal and revered, but up for the dirtiest things I can concoct for you in private. Right now I want you satisfied. I'm not going to just leave you hanging, even if it was only my dream self that got you started."

She could barely speak when he attacked her fiercely, and he had to hold her close in order for her to stay upright at all. Mercury was dripping and needy for him, so it took nearly no time at all before she was moaning his name. She loved his name. His hands. His body. Everything about him, she loved. Especially because she felt loved by him, too. Mercury still wasn't sure how it happened, and it still didn't feel quite real. She had no idea that she could feel this passionate about and toward someone, but she did.

The moment before she climaxed, he held her back so he could look her in the eye as she did, drinking in the pleasure there and the complete vulnerability he felt from her in that moment. Being with her, having her, had been the most incredible high he had ever experienced in his life, but it went beyond just the satisfaction of control. She was his, heart, body, and soul, if indeed either of them had one. Feeling her give herself to him completely was the best part of his day, the dream of his nights. As far as he was concerned, the world became a better place every time she moaned his name. "That should get your day off to the right kind of start."

"Mmmm." She purred in complete satisfaction as she curled into him afterward, since the feeling of his body pressed into hers made the high last even longer. "Being with you makes my day better. No matter what else could happen." She ran her fingertips lazily over his skin as her body attempted to come down from the high that he'd given her. "I'm so in love with you, Logan Bickford."

He held her tight against his broad chest as his hand finally left her to recover, moving his rough caress up over her back to press her into him. "I love you too, Mercury." He leaned in to kiss her neck with a sigh, crushing her to him. "They unlocked the doors this morning. I haven't left yet. Under different circumstances, I think I would be content to stay here with you for at least another . . . year. As it is, I'm still in no hurry to get back to the rest of what's waiting for us out there. What matters is you."

It warmed her in a way nothing else could to hear how important she was to him, and how much he cared about and loved her. Mercury moved just enough in his lap to reach his lips to kiss him soundly with both of her hands holding onto the back of his neck. After that, she pressed her forehead to his. "I don't want to leave either. Though I think we both agree that we have a lot of work to do."

"Yes, we do." He agreed with a sigh as he kissed her again to procrastinate participating in the rest of the world for a while longer. "Go get a shower and wait for me in there. I'm going to finish putting breakfast together for us and then I want you at least once before we go out and see the world again. Take the #7 in with you."

Mercury nodded and snuck a few more kisses before she dared to move away, since she loved the feeling of his lips against hers. It was one of a million things she loved. "I will go get it right away." She stole one more kiss before she moved. "Do you think we'll finally have our baby after being locked up this long?"

That made Logan laugh, and he made no secret of looking her over as she moved away toward the bathroom. He was a very visual person, all in all. "I should fucking hope so. Not that I'm ever averse to finding new ways to get you pregnant, but if none of the ones we've tried so far have worked, some very serious creativity will be called for."

"Very serious creativity indeed." Mercury smiled back at him and made no secret about looking him over either, since he was ruggedly gorgeous. Her gaze flitted over his body and his arms, blushing as she thought about all the things he could do with his hands. And his mouth. "Time will tell." She headed toward the shower with a final smile. "I'll wait patiently for you."

The "quarantine," as it had been consistently termed by all communications from the brass, had left the entire station a quieter place than it had been previously. Doors were opened and people began to return to their tasks, either in various teams of design or in training for their eventual roles on Eleusis, but no one seemed particularly excited to do so. Everywhere they went, visiting the various departments and private residences of certain individuals, Logan and Mercury came across people who were more scared than anything else. Scared to leave their unit, scared to go *back* to their unit, to continue working, scared that they could be the next to disappear.

"They got rid of half my agricultural consultants." He kept his voice low as they headed up a vacant corridor, but she knew him well enough to know that he was fuming. "How the fuck do they expect us to get everything ready for takeoff with half the staff that was already overtaxed? How much of your team is left?"

Mercury sounded calmer, but she was clearly stressed, since nearly half her staff was gone as well. Essential staff. Medical staff was supposed to be essential, but apparently there was an 'accident' and some people had to be evacuated. Mercury didn't believe it, but that was what they were told. "We have five doctors total for all of us. Half the nursing staff." She sighed and shook her head. "Maybe that's the point. Maybe they don't actually want us to be able to get ready for takeoff."

"So they can delay us just a little longer at the time." He agreed, since that kind of strategy made sense, from the Consortium's twisted perspective. He lifted his communicator to his mouth, even though he wasn't interested in having a conversation with the recipient of the message.

"I want department governance meetings set up in the next two days and reports from all department heads about potential impact of lost personnel to readiness timeframes. Set up an Executive Council meeting for Thursday afternoon and request that the Judiciary meet as well once the reports are in." He sent the message to his secretary and shoved the device back in his pocket. He didn't need to hear the woman simpering about how long it would take to get everyone coordinated, he just wanted her to get to work, even if she was more on the Consortium's payroll than his own. "Who's next on your list to visit? Is Fitch one of yours?"

Mercury nodded. "Anna too." She watched his expression closely. They had been in their own world for long enough she wondered how things would go when they were faced with Anna and Orion again. Obviously things had changed since she had last seen Orion. "I have all the women who are pregnant on my roster to visit. I'm the only Obstetrician here."

He thought in silence for a while, but eventually shook his head with a frown. "They've left a single OB to treat hundreds of pregnant women, most of them first-time mothers. That has to be for a purpose. When I requisition the brass on your behalf for more doctors to assist with your caseload, they'll either bring in more of their own or they're expecting some of the women not to get all the care they need for some reason. Whatever game it is they're playing, it needs to end."

"This has been a game from the beginning, it seems." Mercury admitted sadly, since she had worked so hard nearly all her life to get where she was. She had no idea she was born on a chessboard, and she was just another piece to be played. "If it ends, I'm certain that means we won't survive past the end of the game."

"That depends on how it ends." He growled in a lower voice. "Chess is typically between two players. The only difference with us is that we weren't aware that we were being played until recently. Now that we are . . . well, we can fiddle with the rules a bit." He actually smiled to reassure her, since nothing could be completely wrong with the world when Mercury was around. "Who else can we rely on, among your patients? It's a rare woman who will be willing to put herself at risk while she also has her unborn child to think about, but I'm sure we can rely on at least Kameron, as well as Anna."

"Aiko Tanaka and Jessica Rogers. They both have been very honest with me and open, though Aiko more than Jessica." Mercury looked away from him for a moment as she thought about some of her other patients. "Barry's wife. And Barry. We can trust them too." She chewed on her bottom lip for a moment before she looked over at Logan again. "There are some others, I think. But I'm not completely sure." They were headed toward Fitch's unit already so Mercury could check on her, but Mercury didn't know if Logan would get called away again and she was afraid to walk the halls alone. "What if they decide to send me away? Or to send you away? We had no knowledge or warning about the others that are gone."

Logan wasn't sure how to protect against that happening, and all he could do was shake his head. "We'll just have to work quickly, that's all. Now that we're out of lockdown and so many people are missing, they'll expect us to be reeling for a few days, give them a chance to lay some new strings for us to dance on. We need to be faster and better than that." He sighed, since he hoped they would have more time, but circumstances dictated more action and less planning. "When you see Fitch and Jessie, tell them to be up at the dock tonight at nine. It's gonna be busy up there no matter what, but if we can get all the right people in one place and get on the same page, we can move forward. Tell Barry and Erebi too. We'll need everybody we can trust."

"And Aiko and Carl? Anna and Orion?" It sounded strange to say it out loud, Anna and Orion. All of it happened so fast, and it happened in such a way that was definitely not how she would have chosen it. But it happened. She didn't regret being with Logan, but that didn't mean that the situation didn't hurt. "Will you go talk to them, then?"

"I'll visit them." He said shortly, since he clearly wasn't looking forward to it. "I'll have Orion contact Carl, I know they're friends. No need for you to have to go out of your way until Anna's next scheduled exam." The look he gave her was one of understanding, even though they hadn't really talked at length about what happened. He knew Mercury loved Orion, even if their relationship hadn't been as deep or long-lived as his long-time complicated friendship with Anna. But their hand had been forced by the Consortium, and Logan had made his choice. Clearly Anna had also made hers.

Mercury nodded and pressed into Logan so she could pull him into a kiss, since she didn't want to go her separate way without kissing him and letting him know her feelings for him at all times. "I'll be back at our unit as soon as I can be. I have a long list of patients to see."

He returned the kiss, even though there were plenty of other people moving through the hall around them. It was relatively new for them, showing affection in a public place, but Logan no longer saw the point in feeling strange or awkward about it. She was his, and he was hers, and it didn't matter who knew it or who saw it. Besides, if even a few of the rumors he'd heard were true, Anna and Orion had never had any such compunctions against people knowing about their activities in public.

He took out his communicator and let her watch him type a message to her, clearly not for her benefit, but the benefit of anyone who was watching. *Keep me updated with your progress. If I don't hear from you within twenty minutes of contacting you, I'll assume I need to call out the guard to search for you.* He sent the message to her device, then put his own back in his pocket and kissed her again. "Be safe. I miss you already."

Mercury smiled at him as soon as he said he missed her, and she kept her communicator close in a pocket of her scrubs so she could contact him whenever she needed to. She ran her fingers over his cheek once before she headed off without saying anything else, mostly because it was too hard to say goodbye to Logan. It was just easier just to go, no matter what the situation. She had patients that still needed her, even if the Consortium felt she was expendable. Her patients relied on her regardless, and she wasn't going to let them down.

The panel outside Kameron's door glowed a dull red as Mercury walked up to it, but so did most of the units on the corridor. Many of them weren't occupied, but even for those that were, the end of a lockdown didn't mean the end of a human need for some illusion of safety behind a locked door. As she walked up to it, though, the panel turned green even before she could chime to knock.

Mercury was confused as the door turned green before she knocked, but she knocked anyway, since she wasn't about to barge in on anyone. Her communicator said that the unit was occupied, but she'd gone to two other units that day that were supposed to be occupied but weren't. "Lieutenant Fitch, Dr. Finnegan here to check on you." She said through the door, hoping that she would be heard if Kameron hadn't been alerted.

She heard a muffled voice through the door, but it wasn't raised. "Kameron! Kameron, someone's here! It's not them!" There was a sound of some quick movement inside and Mercury could feel someone run across the floor toward the door. There was a loud clattering and the sound of scraping against the floor, but the door opened to show a deeply-bedraggled blonde who was more than a little frantic. "She needs help. Do you have water? Food?"

"Water and food?" Mercury said in confusion but she was quick to act, and she rushed inside the unit and used her own code to request food and water. It required an override, which she had, fortunately, along with her medical kit. At least for the moment. A bottle of water popped down quickly, and the food was en route. At least she hoped. "What happened? What's wrong?"

"It's been eight days, that's what's wrong!" The blonde was frantic as she grabbed the water bottle right out of the dispenser and stumbled toward the bedroom with it as quickly as she could.

When they both got there, Mercury could see that Kameron was in a bad way. She was laid out on the bed looking even paler than usual, in the fetal position. Both of them were showing every textbook sign of dehydration and sleep deprivation, circles under their eyes, shaking extremities, and the scent of the room told Mercury that they had been denied so much as the necessary water for bathing.

The blonde attempted to hold the bottle to Kameron's lips, but it was clearly getting difficult for her to get a response from the somehow-still-pregnant woman. "Come on, girly, drink. Doctor's here, we can get more now, the door's unlocked. We'll be alright, please, just drink it. Please."

Mercury had no idea why the women had been denied food or water, but she didn't have time to think about it. She immediately went to the side of Kameron's bed as Kameron's friend attempted to help her drink, and she set the case of medical supplies on the floor. The case flew open easily and Mercury pulled out the one bag of IV fluids and started it immediately.

Kameron was mostly immobile, and Mercury would need to get a doppler on her to check on the baby as soon as Kameron was stable. "Has she had any bleeding?" Mercury didn't really know who the other woman was, as any other time she had visited Kameron or been visited in her clinic, Kameron would talk about Kazuo. After he died, Kameron was entirely focused on the baby.

Mercury was able to get the IV into Kameron flawlessly and she found a pin in the wall to hang it from. "When was the last time she ate?" The fluids had electrolytes and vitamins, as well as a standard dose of anti-nausea, just in case.

"They've been sending some . . . nutritional ration shit. Comes in a bar, tastes like dog shit. They've been giving us one a day." Melissa said without taking her eyes off Kameron. "One of those and two bottles of water this size every day. That's all they've been sending. That's all she's had."

"What? Why . . ." Mercury kept her attention on Kameron and went digging through the medical kit. She pulled a tube out of it and she had to gently nudge the blonde out of the way so she could get to Kameron's mouth. "Kameron? Can you hear me? I need you to talk to me, if you can."

Kameron just groaned at first, everything hurt, she felt so tired and weak that nothing felt right. She couldn't even think, but she tried to open her eyes. There was a blurry vision of red hair until her bleary eyes opened a little bit more. "Doc?" She said softly, but she couldn't keep her eyes open for long. "The baby . . ."

"I know, I'll check on her right away, I promise. I just need you to eat some of this, okay? It's supposed to taste really sweet, but it's high in calories for a purpose. It'll spike your sugar at least. I just need you to have some quick energy and I need to get a response out of the little girl, okay?" It looked like Kameron nodded but she wasn't quite sure as she put the tube of paste up to Kameron's lips. Kameron attempted to eat the paste, but not without a few gags here and there, though no complaints.

Once half the tube was gone, Mercury left Kameron alone for a few moments before she let the blonde go back to giving her water. "I'm going to check her blood and then I'm going to check the baby. Are you all right, Miss . . .?"

"Melissa. And I'm not the pregnant one, she is. I'll be fine." She really did appear to be in much better condition than Kameron, but that wasn't saying much. "It's not the first time I've had to go hungry, and it won't be the last."

There was an alert to let them know that the food Mercury ordered was delivered to the dining area, but Mercury didn't even look back or get up. She would have to order something else for Kameron once she was able to actually eat. "You need to eat also. You won't be much help to her much longer if you don't." Mercury nodded back toward the dining area, but the woman wouldn't budge. "I'm going to look her over and check on the baby, I'm not sure she'll want you . . ."

"She can stay." Kameron said between small sips of water, but her eyes didn't open again. All it took was once. One time after lockdown that Kam gave in to Melissa's persistence about getting naked, and then the water and the food stopped coming. No showers. No lights or flowing electricity into the unit except for a few hours a day, and to keep things on that they needed to survive. Kameron knew why they were punished, but the Initiative had locked them in the unit in the first place. They had been punished for being together, but they weren't the ones who had trapped themselves in the first place. "I don't care what she sees. I want her to stay."

"Even if you did, I'm not leaving." Melissa said fiercely from the side of the bed. "It's my fault. I should have known. I'm so sorry, Kam. I should have . . ."

"Known? That they're fucking perverts, watching . . ." Kameron broke into a fit of coughing, but more water seemed to help, and it was a little while before she could say anything else. "They want you to get back with your match. That's how it works." She opened her eyes just a little and stared at Melissa, still beautiful, even though she was just as bad off as Kameron was. "You wouldn't want to be with me anyway, hot stuff. I'm way too possessive." She coughed a little bit more and closed her eyes as the doctor kept checking on her.

Mercury didn't need any more explanation than that to know why they were mistreated. They had gone against the Initiative. She wasn't sure how it was at all fair to lock the women up and punish them for it, but the Initiative wasn't fair. It was cruel.

Mercury worked at getting Kameron's shirt off so that she could check on the baby, but she took a few blood samples first. There were a lot of issues that needed to be addressed based on her readings, but she pulled out her fetal scanner before even thinking about that. She had to check on the baby.

Mercury stood up so that she could hold the framed piece of opaque glass above Kameron, and when she tapped a button on the side, the glass turned into a scanner. Mercury bent down to get closer, checking for the baby's heartbeat and checking vitals as she also looked at the amniotic fluid all at once.

"There's still a heartbeat. Slower, much slower, than I would like, but you've kept a surprising amount of fluid in there for her. We need to get more food and water in you to help little miss, or there's going to be serious issues. I don't know what kind of long-term impact this will have on her, but those are the only immediate actions we can take."

"She'll be alright." Melissa said from where she still knelt at

Kameron's side. "She has an amazing mom." Melissa was holding one of Kameron's hands as tightly as she could, and leaned in to kiss her cheek as well, though it was clearly an effort to do so. "I might get back with my match just to get a decent meal," she whispered against her cheek, "but I would love to be possessed by you."

"A decent meal? Is that what they're calling it now?" Kameron attempted to tease, but she wasn't even smiling. "They'll kill us if we give them the chance. When the doctor leaves, you have to go with her. And don't come back." Kameron said in a shaky voice, since she didn't want Melissa to go, but she wasn't about to see the woman die on her behalf. "Falling for your gorgeous ass would end up being the worst kind of heartbreak."

Melissa knew what Kameron said made sense, but she didn't move away as Mercury did her work. Instead she leaned in and kissed her again lightly, resting her forehead against Kameron's afterward. "I'm not done with you yet, girly. We're gonna get out of here, we're going to get somewhere they can't fuck with us. We're going to get away from them, because I don't want you getting away from me."

"You're fucking persistent, has anyone told you that?" Kameron whispered as Melissa kept her forehead close. She wanted to reach her hand out to touch her, but her arm felt so heavy. "Kiss me again. Please." If Melissa was going to leave, she wanted to kiss her as many times as she could manage. Even if she was technically still dying on the bed, since it definitely felt that way.

Melissa pushed herself up onto the bed, even though she bumped the scanner in the process of laying herself against Kameron. Now that a doctor was in residence to take care of her, Melissa wasn't worried that she would recover. Kam was a tough one. She kissed her deeply, a few lingering water droplets on her lips, and reached up to caress her face afterward. "I'll see you soon, girly. Don't die on me, and take good care of that baby. You're gonna be fine."

Kameron looked into Melissa's eyes once the kiss broke and she forced her arm to move so she could actually touch Melissa just once. She ran her fingers weakly across Melissa's face and didn't look away from her, but she still whispered her response. "I told Kaz I can't do this whole parenting thing by myself. It's still true. She can be your baby too, if we get the hell out of this nightmare."

That elicited a grin from Melissa and another slightly more scandalous kiss, considering that they were both on the edge of starving to death. "As long as you're my baby first." She kissed Kameron a few more times and slid off the bed with a groan, pushing herself slowly to her feet. It was hard to leave Kameron after so long together, sharing so much, being so close to the edge together, but if the past week had taught her anything, it was how much she had to leave. For everyone's safety, they had to make the bastards running the station happy, if only for the time being.

Kameron hated seeing her tattooed angel leave, but she didn't even try to stop her as she watched Melissa walk out of the room. "I thought I could keep her safe." Kameron eventually said out loud as the doctor worked quietly. "I thought nothing could stop me from taking care of someone. The universe keeps showing me over and over what shit I am at protecting people."

Kameron was sure she was teetering over the line of breaking down completely. Her whole life she'd been the tough one, and in such a short time she had been shown how tough she wasn't. Kaz died, despite her efforts. Melissa and her baby nearly died, despite her efforts to protect them both. "They did it on purpose. The fuckers did it on purpose. They wanted to punish us, they probably wanted my baby dead. Twisted, disgusting motherfuckers."

Mercury let Kameron talk, let her say what she needed to say, keeping watch on her vitals as well as the baby's. When she went quiet, Mercury looked at Kameron again. "We're working on a way to get out." She said softly as she examined the IV and the fluids. She definitely needed more for Kameron, and it would be easier if she just transported Kameron to the clinic. "Logan and I and some others. We'd love your help."

Kameron raised an eyebrow as she looked the doctor over and kept her head in her pillow. "I don't know if I can trust you. Or Logan. But I guess I don't really have much choice. Orion trusted you, so I guess I can try." She looked down at herself and back up at the doctor. "My baby is going to end up dead if they keep me trapped here. I think that's what they want."

"I'll do my best to take care of you both. I promise." Mercury said with complete sincerity before she pulled out her communicator. "I'm going to need someone to help me transport you to the clinic. You need more fluids and more care than I can provide from a small kit. I don't trust very many people, so . . ."

"Call Orion. Or Carl. I don't trust very many people either. But I trust them." Kameron put a hand on the side of her belly and then sighed. "Kaz's baby needs to live. He didn't. I can't let her die too."

Mercury didn't know Carl well enough to contact him, so she pulled up Orion's contact instead. This wasn't exactly what she hoped for when considering her first conversation after the dissolution of her marriage, but it would have to do.

When you can, please come to Kameron Fitch's unit. I need your help.

Just as soon as they had been notified that the doors were unlocked, Orion and Anna returned to the dock to make it appear as though they were resuming their duties as normal. They listened to the same bullshit message all morning about a pathogen that hadn't been properly contained and required evacuation and quarantine of crew members.

The crew members in question were telling. Pablo was gone, and a quick round of the rumor mill confirmed that his husband was gone as well. Those who were left were quiet and diligent, keeping their eyes on their work even when their work really wasn't all that interesting.

"According to this, we've missed two supply ships." Orion said to Anna and a few of the other pilots under his command. "Which means we're fine for now, but we're gonna be in a bad way a few days from now unless we make some extra runs. We're on the dark side of the orbital pattern to boot, so that just makes things even more fun for us."

"We're going to run two teams to retrieve supplies from tangential stations during this round. Two pilots each, plus another navigational consultant who'll stay here to coordinate. No mistakes, no risks. Kipling and Adams, you'll take one, Ramsay will consult. Ascuncion and Rosetti, you take the other, with Anna consulting. You've got access to the requisition lists and our current navigational data. We need these to be clockwork. Do not fuck this up." Orion handed out the assignments and lists to Kipling and Ascuncion and sighed as they headed back to their stations.

"What about you?" Anna asked once everyone scattered to prep. "You better not tell me you're going to go out there and leave me here. I'm not going to take that."

"I wouldn't dream." He smiled over at her and pulled up his messages. "No, I got a very clear directive from Gehrig that I was not to leave the station, under any circumstances."

"It's so nice to be targeted." Anna quipped as she looked at the message, but she narrowed her eyes when she saw one from his ex. "And love notes from your ex?" She asked suspiciously, but she wasn't suspicious of Orion. Anna barely knew Mercury, and Logan was still her friend. She hoped he was with someone who would treat him right, but she would be damned to stand by if Mercury was being any kind of shady.

Orion's eyebrows tied themselves in a confused knot as he selected the message. "That one's new. I wonder what's going on with Fitch? I haven't heard from her since before the lockdown."

"I asked Gordon to check in on her, remember? Though they lifted lockdown pretty much right after that. Maybe he didn't see the point." Anna's expression darkened and she looked away from the message and back at Orion. "You better go see what's going on. I highly doubt Mercury would be sending you a message unless it was important. I'll stay here and watch over the flight prep."

Orion nodded, since he agreed that there was no way Mercury would have contacted him outside of an emergency. It had been that way between them for weeks, not just since they had both remarried. "I'll be back as soon as I can." He kissed her once before he started moving away toward the lift, floating through the subdued stillness of the dock between people flowing back and forth to the bar and the zero-gravity storage modules. He hoped Mercury herself was alright.

When Mercury heard a faint knock on Kameron's door, she reassured Kameron that she would be right back before she got up to answer. It was a strange moment, looking up at Orion when she was no longer his wife, but she stepped aside quickly so he could enter the unit and she could lock the door behind him. She didn't want any surprises.

"Kameron needs to be transported to the clinic, and she asked that you or Carl help me do that. They had her trapped in here for eight days with Melissa, who I assume is her girlfriend, but they rationed their food and water to one survival bar and one liter of water total each day. Her baby survived, which is a miracle in itself. I need to get more fluid for her, but I can't access what I need from here."

Orion cursed in Arabic as she gave him the rundown of what happened, and she had learned just enough of it in the time she had lived with him to understand just how foul-mouthed the expression was. He rushed further into the unit with Mercury and stopped when he got to the bed, sniffing a few times as he tried to banish the scent of the room from his nostrils.

"Ugh, Kameron, seriously. We need to work on your stay-at-home skills." He immediately started looking for the best way to transport her, and eventually settled on a clean blanket that had been laid aside on a couch to one end of the room. He started wrapping her up in the blanket so he could pick her up and transport her, but though his tone was light, his face was deadly serious. "What happened with the tattoo artist? She get out okay?"

Fitch groaned when he picked her up, but it wasn't his fault that her whole body ached from dehydration and malnutrition. "She went back to her unit. I was trying to keep her safe, but seems like the only way she's safe is if she's fucking a man." She kept her eyes squeezed tight as Mercury grabbed the mostly-empty bag of IV fluids.

Orion walked as carefully as he could, but clearly Mercury either hadn't trusted anyone else to get a gurney or Fitch had insisted on not having one, which Orion thought was more likely. They were out in the middle of the day, so they inevitably got a few looks from people on their way to the lift to reach the clinic. Looks, Orion could deal with. One of his best friends dying of malnutrition just because the Initiative wanted to play games . . . that was not something he was going to tolerate.

He didn't force Fitch to talk any more as he carried her, but he did look over at Mercury as she carried her medical bag and held the IV fluids high to keep them flowing into Fitch's system. "What else is she going to need? Besides some decent nutrition?"

"Protection." Mercury said softly as she looked over at Kameron and then up at Orion. "The Initiative put us all on mandatory lockdown, including Kameron and Melissa, and then punished them for it. She would have died if she hadn't had someone watching out for her, and they put her in that kind of situation alone. They probably wanted her to die. She needs to stay with someone so that she can be monitored. I'd volunteer to keep her with me, but I don't think she trusts me very much."

"I'll have my people stay with her on rotation until she gets back on her feet." He said with a nod, looking down at Kameron and waiting for a snarky remark like she normally would have given, but she was too out of it to even know she was in a lift, from the look of her. "What's your expectation on how long before that is, do you think?"

"A week, maybe longer, depending on what kind of medication and supplements I'll actually have access to. I never know what I'm going to have anymore." She shook her head, since she felt more and more frustrated and defeated as a doctor. "They limited us to five doctors. Took away half my nursing staff. People will start dying if something goes wrong because there won't be enough people to help them."

"One of my guys has some field medic experience, I'll re-task him over to you to try and help with triage, at least. And keep an eye on Kameron." Orion was starting to see holes everywhere he went, after going to bug the Twist with Anna, and the longer he thought about the organization he'd been in all his life, the worse he felt about it. "I'm glad you're alright. I assume Logan is doing more or less alright as well, after all this?"

It was strange to have Orion ask her about Logan and his well-being, but she nodded in response. "He's alright. He's angry about all of the people we've lost, and because it seems like no matter what we do we're being blocked and caged. He's still working on a way to change that and to get us out." She said the last statement softly and then she met Orion's eyes again. "We should have a chance at a normal, happy life. All of us."

Orion nodded back quietly, but he couldn't look at Mercury for too long. He didn't regret the choice they all made, but a lack of regret didn't mean it hurt any less to see the woman he'd been married to only a short week before. "Should is a pretty iffy word up here. Means a lot to some people, doesn't mean much to others. All I know is I'm not cut out to live in a cage. And neither are you. Neither are any of us."

He was able to meet Mercury's eyes, then shook his head, since he didn't know who could've been listening to their conversation. "We've made some progress, Anna and I. Things should move quickly now. I've got a lot of work to do to be ready, and I was counting on having this one around to help." He lifted Kameron a little in his arms with another look down at her drawn, unconscious expression. "You say it'll take a week, I give her three days before she leaves against your advice."

"If she leaves against my advice, I hope that she'll still be protected, one way or another." Mercury looked at Kameron in his arms and sighed as she reached out to brush some hair away from Kameron's face. "Not only did they try to kill her, but they wanted her to die without dignity. They couldn't shower. They couldn't take care of each other or themselves. What is the point of that? What is the point of stripping someone down to absolutely nothing to let them die when it takes absolutely no effort to let them live?" Mercury's stomach twisted into knots of disgust. "How did I not see it before? How did I fall into this project believing that I was doing something good when these people are so bad?"

"Because it's these people. Not all people." She knew Orion well enough to read more in his tone and expressions than he was ever willing to say out loud, and every time he talked about the Consortium, the conflict in him was the same as the conflict in Mercury herself.

"I took a class once during flight school about security and psychology. It included a few classes on profiling and the psychology of criminal behavior. Something they said in that class has always stuck out to me because it gave me the creeps at the time. They said the most successful criminals throughout history have been the ones who would never have been suspected of being criminals by the people who knew them in their day-to-day life. Had day jobs, friends, sometimes had families, then at night or just once in a while, they would go outside of all of it and commit these terrible crimes with nothing to lead back to them. Some serial killers in the twenty-second century were estimated to have more than three hundred kills before they were convicted."

"I feel like that's what's happening here. The Consortium takes care of millions of people up here in orbit, provides what's needed, runs stations in an orderly fashion so that everything functions as it should, but then there's this twisted little side project that you and I just walked into, thinking it would be . . . good. Like the rest of what we know about them."

Mercury nodded, since what he said made sense, but it still bothered her that she felt like she was made the fool. She hated feeling duped. Or worse, stupid. "Logan seemed to know. From the beginning I remember his attitude toward the Consortium was always reserved and suspicious. How did they know things that we didn't? I didn't think I was that naive. I was just so focused on my own work, my own world, I . . . I didn't have time to think about anything else. I certainly didn't question anything. I didn't question any restrictions or protocols, there was no reason to fight against 'the system' for me. I didn't want to fight anything or anyone. I was happy."

"They didn't have that chance." Orion growled as they finally reached the level with the clinic, but he walked slowly even after he got out of the elevator, since he didn't want to disturb Kameron any more than necessary. "They've had to fight for everything they have their whole lives. That's why they knew. I knew Earthborn always blamed the Consortium for most of their problems, but I always thought it was just them looking to make their trouble somebody else's fault. I don't think it's that simple anymore."

Mercury didn't say anything else until they were in the clinic. Once they had Kameron in a room with all the equipment Mercury needed, she buzzed around quickly to get Kameron hooked up. Only when her patient was comfortable did she look at Orion again. "I'll take good care of your friend. I promise. I'm just glad to see they didn't do something like this to you. It would be terrible to see you like this."

"I don't think I could've gone a week without nutrition. Even if I wasn't pregnant. If I was, I think going without food would be the least of my problems, but that's a whole different conversation." He shook his head as he looked down at Kameron and sighed. "I'll have one of my guys down here in a few minutes for the first shift. As soon as she comes around and you're satisfied that she's fully present mentally, tell her she's under orders to contact me."

"I will." Mercury stared at Orion since Kameron seemed stable enough on the drip for the moment. "I'm sorry we didn't get to talk again before things changed." She didn't want to say the word divorce, but it happened, and Orion had initiated it but she wasn't angry at him for it. She should have been honest with him about Logan but she never could get the courage. "I didn't want to hurt you. Ever."

"I know that." He said without any anger in his voice. "I'm glad that you're happy with him. I know people are usually faking or just full of shit when they say things like that to people they've been close to themselves, but I am. I love you enough to want you to be happy no matter the terms. I couldn't get myself to say that before, but the threat of being blown up or starved to death by the powers that be at any given moment tends to make me not give a shit what I say or when I say it anymore. It's like you said, we should all have the chance to live full, happy lives. That means making the choices for our lives that will make them that way. Full and happy."

She nodded and moved closer to him, and while she hesitated at first because she didn't know how he would receive it, Mercury stepped up to Orion and hugged him without permission or warning. "I didn't know what parts of 'happy' I was missing until you showed me that there was more than just being satisfied with your work. You changed me, you know."

It felt incredibly awkward at first because it had been so long since there had been anything between them at all, but eventually he put his arms around her back and held her lightly, most of him relieved they could at least talk to each other about what happened. He doubted their spouses would have the same ease to it that they did.

"I hope you didn't pick up on any of my less-excellent habits in that whole change process. But there is a lot more to life than just job satisfaction, that's for sure. I'm glad you decided to value that. It makes a difference in a person."

Mercury hugged him a little bit longer than she knew she should, but she was saying goodbye in a way, even if they weren't actually saying goodbye. She kissed his cheek lightly and stepped back to break the hug. "I'll take good care of Fitch, and I'll let you know when she's improved enough to talk to you. Can you check on her . . . friend? Girlfriend? I'm sure she'll want to know Melissa is alright."

"I'll do that myself as my next stop." He let go of her slowly, then immediately placed his hands in his pockets so that other habits concerning touching Mercury wouldn't have a chance to reassert themselves. "Thank you, for taking care of her. I'll see you soon."

She let him go, and she didn't say anything else as she stepped back to watch him leave. As soon as he was gone, she let out a heavy sigh and wiped at her eyes, since tears stained her cheeks. Mercury was happy with Logan and she didn't want anything to change, but she also still loved Orion and it hurt to see him go, despite everything else. Hopefully they could still be friends, at the very least, if they survived all of this. He would still be around, since Anna was still pregnant with Logan's baby. Their lives would always be tangled up together somehow.

Fitch needed minimal monitoring for the next few hours, and her vitals continued to gain in strength. More of Mercury's patients came and went for their post-lockdown appointments, many of them still convinced the Initiative was really looking out for their best interests and asking her about some kind of outbreak on the station. It was nearing the end of her assigned work shift when she was notified of one final appointment, entirely outside of the usual scope of her duties.

Stephen knocked politely on the door of her exam room, even though it was open, and waited on the other side of the doorway for her to acknowledge him. He didn't seem sick, didn't seem perturbed, didn't generally seem to be exhibiting any of the other symptoms of stress that the rest of the station was experiencing. Of course he wasn't. "Is there a doctor in the house?"

It was strange for Mercury to see Stephen's name show up and it was stranger still that he approached an obstetrician for anything he might need, but there weren't many doctors left on the station. The last time she had spoken to Stephen Kaplan was to plead with him to see reason about the matching situation, and here he was again, now that her life was so different. She had chosen the man she'd been matched with after all.

Mercury walked to the doorway so Stephen could come into the exam room if he needed to be seen. "Mr. Kaplan. This is unexpected. Is there something I can help you with?"

"Yes. There is." He gave her what appeared to be a truly genuine smile, but it did nothing to make the situation seem less odd. In her limited experience, the man was genuine about almost nothing.

He stepped inside the exam room and closed the door behind him, then made his way around the small room in a lazy inspection of its contents. "I realize that my wife is the ranking psychiatric practitioner remaining on the station, but I was wondering if you have any training or expertise in that area yourself. If so, you may be able to assist me with a few difficulties I've experienced lately."

Already Mercury felt uncomfortable, but she remained by her station with her communicator nearby. The way he walked around the room made her feel like he was prowling instead of just walking, and it had her on edge. "I have limited experience with psychiatric care, but some training. It's my job to be able to assist women after birth and sometimes that includes Postpartum Depression, Postpartum Anxiety, or Baby Blues. Are you here to talk about that?" She tried to keep the mood light by asking him if he had anything Postpartum, mostly because she felt uneasy.

"No, I'm here to talk about somewhat more chronic conditions. Maria hasn't managed to conceive just yet, so we're still a ways from postpartum anything." He smiled at her again, but kept moving, running his fingers over the exam table slowly. "I'd like to pick your considerable brain about compulsive behavior disorders of a few different flavors. I'd like to know what kind of treatment you would recommend to deal with the obsessive thoughts that can . . . sort of grow out of those kinds of conditions. And by chronic, I mean something that's been going on since childhood."

"A few different flavors?" He was talking about behavior disorders like they were a kind of candy. "I'll give you as much information as I can, Mr. Kaplan. But as you already mentioned, I'm far from an expert in this area."

"If someone, let's say just as an example," he said with a casual shrug, "has been holding a grudge against an individual since a very early age, but is unable due to circumstances beyond their control to actually confront this individual, even as an adult, what kind of therapy would you recommend? If this grudge continues to . . . preoccupy their thoughts?"

"There's absolutely no way to contact the individual?" Mercury asked politely, though she felt strange offering advice to Stephen Kaplan. She wasn't a therapist by any means. "Sometimes people find writing or creative outlets as a way to deal with anger or unresolved emotions. I've found painting to be extremely therapeutic when situations are beyond my control and I need an outlet. Writing a letter to the person, or even creating a video clip could be helpful in assuaging the anger. There are also other physical anger management tools, exercise being one of them. Yoga can calm the mind and body. Kickboxing or boxing can also help. Taking anger out on an inanimate object can alleviate the complications that come with a longstanding anger issue like that. There are a lot of options, really."

"So what I hear you saying is that the main method of processing unresolved issues is by expressing the associated emotion. In whatever form seems most effective at helping to achieve states of calm. Does that sound about right?" He asked the question as if he already knew the answer, and actually smiled over at her as he said so. Something was very wrong with the conversation, it just wasn't obvious exactly what.

"There has to be some kind of release, certainly. Else the emotion goes unresolved, yes." Mercury stared at Stephen for a moment before she turned her attention to her communicator. "I'm sure your wife knows far more about the subject. I don't think I can be of any further assistance to you, Mr. Kaplan."

"That's not the only thing I'm here for advice on. And on the next subject, I think you can be a lot of assistance to me." He glanced over at her communicator when she did, and smiled when it had no new messages for her. "I'd also like to discuss . . . sort of a mob mentality. Who people trust, who people don't trust. What makes a large group of people trust a person as opposed to what makes a mass of people lose trust in that same person. What qualities do you value in your leaders, would you say?"

"You're asking me about leadership? I thought you came here for medical advice." She said with a sharp edge of irritation. "I think it is quite obvious who is a good leader and who isn't. People listen and agree with Logan and people run away from you and your wife. No one likes to be around someone with a superiority complex."

That only seemed to etch the smile firmly on Stephen's face, and he leaned back against the exam table to look her over with an even expression. "We've moved past our conversation dealing with my own complexes, Doctor. Please stay on topic. But since you mentioned superiority complexes, I believe sexual arousal centered around controlling or dominating activities would be considered a variant of a superiority complex, don't you think?"

Mercury felt as though she was frozen in place, but she only let the silence linger for a couple of heartbeats before she responded. "Sexual behavior is separate from public behavior. I would not like to discuss different sexual preferences with you, Stephen. If you want to do that, you definitely need to go find your wife."

"See, this is why I wanted to discuss public perception." He sounded as if he was agreeing with her, his otherwise-charming accent turned dark by the smile on his face. "I think, and I could be completely misreading the public mind on this, that if a person is known to be a certain kind of . . . well, I won't say deviant, since we're all adults here and frankly, I don't care what a person does in their bedroom, but it is still the word that fits . . . well, public perception of that person begins to change. People become wary, distrustful, prone to disobedience, just because they're worried their leader is getting off on telling them what to do . . ." he shrugged and took a few steps toward her with his hands back in his pockets. "It becomes a mess. One that's very nearly impossible to clean up ever again. Things just fall apart, almost overnight."

"The people here don't fall prey to *rumors* that easily." She defended even as he approached her. Mercury held her ground. "That's all they would be. Rumors."

"Would they? I've heard . . . and this, this is just a rumor, of course . . . that there are people who are messing around with surveillance lines throughout the station. Snooping on people's privacy, trying to patch into all kinds of feeds to snoop on the brass . . . there's really no telling what could get out." He looked her up and down as he got closer, but he wasn't quite close enough to touch, just close enough to dirty every part of her with a glance. "The *rumors* I've heard have toys in them, a lot of order-giving and order-taking . . . quite a lot of obedience that seems to be taken for granted. Again, just what I've heard."

"You are disgusting, do you know that?" Mercury replied coldly, though she should not have been surprised that Stephen Kaplan was some kind of pervert, watching her through surveillance just to use it against her. Or against Logan. "Get out of my exam room."

"No." He said as he got a little closer to her. "You take the orders, Dr. Bickford." He said with another leering smile. "You don't give them. Certainly not to me."

"I don't take orders from *you*." Mercury replied sharply, since the only person she would listen to without question was Logan. He was someone she trusted implicitly, and someone she knew loved her and had her best interests in mind. "And I will not."

"Then by morning, the entire station will know that your husband took his position because being in authority gets him off." Stephen said with a shrug. "The Executive Council will be restructured with myself and Maria at its head, he will be removed from his post and reduced to testing dirt samples in a closet for the rest of his stay on this station, and the entire population of the Initiative will have an intimate knowledge of both your sexual proclivities."

He backed her up a step with his next advance, still smiling with the eyes of a demon. "For your part, if your husband's status isn't enough to persuade you, I personally would have mixed emotions about putting my faith in a doctor who places so much of her personal life entirely in someone else's hands. How can I trust someone who doesn't even seem to trust herself? Each patient you see will know exactly what kind of woman you are behind closed doors, and they will find you to be less for it."

"I trust myself. Otherwise none of the rest would be possible." She put a hand out to push him away from her, or, at least, to keep him from getting any closer. Mercury didn't know if what he threatened would happen, if Logan would be removed from his position, if people would stop trusting her as a doctor, but they did sound plausible. Especially because so many people still believed that the loss of Initiates was from an outbreak and not because of sadistic people like the man in front of her.

If they removed Logan from power, their plans might fall apart. He wouldn't have the resources he needed to get them away from the station, and things would get much worse if Stephen and Maria went unchecked. She also didn't know what she would do if she lost patients. Being a doctor was just as important to her as Logan was. "You are threatening me for a reason. What do you want?"

"Nothing outside your usual activities." He grabbed her wrist as she tried to push him away, and actually held her hand against his chest as he continued to push her backward, crowding her against a wall until there were only a few inches left between them. "I want you to do as you're told."

Mercury twisted her arm to try and free her hand, but his grip was a lot stronger than hers would ever be, and she didn't want to give him any reason to damage her hands. Her hand was entirely necessary for her profession. "You're not telling me to do anything, you're just threatening me." She still tried to get away from him, even though she knew she probably wouldn't manage it. He had her cornered in her own exam room.

"Here's an order for you to take, then." He seemed . . . aroused. . . by her efforts to struggle, in a way that she had read about in textbooks but had never actually seen for herself. He gripped her arm harder as the pace of his breathing picked up. "You're to come to my quarters tonight at one in the morning. You will not be leaving before noon tomorrow."

"What? I'm not agreeing to that!" She pulled harder to get away from him, but she just bumped against the wall behind her. There was only one reason why he would want her to go to his quarters, and she wasn't going to do it. "If you want someone to play with, play with your wife. I have patients to see, and I am married. I'm not going to go to your quarters."

He released her wrist when she said that, but he didn't move away, and pressed her back against the wall, one hand grabbing a handful of her scrubs as she squirmed to look for a way out. "You know, there's a part of me, a very small and curious part, that actually hopes you don't. I hope you choose defiance. It makes things so much better in the end. Because if you do, you and your husband will be known for what you are, and when all is said and done, I will still have you every which way I want you."

He took in a deep breath as he lingered close to her, then actually stepped away and released his hold on her shirt as he headed toward the door. "Your choice. It may be the last one I ever permit you to make for yourself."

Mercury remained against the wall as Stephen approached the door, and several things went through her mind at once. She thought about Kameron first, and she knew that no matter what she fought for or what she fought against, anyone could choose to kill her at any given moment. Stephen Kaplan had power, he was in high places, and he could probably walk out of the room and have her gassed in the exam room if he really wanted to. Even knowing that, though, she didn't want to even think about him touching her. "Logan will murder you."

Stephen actually seemed interested in that possibility, and he shrugged with a nod back at her from the door. "He might, that's true. I always enjoy seeing the rage of the offended. There's just something so pure about it. But what would happen to him afterward, do you think? He would be a murderer. There are consequences for crimes like that."

They would lock Logan up, most certainly. Probably send him off to another station to have him tried, and then what? What if she never saw him again? Everything was stacked against her, and the only way to protect Logan and herself was to do as Stephen asked.

He would leave them alone, and Logan would be able to continue to work on getting them away and free from the Initiative. If she didn't do what Stephen wanted, it might destroy everything. Mercury wanted to be free, to live with Logan and to have a happy life with him.

Especially because she was almost certain that after being in lockdown, she was already pregnant. Her fertile week was ending as the lockdown began, but she could just feel it in her bones. She knew she had to be pregnant this time, and her baby needed to be free of the Initiative too. That meant showing up, playing Stephen's game, and moving on. It sounded simple enough, even though she knew it was far from simple.

She could handle it. She could turn her mind off, her emotions, she could do it. She just couldn't ever tell Logan about it, he wouldn't understand that it was necessary. They had to get out.

He stood at the door and watched her think it through, the grin on his face getting wider moment by moment as he saw her spiral down into the no-win situation in which she had been deliberately placed. "No later than one o'clock, Doctor." He reminded her with a final once-over as he lingered with his hand on the door. "And wear something nice."

Mercury didn't hide the disgust that she felt as he opened the door to walk out, and a chill ran down her spine at the idea of going to Stephen's unit to . . . do whatever he wanted her to do. As soon as he smirked at her once more and walked out, Mercury actually felt sick and had to rush into the small bathroom attached to the exam room to empty the contents of her stomach.

33

Logan felt more anxious by the minute as he waited in the bar for people to arrive, and for a long time, he didn't think his messages had reached any of their intended recipients. As he sipped at his drink, he watched the lifts in the distance, perpetually opening and closing with the flow of human traffic.

Had every message he'd sent been somehow intercepted?

Had he sent one to someone he couldn't trust?

The first people to show up were the last people he had expected to arrive first. Gordon and Jessie had been outsiders in most of the dealings of the station, aside from Jessie's work on the Judiciary with Anna, and Logan hadn't had any occasion yet to talk to Tatyana Sery. He didn't remember inviting her, but he had also told those he spoke to that they should bring anyone they thought they could trust.

"Good night for a drink." Logan said as the three of them approached, but he was looking at Tatyana, trying to get a feel for why the usually-quiet woman would have responded to a summons for something approaching a war council. "Their vodka up here is for shit, but this Shine stuff isn't too bad."

"There is better alcohol in my unit." Tatyana responded with a raised eyebrow at Logan before she ordered a drink anyway and sat uncomfortably close to him. She liked to see how people responded to things when they were uncomfortable. "You look nervous. I see it in your jaw. Why are you so nervous?"

He gave the tiny woman a testy look, but didn't move away as he took another sip of his drink. "I'm afraid of heights." He bit off sarcastically, gesturing to the many, many meters between them and the walls of the docks around them. "Puts me a little on edge."

"No wonder you look so angry all of the time." Tatyana replied as a few more people filtered in, Anna included, but without her tall, imposing husband. "Hello, Mrs. Bickford." Tatyana replied with a smirk, before she corrected herself. "I mean, Mrs. Al-Jabbar."

Anna glared at Tatyana, but she didn't spend any more energy than that, since seeing Logan after everything made her stomach twist into nervous knots. It didn't help her sometimes-present pregnancy nausea. "Logan." She said softly, though as professionally as she could, despite the fact that their relationship was everything except professional. She was carrying the man's daughter, for crying out loud.

Logan didn't move from his seat, but he did nod up at her as she approached. He held her eyes for a while, his own unreadable and contradictory as always in spite of the constant storm in his eyes. He flicked a glance down at her stomach before he looked up at her again. "How are you feeling?"

"I go back and forth." She moved to sit down next to him, since she would rather sit next to Logan than anyone else there. "The nausea is picking up some more. Hopefully that shit doesn't last." She looked over at his drink and pouted a bit. "And the anti-booze thing is fucking dumb."

"One of the many injustices of the world, I think I'd agree." He took his drink and finished the rest of it, then ordered water as a refill so that he wouldn't be drinking while she couldn't. "Is Orion coming too, or is he looking in on Fitch?"

"He said he'd be here if he could, it's important to keep someone watching over her. I mean, can you fucking believe that shit?" Anna looked away from Logan and glared at Gordon, since he was supposed to look in on Kameron. "They would have done that to us too. I'm surprised they haven't."

"I'm not. They want you alive." Gordon said as he ordered a drink from the console in front of them. It was less personal than a bartender, certainly, but that was sort of the point. "Specifically, they want your offspring alive, but at the moment, you're sort of attached."

Logan glared at Gordon. He had never liked the man, but he didn't have to like him to know he was useful. "How many more are we expecting from your end?"

"Should be four more, all on their way. Renata said she's going to be a little late." Gordon started munching on a pack of peanuts that appeared on a tree of holders in the middle of the large meeting space they were slowly taking over.

"Renata? My secretary?" Logan hoped he didn't look quite as

surprised as he felt. "She's one of yours? I thought she was an Initiative plant?"

"Oh, she is. But she was ours first." Gordon grinned, since he always enjoyed knowing something that someone else in the room didn't. "Complicated creatures, people can be sometimes. You never know quite where somebody's pointed until . . ."

"My god, do you ever stop talking?" Koskei came to join the rest of the group with a glare at Gordon. The grey-haired man took a perch at a distance from the rest of those gathered and waved a hello at Logan before he punched in his own drink order. "Thanks for inviting me to the club. I wasn't sure what side you thought I was on."

"Pretty sure you're on the side of the living, friend." Logan smiled at the sight of one of the few genuine friends he'd made since coming to the station, for whom nothing ever seemed particularly complicated or even weighty. He had blamed old age for his apathy more than once, but Logan knew he just liked to keep to himself. "Good of you to come."

"It'll be good of all of us if we can make some progress. That's what I'm here for. And you, hand over the peanuts. Age before assholes." He smacked Gordon on the back of the head and used the moment of disorientation to snatch the bag of peanuts from the man's hand, to the general entertainment of most of those present.

"What can we really talk about here that won't get us locked up in our cages again?" Anna asked as she looked around the small group. "This isn't exactly a private location. I thought we were going to make a plan or something like that. You know, to survive."

"This location is as private as it gets around here." Gordon answered with a mildly annoyed look at Anna. "Please, remember who you're hanging out with. Have just a little faith." He took the data core out of his shirt and let it float in the air in front of him by way of illustration. "We do need to coordinate our efforts to get out of here in something approaching relative safety. Complete safety can never quite be guaranteed."

"Not just us." Logan countered, since he wasn't going to negotiate with rebels and terrorists too loosely. "My intention is to get every single person off this station who came here under false impressions of what would happen regarding Eleusis. They need to get to safety, which means getting to Earth. Where nobody can just turn the air off if they decide they don't like something you said."

"I think we can all agree that getting back to Earth is the safest solution for the moment." Tatyana looked back and forth between Logan and Gordon. "Our intention, however, is to get to Eleusis. That means we take down the leadership here, but that also means that we aren't just trying to get out of here alive. We're trying to get out of here armed, with both weapons and information. We need to take control of the entire situation. At least temporarily."

"I'm sorry, who are you?" Logan finally sounded as flustered as he felt, and turned a little in the seat to look down at the tiny near-albino woman who had come in as if she owned the entire meeting.

"The beauty and the brains behind most of this, Mister President. Gordon helps. Mostly with the brains part, but he's pretty attractive also." Tatyana smirked as she noticed Jessie move uncomfortably in her seat, but Tatyana kept her attention on Logan. "I'm one of the leaders of the rebellion. If you want to survive and have somewhere to go without being tracked by the Consortium, you should work on your ass-kissing."

Logan narrowed his eyes at that kind of self-identification, but he inwardly chided himself for not realizing that Tatyana was that heavily involved. "And if you want two thousand more rebels to fall in line and help, it's my ass that's gonna need more kissing."

"Biting is more fun." Tatyana added without missing a beat, and she looked around at the small group again. "We have a lot of things already in place to get as many of us out of here as possible. Anna and Orion were able to get us a lot of information we needed." Tatyana looked at Anna and gave her a nod of recognition before she continued. "What we need now is organization among the people. We need to start collecting health and food items and storing them for transport. We'll need them. We also need to gather more weapons. The Initiative isn't going to let anyone go without a fight."

"They aren't going to let us stockpile without a fight either." Koskei interjected as a few more people joined the group. Carl and Aiko were the most noticeable, just because it was difficult for anyone to picture a more dramatic couple by way of appearance, but they weren't the only ones coming. A sizable portion of the Executive and Judicial groups were represented, and people outside the gathering were beginning to look over and whisper to themselves. Logan couldn't bring himself to care. "As soon as they notice we're trying to stockpile supplies," Koskei continued, "they'll begin cracking down on those supplies or they'll just raid and remove the stockpiles themselves."

"If they can find them." Gordon suggested. "There are several natural blind spots already on the station. I can help create a few more where the Initiative won't be likely to look for them. And I can tweak some of their inventory tracking to trick them into not noticing when things go missing. We just need people to do the work, and lots of it."

"And it needs to be quick." Jessie added, even though she knew no one cared to listen to her. She wasn't a leader, she was a follower, but she had been around Gordon long enough to know what she should say. "The Initiative wants to eliminate us as quickly as they can, and clearly they've already started that process with their pathetic excuse of an 'outbreak'. If we want to survive, we have to be sneaky, and fast."

Tatyana looked at Jessie, then Gordon, then over at Logan again. "Do you think you can gather enough people that will trust you to lead them in a quiet rebellion until we have enough to make it a loud one? You make it sound like you do, but I'm not convinced you're nearly as popular as you think you are. You and Anna chose your matches instead of each other. That makes it look like you would choose to bend to the will of the Initiative."

"If you knew or cared much about public perception, you wouldn't come off as quite this much of a cocky bitch. You should leave that part to the experts." He snapped back at her, since he didn't appreciate her walking in and immediately challenging his authority on things he'd been dealing with for months. His comment got a few chuckles from around the gathering, but most people were in too solemn a mood to laugh.

"The people in this Initiative know that everything I'm going to ask them to do is going to be in their interests. That's enough for most. The rest will come if they choose or they'll do for themselves as they can if not. The people here already are the only ones I trust, with a few exceptions." He looked around at the gathering and managed to get smiles and a few supportive nods back from most people he had worked with before he looked back at Tatyana. "They'll do as I ask, but we need a plan for getting out of here. The ships available in dock aren't nearly enough to transport the number of people we have here at any given time."

"Right now, no." Orion said as he came up to the group and glided in through a few of the others who had come to be a part of the conversation. "But in a few days, we're due to get another supply convoy. They've limited the number of ships they allow near the station at any given time, but the cargo ships are huge no matter what restrictions are placed on them. Even carrying two duffel bags of supplies each, just one cargo ship could hold five hundred people. We figure out a way to get all three cargo ships to stay around the station at the same time and it'll be enough to get everyone out, added to everything that's already standard in dock."

"They're watching every move of anyone who knows how to pilot a ship." Anna replied after Orion, but she smiled at him as soon as she made eye contact, even though she was sitting next to Logan. "That means if we're going to do something to fuck them up long enough to keep them but also to keep them working for us, then we have to rely on people who wouldn't normally know their way around a ship. We need to shuffle around, throw the Initiative off their game. Otherwise they'll stop us at every turn."

"Coming at them sideways. I knew I liked you." Gordon said with a chuckle, which was echoed by only a few others. There was something too sinister about the man's amusement to be truly funny.

"I know almost nothing of ships." Koskei volunteered with a shrug. "It would be easy enough for me to conduct an inspection of the goods we are receiving under Executive Order, and leave something behind to cause problems. It would allow me to visit all three supply ships and even take along a few assistants to help with the inspection."

"I think we can get an order like that passed without much trouble." Logan agreed, looking over at some of the other agricultural consultants he had trusted enough to invite to the meeting. "As long as it isn't proposed by me, we should be in the clear for suspicion." He quickly had a volunteer to submit the order, and he sighed as he thanked the man for his willingness. All eyes were on him, and he felt the weight of it, but it had to be a plan between all of them together for any of it to work.

Anna watched as people volunteered for all sorts of things she didn't think people would be willing to do, which just further proved that everyone was tired of being fucked with. She voiced her opinion here and there, even if people didn't want to hear it.

Eventually a woman that Anna didn't really recognize spoke up, and she asked a question that silenced the group, since no one really knew how to answer.

"Does anyone know what we can expect next from the Initiative? What are they going to do to us? How do we survive it?"

Aiko, who had been mostly quiet, eventually spoke up. "You can expect that things will get worse. They will push harder on your limits to control you and to see how you will behave. They are trying to tap into every response they can get, and they will go to extreme measures. But you have to remember that we have a plan to get away. That's what you can hold onto."

"And if we do manage to get away?" Barry spoke up, even though he and Erebi had been late in joining the large group. "This is the Consortium we're talking about defying. They're everywhere. How do we evade something that's everywhere? That tracks everything?"

"Clearly you grew up in orbit." Gordon interjected with another mirthless chuckle, which no one echoed. "The Consortium believes it tracks everything in the world, controls everything. But that's never been true and never will be. Unless we allow them to win in the colonization of Eleusis. There are places which are shielded from their observation. We will be returning to Earth and taking up residence in such places."

"What if we want to go back to our homes? Our families?" Another unfamiliar face interjected.

"Then you haven't been paying attention." Logan cut off the question almost before the man was finished asking it. "The Initiative intended to kill us from the moment it began recruiting us for this venture. To them, we are already as good as dead. When we defy them, they will pursue that intention, and they will do it with every tool at their disposal. They know where you lived, who your friends were, where you went to school. We are not just fighting for our own survival or rebelling against the Initiative here. We are declaring our own personal war on the Consortium. Because that is what they have already declared on us."

Anna had already been cut off from her family, but she hated realizing that she would have to be dead to them even though she wasn't actually going to be dead. Or, at least, she was hoping she wouldn't end up dead. It had only been a few short months, but already she felt like the whole universe was different. Her life was different. But her family still meant the world to her.

"It's either stay up here and certainly die, or go back to Earth and hope for the best. No one wants to never see their families again, but those are the facts. Dead in name or dead in reality. I would rather everyone think I was dead than actually *be* dead."

There was a quiet murmur of agreement from around the group, most of those present nodding in quiet resignation as they each said their own quiet goodbyes to their families.

"Alright." Logan eventually said, when no other questions were forthcoming. "You've all got work to be doing. Look around. The faces you see here are the ones that are friendly. If you need to pass messages, don't pass them through the same person every time or go to the same person every time you need to know something. Any pattern is going to be something they can analyze and try to control. We have to work it sideways. If you need help getting around the technology, get a message to Gordon. If you want to help with the ships, get it to Orion. If you want to help with the stockpiling, get word to Anna or Barry or Renata. And if someone tries to punish you or intimidate you, remember that you don't belong to them. You belong to yourself. And we're going to show them as much. Very soon."

There was another flurry of questions afterward, but no one wanted to look suspicious for too long. People filtered out when they felt satisfied with the answers they had, such as they were.

Orion was busy talking to Carl and Aiko, and it seemed to Anna she had a moment somewhat alone with Logan. "Can we talk? Alone?"

Logan gave her an apprehensive look at that question, but nodded and moved away from the main group. Mercury hadn't been able to attend, but Logan hadn't expected her to. She already knew her part in things, and she had more patients to attend to than she knew what to do with after recent disappearances. "I'm glad you and Orion didn't have the same troubles Fitch did during the lockdown. And that you didn't disappear."

"I'm glad too." She glanced back Orion's way but she looked up at Logan again after that. There was so much storm in his gray eyes, now even more than before. "Do you hate me? For all of this?" She felt like the instigator for them being in Orbit in the first place, even though they had applied separately. She also felt like she was the one who had killed their failing marriage. A marriage that would never have failed if they had stayed on Earth in the first place. "We promised each other so much, and now . . ."

"I'm not capable of hating you." He cut her off quickly, though he wasn't looking at her. "I've found out that I'm capable of doing a lot more hating than I ever thought before, but you're never gonna be on that list. I've loved you since I was twelve." His voice finally softened a little as he said so. "We both chose this. This program, this . . . fucked-up, twisted life. The Initiative might have pulled our strings for months, but the individual choices we made were ours."

"This is all so fucked up." She said softly, but she didn't look away from his eyes. He was the only thing left that she had from home, and even if he wasn't hers anymore, he still meant the world to her. "I thought a lot about the life we could have had, and what the Initiative did to destroy that. It kills me." Anna just shook her head and she stepped closer so that she could hug Logan, even if he didn't want her to.

She held onto him even as she started talking again. "You're the only person that knows everything about home that I do. You're a part of me, especially now, with the babies . . ." Anna took a deep breath before she continued. "I want to hate you. I want to hate myself. And I still hate seeing you with the redhead." Even after all they had endured, she still had a hard time saying Mercury's name. "You've been my best friend for too long. I can't lose that too. And Lynnette needs you."

He felt immediately and sharply conflicted as soon as she hugged him, but he didn't pull away, and held onto her after a moment. It was a much lighter and less insistent touch than any that would have passed between them only weeks before, but he still couldn't find it in him to push her away.

"We came up here because we wanted to help with something that was bigger than both of us." He finally said, when he could convince himself to speak again. "And as usual, we got exactly what we fucking asked for. Right in the middle of the biggest shit sandwich the world has ever had crammed down its throat. I want to hate myself, or you, for what we've been pushed into, but we don't have time to sit around being introspective. We've made our choices, and we're gonna get shit done. There's nobody I'd rather be on the same side with than you, especially when it comes to a fight."

Anna nodded when she pulled away, even though she could

still feel the flickering twist of anger and pain inside of her, though she did her best to ignore it. He was right. They'd made their choices. There was no reason to wonder what could or might have been, because they were on different paths now. Without each other, but still fighting for each other. "Orion and I saw it, Logan. We saw Eleusis. It's as real as anything else we know. It's beautiful."

That was clearly new information to him, and the look in his eyes said that he briefly wondered if she was stoned. But only briefly. "You saw it? What do you mean?"

If it was possible, Anna's voice dropped even quieter so only Logan could hear her. She hoped Orion wouldn't get the wrong idea, but she had to tell Logan about it. "Gordon sent us into an abandoned arm of this station. They have this fucking crazy-ass portal, Logan. You can *walk* through it and you're on different fucking planet. It's like some kind of trippy window or something. But we could see Eleusis through the portal. It's weird, the sky is weird, the grass and plants look weird, like someone used the wrong crayons out of the box, but it's still gorgeous."

Even in near-zero gravity, Logan had to reach out and grip the sphere that passed for a table in order to steady himself as he closed his eyes and gritted his teeth. "So you're telling me . . ." he asked in a tone that she could barely hear, "that there's no . . . mission. No flight. No ship. No year or twenty of waiting. That they can walk across a station block and step out on Eleusis."

Anna nodded, and she didn't reach out to comfort Logan, even though he was clearly furious. He should be furious. She had been, and she still was, but at least it wasn't news to her at the moment. "I saw Vance and Gehrig walk through, talking shit about how they wished they could stay on Eleusis all the time. They were never going to send us. We've been test subjects since before we even signed up. And now they want to send us off on a malfunctioning ship so the world will mourn over more lost pioneers and progress. Except that's not true."

He grew angrier the more she said, and most of the conversation in the area had died down as soon as Logan's knuckles had turned white. Anna was the only one present who had ever seen Logan really lose his temper before, and on the one occasion that came to mind, Liam had been present to hold him back before he actually killed the target of his fury. Unfortunately, the target of his present fury was nowhere nearby, so when he lost the momentary battle to hang onto his self-control, he had no one to vent it on.

Everyone shrank back as Logan actually dislodged the spherical table and slammed it through the flimsy outer barrier of the gathering-space. He spun his makeshift weapon on panel after panel as he let out a nearly-unintelligible string of curses. In moments, he had laid waste to an entire booth of the bar, keeping his back to the rest of the people who were gathered nearby so he wouldn't inadvertently harm any of them.

Orion watched in wide-eyed disbelief at the tantrum in front of him. He'd never felt anything even approaching the kind of anger that had Logan flailing around like a madman, and in his book, that was a good thing to lack. He was equal parts impressed and disappointed by what he was seeing, and imagined most of those present felt much the same way.

On the one hand, it was impressive to see the man really go off on a destructive streak. He'd always been obviously strong, but seeing that strength in action was very different from just understanding that it existed. Not to mention his obvious acclimation to near-zero gravity. On the other hand, in Orion's mind, he was letting off a fit that was more fit for a toddler than a grown man, let alone one who was supposed to be the leader of thousands of people.

When Logan finally quieted, he held the broken remains of the spherical table in both hands, bracing himself in a window that had previously been a wall as the shards and fragments of his fit floated away through the dock. Small maintenance drones had already been called out of their hiding places to assist in the cleanup.

"Every single person on the planet." He finally said in a low, ragged voice, though only Anna was close enough to hear him. "Every single fucking person on the planet. They could line them all up and march them a family at a time across a room and save them from the planet that's wanted us dead for centuries. They could, and they haven't. And they won't."

Anna didn't move away except to avoid his line of fire, and she only winced a few times during his destruction, but she wasn't afraid. Not of Logan. Anna had seen Logan in all sorts of emotional states, and if that hadn't driven her away, nothing would.

"*They* won't. But we can." She reached out to put a hand on his arm to try and comfort him, and to remind him they still had hope. "We just need to get that fucking thing away from them and then we can decide for ourselves."

He still wanted to destroy something, she could feel that much in the tension of his muscles beneath her hand. But he didn't move again except to close his eyes and bow his head to try and calm himself. "Whatever you and Gordon need from me or anyone else in the Initiative, I'll make sure you get it. We came up here to help humanity get to Eleusis. That hasn't changed. If we can get our hands on that technology, we can change the fucking world. Not an exaggeration for once."

He couldn't bring himself to turn and look around at everyone who was still throwing cautious glances at his back, so he just pulled himself over the window to leave. "I have visits to make. If anyone needs anything, have them go through Renata. Apparently I can trust her more than I thought."

"Alright. Just be careful." Anna called after him, but he was gone before she could say or do anything else. Anna wanted to tell Logan about Eleusis as soon as she saw it, but she should have realized how angry it would make him.

When she made her way back over to Orion, she felt a little ashamed for pushing Logan into causing a scene, even though it hadn't been intentional. "We should go back to our unit, or whatever else we're supposed to do. There's a lot to do."

"Do I want to know what set that off?" He pulled her into his arms, as usual, and did the navigating for them through the docks. Null gravity was just another excuse to hold her tight, as far as he was concerned, and he'd spent more of his life in low gravity than she had. He moved around easier.

Anna easily curled into Orion and held tight, and her body relaxed once he was holding her and guiding them both through the station. She rested her head against Orion's large chest and sighed. "I told him that we saw Eleusis. And I told him how. I don't think he was too happy about knowing for sure that we were never meant to get there."

Orion nodded, since he could understand that kind of anger, even if he didn't feel it the same way her ex-husband did. "Whether we were meant to get there or not, that's not gonna stop us."

Anna kissed Orion's neck as he held her, since she was grateful he wasn't mad at her for talking to Logan or telling him what she saw. "I wanted to tell him because we came up here together to get to Eleusis. I wanted him to know it was real, and what we're going to do is going to help us get there. I hope I didn't upset you by talking to him about it or anything else I did."

He shook his head, and rolled them in mid-air so that he would take the light impact of them reaching the lift with his back against the doors. It wasn't much, and she was plenty tough enough to take a lot more than that on her own, but that didn't stop him from taking it for her. "We still need to work with them. Both of them. If we can keep things civil between all four of us, I think we stand a much better chance of making a decent life for ourselves. Never realized the guy had that bad of a temper, though. Always just seemed like the 'carry a big stick' type."

Anna shook her head. "He's quick to anger, but not quick to act. Not usually." Anna clung to Orion as they moved into the lift and made their way back to their unit to wait for further instruction. "Sometimes I really wonder if he even wants to be Lynnette's father, especially now. And all those times I wonder that, I wonder if you'll resent me because I ended up pregnant by two men instead of one. It shouldn't have happened." Part of Anna couldn't believe those particular words came out of her mouth, since she had been trying, almost the entire time, to get over not being pregnant with Logan's child from the beginning. Now she wondered if it was a giant mistake.

"I don't care about you ending up pregnant by both of us." The rotation of the station began to work, and Orion pressed his feet gently to the floor of the lift as they descended. "For all our sakes, I was hoping the first couple months you would end up pregnant with Logan's baby so that all this chaos could get put behind us. Same on my side of things. But that's not how it played out. Whether they fucked around with us somehow to make it work out their way or not, I've got no idea. But you're the one I married. I'll take every part of you there is, no matter what kind of strings come along. You're worth that."

There was a long silence that followed what he said, which felt a little disconcerting, but Anna was trying to say exactly what she wanted to say. She didn't want to sound trite or insincere.

"I know this sounds strange to admit, but you almost don't seem real." Anna's hands gripped his clothing, since she wanted to remind herself that he was. "I know you have no way of knowing this, but you're very different from any other man I knew on Earth. Even Logan. People fall in love on Earth, sure. They get married. They make families together, they live as happily as they possibly can with the forty years they get. Give or take."

"But people . . . people don't love like you do. They don't love without wondering about the things they might have missed out on, because there is so much to miss out on. Plenty of people cheat, take on more wives, partially out of necessity, partially because they want more. Rarely is a couple as devoted to each other as you are to who you love. Half of them got married because someone got pregnant, not because they love each other. Love on Earth is something that happens second, usually. Not first."

Orion tried, without success, to keep himself from rolling his eyes and shaking his head at that kind of pattern to life, since it just didn't make any sense to him. "I get why, with everything else you've told me, but that doesn't make it any more sensible to me. Two people making a life for each other doesn't seem like it works well when those people are just together because somebody got knocked up. Seems more like a recipe for a whole lot of problems. Especially if you start adding on wives and talking about bits on the side . . . that's how things get miserable."

Anna shook her head, since sure, there were miserable people, but they weren't the majority. "Most people want to live life to the fullest. There isn't time to get miserable over someone knocking boots with someone else." She looked up into his dark eyes and wiggled her way up his body so she could get closer to his lips.

Anna kissed Orion soundly before she said anything else. "When we get there," she emphasized the 'when' and paused but then continued after another kiss. "Married or not, women are going to want you. They won't ask questions, most of them won't even pause to wonder. You're gorgeous and massive and that means a good time and strong babies. I just want you to know what you're getting into, going down to Earth."

He actually laughed at that, and gave her a heated kiss, locking her legs around his waist just to hold her against him as they descended. "I've had women coming after me since I was an overgrown thirteen-year-old. I've had more than a few offers from some of the other women on this station, as a matter of fact, especially after some of them caught you screaming your tits off in the maintenance shafts. That's not new for me, and saying 'no' isn't new either. I want you. Anybody else can come knocking if they want, I'm closed for business unless it's *your* business."

That had Anna smiling, but she wasn't naive enough to think he might not change his mind when they were actually on Earth. Earth was just . . . so very different. Real and raw and beautiful in all of the good and bad. Mostly, anyway. "I like you in my business." Anna said before she kissed him several more times. "All up in my business. There's a reason why I scream so loud."

Orion was never shy about touching her however he wanted to, no matter their surroundings or the potential observers. The lift was no different. His hands cupped her ass to press her against him under the kisses with a promise of wicked business to come. As he kissed her, though, the lift felt as though it was about to come to a stop, a great many decks early for their programmed destination. Their communicators went off a moment later, as the lift began, strangely, to rise.

"What the hell?" He held her against him with one arm as he reached down to retrieve his communicator, but once he read the message, his expression darkened by degrees. Whatever it was, it meant nothing good.

* * * * *

For Logan, it was a long, long walk to get back down to his unit. Mercury told him earlier that she had rounds to do and one woman who was currently going through what appeared to be a complex miscarriage, so he wasn't surprised when she hadn't been at the bar. She knew everything she needed to know about what was going on anyway. Parts of it had been her idea.

He was, therefore, surprised to find her in their kitchen as soon as he stepped inside. The sight of her instantly brightened his mood from the brooding thoughts that had been running circles in his mind the whole way back down the lift. "I thought you said you would be gone for the night?" There was no accusation in his tone, only surprise, since they'd had that conversation only just before he left to go to the bar.

"There's something more important." Her smile was subdued, and there was something that kept her expression darker than usual. Still, she was always happy to see Logan, regardless of any circumstance. Even the worst ones. "I have blood results I haven't opened, but I thought we might want to do it together."

Mercury hadn't even submitted herself for a blood test, and

the only one she could remember being recent was about a week prior when a bot had appeared requesting a routine blood sample. She hadn't thought anything of it, since the whole crew had been giving samples of just about everything since they arrived. Now she realized that someone must have requested it on her behalf, someone who wanted to know if she was pregnant. Logan didn't do it, he would have told her. Knowing who probably had requested it made her feel sick. "We've both had a long day. No matter the results, I wanted to see them with you."

He looked back and forth between her eyes and the tablet in her hand a few times, then carefully took his shoes off by the door and went to their small living space. At the moment, the walls depicted a mountaintop vista overlooking a white-capped range. It was too still and artificial for his mind to really believe the illusion of living back on Earth, just as with every other view they had chosen for their home, but it was still a peaceful view.

He went to a couch along one wall and sat down on one end, tapping the cushion next to him. "Come here. We'll look at them together."

Mercury carried her tablet quietly over to the couch and sat down next to him without saying a word. She had changed out of her scrubs into one of his t-shirts, which he had given her approval to wear, even though he told her that he preferred her naked. Her hair smelled freshly washed, since it was fragrant of the smell of vanilla and something fruity, but her hair was dry as it fell over her shoulders.

"There's something else." She produced a tiny plastic box. As she opened it, inside was a thick silver ring with a few small diamonds and flecks of obsidian nestled in the top. She pulled the ring out and placed it in the middle of her hand. It was inscribed with, *Always and Only Yours* on the inside. "I asked another doctor to cover my last patient and had this fabricated for you."

Logan took the ring from her and turned it over a few times in his fingers, then spun it between them so that it landed on his ring finger where it belonged. He pushed the ring into place over the large knuckles of his hand, and flexed his fist once to get the weight of it comfortably settled, looking down at it the entire time.

"I didn't realize the station would allow us access to these kinds of resources." He spun the ring once on his finger, just to get accustomed to it, then reached out with his newly-ringed hand to pull her into a kiss. He slid her into his lap instead of letting her sit on the couch beside him, and kissed the breath out of her a dozen times before he smiled and looked her own hand over. The calculating look on his face told her that he was plotting something extravagant, but he wasn't about to give up any details yet. "It's perfect. Thank you."

Mercury's pulse picked up after the kind of breathtaking kisses he showered her with, but she tried not to think too much about it as he held her in his lap. "We've complied with the Initiative in their orders, for the most part. They have no reason to stop me from requesting a ring to be made." She ran her fingers over his ring almost delicately.

"It's made from the strongest metal found up here. Created to make these very space stations." Mercury trailed her touch from his finger to up his arm. "You're the strongest and most reliable man I've ever met. The metal suits you." She looked at the flecks of stone before she looked into his grey eyes.

"But the stones are from Earth. Space-made metal. Earth-made stones. Space-made woman, Earth-made man." It was the most romantic thing she'd ever thought up on her own, and she was pretty proud of it. It had taken more effort for her to think up something like that than it did for her to learn anything about the human body.

The uniqueness of the gesture wasn't lost on Logan, and he moved his hand up over her body before he drew her into another heated kiss. "I've wished for a lot of things in my life." He confessed as he leaned back, drawing her with him so that her lips would never be more than a breath from his. "Right now, I wish it was possible for us to go home, back to the place where I grew up. There, I would have the resources to do as I pleased in getting your ring. I know a guy in the South Erie district who harvested a fallen meteor, found a whole stash of diamonds in it from the pressure. Last I checked, the biggest one he still had was four karats." He lifted her hand and kissed the knuckle where her ring would go, still picturing it there even if he knew he wouldn't be able to go back to that life. "I look forward to seeing it there."

"Wow." She thought about what something that large would look like, since she didn't usually wear any jewelry. Mercury had given her ring back to Orion, even though he had insisted that she keep it, it didn't feel right. Whenever she worked she would never be able to wear such a large ring, but anything Logan would give her, she would proudly wear whenever she could. "I look forward to it too. I want the universe to know that I'm yours." Her voice cracked on the last two words because of the turmoil in her head after her conversation with Stephen Kaplan, but she did her best to keep composure. Logan couldn't know, or she was sure they would kill him. "I hope there's nothing that would cause you to change your mind about wanting me."

He actually smiled again at that, and wrapped both his arms around her just to hold her tightly. "Nothing. In this world or any other. You're mine, and the world will never get my permission to be otherwise." He had to shift a little beneath her on account of the effect that her sitting in his lap always had on him, but he didn't move away. "Let's see these results."

Mercury turned her attention back to her tablet even though her thoughts were all over the place. She opened up the message with her results and brought up the file, though she felt overwhelmingly nervous even seeing her name at the top. "I don't know if I can read through it."

"Is this the first time you've tested since we began together?" He didn't have to look over the full report to know what kind of report it was. He'd seen several of them, including the report Anna had received with her own news. He even knew where to look for the results, but his attention was on Mercury, not on the tablet.

"No, it's . . . it's just the first time I've wanted certain results so badly that my emotional response is overriding my abilities to stay calm and focus." She admitted softly. "I want a family with you. I have for a while now."

"If you want it, then you'll have it." It felt like his entire touch on her body was making the promise to every part of her at once. "Today or next month, or the month after that. It is my intention to see to it you have everything you ever want, Mercury. That includes our family."

She still didn't look back at the results, keeping her face buried against his neck and shoulder, since she had slumped down so she could curl into him a little easier. "I want to give you everything you want, too. I wish we could go back to your home, see your family. There are a lot of things I wish for." Mercury kissed his neck and nibbled on it just a little bit to distract herself. "Do we have to try again?" She found herself trembling, mostly because she was afraid of ending up pregnant with Kaplan's baby if she wasn't pregnant already with Logan's. It twisted her stomach up to think about it, but she knew she didn't have any choice one way or another.

He moved the tablet so he could read through the results, then set it down on the couch beside them so he could put both his arms around her. "Do we *have* to? No." She could hear the smile in his voice and feel it against her neck. "Are we still going to fuck like we're trying to get pregnant? You bet we are."

Mercury jumped a little at hearing him say that, but she was careful of his half-erect member beneath her. She looked toward the results and flipped through them as he continued to kiss along her neck. His kisses gave her shivers, but they were the kind she liked. "Two boys! Twins! Finally!" She sighed in relief before she turned her face toward him again and moaned when he caught her lips with his and kissed her deeply. "I was beginning to wonder if it would ever happen." She gripped his shirt as she held onto him. "I thought something might be wrong with me."

"So you're saying you thought I was lying when I told you that you were flawless?" He shot back a playfully reproving tone, his kisses never ceasing.

"No, I don't think you are a liar. I just thought you were complimenting me. Which sometimes can mean exaggerating the truth."

"On the subject of your perfection, I exaggerate nothing." His kisses turned gentler, but no less warm, merely taking his time with the touches so he could savor her and the moment between them. "Twin boys will be a handful. I should know. But that doesn't scare me. I'm just glad they're ours. They're fortunate in their mother."

Mercury wrapped her arms firmly around the back of Logan's neck and pressed her body to his. She wondered what would happen if he ever found out about Stephen Kaplan, but she didn't have time to think about how she could protect him in a different way. "I love you so much." Mercury's heart ached as she said the words, and she held tighter. "I'm scared, but I'm with you."

"Damn right you are." He moved to put his feet up on the couch beside them so he could lie back and take her with him, until he was leaning back against the arm of the couch with her settled in comfortably on top of him. It was easily the most relaxed, the most at peace he had been in weeks, and he sighed contentedly beneath the kisses, knowing that it was only with Mercury that he could find that kind of solace anymore.

* * * * *

Hours passed too quickly and the hour turned late before Mercury was mentally ready for lying to Logan and leaving. She looked at her communicator long after he had fallen asleep, and while she hadn't received any messages, she knew time was not her friend. She turned onto her side and shook Logan's shoulder gently before she kissed his cheek and willed herself not to cry. "Logan. One of my patients sent me a message that she's in pain and needs me. I'm going to go for a little while."

Logan was still mostly asleep, but he turned enough to return the kiss as he adjusted the covers to his liking. "Send me updates, just let me know you're alright. If you're not back by morning, come find me when you're free."

Mercury nodded, her voice was caught in her throat, but she finally forced herself to speak. "Yes, of course." She kissed him one more time before she pulled away. "I love you. I'll see you soon."

"I love you too." He rolled a little, but hung onto her hand a little possessively before he finally relaxed his grip to let her go, almost immediately asleep with one hand over the spot where she'd laid a moment before.

Mercury felt a heavy wave of guilt as she headed over to their closet and dug through her things. She remembered Kaplan's instructions to wear something nice, and she was too afraid of the consequences to fight his orders. She changed quickly in the closet into a revealing green dress and pulled her hair up and back into a bun. She wanted it to be as distanced from herself as she could be, and since Logan liked her hair down, she put it up.

Mercury put a jacket on over her dress and stepped into heels before she quickly left their room and their unit without looking back. She needed to be brave. She could get through it. It was just sex. Forced, but she hadn't exactly been trying to have sex with Logan at first, either. She could get through it. She had to.

The lift opened before she even got to it, as if she needed more reminders that the Kaplans were watching her every move. It drew her up to their level without needing her to press the button to request it, and the only lights on in the corridor at that time of night were guides in the floor that led her toward them. The rest of the station itself seemed inert, almost abandoned, until she was the only soul still alive in the darkness of space. She passed several windows and floor-to-ceiling galleries on her way to their chambers, and even the pale disk of the moon in the distance turned away from her. Only the distant stars watched, and they were too far away to be of any assistance.

Their door didn't open as she moved closer to it, so she knew they wanted her to knock. They wanted her to make that choice, and while she hesitated, Mercury eventually knocked on the door and stood in front of it while she stared down at her heels. She felt sick. Well and truly sick, but she couldn't do a thing about it, and even if she did get sick, she doubted they would let her go. She was their toy and she knew it, but she was trapped anyway.

When Stephen opened the door, Mercury could tell the party had already more or less gotten started before she even arrived. He was dressed casually, wearing only loose shorts. His torso and legs were otherwise bare, and her medical mind immediately identified a number of scars on his bare skin, leading her to wonder about probable causes. None of them seemed at all recent, and clearly none of them were on his mind as he looked her over.

"Welcome, Doctor. Glad you could join us." He held a glass of water in his hand, and Mercury could see a luxurious sectional couch just inside their living area. There was a pitcher of water with extra glasses in an ornate stand on a table in front of it, and Maria waited for them both beyond, lounging on the couch. "Please, come in."

Mercury was quiet as she followed Stephen into his unit, but she couldn't help but scowl at Maria as soon as she saw her. Maria was her colleague. They took oaths to help people, not to . . . rape them. Mercury shook her head a little after she thought about that word, because it made her feel weak and defenseless. She wasn't weak, even if she was defenseless. She was strong. Wasn't she? She was strong enough to walk into this and walk out. She was trapped no matter what she did.

"You make it sound like I want to be here." She replied in her only way of protest, even though the rest of her was not fighting him. Mercury stood next to the end of the couch and shot another disgusted look at Maria. "You should be ashamed of yourself. You are disgusting for being involved in this."

Maria smirked as she looked up at Mercury from the couch. She was in loose pajamas and clearly did not have a care in the world. "I'm disgusting? I've seen some of the things you've done with that earthling of yours. Don't throw stones, sweetie."

Stephen chuckled low in his throat at his wife's barbs and closed the door slowly behind Mercury, taking a moment to lock it audibly. That was one of the most satisfying parts of the experience for him. The moment he knew there was no escape. "I can only imagine the kinds of things you'd like to throw at me, Doctor." He went to the table and lifted the pitcher to pour a glass. "Especially if you actually knew half of what I've been involved in. Even Maria doesn't know the half of it, and I've managed to shock her once or twice." He gave Maria a look that would have been loving on anyone else, but there was too much monster behind his eyes for true affection.

Mercury kept her arms crossed around herself protectively, especially because she was aware of how revealing her dress was underneath. It was meant for Logan, only for Logan, and now these people wanted to defile it. And her. "Why are you doing this? I've done nothing to harm or injure you in any way. In fact, had you needed my help, I would have helped you any way that I could."

"Oh, I'm sure you would have. But in case you hadn't noticed, I'm married to a doctor. If I require medical attention, I'll ask her." He set the pitcher down and approached her with the glass he'd just filled, sipping from his own in the process. "There comes a time, at least for people like us, when the 'why' doesn't matter anymore. Only the 'what' is important." He looked up and down the coat she wore, and just smiled, since her dress was short enough to not even be visible beneath it. She looked like a hooker going to work for the night, only much, much more beautiful than any hooker he'd ever had the pleasure of destroying. "You'll be breaking a sweat very soon, Doctor. Go on and hydrate before we put you to work."

She looked at the cup of water in his hand and she already didn't want to know what that meant. She didn't want to even think about it. Mercury didn't know if she should resist or if she should just submit, since resistance would probably mean bad things for Logan but submission was meant *only* for Logan.

Mercury reached out slowly and took the glass into her hand, but she didn't drink from it just yet. "Did you request the blood test?"

Maria waved her hand in the air. "I did, Red. He didn't want any chance of knocking you up, so we had to check before we asked you here. Good job getting knocked up twice. We like twins around here. Now drink. Didn't you hear him? I thought you were good at following directions by now."

Mercury looked at the water again and kept her jacket closed tightly with her free hand while she took a drink. At least they weren't trying to get her drunk, since she was pregnant, after all. Alcohol could have a negative effect on the babies, though it would take much more than a single glass. Still, what she drank definitely tasted like water. Purified water, actually. It tasted especially crisp and clean, and oddly, the taste made her thirsty for the rest of the glass. "You are hateful, and cruel, both of you." She said after she had consumed half the glass. "Psychiatrists are supposed to be kind and attentive and caring."

"Only when we're on the clock." Maria sat up and watched Mercury drink. "Why don't you sit down? But take off the jacket first." She looked Mercury over and then back at Stephen. "Actually, do you want to help her with her jacket, my dear?"

"I'd be happy to." He said pleasantly, then stepped up to Mercury as she finished the glass, grinning like the demon he was. His touch was light as he reached out to take her arm and slowly move it away from her midsection where she'd had it wrapped around herself. His fingers were disconcertingly gentle as he reached up to unbutton the two buttons holding the coat against her, his eyes never leaving hers.

When the coat hung open in front of her, he reached up to take the glass for her, then pushed the coat back over her shoulders. His fingers were like a caress on her skin, and it . . . tingled, where he touched her in unexpected ways. "I approve of your taste in scandalous dresses, Doctor. You followed instructions very nicely."

Mercury didn't look down at herself, and instead of staring into his eyes any longer, she closed hers. She remembered how Logan had also approved heartily of the dress, since her ample cleavage was on display, and her long legs as well.

She didn't know why Stephen's touch tingled, but she wondered if it was just her nerves overreacting to his unwanted touch. "You said you would leave Logan alone if I complied. So I complied."

"And you're going to keep on complying." He growled, before he walked around her to get a good look at her from every angle. "The fun part, though," she heard her glass clink down on a table nearby as Stephen ogled her, "is that pretty soon, you won't be complying out of fear, or love for your husband. You'll be complying because you want to. More than anything else in the world, every perfect curve of you is going to want to do exactly as we say."

"Why would I ever . . ." The clinking glass made her look back, and she looked at her empty glass before she looked up at him again. There was terror in her intensely green eyes. "What was in the water? Did you poison me?" She hadn't even considered someone would put anything in her water, mostly because she was there, doing what they asked her to do. Why would they do that? With what?

"Poison usually denotes something that hurts a person." Stephen's grin was even wider than before, since he could see that she was catching on, if a little too late. "Nothing I've given you yet is going to hurt you. Or your babies. At least not in the testing we've done so far. Welcome to the experiment." He walked over to her and reached out to caress lightly up her exposed arm, a mere whisper of a touch. "I admit, I didn't expect you to drain the whole glass, but I'm very, very glad you did."

"I'm going to be sick." She replied as she pulled her arm away from his touch, since she didn't like that it felt good because it tingled again. Mercury knew that she shouldn't resist, but she couldn't help herself. "You are disgusting. I could never, not even once, want you to touch me."

Maria just smiled from the couch. "You *do* have some fire in you. I was wondering if you did, you hide it so well. But an Irish redhead always has some fire. It's in the blood. Irish can't help themselves, can they, dear?"

The next touch Stephen gave her, while she was busy glaring at Maria, was a violent grip on the back of her neck, as if he was about to pick her up like a kitten. He was stronger than he looked, but he was no Logan. Nevertheless, his touch was firm, and while she knew her nerves were giving her some discomfort, there was too much interference from whatever they had given her for the discomfort to register in her mind.

All she felt was the drug, and the tingling sensation that grew even more powerful and more pleasant the more firm the touch.

"You can feel free to fight if you want." He whispered near her ear. "You're here, and you're not leaving until we've had our fill of you. You can fight, kick, scream, try and run, do what you want. It won't make any difference. And soon you won't even want to. So go on. Fight while your mind is still deluded into thinking you can. Your body knows better."

Mercury reached back to try and dislodge his hand from the back of her neck, but her body was so conflicted. Why did it feel good? What kind of drug did they give her? She'd never heard of such a thing, not like this.

"Don't." She knew resisting him was useless, but she didn't want him to be right. She didn't want to want anything from him. "I would have done whatever you asked without the drug. I came here, didn't I?" She still tried to push his grip away, and in her distraction, Maria came up and touched her, which also felt good and made her feel nauseous at the same time.

Mercury fought. She tried so hard to keep her mind in focus, to keep herself hating the people who had her captive, but every second that passed with the drug in her system meant that her body was getting further away from her control no matter what she wanted.

She didn't make any noise, in spite of the drug, though it had taken all of her effort to do so, and a thin trail of blood from her lip trickled down to her chin. They just stared at her. Why were they just staring at her? Mercury felt uncomfortable for so many reasons, and she hated most of them, but she refused to say anything or even move. She wanted to think about Logan but the drug meddled with her mind and all of her sensations. "I've done . . . as you've asked. Just . . . get it over with." Mercury desperately wanted to be stronger than the drugs, but she was a doctor. She knew better.

In the end, no one was stronger than their own chemistry. Not in the moment. After . . . would there be an after? She could recover, she could go back . . . she wanted to go back, but the drugs kept her mind fixed on the moment, incapable of constructing a future free from their chemical hold on her.

Stephen went back to circling her like a predator, pausing only to give his wife a heated kiss along the way. "We invite you here, drug you like this, and threaten your husband, and you think this is going to just be gotten over with?" He moved behind her, but she could feel him shake his head. "We're going to take our time with you, Doctor. We're barely getting started." He leaned in and pulled his hand back and slapped her ass harder than Logan ever had.

It should have hurt. She knew it should have hurt, but it didn't. The sensation that should have stung lingered against her skin in a pleasant way. Why did something that logically should be painful feel so good?

"It alters the pain receptors." Mercury's legs wobbled from the intensity as she tried to think. "Pain receptors are all over our bodies . . . Your drug tricks them."

"Elegance in simplicity. Usually best when dealing with the human body." He agreed, before he repeated the slap, hard enough to shove her half a step forward and drive her to her knees. "The effect takes a long time to wear off, and it's going to get a lot worse."

As Mercury fell to her knees she somehow hated it a little bit less. Not because she wanted it, but because her mind was losing focus and control to the strong drug. "I can't . . ." She couldn't even finish a thought. "I'll . . . still remember. After."

"Perfectly." She vaguely felt him kneel behind her. The image of Maria coming down in front of her was equally hazy, but somehow crystal clear at the same time. "Leaving memory intact was one of the most difficult parts of designing this beauty, but we finally managed to get it right. Your recall should be . . . exquisite."

Mercury couldn't think at all as they both started to play with her like she was their toy. She wanted them to stop, and tears built in her eyes, streaming down her face.

Whatever hell she had imagined, that night was worse.

34

Anna hopped down from being held up against Orion once the lift stopped moving, but she didn't want to go out the doors when they opened. The message that Orion had shown her on his communicator made her worried, but there was little they could do about it. They were being watched, so there was nowhere they could run.

Your presence with Director Vance is required immediately. Any delay would be discouraged.

"It still sounds like a threat." Anna said softly as they eventually stepped out of the lift. "Why the hell would Vance want to talk to either of us? I mean, I know I'm involved with the Board and the Council and all that shit, but we're not Mercury and Logan. You'd think he would summon them."

"Well, I doubt he's having us over for tea." Orion walked slowly down the corridor in spite of the warning about delay, but he slid one hand into the pocket with his communicator nervously, as if checking to make sure it was still there. "We try to break for it, he sends goons after us, we go along, well, that conversation is gonna depend on how well-informed he is, I suppose. If he knows about those terrible cartoons of him that I laughed at the other day in the mess hall, we could be in deep shit."

"Hopefully there's not too much video evidence out there of all the things we've been doing in places where we shouldn't be doing things." She was smirking despite knowing that she shouldn't, but she couldn't help herself. "I mean, they put us together. They can't be that mad at us for fucking like rabbits."

"I shouldn't think so. A penchant for exhibitionism was in both our sexual profiles. No surprises that we actually acted on it." He smiled back down at her, even though they both knew having sex in maintenance corridors was far from the worst offense they had committed against the Initiative.

By the time they were standing in front of Vance's door, Anna slipped her hand into Orion's and squeezed it, even though Orion's hand more than swallowed hers up. "At least you're with me."

He wasn't satisfied just looking down at her, so he leaned down to kiss her once, ignoring the fact that they were right in front of what might very well be death's door for them. "Better or worse, thick and thin, something along those lines. Boils down to partners in crime. Nobody else I'd rather face the world with."

"The world I can handle. It's being up here that has been a challenge." She pulled him down for another kiss as the door opened, and they walked in to Director Vance sitting behind his desk like he was sitting on a throne.

"If it isn't the king of the castle himself. Nice to see you, Director." Anna was scared one moment and sarcastic the next, but she knew no one would expect anything less. It was how she dealt with her fear and her anger.

"Likewise, Mrs. Al-Jabbar." He turned his chair to face them directly, indicating the two chairs on the far side of his desk. "Please have a seat. I don't expect our conversation to take too much of your time, we'll have you on your way again shortly." He tapped a few parts of the hologram in front of him and then reached down below the desk off to one side to shut down the base that powered his system, since he apparently didn't need it for their interview.

Anna was tempted to wait for Orion to sit down so that she could just sit in his lap as her own form of quiet rebellion, but she took a seat to herself even though she never let go of Orion's hand. She refused to. If they were going to separate her from Orion, they would have to cut her hand off. "Is this going to be a short, *fun* conversation, or not so much? Your expressions are habitually hard to read."

"Thank you. I've practiced for a long time to keep them that way." He looked back and forth between the two of them with a sigh, looking mildly sad or annoyed by whatever they needed to talk about. "How is your pregnancy progressing, Mrs. Al-Jabbar? I see the medical reports every day, but they're always so sterilized and clinical. Especially from your doctor. I prefer to know the human side of things. How have you been feeling?"

"You've been reading my medical reports every day?" That

was definitely shocking to hear, since that was closer tabs on her than she ever imagined. "Talk about boring reading material, Director." Anna looked down at herself and then touched her still-flat stomach with her free hand. "I still have trouble with smells and foods sometimes, but I'm looking forward to actually feeling evidence of their existence in here. I feel fine, really. I still feel like not much has changed."

"And yet so much has." He grinned as he looked down at her hand on her stomach. "Well, I can tell you that we're all very excited about your twins, and we look forward to meeting them. But of course, you knew that already." His tone darkened toward the end of the statement, though he didn't move from his chair, one knee crossed over the other as he looked back and forth between her and Orion.

Anna ignored his darkened look, because she knew that they weren't being called to Vance for no reason. She'd been interrogated enough times (even on Earth, she was good at lying her way out of legal trouble) that she knew acting dumb was probably best so that no one would incriminate her of things that they didn't have solid proof of already. "Who wouldn't be excited about meeting my babies? Though I'm surprised you're so interested in them that you would check on their well-being daily. Even Orion doesn't harass me about them that often, and he's their father."

"In my defense, harassing her about anything is usually a bad idea. I avoid it as much as possible." Orion was as relaxed as he could be under the circumstances, matching Vance's posture with one ankle over his knee as he leaned back in his chair. "I figure if there's something that needs my attention, she'll yell about it. Until then, there's no point worrying."

"Usually a good policy with women. Especially pregnant ones." Vance agreed with a grin, then reached into a drawer under his desk and pulled out a tiny object, no bigger than a coin, and set it on the desk between them. A moment's examination confirmed that it was one of the bugs Gordon had given them to plant in the Twist rooms. "This was found recently in the maintenance bridge between this arm and Arm Four. There were no fingerprints, of course, since it's too small to carry such things, but the systems there reported some unexpected debris on a recent cleaning sweep. The debris was identified as a few human hairs. Specifically yours, Mrs. Al-Jabbar."

"Huh." Anna said with feigned confusion, and she leaned forward to examine the bug as though she had never seen it before before she leaned back and looked up at Vance again. "I have to admit, I never thought my hair would get that far. Orion and I have a particular enjoyment for odd places to be intimate. They must have carried in a draft or something."

"Drafts can be tricky things, to be sure. But our maintenance systems for each arm are distinct one from another." He picked up the bug again to work it between his fingers casually as he spoke. "As are those for the dock. So you can only imagine my utter confusion when your hair also showed up in a cleaning sweep of Arm Four."

He fixed her with a look that she'd gotten a number of times in her life, mostly from her father or Ben, which said plainly that he wasn't buying what she was trying to sell. "Now, I can understand an enjoyment of the novelty that new places provide, but violating protocols to move through evacuated arms of this station is something else entirely."

"What's a little bit of fun without risks?" She looked at Orion's hand in hers and realized quickly she could go down by herself. They didn't have any evidence on him that she knew of, and he could find a way to bust her out. Maybe. "I like to investigate places I've never been before. What did my file say? 'Dangerously and sometimes recklessly curious'? I think those were the exact words."

"Yes, well, occasionally that danger comes with consequences. Otherwise it wouldn't be dangerous, would it?" He set the bug aside on the desk next to him and sighed as he looked back at Anna. "The two of you are to be detained on charges of violating Initiative protocols and violation of Consortium property. You will be held in isolation while your case is under review, though these kinds of cases are generally pretty straightforward. Once sentencing comes back, you will in all likelihood be transferred to a Lunar penal colony to serve your sentence. The details are, of course, out of my hands."

"Transfer to a Lunar penal colony because we decided to get freaky in an unauthorized area?" Orion had slipped his free hand into the pocket with his communicator again as he listened, but Anna could feel his hand tighten on hers as his free hand came out balled in a fist. His voice trembled with outrage and indignation. It wasn't like the man she had married at all. "We didn't do *shit* to Consortium property that couldn't get cleaned up with a fucking wet wipe."

"Captain Al-Jabbar, that's really not the way to address a superior, especially in your current circumstance." Vance's tone retained every bit of its condescension and calm in spite of Orion's apparent rising temper. In fact, the man seemed almost amused.

"He's just standing up for me, he didn't go into Arm Four. I did." Anna kept her hand just as tightly connected to Orion's as he held hers, though she was also surprised by his anger. It wasn't like him, though she wasn't exactly against him getting angry, especially in a situation like this. "Let me guess. You want to lock me away and then take my babies from me because I'm serving some sort of ridiculous sentence when you don't have any actual proof of anything? A couple of hairs? Where's social media when you need it? People would have a field day with that."

"Oh, people have been having fun with the Evil Consortium social media commentary for centuries. You understood the rules and broke them wilfully, by your own admission just now. Thank you for that, by the way. It will make sentencing a great deal easier." Vance uncrossed his legs, about to stand up. "As for your Captain husband, we have cellular evidence of another nature from him. So you will not only be serving for violation of property, but obstruction of justice, having lied in this interview about being alone in your break-in. The penalties for that are a good deal stiffer than just violation of property."

"No one's taking my wife anywhere, you son of a bitch." Orion actually growled from his chair, before he unexpectedly launched himself across the desk and landed a single bone-crunching punch straight across Vance's face. The older man hadn't even had time to blink.

The two men went down in a heap as Orion's weight carried through, even in lower gravity, and as Vance began to get his wits about him again, it was clear the fight was anything but a foregone conclusion. He was no slouch himself when it came to personal violence, but Orion was younger, much taller, and much faster, though Vance seemed a good deal stronger from the way Orion grunted when a few of his hits landed. They sent his chair crashing through the room and Orion managed to crack the man's head and shoulder against his desk before getting kicked back against Vance's computer console. Orion put a hand back to stabilize himself against it briefly, but then launched himself at the director again, just as they all heard booted feet pounding down the hallway toward the office.

Anna moved quickly to give Orion more time to beat the shit out of the asshole director, and she grabbed one of the chairs she and Orion had been sitting in to wedge it against the door, which surprisingly actually had a handle. She busted the computerized locking/opening panel with the heel of her boot and then stood aside.

The guards would bust through, that was obvious, and she was going to get thrown into a cell. That was obvious too. But she was all about maximum damage even when she was going to get in trouble for it. She would have tried to land a few punches on Vance herself if it wasn't so difficult to get between them, but instead she just watched in appreciation. "You're a lot more badass than you appear most of the time, babe. I definitely like this whole defending my honor thing!"

"I'm only . . ." he had to duck a hit from Vance, but managed to get a knee to the man's collarbone for his trouble, "mild-mannered when I'm not on the clock. This," he got an elbow to the midsection himself that sent him flying, but he threw himself back at Vance with the bounce off the wall, and got his boot to the side of the older man's knee with an audible crack. "This is me when I'm on the clock."

He also appeared to be about maximum damage, from the way he was picking the older man apart, but Vance managed to roll back away from the assault and grab a gun that he had hidden in a compartment of his desk. The struggle turned quickly from a brawl to a contest for control of the gun, and Vance's strength worked quickly against Orion as the guards outside began trying to beat down the door.

Once there was a gun involved, Anna's joking attitude disappeared, and she went lunging since she wasn't about to let Orion get shot for defending her. She heard a shot go off just as she got close, but she didn't feel any pain, only debris from the ceiling. Anna slammed her foot against Vance's wrist to loosen his grip on the gun. "You fucking psychotic bastard . . ."

Just as Anna got involved and it looked like the two of them might have a chance at getting the gun away from Vance, the door burst open and four guards streamed into the tight space. Orion had nearly wrenched the gun into position to blow Vance's head off when the guards reached them and began ripping them away from each other.

It took two guards each to restrain them, leaving Vance standing over the remains of his office chair on one leg as blood streamed from his destroyed knee. His face was twisted in pain and filled with more genuine anger than Anna had ever seen there, and his grip tightened around the gun in a way that told her he was considering using it. "I admit . . . I'm a little impressed, Captain." He waved the gun over at Anna dismissively. "I knew this wildcat had it in her, but I thought you had a little more discipline."

"I've discovered lately that discipline is overrated." Orion breathed heavily, but not obviously injured aside from a few cuts on his face and arms. "Given recent events and revelations, I think I've given it up entirely. From now on, I aim to misbehave."

Anna was breathing heavily from getting into the fight, but she still fought against the guards that held her like an animal, since she wanted to get to Vance for even trying to threaten Orion's life with the gun. "He's doing what you trained him to do, you motherfucker. Taking down the bad guys, making murderers pay for their crimes." She glanced down at his completely destroyed knee before she spit in his direction. "You'll get yours."

That brought the amusement back to Vance's face through the obvious pain he was in, and he put the gun down on the desk before motioning to the guards. "Lock them up and keep them dark until I get out of surgery. Victoria will be along to question them in an hour."

They didn't make it far out of Vance's office before Anna managed to take one guard down by kicking him right in the crotch, but there were other guards to take his place and haul her along with Orion toward a cell. They weren't gentle with Anna as they tossed her inside a dark room with the barest flicker of light. Landing on her ass was enough to send pain up her spine.

Orion came flying in after her, narrowly missing her. That would have hurt too. "Fucking assholes." She attempted to move closer to Orion. "Are you okay?"

He let out a groan when he hit the wall beside her, but afterward, he fell slowly to the ground with what sounded like . . . laughter? They had been taken up to a cell with exceptionally low gravity, normally used for storage because it drove people crazy after living in it for too long. He rolled over on the floor and took a moment to check over his arms and legs to make sure nothing was actually broken, laughing the entire time.

"I'm fine. Just a little scratched up. Nothing that won't wash off." He could barely talk, he was laughing so hard, but eventually he had to cough and rolled over on his side to spit blood out of his mouth from where his cheek had been cut in the fight.

"Okay, are you broken?" She asked as she finally managed to find her way to him in the nearly-complete darkness. "You're laughing? You sound a *little* bit crazy. He was going to fucking shoot you."

"It's not the first time I've been shot at. And I hope it's not the last." He laughed a little longer after he spoke, but just reached out to hold onto her and pull her close, his hands wandering over her to make sure she was alright after getting thrown around by the guards. "I'm not broken, I promise." He chuckled, but finally managed to calm down and took one of her hands with his and led it down toward the pocket of his pants as he kissed her.

"I've never gotten to use that whole knee-break thing. Ever since training, I've never had to fight somebody stupid enough to give me the opening. That was satisfying. And at least I got to tear up the bastard's office pretty good in the process."

"You better not be looking for a hand job right now." She said as he led her hand toward his pocket. "That was sexy and everything, but I don't think that's wise. Also, one of those fucking guards was grabbing my ass and poking himself into me as he restrained me like a disgusting fucker, which was why I took him out cock-first."

"He had it coming. If you see him again when I'm armed, point him out and I'll make sure he gets more than your boot in his formerly-happy place." He pushed her hand into his pocket, and as soon as she got to the bottom of it, she found what he wanted her to know he had. He held her eyes with a knowing look, waiting for her to process things along with him. "That was a good hit, you taking out that guy. I was impressed. I think the best I was able to do that whole fight was hit Vance's data server. I didn't see the indicators go off on it, so I'm pretty sure it still works, but if he's paying attention, he'll notice where I left a mark."

"Violence for show?" Anna just sighed. "And here I thought you were doing it for me." Anna slid carefully into Orion's lap and pulled her hand out at the same time so that she could slide her hand across his groin anyway. "They won't leave us behind. At least, I hope they won't."

"I was doing it for you." He held her tightly as he got them situated against the wall, and he leaned down to kiss her once she was firmly in his grip. "And I know they won't leave us. If they don't already know what's happened, they will within the hour. We just have to sit tight."

Anna kissed him back harder and wrapped her hands behind his head carefully, since she didn't want to bump any injuries. "I love you." She said against his lips. "I should have been more afraid and cautious, but when they've already threatened everything you hold dear and they're still planning on killing you anyway, everything else doesn't seem to matter so much. The worst is already right in front of you."

He nodded under her hands, and kissed her neck as he held her, his head resting against her shoulder. "As soon as he said we were gonna be detained, I knew anything else was pointless. We're already detained in this place, they just don't call it that, so most people can't even see it yet. Waiting to be put in a hole they can't climb out of." He sighed, since he didn't like feeling helpless, but he had done what he could to help. It was up to the rest to finish the job. "Now we just have to be ready when time comes to move."

"I'm ready. You're here. We did what we could. Now I just want to go home. Well, Earth anyway. None of us will be able to go home."

"Home is where you are, from now on." The last of the mirth vanished from Orion's tone at that declaration, but it was back again quickly. "Which means for the moment, home is right here in this cell. Not the square footage I would prefer, but it'll do for the time being." He kissed her again and reached up to wipe away some blood from a cut on his face that felt like it was finally starting to close up. "We'll be alright. We just have to get out of here first. Once we're back on Earth, we'll give them a hell of a time trying to find us."

* * * * *

Jessie looked at the message on her communicator a few times before she went to find Gordon in their room. He was working away, as usual, but she didn't mind interrupting him for this. He needed to know. "Orion and Anna were called up to talk to Vance after the meeting. Word has it they're in a cell and Gehrig is going to interrogate them in an hour."

Gordon paused in his work to put his head down on the table in front of him with a heavy sigh. "What have they said they were charged with? Or has that not been released?" Jessie was accustomed to seeing Gordon at work, usually with a tall wall of holograms surrounding him, but the last few days since Anna and Orion had found the Twist had been something else entirely. The entire room where he was working was filled to bursting with information, some of it intelligible and some of it intelligible only to Gordon. It was chaos, but it was chaos with a purpose, and Gordon was at the center of the storm of lights.

"They found some of Anna's hair on Arm Four. That's what one of the guards heard him say." Jessie went through her own programs on her hacked communicator, courtesy of Gordon. "Gehrig is not going to be nice about it. They injured Vance somehow. He's requested medical attention."

"They fought Vance? Were they stoned?" He was already incredibly stressed, from the high pitch of his voice and the dark circles under his eyes that no amount of caffeine could erase. "What were they thinking?"

"They are tired of feeling like they're marching to their death. We all are. Except they're more violent than most." Jessie sighed and then looked around at the chaos in the room. "How are we going to get them out?"

"I don't know." He put his head down in a hand again and gripped his hair in aggravation. He had spoken over and over again about how he needed every single person who was involved in their plan of escape, but Orion and Anna were more central than most, as rebel-friendly pilots. "I haven't been able to get access to the central brass systems, I've just got the public sectors of the arm we're on and the patches into the Twist systems." He looked up at the holograms around him and swept most of them out of the way before she saw him drill through the station access to the pieces of the private security system he had been unable to break.

"If I'm going to pop their holding cells, I would need to get around their protocols and get into his office to get through his server directly . . ." he made an attempt and stopped, as systems began popping up. "Wait . . . I didn't do that." He was incredibly confused for a few seconds, but then let out a weak laugh, since he simply didn't have the energy to put much effort behind it.

"That crazy, gigantic, fucking bastard. They bugged Vance's system." He started moving frantically through the systems, grabbing pieces of code from all over the room like a kid on Christmas morning throwing wrapping paper in every direction.

"It's all of it. It's everything. The whole . . . not just . . ." the interface that he manically probed through expanded to show all the systems of the station, then all the operative systems of the ships and satellites around the station, then expanded to the entire orbital map, showing systems for hundreds of stations of various sizes, spinning and dancing through their living room. "That son of a bitch got it all. I've got all of it! All of it!"

Jessie had no idea how to identify the vast majority of what was pouring out all over their living room, but she had almost never seen Gordon so excited. The man was manic, and not just from caffeine. It was infectious. "I guess they're smarter than we give them credit for. Save as much as you can! Hurry! We've got to work on getting them out before Gehrig decides to use slow torture on them or something."

"We can't get it done in that kind of timetable." Gordon's elation had disappeared quickly as he thought about their friends again, and though his fingers were working furiously through the station's full systems, he shook his head and had to pull his own hands away from the security protocols before he went and released Orion and Anna from their cell. "If I show my hand now, that I can do whatever I want with their systems, then they'll know I've got the access. I don't know enough yet. I need to . . . I have to . . ." he was trembling from the number of needs running through his mind, and his fingers went back to pulling at his hair as if each strand lost was one less thing he had to worry about.

Jessie went up behind him and covered his eyes with her hands before she said anything else. "I'll talk to Logan. Maybe he can help. You focus on this, we'll take care of moving things up as quickly as we can to get out of here. Maybe we can even distract Gehrig and they'll just leave Anna and Orion alone for a day or two. Okay?"

"Distract Gehrig. Right. Distract. We can do that." He reached up to hold onto her hands as they covered his eyes, keeping them there and keeping her close to him. The world made more sense with Jessie near him. She didn't give it a choice, everything she touched for him just worked better. "Distract her from two suspects who may have discovered something they desperately want hidden . . . does anyone higher . . . if they don't, and if they do . . ." He went back to forming incomplete sentences, but at least his brain was moving in a certain direction again, and he broke off after a few nonsense syllables to turn around and face her.

His eyes looked into hers, since the reflection of the world in her own expression seemed more real than anything he had ever seen for himself. "I love you. Thank you." He kissed the back of her hand then used it to pull her down into a brief kiss. His lips stung with the taste of black coffee and overcharged energy tonics, but it had been the same for several days. He had been on overdrive for so long it was just a matter of time before he broke apart at the seams. "Talk to Logan. Work out what you can. I can crack this. I'll keep them out of circulation for as long as I can."

"I will be back in one hour." She pulled him into another kiss before she let go. "You will take a break and get some rest when I come back. Don't fight me on this. You need sleep desperately."

"We need to get off this station." He countered, but he clearly didn't have the mental energy to fight her when he knew she was right. "If I can dispose of Gehrig and the others for a few hours, then I'll . . ." he broke off and shook his head while he took a deep breath to still the ever-rising anxiety of the situation. "I'll get some rest when you get back."

"Good. If you won't do it willingly, I'll get drugs from Mercury to force you." Jessie threatened, but clearly she meant it. She was worried about him, no matter how dire the situation was in front of them. "I'll be back soon."

"I'll be here." He promised, since he certainly wasn't going anywhere else with all that was going on. He managed to give her a smile on her way out the door, but when it closed behind her, he slumped back in the chair with his hands over his face.

There was just too much. Too much at his fingertips, too many possibilities, and it was such an overload of information and access that he didn't know where to start. With the access he had, he could get inside the Consortium and bring everything down. Everything. All of it was just a collection of the right keystrokes.

The goal was Eleusis. He had to keep the goal in mind. The goal was freedom, and life, and health, and peace.

That was the real war. The real struggle of the world. The struggle between those who wanted such things for everyone and those who wanted such things only for a select few.

But that puzzle was too big, there were too many moving pieces. The Consortium was a vast organization, with its fingers in

every single dealing on Earth and in Orbit. It was too big, too big
. . .

The goal wasn't Eleusis, he realized as his mind spiralled out of his control. It had been Eleusis once, and was still Eleusis in the long run, but the past few months had made the goal much simpler.

The goal was Jessie, and their daughter, living long and healthy lives in peace. That was the goal. That was all that mattered. If he concentrated on that single goal, that single point of light, then the path toward it became clearer.

First, he had to get them off the station, then he had to get them to safety in the short term, then he had to get them to Eleusis, then he had to make sure the world was secure for her and their daughter to live in. Everything else was in the details.

That was a world that he could work with. That was a goal he could manage.

His fingers tapped on the interface once he had a path in mind, the top priorities that needed to be addressed before all others falling into place like building blocks of a better world. He was going to make it happen. Not for the war, not for the rest of humanity, not for his brothers or Tatyana or himself, but for Jessie.

* * * * *

It was hard for Jessie to track Logan down, but once she found him, she was quick to act so he wouldn't brush her off or yell at her or something. He was talking with Renata when she approached, but she wasn't apologetic when she interrupted him. She was working on a time crunch. They all were. "Logan, I need to speak with you. Now." She paused and then sighed. "Please."

He was in the middle of a hallway headed toward the clinic, and though he looked worried, the urgency in Jessie's tone caught him off guard enough to get a second look. He turned back to Renata briefly to send her on her way. "Go see if the other doctors have seen her and if not, go through her messages. I want to know where she is." He spoke like a man who was accustomed to being obeyed, and didn't even wait for Renata to respond before he turned back to Jessie. "What's happened now?"

Jessie wasn't about wasting time, her own or anyone else's, so she didn't hesitate to get to the point, though hearing he was concerned about Mercury's location made her want to question that. She didn't, though, since he was perfectly capable of keeping tabs on his wife, and Mercury was a capable woman even without Logan. "Anna and Orion are being held in custody awaiting interrogation and then probably no trial before they're shipped off to some random location. I need your help to delay Gehrig from her interrogation, because she's known for being ruthless."

"They just told me they were taken a few minutes ago." Logan said with worry creasing his face. He looked older than he had just half a year prior during the information sessions where they had met, but they had all been through a lot in the meantime. "I've got a couple of our legal minds on their way up to claim representation for Anna and Orion under the Initiative's own protocols, but I doubt they'll even be allowed through. What can Gordon do about breaking them out?" They were still walking as they spoke, since Logan didn't want to make it any easier for the Initiative to spy on them.

"I don't think there's much Gordon can do right now. He's trying to figure out how to get us all out of here in relative safety." She stopped the bigger man and pulled him down by his shoulder to whisper in his ear. "Orion managed to bug Vance's servers. Gordon's working through a flood of Consortium information. He's good, but he can't do everything at once." She let go of him and continued walking. "If Anna and Orion are going to get help, it has to be from you."

"Oh, great. First he spends all his time shoving everything he can do in everyone's face and now he's too busy to help take care of the people who risked their asses for him?" Logan reached up to rub at his forehead and scrolled through a list of contacts on his communicator with his free hand. "Real quality man you've got there."

"Lay off, Bickford." She said sharply as she looked up at the man without backing down even though he was bigger than she was. "He would do something if he wasn't trying to save *all* of our asses. They knew the risks. He's no angel, but he's not trying to leave them out to dry."

Logan wasn't mollified by that defense, but he was a little surprised by it. He knew Jessie was pregnant, but he thought she had just been doing as the Initiative had forced them, just like most of those involved. "He's a cocky asshole, and he's looking out for his own interests. Him and Tatyana both have their own agenda in all of this and fuck everybody else if they don't fit into it."

He finally got to a name that seemed to be potentially of use to him, and he let out a brief sigh. "If he can't actually help, can he at least assist in blowing something up on the other side of the station? If I get something to go haywire, even on one of the way lower decks on our own arm, then I can dispatch security crews to handle and repair it, and hold Gehrig personally responsible for overseeing it. It's the only pull I've got, where she's concerned."

"You're wrong about him." She defended first and foremost, even if she knew it was probably pointless to do so. "He is an asshole, but he's not here to fuck everyone else. He's here because he wants people to be able to get to Eleusis." Jessie just shook her head. "I'm sure we can get something to go haywire. I'll go back and see what he can do. He's the best chance we have at actually surviving. And he does have some feelings. He cares about our baby. Me too, most of the time, I think."

That got Logan's attention, since he hadn't thought she would actually defend the man, and she could see him attempting to alter his own perception of Gordon according to what she was saying. Gordon just didn't make that easy on other people. "I'll be on the lookout for some kind of shit to go haywire. I hope you're right about him. For all our sakes."

"I am. You'll see." Jessie said confidently, since she knew that Gordon was capable of doing good and being good, even if he was just as capable of being cruel. She turned away and headed off after that, since she didn't want to linger. There was too much to do.

* * * * *

Mercury wasn't sure how long she'd been asleep, but there was some kind of ringing noise that eventually woke her up. Her whole body ached, and she didn't want to even reflect as to why. She knew why. She didn't need to think about it. She didn't want to think about it. Ever.

She opened her eyes slowly only to see someone approaching her, and she flinched as the person stopped next to her, but the ringing got louder. When she tilted her head to look up, it was Stephen Kaplan, still naked, but holding a communicator. She was similarly naked, but she didn't attempt to cover herself or even move, since there was no reason to. He'd seen and done everything that Mercury could and couldn't handle, and the weight of all her unwanted memories were enough to immobilize her in place. If he wanted more, he would take it regardless.

Stephen stood over her with the communicator for a moment, enjoying her refusal to respond in any way, then lifted the device to his ear. "Yes, Director." He said in as jovial and relaxed a tone as she'd ever heard from him. "I see. Well, that's not quite as we expected from them, hopefully surgery goes quickly. Yes, I understand. No, I'll handle it. And I'll inform Maria. I'll take care of it, Sir, don't worry. Alright, keep me posted."

He disconnected the line and then laid his communicator down on her breasts as if she was nothing more than a table for his things. He crouched down beside the low couch where she'd fallen asleep. "No going back to sleep for you, precious. You're too good when you're awake to let you go back to sleep. I had you both ways, and I definitely prefer you awake."

Mercury felt even worse, knowing that she was violated when she was asleep, even, but she didn't do anything other than open her eyes and stare at him. The things she did remember were bad enough. The man in front of her did not have a single redeemable quality, and the whole universe would be a better place if he wasn't in it. Still, she didn't move, even though he told her to wake up. Mercury wanted to leave, but she'd wanted to leave for so many hours now that she was beginning to wonder if they would ever free her. Even if they did, she was certain that they would find some way to haunt her once she had gone. What could he possibly want from her now? He'd already destroyed her pride, her mind, and everything else along with her body.

"Get up." He commanded afterward as he stood up again, drawing her body up with a touch. His touch didn't tingle the way it had before she'd fallen asleep, and the world was beginning to feel something like what she remembered as normal, but there was still something overall wrong about the way her nerves were acting. "It's time for you to get back in your jacket and heels and be on your way like the whore you are."

Mercury got up after flinching from both the pain and the hateful words that he hurled at her. How did she end up this way? How did she go from a smart, talented doctor that was well-respected and honored to this? To a woman who was as good as drunk and destroyed on a disgusting couch with a horrible man yelling at her as though she was nothing? Maybe he was right.

He'd told her over and over all night long that women like her were meant for pleasure and nothing else, that her career was a joke, that she was only a doctor because her father made it happen. He talked about her father a lot, he told her how ashamed she should be, that her father would hate her, that she was nothing to him or her mother, the verbal abuse had been just as bad as the rest of it. Mercury stumbled her way to her jacket and shoes, and her limbs were shaky with pain as she attempted to put her heels back on and close the jacket over her naked body.

She believed before that she was in a respectable relationship with Logan, even though it had been a strange concept to most, but now she didn't know. Maybe all he saw was a pretty, perfected face and body. Stephen told her that no one could resist her, even a married man, who she stole from his best friend. All of it was clear in her mind, and she hated it, just as much as she hated herself at that moment.

He hadn't moved from where he stood the entire time she attempted to put herself back together, but when she was finished with her coat and started to put her hair back up, he caught her sharply by the back of the coat and held her back against him. He was still bare from head to toe, and the predatory nature of his touch was more than apparent in the way he was holding onto her. "I have one more parting gift for you, Doctor, to send you on your way."

Mercury's hair fell out of her hand as he pulled her back, and she couldn't stop the involuntary whimper that escaped her as he held her body against his. She was grateful, at least, for her jacket between them, even though it wasn't much. "Yes?" She said weakly, though she had avoided speaking as often as she could, partially because she didn't want to, and partially because her throat hurt as badly as the rest of her body.

He moved in to whisper against her hair as his free hand moved freely over her body, the last vestiges of violating ownership to endcap a horrific night.

"You were designed, prior to your conception, with many and sundry gifts. Your body is a work of art seldom surpassed in the history of our species. You know you're unnatural. You've known it your entire life. But in the time you have left before you die, I want you to ask why. I want you to ask what you really are, what you're made from. What the purpose could have possibly been behind your creation."

"Everyone would prefer their children to be beautiful and graceful creatures, sure, but the artificiality of your construction doesn't end with these perfect tits. I want you to ask why your parents made you what you are. Because when you understand that, you'll know that everything I've told you is true. You are an experimental goddess, shaped by those who thought they could play god."

His free hand went up to her throat one last time, bringing all her memories of the time he'd spent choking the life out of her the night before roaring back through her mind. "Now, tell me you'll be an obedient bitch and investigate as I say."

Mercury wasn't sure how she could still have enough emotion or fear to create tears, but his hand on her throat again made her vision instantly blurry. There was no more powerful drug in her that confused her senses. It was just the harsh reality.

"I'll investigate." She had no idea what he was trying to point her toward, or why it mattered, especially now, but she knew he would find some way to punish her if she didn't do as instructed. He had all the power he could ever want, even over her life, and she had none. Not as long as she was trapped on the station, and that could still be months. She had no idea.

"Good girl." His grip on her neck turned into a caress, and his hand violated her her body again before he slapped her ass, hard, to push her toward the door. "Go on back to your cell. I'll miss you. But only until the next time. Make sure you come thirsty."

Next time? The tears slid down her cheeks as she looked back once, only to see Stephen smiling at her and Maria standing in a doorway behind him, also to watch her go. "Next time?" Mercury didn't know why the words came out, but she was so horrified to think that there would be a next time that she couldn't stop herself from asking.

"You'll be begging for it before it gets here, Red." Maria said with a grin as she continued to lean against the doorway. "It's highly addictive. It's made to be. You're going to want to come back, believe me."

"When you start to feel it, the pull. . . you know where to find us." Stephen put his arm around Maria's shoulders as Mercury headed for the door. Even though he wasn't actually pulling her back in physically, she could feel their hooks in her nonetheless, spiked through every single nerve. She was a lab rat with no defense.

Mercury didn't stop the tears as she walked out without looking back again, but she didn't allow herself to sob. She had to be strong enough not to break down, even though it was taking everything in her not to break in a public hallway. She was already worse than broken.

"Do you think she'll keep her mouth shut?" Maria said as she looked up at Stephen, and she stepped up onto her toes so that she could kiss his cheek. "That was fun."

He grinned down at the perfection that was his wife and kissed her again, grabbing a luscious handful of her ass in the process. "It was. I'm gonna say she'll be back in . . . two weeks. After one, she'll be feeling it, but she's got more willpower than I thought she would. She'll hold off until she absolutely can't anymore."

"Two weeks. That's a long time to be patient. We might need to go after her before that." Maria smacked at his hand after he grabbed her ass, just because she was so accustomed to fending him off because he liked the resistance. "I don't know if I can wait two days. I'm insatiable after last night."

"This is what I get for introducing you to my experiments." He grabbed her wrist as she pulled away, since he was used to her being contrary, and enjoyed it just as much as she thought he did. "You're just as much of an addict as she is, just in a different way."

"You're right." She looked into his eyes. "We all are. That's how the human mind is ruled, by what it wants and how badly. The flavor just varies from person to person."

"I like your flavor." He said with another kiss, pushing her back toward their bedroom. "Now, with her out of the way and you all to myself, it's time to put you back in handcuffs."

"Oh, really?" Maria couldn't help but smirk as she looked up at him once more before she turned and ran. "You have to catch me first, Mr. Kaplan."

* * * * *

Logan was going insane with everything that was happening at once, and he had to take a moment to walk off around the bend of a corridor to get a moment to himself. Renata hadn't been able to find any trace of Mercury anywhere in the station, and neither could anyone else. Even Gordon had been unable or unwilling to find any trace of her.

He was going to have to go to the brass, about Mercury and about Anna and Orion. He had no idea what he was going to say to them, no idea what he was going to even try to do to get them back, but he had to get them back to safety somehow. They had to get away, all of them. He just had to attempt to get a breath and get his head back on straight first.

Before he could hit the bottom of his downward spiral, his communicator beeped with a message. From Mercury.

The battery of my communicator died. I am now at our unit. I am going to take a shower.

Logan was immediately confused at the apparent flippancy of her message, but he couldn't waste any time wondering if it was some kind of trick from the brass. If there was even a chance that she was back in their unit, he needed to be there. He rushed off toward the lifts as quickly as his legs would carry him, ignoring everyone and everything in his way.

Mercury couldn't get the water hot enough. She couldn't use enough shampoo, she couldn't use enough soap. Her body was red and raw by the time she stopped scrubbing, and she couldn't even feel the tears underneath the water. She slid down the wall to the floor and rested her head against the tile.

They were in her head. She could feel their hands. Their bodies. Everything. How would she ever get them out of her head?

She had waited until halfway through the shower to send him the message in the first place, and she had been down in the corner of the shower for a while before she finally heard the door to their unit open. "Mercury!" Logan's voice sounded frantic, and he had every right to be. She had been gone for a total of almost nine hours. Well beyond anything that one of her patients might have required.

Mercury heard Logan call out for her, but she felt more guilt than anything else. She was nothing. Especially if he didn't care about her. Were they right? Did he only care about her appearance? That was the beginning of it all. Their entire relationship started on a sexual agreement. She knew that wasn't normal. Instead of attempting to get up, she just sat under the water and kept her eyes closed. Even if he was angry, she didn't have the energy to do anything.

She heard him calling her name over and over again as he ran through the unit, but it didn't take him long to get into the bathroom. He tore in and heard the water running, then ripped back the shower curtain quickly and gave an audible sigh of relief. "Mercury." He rushed in beside her, fully clothed, and was immediately down on the floor of the shower with his arms around her, as if he had to clutch her against him just to make sure he wasn't hallucinating her safe return.

Mercury was surprised that Logan rushed into the water to hold her, but she couldn't stop the flinch that escaped her as soon as he did. He would hate her if he knew. He would be so angry. He wouldn't want her anymore, but she wondered if that was for the best anyway. "I'm sorry." It was the only thing she could say about so much.

"All I care about is that you're alright." He said as he held her, his breath slowly returning to normal. "I've been all over this station looking for you. I ran through most of your patients, I had all the nurses looking for you . . ."

She kept her face close to his shoulder but she had a hard time allowing him to be close to her. Mercury had no idea what he would see, if there would be bruises or not, but just remembering Kaplan choking her made her cry a little harder. "I'm . . . not."

"Are you hurt?" He released her just enough to look her over, but if anything the Kaplans had done to her should have left a mark, it wasn't visible over how red her skin was beneath the scalding hot water. "Do you need help? What can I do?"

Mercury shook her head and forced herself to pull away from him and stand up. No one could help her. Especially not Logan. "You can't do anything." She turned away from him to turn off the water. "I'm sorry I worried you."

"What happened?" He got up and moved away from the water once she put some distance between them, but he was mostly confused. She was pulling away and acting like she wanted nothing to do with him, when only hours before, they had been committed to working together on getting free of the station. "Where were you?"

"I can't tell you." She stepped out of the shower and snatched a towel as fast as she could to cover herself up. "I . . . can't. You need to focus on other things."

Logan was so surprised by that answer that he just stood, soaking wet and confused, and stared at her for a moment. "Focus on other things? You were just missing for nine and a half hours! I'm not focusing on anything if you're not alright. There's nothing else to focus on!"

"I'm here. Clearly uninjured. We have to worry about getting away from here." She kept her voice as calm as she could before she looked back at him once. Her face was swollen from all of her crying, but her voice sounded sullen and dead. "We have only been together for a few months. There are bigger things than us. You didn't choose this."

"What are you talking about? Where is this coming from?" He knew she was trying to put some distance between them, but he couldn't help taking a few steps closer to her. "Nothing you're saying is making sense, Mercury. I love you. If they gave me the option between going back to Earth without you and staying here with you, I would stay here, fucked up as everything about this place is. Nothing is a bigger deal to me than you."

"Did you say that to Anna too?" Mercury knew she was lashing out, but she had a hard time believing that he wanted her for all of the reasons he wanted her to believe. "Our relationship isn't normal. You didn't want this before, we both didn't. But you agreed because of the way I look. How could anything good come from something that you hated about yourself? You still do. You don't want this." Mercury could hear Stephen and Maria's voices, but she couldn't deny that they were probably right. Mercury couldn't mean more to Logan than Anna. He had known Anna his whole life.

Mercury hurried to get dressed, and she did not care about the rules for their unit. She was going to wear as much clothing as she could.

It was so completely out of character from anything else he'd ever heard from Mercury that he wasn't sure how to respond at first. It was like she had been speaking another language and it took him some time to translate. He shook his head, even though she wasn't looking at him, then went back into the bedroom with her, dripping all over the smooth tiles of the floor.

"I don't know where you were, or who you were talking to, but whoever they are, they're full of shit, and you know it. I didn't agree to this between us because of the way you look. I agreed to this in the first place for the same reason you did. But those reasons have changed. So have I. We all have." He took a deep breath to calm himself, but it was getting harder and harder to do the more she flung at him. "I want this. I want us. No bullshit anybody else can spew is gonna change that."

Mercury shook her head and continued to dress until she had as many layers as she possibly could. "You won't want me anymore. You just don't know it." She didn't know how she could continue crying, but more tears fell. "People know, Logan. People have been watching us. People know about us. More people will know if you don't just keep moving forward. If people find out, they won't support you. We won't get out."

He was still more confused, but he understood that part of what she was saying at least. "Someone blackmailed you? Because of our relationship?"

His question was met with silence because she didn't want to confirm it and make him angrier. They needed to get out or she would continue to live in her worst nightmare. "I didn't want you to be exposed. We need all the help we can get . . . they were going to lock you away . . ."

"Nobody's locking me anywhere." He said quickly as he got closer to her. He hoped she would be a little more open to him being close once she was clothed. "Nobody's locking you anywhere either. And if they want to put it out there that you and me have an outside-the-box relationship, then fucking let them. I'd rather risk people's perception of me than let you go through . . . whatever it is you've gone through the past nine hours." He didn't touch her as he got close to her, but he did his best to meet her eyes, wanting nothing more than to hold her and tell her that he was going to kill whoever had hurt her. Slowly. "Nothing else matters besides this. Besides us. Not to me."

She met his eyes briefly, but as soon as she looked into those steely eyes, she shook her head and stepped back away from him again. Even with underclothes and her scrubs, which were her safest clothing, she felt too exposed. "If you knew . . . If you had any idea . . . what they made me do . . . what they made me *think* . . ." Mercury tried to cover her eyes with her hands but she just saw Stephen behind her eyelids and her hands instinctively went to her own throat protectively as her pulse quickened. "I begged. All night long. I couldn't help it. It was in the water."

"In the water . . . what . . . they drugged you?!?" He took a step in for every one she took away, but he didn't touch her against her will. He could feel the rising fury boiling inside him at the thought of anyone tampering with Mercury in any way, especially the kind of violation she was talking about. "They . . . Mercury, I'm so sorry. Whoever they are, they're going to pay for what they did. And if they drugged you, then it wasn't you. Whatever happened, it wasn't your fault."

"I agreed to go. I agreed that I would go there to do whatever they wanted me to do as long as you were left alone and safe." Mercury didn't want him to reach out and touch her, she didn't want him to defend her or care. She felt like a waste of life, a lie, a fraud. "I didn't know what they would do. I lied to you to go. I thought I was doing the right thing."

"I know. You've never done anything else." He could feel his heart breaking as she told him why she had done what she had done. What she had endured, because of him. "Just because you agreed to go doesn't make any of what happened your fault." The breaths he took were slow and shuddering, just because he was trying to keep himself from running out and hunting down the ones who had hurt Mercury there on the spot. "I don't care what they do to me. What happens to me. You deserve to be safe. More than anything else in this universe."

"The only way we're going to escape here is if you aren't thrown into a cell because of me. Because of something that I suggested in the first place." Eventually Mercury hit a wall and she couldn't back up any more, and she looked panicked as she looked back at it. She felt trapped all over again, but she knew Logan wouldn't hurt her. "They want me to go back." She admitted out loud, but it was followed by a sob and her hands went to her neck again. "I thought he was going to kill me. Sometimes I wanted him to kill me just to make it stop."

He saw the panic in her eyes and finally took a step back, so she knew that he wasn't going to force anything on her, but it took a huge effort to do so. "They're not going to have time to throw me in a cell." He said quietly, since a lot had happened in the time that she had been elsewhere. "They've put Orion and Anna into custody on an upper level near the dock, but Orion managed to bug Vance's servers in the process. Gordon has access to everything now, and he's digging through it as fast as he can. It's not going to be a matter of weeks or months that we're going to get out of here. It's going to be hours."

There was some relief in her eyes at hearing how quickly things were supposed to change, but she still wasn't certain that Stephen or Maria wouldn't come after her whenever they wanted to anyway. As soon as Mercury was against the wall and there was nowhere to go, she slid down to the floor again. "I'm so sorry." She repeated again. "I . . . I can't get it out of my head. I can still feel it. I couldn't get the water hot enough. I used all of the shampoo. I can still feel them. I feel like nothing. Useless. Weak. Stupid."

He went down to the floor along with her, but didn't get any closer, fixing her with a look that was as desperate as she felt. "You are not nothing." His voice was as commanding and insistent as it had ever been with her in other circumstances, but there was nothing of the expectation of obedience in it. He was merely stating a fact, something he knew beyond any doubt. "You are a woman I'm proud to know, proud to share my life with. You're an incredible doctor and one of the most talented, kind people I've ever met. You are amazing, Mercury, and whoever was empty enough to do something like this to you . . . they are the ones who are nothing."

Mercury looked over at him after so much avoidance. "How can you care about me enough to say that? After all of this? You don't know what happened. What I did. What they did. I was supposed to be yours only. They . . . I can't . . . I don't know what to do now. What if they were right? What if I'm only a doctor because my father made it happen? That could be disastrous."

Logan looked confused at that claim, and shook his head. "I've seen you with your patients. I've heard your patients rave about you, and I've seen your research. You're brilliant, Mercury. Everything you have, you have because you earned it. Your parents had the means to support you while you did it, sure, but that doesn't take away from your achievements. You're an amazing doctor. You take care of people. You know more about the human body than I ever will in seven lifetimes. As for what you're good for . . ." he looked incredibly angry at that, but it wasn't at her, it was directed at anyone who would try to tell her she was nothing. "I love you. Maybe I don't say so often enough under the circumstances we've been in, but I do. I want you with me in whatever life is waiting for us after this. Wherever we go, whatever we do, I want to spend it with you, and our children."

Mercury hadn't thought about the babies, she was too afraid, too drugged, too much of everything to think about anyone other than herself and Logan. Slowly she crept to Logan's side and she touched him so tentatively it was clear that she was afraid to be close to anyone. "I can't go back. I'm so scared, Logan. Please. Don't leave me."

"You don't have to go anywhere." He held her hand tightly when she reached out to him, and leaned into her a little, wanting nothing more than to hold her and make sure she knew everything would be alright. "I'm right here. You're not leaving my side again, even for a minute. Not until we get the fuck off this station and away from these . . . pathetic excuses for human beings."

Mercury didn't want to be alone, even though she knew Logan shouldn't want to take care of her or care about her after what happened. She started sobbing again as he held her hand, and she nearly collapsed into his side and lap, since she wanted to be held and told that she would be okay even though she didn't know how it was possible to be okay ever again. "Will you . . . hold me?"

She didn't have to ask twice, and he pulled her forcibly against him, gathering her into his lap against his part of the wall as if she was a child that needed to be completely enveloped. He tucked her head against his shoulder and locked his arms around her so tightly it actually hurt a part of her upper back. As it did, though, she could feel her back crack as the pressure popped it, and a jolt of pure, drugged pleasure ran through her entire body as a last vestige of the effects she'd been under, lingering in her spine.

A moan escaped her lips first before another sob and then she buried her face into his chest as she clawed at his shirt to keep him close. Could he really protect her? Did he really want to? Would he? She didn't know for sure. In his arms, though, she felt safe, as long as he didn't trap her hands or try to touch her throat. "I hope you don't regret protecting me."

He shook his head against her hair, taking a few difficult breaths. "I would die before I let anything happen to you, Mercury. Or to our children. You're my family. I will never regret being here for you."

Mercury closed her eyes tightly, though she wondered if she would ever be able to sleep again without the right sedative. She tried to take calm, even breaths to force herself to relax, but it wasn't working very well. "I'm so tired, but I can't stop thinking about it."

"Think about us instead." He offered, not as a command, but as a suggestion, running his hands over her shoulders. "Think about the home we're going to have. Away from everything, away from all of this."

She nodded and tried to do as he suggested, but it was the sheer exhaustion and the unending tears that finally forced her into sleep.

He held her through the tears, even as the exhaustion in her body began to finally overcome the trauma. While she was still barely conscious, he stood and moved just a few steps to place her on her own side of the bed, but didn't let go of her even after he had laid her down.

He waited until her breaths began to even out from the continual sobs, and slid his arms out from under her bit by bit until she was resting on her own. She seemed much more sensitive even to the smallest touches than she ever had been before, but he took his time to make sure she was settled comfortably with a blanket pulled over her.

He stopped beside the bed to write her a note that said that he was just out in the living room if she woke up and needed him, that he wasn't going to leave the unit, he just wanted her to get some rest. He left it on his pillow beside hers, and snuck out of the room as quietly as he could, leaving the door cracked with a pillow to wedge it open. He wasn't going to take a chance of some sick fucker closing the door remotely just to torment his wife any further.

He went to the kitchen portion of their unit and poured himself a drink from the pathetic excuse for whiskey brewed in orbit, and downed a tall shot of it just to feel the burn of it down his throat. It did nothing to cool the rage burning inside him that someone would . . . that someone had . . .

He eventually turned away from the kitchen counter and went to the computer interface for the unit, where all the updates and requests for information came through when people tried to reach them. There was a small aperture near the center that was designed to take in images in the greatest possible resolution to facilitate video communication, but there was nothing lit around it to indicate that it was active.

"I hope you're watching." He whispered quietly as he faced it, a second shot already poured in his hand. "I hope you're getting all of this, and that you're enjoying the show. I hope this, all of this, the Initiative, the charade with Eleusis, the constant games you've played with everyone here, has been good for you. Because it's going to end. Soon. And if I have anything to say about it, it's going to end with you begging for mercy as you die one piece at a time."

He downed the shot in his hand as he glared into his reflection in the camera. It didn't matter if no one was watching. He knew who was on the other side.

"That woman, these people, this world, is not your toy to fuck around with as you see fit. It's the animal you've prodded one time too many, and if it's in my power, it's going to rip your fucking heart out and feed it to you."

35

Tatyana looked across the table at Gordon as they reviewed the map of the station and all the schematics they could get their hands on. She let out a sigh with a multitude of meanings behind it before she stood up a little bit straighter. "I think we have covered everything. Now all that is left is to put it in action."

"Right. Sure. It's just that simple." Koskei said from the far side of the room, shaking his head. A quick glare from Logan served to give the man pause, but didn't deter him completely. "I'm no expert on statistics, but with all the pieces of this plan that have to fall into place at the right moment, in the right way, I'm seeing the most likely result here as suicide. And not the honorable kind."

"The variables we haven't accounted for will be dealt with by everyone overseeing their portion of the action." Gordon explained calmly. The world really did feel like a much better place after six hours of uninterrupted sleep, even though he had been initially irritated about being allowed to sleep twice as long as he had agreed to. "Some improvisation on all fronts is going to be necessary. The main point is that we have our goals identified and tasks set to accomplish them. Can you get people moving or not?"

Koskei didn't like to admit when he had been overruled, but he eventually nodded. "They'll move. I can't promise people are going to be happy about it or that people will keep from causing their own kind of chaos through all this, but they'll move."

"If they understand what's at stake, they'll do as they have to." Logan growled from his side of the table. Mercury was there in the chair beside him at the table, but he hadn't stopped glaring from one set of eyes to the next the entire time they'd been meeting. Everyone in the room knew he was out for blood and something had changed, but no one had cared enough or been brave enough to ask why. Gordon just assumed it was due to

Anna's imprisonment.

"We do not have the time or the resources to be bleeding hearts about this." Tatyana replied. "We want to save everyone that we can, but those who resist despite being given assurances will take their own risk. Each second we have is necessary and vital." Tatyana looked around the room at the group gathered, even though no one looked particularly happy to be there.

"Only a select group of people have any knowledge of where we will be going, and the coordinates will not be put into the shuttles until we have full control of the operating systems and can keep the Consortium from accessing our information. Many of you have been gathering supplies. We will need everything we can get. If any of you see anything valuable, grab it. We will be met by others in the rebellion down on Earth, and they will need some of the supplies just as badly as we will. Medical supplies as well. Dr. Finnegan? Do you think we have enough gathered?"

Mercury was surprised to hear her name and she looked up slowly to meet the eyes of the Russian woman across the room from her. "We have enough supplies and then some. We will run out of CV treatments eventually, so in order to keep everyone from beginning to deteriorate as they would have otherwise, we'll need to find access to the treatment medication eventually." Her voice sounded hollow, her eyes looked empty, but she was responsive.

"Hopefully we'll be roasting marshmallows under an Eleusis sunset before that happens." Barry was eternally the optimist of the group, though most of those present seemed only to tolerate his presence for that exact reason. He and his wife were constantly trying to help everyone look on the bright side, not because they didn't understand the gravity of what was taking place, but because they needed to remember the reasons for their actions.

"Have you ever even seen a marshmallow?" Melissa piped up from across the room, easily the most out-of-place person there, but she was present on Kameron's behalf, with her match standing behind her looking ridiculously overwhelmed. "You're like a stick wrapped in a medical coat."

"We can hope things will move that fast." Logan interjected, which had Melissa and just about everyone else backing down in a hurry. "For the time being, we need to focus on moving quickly and effectively. The moment those ships dock, things are going to go a little haywire. Melissa, are you sure Kameron's up to this?"

Melissa just smiled back, shaking her perfectly-blonde hair over a beautifully-inked shoulder. "If you knew her better, you wouldn't ask that question. She's ready to kick some ass, just as soon as some ass presents itself. She'll get it done."

"Alright, then." Logan said with a last look at Tatyana. "Supply ships dock, then we wait for Gordon's cue. We've all got work to do and bags to pack. Let's get moving."

Most people moved out quickly, Logan among them with Mercury at his side, but Aiko and Carl lingered until they were some of the last people left with Gordon and a few others. Aiko didn't want to talk to anyone, especially not Tatyana, but she wanted to talk to Gordon.

Carl stayed by her side as she approached, but she wasn't shy as she made eye contact with the man that used to be a close friend. "I made an emergency kit for you and your wife." She held out two small pouches. "If you need to clear an area in advance of entry, use the little blue devices. They have a gas in them that contains a heavy sedative. Wait at least twenty seconds after you pop one if you need it and cover your face. Short-lived but powerful." She chewed on her bottom lip before she said anything else. "Everything else in there is some kind of poison, and there are darts and needles if necessary. If you get caught, this little kit just might save you. You're the brains of this operation. We need the brains."

Gordon took the small pouches from her, and immediately handed one over to Jessie beside him. He didn't need to look through it first. It was Aiko. She was one of a very small group of people in the world he trusted. "You really shouldn't call me the brains of the operation. My brain typically ends up in very dark and cobwebbed places that I would prefer the operation stayed out of." He put the pouch into one of the large pockets on the side of his pants without breaking eye contact with his old friend. "Thank you. For this and for everything else I know you'll be doing to make this plan work."

"I'm doing this for the future. For all these babies and for my brother. Kazuo should be here right now, and he's not, and I'm going to make sure my niece gets to live his dream. Someday we're going to get to Eleusis." Aiko looked between Jessie and Gordon and then she turned back toward Carl. "Let's go. You're the strongest person we've got and your best friend is in confinement."

"You've been spying on me while I'm working out again." Carl said with a grin down at Aiko. Beneath the coat he was wearing, the man was armed to the teeth, though the extra bulk of all the weapons he was carrying was barely noticeable beyond his already-gigantic stature. His look turned to Gordon after lingering on his wife, and his eyes narrowed in a distinctly predatory glare. "You'd better hold up your end, White. I get killed in all this and I'm gonna be a fucking mean ghost."

"Duly noted." Gordon wasn't fazed by threats, even from the monstrosity in front of him. "Ships will be hitting the dock in thirty-eight minutes. Loose ends need to be tied and trimmed in thirty-five. I'll see you both at the docks." He had protested against Aiko joining him and Tatyana on the team going to retrieve the Twist, but she had argued her way past his concerns. He had to admit that she would be an asset when it came to the technical aspect.

Aiko took Carl's hand as they walked out, since she was aware that it might be the last time either of them held hands, and she wanted to take the moment while she still could. "No dying." She reminded him as they walked out of the room. "If you die, I can't spy on you working out anymore, and I need that in my life."

Carl grinned and spun her once as they walked. He knew exactly what they were walking into, but the difference between him and everyone else involved in the operation was that he actually enjoyed the danger. "You'll get everything you can stand and then some. You already know better than to think that anybody can kill me without my permission."

In the weeks since Aiko had really made breakthroughs in understanding Carl's physiology, no fact had stood out quite as starkly as that, since it really wasn't an exaggeration. Examining the man's scar tissue had told her that his cells didn't just heal damage, they actually went into regrowth mode to restore the lost tissues in as close to an original state as possible. There was no sign of aging in his joints, no sign of the wear and tear associated with his rigorous lifestyle. As long as he took his daily regimen, all the results pointed to the man living very nearly forever. "You and the little one just stay out of the way when shit starts flying. I need you two in my life too."

Aiko looked down at the smallest of bumps she knew most women wouldn't be able to see, but she was tiny and surely a baby with Carl's genes was going to be bigger than most. "We'll be okay." Aiko yanked Carl down into a kiss, even though it was more like yanking his arm to request a kiss, since she in no way had the strength to yank him anywhere. Aiko kissed him intensely and paused to do so, even though they didn't really have any time to burn. "Let's go grab our bags. We're not gonna have time after this to get back to our unit to grab them."

As the group scattered in every direction, Gordon was left behind with Jessie, neither of them in a particular hurry to go anywhere, since their portion of the plan entailed waiting for several other people to get themselves in motion after the ships had docked. Half an hour was plenty of time to reach the docks.

He walked at a sedate pace, a little gratified to see one of the Consortium-loyal Initiates coming down the corridor toward them looking suspicious. He gave the woman a pass-in-the-hallway smile, and she went on her way, though Gordon swore he could feel her looking back over her shoulder every now and then. "Are you scared?" He finally asked, squeezing her hand as he did.

"Yes." Jessie admitted without hesitation and he could feel it in her grip as she held onto his hand, since she didn't want to let him go even though she knew eventually they had their own parts to play. "I'm scared of losing you. Or the baby. Dying, too. I'm not really ready to die. I came up here so I could live."

"I came up here knowing I might." He said matter-of-factly, but there was a slight tremble in his hand nonetheless that she knew had nothing to do with the ridiculous doses of caffeine he'd consumed. "That didn't mean I was excited about it, or ready for it. Strangely, I feel much less ready and less excited about it now than I even felt then." He offered her a hesitant smile, since it wasn't exactly the time to joke about anything, but he hoped it would at least get a smile from her before they descended into chaos. Chaos was never perfect in its predictability. A thousand things could go wrong, and at least ninety percent of those wrongs could get them killed. "You're not going to lose me. I'm widely regarded as being too stubborn to die."

"Do you promise?" Jessie asked hopefully as she looked over at him again. "I don't think you understand how much I need you. Even if I'm still a little scared of you."

"You've got me. From now until whatever end we find." He stopped and pulled her into a kiss, holding onto her tightly by the sides of her shirt. "The situation is never going to be any more controlled than it is right now, tonight. If we wait longer, there's more chance of them finding out how much we know or narrowing their problems down to me. If we had moved before now, we wouldn't have all the access we have. It's now or not-advised. Which means this is the option we've got. Stick to the plan and I'll see you in the sky."

Jessie nodded and kissed him back intensely before she pulled back just enough for him to see there were tears sliding down her cheeks. "I didn't know that I would ever have the chance to actually love someone. But I love you. Don't fuck this up."

That kind of warning and the fire that was never entirely absent in his wife brought a smile to Gordon's face. "I love you too. And I won't. I was made for this. In a more literal sense than I typically like to contemplate."

* * * * *

Mercury was quiet as she loaded up yet another case with medical supplies, since she didn't want to have to go without anything if they could steal as much as possible. She didn't know if she had unrestricted access because the Kaplans didn't think that she would rebel against them in any way, but she was grateful that she wasn't finding any difficulty in requesting and taking whatever the station had to give. Logan was handing off each case and bag as soon as they were filled, each one quickly taken away so they could be loaded into one of the shuttles.

She still wondered if they would be able to escape and live to tell the tale. "I thought Anna and Orion would be here to help." She said flatly, since she had resorted to allowing herself to feel as little emotion as possible.

"So did I." Logan said just as quietly, trying to keep his own emotions on a tight leash for an entirely different reason. "I thought . . . well, I thought a lot of things would be different about today." He handed off another case to one of the workers Renata managed to round up, and tried to ignore some of the suspicious looks they were constantly getting from the rest of the Initiates.

They had told as many people as they could, as quietly as they could, that they advised going home and packing. If word of their advice got back to the brass, it didn't matter anymore. It was too late for the brass to do much of anything to prepare for what was coming. "We'll get to them soon. Right now I just hope Gehrig stays occupied with the conduit problems Gordon fed her the other day."

"I don't think Orion would let anything happen to Anna." Mercury glanced over the vials of treatment as she stashed them away, but her focus was nowhere near where she knew it should be. "Do you know where we're going down there?"

"They told me last night." His voice darkened a little and he sighed afterward. "I'm not happy about it, but they insist it's the location where they're best equipped to provide security." He hefted another case into a cart for transport, but turned back to her afterward, trying to meet her eyes even though she wasn't looking at anything but the floor. "You'll like it there, I think. Based on some of your paintings, I think you'll enjoy the scenery."

"I hope so." Mercury said softly, though she only briefly looked at him before she continued working. "It's a very different life. I'm not against hard work, I'm just not used to life on Earth where you can't just push a button to get what you need." She sighed as she held another vial of treatment. "I thought I could cure Earth of CV, and now I might die from it. Interesting how that goes."

"You're not dying of anything." She could hear the command in Logan's voice, but it wasn't directed at her. It was as if he was ordering the universe itself not to permit her to die just because he said so. "You and our children are going to lead long lives on the far side of all this. There's a chance of that now. For us and for everybody. We're going to make that happen."

Mercury didn't contradict or agree with Logan, she didn't even look at him as she finished the last of the medical supplies and closed up the case before she turned toward him and handed it off. "Every time I think something is going to be one way, it changes. It's overwhelming. I can't believe in or trust anything anymore."

He put the case on the cart where it belonged and turned back to her. "Not even me?"

She finally met his eyes after and stepped up to him, even though there was a war in her whenever she did that. Mercury wanted to feel protected by Logan, but she still had anxiety about being touched or held that didn't feel like it would ever go away. "I trust you." She said softly as she slowly reached out to touch his cheek. "I know you won't hurt me and you will protect me. I hope I mean as much to you as you've said that I do. It's still hard to reconcile."

He reached up to hold her hand as she touched him, but it was a light touch, like all of his ever since she'd come back to him. He could feel her shy away if it was anything else, and it killed him every time. "Sometimes things work out that way. It's not about time, it's not about any one thing. It's just about the person you're with. Relationships come in a lot of flavors and fascinations." It was something he had taken for granted, after as many relationships as he had from such a young age, and something he had to remind himself that she had no way of knowing with her own history. "I love you. If that was the only reason I had for doing all of this, fighting for Eleusis, getting away from here, it would be enough."

Mercury stepped a fraction closer, but she was grateful when he only loosely wrapped his arms around her. She closed her eyes and took a few deep breaths to try and chase away the anxiety she felt from being held. "Please don't die. You're the only thing I have left to hold onto, or I'll be all alone."

"Hold on tight, then." He leaned down to kiss her cheek lightly as he held her. "It's going to get bumpy before it gets better. Just stay close by me and we'll see this through. All the way."

She nodded and looked back at the clinic space that had been hers for the last several months. "That's everything I can get, anything else would take fabrication time we don't have." Mercury squeezed his hand and then let go slowly. "We should go back to our unit and check if there's anything there we want to grab."

Logan agreed and hurried out of the clinic with her, giving a few last directions to those who had come to help loot the clinic. Nurses were already beginning to move through those patients still waiting to be seen and give hurried, low-voiced instructions to do likewise, go home and pack. It had people responding in a number of ways, not all of them good. Tensions had been high since even before the lockdown, and Logan knew it wouldn't take much of a push to reach mass panic.

As they went, he gave the same directions to everyone they saw who had been with the Initiative the whole time. The newest batch of Initiates still walked the corridors looking confident as they surveyed their kingdom, but Logan saw a glimmer of worry in some. They knew something was going on, but they were distrusted by most of the original crew, and Logan knew they would all be dealt with individually if they tried to board the shuttles. They weren't his contingencies to monitor. His concern was his own people.

As they approached their unit, though, crossing the gallery filled with high glass windows to look down on Earth, Logan slowed down as he saw four men loitering near their door. It was still locked, but he could see that the panel had been broken open and one of the men looked like he had been tampering with it and was talking on his communicator in annoyed tones. All four men turned quickly as soon as Logan and Mercury came in sight around the corner, and the man on his communicator ended the call quickly.

Logan slowed and adjusted the coat he wore in the same motion as he pulled Mercury slightly behind him. "Evening, gentlemen. Maintenance crew for the door lock, I'm guessing?"

"There's a lot that needs some maintenance around here." The one who'd been on his communicator said as he stepped through his companions. "A lot of things are broken, not acting the way they should. Makes a person curious."

"Must be a terrible state of being for you. I sympathize." Logan said with all the sarcasm he could muster. "Now, are you here to try and fix something specific, or should we keep being vaguely ambiguous about our intentions until one of us throws a punch?"

"There's no reason for a fight." Mercury had both of her hands on one of Logan's arms from where she stood behind him. "We're just trying to get into our unit, gentlemen. There's nothing in there that you want or need, unless you're a collector of my art."

"Maybe that's what we are." One of the other men said as they fanned out to make as much of themselves in the broad corridor. "We heard you were a real artist. Wanted to get a look at some of your handiwork." From the way the man leered as he said it, art was the farthest thing from his mind.

Mercury could feel Logan go eerily still as he looked back and forth between the four men with dismissal on his face. "Have you been looking forward to dying since you woke up this morning, or did you only get that way late in the day?" His jovial tone seemed to strike exactly the wrong chord in one of the men who hadn't spoken, and the man rushed Logan in a fury, hoping to catch him off guard.

Instead, Logan caught the man mid-rush by the throat, and held him up off the ground at arm's length while he crushed his windpipe with one hand, still holding onto Mercury with the other.

He held the man up as he kicked and struggled as if he was showing some kind of prop to the other three, but the man didn't struggle for long. He passed out after only a few seconds without any blood or air supply, and Logan didn't release his grip, as he stared past him at the other three men, none of whom wanted to be the one to go first.

"Apparently he just woke up that way." Logan waved the man back and forth one more time, then threw him aside until his skull and shoulder made a sickening crack against the glass. An angry smear of blood was left in the man's wake as he slid to the floor, but Logan never broke eye contact. "At least one of you should've brought a gun, if you want to really threaten somebody. Be on your way, now, and you'll live to be pathetic for at least another hour. Stay, and I don't make that guarantee."

None of the men made any move to assist their fallen comrade, and all three exchanged looks and began moving away from Logan slowly down the corridor. The one with the communicator was still looking at Mercury. "Pretty soon, Doc, I'm gonna see some of that art. Keep it warmed up for me."

Mercury's green eyes lingered on the man who threatened her before she looked at the floor again, even though she was clinging to Logan as hard as her fingers could manage. She couldn't help but wonder what the man knew, especially if he was loyal to the Consortium. Was he friends with Stephen Kaplan? Did he know about her, about what happened? Or was Stephen right? Was there no way for anyone to take her seriously? Did she just look like a cheap whore, made for that purpose?

Mercury's horrors and nightmares lessened the impact of seeing a dead body in front of her, even though Logan had killed the man right in front of her. Logan had protected her once with violence, the very first day she'd met him. He hadn't even known her then, and he had still protected her.

"We should hurry." It was all she could say, though her thoughts were in turmoil.

Logan couldn't begin to guess all the things going through her mind, but when he turned to face her, his touch and his eyes were gentle, with no lingering ghost of the violence that had taken place. Whatever he had to do for her, he would do, without regret and without remorse. "They won't be the last we have to deal with tonight, I'm sure. Just stay with me." He held her hand and pulled her in to kiss her forehead, then rushed into the unit to look through the life they were leaving behind one last time.

* * * * *

"What the fuck is taking so long?" Vance growled into the communicator, glaring at Victoria on the other side of the screen. "I thought you said that ballast conduit was going to take an hour, maybe two, to get back within specs. We're on days, what is holding up the process?"

"Things keep breaking, Director. It's incredibly suspicious, but there's nothing I can do about it other than keep crews on it and watch the area." Victoria replied with as much annoyance as was getting thrown at her. "What would you like me to do about it, exactly? I can't get in there myself."

"If things are incredibly suspicious, that means we have a leak you haven't plugged, Victoria." Vance's voice calmed somewhat, but he was pushed beyond the limits of his tolerance. "You're head of security for this Initiative. We knew there would be rogue elements, and you said that after the lockdown, everyone who needed to be removed had been. Clearly you were mistaken, or we have outside influences we haven't accounted for."

"Or the people we know we can trust are getting lazy." She replied sharply before she pulled back a little bit. "We'll do another sweep. I haven't even heard from Stephen or Maria for days now. We'll find out who is creating the problem and instead of being polite about it, we'll use force."

"I'm no scientist, but if my own observations of this batch are of any consequence, it seems to me as though we should have begun with force in the first place." Vance glanced away as a few notifications popped up to let him know that the routine maintenance drops were in the final stages of docking, but he barely paid it any mind. They were due to get a few more shipments before dropping the entire population, and he would worry about all of them when he had the time to do so.

"Find someone you can delegate the conduit situation to, I need you back here on other things. The Al-Jabbars are still waiting in confinement and no one else has been able to get them to crack. They're going to need you, like I said in the first place. When you're done with them, I want you to . . ." he broke off as his screen began to short out, which only made him angrier and had him checking the linkup quality on his own server nearby.

He could barely make out that Victoria was doing the same thing on her end, speaking inaudibly. "Victoria? What's going on? I don't have a source for that interference. Victoria?" He continued attempting to restore the connection for a few more moments, but as he did, the entire world around him went dark, leaving only the evening sky of the Earth below to provide light in tiny fits of existence scattered across its surface.

His tablet was dead, his server appeared dead, the screens monitoring all ship systems were dead all around him. The lights and vents all appeared to have stopped working, all at once. It was a failure on a scale he had never seen in his entire life in space, and it succeeded in stopping him in his tracks.

Greetings, Humanity.

Vance looked around his darkened office at the disembodied voice, until he realized it was coming from all the speakers on his apparently-dead technology. What the hell was going on? Who in the world could have engineered that kind of failure all at once?

I'm sure, the voice continued, sounding more and more familiar the longer it went on, *that the majority of the human race is right now wondering who I am and how it is that I'm speaking to every single member of our species within range of the appropriate technology. For tonight's purposes, I will introduce myself only as White. Speaking to all of you on the whole, I am a friend. To some of you who will become obvious shortly, I am decidedly otherwise.*

Vance could feel his blood boil the moment White identified himself, and he jumped up from his chair in the dark to head for his door, only to find it locked. One more thing he certainly hadn't done. "Damn you, White." He and Victoria had talked about the potential threat of Gordon White when he first arrived on the station, but they had been convinced since his arrival that he was nothing more than a mild-mannered programmer who had married above himself and managed to knock up his assigned match. Damn him. Damn them all.

Well, not everything in the station obeyed computerized commands. Vance set to work on one of the floor panels in his office, accessing the escape conduit that had been built into the station at its design. White was going to get what was coming to him, no matter what kind of game he was playing.

I'm talking to you tonight because there is a story you all need to hear. This story is our story. Just the part of it that no one is allowed to talk about.

I am speaking to you tonight from the corridors of the Eleusis Initiative,

Station Nine. Some of you may have heard of us. There are more than two thousand of us here, and the Consortium intends, very soon, to kill every last one of us, just as they killed our predecessors.

Anna wasn't sure how they could hear Gordon's message in the dark room, but there had to be speakers somewhere, there were speakers everywhere. She clung to Orion, careful of some of the wounds on his arm. Both she and Orion had been mildly tortured for information, but nothing they couldn't handle. They were far from broken. "I guess the word is out."

Orion was smiling, in spite of the exhaustion they both felt. Sleep deprivation had been a part of the torture routine. "And it sounds like he noticed the plant. There's some comfort in knowing that you're not getting the living shit beaten out of you for nothing." He took a deep breath as Gordon continued, trying to tell himself that he was going to have to get up and get moving, but his body wasn't excited about listening. "If he's talking, that means the shit is en route to the fan. We need to be ready to move."

You all remember, Gordon's voice continued, over everyone and everything on Earth and in Orbit, *a few months ago when we collectively mourned for the tragic . . . "accident" that befell this station, when an arm fell to the ground, killing thousands of people.* Gordon restrained the sarcasm in his voice, but the air quotes were audible nonetheless. *Information is being relayed in parallel to this audio feed to every available computer system which includes detailed message logs between various Consortium leaders, detailing their plans and methods of execution leading up to the intentional release of the arm.*

Let me say that again: the intentional release of the arm.

"Ben?" Susan put aside the ingredients she was working with and wiped her hands on her apron before she went to find her husband somewhere in the house. He'd taken their son to occupy him while she cooked, but she found him glued to their main television with his father sitting at his side. "What is this broadcast? It interrupted the news . . . isn't that where Anna is? Station Nine?"

Ben tended to be quiet and brooding by nature when he wasn't snapping at someone in a foul temper, but it wasn't often that he was actually rendered speechless. He barely looked up at her as she came into the living room, but reached up to take her hand and pull her in to watch with them.

Both he and Joseph, Susan's father-in-law, leaned forward on their knees to take in the barrage of images shown through the pirated broadcast. The message began with pictures Ben assumed were of the station itself, sterile, empty corridors with red lights outside of doors, people lying in clinic beds sick, one woman pale and sickly with sunken cheeks, one Japanese man coughing up blood as he got closer to death.

Anna appeared in some of the images as Susan watched, a brief flash of her being thrown into some kind of holding cell with a ridiculously tall, dark-skinned man. Both looked as though they had been recently abused, with cuts and bruises showing on their faces and arms. The overall picture the images painted of the station was horrifying even without the mysterious White's narration.

You see, the prior occupants of this station, whose remains are now fertilizing a midwest corn field, were some of the original minds behind the Eleusis Project. They conceived much that has been utilized in preparation for colonization, and they were told, like us, they would be among the first to leave our solar system and make a new life for humanity among the stars.

If that idea sounds noble and uplifting, you can imagine how noble and uplifting some of those who worked on such a project were as people. They were some of the finest minds and hearts that our species has ever produced. Their names are also being sent along with this transmission. But all we have left are their names and their ideas, because this is what the Consortium did to them.

White's narration broke off momentarily, and the video and audio went to that of an older Russian man, running for his life and screaming in grief at his own death the entire way to Earth.

Susan was quick to grab her son and cover his eyes and ears by wrapping him up in her arms, since she didn't want him to see what was on the screen, even though he was really too little to understand anyway. She looked away herself, but the man's panic and screams were still ringing in her ears.

"Oh god." She said softly, since there was little else to say about watching someone die because the Consortium was finished with them. "Ben, you don't think . . ." She had clearly seen Anna, if only briefly, beaten and abused. They hadn't heard from her in months, but they figured it was because she was so busy she just didn't have time. It was the simplest and easiest solution to think about, but Ben and Cory had been absolutely convinced that something was wrong. Clearly they were right. "If this man is speaking to us, she'll get out, right?"

"If he's speaking to us, then they're in trouble." Ben said in a low voice, not wanting to miss anything, though he imagined it was going to be all anyone in the world talked about for the next year. "This doesn't sound like somebody about to save anyone. It sounds like somebody throwing out a call because they think they're about to die."

"Have more faith in your sister than that." Joseph said from his chair nearby, his eyes glued to the television screen, on the off chance they showed another image of his eldest child. "If there's trouble to be had and she's getting . . . if they're giving her a hard time for it, you can be sure she's not taking it without a fight."

The broadcast didn't stop even though the Consortium was trying to end it, though there was no going back now. The Consortium and the Initiative were exposed.

"Babe!" Brianne pounded on Liam's personal bathroom door, where he had escaped to shower in peace, since multiple wives was bad enough, but multiple pregnant wives was enough to drive a man insane. "Get your naked ass out here! They're talking about Logan on the TV, the computers, it's even coming out of the fucking radio!"

She heard a vague yell of compliance from the bathroom, and seconds later, Liam's naked ass came out as requested, pulling a bathrobe with him as he ran a hand through his hair. "What the hell are you yelling about? What are they saying about Logan?" He ran after her as he pulled the robe on, not caring about the fact that he was still partly soaped and flapping in the breeze. It was him and his three wives in the house. There was nothing about him that any of them hadn't already seen.

This was the experience of the previous members of the Initiative. The voice on the television continued, as images of the crash and the footage of Anna and Logan's rescue attempts played yet one more time. *They died screaming, cast off by those in power over them. The pertinent question, of course, is why. Unlike so many other occasions in life, I have the answer to that question, which I want nothing more than to share with you tonight.*

The next images that came across the screen were staggeringly beautiful, but . . . wrong . . . in ways that didn't immediately jump out to the casual observer. Liam was confused and annoyed as he and Brianne got to the living room with Rachel and Margo to watch on their largest screen. The sky of the landscape on the screen was just barely the wrong color for how brightly lit everything was. The underbrush was a darker green than it looked like it should have been. And the sun . . .

"That's not Earth." Liam said as the video moved over the landscape, capturing various angles of trees and plants and alien flowers in its course. It became obvious that it was a probe of some kind, flying low above the ground just to capture video imagery of the area.

The previous members of the Initiative died screaming for this. For Eleusis. It is real, it is not a fabrication, not a myth, not a conspiracy, at least not in the sense you may have believed. It is a habitable, Earth-like planet, with a breathable atmosphere, edible vegetation, and abundant liquid water. It is not all this beautiful, but then again, neither is Earth. It is still appropriately termed a paradise. Specifically, it is a paradise which the Consortium possesses the means to reach, and no one else does.

The previous members of the Initiative died because it is in the Consortium's interests to maintain control over access to paradise.

The worthy may enter, the unworthy can rot, and the great and powerful Consortium will judge the difference.

"They showed video of people being abused." Rachel said as she glanced over at Liam, but she didn't want to look away from the television for long enough to miss anything. "You could see Anna with someone I didn't recognize, he looked too pretty to be anything but modified."

"And he was a fucking giant." Brianne added as she sat on one side of Liam. Margo was on the other side, and Rachel was on the other side of Margo. "Anna didn't look like she'd been beaten to hell, but she definitely didn't look great."

"There was a brief shot of Logan." Rachel continued after Brianne, and of course, Margo had little to add, since she was usually the quiet one unless Liam was attempting to engage her in the conversation. "He was wearing that jacket Larissa gave him. But he looked different. Harder. Angrier. I've never seen him look that way." She chewed on her bottom lip as she stared at a few more images of Eleusis on the screen. "No one would be broadcasting this from Station Nine if they thought they could do it from a safer place. This White person said that the Initiative wants them dead. I don't know . . . it looks bad . . ."

"If somebody pissed Logan off, then they're gonna have a bad fucking day." Liam said, supremely confident in his brother, as always. "I'd like to be happy this place is even fucking real, but it doesn't look like that's really an option." He watched the probe's video as it skimmed over the landscape, and he opened his mouth to talk again when it looked like they were going to get nothing more than just a guided tour. He closed it again when the probe cleared the next hill.

A massive complex came into sight, nestled against the foothills of an abrupt mountain range. Low, modular buildings crowded one space, while more permanent construction was still in the process of going up at a distance up the slope, some kind of large government-style building of steel and glass. They all looked so out of place on the pure Eleusis landscape that it was almost painful to look at them.

Liam's jaw fell open in confusion as he leaned forward to get a better look. "What the . . ."

"The fuck is this?" Marcus was in his office as the broadcast continued to play on every screen, every wall, every speaker in the entire sector. He could see his entire staff watching in rapt attention, and all life on Station Six had come to a complete halt to take in the information. He left his office and stepped out to be with Claire at her desk nearby, both of them watching the same thing pouring through their world.

"They told us they were still years out!" His Irish accent became more pronounced when he was aggravated, and he gripped the back of his wife's chair in both panic and anger over the circumstances it looked like their daughter had walked into.

Claire wanted to stand up to get closer to her husband, but all she could do was stare. Mercury was there, her life was at stake, and Claire couldn't feel anything but anger and despair. They had tried to do everything in their power to protect Mercury, even though clearly they had been unsuccessful. Every choice they made, even before Mercury's birth, was a well-thought and planned decision.

"Is there any way we can get to Nine?" They hadn't been able to even communicate with their daughter for months, but she was about to do whatever it took to somehow get to her daughter. "She's . . . we can't lose her, Marcus. Did you see what the others looked like? Sick? Dying?"

"Bastards 'ave had Nine locked down for weeks now." He shook his head at first as he thought through the situation, but the more he saw, the angrier he got at the things he hadn't been told. "But we can bloody try. Come on. Cooper's on shuttle duty at the docks, and she's crazy enough to give a run for it. Let's go." He was generally all about thoughtful decisions, planned steps, careful measures, but if the Consortium had kept him, one of their own elite Station masters, in the dark for so long, then some recklessness was called for.

The Consortium has been lying since it was organized. Gordon's voice continued over the whole world, set against the backdrop of the Consortium's own facilities already standing on Eleusis. *They've lied about Earth, they've lied about themselves, they have lied more times than I have time to tell you about tonight.*

But right now, the biggest lie that affects you, every single one of you, is the one you see on your screens. The Consortium has already reached Eleusis. They are already building their systems of control on a new world, without the knowledge of any other organized body of our species. Contrary to what they have been saying for decades, they have claimed Eleusis for themselves, and kept the knowledge of it from the rest of us.

More than this, they can get there as easily as you on Earth cross the street, as simply as you in space cross a sector bridge. It would not take years and countless resources to transport humanity to Eleusis. The entire planet could be there in a matter of days, with the right preparation.

But the Consortium controls the door, the Twist, as it is called, which enables them to cross the galaxy in a single step. They control the path to paradise.

I can't speak for the rest of you, but I am of the strong opinion that that needs to change.

Gordon and Jessie were supposed to be the last ones to arrive at the Twist, since obviously the authorities would go after them first for blowing the lid wide open. Aiko followed the instructions given on her hacked communicator, and when they burst into a room with a lot of tech she'd never worked with, Aiko was stunned, and she could hardly convince herself to keep moving toward the Twist and work on getting it disconnected.

"Holy . . . moly." She added chastely before she looked over at Carl. "I've only ever seen design drawings, Kazuo saw a few of the very early designs. He showed me." Aiko was quick to shake off her awe, though, since they didn't have a lot of time. Logan and Mercury were in charge of attempting to bust Orion and Anna out, Renata and the rest were supposed to load up the shuttles, and Tatyana, her team, Carl, Aiko, Gordon and Jessie were going to get the Twist. Somehow.

"I think he thinks he's funny when he calls this the little one." Aiko ran up to the ring of metal and then to a large computer screen so she could start assessing the status of the Twist. They didn't want to break the thing, after all. "Any computer or other tech that isn't hard-wired into this thing, start destroying it. I'm sure they have backup controls and we don't want to give them the option to use them."

"A woman who carries my kid *and* tells me to destroy things. God, I love this woman." Carl didn't have to be told twice to get to smashing things, and he started with the security monitoring systems near the far side of the room from the Twist, wrenching free a stretch of metal piping from the wall that held electrical wiring to use it as a club.

Several of the others on Tatyana's crew fanned out through the room, assisting Aiko and others in doing diagnostics and downloading the current software to go with the device. "Honestly, I'm a little disappointed." Carl said as he came back from smashing some of the surveillance, just to get a closer look at the device itself. "If I had one of only three of its kind in the universe, I think I'd have some guards on it or something."

"Response time for security's been delayed." One of Tatyana's goons said without looking at Carl. The man was odd-looking at best, and seemed even more nervous than their situation warranted, which was saying something. His head was completely shaved and he had a perpetual twitch to his features that came from being on too many artificial stimulants. "White got everybody locked down as much as possible, but they're starting to slip through and head this direction. ETA is four minutes."

"Four minutes?" Aiko's voice increased in panic as she hurried through the programming, instructing the Twist to prepare for removal. They were made to move, just not easily. Aiko was starting to get things to finally disconnect when the Twist started to power up. She had definitely *not* instructed it to power up. "What is going on?" There were only so many times that she could hit abort, and it wasn't responding to what she was trying to do any longer. "They probably knew we would come in here after this thing."

"Yeah, after White broadcasted it to the entire universe." The high-strung guard said before a look of true alarm crossed his face. He looked up and yelled across the room at Tatyana in Russian before he did anything else, but whatever he said had people scattering away from the Twist as it began to resonate with power. Finally, he turned back to Aiko, beginning to run for it himself.

"The initiation came from the other side! Take co-" whatever else the man said was choked off by an electrical discharge from the Twist, one of many in what looked like a small storm around the opening, getting larger as the power to it increased.

Carl was there beside Aiko in a moment, picking her up bodily and dragging her clear, but the only space for them to hide was in the corner just a few feet behind the side of the Twist itself. He covered her with his own body against the corner, and she could feel him twitch and groan a few times as shocks hit him, but he didn't move from his position shielding her, even as the light and the heat in the room increased to scalding, blinding heights.

Aiko clung to Carl from beneath him, afraid that she was going to see a dead body on top of her as the room got hotter, but she just kept trying to talk to Carl instead of crying like she wanted to do. "It'll stabilize, baby. Just hang on. Please." She gripped his shirt before more loud popping filled the room, and then all went silent for a moment.

Her ears were ringing by the time the Twist actually stabilized, but she could see that Carl was still breathing at least. "You gotta wake up. They're going to send people in here, it's the only reason why they would activate it . . ."

It took a few seconds for Carl to get himself back into focus, but he shook his head and stretched to make sure everything still more or less worked. "Holy shit. Remind me to tell that fucking spa I had some shitty service." When he turned around, part of the long coat he wore was badly singed, and she could tell the backs of his arms had been scalded as well, but he was mostly unharmed. For Carl, it might as well have been a mosquito bite.

As he turned, he caught sight of the fact that there was another world impossibly open to view nearby. Instead of rushing toward it, he placed himself again between it and Aiko, brushing back his coat to pick out a few of his weapons. Tatyana's guys preferred guns, and he had a few of those, but Carl had been working street-level security most of his life. He was more comfortable with his fists and nightsticks. Instead of either, he drew a pair of nightstick-sized knives made of dark, non-reflective steel. Clearly he wasn't interested in just keeping the peace.

He drew a gun from the back of his waist, though, and reached behind him to hand it to Aiko. "I'm not going far, but I don't know what they're sending through that gate. Hang onto this."

Aiko looked at the gun in her hands, and for all of the things she knew how to do, she did not know how to use a gun to protect herself. Not really. Carl had given her a few lessons, but that wasn't enough to face whatever was going to come through that portal.

Aiko looked up just in time to see Gordon and Jessie come running into the area, and it only took seconds to see his reaction to the Twist being on and open instead of separated from the floor like it should have been by now.

"Shit." Jessie said as she skidded to a stop next to Gordon. "The Initiative must have activated it. What the hell do they have on the other side? Are they going to send over alien animals to deal with us?"

"No, the other side comes out in a . . ." there was a final flash as the Twist stabilized its connection entirely, and the entire room could see the ramp on the far side under the dim Eleusis sun. The ramp was nowhere near as grand as the one descending from the larger Twist a few rooms away, but it did offer a much more direct look at the compound beyond.

It was situated in a secondary holding area just outside a tall wall that enclosed the compound, with a wall of its own protecting it both from the compound and from the rest of Eleusis. At the moment, it was a staging area, with an entire squadron of armed guards running down from the walls heading for the ramp, shouted on by officers looking nervously into the newly-opened Twist. Gordon had to duck and pull Jessie aside as a few of the guards began firing through the opening into the station control room, and bullets started ricocheting everywhere.

Jessie stepped back but turned her gun on the guards as soon as she could get a clean shot past Gordon, and one of them went down as she shot him in the side of the head. She was a little stunned her aim was still good, but she had been raised on a farm, after all. She looked over at Gordon only to turn her attention back to the attack and take aim again. "It's them or us."

He was a little impressed too, but he did his best not to take too long showing it as he got back up to crouch behind a console. "Keep them busy." He said in a hurried voice, digging out an interface to patch directly into the controls so that he could manipulate it. "I can shut it down, just keep them busy in the meantime."

Tatyana's guards recovered from the blaze of the Twist's opening, and returned fire along with Jessie. A few of them moved to her side to share her vantage point and the relative cover of the consoles. Most of the guards were still on the Eleusis side, but a few brave souls had managed to storm their way through onto the station, dodging the gunfire that was starting to rain down from the back of the control room.

Carl got a knife straight through the throat of one of them, which got the attention of another who got riddled with bullets for his effort. Carl was grateful for the support, but for the moment, it meant there was no safe way for him and Aiko to get back toward the door, and more guards streamed through.

Aiko was just as worried about Carl as he was about her, though he had yet to be hit by anything other than a few stray bullets to his arms, which didn't seem to bother him. Aiko was trying to shut the Twist down even though she could see Gordon was doing the same thing, but a guard taking aim at her forced her away from the console as she dove onto the ground, which put her even closer to the portal opened by the Twist. She landed on her side to protect the baby, but she was exposed halfway while Carl stood in front of her. "We're getting pushed the wrong way!"

Carl took a step back to cover her directly at her cry, but as he looked around, he could tell from the flow of the fight that she was right. Tatyana's people could hold the guards coming out of the Twist from their cover, but the entire complement of the guards on the Eleusis compound wall emptied out and poured into the room. No more were coming, but there were too many for them to fight their way through, even with Carl laying about with his knives and dodging bullets in favor of hand to hand combat.

"I can't shift it!" He yelled back at Aiko, doing his best to be in three places at once to fight, but the two of them were getting pushed further and further as the fight went on, just to avoid stray bullets, friendly fire and enemy fire alike. Aiko was only a few feet from the corner of the narrow portal. "And I don't think we want to be next to this thing when it shuts down!"

Aiko looked back through the portal to Eleusis and she looked over at Carl again. It was riskier for them to try and push through, Carl would probably end up dead, or maybe even both of them. Once she was able to get up and press herself against his back, she squeezed her arms around him as far as they would go. "There's only one way to go, big guy. Otherwise we're going to end up dead!"

Carl actually found it easier to protect Aiko when she was strapped to his back, but he still had to admit that he felt a slight sting of panic at her suggestion. During a spare moment after punching a guard to the ground, he looked back over his shoulder at the open portal. He could feel the heat from it, and wasn't sure if that was some kind of heat generated by the portal itself or if it was just hot on Eleusis that time of year. He had no idea. The look only lasted a heartbeat before he turned to wrench a gun from a guard's hands.

"Which one's the frying pan and which one's the fire?" He yelled back to Aiko over the chaos of the fight, since he wasn't honestly sure himself.

At that moment, Aiko was never happier her parents had always warned her to be prepared for anything. If they hadn't gone back to get their own backpacks of supplies, she knew for sure they would be dead one way or another. Maybe this way, they might survive. She had no way of knowing.

"The fire is in front of us. The frying pan is the unknown. But at least we won't die right now!" She looked past Carl and saw Gordon, and she let out a heavy breath. The portal wouldn't be closed in time, and Carl could only do so much. They didn't have any other choice.

"White!" She yelled out, but she doubted he could hear her as Carl took another couple of steps back. Aiko could already feel more heat from the portal against her back, but she was trying to convince herself it would be okay.

They were headed toward Eleusis, just sooner than she ever imagined.

Gordon couldn't hear Aiko at first in the middle of the chaos and outside of his focus on getting the Twist shut down, but when he finally isolated the proper procedure and began the sequence, he looked up just long enough to see her and Carl backing up through it. The behemoth of a man caught a guard by the front of his uniform and hurled him against the side of the Twist, but the device itself didn't even wiggle. The man, however, was cut seamlessly in half at the ribcage, his top half falling sputtering inside the control room while the rest of him fell off the ramp coming down from the Twist on Eleusis. It seemed to shock everyone nearby, but Carl reached back with one arm to hold Aiko tighter against him and continued backing up through the gateway to get away from the guards.

He hated how clear the choice in front of him was, the fact that it wasn't a choice at all. That he didn't have to agonize and torture himself over it, even though he could see the agony coming in his future. The Twist had to be closed. They had to get it off the station. He could see Aiko watching him, though he wasn't sure what for. She knew better than to expect miracles from him, of all people.

"I'll find you." He mouthed at her through the chaos, adding no audible sound to the tumult. "Survive. I'll find you." He promised quietly, then pointed at the console with his finger poised over the right command. "Run. Now."

Aiko nodded and grabbed harder onto Carl's arm to pull him backwards so that they could move the rest of the way through the portal that was forced open by the Twist. They had no way of knowing if another wave of guards would be coming up behind them, so they had to move fast. "Come on, we have to get away from the portal!" As long as he was with her, she had to believe that they would be okay. She couldn't do it alone, but with her knowledge of the planet and Carl's strength, they had a chance. Maybe.

Gordon's emotions were screaming in the background as most of his brain watched their departure carefully, calculating the average event horizon for the startup and shutdown of the Twist to ensure that they had reached minimum safe distance with the appropriate velocity to ensure significant odds of survival. He saw a few more guards on the other side, latecomers from farther along the wall, rushing toward them, but Carl leapt aside and was lost to Gordon's view, still clutching Aiko against him as he went.

A few of the guards inside the control room moved to follow, and Gordon turned the control to begin the shutdown. The field glowed white-hot between the crystalline mechanical filaments of the Twist, and several of the trapped guards shrieked in pain as the force of it tore through them, leaving half-people in its wake as the machine went dark.

The remaining guards were so disheartened by the apparent lack of more reinforcements that they were distracted just long enough for Tatyana's people to finish mowing them down, after which the room fell silent.

"Get it disconnected." Gordon growled through the silence. "Move your asses! We've got a shuttle to catch!"

Jessie was as stunned as some of the rest of Tatyana's people but she was trying to help in any way she could, even though the Twist itself wasn't something she would be any help with.

"Gordon." She said softly behind him, even though she didn't know what was going through his mind. Jessie touched the back of his arm gently to reassure him she was still there. "It wasn't your fault. Carl will protect her."

"I know he will." He allowed himself a moment to lean over the console and heave a sigh, since Tatyana's people were doing most of the physical work of disconnecting the Twist architecture and his data core was hurriedly downloading everything it could get its electronic hands on without his help.

"Once we get it working on Earth, we can go find them. We just have to get there first." He took a deep breath to steel himself for anything else that could come, and reached back to squeeze Jessie's hand, grateful that she had stayed near him through the fight. "Are you hurt?"

"My arm got grazed a couple of times." Jessie looked over at her arm where her sleeve was stained with blood, since she'd been hit a couple of times by rogue bullets but she couldn't feel the pain yet. She was both too afraid and too worried about Gordon that the pain was far away, though she knew it would hit her hard shortly. "I'm okay. Better than dead. I . . . I wasn't expecting them to open it from the other side. That was crazy."

"I'm hoping that's the last thing we haven't planned for." He grumbled, and as he turned around, she could see that he'd been shot in the side, his shirt quickly soaking through with blood. He had one arm clamped against it, applying pressure on his own wound, but it was a testament to just how accustomed the man was to pain that he was still speaking evenly. "Can you still shoot? Once they have that thing free, we're going to need to get out of here in a hurry."

"Yeah, I can still shoot." Jessie was focused on Gordon, though, since the last thing she needed was for him to bleed out and die before they could get on a shuttle and get away from this hellhole. She quickly ripped off a large piece of her shirt so she could wrap it around him and tie it tight to help slow the bleeding. Jessie was almost always aware of her appearance and how exposed she was at any given moment, and so the fact that she had ripped at her own clothing for him without a second thought said a lot about how focused she was on him and how much she cared about him. "They're almost done. Don't pass out or die before I can get you to Mercury for help."

"She'll have worse off to see than me before we get out of here, I'm sure." He accepted her help without any other complaint, though, and encouraged her to tie it even tighter when it felt like she was going to break his ribs in the first place.

One of Tatyana's people gave a triumphant whoop as they severed the last cable connecting the mechanism to the Station, and the entire group moved like a kicked wasp nest to lay the portal in a conveyance sled for transport, along with all the other cabling and equipment they could cannibalize from the room.

"Internal response will intercept us in a few minutes." Gordon plucked his data core from the console and tucked it beneath his bloodied shirt. He was talking mostly to the fighters under Tatyana, but also partly to Tatyana herself. "We knew coming into this that we were going to have to shoot our way out. If I was them, I'd rather sink this station than let me take this back to Earth."

"They can try." Tatyana said as she looked him over, and then nodded toward the pouch he had been given by his tree-hugging friend. "She didn't give you anything to help you if you got injured? That seems short-sighted."

"She came to fight, not to patch people up, and she might have just died for what we're trying to do here. Don't be jealous just because she gets to be a martyr and you're still alive." He clutched at the pouch as the last thing he might ever have from his friend, and moved out of the room behind the first rank of Tatyana's goons. "I'll be fine. Leave the dead and advise the wounded to keep up."

36

Back at the shuttle, Mercury was surprised to see as many people showing up as there were, but she kept reminding herself that at least half of them were just like her. People who once believed and supported a cause and a government that had deluded and abused them. Once she remembered that, she didn't feel quite as surprised. People wanted out, just like she did.

Logan was helping people load up while Mercury was tending to small wounds here and there, and so they were separated but still within sight. Mercury was on edge, of course, jittery and scared, but she was doing the best she could to remain grounded in the situation.

At least, she *was* doing her best, until she saw Stephen Kaplan and Maria Santos at a distance, and Stephen took his time to wait until she saw them before he met her eyes and smirked at her.

Instantly Mercury wanted to run, but she finished working the suture she had in front of her. How did they know where to find her? Were they going to attack her or something equally terrible?

Logan directed traffic between the different shuttles, giving instructions to a few intermediaries to make sure people and their things were secured and people were brought on board as quickly as possible. The docks were no place to keep things secure, as the attack from Carmina had shown them, and Logan wanted no repeat of that particular encounter. The brass would eventually get around the lockdown that Gordon had enforced, and Logan hoped they would all be well on their way before then.

As he sent off the most recent group, there was another waiting to talk to him, but he looked over to check in on Mercury instead, as always, just to make sure she was alright. The pale look on her face was enough to tell him that the answer was no.

"Mercury?" He pushed himself over to her in the null gravity, but he couldn't tell from the direction of her staring exactly what was the problem. "What happened, what did you see?"

Mercury just shook her head, since she didn't and couldn't really speak, not when she knew that the Kaplans were close. They were probably watching her, and just thinking about them smiling at her as she looked visibly uncomfortable and upset made her tremble. However terrified she was, though, Logan couldn't know. He couldn't lose control. He was the one keeping everything together and moving when they didn't have a second to lose. "N . . . nothing. I'm alright."

All around them, people were rushing, panicked looks on their faces at the message that Gordon sent out and the revelations it contained. The dock buzzed with hurried, frantic conversations, arguments between people who were no longer sure if they could trust each other as the news of the Consortium's intentions escalated tensions in Earth-Orbital friendships.

But as Logan followed Mercury's look through the crowd, he caught sight of Stephen and Maria, both of whom looked as comfortable and peaceful as if they were sitting on a porch drinking tea on a warm summer day. They were looking right at Mercury from time to time, with smiles on their faces that would've made the devil himself blush with pride.

It was their smiles that caught his eyes, and made his breath catch in his throat.

He looked back at Mercury, obviously shaken to a degree he hadn't seen since she came back to him from being missing, then looked back at the Kaplans.

The only warning Mercury got was a quick tightening of his grip on the fabric of her scrubs at her waist, then he had pushed off in the Kaplans' direction, moving faster than was advisable in near-zero gravity. They were mid-jump themselves, and at the speed he was going, Logan was going to intercept the two of them like a human car accident. It was clear by the look on his face that that was his entire intention.

Mercury didn't know what she gave away in her silence, but she couldn't stop herself from yelling out. She didn't want him to fight for her, not now, not when fighting meant he could get left behind. "Logan!"

Maria looked up at the sound of Mercury's voice, which she found quite pleasant. Her mind didn't get to linger on that thought for long, since in the next second, a body came crashing into her like a bulldozer and sent her flying away from Stephen, back toward a wall at an inadvisable speed. She barely had enough time to turn in a way that impact wouldn't leave her paralyzed, but she still cried out in pain as several of her ribs audibly cracked from the impact. Confusion prevailed through the pain, but she was still trying to think through the haze in order to see Stephen and to understand what the hell just happened.

Screams erupted throughout the dock at the chaos that followed. Even those who knew both men well could only distinguish Stephen and Logan by Stephen's blond hair and Logan's dark beard. Otherwise they were a jumble of violence careening through the air attempting to rip each other to shreds.

Stephen had seen Logan coming just an instant before Maria had, and was fighting for his life. But Logan was the larger of the two of them, if only by a small margin, and the ferocity of his attack wasn't something that anyone in the dock had expected. Every time Logan caught Stephen by the shirt or by an arm, he flung Kaplan against a column or a wall, every impact leaving stains of blood and the crack of broken bones. People shrieked and rushed past the brawl to get toward the ships, but Mercury could see the panic on many faces at the sight of her suddenly-feral husband.

She had known Logan was strong, she had felt it from him every day they had been together. He told her once or twice about playing football back on Earth, about some of the fights he got in during his days in school, he and his brother's proclivity for boxing and generally beating up any competition. It had all sounded innocent, the stuff of children and clearly outgrown with the stature he had attained in the Initiative leadership. She had even seen him kill just a few minutes before, in defending her from strangers. It had been efficient and cold and clean.

But what she was seeing from him in that dock was something else entirely. He wasn't trying to kill Kaplan, he was trying to maim and disfigure him. To make him feel as much pain as one human body could inflict on another. At one point, he caught a wild punch Stephen threw at him, and Mercury could hear Stephen's choked sobs as Logan slowly crushed the man's fist inside his own, snapping every bone in both his hands and watching as the agony of it contorted what was left of Stephen's ruined face.

The punishment seemed endless, suspended in a screaming moment from which Logan wouldn't allow her attacker to escape. Stephen was still screaming when Logan finished shattering his hands and wrists, and the screaming only stopped when Logan took a handful of the back of Kaplan's shirt and slammed him chest-first over a column, crushing the man's sternum.

With his lungs collapsed, the man was no longer able to scream, and Logan drew him back just to get a look at his bloodied face, watching the expression there for any sign of life. Seeing none, he looked around for Maria, and braced himself against the column to throw Stephen's body at the broken man's wife, trails of blood streaming in the air.

Maria wasn't prepared for what she saw as soon as Stephen's body made it over to her, but she had tortured enough people to at least keep her wits about her even in the face of such complete destruction. Her own pain was easily overshadowed by looking Stephen over, but she had to do something.

Maria looked across at Logan as he made his way back toward the shuttles, and though she was struggling to breathe with broken ribs, she swore she would find Logan Bickford and make his life a living hell again, no matter what happened to Stephen. She did not like being a victim.

Maria shuddered as she dumped the contents of a vial into Stephen's mouth, hoping that he didn't feel anything. A faint pulse said he wasn't dead, but he wasn't far off. "Don't die, you fucking bastard." She moved him through the null gravity and wheezed as she reached for her communicator, immediately calling for help. "Our position has been compromised. Send every fucking gun you can to the docks."

Logan did his best to ignore everyone streaming around him, avoiding him like the plague. He didn't need other people to understand what he had done. All that mattered was that it had been done. It wouldn't undo what had been done to his wife, but he hoped it would stop Stephen from doing the same to anyone else ever again.

He got to Mercury's station and picked up a shirt that someone had already taken off because it had been stained with blood in a firefight down below. He started to wipe his face and his knuckles, wondering if some of the gashes from Stephen's broken bones would need stitches. He couldn't quite look at Mercury, but he stayed nearby as he attempted to clean himself up.

"I didn't know it was him for sure." He eventually said quietly. "I thought it might have been Vance. Even if it had been, it wouldn't have stopped me. Vance has the same coming to him or worse."

Mercury didn't look up from his hands, though she knew he wasn't looking at her either. She wasn't afraid of him, though she knew she probably should be, considering what he just did, but she wasn't. She was afraid of what he would think of her now that he knew who she had been with, who she had agreed to sleep with, even if it was drug-induced rape. "Let me get some bandages on your hands at least. I can see bones in some places."

He nodded quietly and let her work on his hands, though he still couldn't even feel the pain in them from all the anger still raging through him. "I knew they were assholes, but I didn't know he would . . . I would've done that a long time ago if I had known. I wish I had. I could have stopped it before it happened. To you or anyone else."

"I agreed to it." She reminded him softly as she used some medical glue to bond the gashes and stop the bleeding so she could stitch him up later. Mercury didn't dare look up from his hands. "I'm not saying he didn't deserve it. But I agreed. I showed up there. I drank the water. I let it happen to myself, even though I didn't know it would happen." She took a deep breath as she very carefully tended to one hand and then the other with the glue and an antibiotic to prevent infection. "He said I was genetically made for the purpose. And maybe that's true."

"You were not made to be abused." The violence in his voice flared up again, and it was there in full force behind the grey storm of his eyes. "No one is ever made just to be somebody else's slave. Least of all you."

"I don't know if that's true, that no one is made just to be someone else's slave. It seems like a lot of people are made for very specific purposes and nothing else. At least here. I don't know how it is on Earth." Mercury felt like she had allowed herself to live in a bubble, and after what happened with the Kaplans, everything had burst. All she could see was the cruelty of the Consortium when once she adored the government for everything they had given her.

Mercury finished binding up Logan's hands before she focused on putting the supplies away without looking at him once. "We're running out of time."

Those nearby who waited for instructions from him numbered a great deal fewer than those who had been waiting before he'd gone after Stephen, but he turned and continued giving orders as if nothing had even happened.

People were concerned about which shuttle they were on, where they were going, where the Consortium's response would be, what to expect from Earth, and a hundred other questions to which Logan didn't have the answers. The answers he could have given, he didn't want to give, since there was no telling who might be a plant for the Consortium among them anymore. Once they were away, things would take a slightly different flavor, but he had to focus on what was in front of him.

He caught sight of Koskei shepherding one batch of Initiates up from the lifts toward the shuttles, and moved toward him without taking his eyes entirely off Mercury. Wounded were beginning to come in from various parts of the arm, the result of engagements with the Consortium's guards on the outer levels, but she was handling them as well as she could under the circumstances.

"Where are Fitch and the tattoo artist? They should have been back by now!"

"I've had nothing from them. I tried to radio Fitch ten minutes ago, but there was no answer." There was sympathy in Koskei's eyes, but he had his own small flock to tend to at the moment, and couldn't be bothered to stop and deal with Logan's priorities.

Mercury didn't like hearing anything that made it sound like Orion wasn't going to make it, but there was nothing she could do to help Orion. No matter how much she wanted to. "How much time do they have until we have to go? Do we even have a pilot?"

"We've got dozens, just none as good as he is." Logan admitted quickly, since he had always been impressed with the man on a personal level, even if he was at odds with the man romantically. "Last check-in from White's unit said they were taking fire, I haven't heard from them since. We can give them another ten minutes, maybe fifteen, but the arm is just about cleared of non-Consortium personnel from the last check-in. I don't want to give Vance and his goons any more time than that to get around White's safeguards."

"Ten minutes? Then what, we are just going to leave them behind?" Mercury had chosen Logan, but she still loved Orion. She still wanted him to be happy and safe. Not stuck in eternal hell on the space station. "We can't just leave them behind. Orion . . . and Anna . . . she's pregnant with your daughter, Logan, you can't just . . ."

"If we don't get off this station soon, everyone here is going to die." Logan said quietly, not wanting to disagree with her, but the situation was more complicated than just waiting for two people. "The longer we stay, the longer the Consortium has to send reinforcements and make this place into a . . ." a shot rang out closer to the lifts that made him flinch and grab at Mercury to shield her with his own body as he tried to identify the source.

Half a dozen Consortium guards had made it up the lift and opened fire on the crowd. A few of their own people fired back, but with so many people in one place, it was chaos. "Get into the shuttle! We'll hold as long as we can here, but we need to get the fuck out of here." He drew a rifle from where he'd left it near her medical supplies, and braced himself against a column to take aim at the new attackers.

Mercury moved to get into the shuttle as Logan advised, but she didn't sit down and strap in. She was watching him. He was all she had left. It looked like he took a bullet to the arm, but he didn't stop, even though it looked like the guns on their side were vastly outnumbered by the guns on the other side.

Anna heard the gunfire in the corridors long before they could actually see the fighting, but she had her gun ready, even if her body wasn't quite up to the task. She looked over at Orion who looked just as ragged and beat up as she did, moreso, since he had thrown himself into harm's way several times to protect her.

A piece of floating shrapnel sliced into Anna's cheek before she knew to look for it, and she glared at the wall as if it had offended her. They had to get out. She would shoot as many people as it took. Fortunately, the guards weren't expecting anyone but their own to come up behind them, and the element of surprise was on their side.

Anna saw Orion take a shot from one of those defending the dock, since he was still in his uniform. The hit to his leg sent him spinning wildly against the lift doors, but he pressed himself into a corner and took aim on some of the other guards nearby, shooting just behind Fitch and Melissa as they assaulted those who were assaulting their friends.

Orion wasn't sure what to make of Melissa in the middle of everything, since she had turned downright scrappy in the process of breaking him and Anna out of confinement. The girl looked like nothing more than a technicolor bombshell, but she had proven agile and lethal, even if she was shrieking like a demon the entire time. Every time anyone threatened Fitch, Melissa was on their back clawing at their eyes and pulling hair until Fitch could finish them off.

A few more shots ricocheted off the lift platform beneath him as more of the Initiates shot at him, and he had to cower and wave his hands. "I'm on your side, asshole!" One of the Consortium guards floated into range from where Anna had put her knee most of the way through the man's chest, and Orion took the headshot that offered itself and looked back up at the ones who had been shooting at him. "See?!"

Anna was quick to get to Orion's side so that she could help defend him from the fucking idiots who didn't even recognize one of their own. She took a small knife Fitch had given her and started cutting at the insignia of the Consortium and the Initiative on his uniform between shooting at the dumbass guards who wouldn't fucking die or run away.

Fitch and Melissa had saved her ass more than a couple of times, and the four of them kept close while they inched their way to the shuttle. More guards were starting to show up as reinforcements, and as soon as they did, she heard Logan yell out the command to close the shuttle doors. He was fucking going to leave her there in the middle of gunfire to die to save his ass and his pretty little redhead? Fucking asshole.

The fury that built up in Anna had her shooting the enemy like a wild woman, and they barely managed to make a path that would last all of a minute so they could attempt to make it to the shuttle. "Come on! They're closing the doors! We're going to get left behind!"

Logan couldn't get a clear view of the fight through all the chaos and debris. Bullets continued to ricochet indefinitely until most of them were buried in the softer plastic of the pods near the bar, but there seemed to be bullet wounds everywhere he looked, blood hanging in the air like curtains of lost life.

Between volleys of gunfire, he admired the courage of some of the strangers he had never spoken to in the Initiative, risking their lives to search the rest of the docks for stragglers and wounded so that they could ferry them into the shuttles. The bartenders hid out behind their inventory and were shepherded onto shuttles, the drifting wounded were pulled out of the air so that the Consortium guards remaining could no longer use them as target practice.

Finally, he caught sight of Anna and Orion, keeping themselves behind a wide column as much as possible so that they could get closer to a shuttle without getting shot.

"Hold Shuttle Four!" He called out as they approached, himself still out in the middle of the firefight. The doors stopped closing, though the attendants on it looked more furious than hopeful at the command.

Logan stayed out of the line of fire long enough to lock eyes with Anna, but she was too far away for him to talk to. She was alive, though. That was what mattered. She was alive, and she was going to be safe, if he had anything to say about it. They had one long jump remaining between them and the shuttle, though, and the rest of the gunmen fighting for the Initiates were starting to run out of ammunition. "Go, we'll cover you!"

Anna didn't hesitate as soon as she heard Logan tell them to go, and she was the first to move, hoping that Orion, Fitch, and Melissa wouldn't hesitate either. Anna pushed herself as quickly as she could through the fight, but she wasn't without injury, since a few more bullets found their way into her arms and one in her thigh. Relief flooded her when Logan reached out to pull her the rest of the way, though, and Orion came in behind her.

The shuttle itself was a mass of chaos, with wounded everywhere and people rushing to bandage every injury, only in tightly constricted space. They were all scattered in the ship's cargo hold, with canisters and bags and crates and boxes shoved every which way with all the supplies they could steal from the station. The churn of humanity inside was enough to make a person lose their lunch, and everywhere there were people crying over those they had lost, screaming for a friend or a lover who couldn't be found, who may or may not have made it to another shuttle.

Near the door, Anna watched as Logan took a bullet in the shoulder and twisted away from the hatch in pain before switching hands and returning to the fight, but a moment later, he stopped shooting. Through the hatch, Anna could hear a massive roar of firepower being unleashed, coupled with a dozen screams from the Consortium guards, and then, from the door if not from inside the shuttle, silence.

Logan stared down out of the hatch with murder in his expression, but he eventually engaged the safety on his gun and stowed it in a large pocket of his coat. "Five fucking minutes! You couldn't have gotten here five fucking minutes ago?!? I should have left you here."

Tatyana glared at him but she didn't care what made the man angry, they were alive and they had the Twist. That was all that mattered. For now. "We need to hurry." She was still in action, even though they were safe enough from guards for the moment. "They'll blow us up if we give them too much longer."

Fitch was in the best shape of the pilots, so she moved as soon as she could to get through, up to the controls. Whoever was up there was not going to be able to handle the shuttle like she could. "Come on, Liss. I'm not going anywhere without you. And the view is better up top."

Anna was looking over Orion's wounds as they tried to find somewhere to strap in, but it was difficult in all the chaos. She was bleeding profusely from all sorts of different places, but she was both too tired and achy to notice as much pain as she knew she should feel.

She looked away from Orion for a moment and up at Logan, even though he was barking commands. "Thanks. For not leaving us behind." Anna was genuinely grateful, since as banged up as they were, they would certainly be dead if he hadn't waited for them.

"Thanks for not getting yourself killed." He said in a low voice as he looked her over, though he was too exhausted and wounded himself to do much for her. Mercury had wrapped up his shredded hands until he had little left but a grip and a trigger finger by way of mobility, but he managed to grab a piece of shirt that someone had already shredded and wrapped it around her leg, where she seemed to be bleeding the most.

Mercury was a few feet away tending to someone else so they didn't die right there on the spot. All he had to do was make sure Anna could hold on until Mercury could get a look at her.

Behind him, Gordon and the rest of the crew maneuvered the Twist into the center of the chaos and cleared out a space along one wall of the cargo hold to brace it for transport. Gordon was one of the last to clear the cargo hatch, moving slowly and awkwardly from the amount of blood he'd lost. He twitched violently once when another gunshot went off, since more guards were coming, but he rolled clear of the hatch and looked at Logan through the pain in his eyes. "Is everyone loaded? Are we the last?"

"If you've got all of yours, we've got everyone else. Most of the shuttles have already launched." Logan didn't spare the man more than a glance, since Jessie seemed to be taking good enough care of him, helping him maneuver in the null gravity to get away from the hatch.

"What about Carl and Aiko?" Orion managed to groan from nearby, holding in a wound on his stomach that was trying to kill him. "They were with you, weren't they?"

"They were." Gordon said sadly, then went digging in the pouch that Aiko had given him. She was halfway across the galaxy, but she was still helping him. That was always going to be the way with them, trying their best to help each other while maintaining as much distance as humanly possible.

He took some of the small items she had placed in the pouch and threw them almost blindly through the hatch. With any luck, so long as everyone was evacuated, the contents would spread through the entire dock in the maelstrom of currents left behind by the chaos, and it would incapacitate anyone trying to follow them.

"What does that mean?" Anna asked, even though she could already tell that Orion didn't want to hear the answer. "Are they dead?"

Jessie answered for Gordon, since she didn't want him to have to talk or do anything more than he absolutely had to. She wasn't about to watch the man she loved die. "They're on Eleusis somewhere, hopefully alive. The Consortium opened the Twist to send in reinforcements. They got pushed through and we had to close the link." We. She and Gordon were a 'we' even though he was the one who had made the decision, but she could take the anger and blame on his behalf.

Orion just closed his eyes and rested his head back against the bulkhead, since there was nothing he could do for his friend if he was halfway across the galaxy. He just hoped they would be alright. Hell, he hoped *he* would be alright. They were far from out of the woods. "But they were alive the last you saw them? They had a shot?"

"Aiko was ready for anything. She had supplies with her, and the woman knows Eleusis better than any of us." Jessie took a deep breath and looked down at her husband again, ever-conscious of his every wound. "They were alive when the Twist closed. If we make it down to Earth alive, then we'll see what we can do for them."

Kameron's voice came over the speakers and though she didn't sound as rough as she probably intended, she did mean business. "Even if you're bleeding or beat up, everyone strap in. Otherwise you'll be even more of a stain on the walls than you already are. We're drifting for five minutes to clear the station. Five minutes, people."

Anna looked up at a speaker and over at Orion again. "Thank god she didn't decide to be a doctor. Talk about terrible bedside manner."

"She's better at making holes in people than making people whole. She picked the right career path." Orion groaned and tried to push himself toward a set of straps nearby, though every part of his body hurt and he knew he was likely to pass out soon. "I should be up there. She was supposed to pilot one of the others . . ." He coughed and gritted his teeth against the pain, since obviously he was in no condition to be of help to anybody.

"She's fine." Anna said sharply as soon as she saw him struggling and she moved quickly despite her own wounds to get him strapped in. Anna looked down at his stomach wound and the other holes he'd taken just to protect her. Her own wounds were still bleeding, but they were nothing like his.

"Thanks for being our human shield, you giant." She pressed her cheek to his and kissed him gently afterward as she finished the final buckles. "Leo, Lynnette, and I appreciate it." She pressed her forehead to his and looked back just in time to see Mercury making her way over to him. "Your redheaded ex has some good drugs for you, I'm sure. She's on her way over. I'll be right here."

Orion didn't open his eyes as he felt Mercury tending to his wounds, even though they were all being tossed around by Fitch's "drifting" maneuvers to get away from the station. He knew it was Mercury just by the way she was handling him and the quick way her fingers moved to apply pressure where it was needed.

He hissed in pain a few times as she performed some very quick and probably-dirty surgery to extract the bullets lodged inside him, but the adrenaline in his system was still blocking most of the pain. "I'm glad you're alright." He said without even opening his eyes.

"I'm alive." She said in response, since she was far, far from alright. She didn't know if she would ever be alright again. Once the bullets were removed, she felt better about patching him up, but she would have to use the surgical glue like she did with Logan until she had more time. Her main priority was to stop the bleeding and the pain. "Being 'alright' means something else entirely, I believe."

She knew she was crunched for time, but she wasn't about to let Orion just bleed out on the way down to Earth. Mercury didn't want anyone to die on her watch, but realistically, she had to choose who would live and die in that moment. Orion was someone she was choosing to save over others. "As soon as we get down to whatever facility is housing us, you need surgery. And proper nutrition." She ran a thumb over the circles under his eyes. "And sleep. That, I can help with, at least."

"Sleep might help." He was strapped in right beside an observation window, and he opened his eyes when a flash through the glass was bright enough for him to perceive through his closed eyelids. "What the fuck?"

Logan was at the same window in a moment, and people were scurrying all over the space, watching what happened outside in the vacuum with open-mouthed astonishment. Several of the other shuttles were engaged in a firefight with weapons systems aboard the station itself that Logan hadn't been aware of. The lasers that were normally used to combat space debris had been turned to a very different purpose, and were lashing out at the other shuttles to try and disable them, and the shuttles returned fire for the same reason.

"We didn't account for this." Logan said quietly as everyone in the cargo hold started screaming and rushing away from the windows. Fitch appeared to be fighting back as well as she could, but they were in a cargo ship, and the lasers were meant for maintenance, not offense.

Anna didn't look away from the destruction out the same window at first, but suddenly she pushed away from Orion's seat so she could make her way to the control room. "I'm going to help her. Even if we're the last fucking ship standing, we're getting away from here." Anna pushed people aside and took control when she usually was content to let someone else control, but clearly she was capable of being a leader when she was forced into it.

She yelled at people to buckle in or prepare to die, and nothing about her voice sounded kind. She looked back at Logan and Orion before she kept pushing her way to Fitch, but she remembered something and went to where Jessie had strapped Gordon in. "You said there was another one."

Jessie looked up on Gordon's behalf, but he had lost too much blood, and so she just shook her head. "Who the fuck cares about the other twist?"

"I do!" Anna said loudly before she grabbed at Gordon and Jessie pushed her off. "I need his data thingy."

Tatyana wasn't far, and instead of buckling herself in the rest of the way, she came between the bickering women and grabbed Gordon's data core for herself and ignored Jessie to look at Anna. "Why do you need this?"

"He was patched in." Anna said quickly. "They have fail-safes, everything does. This one is disconnected, but that other Twist won't be. Self-destruct. Fucking push the self-destruct! They'll shoot us out of the sky if we don't destroy them first!"

"Activate it." Gordon rasped, clearly struggling to stay conscious, but he managed to keep his eyes open by sheer force of will. "Tatyana . . . Activate the larger Twist. Once it's active, target the beams on that sector."

That got Orion's attention nearby, and he started, breaking some of the bandaging Mercury had already put in place. "That thing looked like it was going to destroy the station even when it was working. You disrupt it mid-process . . ."

"And it will succeed in destroying the entire station." Gordon shot back with a tired glare. "At least."

"At least?" Logan didn't like the sound of that, but he didn't know enough about the science involved to know how worried to be. "What does that mean?"

"Just do it!" Gordon said with a cough, clutching at his side. "It'll work. We have to get away from here. Can't do that with the station firing at us. Just do . . . just do it."

Anna looked around at the people still getting strapped in, and once Tatyana had the order to essentially destroy the station, she pushed herself through the ship the rest of the way to get to the control room. "Drop us. Kill any lateral thrust, just push us toward the planet." If debris was going to go everywhere, it was more likely to thrust up and out than down, even though she knew the debris would go everywhere.

"We're not ready to go down yet, Anna, not this fast . . ." Fitch started to say, and Anna just shoved in and sat down on top of Fitch, even though Melissa and Fitch thought she was clearly crazy. "Hold onto me, you're strapped in, I'm not, and I don't want to be a smear of AB positive on the ceiling. Just trust me!"

Mercury couldn't help anyone else after she had gotten as far as she could with Orion, so she took the seat Anna vacated and strapped in as quickly and hastily as she could. She could already feel the thrusters had been killed, leaving them floating for a moment while the shuttle adjusted, and Mercury couldn't help but reach out and grab onto Orion's hand. Whatever was about to happen was not good. "I remember the day I received my acceptance. I thought it was the happiest day of my life. I didn't think that it would lead . . . here."

Orion wasn't sure where Anna had gone through the pain he was in, but he held onto Mercury's hand as tightly as he could. "We've been nothing but a game to them for most of our lives." He closed his eyes and winced in a renewed wave of agony, but he looked out the window at the fight and shuddered along with everyone else when a blast hit their ship. It didn't appear to cause catastrophic damage, but it had been enough to shake them. "I thought I knew what I was supposed to do. Who I was supposed to be. All I was to them was a warm body and a skill set. We're better than that. Both of us."

Mercury knew Orion didn't know that telling her that she was more than just a body and a skillset meant a lot to her, but she needed to be reminded that she was worth more. That she knew more than what Stephen Kaplan let her believe. Tears flooded her vision and she leaned in to kiss his cheek gently as their shuttle started to freefall and the thrusters started to push them downward. She just held his hand tighter.

Maybe this was the end. Maybe it was impossible to actually beat the Consortium.

The shuddering fire between the station and the shuttles changed as Tatyana finished her work. The interior lights on the shuttle went dark as Anna refocused the shuttle's power reserves into a singular, station-killing beam, concentrated on a single arm of the station to batter through multiple bulkheads. When it reached its destination, there was a singular, fluttering flash of light, before the entire station was ripped to shreds by blinding incandescence.

Fitch kept a solid hold on Anna, and Anna was grateful as they continued to fight against the ship to keep as many people alive as possible. "Never thought I'd want you to hold me as bad as I do right now, but thank god you're a freakishly strong woman, Kameron."

Anna turned her attention out the window again and looked up to see the station still blowing up as heat and fire consumed it bit by bit. "They're sure as hell going to come after us now. We took their Twist and blew up the other one. All we need to worry about right now, though, is getting down to Earth before more people bleed to death on this ship. Where are we going, Kam?"

Kameron looked down at the coordinates that had been patched in last-minute, pointing them out to Anna. "You know better than I do. I'm not from your planet, sweetie."

Anna looked at the coordinates and felt a pang of regret. She wasn't going home, but she was going close enough to make it hurt that she wasn't going home. "Well, ladies. According to the Consortium, we'll all be officially dead now. Welcome to the afterlife."

Logan watched out the observation window as ship after ship finally laid in their own courses and sped away into the void toward their own destinations. Against the wall, Tatyana helped a barely-conscious Gordon finish the last of his programming tricks that would hide the lot of them from Consortium detection both during and after re-entry. Logan just hoped it would actually work.

"Renata." He said quietly, since peace had more or less settled over the entire cargo hold in the wake of their messy escape, and he had no desire to disturb it.

His former secretary wasn't far away, and he found himself feeling grateful that she didn't seem to be as badly injured as many. "Grab a couple people to help you and coordinate with the other ships, I want a full census of everyone who got off and which ship they're on, before any of us land. People are going to want to know who made it and who didn't."

Renata nodded and looked him over once before she moved away. "Are you alright, Mr. Bickford?" Even now, she was ever the dutiful employee. She knew that leadership was especially important in such times, and if she continued to treat him as their leader, other people would fall in line. "Is there anything I can get you?"

He gave her half a glare for being so deferential, but he couldn't entirely fault her for it. He understood the stakes of what was going on just as well as she did. "I'm well enough. There's plenty worse off than I am right now. See to the census and let me know when you have the results."

"Of course, Sir." She said with as much of a warm smile as she could muster before she went about her work.

Anna passed Renata as she left the control room and left Fitch and Melissa back in charge. She saw Logan first and went to him, even though she looked at Orion's seat and saw he was sleeping. At least it looked like he was sleeping, since she knew the dead people had each been covered up by now. Orion wasn't dead. Mercury wouldn't have been calm nearby if Orion was dead.

Anna's bleeding wounds had slowed to a trickle, mostly because all the shots had been clean and had gone all the way through, leaving the makeshift tourniquets to do their job. "I saw where we're headed." She said as soon as she was close enough to Logan to talk quietly, but she didn't say anything else before she recklessly pulled him into a hug. He was injured, she was injured, but her emotional state had held off until that moment. Mostly. "It's not home, but at least we're headed back to Earth."

He groaned as she held onto him, but he put his arms around her as well as he could in response, even if his hands were too shredded to actually hold onto her. "It'll be more home than that fucking place ever was. And we'll be close enough to keep an eye on our families. Quietly."

Anna nodded against his chest and closed her eyes. "Seeing you makes this easier. You're still home to me."

Logan closed his eyes against the conflict that kind of statement elicited in his thoughts, but Anna had been the one to initiate their remarriages. Brief as they had been so far, he had accepted them, and begun accepting the changes in himself. "Home is going to mean something different in the days ahead. Home is going to be where these kids are. Wherever we can make a good life for them. All of them." He looked down at her stomach and then over at Mercury, though his wife didn't appear to be watching them, just keeping her eyes on Orion's chest to make sure he kept breathing.

"Promise me you'll be there when they're born." She said desperately, since even though Orion was her husband, Logan was still a part of her past. And with Lynnette, a part of her future. "These babies give me hope. I need to cling to it."

"I'll be there. Provided that Kameron doesn't crash this thing and kill us all." He hugged her one more time and let her go just as Kameron engaged some maneuvering thrusters that threw him a little off balance.

Gordon looked up at the shaking of the ship and Logan nearly crashing down on top of him, but he was so exhausted that he couldn't bring himself to care if the larger man had actually fallen on him. Not after everything else that happened.

He could feel that he had lost enough blood to be worrisome, but Mercury had done as good a job of patching him up as she could under the circumstances. He would live, if only by his own stubbornness. That didn't stop him from shivering as his body continued to panic under his injuries.

"I told you." He said quietly, attempting to look up at Jessie through half-open eyelids. "I told you we would make it. That I would get you away from that place."

"Shhh." Jessie said gently as she ran her fingertips tenderly across Gordon's face. "You're my hero, Jason." She said softly with a warm smile that was reserved only for him. Otherwise she was still pretty much a bitch to everyone else. "You saved me and Rebekah both. Now you can't die. That's all I care about."

He closed his eyes completely under her touch, still taking labored, shallow breaths. His head was starting to nod as he lost consciousness, but he was still fighting to hold on. There was still so much to do. "Don't be . . ." he rasped with some difficulty, having to gulp a few breaths to get enough air. "Don't be afraid." He finally managed to say, though he was clearly losing his fight to stay awake. "Don't . . . be afraid . . . of me."

"I love you." She said calmly and confidently and she ran her fingers over his lips a couple of times. "I'm going to take care of you and we're going to have a beautiful house in the mountains and make lots of babies. I'm only afraid of losing you. You've never done anything to hurt me. I don't even understand why you love me, but you can explain it to me later."

That got a subdued smile from him, in spite of the struggle he was going through, but though he opened his mouth to speak again, he lost consciousness before he could force any sound out. There was so much he wanted to tell her, so much he wanted to share. It would take time. Time he hoped they had.

"And you're sure this will keep us off the Consortium's radar?" Logan returned to a seat near Mercury, where Tatyana worked on a holographic projection from the data core Gordon gave her. Anna rejoined Orion, unconscious as he was. The programs Tatyana utilized made sense to Logan in theory, but believing that Gordon had the kind of global access Tatyana claimed was stretching the limits of Logan's faith. "All of this is pointless if they can just nuke us from orbit as soon as we land."

"The most they will be able to do is narrow down which continent we will be on." Tatyana continued to work without looking up at Logan. "The other shuttles are all going to other places. They cannot *nuke* us all at once, and anyway . . ." She paused to bring up some internal messages between Consortium leaders and the remaining Initiative leaders still alive after the exploded Station Nine.

The Eleusis project is officially disbanded. All personnel still alive and associated with the project will report to Station Three for questioning.

Thousands dead. A breaking news report read. *Eleusis footage believed to be a hoax. The project is no longer.*

Eleusis: Does humanity deserve it?

The Consortium shuts down the Eleusis Initiative. Press conference forthcoming, Consortium leaders 'deeply saddened' by the devastating loss.

"The Consortium has to answer to the rest of humankind. They can't come running after us right now."

Logan couldn't help feeling a deep sense of satisfaction as he looked through the headlines, and he eventually dismissed them with a nod. "Humankind isn't going to like their answers. Especially with the entirety of White's speech and all the data he just dumped out on the world." Logan's voice didn't often showcase the country twang of his heritage, but in his more relaxed moments, it was more pronounced, and it came out more as he spoke. "I expect the rest of the world is gonna be a little more inclined to call bullshit when they see it with all that data hanging around."

"They'll come looking eventually." Tatyana's words were sure that they wouldn't be safe forever, but they would be safe for a while. "We have their Twist. But hopefully we will be prepared when they come knocking."

"We will." Logan said resolutely, before looking back at Anna and Mercury in turn.

He was in pain, they all were, in one way or another. It would be some time before all of them were back to themselves, but for the first time in months, it seemed likely that they would actually have the time they needed. To heal, to recover, to rest, to be with each other. Outside of the Consortium's control, outside of the constraints the Initiative had placed on them, outside of everything but their own decisions.

It was a kind of freedom he had taken for granted his entire life, but he felt gratitude for it consuming every part of him as a shadow to the pain he had endured to obtain it.

They were rebels against the single most powerful government in the history of humanity, but Logan wouldn't have had it any other way. Eleusis was real. Humanity still needed it just as much as the day he and Anna had chosen to go into space. He was alive, Anna was alive, and Mercury . . .

His eyes settled on his wife with a lingering sigh before he approached her and took the seat beside her. With slow, anguished movements, he put out an arm to fold her in against him. He was going to be unconscious soon, he knew from the weakness that crept through his limbs and the radiating pain from his hastily-bandaged gunshot wounds.

"I love you." He said quietly once she was against him. "We're going to be alright."

Mercury didn't know why tears burned in her eyes as soon as he said that, but she closed her eyes against the tears as Logan held her. She wanted to believe him, but it was hard to believe that anything would be alright. Everything Mercury had ever known and loved, other than Logan and Orion, was up in orbit. Her parents. Her childhood home. Station Seven and her practice. She was leaving her whole life behind, and it was terrifying, even if escaping the Initiative was liberating.

"Do you promise?" She eventually asked, her voice small against the empty terror of the future.

He nodded against her hair and held her a little tighter. "I promise. Whatever happens, we'll handle it together. No matter what the future throws at us."

EPILOGUE

Eight months later

Anna looked a bit crazed as she leaned back on the bed, her face covered in sweat, brown hair clinging to her face. Labor was a bitch, and she had not been quiet about it, even though her also-incredibly-pregnant Doctor looked freakishly calm.

How did Mercury look so good pregnant? Was that even a thing, beautifully pregnant? Orion made Anna feel that way, since he couldn't get enough of her, but she was also fairly certain that his need for pregnancy sex had pushed her into labor in the first place.

"What do you mean I'm not ready yet?!?" Anna had a death glare fixed on Mercury, but her nemesis-friend was not fazed.

"I meant what I said. "You're at a nine. You can't push until you progress one more centimeter. You're almost there, Anna. It won't be long now."

"It won't be that long?!? These contractions feel like someone gave my babies knives and they're going fucking psycho on my insides! I can't wait any longer!"

"You don't have any choice. And you refused the drugs. I can't even offer them to you now." Mercury responded placidly. She had been threatened and yelled at by a lot of expectant mothers, which was why she encouraged the epidural, but Anna had been insistent about having a drug-free birth.

"First you offer them several times and now you can't give them to me? You . . . gahhh!!!" Anna only looked away when she heard a door open and Orion peeked in. "You! Get in here! Find the drugs!"

Orion's face fell a little at that order, but he did enter and head for the side of the bed where Mercury had inserted the IV. Anna was right-handed, and it was her right hand that had a needle shoved in it. He had better odds of dodging her left cross. He'd learned that from past experience. "Can't find the drugs, I'm sorry. Promised my doctor I would quit. Only way out is through, baby."

"Through? Your monstrous son is going to tear me wide open! My vagina will never be the same!"

"I will fix any tearing." Mercury reassured, but she knew Anna didn't want to hear it. "How about I step out for a bit? I will come back and check on you in ten minutes."

Anna was conflicted. Of course she didn't want Mercury in there, but she couldn't get the babies *out* without Mercury there. "Ten. Minutes." She agreed through gritted teeth. "But then you're gonna come back in and drag these babies out of me."

"Just take a few deep breaths, Anna. They'll be here as soon as they are ready." After that, Mercury stepped out and let out a sigh. Logan was standing outside the room, obviously waiting for an update. "Do you want to go in? Orion and I wouldn't mind sharing the verbal abuse. You don't have to stay out here when your daughter is nearly here."

Logan chuckled at the comment about verbal abuse, but nodded as he stepped up to Mercury. "I'll go in shortly. I'm sorry it took me so long to get here." He pulled her into a brief kiss, holding onto her by the sides of her shirt. They hadn't been able to get official scrubs for anyone for a long time, so he'd become accustomed to seeing Mercury at work with nothing more than her white doctor's coat over her everyday clothes. "Tell me how you're holding up."

"Holding up? I've been yelled at by many a laboring woman. I'm alright." Mercury kissed him again, even though she should have been less selfish with him when his first child was about to enter the world. "Being on my feet for this long isn't as easy as I had hoped." There was a feeling of jealousy she didn't really want to admit either, but it was easier to tell Logan everything than to keep quiet. "And she's having your baby. I'm delivering your baby. I feel jealous also."

His smile left his face at the mention of jealousy, but that kind of feeling was something all of them had been living with off and on for most of a year since the destruction of Station Nine. "Half of me wishes the boys had come early, so that they could be first, but the other half of me knows you would yell at the first half for actually hoping for a premature baby. Let alone a premature set of twins."

"Anna and I have been lucky to carry our babies this long.

Hers to term. I'm glad her babies will be healthy." She sighed as she glanced back at the door leading to Anna's room. "Delivering a baby is such a beautiful thing. And knowing that one will be yours . . . I'm sure she will be so beautiful."

"Well, when she first comes out, she's going to be a screaming, goopy mess. You know that better than any of us." He teased her with another kiss and reached up to caress the side of her face. His hands were covered with scars that had taken most of the preceding eight months to heal, but the scars had become just another part of the jumble of calluses and hardened skin that his farmer's hands had been even before the space station. "If there's something you need or something that would help, I'll go get it for you before we go back in. I heard you mention it won't be long now."

"There's a knot in my neck and my shoulders." She turned slowly so that her back was facing him, her hair pulled up since she was working. "If that's okay with you. I don't want to go back in there until she's ready."

"Wise choice." He stepped aside and pulled up a chair from nearby to sit her in it, after her comment about being on her feet all day. Once she was seated, he went to work on her neck and shoulders, moving slowly and methodically against the muscles that had been bothering her for most of the last few months of her pregnancy. "I saw your roster back outside your office. You've got a hell of a line-up these next few weeks. I hope your trainees are ready for it.

"They don't really have a choice. I'll need some time when the boys get here." Mercury looked down at her large belly and closed her eyes again as Logan kept massaging her muscles. It did make her feel a little better that he was making her his priority instead of Anna.

"Can I ask you something?" She paused only slightly before she continued. "Do you think that we could deliver the boys by ourselves?" She knew that Logan wasn't a doctor, but she knew what she was doing. She could tell him what to do. She didn't want anyone else there interfering with their moment, their boys. Not if she didn't have to.

She could feel his surprise in the way he touched her. The slight pause in his massage was enough. "I know I helped deliver the Montoya girl a few weeks ago in a pinch, but I hadn't thought to make a career out of it. We'll do things however you want to do them, but do you really want just me?"

"I don't want someone interfering with our moment with our boys." She tilted her head back to look at him but she took a deep breath and admitted another thing that she was afraid to say out loud. "I don't want to be vulnerable and exposed to anyone else. If someone has to be there, that's one thing. But I think we can do it alone."

He nodded and leaned down to kiss her forehead. "It'll just be me, then. Unless one of the other doctors becomes necessary. No one will interrupt. I'll see to it." He had that kind of authority. The last months on Earth had made that clear. If anything, his position had only gotten stronger the longer they stayed on Earth.

After a few more minutes of Logan's hands on her shoulders, Mercury stood up slowly, wobbled a little, but looked over at Logan with a small smile. She pulled him into a gentle kiss. "I love you. Let's go meet your little girl."

He held her back with him a moment longer just to keep the world between them, then nodded with his forehead against hers and headed into the room, just as Anna was letting out a grunt of relief at the end of a contraction. Logan squeezed Mercury's hand before letting her go to check Anna's monitors, then moved to the opposite side of the bed from Orion, nodding at Anna. "She threaten to castrate you yet? Or should we look forward to that a little later on?"

"Couple threats." Orion answered, still holding Anna's hand. "We made sure all the sharp objects are on the far side of the room, though, so I think we're safe for the time being."

"Temporary state." Logan agreed, taking a stool already set in place for him. "You want to catch me up on the threats, or should I get the notes from Orion later?"

"I can't threaten to castrate you." Anna said in clear exhaustion, since she had been laboring for the better part of a day. "My doctor has claim on your dick, and I really don't want to piss her off before she gets these kids out of me." She looked over at Orion after that. "I don't want to castrate you either. That would just ruin all of my fun later." She couldn't even finish her quips before another contraction started, and this time she reached a hand out for Logan too, even though it was the strangest situation to have both men at her sides.

"Alright, Anna. You're definitely ready now. It looks like big brother is coming first, I see a full head of very dark hair." Mercury glanced up at Orion and gave him a small smile before she got back into position. "Okay, Anna. Get ready to give me a big push."

Anna was already crying from the contraction, and her hand felt numb from squeezing Orion's so hard, but she couldn't talk. All she could do was what her body needed her to do.

Logan had sat with laboring women before. He remembered his mother in labor with Larissa, though he had been very young at the time. He hadn't been able to help and hadn't completely understood what was going on. Labor didn't scare him or gross him out as he'd seen on some of the other new-made fathers in the last few months, but Anna was the one suffering through it, and that made everything very different.

Mercury was a master at her craft, though, and however Anna raged about the contractions or groaned through the moments between, Mercury was right there with her to coach every moment and guide her through it. He had to admire both women in the timeless struggle that followed. For different reasons, certainly, but both were strong, each in their own way.

As soon as Leo was born, Anna wished that she felt a sense of relief, but with another baby still waiting, all she could do was laugh and continue to cry at the giant boy that was laid on her chest by Mercury. Mercury immediately helped Anna by cleaning Leo up a little bit and suctioning his nose and mouth so that he would cry. And cry he did. He wailed as Orion cut his cord, but Anna was still impressed at how strong and beautiful her little boy was. She didn't get much time to admire him, though, before another contraction hit her.

Mercury had enough time to hand off a towel to Orion so he could clean up his son before instructing him to pick up the boy so that Anna could focus on her next baby. "Okay, Anna. Here comes your little girl. Just like you did with Leo. You're doing great. Even breaths. Big push."

Orion took the little boy and wrapped him up tightly, focused more on keeping him warm and secure than getting him clean right away. He needed to know the world was a safe place more than he needed to look like he hadn't just been doused in cottage cheese. "You've got this, baby. Halfway there."

Logan hadn't moved from Anna's side throughout Leo's birth, but he did hold Anna's hand tightly as Mercury checked her to make sure Lynnette was in position. "If she's got lungs like her brother, the pair of them are gonna bring this whole place down on top of us."

"I'm okay . . . with that." Anna didn't know why she couldn't stop crying, but she turned her attention to Logan for a moment before she was pushing again. She was clinging to his hand this time, and after only a few pushes more, the cries of Leo's sister filled the room. She wasn't as loud as her brother, but Anna fell back onto the bed in exhaustion as Logan took his turn to cut a cord.

She closed her eyes as both babies cried, just happy to hear that they were crying. "Are they okay?" She asked between her own tears, since she was both happy and exhausted.

"They're great." Logan said as Mercury helped him clean Lynnette off. The girl was bright red and her eyes were closed tight, but she was shivering less than Leo had while she cried. "Looks like she got your hair." He sat back down, bringing Lynnette a little closer to Anna as she relaxed against the bed.

Anna opened her eyes just a little and looked over at Lynnette and smiled. She looked over at Leo afterward, and smiled a little brighter. "They're so perfect." She mumbled before she looked at Logan and then Orion. "You both gave me beautiful babies. Thank you." Was she ever going to stop crying? It didn't feel like it.

Logan wrapped Lynnette a little tighter in the blanket, and smiled when the action seemed to calm her down just slightly. He held her close against the side of the bed near Anna, but as she looked over at Leo and Orion, Logan looked back at Mercury, who was still busy with the final details that came with the birth of children.

"Everything alright?" He mouthed at Mercury, not wanting to alarm Anna by even inquiring, but also wanting to make sure there were no surprises waiting for them on the other side of such beautiful children's entrance into the world.

It was clear that Mercury had been working hard to help Anna through, since a few strands of her red hair clung to sweat on her forehead, but she gave Logan a reassuring smile and nodded. Mercury helped Anna through the afterbirth and stitched her up from the minor tear, and she was working on getting everything cleaned up.

"You did a great job, Anna." She said warmly, since Anna was her patient, even though things were far more complicated than that. "Just a little bit of tearing from that big boy of yours, but you'll bounce back quickly."

Anna looked at Mercury and then nodded before she leaned her head back again. She was so tired. Nothing seemed to matter except that both babies were okay and she wasn't dying and now she could finally go to sleep. Maybe. "So they're really okay?"

"Perfectly healthy." Mercury reassured Anna quickly. "You go ahead and rest if you want to. We'll get them weighed and cleaned up. I can help you figure out how to get them latched later, if you want me to help."

Awkward. So awkward. The last thing Anna wanted was to have Mercury grabbing at her boobs to help her feed her babies, however, she was sure Mercury knew more about it than she did. She didn't exactly hang around to watch her mother feed her siblings after they were born. "Yeah . . . let's cross that bridge made of awkward after I've had a nap. I don't want to put any fantasies into either man's head right now, thank you."

Both Orion and Logan glared at her for that comment, since the thought of both women in the same room was far from a fantasy for either of them. Orion was the one who spoke up afterward, leaning in to kiss Anna on the cheek as she settled against the bed. "Only fantasies in my head are your sole property. Get some sleep, baby. You were amazing."

"I love you." Anna replied sleepily as she looked up at Orion with a smile and kissed him again when he obliged to lean in closer to her. She ran her fingers over Leo's face in Orion's arms and then closed her eyes. "He looks a lot like you."

"Poor kid." He said with a smile, then held Leo up a little closer, since the boy was quieter the closer he was to his mother. His skin looked to be nearly the same shade as Orion's, but he was still mottled and ruddy from the birth. He was already larger than Orion expected him to be, and it explained a lot about the discomfort Anna experienced the final few months of her pregnancy.

"You're prettier than me. Don't even start." Anna said with a laugh that was followed with a groan because she was still all sorts of achy.

Mercury helped Logan with the little girl as Orion and Anna had their moment with their son, and she smiled as she looked down at the content little girl. She ran her now-clean finger across Lynnette's cheek before she looked up at Logan again. "She's beautiful, Logan. Congratulations."

Logan was smiling from ear to ear as he held the girl, glad that she seemed a little less angry at the world than she had when she first came out to meet it. "You told me once that this is your favorite part." He looked up at Mercury, running a rough finger over Lynnette's cheek reminding her that someone was there with her. "Would you say that's still the case?"

"Even more right now. Because this baby is yours and you look so happy." She squeezed his arm gently, since she really was happy to see Logan so content for once. To see his smile. He didn't always have a reason to smile, but he smiled more now that they were down on Earth. Even eight months after their arrival, eight months after fleeing the Kaplans, Mercury still didn't feel right. She didn't feel like herself.

He took one arm off Lynnette to hold onto Mercury, and pulled her down into a brief kiss. "Thank you for taking such good care of them. All of them." Things had been difficult for them since coming back to Earth, and Logan expected things to continue to be difficult, with children entering their lives. Shadows seemed to hang over all of them at all times, waking and sleeping, waiting to descend and disturb the life they had tried so hard to build. "No one, baby or otherwise, ever had better care. I love you."

Mercury was glad to be in Logan's embrace, and she savored it for a moment as he held onto her with a baby between them. There was a sting of jealousy that the baby he was holding wasn't hers, but the ones kicking inside of her were both his and hers together, and their moment would come soon.

Mercury wondered if she would feel more like herself again someday, if having her own babies would make things easier or harder. "Go on, take this little girl back to her mother. I'll go check on the little boy and get him weighed." She kissed Logan once more before she pulled away, even though she didn't want to. Being close to him was the only time she ever really felt safe. It was hard adjusting to their new 'normal'.

Mercury walked over to Orion with a small smile back on her lips. "You look like a professional Dad already. Do you want to bring him over so I can get him weighed and measured? You'll want to remember how small he started someday when he's taller than you are."

"Don't curse the kid when he just barely got here." He said with a playful glare. He carried the boy over to the scale and set him down tenderly, though the boy cried heartily when the blanket was taken away so that they could get accurate measurements. "I remember back when we met, you told me you doubted I would keep growing beyond my height at the time. That was . . . about three centimeters ago. And counting."

Mercury laughed softly and kept her attention on the scale, recording the weight on a tablet before she scooted the little boy to the top so that she could measure his length accurately. "You have to stop growing eventually. And you will. I've seen your genetic code, remember?" She glanced up at him and then turned her attention back to his squalling child. "I'm a little amazed that Anna didn't explode with these two. This boy alone is over three kilograms. I don't know how she had room for them. Though his sister looks significantly smaller."

He smiled as he looked back at Lynnette, even though Leo was still screaming on the scale. "Well, at least now she's got some room to run away from him so he can't beat her up all the time. Just some of the time." He put a massive hand over the boy's chest, which seemed to help him panic less, but he still clearly wasn't happy. "Yours will be out here before too much longer. Can't be doing you too many favors to be having women giving birth on a daily basis when you're so close yourself."

"It's part of the job. Even if I was in early labor, I still would have been here for Anna." Mercury said without any hesitation, and she wrapped Leo up in a fresh blanket once she had done enough measuring and documentation.

She really made him angry when she had to give him his first round of vaccines, though, since they were safe and made to give to newborns so they were protected almost instantly.

Especially living on Earth, underground.

The babies would need their first treatments after they were a month old, unless Mercury found they were resistant to CV after an initial blood test, but she doubted that would be the case.

"How are you doing?" She bandaged up Leo's tiny foot where he'd been pricked and handed him back to Orion. "Most people forget to ask the father how he's doing after a long labor like this. But you've been awake nearly as long as she has."

"Yes, but I got the luxury of caffeine during that time. She didn't." Anna had fallen asleep while looking over Lynnette, and Orion couldn't blame her. She'd been through twins, and he couldn't even imagine how exhausted she had to be. "So I'm fine, but thanks for thinking of it. I just see a whole lot of artificial stimulants in my future where these two are concerned. Especially this loudmouth." The boy had yet to calm down again after being wrapped up, but he was at least starting to settle a little once he was back in the crook of Orion's arm.

"He's just not used to this place yet." She looked up and around with a sigh, since she wasn't used to it either. Her makeshift clinic was far from what she would expect or want from a clinic, but at least it was clean and stocked with supplies. "I'm not either. But we'll all get there." She reminded herself to be patient more than anything, but then she turned her attention back to Orion and gave him a side-hug as he held onto his son. "Congratulations. You have quite the little family. And you look happy."

He nodded and returned the hug before he was back to focusing on holding Leo. The look he gave her over his smile, though, was more pensive than most people expected from Orion. He was too lighthearted and too prone to make jokes to be taken too seriously. That didn't mean he was incapable of being fully serious when the time called for it. "Happy is a complicated thing anymore. I didn't think it would be, before all this, but lessons learned, I suppose."

Mercury nodded and gave his arm a squeeze before she stepped away. "I'm going to go steal your daughter now and make her cry too. They're just going to love me." She teased before she gave him another smile. "I can just see our whole mess of kids creating a lot of trouble someday. I'm already blaming you for part of it."

"I accept this blame. Not a problem." He smiled at her as she headed away, and went to the side of the room to try and quiet Leo so he wouldn't wake up Anna.

Logan brought Lynnette over to Mercury once Orion stepped away, and set the girl down on the scale slowly enough that she wasn't terribly disturbed through the process. Unwrapping her from her blanket made her less happy, but she seemed more tired and curious than cranky even when she was exposed. "I wish Larissa had been this calm as a baby. I think she screamed for about half a year straight before she eventually shut up."

"One of them had to be the calm one." Mercury looked the baby over and gave the tired little girl plenty of smiles and coos because she was more attentive than her brother had been. She ran a finger along Lynnette's cheek before she weighed her. "She's almost a full kilogram smaller than her brother." Mercury said with a laugh before she shook her head. "And shorter too. She's probably going to be just as scrappy as her mother to make up for it, though." Mercury looked down into the tiny baby's eyes, which were just as grey as her father's, though Mercury knew that Lynnette's eyes could easily change colors even by the time she was a year old. "Her eyes look like yours."

The little girl didn't seem to enjoy having her eyes opened on such a new world, but she didn't cry for long as Mercury examined her. "I hope that's where the resemblance to me stops, for her sake." He smiled at the girl as she flailed for no apparent reason and upset herself a little, but Mercury's examination didn't last long before Lynnette was permitted to go back into a clean blanket.

"I had a dream about them the other night while you were away." He said quietly, since he didn't want to disturb Orion and Leo on the other side of the room or Anna sleeping in her bed. "We were in front of a house that was being built somewhere and we were yelling at our own kids to stay off the construction blocks. These two kids were just sitting back and laughing. Not sure what that means and I don't think I want to get too deep into my own subconscious to figure it out. But they were cute kids, all of them."

"It won't be easy, trying to raise them up together so that they feel like family." Mercury admitted as she finished wrapping Lynnette, then picked her up and held the baby girl herself. Lynnette wasn't her daughter, but Lynnette was a part of Logan. She loved both babies just a little bit more because she loved their fathers. "I want you to be able to be a part of her life, and I want our boys to know their sister. It just won't be easy." She watched Lynnette's face for a moment before she looked back at Anna who was still asleep.

Mercury continued softly as she considered their future. "Anna and I will never be friends. I don't think it's possible. She doesn't want it, and I don't think I'd be good at it. Though I would try, if you want me to." Despite Mercury's horrific experience with the Kaplans, her relationship with Logan was still more or less the same, though she struggled with physical intimacy. Logan was someone she always wanted to defer to, since doing so made her happy. "We're very different people. We'll be different mothers. Different wives. Different everything. It is difficult."

"I gave up thinking that anything about life would be easy a long time ago. A long time before I even went up to the station, actually." His smile was overshadowed by the ghosts of the different choices he'd made along the course of his life to reach that perspective.

"I respect Orion, but I don't think either of us imagine we'll ever be friends. Things are just too complicated. What's important is that we're all . . . committed . . . to being in this together. Whatever comes." There had been a lot of rumors going around lately about what could be coming, but nothing concrete enough to rely on yet.

"I made up my mind a long time ago." It felt like a long time ago, anyway, that Mercury had decided Logan was the one and only for her. Still holding Lynnette, Mercury stepped in to kiss Logan warmly. "Orion is my friend, I'll always love him, but you are the man that I want." Mercury pressed her forehead to his, a baby and her bump between them. "I hope I'm enough for you. I can already see some things are different here on Earth as far as marriages go."

That comment made him laugh once, in spite of the serious moment, and he shook his head against hers. "You're more than enough for me, Mercury. I've never been interested in having more than one wife. It's not something I'm suited for." He reached up to run a hand along her cheek to reassure her as he held her. "I'm yours."

She smiled back at him after his laughter and pressed her hand lightly to his. "I'll be myself again someday. I promise. I know things haven't been easy for us."

He shook his head to wave off her concern. "Whatever you need. I told you that when we first got here, and I meant it. I expect you to tell me when there is something you need or something you need to be less. So long as you're mine, nothing else matters."

"I'm yours." Mercury replied softly before she kissed him again, though it was a careful, featherlight kiss. The little baby girl between them didn't move or squirm, in fact, she seemed calmed by the closeness of Mercury and Logan, and that gave Mercury hope in turn. If a newborn could feel at home on Earth, maybe she could too.

The story continues in

The Fugitives

ABOUT THE AUTHOR

D. Brumbley is a husband/wife duo from Kansas City who spend most of their time in each other's heads. In suburbia the duo lives in a simple house with a dog and two feisty kiddos. One half of the duo loves football, baseball, libraries, and romance. The other half of the duo likes D&D, Fantasy novels, Marvel Comics, and cheesecake. A country girl and an east coast boy met online, became best friends, fell in love, and somewhere along the way decided that telling stories together would be fun.

Best. Decision. Ever.

www.ingramcontent.com/pod-product-compliance
Lightning Source LLC
Chambersburg PA
CBHW060556300726

48975CB00005B/1342